DEDICATION

For Mom, the wonderful woman who brought me into this world, and gave me two of the best gifts that can ever be had: a mother's love, and the love of reading

CONTENTS

Part Two

FAMILY TREES THROUGH JULY, 1815

A printable version of the family trees can be found at sophie-turner-acl.blogspot.com.

Notes: Because the events of *A Constant Love* were moved forward one year from when *Pride and Prejudice* is commonly thought to have occurred, the death of George Darcy has been similarly adjusted. Because the families lack an additional courtesy title, George Stanton and Andrew Fitzwilliam take the style Lord [Lastname], and have the precedence of viscounts.

1

Bennet
Esquires
Seat: Longbourn

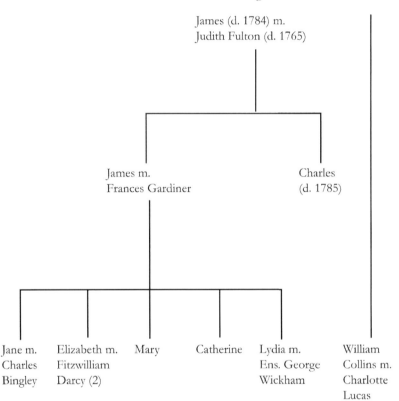

James (d. 1784) m.
Judith Fulton (d. 1765)

James m.
Frances Gardiner

Charles
(d. 1785)

Jane m.
Charles
Bingley

Elizabeth m.
Fitzwilliam
Darcy (2)

Mary

Catherine

Lydia m.
Ens. George
Wickham

William
Collins m.
Charlotte
Lucas

Darcy

Esquires

Seat: Pemberley

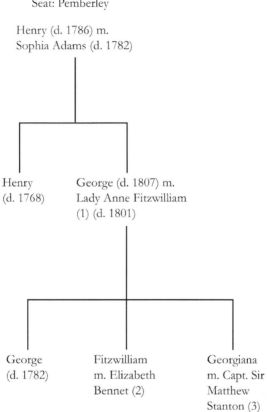

Henry (d. 1786) m.
Sophia Adams (d. 1782)

Henry
(d. 1768)

George (d. 1807) m.
Lady Anne Fitzwilliam
(1) (d. 1801)

George
(d. 1782)

Fitzwilliam
m. Elizabeth
Bennet (2)

Georgiana
m. Capt. Sir
Matthew
Stanton (3)

Stanton

Earls of Anglesey
Seat: Rutherford Abbey

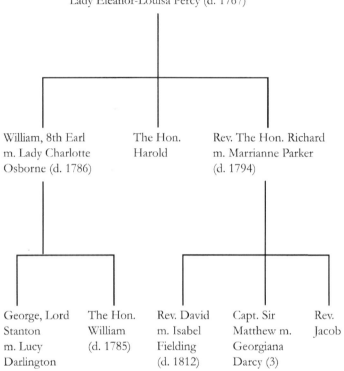

William, 7th Earl (d. 1782) m.
Lady Eleanor-Louisa Percy (d. 1767)

William, 8th Earl
m. Lady Charlotte
Osborne (d. 1786)

The Hon.
Harold

Rev. The Hon. Richard
m. Marrianne Parker
(d. 1794)

George, Lord
Stanton
m. Lucy
Darlington

The Hon.
William
(d. 1785)

Rev. David
m. Isabel
Fielding
(d. 1812)

Capt. Sir
Matthew m.
Georgiana
Darcy (3)

Rev.
Jacob

Fitzwilliam

Earls of Brandon
Seat: Stradbroke Castle

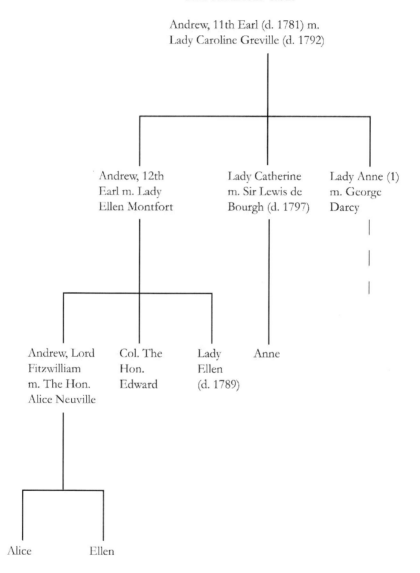

Andrew, 11th Earl (d. 1781) m.
Lady Caroline Greville (d. 1792)

Andrew, 12th Earl m. Lady Ellen Montfort

Lady Catherine m. Sir Lewis de Bourgh (d. 1797)

Lady Anne (1) m. George Darcy

Andrew, Lord Fitzwilliam m. The Hon. Alice Neuville

Col. The Hon. Edward

Lady Ellen (d. 1789)

Anne

Alice

Ellen

Part One
September, 1815

CHAPTER 1

"My dearest, I love you too much to wait another day," he said, caressing her cheek. "Let us leave for Gretna Green tonight."

"I cannot – I do not – I do not think I am ready to leave so soon. This is all so sudden. I wish to be married to you, but I do not think I am ready."

"I own it may seem sudden for you, but I have been in love with you for so long. So very long, my dearest." His thumb brushed over her lips, and Georgiana could hardly bear the sensation, so wonderful and yet so overwhelming it was to her. "I cannot wait; I cannot brook any sort of delay. There is nothing I wish for more than to be married to you."

"I would like to at least speak with Fitzwilliam, first – "

"Oh, my precious Georgiana, I understand, but it may be some time before he visits. Come away with me tonight."

"I think it might be better to at least wait until Monday, as we planned."

"It pains me that you wish to wait, my darling," he said. "Speak to Mrs. Younge; I am sure she will agree."

"But – my brother – "

"I am sure your brother will be exceedingly happy to find we have wed. After all, he and I are nearly brothers ourselves, so close were we as children. And think of how much easier it will be on him, to not have to support your coming out into society. All those London seasons – they cannot be something a single gentleman wishes to devote his time to."

"Fitzwilliam says I am still too young to come out into society."

"Of course, he would be too kind to tell you that supporting you through a season will be a great burden to him, when he is entering a time of life where an established gentleman should be considering his own marriage. It will be so much easier for him if you marry without any effort on his behalf."

"Do you think I am a burden to him?"

"My love, of course you are, but I promise you shall never be a burden to me."

"Let us go tonight, then," she said. He loved her so, and he was right, that she was a burden to her brother. Fitzwilliam had not sought her guardianship, but it could hardly be avoided, after the death of their father. She might marry the man she loved, and relieve her brother of this duty, all as soon as they could reach Gretna Green.

"I knew you would see things as I do," he said, taking up her hands and kissing them. "Go to Mrs. Younge – she will help see your things packed. I will go and hire a post-chaise."

"But we already have a carriage here in Ramsgate – may we not just ride in it?"

"Mrs. Younge will need to return to London – after all, once you are a married woman, you will not have need of a companion. And it should be returned to your brother's home – when we are married, we shall set up our own carriage."

"Oh, may we get a landau? I have always loved our landau at Pemberley."

"We may purchase whatever sort of carriage you choose, but I adore the idea of riding through the country in a landau, so all England may see my beautiful bride."

He smiled deeply at her, and Georgiana skipped off, calling out for Mrs. Younge to help her. There was so much to do!

So much to do, and all of it done so quickly that the packing of her trunks and those first few days in the carriage seemed like nothing but a vague memory she could hardly grasp, when she attempted to think back on them. But Georgiana thought of the future, of the man asleep on the seat beside her, for Mr. Wickham had desired they drive through the night, saying he would rather marry his darling Georgiana sooner than stop at an inn, and she found this terribly romantic.

Whenever he spoke of such things, it gave her a heady rush of happiness. George Wickham, who had always been so kind to her as a girl – secretly in love with her all these years! She could never have thought it, and yet she had felt such pleasing emotions when he admitted it to her.

Then Mr. Wickham was grasping her hand, and murmuring that they had finally entered Gretna Green. He eschewed the blacksmith as not nearly good enough for his Georgiana, and so they found an inn where the innkeeper promised the marriage could be done, and a room provided for them. This sounded well to the both of them, and Mr. Wickham ordered their trunks unloaded, and handed his betrothed down from the carriage.

The ceremony itself shocked Georgiana in its brevity. Two of the inn's servants were gathered in the common-room with them, and the innkeeper looked to Mr. Wickham, and said: "Do ye, sir, declare yerself inna desire to be married to thee lass?"

"I do."

"And do ye, lass, declare yerself inna desire to be married to thee lad?"

Georgiana hesitated. This all suddenly seemed so wrong, to be here without her brother, to be so far from home and family. But Mr. Wickham looked at her pleadingly, and she finally whispered: "I do."

"Then by the laws of Scotland, I pronounce ye man and wife," the innkeeper said. "Ye may kiss the bride."

Mr. Wickham – Georgiana realised she must call him George, now, for they were married! – had always teased her with the idea of kissing, caressing her face or touching her lips with his fingers, but he had never actually followed through. He did so now, and it was a slovenly experience that left her thoroughly disgusted, and relieved when it was done.

"Ye must needs sign this paper, as a way of documentin' the marriage 'tis done," the innkeeper said. "Then Brenda ken show ye to yer room."

In their little room, they found a tray of cold meat and bread on the table, and George ate hungrily, with no time for the sorts of endearments he was usually giving her. When he finished, he looked up at her with a strange smile, and said, "So are you ready for your wedding night, Georgiana?"

"Yes?" she said, although she was not entirely sure what he meant by it.

"I shall go downstairs for another drink, then, and you may change into your nightclothes."

She did as he instructed, struggling to free herself from her dress and untie her stays. She missed the help of Miss Hughes, who had been nominally acting as her lady's maid for years, even though Georgiana was not a married lady. They would need to employ Hughes now, she realised; she would have to speak to Fitzwilliam about it, once they returned south.

She was wearing her nightgown and sitting on the edge of the bed when he returned, seeming as though he had consumed several drinks, rather than one. He closed and locked the door behind him, and smiled that strange smile again, taking the few steps required to get to the bed. Then he gave her another of those slovenly kisses and pushed her back on the bed.

It was only now that Georgiana felt herself to be suffocating under the weight of him, under the strange firmness between her thighs, and his hands slipping into places below her nightgown that left her squirming in discomfort, and then fear. She whimpered, then cried out, pushing against his shoulder.

"What are you doing, George? What are you doing to me? Stop. I don't like this. Please, stop." She might have said it aloud; she might only have thought it, but suddenly, mercifully, the weight was gone.

"You know, I would be well within my rights as a husband, *dear*

Georgiana," George said, rearranging his breeches. "You're lucky I only go for willing girls. The damage is done, so far as your brother is concerned, whether or not the marriage is consummated. Indeed, now that I think on it, this might be useful as leverage. Although I shall have to find a more pleasant bedfellow, for the evening."

"I do not understand. George, what are you talking of?"

"Oh you poor, innocent child. Do you not understand what this is all about? No, if you did, you would not be here, and I would not be awaiting my thirty thousand pounds. I suppose if your father was still alive, he would have warned you against those who would use you for your inheritance. Your worthless brother, on the other hand, clearly has not."

Georgiana was young, she was not well-versed in the ways of the world, but with an encroaching feeling of the most horrible dread, she began to understand why he spoke of her inheritance. When she looked up at George – nay, Mr. Wickham, for there was no reason to address him so familiarly – she did not find anything to reassure herself.

"Thirty thousand pounds! There is no way he will get out of it now," Mr. Wickham said, triumphantly. "He will hand over the money, and then our business together shall be done, Georgiana. I only hope for your sake it will happen quickly. For now, though, we must see you secured for the night, for you are very valuable property, and it would not do to lose you."

He produced a long piece of fabric – perhaps such as a gentleman used for his cravat, although she could no longer think of *him* as a gentleman – and she eyed it with suspicion and fear, finding she was correct in both concerns when he pulled her jaw open and yanked the fabric back against the corners of her mouth, tying it behind her head. When this was done, he took up more fabric, and tied her wrists and then her ankles together.

When she was left, thus trussed, lying on the bed, as Mr. Wickham went out in search of his more pleasant bedfellow; when she was left, lying there in her fear and unable to do anything to alleviate it, Georgiana began to consider how rapidly things had gone wrong.

This was not right, this could not be! George had loved her! He would not leave her in this way; he would not tie her up like a pheasant to be cooked for dinner! He would not use her for her fortune! And yet he had. There was no denying that he had. She tried to scream against the fabric in her mouth, but the sound she made was barely a whimper, and she knew a fear far beyond what she had ever considered possible.

Georgiana woke painfully, up through the deep, deep layers of sleep, fleeing the dream. Her heart was pounding, her breathing panicked, and she took some time to reorient herself, to reassure herself it had not been real.

It had not. There was the presence of her husband – her *real* husband, the one she truly loved and had married little more than a month ago – in the bed beside her. His arm, with the horrid pink scar that had shocked her so when she first saw it, was draped over her stomach, and they were both in a state of undress that would have completely appalled her to even think about before her wedding. It might have continued to do so, had they remained in England, but they were in Paris, a city that even now, in defeat, had its own standards and morals. Georgiana had begun their residence here in the belief that none of her own standards should be undermined, and yet she liked the warm, firm nakedness of the man who shared her bed, although the thought of this still made her blush.

She slipped from his embrace and pulled on a dressing gown, walking over to the window and looking out across the rooftops that comprised the view from their room, in the low haze of the city's remaining light at the present hour. It still seemed strange to her to be here, in the country England had been at war with for most of her life, without peace even formally declared. Yet it would be – this was clear even to someone so loosely connected with the negotiations as she.

Georgiana opened the window, and was reminded that the air was no less foul than that of London, although it still calmed her. She knew full well what had prompted the dream. There they had been yesterday, walking along and enjoying this unexpected honeymoon, discussing their engagement for the opera that evening, when she had thought she glimpsed George Wickham. It was an impossibility, of course: Mr. Wickham had gone missing after the battle at Waterloo, and was most likely dead. Yet whoever this gentleman was who bore such a resemblance to him, he had been enough to prompt a most horrible dream.

The church bell down the street rang, a fine, pure tone through the window, and Georgiana watched as her husband stirred slightly, ran his hand languidly across the space in the bed where she should have been, and then woke immediately, looking troubled at her absence. She felt a surge of fondness for him, before he spotted her by the window and said, "Whatever are you doing over there, Georgiana? Will you not come back to bed?"

"Nothing, just thinking on a bad dream," she said, walking back over to the bed, and slipping out of her dressing gown.

"Do you wish to talk about it?" he asked, in a tone of concern.

"No, it was one of those dreams that will never truly happen," she said. "I was only a little disturbed when I woke."

It could have happened, but it would not, now. Georgiana had been the innocent girl of her dreams, back then, but she was older, and – more significantly – a married woman, now. She understood fully what Wickham had been about in her dream, and was most thankful to be married to a man who had gone about things much more delicately their first night together, and most nights thereafter, a man who loved her most earnestly, and whose love she fully returned. She blushed again, to think of their activities in this bed, and those before it, and relaxed back into his embrace, pulling his arm very tight against her chest.

It could have happened, though. If George Wickham had convinced her to elope before her brother arrived in Ramsgate, her fate might very well have been that of her dream. She shuddered at the thought of it – she could not help herself – and was once again asked if she wished to speak about her dream.

"No, I don't think so," she whispered, turning around to face him. "Will you help me forget about it?"

Georgiana had always been shy, and she suspected most of her acquaintances would still describe her as such. Over the brief course of her marriage, however, she had gained enough confidence to be able to say such a thing to her husband. She did not understand how her mind had even conjured those terrible kisses, for every one she had ever experienced had been so very pleasing, like the one she gave him now and found returned most tenderly.

Her request was met with the degree of enthusiasm a gentleman who loves his wife will generally feel, upon being invited to an unexpected round of marital relations in the midst of the night. And Georgiana did find herself able to chase nearly every thought of George Wickham from her mind, in the comforts of Matthew Stanton's attentions.

CHAPTER 2

Elizabeth Darcy had desired a large summer house party, and she had brought it about, along with a ball and a wedding, and as much as she had gained enjoyment from hosting these events, she now experienced enjoyment at having reached their completion. The last of the guests – Mr. and Mrs. Bennet, and their two unmarried daughters – had departed three days ago for Longbourn, and now she could stroll Pemberley's gardens in the knowledge that her demands as mistress of the house were significantly lessened.

Of course, there were still Pemberley's more permanent guests: Jane and Charles Bingley, and now their daughter, little Elizabeth Bingley, who, for a child of such amiable parents, did a remarkable amount of screaming. Such continual fussing must have been loudest for the child's nurse, in Pemberley's freshly scrubbed and painted nursery, but could be heard through much of the house, and Elizabeth hoped her own child would be quieter. Not that this would be entirely beneficial, as the Bingleys would still be staying at Pemberley for some time, while they built a new house at nearby Clareborne Manor, and so long as young Elizabeth remained, there was to be little peace at Pemberley.

Elizabeth smiled; she still thought tenderly of her own namesake, although she believed her husband, who generally looked rather disturbed by the sounds emanating from the nursery, was not nearly so sentimental. They both suspected it of having driven the newly married Stantons from Pemberley sooner than had been expected, although it could not be denied that the opportunity to spend a honeymoon in Paris held independent appeal.

Jane's birth, at least, had been as quick and painless as could have been hoped for; Dr. Alderman had hardly arrived before it was time, and Elizabeth hoped this boded well for her own birth. Jane had been certain through her entire pregnancy that she was carrying a girl, and had seemed quite content upon learning she was correct. Mrs. Bennet had been unexpectedly helpful and calm through the whole event, although perhaps this should not have been so unexpected, she having borne five daughters of her own. Upon learning the sex of the child, however, she had not been able to help herself in pronouncing: "Well, Jane, I suppose we should not take it as a surprise. I only hope you do not have four more."

Charles, thankfully, upon being handed his daughter to hold, had seemed ready to faint regardless of the sex, but he had held himself upright as a look of delight several times that of his usual happy countenance overtook him. He had said she was an angel, and he had no doubt she should grow up to be as beautiful as her mother. She might still grow up to be as beautiful as her mother, but no one could call the child an angel at her present age, and the Darcys continued to receive profuse apologies from the Bingleys regarding the disruption of their peace. They assured the couple they were still welcome, although both Darcys found frequent reason to be as far away from the nursery as possible. Elizabeth walked in the gardens as often as her present state allowed, and made use of the most distant sitting-rooms in the house. Darcy, meanwhile, occupied himself with riding the estate grounds, and took more zealously to shooting with other gentlemen from the neighbourhood than he might have otherwise. Charles, in solidarity with his wife, would not go out with them until after Jane was churched, but following that event, he, too, seemed to have a most eager anticipation for such outings.

"And how do you find the gardens today, Mrs. Darcy?" asked her husband, entering on one of the paths that led from the kennels, and still dressed in his sporting clothes.

"I find them very peaceful," she said, giving him a little wink.

"At least no one need accuse that child of not having a healthy pair of lungs," he said, drily, settling in to walk beside her.

"Jane already wishes her to learn the pianoforte. Perhaps she shall have to engage a singing master, as well. We may well have the next opera diva here, under our roof."

"I suppose that would be a productive use of so much vocal power, although at present she wants a great degree of tone. Should we be quite certain there is nothing wrong with the child?"

Elizabeth took up his arm. "Dr. Alderman says she is perfectly healthy, and my mother claims we were all rather vocal, in our infancy."

"So you mean to tell me we will soon have two babies, making such noise?"

"You will feel differently, when it is our own child. Surely you must remember when Georgiana was born – did she not cry?"

"You are likely right, about it being our own child. But I do not remember Georgiana making such noise. She was rather feeble in her early infancy, and I expect she was shy, even as a baby."

He sounded a little wistful at the mention of his sister, to whom he had been more like a father than a brother, for so many years. Darcy had happily given his consent to the match, yet Elizabeth could not forget the shocked expression on his face, when the Stantons had spoken of their invitation to Paris over dinner, and said they would be going. By Darcy's countenance, it had been clear he still expected to be asked permission, and had realised abruptly that permission was no longer his to give.

"Georgiana and Matthew have arrived safely, and I expect we will each have another letter from her soon," Elizabeth said, soothingly. It still felt strange for her to call her new brother Matthew, for they had known him as Captain Stanton before, and he should by rights have at least been Sir Matthew, but he insisted on plain Matthew, among those that were now his family.

"I know," said he, "I just cannot help but think of all the other times, when we thought there was peace with France and then war broke out, and many of our countrymen were trapped there."

"They are there with the official delegation, Darcy. You know there are ships waiting to carry them off if such a thing happens. Failing those, I expect he would steal a boat and sail it across the channel himself, if that was required to get Georgiana to safety."

Darcy did not respond, but Elizabeth knew he was aware that she was right; in consenting to her marriage, he could not have given Georgiana over to anyone more concerned for her wellbeing, nor so capable of seeing to it. And she could not help but smile; by his behaviour towards his younger sister, she was certain he was going to be an excellent father.

They walked on for some time, enjoying the very many pleasures a well-tended garden in early September could provide, before Elizabeth found herself overcome by the strangest sensation.

"Oh!" she exclaimed, halting and clutching her belly.

"Is something the matter, with the baby?" Darcy asked her, immediately concerned.

"No, it is very strange, like a little tickling inside," Elizabeth said, suffused with a feeling of the deepest happiness. "I believe it is the baby quickening."

Her pronouncement caused some confusion of actions by her husband; he made as though he was going to embrace her, seemed to think better of it, and finally gave her a very deep kiss, through which she could sense he was every bit as joyful about the event as she. Elizabeth had seen an accoucheur in town, and Dr. Whittling had warned her that the quickening might come later in her pregnancy, this being her first child. This had reassured her, as had the continued thickening of her belly, but it was still a relief to have it happen; nay, something beyond relief, she realised, for there was a certain wonderment in this feeling of life stirring inside her.

"I do not think the baby will mind, if you embrace me," Elizabeth said, for she could not resist teazing her husband.

"I did not want to make it stop. Has it stopped?"

"No, not yet. I wish I knew better how to describe it to you."

"I would imagine it to be rather indescribable," he said. "Still, I am glad I was here when you experienced it. The look on your face was absolutely beautiful."

"I cannot say the look on yours was so. Will you ever cease worrying?"

"I believe I will, when the child comes of age."

Elizabeth chuckled and took up his arm again, and as they walked on, she thought they could not possibly be happier than they were now, but then realised they very likely would be, in just a few months.

CHAPTER 3

Like many young women, Lady Stanton had married her husband after a short acquaintance. Thankfully, Georgiana had married for love, and joined herself to a man whose fortune and family had been compatible with her own, but she was still learning that he was not quite so perfect as she had thought before their wedding.

She had, of course, known he was a naval captain who had been at sea for five years in command of HMS Caroline, and that he had returned to England for just enough time to fall in love with her, then go back to sea during Napoleon's Hundred-Day War. Georgiana preferred not to think of the grave wounds that had sent him home, although her new title was a constant reminder of the baronetcy he had earned in a nearly impossible victory, capturing a seventy-four gun ship with the fifty-gun HMS Jupiter.

What she had only realised after they were married was that he had generally only encountered women in drawing-rooms, and even then only infrequently for most of his life; that he was used to much rougher conditions than she; and that he had mostly been at sea after he had earned his fortune. He had spent the beginning of their marriage perpetually shocked at how long it took a lady to prepare in the morning, and only of late had they settled on a solution, that he should go down to the coffee-room of their hotel and read the latest English papers until she was ready, rather than pacing around their apartment, making both her and Miss Hughes nervous.

His absent-minded frugality they had still not solved, for Georgiana had yet to raise it as something that required solving; here, she thought more subtle measures might be required. Matthew had a high regard for cleanliness, but it seemed he would otherwise willingly sleep anywhere with enough walls for a hammock to be slung. Fortunately, he was observant enough to note her concerned countenance, upon seeing the apartment at their first hotel in Paris, for although it was indeed clean, it was very small and shabby, and not remotely what she was accustomed to. He had been most agreeable when she asked if they could perhaps try somewhere else, and they had taken on a much finer and larger apartment in this hotel, which was still less than they could afford, but at least sufficient for them to present themselves respectably when people from the delegation called on them.

It was not as though he was not generous, either; he had been exceedingly so with her pin money, when drawing up the marriage contract with her brother, and more often than not he had paid for her purchases here, anyway. No, it seemed to Georgiana that he simply did not consider how one could live on land, with nearly five thousand pounds a year. It would be her part to continue to recall him to it; for some time, she had been giving little hints of their setting up a carriage once they returned to England, as yet to no avail, and so perhaps she would have to be more direct about it.

Still, she loved him very much, and could not deny she was happy in her marriage; after all, it was not as though she had married a man of little fortune, merely one she needed to remind to spend a little more of it.

Hughes finished her hair, and asked, "More shopping, today, my lady?"

"Yes, I expect so. Have I reached the point where I shall need another trunk, to bring it all home?"

"You are coming very close, if you don't mind my saying so, ma'am."

Georgiana was typically not one to shop so much she required an additional conveyance for her purchases, but presented with the opportunity to buy that which had been so recently unobtainable, she had been unable to resist some purchases for herself, and a great many gifts. As well, although she had forgone most of her wedding trousseau, having been married so soon after coming out into society that she could hardly justify a whole new set of dresses, she had opted to have a few made for herself in the latest French style. She told Hughes she would ask the hotel to arrange the purchase of an additional trunk; usually it was the sort of thing her maid would have seen to, but poor Hughes had spoken nary a word of French when they arrived, and had learned only a few thus far.

Georgiana made her way down the stairs to find her husband sitting not with a newspaper, but instead a small piece of paper in his hand, and she asked him what it was.

"It is Marguerite Durand's address. They have located her, finally."

"Oh – do you wish to call on her this morning?"

Georgiana was not looking forward to calling on Marguerite Durand, and she expected her husband was not, either, although she found it honourable that he wished to. Charles Durand had been the captain of the

Polonais, the French ship Matthew had captured, and Captain Durand had not survived the engagement. Matthew had brought the captain's belongings with them, in the hopes of finding his widow and returning them to her, but her current address had proved elusive.

"Would you mind terribly? I know we have the dinner this evening, and I hate to make you spend an entire day where much of our time is not our own."

"I do not mind at all. I would not wish to make her wait a day longer than is necessary, and I know we would not be here, were it not for the dinners."

Their invitation to visit Paris had come through Matthew's uncle, the Earl of Anglesey, who had spoken to someone in the peace delegation and suggested his nephew's presence might be useful, although Lord Anglesey's aim had been more towards an intriguing honeymoon, for the couple. They were, as such, nominally part of the delegation, but primarily there to attend dinners and remind the French of British naval superiority: everyone at the dinner table knew who Matthew was, and what he had done, although the French were unfailingly polite. Georgiana, as she had indicated, did not mind the dinners; although shy, she liked having some manner of society, and the food was so good she felt certain she had become a little heavier since they had arrived here.

"That is very good of you." Matthew smiled, and handed her the paper. "Will you see whether we need a carriage to get there, and have them send Hawke up for the chest, and the sword?"

"I will. It is such an annoyance, to have to hire a carriage instead of being able to come and go as one pleases, but of course it cannot be helped, since we are here for such short duration," Georgiana said, to which he only nodded in agreement.

Georgiana approached the maître d'hôtel, who by now knew her to be the more fluent in French of the couple; Matthew's education had tended more towards mathematics and navigation than foreign languages, although he seemed to get by with his few phrases and hand gestures, when Georgiana saw him communicating from afar. The need for a carriage was confirmed, and she asked that one be hired for them for the day, and the items retrieved from their apartment.

Georgiana did not know Paris well enough to anticipate the quality of the neighbourhood they travelled to, but it became readily apparent that it was a poorer part of the city, for their route there took them through a great crowd of beggar children, which only dispersed sufficiently to let the carriage through when Matthew had thrown a handful of coins toward the side of the road. This was the only threat they encountered, but Georgiana was glad it was a fine, bright morning, for it was not the sort of place one would want to be in darkness. The carriage pulled to a halt in front of a building no more or less dark and decrepit than the rest on the street, and as he handed her down from the carriage, Matthew asked her to remain close to him, although he needn't have – Georgiana would have done so, anyway.

They made their way into the building, followed by Hawke, who carried the battered old sea chest that had been sitting in a far corner of their apartment all this time. The entrance-hall was dim, and this may have caused it to seem less squalid on the whole than Georgiana had expected. They made their way up to the first floor, to the sound of a couple arguing in the ground floor apartment, speaking so quickly Georgiana could not understand much of what they said, although it was clear they said it angrily. With some relief, she watched the door to Madame Durand's apartment open in response to Matthew's knock, and found herself facing a harried-looking maid.

"Bonjour – Sir Matthew et Lady Stanton pour Madame Durand, s'il vous plaît," Georgiana said, wondering too late if she should have introduced her husband as a naval captain, instead.

It did not seem to affect their entry, however, for the maid stood aside, motioning that they should enter, and called out, "Deux Anglais!"

A woman came in, then, looking tired but otherwise wholly beautiful, a full head shorter than Georgiana, and of more voluptuous figure, accentuated by a dress at least three or four years out of fashion, even to Georgiana's *Anglais* eye, and dyed black. She was followed by a boy of perhaps three years of age, also dressed in mourning.

"Good morning," she said. "I am Madame Durand, but I do not know to expect English callers. Please have seats. This is my son, Jean-Charles."

Like Matthew's first choice of hotels, the room was clean, but undeniably shabby. It appeared there were only two rooms to the apartment, and that Madame Durand and the boy had come from the only bed-room; perhaps the maid slept on a pallet on the floor. They sat, as the maid ushered the boy back into the bed-room, and Hawke deposited the chest in the middle of the floor.

Madame Durand might not have known to expect English callers, but she knew full well what had just been placed in the middle of her little room; the worn sea chest had "C. Durand" painted in the centre of the lid, and down one side, a long list of ships's names, ending with the Polonais. She looked up at them with an expression of grim sadness before kneeling in front of it, laying her hands down on the worn wood. Georgiana was not certain whether she reached for her husband's hand first, or he hers, but for some time they sat clasping hands on Madame Durand's worn sofa, watching her wipe a tear from her face.

"Lillette did not say your names," Madame Durand finally said. "I should think, why else would two English call on me, but to return this. I

19

thank you very much for not sending only servants."

"Madame Durand, my name is Captain Stanton, and this is my wife, Lady Stanton. I was – I commanded – I was captain of the Jupiter, the ship which captured the Polonais. I am very sorry for your loss. I have also your husband's sword."

Matthew made to hand her the sword, but Madame Durand looked up at him with an expression of fierce anger, saying, "I do not want his sword. I have no desire for pieces of war. I hold no anger for you, for you do your duty, as do Charles, but I do not wish to have that in what home I have left."

Matthew nodded, and pulled the sword back. He and Georgiana watched as Madame Durand pulled the lid off of the chest and began removing its contents: simple, mundane items, shirts and books and writing things. Then a packet of letters, a fob watch, and a miniature, of her. Madame Durand looked up at them with a startled expression as she pulled out her late husband's purse, which sagged with coin.

"You do not take his money?"

"Of course not, madam, it belonged to him. We only took that which belonged to Napoleon."

Madame Durand opened the purse and placed her hand inside, seeming to count the coins with her fingers, then whispered, "Dieu soit loué."

"Madame Durand, I hope I do not offend when I ask if your situation is such that you do not have enough money to live on, and if there is anything I may do to assist?" Matthew said.

"I have enough money to live on, for now, although there was time in my life I would not call *this* living," Madame Durand said, motioning to the room around her and then holding up the purse. "This is welcome all the same. I use care with what is left of my husband's money, and with help of God it will last, until I am gave my father's lands."

"You have land that is owed to you?"

"It is my hope. My father was killed in terror, and I have no brothers or sisters living. I am hopeful with King restored and peace near, I may claim some of my father's lands, but no attorney has time for a poor widow."

"We are here with the British delegation for peace, and are acquainted with several attorneys on the delegation. Will you allow me to speak to them on your behalf?"

"You do this for me?"

"Of course. You must let us know if there is anything else we may do, to assist you."

"Thank you," Madame Durand said, looking a little embarrassed. "You must know Charles did not like you English at all. I think where he is, he must feel a little poor now, at how kind you treat me."

They sat in silence for a few minutes following this, Madame Durand occasionally glancing down at the trunk. Georgiana looked at her sadly, and could not help but think of how she herself would react, in such a situation. Could she be kind, and polite, to the man who had brought about her husband's death?

"Madame Durand, I expect you have been wishing for our absence, so you may better acquaint yourself with the contents of Captain Durand's trunk," Georgiana said, finally. "Perhaps we may call again in a few days, when Captain Stanton has had a chance to speak with the attorneys?"

"I would have pleasure to receive you," Madame Durand said.

It was only when they had both been seated inside the carriage that Matthew took up Georgiana's hand and said, intensely: "Your brother did show you my will when you went over the marriage papers, did he not? You know you will never be in a situation where you are so relieved over a small purse of coins. You will always have security in life, if anything should happen to me."

"He did, and I am very grateful for how concerned you both were for my welfare, although I do not like to think of the event that would cause need of it."

Georgiana knew that if what she most feared did ever happen, she would never be reduced to Madame Durand's circumstances; even if Matthew had not won his own fortune, as it seemed was the case with Captain Durand, she had brought her own inheritance to their marriage, and would always have a home at Pemberley, if she needed it. Yet Matthew did have a fortune, and he had been exceedingly generous in his will; if anything should ever happen to him, she would not have a thought for one purse of coins, for she would be a tremendously rich heiress, with most of their combined fortunes. And yet not as happy as she would be on this day, to be in the carriage with her beloved husband.

"I am sorry. I know this visit must have made you think of it, but I cannot tell you how grateful I am that you came with me," he said.

Georgiana squeezed his hand, in acknowledgement of what he had said, and they were silent for some time.

"Madame Durand is very beautiful, do you not think?" Georgiana asked, eventually.

"Hmm?" Matthew said, for he had been staring out the carriage window.

"I said Madame Durand is very beautiful. At least she has that in her favour – when her mourning is complete, I do not think it will take her long to find another husband, even if she does not regain her father's land."

"I suppose she is, for the sort of man who has an inclination for petite women," he said, slipping his arm around her waist and pulling her close to him. "I happen to prefer women of very different proportions. She is not your match in beauty, so far as I am concerned."

"Now you go too far. I am hardly beautiful."

"You are very beautiful to me," he said, kissing her, and then noticing her look of scepticism: "When you play the pianoforte, you have this look of both immense concentration and joyfulness on your countenance. I assure you, it is very beautiful, particularly when the sound is also so beautiful."

This soothed Georgiana, for although she was not at all the vain sort, and barely counted herself as pretty, she was capable of any manner of jealousy, and found his statements precisely what she needed for reassurance. Following them, she was very much inclined to find more ways in which they might assist Madame Durand.

CHAPTER 4

With only two couples remaining at Pemberley, dinners had settled into rather casual affairs. Elizabeth planned soon enough to begin inviting a family or two from the neighbourhood to join them every evening, but for now she was enjoying having only herself, her husband, and the Bingleys gathered in the small dining-room to eat whatever of the day's shooting had not been sent home with the other gentlemen.

After dinner, they would repair to the blue drawing-room, there to sit in private occupation, unless someone – usually Charles – might grow so bored as to suggest cards. The Darcys generally read, and Jane preferred needlework, although she went about it slowly, with an exhausted countenance that indicated how much she attempted to spell the nurse, poor Mrs. Padgett, from young Elizabeth's squalling.

On those few evenings when the baby was quiet, such as this one, she was brought down by Mrs. Padgett, so they all could spend some manner of peaceful time with her. Elizabeth held little Bess – they had settled upon this as a nickname, when it became clear that having two Elizabeths in the household should prove confusing – and was tempted to ruffle the baby's little fluff of fair hair, but would not. Bess was sleeping, and they all spoke softly, when at all they spoke, for fear of waking her.

It was not to be, however. With no apparent cause, the baby woke, scrunched up her face, and emitted a shriek seemingly loud enough to be heard in Lambton, if not Derby. For Elizabeth, the only fortunate thing about the situation was that no one looked at her, with her own rounded belly, and made any judgments about her fitness to be a mother. This was simply what Bess did, and Jane rushed over to pick her up, apologising wearily, and checking to see whether the baby was wet, which she was not.

Poor Mrs. Padgett was about to return her to the nursery to see if perhaps she was hungry, but Jane did not hand the baby over immediately.

Instead, she waited for a break in the crying, and said: "Lizzy, will you humour me, just for a few minutes, and play the pianoforte?"

Elizabeth gave her sister a look she hoped indicated just how very much she felt this was the oddest thing that had ever been requested, by Jane, and saw her sister was very much in earnest. Nor could Elizabeth make much in the line of argument, for she would be required to compete with her namesake in being heard, and Darcy and Charles were both looking at her in desperation. Any argument would only prolong things for all of them.

Before Elizabeth had married, she would have been the first to name herself but a mediocre player of the pianoforte. It was a useful skill in her Hertfordshire neighbourhood, to be able to assist in providing the entertainment for an evening, and so she had kept with it, but had never possessed the passion for it that might have seen her put in the hours of practise Georgiana and Mary did each day. Given the choice, she would always much prefer to be out for a country walk, rather than practising her music.

After she had married, with two fervent pianoforte players in the household, Elizabeth had rather assumed she should become one of those ladies who gave up the instrument upon marriage. Now, with some degree of horror, she was required to open up the cabinet beside the pianoforte – an older model that had been moved from the music-room in favour of Georgiana's magnificent grand – and sort through the music within, to find something she had at least once been able to play.

With only the thought that she was about to add even more to the cacophony, Elizabeth seated herself at the bench and launched into the song. Her fingers were stiff, and she felt she stumbled more than she got right, and yet after a minute or so, Elizabeth realised that all she could hear was the sound of her own poor playing. She risked a glance at her sister, and found her still holding Bess, with the nearest thing to a triumphant smile that might ever be seen on Jane's face.

"I knew it!" she exclaimed. "When I was carrying her, and she would take to her kicking, she always stopped when I sat in the music-room with Georgiana or Mary. And do you recall that day, when she was quiet?"

"Of course!" Charles said. "Our sister Mary said she had been neglecting her practise, and sat down for several hours. Do you think Bess could hear it all the way from the nursery?"

"It appears she did," Darcy said. "I congratulate you, Jane, on finding the solution, although I am rather afraid of what my wife thinks of it."

"I must admit that right now I am wishing you had withheld your consent for Georgiana's marriage, so she might be here to perform this duty far better than I am able to," Elizabeth said, slurring her way to the end of the song and frantically flipping back to the beginning to play it again. "We must send for Mary tomorrow. Perhaps in a year or so she may be allowed to leave."

They all laughed, Mrs. Padgett included, but it was the exhausted, relieved laugh of five people who had not slept nearly so much as they should have for several fortnights.

It seemed the hour of playing had some manner of lasting effect on little Bess, for even when Elizabeth went upstairs to be changed, it was to the sound of a goodly silent house, Pemberley as it should be.

"If you don't mind my asking, ma'am, I have a great curiosity as to what it was that finally quieted the bairn," said Sarah Kelly, Elizabeth's lady's maid, as she finished removing the pins from Elizabeth's hair.

Some ladies might have minded their maid asking about anything at all, but Elizabeth was very fond of Sarah, and would have forgiven any manner of transgressions far beyond what Sarah herself – who was as steadfast as could ever be asked for – was actually capable of committing.

"I do not mind at all, Sarah," Elizabeth said. "Mrs. Bingley asked me to play the pianoforte – she had a theory that it would quiet Bess, and it seems she was correct."

"I did not even realise you played, ma'am."

"You might not have, were it not for this. With my sisters in the household I had no need for it, and had thought I might give it up permanently."

"But you have the ability to create music, ma'am – that seems a rather powerful ability to give up."

It would be, Elizabeth realised, for Sarah, who had grown up on a small farm outside Galway, and certainly would have had no opportunity to learn a musical instrument.

"Should you like to learn the pianoforte, Sarah? I expect we will be enlisting anyone who has interest in learning, so long as it continues to appease the baby."

"I would like that very much, ma'am," Sarah said, her voice indicating she was attempting to contain a degree of enthusiasm even beyond what her words indicated. She finished brushing Elizabeth's hair with a particular happiness, and they said their good nights.

Although she was nearly three months away from having her own child, Elizabeth still made her way to her husband's bedchamber, for she did not sleep well without him. She knew this was the largest factor in their inability to give up marital relations, even this far along in her pregnancy; it was far too easy, when they slept in the same bed, for a kiss and a caress to stoke her ardour, or his, and from there things would progress much as they had before Elizabeth had become with child.

After Elizabeth had come in and kissed her husband, she felt the need to speak, once the kiss had wound to its lovely, lingering end: "Do you think we should stop, now that I have had the quickening?"

Darcy groaned. "I suppose we should. We have been intending to stop for some time now. Did we not say we were going to stop in September?"

"I believe we did. What is the date, today?"

"September twelfth," Darcy said.

Elizabeth laughed heartily, at this, and found herself joined by her husband. The truth was, although she knew at some point it should become uncomfortable for her, once her belly grew too large, she was not yet at that point, and until she was, they would continue to struggle to find some *last* day.

"This Saturday is the sixteenth," Darcy said. "Given the Sabbath is the next day, perhaps we should make the sixteenth our last?"

"It is a nice date to aim for. I cannot say I have any degree of confidence we will succeed."

"Perhaps I shall have to lock you out of my bedchamber."

"You would not."

"You are correct, and that is why we find ourselves in this predicament."

"Well, perhaps we should move this *predicament* along, given we only have until Saturday," Elizabeth said, laying her hand upon his thigh, and then touching him in more sensitive places. "I am rather tired, after so much unexpected playing."

"I could not agree more, my love. And I must admit I am glad to hear you play again. I quite missed it."

Darcy, wisely, kissed his wife before she could make any manner of retort.

CHAPTER 5

For the Stantons, life in Paris had begun to take on some semblance of normalcy and habit. Evenings were spent either in long, lavish dinners with the rest of the delegation, or, if they were not required for the evening, in quick dinners at one of the Parisian restaurants, followed by the opera or a concert. Both Georgiana and Matthew were terribly fond of music, and had been indulging this fondness as much as possible, now that they were married.

During the day, if the weather was poor, they would take callers or call themselves, for many of the delegation stayed in their own hotel or one of those nearby, and so no more than a short walk with an umbrella was required of them. On fine days like this one, however, they would most often walk out and wander, exploring the city, and only occasionally going so far or becoming so lost amidst the narrow, winding streets that they were required to seek out a fiacre to return them to the hotel.

Georgiana enjoyed Paris, although she did not think she should ever like to live here. Currently everything was novel to her – the gardens and the architecture were different from what she had known all her life, and therefore interesting. Even as the city intrigued her, however, she had a sense that as she came to know it better, the novelty would wear thin, and she would wish to return home – although *home* was a somewhat ambiguous word for her, presently.

As well, there was a grim sadness to Paris that made it difficult to love; it was a city in defeat, and one whose citizens must have seen Georgiana and Matthew as reminders of this defeat every bit as much as the British soldiers in the streets. Everyone was polite to them, but then, everyone they met with – aside from Madame Durand – was either involved with the peace negotiations, or had some want of the Stantons's money.

Their strolls through the city often took them into the more commercial areas, a riot of signs competing for attention, and they preferred the bright, glass-covered passages filled with more refined shops. Matthew had waited patiently through any number of modistes and perfume houses, while they were both capable of becoming hopelessly distracted anywhere music could be found to purchase, and thus often required to rush home to change for dinner when they noticed how late it had grown.

Today Georgiana's mission was not to shop for herself, or even family and friends, but instead for Madame Durand, for she had suggested to Matthew that some little gifts might be procured before their next call on the widow. Fine things, but useful things, so Madame Durand would not think them to be overreaching themselves, but pleased to have her burdens eased a little. Thus added to the rosewater Georgiana had already purchased alongside her own perfume were bolts of black muslin and crepe, soaps, candles, and some fine claret, of which they could not resist ordering more for themselves, and family. These items were all to be sent back to the hotel, so they could continue to walk unencumbered, and as they approached a tailor's shop in the passage, Matthew said:

"I suppose I should purchase some new shirts – a few of mine are grown quite worn. Hawke has been threatening to sew me new ones if I do not, and there are few things Hawke likes so well as a foppish shirt."

"You wish to *purchase shirts in a shop?*" Georgiana asked, incredulously, so strange the concept was to her. But then, she realised, he had no mother or sisters living to sew his shirts for him, and so his shirts must have been procured in some manner.

"I did not think it so outlandish. I have been purchasing shirts since I was a commander, and it was no longer appropriate to sew my own."

She stared at him, even more incredulous. "You can *sew?* But you are a man!"

"Dearest, when we men are at sea for months at a time, do you think we let our clothes fall to pieces for want of a woman on board?" he asked, his countenance amused.

"No, I suppose not, but I had assumed Hawke does all of your mending for you, as he would do on land."

"Indeed he does, but he was not my servant until I achieved sufficient rank, and so I learned for myself."

"Yet you would purchase your shirts now?"

"Do you know of any other gentlemen who sew their own shirts?"

"No, of course not. I sewed all of Fitzwilliam's, until he married Elizabeth."

"It is appropriate for a lady to make shirts, then?"

"Yes, and I shall make yours, if you would like. Let us purchase some fine cambric and linen, instead of completed shirts."

"If you do not mind doing so, I rather like the idea of wearing shirts that have been made by your hands."

"I do not mind at all. If you like the fit of one of the worn ones, I shall take it apart and use it as a pattern."

Matthew replied that he had one he preferred, and they purchased the fabric, then walked on down the passage until they reached the modiste where Georgiana had ordered several dresses. Matthew asked if she would like to inquire about her new dresses, and Georgiana readily agreed. She was eager to see how they were progressing, for she liked the fabric very much – it had taken some degree of convincing to make Mademoiselle Barteau believe she would never wear any of the more diaphanous options presented to her at first, and then finally some silk of appropriate weight, but still very high quality, had appeared.

Georgiana was pleasantly greeted by Mademoiselle Barteau, inquired after the dresses, and learned one was ready for her to try. She was sent into a room in the back of the shop with an assistant, who tightened her stays severely, then helped her into the dress. Georgiana emerged with some degree of embarrassment; even in this fabric, she felt too much on display. Mademoiselle Barteau inspected the fit of the dress, and pronounced Georgiana to be a little bigger than when she had come in for her fitting, although nothing that could not be compensated for, to which Georgiana blushed, and was thankful that if her husband could overhear what had been said, he would not understand it.

She vowed to be more cautious about her selections at dinner, and to attempt to spend more time walking and less time shopping, then made her way to the front of the shop. There she spun so Matthew could see the full gown, which *was* very finely done, even if it did leave exposed far more of Georgiana's bosom than she was comfortable with.

"What do you think of it?" she asked him.

"I think you look very well in it, although I cannot say I like the idea of any other gentleman seeing you in it."

"I know precisely what you mean," she replied, then leaned close, and whispered, "I shall trim it with some lace, when we return to England."

With her stays still uncomfortably tight, but returned to her original dress, Georgiana took up Matthew's arm, and they exited the shop. They were not but two paces down the passage when she halted completely, and breathlessly exclaimed: "Mr. Wickham!"

For there, approaching them in the passage, was not a man who looked like George Wickham from a brief, faraway glimpse, but instead a man who was unmistakably and undoubtedly George Wickham. He heard her, recognised her, and made, with a panicked look on his face, as though he meant to evade them. There was nowhere he could go in the passage except into one of the shops, however, and those convenient to him were not ones a gentleman would visit, without being accompanied by a lady. He must either greet them, or turn and walk the other way, and Georgiana watched as his face settled into an attempt at an amiable, charming smile, and he closed the distance between them. She tightened her grip on Matthew's arm.

"Miss Darcy! How very good – and most surprising – to see you here. And how have you been?" Mr. Wickham asked.

"I am well, although I am Miss Darcy no longer. I am Lady Stanton, now."

"Ah, so you have married – my congratulations," he said, in a tone completely belying that he had once attempted to make her his own wife, and just enough of a drawl to indicate he was at least a little drunk. "This must be your husband."

"Yes, Captain Sir Matthew Stanton." Georgiana and Matthew both agreed his full name was rather long and awkward, but even though Matthew had not requested an introduction, she took a great deal of enjoyment in saying the whole of it now, slowly and deliberately. "This is Ensign Wickham."

"Lydia Wickham's husband?" Matthew asked.

Wickham blanched at the question, looked briefly as though he wished to escape their company again, and then said, "Yes, Lydia Wickham's husband."

"I met Mrs. Wickham at Pemberley, in the summer," Matthew said. "However, it seems she was mistakenly in mourning."

"Yes, well, I had been trying to determine whether I should send word to her. I will not be returning to England, I do not think."

"You *will not* return, or you *cannot* return?" Matthew asked. "You seem to have come out of Waterloo rather unscathed for an ensign. I am less familiar with the workings of the army, but I had understood your role to be carrying the colours into battle."

"Yes, well – " here, something in Wickham's countenance seemed to give way, as though he was acquiescing to whatever amount of drink he had consumed. "As you say, I was a rather conspicuous target. People around me were falling, so I opted to fall, as well."

"You played dead, while your countrymen fought."

"It does sound rather poor, when you put it that way, but what do they truly need an ensign for? If I had been able to wield my own gun, perhaps things would have been different."

"Somehow I doubt it, given you decided to desert, after the battle," Matthew said. "That is why you cannot return to England, is it not?"

"Perhaps."

"Paris is a good place to hide oneself, right now, although it may not be for long, as the occupation army settles in," Matthew said. "And here you are with a nice new coat, and fine French brandy on your breath. Where did you get the money, for these things?"

"How I came into funds is not your business."

"You robbed your fallen comrades, did you not?" Matthew's voice was angry, far angrier than she had ever heard from him. "All those dead men on the battlefield – it must have been very easy to lift their purses."

Wickham paled again, and said nothing to deny that he had done so.

"You damned coward. Men like you disgust me," Matthew said, and now it was Georgiana's turn to grow tense, for such an insult would have been grounds for Mr. Wickham to call him out.

Matthew was right, however, in calling Wickham a coward. His face turned furious at the insult, and he even seemed to contemplate his gloves for a moment, but then he shrugged, and said, "Think as you will, for your opinion makes no difference to me. Lady Stanton, you look very well – marriage must suit you."

Mr. Wickham stepped around them, and made his way rapidly down the passage, leaving the Stantons to turn and face each other, Georgiana's countenance shocked, Matthew's furious. He knew the whole of Georgiana's history with Mr. Wickham, and that the man's last comment had been a subtle reference to Georgiana's nearly having eloped with him.

"I do not think it is possible for any one man to come up with more ways in which he might infuriate me," Matthew said.

Georgiana had seen her sister, Elizabeth, diffuse any number of uncomfortable situations with her humour; she should never have thought it required now, that she should be the one less affected out of an encounter with Mr. Wickham. Yet it seemed the best thing to attempt, and she replied, "It might have been worse. He did not insult the King, or kick a puppy."

He stared at her for a moment, before endeavouring to smile, taking up her hands, and saying, "Oh, my dearest Georgiana, if you can be so complacent after seeing him, I must attempt to follow your lead."

"I cannot say I am fully complacent, but I do not wish to allow him to ruin our day," she said, soothingly. "Let us go and have a nice dinner, and listen to our Vivaldi concertos tonight, and not think about someone who does not merit our thoughts."

"We must think of him a little more, though. Surely one of us must write to your brother and sister, and inform them that he lives."

Georgiana sighed. "You are right, although I wonder if it would be better for Lydia if he was still thought dead, particularly if he shall never return to England. She would go through a year of mourning, but then she would be free of him."

"If she remarried, though, she would be a bigamist. If her first marriage was ever found out, her second would be dissolved, and any children from that union declared bastards. It is unfortunate, that she shall have nothing to live on while he flounces around Paris spending dead men's money, but I do not see any way around it that is not fraught with risk."

Georgiana fell silent, for now she could not help but think that it had very nearly been her, in Lydia's situation.

"I will write to them of it," Matthew said. "You need not be faced with any more reminders of that man."

"No," Georgiana shook her head. "They will worry if they read we have met with Mr. Wickham, and the news does not come from my own hand. I will write to them; it will be no trouble."

He asked if she was quite certain, and Georgiana assured him she was, taking up his arm and indicating they should walk on.

"I am impressed you are able to remain so calm. Is this the first time you have seen him, since that summer?"

"It is," Georgiana said. "I would not say I am calm, but I find I am mostly relieved, that I did not make the mistake I might have, and very happy I married a far better man."

"I suppose I shall take that as a compliment," he said, reaching over and covering her hand with his free one.

"Yes, and I will own it is not the compliment you deserve, to be compared with such a man. You are all that is good and handsome and brave, and I feel my good fortune independent of relief, I assure you."

They travelled south. In Georgiana's trunk was a cloak she could not remember having packed, and she was made to wear it in the few times she was allowed out of the carriage. Mr. Wickham held a knife next to her side while he walked with her, hidden by the cloak, and told her that he would not kill her – for all her worth was in being alive, as his wife – but if she did not make matters easy for him, he would hurt her. Georgiana believed him, and doubted in her ability to run away, anyway; she had felt sodden since her wedding night, and it seemed time was moving too quickly, while she herself had become sluggish.

Nor did she know where in the country she was when they stopped finally at a run-down inn, where Mr. Wickham took her to a room, tied her up as he had done at Gretna Green, and left her. The days and nights seemed to run together in a continual stream of despair, broken only when he untied her, which he did not do frequently. Once, almost kindly, he promised her that this would not last forever, but generally she came to understand she meant less to him as a person than as thirty thousand pounds, and all her hopes were in things being resolved between him and Fitzwilliam as regarded her dowry, so she could go home to Pemberley.

But she did not go home. Mr. Wickham came in, and told her to put on her cloak, for they were going somewhere more permanent to wait on her stubborn brother. It was a silent, short ride in a hired carriage, which passed through a village, drove on for some time, and finally halted in front of a small cottage. The cottage had only two rooms: one quite large, an L-shaped space containing a hearth, dining table, and bed; the second much smaller, with another bed, a battered old wooden chair, and little else.

Georgiana was pushed into the smaller room by her husband, who locked the door behind her. She pleaded with him through this door, asking him to let her go home, telling him she was certain Fitzwilliam would give over her dowry, if she was allowed to go home.

"I hope your brother will be forthcoming with your dowry, Georgiana," Mr. Wickham said. "As soon as he releases it, I shall release you, and I hope you know how I wish to. I have no desire to keep you here, while you long to be home. You might assist a resolution in the matter, were you to write to him indicating you are unharmed, and untouched, insofar as the marriage bed is concerned, and very desirous that he release the funds I am owed."

Georgiana told him she would write the letter, and pen, ink, and paper were given over to her. Lacking any sort of desk for the chair, she was required to kneel on the floor, and there wrote a most desperate and sorrowful letter to Fitzwilliam, apologising for her folly, and begging that she be allowed to come home, in exchange for her inheritance.

In the days and nights that followed, as she took up residence in the miserable little room, she was never informed if Fitzwilliam had responded to her letter.

This time, Georgiana woke softly, although chased by a lingering sense of dread, that her dream had been true, that her real life was existing in sad wretchedness in that cottage, praying she should be released and returned to the safety of Pemberley.

No, no, no, no. She had married Captain Sir Matthew Stanton; she had delighted in every note of the Vivaldi concert with him earlier in the evening. They had separated at some point during the night, and she did not have his scarred arm draped over her side as proof, but she turned to face him, and was reassured.

No doubt seeing Mr. Wickham that day had prompted a return of her nightmare, for that was what she must call it now; it had long since surpassed a bad dream. Matthew had called her complacent, after the encounter, but clearly it had affected her, and she did not at all like that it had, that he could still have such power over her.

Georgiana wondered if her dream was how it would have been, if she had eloped with Mr. Wickham. Would he truly make no attempt to live as man and wife, and simply act as he must to collect her dowry? He had seemed – at least for a time – to attempt married life with Lydia, and yet here he was in Paris, alive, with no attempt made to inform his wife of his fate.

Georgiana frowned; she had told Matthew she did not want Wickham to ruin their day, and they had endeavoured not to allow him to do so, and yet here she was allowing him to ruin her night. She should not allow him any more of her thoughts – her waking thoughts, at least. Her dreams she could not control, and she found herself in no rush to attempt sleep again. Instead she laid there, watching Matthew's sleeping face, far more peaceful than it had been earlier that day, hoping his calmness would make her feel the same, that when she did drift into sleep eventually, it would be free from any dreams.

CHAPTER 6

Elizabeth had said it in a jesting tone, but she had been entirely serious that they should send for Mary, after their discovery that little Bess was placated by the sound of the pianoforte. When several sessions in the music-room successfully halted the baby's crying, she raised the topic again, and everyone was in agreement with her that it should be done: the difficulty was in arranging the matter.

Mary, the lone Bennet sister not engaged, married, or possibly widowed, could not travel without a suitable companion. If the distance were shorter, a male servant might have been sufficient, but everyone was in agreement that she should not stay overnight at a coaching inn with so little protection. Mr. Bennet's accompanying her back north was quickly eliminated; Elizabeth's father was not of an age to bear another round trip to Pemberley so soon.

This left Darcy or Charles to journey down and accompany her, and given Charles had a child already in being, Darcy was the logical choice. Elizabeth was not particularly happy with this, although she saw it was the best option; she had vowed not to be parted from him after a frightening experience during the Corn Bill riots, when he had been away from their house in town, but felt herself too far along in her pregnancy to travel with him.

She shared these misgivings at the idea of his leaving as they made their usual – now much shorter – walk along Pemberley's grounds that morning.

"I know, my love, I hate to leave you, particularly when you are so far along," he said. "Yet perhaps it is for the best to be required to do so now. I believe I will go to town, first, and stay a day or so. I can ensure all of our accounts are in a settled place, for I expect we shall not be back to town for a half-year, at least, once the baby is born. As well, it will be easier to find good candidates for a wet nurse there."

"We have no need of a wet nurse," Elizabeth said. "Certainly someone to help care for the child, particularly if it should prove so difficult as little Bess, but I wish to nurse the baby myself. My mother – and perhaps you – shall object to it, but it is what I wish."

"I have no objections to it, and I do not know why she should," Darcy said. "My mother nursed Georgiana and me, as did my aunt Ellen and my cousin Alice, for their children."

"It was not common in our neighbourhood," Elizabeth said, a little embarrassed, but secretly pleased with this fodder for convincing her mother, for if it had been done by her noble relations, this would be the final word in any argument with Mrs. Bennet. She only wished she had known of this before Jane's birth, for perhaps young Bess would have been made more content by her own mother's milk.

"I believe my mother's generation was greatly influenced by Rousseau."

"He has been my influence, as well," said Elizabeth, who had been reading everything that could be found in the library on childrearing, as well as several newer volumes she had ordered from London.

"I will still seek out candidates for a nurse while I am in London."

Elizabeth shook her head. "There is no need, Darcy. We may find someone closer who is able to help mind the child."

"Of course, if you would prefer to interview the candidates, perhaps we should post advertisements in Matlock, and even Derby, after I am back."

"Yes, I believe I would prefer that. It is not that I do not trust your judgment, but this woman will look after our child – I would rather we interview her together."

"I understand completely, Elizabeth. But I do wish to point out that she must be a wet nurse. I respect your choice, and moreover, I am glad of it, but I must insist on this. She need not nurse frequently; just enough to maintain her livelihood."

"I do *not* understand – if you respected my choice, you would believe she should not need to nurse at all. The greatest importance is that she be skilled in caring for the child, not that she be able to serve as a source of food."

"I agree that the care she provides is of the greatest importance, but she should also be able to nurse the child."

"I do not know that we shall be able to find someone so capable of both in Matlock, or Derby."

"That is why I wished to find someone in town," he said.

"If you were not so insistent on her being a wet nurse, I do not believe it would be so difficult."

"I cannot yield on this, Elizabeth. I wish that I could, but I cannot."

Darcy exhaled sharply; Elizabeth could sense he was growing frustrated, and yet she felt her own ire raised, which was exacerbated by the moods she found came with her present state.

"I do not understand why you cannot. I shall nurse the child, and we will find someone to look after her, or him, and manage the nursery. The right candidate might see all of our children raised to the appropriate age."

"That would be a fine plan, but I must insist on this."

"You cannot insist on this without giving me a reason!"

"I would prefer not to."

"What sort of answer is that? You would *prefer not to*. This child is growing in my own belly right now. Do not my own preferences matter?"

"They do, Elizabeth. They are of the utmost importance."

"If they are of the utmost importance, you might respect them more! You might give me some reason, rather than pretending to listen, and then continuing on your own path."

"Is that what you think I am doing?"

"Did you think you were doing something else? For I cannot think of any other reason why you should insist we must hire a wet nurse!" Elizabeth stopped walking, upon exclaiming this, and turned to face him, defiantly.

"I insist, because if you die, the baby must have some means of nursing!" Darcy spoke in the agitation they both felt, he said it with an angry countenance that all but crumpled as soon as the words were out, and then he looked wholly overcome.

Elizabeth caught the full force of his words, and of his turmoil. Of course her planning for the baby had been simpler – she had assumed she should live. All of her thoughts had centred on a relatively simple notion: she would have a child, and she would live. Any alternative outcomes were possible, surely, but she had not brought herself to plan for them, or even to think of them, for after all, in such a scenario, she would be gone. Darcy, clearly, had not allowed himself the luxury of ignoring this possibility.

"I am sorry, Elizabeth," he said, hoarsely. "You know how much I hate to bring about this topic, and I certainly did not mean to do so in such a way."

"It is I who should be sorry," she said, laying her hand against his cheek, and then kissing him gently. "I did not have that possibility in mind. Of course we should hire a wet nurse, to be prepared, if – "

"You need not say it. I do not even want you to be required to think of it. It pains me deeply to consider it myself, but I would gladly bear the burden of it, rather than have it be on your mind. You should think of your mother, and your sister, and that they have had six healthy children between them, and both live still."

"Six healthy girls."

"If I find myself spending this Christmas with a healthy wife and a healthy daughter, I can tell you with certainty it would be the happiest Christmas of my life."

"Mine as well," Elizabeth said, kissing his cheek and then taking up his arm, as they resumed their slow pace along the stream. "Although if her lungs were not *quite* so healthy as little Bess's, I would make no complaints, there."

He chuckled softly, and said: "Thank God your sister has come up with the solution for that particular problem."

Darcy's preference would have been to leave for London at dawn the next morning, for he liked the earliest possible start for travel. However, in deference to his wife's needing to sleep later as her pregnancy progressed, and her wish to see him off, his actual departure was a full four hours after he had broken his fast. The Bingleys bade him farewell in the entrance-hall, leaving him and Elizabeth to some privacy out in the drive, as they stood next to the carriage and made their own good-bye.

"You will remember the sheet music, will you not? Simple pieces, that Jane and Miss Kelly may learn with."

"You have reminded me of the sheet music at least thrice already, Elizabeth, and even if you had not, I would have remembered for the sake of preserving the peace of our household, not to mention my own sanity." He smiled, to indicate he was teazing her, although he was right; Elizabeth feared she was beginning to sound as fretful as her mother.

"I do feel badly that we have sent you on so many errands, in addition to so much travelling. I do not know how you shall bear it. The mere thought of it exhausts me."

"I cannot say that I am eager to go, but it must be done," he said, then murmured: "Perhaps this shall solve our dilemma as to when to cease marital relations, if you are notably farther along when I return."

"Perhaps you should delay your departure for another night, then. I was not thinking properly that last night would be our last time, until after the baby is born."

"Do not tempt me, madam."

Elizabeth smiled. "Maybe it is for the best."

"Maybe. Now kiss me good-bye, or it shall be time for dinner before I set off."

Elizabeth did as she was bade, trying not to think of how many days must pass before she could kiss him again. They embraced as best they could, given her belly, and she whispered, "Be safe, please."

"I will do my utmost. I love you, my darling Elizabeth."

"I love you, too."

With that, he climbed into the chaise, and ordered his postilion to ride on, looking out the window to where his wife stood, until the carriage made its turn. Elizabeth watched it roll down the drive with tears in her eyes, and only when it was out of sight did she sniffle, blame her excessive sentimentality on her pregnancy, and make her way back into the house.

CHAPTER 7

Georgiana awoke from what had thankfully been a shallow slumber, and found her husband still asleep beside her. She had not been sleeping well these last few nights, and found herself excessively tired during the days; last night, dinner with the delegation had seemed to wear on interminably, and she had feared she might lapse into slumber over the vol-au-vent. Fitful sleep, at least, was not deep enough for dreams, and she had not experienced any return of her nightmare of having eloped with Mr. Wickham.

Mr. Wickham. They had not seen him again, thankfully, although occasionally her thoughts would flit towards him. On this morning, she was struck with the vision of him on the battlefield at Waterloo, making his way among the corpses of the other soldiers, stealing their possessions. How long had he been about this task, picking his way through broken, bloodied bodies and severed limbs, reaching into the coats of the dead to take their purses? The thought made bile rise in her throat, and she was startled to realise it had no intention of returning to her stomach; she only barely made it to the voilder before she was sick.

Her rush from the bed had been neither graceful nor quiet, and she was still heaving when she felt Matthew beside her, holding her braid back away from her face, as she was sick again.

"You are unwell," he said. "Should we call for a physician?"

Georgiana felt the lingering embarrassment of having done such a thing in front of a man, even if he was her husband. Leaning back against his arm, she assessed herself. "No, I believe I am fine. I simply made myself ill. I was thinking about Mr. Wickham, robbing those corpses on the battlefield."

"Ah. The thought of that makes me a little ill, as well, but I wish he would not trouble your mind, Georgiana. You encouraged me not to allow him to ruin our day when we first encountered him, and he has surely ruined your morning."

"It is still early. Perhaps the morning may be recovered."

"I admire your spirit, dearest. Let us have a fine morning," he said, kissing her temple and then helping her to rise.

They broke their fast as they usually did, at the little table in their sitting-room, still wearing nightclothes and dressing gowns. They had planned on this day to call on Madame Durand, now that the basket of gifts they had prepared was full, and Matthew asked her if she still wished to do this. She replied that she did; she was feeling well, aside from still being a little unsettled in her stomach.

Matthew was dressed in what seemed a few minutes. His valet, Hawke, was a seaman who had been with Matthew from his first command, and held the role of steward on his ships, which had somehow translated into valet by land. He dressed his employer with brisk, seamanlike efficiency, and Hughes was still lacing Georgiana's stays when Matthew called out over her dressing screen that he would take the basket downstairs and meet her there.

Hughes finished dressing her lady at a more natural pace, and by the time Georgiana emerged from the screen, both her husband and Hawke had left the sitting-room. Bidding Hughes a good day, she made her way into the hallway, idly thinking of how much nicer this space was than the dim, narrow corridor of their first hotel. She turned the corner toward the stairs, and there found herself pushed against the wall, a hand clapped tight over her mouth.

Mr. Wickham! So startled was Georgiana, she surely would have screamed if she had been able to, but it died deep in her throat as the slightest little yelp. She trembled and felt her pulse quicken; it seemed her dreams come to life, and she willed herself not to allow him to see how frightened she was.

"A few minutes of your time, please, Georgiana," he said. "Oh, I am sorry, *Lady Stanton*. I am going to remove my hand. Do not scream, or you will regret it."

He removed his hand. Georgiana screamed, anyway, although she had not enough breath to make it very loud. She found herself slapped hard across the face for it. Shocked, she brought her hand up to her stinging cheek, and saw that he had produced a knife from somewhere, not so very different from the one in her dreams, and was pointing it at her throat.

"I would not try that again," he said, in a hardened voice she knew too well.

"Whatever it is you want from me, I suspect you will not get it if I am dead."

"You are much feistier than you were when we courted, Georgiana.

Perhaps I would have enjoyed being married to you. Certainly your figure has matured into that which is quite fine. There is not a dolly at Madame Levéfre's who could best you."

Georgiana glared at him as best she could, supported as she was by violently shaking knees. He was not holding the knife so close to her that she felt it an immediate threat, but she remembered him from her dream, saying he would not kill her, but he would hurt her, and thought it best not to attempt another scream, or to try to run away.

"So let us get about our business," he said. "I find I've had a few poor nights at the gaming tables, and I am rather short of funds. So you are going to get me five hundred pounds, and in exchange I shall not tell your husband of the more *intimate* details of our past."

"How do you think I should be able to get five hundred pounds, without my husband knowing about it?"

"I think with such motivation as I am providing, you will be able to find a way."

"Even if I could, and cared to, Captain Stanton is already aware of my history as it regards you."

"So he is aware, then, that we anticipated our wedding vows, is he? That we laid together as man and wife several times?"

"That is a lie, and you know it!" Georgiana protested hotly.

"Perhaps it is, but will your new husband believe it? I will tell him in very great detail of all of our escapades as we anticipated the marital bed."

"He will not believe you. He knows me, and he knows I would never do such a thing!"

"I would not be so sure, Georgiana. I see that fine little bosom of yours has increased with your womanhood, but I shall delight in telling your husband of how it was, in your younger days. And of course, those long, lovely legs. How very nice it was to be between such a pair."

"Step back, away from her, or I will relieve you of your hand," said a low voice, one that most certainly was not Georgiana's or Mr. Wickham's.

Georgiana realised with an overwhelming rush of relief that it was Matthew's, that there was now a sword blade between her throat and Mr. Wickham's wrist, such that there was no way he could cut her with the knife. Matthew had come upon them so quietly she had not even noticed the sword until it was there, a few inches away from her throat, but its proximity did not frighten her; the blade did not waver at all, and when she moved her eyes to look at Matthew's countenance, she saw a determination there that matched the steadiness of his grip.

Slowly, Mr. Wickham stepped away from her, followed by the sword's blade, and Georgiana felt her knees finally give way; they could no longer support her, and she sank heavily to the floor. When she looked up, she saw Wickham's back was now against the wall opposite her, and Matthew had the point of the sword – Captain Durand's sword – pressed against Wickham's throat.

"Drop the knife," Matthew said, and Mr. Wickham did as he was bade, now looking every bit as frightened as Georgiana had been, minutes earlier.

Matthew continued, in a calm, cold voice that startled Georgiana: "Allow me to make this very clear to you – if you slander my wife again, or lay so much as another finger on her, I will have you on the next naval ship bound for England, so you may hang as a deserter."

"I doubt the French government will simply allow you to take a lawful inhabitant home to be hanged."

"The French government knows not that you are here, and it will know not that you are gone, bundled up and smuggled into the hold, where you may contemplate how many days you have left before the gallows, down there with the rest of the rats."

Mr. Wickham made no response to this; he gaped stupidly for a little while, and then Matthew said, "Leave this place, and give us a wide berth, if you are to stay in Paris."

Thus dismissed, Wickham slunk away from Matthew, who continued to point the sword at him. Only when Georgiana could hear the pounding of Mr. Wickham's boots down the stairs did Matthew turn to her, and with a rapid return of tenderness to his countenance, kneel down beside her.

"Are you hurt?" he asked, taking up her hand.

"No, just a little overwhelmed."

He reached out to caress her cheek, and had the misfortune of choosing the one Mr. Wickham had slapped. Georgiana started, and found his hand instead on her chin, tilting her head so that he could see her cheek, which must have held at least some degree of redness, more clearly.

"Georgiana, did he hit you?"

"He slapped me," she whispered.

All of the anger returned to his face, instantly, his eyes hardening. "I will have to call him out; it must be done, although he is even lower than I thought, to have done *that*. I will cut his cheek to the bone for it, if ever I can, and every time he looks in the mirror, he may be reminded why he is the worst of men, to have struck a woman."

Georgiana had, until now, been too stunned for tears, but she found herself crying as she pleaded: "Please do not! He will know you shall beat him if he chooses swords, so he will choose pistols, and anything may happen with pistols. He is too low a man for you to die over. Please, Matthew, do not fight him – "

She might have continued to plead, but she found herself taken up in a tight embrace, so that she sobbed against his shoulder as he said, "If you wish it, I will not, my dearest, but I will make good on my promise to him, if he so much as touches you again."

Georgiana felt soothed, but she continued to cry for some time, overwhelmed by all that had happened, and relieved that it was over. When finally she stopped, Matthew said, "Let us return to our apartment. You should rest; you have had quite the ordeal this morning."

He laid the sword down against the wall, and then assisted her to standing. Georgiana found, however, that she could not remain so. It was no longer that her knees could not support her, but instead that she found blackness encroaching rapidly on the edges of her vision, and that she was overcome by dizziness; she would have sunk back to the floor if he had not caught her.

"You are unwell," he said. Supporting her heavily, he helped her back into the apartment, and over to the sofa in their sitting-room. Georgiana laid down there, still feeling exceedingly light-headed. She was not of a constitution prone to fainting; this was the closest she had ever come to doing so, and it troubled her greatly.

She now found Hughes, in addition to Matthew, leaning over her with an expression of concern. Hughes, however, had smelling salts, and was holding them under Georgiana's nose, a sharp tang that made Georgiana nauseous again. She waved Hughes off weakly, feeling once again overcome.

"Thank you, Hughes, but I do not believe I have need of those. I am a little better now."

"You should be seen by a doctor," Matthew said. "I will go down and ask that one be sent here. What is the word for physician, in French?"

A thought came to Georgiana as she recollected how she had felt over the last few days, and the symptoms she must impart to a physician, if she was to be seen by one.

"Not just yet," she said. "Will you bring me my letters?"

Matthew looked at her as though she was not right in the head, in addition to being ill, but did oblige her, bringing the little bundle of letters Georgiana had received since arriving in Paris. Georgiana untied the ribbon that bound them, and sorted through the letters until she found the one she sought. She skimmed Elizabeth's slightly wild, yet elegant hand, until she found the passage she had recalled:

"My dear sister, it has occurred to me that there is more about the married state that I should have shared with you before your departure, and did not. No one shared it with me in detail, and I was only fortunate that Miss Kelly recognised my pregnancy, or it would have been some time before I recognised it myself. So please do allow me to share the symptoms you might encounter, if you are to become in the family way.

"You may find yourself ill in the mornings, perhaps even so much as to need to evacuate your stomach. Fortunately, this does not last the entire course of the pregnancy, but it may be rather severe in the beginning. I experienced this, as did Jane. She complained a great deal of dizziness, and I have felt it occasionally myself. I feel even more a great pervading tiredness, regardless of how much I sleep, and this may sound odd, but I have found my dreams to be far more vivid. You will also likely grow fuller in the bosom; that is how Miss Kelly noticed it, at first, for me. She said my stays did not lace up as tight as they had before. You may already know this, but the surest sign is that you miss your courses, although you may experience these other symptoms even before you have such a confirmation of your state."

Georgiana rested the letter on her lap and exhaled, deeply. "How long have we been in Paris?" she asked.

"A day shy of three fortnights, I believe," Matthew said.

"I am at least a week late for my courses, then – I had lost track of time," Georgiana said. "Elizabeth wrote to me of the symptoms I should expect, if I was to become with child. I am not ill – I am pregnant."

Matthew's face showed every bit of the shock such a revelation must cause, and he asked, "So soon?"

"I suppose so. I thought it would take much longer, as it did for my sister." Georgiana was still stunned by the thought that she should have a child, and she wondered if she should be worried that the news did not make her so happy and serene as it had Jane and Elizabeth. Matthew, as well, looked more stunned than anything.

Georgiana was vaguely aware of Hughes slipping from the room, leaving them to privacy, and then Matthew asked, quietly, "Does this please you, being with child?"

"I find myself more overwhelmed, than anything," Georgiana admitted. "I suppose I presumed we should have children, and I would be a mother, but later, when I was older. I am not even nineteen, yet."

"I know what you mean," he said, clasping her hand. "And between us, we have only one living parent, who stands as a most dreadful example."

He referred to his father, The Honourable Richard Stanton, a rector who believed in a strict and – so far as Georgiana saw it – cruel interpretation of the Bible. She had witnessed first-hand the father's heartless treatment of his son, and had only then truly understood what had caused Matthew to leave home at a terribly young age, to join the navy.

"You will surely be a much better father than him," Georgiana assured him. "Anyone who may lead men as you do can surely lead a child on the right path."

"And you, who are all that is kind and gentle, will be a wonderful mother," he said, leaning over to kiss her forehead. "But right now you should rest, my dearest."

"Will you stay here, in the apartment?"

"Yes, of course. I assure you, Georgiana, so long as we might be in the same city as that miscreant, you shall never again be left unattended. I regret

I did not anticipate such a thing could happen, after we first met with him, so I might have saved you this distress."

"I do not see how you could have," Georgiana said. "And he might not have done what he did, if he had not gambled away his ill-gotten fortune."

"Is that what prompted this? I wondered what had caused him to impose on you."

"Yes. He wished to blackmail me."

"That much I gathered, from what I heard of your exchange. How he thought I should believe such a thing, I do not know. Beyond what I know of you, and your honesty, did he not think I was a participant in my own wedding night?"

Georgiana thought back to that night and could not help but flush in remembrance as she thought of how oversensitive she had been to each and every one of his caresses, and how nervously she had come to the marriage bed, given the differing accounts she had received from the women of her family. Elizabeth and her aunt Ellen had seen it as their duty to prepare her, but had been vague about what was to happen, and given their accounts with a goodly amount of discomfiture, although indicating the act would be pleasurable, with a husband who loved her so. Her aunt Catherine had been far more explicit about what was to happen, but had also indicated she would not like it at all, although she was to lie there and allow her husband to do whatever he pleased. Thankfully, the better parts of each account had been correct, for Matthew was not pleased unless his wife was, as well.

Georgiana had become lost in her recollection, but Matthew did not seem to expect a response. Finally, she asked how he had known to come to her aid, and he said Hughes had heard her scream, and snuck down the servants's staircase to inform him. Georgiana then asked how he had come by the sword so quickly.

"I had Hawke bring it down, with the basket," he said. "I handled things poorly with Madame Durand, when we called on her. I understand her sentiments regarding the sword, but her son will have little to remember his father by, as he grows up, and should certainly have his father's sword. That is what I should have told her, and I thought to make another attempt. I shall, when we do call on her, but we must save that for another day. For now, you should rest."

Georgiana herself felt the need to rest, even beyond the events of the morning. Her exhaustion seemed even greater, now that she had a true cause to attribute to it, and after Matthew kissed her temple again, and then moved away, she closed her eyes and quickly drifted off to sleep.

The days passed in what seemed an endless blur, until after some time, Georgiana began keeping a tally, notched in the wall plaster with a sewing needle. She took special care to increase it every morning, and yet it seemed to increase of its own accord. One morning she rose from her bed to find the count at three hundred and twenty, and this seemed to confirm what she had sensed before – that she had lost control of time, and it was spinning away from her.

Yet when she saw the count, she felt truly that she had been there for so long, and all the despondency that such a captivity must engender overcame her. She recalled glimpses of how her days had been passed, by reading the books packed in her trunk, or lying on her bed on the days when she felt too weighted down by despair to do anything else. She recalled her meals, of bread and a jug of watered wine, and those occasional times when Mr. Wickham was feeling generous, and would give her a little fruit or meat. She recalled being made to empty and wash her own chamber pot, and to do their laundry in a great cauldron in the main room.

She recalled all of the ways in which she had attempted to escape, and the punishment meted out for those attempts Mr. Wickham witnessed. She recalled her more subtle attempts at making her presence known, when Mr. Wickham brought girls home from the local inn, and how he told them he was required to care for his wife, who had gone insane after their wedding and should not be listened to. She recalled watching him with one of the girls, through the keyhole of the door, and better understanding what he had wished to do on her wedding night, although she could not see why this girl should like it so much. She recalled a few times when Mr. Wickham looked at her as he had on their wedding night, and how she had feared he would decide to claim his rights as a husband.

She recalled the day he violently pulled a section of hair from her head and sliced through it cleanly with his knife, mockingly telling her that he wished for a lock of his wife's hair. She recalled his impatience at what he referred to as her brother's stubbornness. She recalled begging to be allowed to write to her brother again, or even just to read his letters, and being slapped in response, and told to be silent.

It was not as though Mr. Wickham was not earning money, for she remembered as well that he had lied his way into a position as a steward for an elderly estate owner, Mr. Thornfield, and had somehow managed to keep it. Yet Mr. Wickham lost his money as easily as he came by it, and Georgiana suspected he was in debt, although he would never speak of it to her. He spoke to her rarely of anything, except to command her to do something, and to complain of his missing thirty thousand pounds. Georgiana would have gladly given it up to him, for she desired nothing more than to return to Pemberley, to have those luxuries she had never considered luxuries: a hot meal, a bath, a comfortable room to sleep in.

The cottage door slammed shut, and Georgiana pretended to continue to be interested in her book, lying there on the bed and waiting until the door opened and he appeared, holding a jug and the plate containing her bread, and a handful of blackberries. He picked up the old plate and jug from her previous meal, and said:

"Mr. Thornfield thinks to send me to Jamaica, to look after his plantation there, and that means you shall have to go as well, given your brother remains so obstinate. I look forward to it, actually. A man might make a fortune in the West Indies, and the fortune I am rightly owed is still not forthcoming."

"Mr. Wickham, I beg you, please do not make me go with you. Will you keep me in captivity forever? Your object is achieved, but your aim is not met. Fitzwilliam can be very stubborn; he will not move on this. You will only have to bear the additional expense of my passage, and board, once we arrive."

"You are right that your brother is very stubborn, but so am I. So long as he is alive, you shall not see him, unless he gives me my due. As for the cost of your passage, Mr. Thornfield has provided for yours as well, knowing as he does how I care for my poor, crazy wife."

Georgiana knew she would cry – she could hardly avoid it, at the thought of being forced to leave England, and taken farther away from her brother – but she willed herself not to do so in his presence. "Is there anything I might do to change your mind? May I write to Fitzwilliam again, to persuade him?"

"No, you may not. He will have no more word from you until he is serious about handing over your dowry. You may begin packing your trunk, however. We leave in three days." With that, he closed the door and locked it.

Georgiana was too preoccupied with this change in her situation to eat, or pack her trunk. If she left England, she felt certain she would never return home, but the journey might provide some opportunity to escape. If she could not escape, perhaps she could at least get a letter to her brother, so Fitzwilliam would know of her removal to Jamaica.

If there was to be a letter sent, however, there would have to be a letter written, and she had not been allowed ink and paper since that lone letter to her brother. Glancing down at her plate, however, she realised she had what she needed to make an ink.

Such an operation was too dangerous to conduct while Mr. Wickham was at home, so she hid the blackberries in a corner of her trunk. When next he left the cottage, she removed them and set about mashing them into an ink, using the lip of the jug so as not to stain her hands. This took a very long time, but eventually did produce something resembling an ink. Paper was not such a difficulty, for several of her books had empty pages, but for a pen, a hair pin was her best substitute, and it took a painful amount of time to write even "Dear Fitzwilliam," but she did manage it, and then continued:

"I can think not of how to begin this letter, other than to say I am very, very sorry for what I have done. I have paid the price for my mistake, and will continue to. I know how poorly you must think of me, but if I am able to get this letter to you, I must beg of your brotherly love and assistance.

"I have been locked in a room in a little cottage since shortly after my marriage. I know not where the cottage is, but Mr. Wickham has been working as a steward for a man he calls Mr. Thornfield, although this may not be his real name. Mr. Thornfield now intends to send Mr. Wickham to Jamaica, and I am to pack my trunk to leave.

"Dear brother, if ever there is a way for you to intercept us, I beg you to do so. I care not for my dowry. I want only to come home to Pemberley and see you again, if you can still be brought to have any affection for me, after what I have done.

"Your devoted and regretful sister,

"GEORGIANA"

The watery blackberry ink had bled through the paper, and so Georgiana wrapped it in another page torn from her book, addressed to her brother at Pemberley, and folded them together. She had no wax to seal the letter, and so stitched it up carefully with a needle and thread – then hid it within the pages of the book. When it came time to leave the cottage, she would tuck it into her stays, along with the few coins she had managed to keep hidden from Mr. Wickham, and hope for some opportunity to post it during the journey.

Now that the letter was done, she turned her mind to escape, searching the room again for any means to do so. But the door and its lock were firm, and the windows had been boarded up, leaving only an opening far too small for Georgiana to fit through. She stood on the chair and pulled at the top plank with all her strength, anyway, but it did not yield. It never had.

Mr. Wickham returned home, and once again unlocked her door and stood there with her dinner. Instead of exchanging the plate and jug, however, he placed them on the floor and locked the door behind him. Georgiana sat rigidly on the bed, afraid of what he would do next, but he did not touch her. Instead – and far worse – he went to her trunk, and opened it, rifling through the contents.

"You don't seem to have packed very thoroughly, Georgiana," he said, his tone mocking. "But I suspect you have something new packed away here."

"I do not know what you mean," she said.

"I believe you do. You had sufficient means, and motivation." He reached her books, and placed them on the floor before him, opening one, rifling through the pages, and then another, doing the same. It was the third in which she had hidden the letter, and when he picked it up, she jumped up and grabbed his arm, crying out: "No, please!"

He threw her down with remarkable force, but although she was stunned, she heard well enough his triumph as he extracted the letter. Georgiana waited for him to tear it to pieces, but he did not.

"And here it is, in your sad little hand."

Georgiana sat up on the floor, staring at him and knowing she would never see her brother again, never return to Pemberley. The letter had been her only chance, and she should have kept it in her stays constantly, should have thought he would search her room.

"What do you wait for?" she asked. "I know you will not deny yourself the pleasure of destroying it in front of me."

"Destroy it? Why should I destroy it, Georgiana, when I have worked so hard for its creation? Oh, no, I shall absolutely post it, although I will wait a few days, so the date I am sure you have included gives it additional urgency."

"I do not understand. Why should you post it?" she asked, fearfully.

"*We* are not going to Jamaica, Georgiana. But since your brother will not release your inheritance, I have set my sights on a larger prize – Pemberley."

Georgiana trembled at the way he said it, and waited for him to continue, which it seemed he could not resist, in his triumph.

"I have an acquaintance, in the militia," Mr. Wickham said. "He thought to join the regulars once, but do you know what he said they toast, there? *To a bloody war, or a sickly season*, he said, and he rightly wanted no part of that. And do you know where some of the sickliest seasons are to be had? In the West Indies. So when your brother finally receives a clue as to your whereabouts, and it is in Jamaica, he shall hardly be able to resist going after you there. It is likely a man like him, never exposed to the common diseases of those parts, will have no resistance. If he takes sick and dies, then you, my *dear wife*, shall inherit Pemberley. Which means I, as your husband, shall control it."

Georgiana's shock and horror at this revelation were complete. She could never have suspected this had been his plan, in telling her they were going to Jamaica, and that he had intentionally given her the blackberries with her dinner, so as to provide her with the means for making an ink.

"Please do not do this," she whispered. "Please."

These were all the words she could manage, before she collapsed, sobbing, on the floor.

"Georgiana! Georgiana!"

This time, she was pulled violently from the dream, waking so disoriented that at first she did not know how she had come to be in a rather nice room, and who was shaking her shoulder so. In a few moments, she recollected herself. Of course it was Matthew shaking her shoulder, and they were in Paris, and he loved her, and George Wickham had merely accosted her earlier that day. She emitted an actual sob of relief, and sat up rapidly, so she could pull him into the tightest of embraces.

"Thank God it was not real," she murmured.

"You were becoming ever more agitated in your sleep," he said. "I did not know if it was right to wake you, but I could not bear to watch it any longer."

"It was very much right to wake me. It was a most horrible dream."

"This is not the first nightmare you have had," he said, pulling away from the embrace so he could look her in the eyes, concerned. "Would you like to talk about it?"

The thought of sharing even the subject of her dreams made Georgiana's stomach sink in shame. Yet while such an entreaty could be set aside once, in the darkness of night, Georgiana knew she should not avoid it now. They were not so long married, and she expected it would be hurtful to him, if she was not willing to share.

Georgiana sighed, and moved her legs so he would have more space to sit beside her, then said, "I have this recurring dream, which began with Mr. Wickham convincing me to elope before my brother arrived in Ramsgate. We go to Gretna Green, and are wed, and all that happens after is simply awful."

"My God," he said, taking up her hand and clasping it tightly. "He does not – "

"He does not force me to share the marriage bed, if that is what you were thinking. There is no sharing of the marriage bed at all, thankfully."

"It is what I feared, yes. It would have explained the degree of distress I saw, and it made me wish I had woke you at the first sign of it."

"If you have opportunity to do so in the future, please do," Georgiana said. "But my distress was of a different sort."

She proceeded to tell him of the nature of her captivity, of being deprived of nearly every physical and emotional comfort, culminating in Mr. Wickham's manipulating her in to writing the letter.

"It seemed so real," she said. "It felt as though all hope was truly lost."

"It must have been beyond horrible for you, particularly to follow what happened this morning. I did not think it possible, but I believe I hate that man even more, now."

"You would hate a man for what he does in dreams?"

"In his case, I do, for I can see it in his character to do all that you described, and I believe you can, as well, which must make the dreams feel all the more real."

"But they are not real," Georgiana said, firmly, as much for herself as for him.

"No, of course not. And I promise I shall wake you at the first sign of any distress, if it happens again, although I dearly hope it does not."

"Yes," she said. "Please do wake me. Please bring me back to you."

CHAPTER 8

Elizabeth sighed over her book, and wished yet again that the saloon was not so near to the music-room that the sounds from within were unavoidable. She supposed herself ungrateful for thinking such a thing, for the sound emanating from that room was the reason for Pemberley's no longer being exposed to the shrieking of Bess Bingley, and that the sound was produced by others was the only reason Elizabeth could even be in this room, instead.

The sound was the melody to "Twinkle Twinkle Little Star," which had been hummed by poor Mrs. Padgett as one of the few things that seemed to calm Bess, and then painfully transcribed to pianoforte by Elizabeth. Hummed, it gave the baby some comfort, but on the pianoforte, it utterly captivated her, even when played poorly.

It was played poorly with great frequency, for Elizabeth had – recognising its simplicity – made it the first piece that Jane, Charles, Sarah, and Mrs. Padgett were to learn on the pianoforte. This freed her from the need to be called urgently into the music-room every time Bess fussed, so she could play and calm the baby. Yet it meant she was instead subjected to the song on a continual basis.

Based on the current style, Elizabeth assumed it to be Sarah doing the playing, for it spoke of some attempt at refinement and proficiency, rather than the plodding, hesitant searching of notes that characterised both of the Bingleys. Elizabeth knew it would be several days more before her husband returned to Pemberley with Mary, but she hoped they would arrive as soon as possible. Sarah, at the least, would soon require new music and additional instruction, and although Elizabeth had initially taught Mary, she suspected her younger sister would take some measure of enjoyment in being applied to as a teacher, and thus have more patience for it than Elizabeth did.

As well, Mary's arrival would also mean the return of Darcy, and

Elizabeth missed him deeply. She had written to him – a tender letter containing little in the way of news, aside from the intelligence that the pianoforte continued to placate the baby, and that she had been instructing the new music pupils. His contained more, although much of it mundane. He had concluded his business at both Hoares and Drummonds, thoroughly reviewed all of the accounts at their London house, and called on those acquaintances who were presently in town. With all of these things completed, he was ready to depart for Longbourn. Although Elizabeth appreciated all of the news contained within, it was only the sentiments closing the letter that she reread frequently, filled with both love and longing as she did so.

Sarah's rendition of "Twinkle Twinkle Little Star" had ceased, and Elizabeth decided to take her book to the music-room, which was now the most popular room in the house. In that space, Jane was sitting quietly, with little Bess sleeping in her arms, and Sarah had already left the room. Elizabeth realised there must be some degree of awkwardness for Sarah, to be playing an instrument in a room where she was not invited to spend her leisure hours, and that if Sarah continued to be as dedicated a pupil as she was now, some accommodation should be made for her in the servants's hall.

As though Mrs. Reynolds had been reading her thoughts, Pemberley's housekeeper appeared in the door to the music-room, curtseying, and, upon noting the sleeping infant, making her way over to where Elizabeth sat with very soft steps, and handing over a letter.

"There's a letter come from Miss – from Lady Stanton," she whispered. "I thought you should like it at once."

"Yes, thank you, Mrs. Reynolds."

Mrs. Reynolds looked as though she wished to wait for the opening of the letter, to learn whatever news it might contain – Georgiana was well-loved among Pemberley's staff, particularly its housekeeper, and Mrs. Reynolds had not been entirely enthusiastic about the idea of the young lady's leaving home and eventually setting up a household of her own. Recollecting herself, however, Mrs. Reynolds made her curtsey to leave, but Elizabeth stopped her.

"Wait, Mrs. Reynolds. I had wanted to ask – is there a pianoforte, somewhere in the servants's quarters?"

"There was, ma'am. My predecessor, Mrs. Woburn, liked to play very much. But none of us plays now – excepting Miss Kelly, I suppose, now that she's learning. It's been moved into storage, these fifteen years or so."

"Do you think it might be brought out, and tuned and repaired, if repairs are needed? I should like for Miss Kelly to have an instrument more convenient for her to practise on, in addition to her assisting us with Bess."

"Of course, ma'am. I shall have it brought out, and send for the tuner in

Derby. Should you like me to have the pianoforte in the state rooms tuned as well? The music-room and blue drawing-room were just done."

"Oh, yes, I suppose so. Thank you for thinking of it, Mrs. Reynolds," Elizabeth said, by way of covering that she had entirely forgotten there was a pianoforte in the state rooms.

The state rooms were not something Elizabeth – or anyone else in the house, excepting the maids who cleaned them – gave much thought to. They had been converted over from other spaces by Darcy's great-grandfather when construction on the house was completed, under the hopes by that man of someday hosting the royal family. Such a visit had never occurred, nor was there any likelihood of it, unless there was some falling-out of significance between that family and the Cavendishes, which would preclude their staying at Chatsworth, and so the state rooms sat generally empty but for two purposes. The first was to provide those who applied to see the house with spaces that could be viewed when the family was in residence, and the second was to house any nobility who came to stay with them. Thankfully, the apartments had two bedchambers with separate entrances, otherwise Elizabeth was not certain what she would have done for her last house party, with two earls in residence; even determining precedence for dinner had required a look at Debrett's.

Once Mrs. Reynolds had left, Elizabeth turned to Jane and gave her a silent smile, for she had hardly greeted her sister upon entering the room. Jane's countenance was finally formed of the serenity that should be expected of her, that of a most kind-hearted mother to a baby who was not constantly terrorising the whole house. Jane was also as understanding as ever, and encouraged Elizabeth to read her letter, and share whatever news Georgiana should have.

Elizabeth thought it odd, upon looking at the letter, that it was addressed to both her and Darcy, for Georgiana usually wrote to them independently – although surely knowing that all the news of her letters should be shared between them – as they each preferred observations on different aspects of Georgiana's travels. It was also rather thin for a letter from Georgiana. With curiosity and a little concern, she read:

"My dear brother and sister,

"I hope I do not alarm you by writing to both of you together, but I have news which should not be delayed. Mr. Wickham is alive – Matthew and I encountered him while shopping today."

Elizabeth gasped, thankfully not waking Bess, but it was a sound that could not go without some manner of explanation to Jane.

"She writes that Wickham is alive – they have apparently seen him in Paris."

"Oh my – what does she say? Was he badly injured, in the battle?"

Elizabeth was hesitant to read the letter aloud before she had read it herself, for anything Georgiana should write to her regarding George Wickham would by its nature be sensitive. Jane knew the full history of Wickham's wrongdoings, but anything that dealt with Georgiana's feelings upon seeing him again, and was addressed only to her and Darcy, must be kept private. Therefore, Elizabeth paused occasionally to summarise for Jane, as she continued to read:

"He was very surprised to see us, and I believe if he could have avoided us, he would have. Matthew was not shy about pointing out to him that Lydia was in mourning, and Mr. Wickham said he had been trying to decide whether to send word to her that he lived, but I do not think he ever had serious intent of doing so.

"He did not receive any injuries in the battle at Waterloo. It seems instead that he decided to fall as his comrades were falling, and pretend at being dead for the course of the battle. When it was over – I hate to think of this, but I shall tell you of it – Matthew indicated he had robbed the dead of their purses, and Mr. Wickham did not deny that he had done so, which I can only take as an admission that he did, for he was dressed very fine, and gave no evidence of having any other source of income. Even if he did not do this, there can be no doubt that he is a deserter, having left the army following the battle and then making no attempt to re-establish contact.

"I hate to be the bearer of this news, although it will release your sister from her period of mourning. I suspect you would agree with me in thinking it might have been better for her had he been truly dead, and you must know it weighs heavily on my mind that I narrowly escaped the fate she now faces.

"Aside from that, however, seeing him again has not injured me in any way. I am merely glad once again for my brother's intervention, and that I find myself in a far happier marriage. Matthew and I are both well, and I expect we shall not see Mr. Wickham again.

"I hope this letter also finds you well, and that little Elizabeth is by now doing better. Please give the Bingleys my best wishes.

"Your loving sister,

"GEORGIANA"

Jane did not seem to mind that Elizabeth read the last few lines of the letter silently, so shocked was she by all that had come before.

"I can hardly believe it," Jane said. "There must be some misunderstanding. Perhaps they did not fully comprehend him, and he has been trying to make his way to Lydia."

"Oh, Jane, I wish for Lydia's sake that you were right, but I do not think so. Lydia and the Fitzwilliams spent a great deal of time searching for Wickham, after the battle. If he had wished to be found, he might have been found then, and if not, he has had ample time to make his situation known to her. Georgiana indicated he was well-dressed – surely he could have spared a little money out of what he devoted to his wardrobe to send word to her. Georgiana has no difficulty in getting letters to us."

"But Georgiana is with the official delegation."

"Yes, and perhaps I would feel more lenient towards Wickham if he had asked for her assistance in sending a letter to Lydia. But he did not, and I assume he will not. Jane, we must face that our sister shall – for as long as he lives – remain trapped in a marriage with a man who has no intention of supporting her, or even living in the same country as her."

"Poor Lydia! Will you write to papa with this news?"

"No. Lydia is a married woman, and perhaps if we treat her as an adult, she shall act more like one," Elizabeth said, hoping this was true, although not entirely sure that it was. Lydia *had* been quieter, since going in to mourning. "I shall write to her directly with it."

"But what if she decides to join him in Paris?"

Elizabeth could not imagine doing so; if she had been in Lydia's place, she would have been furious. Yet Jane did have a point – Lydia might very well find some rationale to justify his actions, as Jane had initially, and decide to go to him in Paris, just as she had followed him to Brussels when war had once again broken out.

"She might do so. At least if she does, Georgiana and Matthew are there. Perhaps Lydia's presence would convince Wickham to act more honourably, although it would mean we might not see much of her again, if Georgiana is correct that he cannot return to England."

"Oh Lizzy, I cannot imagine having to make such a choice."

"And you will not have to, because you did not elope with such a man," Elizabeth said.

Jane had not even once held a tendre for him, as Elizabeth had. She shamefully recalled having been taken in by his lies every bit as much as Georgiana must have been, although the lies he had told her were of a different nature, and had, for a time, helped to poison her mind against the man she now loved with all her heart.

"I hope you will be more sympathetic in your letter, Lizzy, or you should let me write it."

It was very tempting, to allow Jane to bear the burden of giving the news. Jane would likely be more kind in doing so, but also much less firm in indicating that Wickham had done wrong, and with Lydia receiving the letter, firmness would be of the utmost importance. Still, Jane's admonishment was a goodly reminder to be sympathetic, while also being firm.

"I will, I promise, Jane. I had better do so now."

Elizabeth considered writing to Darcy, as well, for he would want to know as soon as possible. In addition to his longstanding enmity with Wickham, that Georgiana had been the one to discover him alive would be very troubling to him. Elizabeth was glad Georgiana had given her reassurances at not being injured by seeing him, and that she had written so in her own careful hand. Perhaps it was better, though, that Darcy be able to see this for himself, and given he and Mary had likely already departed for Pemberley, or would well before even an express reached Longbourn, she would have to wait to inform him in person. For now, however, she had a most unfortunate letter to write.

The letter was written, and even given over to Jane for review, before it was sent into Lambton with a servant the day following, to be posted. That servant returned with not one but two letters from Lady Harrison, formerly Caroline Bingley, one addressed to Jane, and the other to Charles. There was no time for these letters to be read before dinner, but they were brought out following it, after Elizabeth had taken her turn on the pianoforte.

"Caroline writes that all is wonderful at Hilcote, and she is entirely settled in as mistress of the house," Jane said. "She is planning to redecorate the drawing-room first, in the style of Mr. Hope, and then the mistress's chambers. The rest of the house will follow."

"That is strange," Charles said. "She writes that her decorating budget will not cover a quarter of what needs to be done, and she is unhappy that Sir Sedgewick intends to put so much of her dowry into improvements on the estate, rather than the house. Oh – I suppose I was not meant to share all of that," he finished, his face falling.

"I do not know how Caroline would think you would not discuss it with me, at least," Jane said. "Will do you anything to intervene?"

"There is nothing I can do," Charles said. "Sir Sedgewick is her husband now, and the marriage contract *was* fairly generous, as regarded her pin money. I expect Caroline wishes to make more changes to the house immediately than they can afford. She would have attempted to do the same at Netherfield, if she had continued on as mistress of the house. And I can hardly argue with his putting more of the money into improvements on the estate."

"Still, I feel badly for her," Jane said. "She was so happy about moving there and setting up her household."

Elizabeth had never believed that true happiness could come about from marrying for the purpose of setting up a household. Still, like Jane, she could not help but feel a little sympathy towards Caroline, who had, perhaps concerned she was running out of opportunities as she grew older, married an ill-looking man without even seeing his estate.

Not too much sympathy, however. This was Caroline, after all, and Elizabeth suspected the rooms at Hilcote were more than sufficient, and Caroline simply wished to show away by redecorating them all, instead of seeing the money spent more wisely. Caroline would favour furniture such as that in Elizabeth's overdone bedchamber, one of the remnants of Lady Anne Darcy's more grandiose taste, although at least Lady Anne had been able to afford her own taste. Elizabeth thought again idly that she should begin her own redecoration of those rooms; perhaps she would make her start after the baby was born, for she was not in such a rush as Caroline seemed to be, perhaps because she spent far more of her time in the master's bedchamber.

CHAPTER 9

For four nights, Georgiana had gone to bed in the company of an exceedingly solicitous husband, who was as worried as she about the return of her dreams. For four mornings, she had been asked in his most concerned tone about whether they had returned, and thankfully her answer was in the negative, although usually followed by an unfortunate bout of sickness.

This fourth morning was marked with a steady drizzle, so that even later, when Georgiana was feeling better, they had determined they should stay in for the day. Georgiana decided she should apply her time to making her husband's shirts, while Matthew occupied himself with one of the pamphlets he was always reading, perhaps some treatise on navigation, or an account of some voyage or battle – Georgiana could not see the title from where she was seated, but assumed it was something of the like. They were thus when one of the hotel's footmen knocked on their door, and delivered a note.

It was from Madame Durand, its contents unsurprising. She thanked them again for calling, for their kind gifts to her, and for their assistance in the matter of her lands. As well, and as emotionally as Madame Durand's limited English could convey, she thanked Sir Matthew for making her reconsider her husband's sword, and what it should mean to her son someday. For now, it was packed away in what little storage space Madame Durand's apartment held, and the Frenchwoman had no notion that it had been used to threaten George Wickham's limbs and life, the day before it had been given to her.

Georgiana handed the note to Matthew to read, and he had only just finished it when two gentlemen from the delegation were announced. They were Sir Frederick Walcott, who had earned his knighthood in foreign service, and whose wife was among those in the delegation who had befriended Georgiana, and Mr. Roberts, the attorney with whom Matthew had been consulting on the case of Madame Durand's land.

"As I looked at the particulars of it, I believed it to be beyond my knowledge of French law," Mr. Roberts said, once they had completed their greetings, and Matthew had asked about the case. "However, I have found a French attorney willing to take on her case; Monsieur Laquerre's credentials are excellent, he has handled several cases of this nature, and his fees are reasonable. I will arrange for you and Madame Durand to meet with him, if you wish."

"Yes, please do," Matthew said. "Lady Stanton and I thank you greatly for your assistance in this matter, as will Madame Durand, I am certain. And we shall be paying his fees, as well as yours."

"The time I have spent on it is hardly worth a fee," Mr. Roberts said.

"Perhaps some French brandy, then."

"Now you know that is hardly a thing I can turn down," Mr. Roberts said, laughing.

"We came for another reason, as well," Sir Frederick said. "We have heard of an exceptional French gunsmith, across town, and hired a carriage so we might pay a visit. Should you like to come?"

Matthew looked to his wife with a guilty countenance that indicated he did indeed want to come, but did not wish to leave her alone.

"You should go," Georgiana encouraged. "You have spent more than enough time visiting all manner of ladies's shops; you deserve a morning spent in more masculine pursuits."

"You see, your wife can spare you," said Sir Frederick. "And I expect eventually Lady Walcott shall brave the rain and come to call on you, Lady Stanton, so it is not as though you will be without company."

In the face of such encouragement, Matthew indicated he would go with them, but not before he had summoned Hawke up to the room to attend his wife, which Georgiana was glad of. They both had lingering concerns of Mr. Wickham returning, but Hawke's burly presence made her feel as safe as she would have if her husband remained, although not so comfortable.

The gentlemen left, and Hawke went to stand in the corner, eyeing her work on the shirt with some manner of jealousy. Matthew had told her that Hawke had grudgingly acknowledged her right as his wife to make his shirts, but Hawke was not particularly happy about it.

When the footman once again knocked on the door to announce a caller, Georgiana assumed it would be Lady Walcott. Instead, however, he said: "A gentleman, is to call on Sir Matthew and Lady Stanton."

Georgiana grew tense, fearing Mr. Wickham had returned – for who else should refuse to give his name? – and was glad Hawke moved to stand by the door. She informed the footman in her best French to tell the gentleman they were not receiving unidentified callers.

He nodded and closed the door, and Hawke remained standing beside it, in case Wickham should now attempt to force his entrance. After what seemed a long time, the footman once again knocked, and now said: "Colonel Fitzwilliam, is to call on Sir Matthew and Lady Stanton."

"Oh! Please send him in!" Georgiana exclaimed. She repeated herself more properly in French, and the footman withdrew.

It was only when Hawke said to her, "If he ain't wearin' a colonel's uniform, you say the word to me, and I'll throw 'm out," that Georgiana felt any degree of concern over this being a new attempt by Mr. Wickham to gain entry. After all, she had received no word from Edward or any of the Fitzwilliams that he should be in Paris; the last she had heard of him, he was still on leave and living with the family at Stradbroke, trying to determine whether he would sell his commission.

The man who came through the door, however, was most assuredly Edward. He was dressed in his uniform, with the left sleeve pinned to his coat, owing to the arm he had lost at Waterloo, so that Hawke should have no need of any reassuring word from her. Georgiana ran forward and embraced him, ignoring the wave of dizziness that came from moving too quickly, and by the time she released him, Hawke had quietly removed to the corner of the room.

"Edward, this is quite a surprise! How have you come to be in Paris?"

"I had meant it to be even more of a surprise, but I see you are taking caution in a strange city, which is wise. I should have thought of it, and not attempted to call in a way that might distress you. Is Matthew out?"

"Yes, he is, and we have been taking greater care for caution, of late," Georgiana said, motioning for him to take a seat with her. "I do not think you will have heard yet from my brother that Mr. Wickham is alive, and here in Paris. It seems he deserted the army and found his way here."

Edward did not look entirely shocked by this intelligence. "I had always thought that a possibility. Not, particularly, that he should surface in Paris, but that he would desert and abandon his responsibilities. Waterloo was quite an opportunity to do so. But how has this been cause for caution on your part? Has he imposed himself on you?"

Georgiana sighed and said that he had, and then told Edward in more detail of both of their encounters with Mr. Wickham – leaving out, of course, all of her dreams. When she had finished, Edward looked as furious as Matthew had been, and said: "Well, I expect your brother will be pleased to know he granted his consent to a man who would threaten Wickham with a sword, but still, it must have been very distressing for you."

"I cannot deny that it was, although I have not written to Fitzwilliam about his accosting me, and I hope you will not, either. I do not wish to worry him. The moment was frightening, but it has passed, and I believe Matthew scared Mr. Wickham well enough that he shall not return to bother either of us."

"I hope that is the case," Edward said, not looking entirely convinced that Fitzwilliam should not be told of the incident.

"Let us speak of other things," Georgiana said. "You still have not told me how you came to be in Paris."

"It is certain the peace treaty will include an army of occupation," he said. "I would not have thought I qualified, but it seems that so long as I am able to write, I am of some use at present, and so I was encouraged to return to my duty here. I harbour no illusions that this can continue to be my life's career, but I am happy enough to earn my pay here for now, until my future is a little more decided."

Georgiana gazed at him with sympathy, and was glad she had not told him Matthew was absent because he had gone off to a gunsmith's shop. "What are you considering, for your future beyond the army?"

"It is not so much what I am considering, as what is being considered for me," Edward said. "There is fairly serious correspondence between my parents and Lady Catherine, that I should marry Anne."

"Marry my cousin Anne?"

"It surprises you as it surprised me, when it was first put to me. But you must admit, there is a great deal of sense in it. I must marry an heiress; Anne must marry someone sensitive to her health. Rosings has not had the returns it should for some years now, and I believe I could set it to rights, if I could live there full-time and give instructions to the steward that could not be countermanded by my aunt. Thankfully, it has a dower house, so Lady Catherine would establish her own household there."

Georgiana had always been sympathetic to Anne de Bourgh. While Georgiana had, by her father's account, been born a sickly baby, she had recovered and soon gained a healthy constitution. Anne, meanwhile, had been Lady Catherine's only healthy infant, but had succumbed to ongoing sickness throughout her life. At present, however, Georgiana found herself far more sympathetic towards Edward, who seemed to be very well convinced of the sense of marrying her, and it pained Georgiana – who had married for love – to think about it.

"Do you know what Anne thinks, of the possible arrangement?"

"She and I have written to each other of it – I am thankful we are cousins, for I know most people in our situation do not have such a luxury. Anne likes the idea of more freedom from her mother's influence; she has always longed to try the waters at Bath, and sea-bathing, to see if they might improve her health, but Lady Catherine's physician insists she would gain no benefit from either treatment. And Anne is very realistic in knowing she cannot bear a child; as long as I do not risk her life by requiring her to share the marriage bed, she is open to my – uhemm, seeking comfort – elsewhere."

"You are considering taking a mistress before the marriage is even arranged?"

"I forget you are a married woman, Georgiana, and not an innocent young girl, now."

No, Georgiana reflected, she was certainly no longer an innocent young girl, and almost certainly carrying her own child. She determined she should wait to tell him of that, though, for she wished to know more about this possible marriage to Anne, and news of her pregnancy would surely divert them from that topic.

"Anyhow," Edward continued, "the matter is far from settled. Alice is in the family way again – I do not believe you will have had that news, yet."

"I had not – that is wonderful news."

"If she has a boy, I expect things will move quickly. If it is another girl, matters will be more complicated."

Alice, Lady Fitzwilliam, the wife of Edward's elder brother Andrew, Lord Fitzwilliam, had borne two very healthy young girls in their five years of marriage, and so the family had every expectation that at some point a boy, who would be heir to the earldom of Brandon, would be born. This next child's being a boy, however, would make them all easier of mind. If Alice never did have a boy, and Edward married Anne, the earldom would die out with Andrew, or Edward, whichever of the brothers died last, unless Anne died young – which was a distinct possibility, Georgiana morbidly admitted to herself – and Edward was able to remarry and father a son. Such a line of reasoning led Georgiana necessarily to her own situation, and the thought that she was married to a baronet.

"I had not even thought about an heir," she murmured, only aware after she had done it that she had placed her hand over her belly.

"Georgiana, is anything the matter?" Edward asked, looking at her with concern.

"Nothing is the matter, I just – Alice is not the only person in our family newly in the family way," she said. "I am, as well."

"So soon?" Edward asked, looking quite shocked at her news.

"It is my understanding that it only takes once," said Georgiana, blushing furiously.

"Of course," Edward laughed. "Congratulations, cousin. I am certain you will be a wonderful mother."

"Thank you, Edward."

"Have you decided where you shall settle? I will confess that Lady Catherine is very vexed you and Matthew have not purchased a home yet."

"Yes, *the baronetcy must have a seat*," Georgiana said, quoting her aunt. "She has written to me about it as well, most vehemently. And no, we have not. We shall wait until we return to England."

She would not admit it to Edward, but Georgiana thought they were still very far from purchasing a home; she had not even convinced Matthew to set up a carriage. It would come eventually, she thought, and until that time, Pemberley would always be there for them, but she was glad to learn she was not the only one who thought things could be settled more quickly than they were likely to be.

"Yes, of course – I am sure you are enjoying Paris too much to turn your minds to such things. And I must admit a certain delight in that which vexes my possible future mother-in-law."

Edward stayed for some time, hoping he might catch Matthew upon his return; in their brief acquaintance, the two had become fast friends on the basis of their shared military backgrounds. When Lady Walcott was finally announced, however, he took his leave after the briefest of pleasantries, although promising to call frequently on the Stantons.

Matthew returned much later, carrying a case from the gunsmith and looking rather guilty over the length of his absence, for he had been talked in to stopping to drink a few tankards of champagne by Sir Frederick and Mr. Roberts. Georgiana assured him she did not mind, and surprised him with the news of Edward's having called. He reacted with dismay at having missed Edward, although it was likely they would meet frequently in the future, and Georgiana shared with him all the news Edward had imparted, finding he was, like her, most struck by the negotiations for Edward to marry Anne.

"I feel for him, poor fellow," Matthew said, "and yet I cannot help but be thankful I was not in his place. I suppose I could have been, if I had not been able to win my own fortune."

"I do not think so – I would have had enough that we should have been able to live fairly well. Not so well as we can, now, but well enough."

"Ah, yes, but would your brother have consented to such a match? And would you have believed me sincere in my attentions, if I had no fortune?"

"I believe he would have. He indicated to me early on that I was free to marry for love, although he encouraged me not to fall in love with a chimney sweep if I could help it."

Matthew laughed. "Well, I suppose I now know where I rank, as better than a chimney sweep and George Wickham."

Georgiana smiled, and considered his second question, recalling the three men who *had* pursued her because of her inheritance.

"As to whether I could have believed you sincere in your affections – I believe so, but I think it would have taken a very long time. Longer, even, than it did take us. But I believe your sincerity would have won out, in the end."

"I hope it would have, as well, although I am glad we do not need to test that scenario," he said. "I feel very fortunate to have married for love."

CHAPTER 10

When the post-chaise containing Darcy and Mary finally arrived at Pemberley, Elizabeth was the only person able to come out to greet them, aside from Mr. Parker, Pemberley's longstanding butler. Bess had been exceedingly fussy that morning, and they had all been taking turns at the pianoforte, playing to keep her calm, so that when Mr. Parker announced the carriage, only Elizabeth had been able to slip out.

Darcy exited first, and then assisted Mary down. No sooner did Mary have both half-boots on the ground than she said, "I shall go to the music-room immediately," and with a determined look on her face, and a thick sheaf of music under her arm, set out thither.

Elizabeth smiled, watching her, and Darcy said: "She has been most eager to provide her assistance."

"It must be rather like a dream for Mary, that her playing should prove so necessary."

The carriage pulled away, and Elizabeth found they were unexpectedly alone there in the drive, although Parker was likely just inside, waiting to open the door for them. Elizabeth took the opportunity to step closer to Darcy and tilt her head up for a kiss, and then an embrace.

"I missed you," she said, her tone indicating just how much this was so.

"And I you," he said. "You look very well."

"I *feel* enormous, and with the knowledge that I shall only grow larger still."

"Yes, I believe that is usually how it goes, when one has a child."

"Fitzwilliam Darcy, sometimes I regret that I taught you to teaze so well," she said.

"You could not help it, even if you tried. Someone who is by nature so good at teazing must necessarily teach those close to her, so long as they are receptive to the teaching."

"You were not always so receptive, but you have undoubtedly made up for it since we married."

"Well, allow me to make some manner of apology for it," he said, reaching into his coat, and pulling out a jeweller's box, which Elizabeth knew meant their jewellers in London had finished resetting another piece from the Darcy family jewels. "I had thought to give this to you later, but since we are unexpectedly alone, I cannot resist."

The jewels this time were garnets, set exquisitely by Hadley's into a necklace and earrings. Elizabeth found herself a little surprised that there was not some additional piece with the set – Lady Anne Darcy's penchant for more substantial jewellery had meant that usually what began as a necklace and earrings were turned into necklace, earrings, and hair clips, or a bracelet, or a brooch.

"This must have begun life as a simpler piece," Elizabeth commented.

"What do you mean?"

"Usually they have enough left over to create some additional piece. Is it you who suggests what the piece should be?"

"It is not – I leave Mr. Hadley to do as he pleases, particularly now that he knows how well you have liked his work. I only told him in the beginning that I thought you would prefer more delicate and refined pieces, and indicated some in the shop that aligned with what I thought your preferences would be."

"I do, I like his work very well, these pieces included," she said, kissing him again. "Thank you, my love, for I would have been pleased merely to have you home again, but that you have come bearing jewellery makes your return all the more wonderful. Now you must be tired; come inside and change, and I shall meet you in our sitting-room, and tell you of some news I received while you were gone."

She took up his arm as they began their walk inside, and he said, hesitantly, "Is this news of yours good, or bad?"

Generally when such a question is asked, there is no reason why an answer should not be immediately forthcoming. Yet Elizabeth had no ready answer for him. It likely would have been best for Lydia, if Mr. Wickham had remained presumed dead. Yet could it really be considered bad news that a man who had been thought dead was in fact alive?

"I hardly know," Elizabeth said, finally.

"You hardly know? Then you must not keep me in suspense. Let us go upstairs and sit, but I shall change later."

Elizabeth could sense his concern as they made their way up the broad entrance-hall stairs, and over to the wing that housed their chambers and the private sitting-room that connected them. When they were in that room, and seated, she said, simply: "George Wickham is alive."

"Ah, now I see why you could not tell me whether it was good news or bad. He has written to Lydia, then?"

"No, unfortunately. Georgiana and Matthew encountered him in Paris. She did not know you would be from home, and wrote to us of it."

"Georgiana! Is she – may I see the letter?" His words came out in a rush of concern, and Elizabeth was glad she had succeeded in having this conversation here, where she might readily go and get the letter from the secretaire in her room, where she had placed it for safekeeping.

"I will go and get the letter," she said, soothingly. "Let me assure you, though, that she does not seem to have been affected by the encounter."

Elizabeth moved as quickly as her present state would allow, in retrieving the letter, and giving it over to him. He was silent for a while as he read, and then finally he said, "I suppose this is the sort of thing we should have suspected of him, and I wish deeply that he could have resurfaced somewhere else, so he and Georgiana would not have crossed paths. She has not seen him since Ramsgate."

"She is a very different young lady now than she was then, Darcy. She has married well, and for love, and I hope Wickham is but a bad memory for her."

"I hope so as well," he said, dubiously, placing the letter on the little table beside the sofa, and then seating himself on the latter. "Will you sit with me a little while? There is something else I wish to speak to you of, and I hope to go about it better than I did last time."

She did as she was asked, wondering if he was going to inform her that he had engaged a wet nurse while in London, and that the giving of the jewellery earlier had been an attempt to soften her on the subject. She felt sympathetic towards him, however, when he began to speak in a most agitated manner:

"Elizabeth, part of the reason I have been so concerned over your birth is that we are so remote here at Pemberley. I understand most births take place in town, these days, where the best accoucheurs are readily available to attend them." He held up his hand; he must have known she was about to protest that she absolutely could not live in town for the final months of her pregnancy, and then her confinement. "I know in your case it would be detrimental to your health, and therefore that of the child, to have your birth in town – I would never desire you to do so. Yet in London, every possible assistance can be had. If a wet nurse is – is found to be necessary, I expect one can be engaged within hours, well before the child's health would suffer from the lack of sustenance."

"I understand," Elizabeth said. "Now that I know your reasons, I agree the responsible thing to do would be to hire someone before the birth."

"Then I hope you will agree that the responsible thing was also to do what I did while in town, which was to inquire with Dr. Whittling on whether he would be able to attend you here at Pemberley. He was not willing to leave his London practice for more than a month, and so I have engaged him for a fortnight before and a fortnight after the date he believes you due to have the child. He will bring with him an experienced monthly nurse – I understand he has several he works with – to aid in the birth, and then assist you after he has returned to London."

Elizabeth had assumed their local physician, Dr. Alderman, would attend her birth, as he had Jane's, and although Darcy must have thought she would react angrily over his engaging her accoucheur for the birth, in truth she was touched, rather than angry. Touched, and staggered over his willingness to engage someone for a month who received a substantial sum for one appointment.

"Darcy, the cost of his services for so long must be incredible," she said.

"Have you no objections other than the cost? It is well within our means, and even if it was not, I would consider it a good and prudent expenditure."

"No, I have no other objections. If you are willing to bear the cost, it would make my mind easier to have someone with his experience attending me."

"Mine as well, as you might have presumed," he said, smiling faintly. "I promise, I shall vex you much less with my worries if they are alleviated in this way."

"You are fortunate to have such an income to spend, in alleviating your worries. Most men do not have such a luxury."

"I am well aware of it, and I sympathise with them, yet I *can* spend such sums, and I would not hold back one guinea or a thousand, to be spent on the protection of those two creatures most precious to me in this world."

Elizabeth felt tears spring to her eyes at his words – she had no teasing retort for this, and instead, laid her hand upon his cheek and kissed him deeply. Her kiss was most passionately returned, but rather than push her back to make use of the sofa as they might have even a fortnight ago, Darcy restrained himself to pressing his cheek against hers, and slipping a hand between them, to rest upon her belly, and they remained thus for quite some time.

Mary finished Mozart's Twelve Variations on "Ah vous dirai-je, Maman" with some measure of triumph, for she had arrived in the music-room to find little Bess fussing, and Jane plodding away at "Twinkle Twinkle Little Star," and now, happily, the baby was sound asleep. Mary had included this song with the music she had brought, thinking it was well-suited for playing to a baby, and was pleased to see she was correct, and that the baby was better placated by this more sophisticated rendering of the song she had been hearing so frequently over the last week or so.

How strange it had been, to receive the letter summoning her back to

Pemberley, where her skills on the pianoforte were desperately needed. There was something very pleasing about knowing her playing was not only appreciated, but necessary, and then to come in and take Jane's place at the very fine pianoforte and calm the baby in less than a quarter-hour's time. It felt perhaps a little heroic, to Mary.

It was not as though she was what most people would consider an hero, someone like Captain Stanton, out fighting French naval ships, but still, she did feel herself to be a bit of an heroine, and rather liked it. The thought of Captain Stanton, however, made her blush. Mary had no feelings towards him aside from familial friendship, but thinking of Captain Stanton necessarily led her thoughts to his elder brother, David Stanton, and her feelings towards him were quite unsettled.

In her more honest moments with herself, she knew that while she would have come to Pemberley anyway – she could hardly say no, when her sister had written in such a flattering way to ask – she had come eagerly because it would put her within less than fifty miles of his living at Wincham. She had come with no promise that she would see him at Pemberley, although Elizabeth *had* noted how often the two of them conversed, during Mary's last visit here, and indicated she would look for opportunities for them to be in company again.

Mary had never expected herself to be like this, hoping deeply to be in company with a gentleman of her acquaintance. Of her sisters, Jane had been the one expected to make a great match, and had; Elizabeth had entirely surprised them all by marrying Mr. Darcy; Lydia had not wholly surprised Mary, at least, by eloping; and Kitty had, as should be expected of her, become betrothed to a man who wore a uniform, although Mary did think she was much more rational now than she had used to be, and would marry a good, respectable man.

Of all of them, Mary was the one who had seemed destined for spinsterhood, unless her idle hope to meet a country clergyman she could be brought to marry should happen. She had a dowry, now – her brothers Charles and Fitzwilliam had increased her portion so that she had five thousand pounds – but she did not like the actions required of making a match, nor most of the men she would have met in the places where it was expected matches would be made. Mary was not one for flirtations in drawing-rooms, and she did not care for balls and dancing. She had come up with her parents and Catherine for Georgiana's wedding and Jane's birth, and had been content to quietly blend into the background of the ever-growing house party, unless she was invited to exhibit in the music-room.

To her surprise, however, she had found herself accompanied quietly there in the background by Mr. Stanton, and eventually they had begun talking to each other. From there, it was not long before they were seeking each other out for conversation, and Mary came to realise there was no one she enjoyed talking with so much as him. For so long, she had sought someone who would be willing to do something so simple as discuss Fordyce's Sermons with her, without placating her opinions, and he had done that, at great length. He had followed these discussions by recommending a few other volumes for her to read, and they had enlisted Mr. Darcy to help find them within Pemberley's vast library, pleased to encounter two of the books almost immediately.

Mary had read them both, and brought them back with her so they could be returned. Yet what she really wanted was to be able to discuss them with the man who had recommended them, and this she could not do. She could not write to him, and this frustrated her a great deal, for she suspected they could have carried on a very extensive correspondence. No, her only hope was that they should find themselves in company together again, and this was the hope that had brought her to Pemberley with the deepest anticipation, and – if she was fully honest with herself – the knowledge that she had met the country clergyman she could not only be brought to marry, but might very well find herself in love with.

There was a matter of some delicacy to be settled that evening, when Sarah had finished helping Elizabeth into her dressing gown. In Darcy's absence, she had been sleeping in her own bedchamber, and was not sure if she should continue to do the same. They had agreed to give up marital relations upon his return, but she was unsure whether she wished to also give up sleeping beside him, and of his feelings on the matter.

She decided that regardless of how their sleeping arrangements should be settled, she would wish him good-night at the least, and made her way into his bedchamber. Darcy looked surprised, but pleased, at her entrance, and said, "I was not sure whether to expect you, given our conversation before I left."

"I am not sure whether I will stay, but I thought I would at least say good-night."

"Do you wish to stay? You are not doubtful of my ability to hold my hands to myself, are you?"

"I am not doubtful of that," said she, smilingly. "I know if you set your mind to it, you would be able to. I am not certain of how torturous it would be for you, though, and to answer your first question, I do wish to stay – I have missed you terribly."

"If you keep teazing me with that look upon your face, it would be very torturous indeed."

"I was not aware there was a particular look on my face. How horrid."

"There nearly always is, although it does not follow that it is horrid. If I did not find you beautiful when you were teazing, you can hardly imagine I would have asked you to marry me, twice."

"If I kiss you right now, do you think we will be able to hold firm to our resolution?"

"I think it would be a worthwhile test of our ability to do so."

Elizabeth needed no further convincing, and they shared one of those lingering, private kisses which are only for the bedchamber, and afterwards stood there awhile in each other's arms. Darcy murmured, "I have missed you terribly as well, my darling Elizabeth," and without any further discussion on the matter, they both got into bed, although Elizabeth was careful to keep to her own side.

"How did you find things at Longbourn?" she asked.

"I told you all of it at dinner."

"Yes, but with the rest of our family there. I was not certain if there was anything you held back, for the sake of Jane and Mary."

"No, nothing. I will own that I am glad your letter regarding Wickham did not arrive while I was there, however. I can hardly imagine what sort of reaction it will provoke, but surely it will not be a peaceful one."

"Very true. I do not know whether Lydia will be angry, or heartbroken. Perhaps both," Elizabeth said. "Poor Lydia; her punishment has been far greater than her mistake."

"I am inclined to agree with you," he said. "I cannot believe I would come to wish a man dead, but I would rather he died at Waterloo than live and shirk his responsibilities as he does now. He is lower even than I thought, and I had already thought him the lowest of men."

"I suppose the only good thing to come of it so far as Lydia is concerned is that my mother will feel compelled to buy her new dresses, as I am sure she has dyed a great many of hers black, if not all of them," Elizabeth said. "And before you say anything, Darcy, if you are bothered by the look on my face right now, I shall turn over and face away from you."

"Please do, madam. You are a very cruel creature, but I love you anyway."

CHAPTER 11

After another week of dreamless nights, Georgiana was beginning to feel she was safe of her nightmare, so long as they did not see Mr. Wickham again, for doing so always seemed to prompt its return. She wondered if he had left Paris by now, although she supposed he would have to somehow acquire the funds to do so.

Although she had no stomach for breakfast, Georgiana still preferred to sit with Matthew as he ate his, taking little sips of her tea so as not to aggravate her morning illness. They were thus when Matthew said: "There is something Sir Frederick told me of, last night, which I wanted to speak with you about."

Georgiana encouraged him to continue.

"He said that once the treaty is signed, despatches will need to go to many of our foreign ministers, with new instructions. He suggested that by calling on the Admiralty at the right time, I might have better hope of a command – particularly a frigate command – as my leave runs out."

Matthew had no need of a command, frigate or otherwise; they could live easily off of their fortune, or perhaps purchase an estate. Yet Georgiana had known even before they were married that this was not something she would suggest. Since, she had seen with what an attentive eye he had examined the ship they made their passage here on, she had seen him reading his pamphlets during most of his leisure time, and she knew she could no more ask him to give up the navy than he could ask her to give up the pianoforte. So instead, she said:

"You do not think having two earls inquiring after you, as well as the Prince Regent indicating you should have the Caroline again, to be sufficient in ensuring you are given a frigate command?"

"You believe Lord Brandon will inquire after me, as well?" he asked, for the other earl Georgiana referenced, his own uncle, would undoubtedly do so, as he had in the past.

"I believe my aunt will remind him to, if he does not think to do so on his own," Georgiana said. "You very much endeared yourself to her in finding passage for them to go and search for Edward, after Waterloo."

"I did not do so for that purpose."

"I know you did not, and so does she, which is why she will do it gladly," Georgiana said. "But let us return to what you said about calling on the Admiralty at the right time. Do you wish to return to England?"

He looked relieved that she had asked it, and said, "If you do not mind. I know we did not set a date for our return, and I should hate to make you leave before you are ready."

"I would be ready to return. I have enjoyed Paris, but I find I have had my fill of it, and there are things about England I begin to miss."

"I feel the same way. Since we are in agreement, I shall begin inquiring about our passage back," he said, smiling. His face then fell, however. "There is one thing I wish we had been able to see settled before leaving. Madame Durand's legal case looks as though it shall take some time to be completed."

"She has Monsieur Laquerre working on it now. Surely he can see it settled."

"I hope so, but I should much prefer to be able to check on him periodically and ensure he is making progress. After all, we are only just acquainted with him. Perhaps Mr. Roberts will do so, although he is not of much longer acquaintance."

"You are forgetting we have a close acquaintance here, whom we may trust thoroughly."

"Edward! You are right, I should have thought of him. Do you think he would be willing to lend his assistance?"

"I feel certain he would, but let us ask him the next time he calls."

Edward called that very morning, and his assistance was requested, and granted, for he too thought it honourable to look after Captain Durand's widow. They all agreed to call on her the day following, and made their way thither in another hired carriage.

Madame Durand was sewing a coat for her son when they arrived, out of what appeared to be some of the fabric the Stantons had given her. She greeted them in a friendly manner, and was surprised to learn they had brought a third with them.

"I am having the whole of English military to call on me, am I?" she said, although smilingly, so they could see it was but a poorly worded jest.

"Good day, Madame Durand," Georgiana said. "This is my cousin, Colonel Fitzwilliam."

"Please to meet you, Colonel Fitzwilliam," Madame Durand said.

"And you, madame. I am very sorry for your loss."

"I thank you," Madame Durand said, nodding and indicating they should all be seated.

"We wished to introduce Colonel Fitzwilliam to you, because we will be leaving Paris in a week or so," Matthew said. "He will assist you with your case, and anything else you should need, once we are gone."

"That is much kind of you, Colonel Fitzwilliam, when you have less connected to me even than Sir Matthew and Lady Stanton."

"It is nothing," Edward said. "Were I better able to seek out those affected by my own role in the war, I would wish to do the same for them, but since I cannot, I would gladly assist someone connected with my family."

"Yes, on battlefield it is much more mêlée, all the people shooting at all the people," Madame Durand said.

The accounts Georgiana had heard, of the Jupiter's battle against the Polonais, had made it sound like it must have been a complete mêlée, at least for those on the deck of the Polonais. Yet this was hardly a thing she would correct Madame Durand on. If the poor widow had a gentler notion of how the battle had been, Georgiana would let her continue to believe in it.

"Mêlée is very much how it was, Madame Durand," Edward said. "Now let me ensure I understand the essentials of your case. You had land that was willed to you by your father?"

"My father did not have will, or if he did, it has not been appeared. He was taken up and killed in terror."

"I am very sorry to hear that."

"Thank you. So my father left no will, but I have no relations living, so it seem the land will belong to me. No one make claim on it, but nor can I sell it, with no proof it is mine. Those lands should have worth of six thousand of your pounds, I think. Enough so I can live more comfortable than this."

"Well, I promise you I shall do everything I may to be of assistance, while I am stationed here."

"Again I thank you, Colonel Fitzwilliam. And to you, my English friends. You have been much generous."

Georgiana and Matthew both nodded, and they all took their leave, promising to call at least once more before they left Paris. When they had returned to the carriage, Edward said: "You both neglected to mention how beautiful Madame Durand is."

"Is that an issue?" Matthew asked. "You need not take on the commission if it will cause you any discomfort."

"No, it is not an issue," Edward said. "I know an impossibility when I see one. Someone so beautiful as her should have no difficulty finding a whole husband, and one with more fortune than I, when her mourning is over. And by then, I may well be married to Anne. No, I mentioned it only because it shall make it far more pleasant to call on her. I know my expectations: I have become rather adept at admiring a pretty face, while knowing I may do nothing but admire."

CHAPTER 12

Upon Darcy's return to Pemberley, he and Elizabeth had sat down together and determined the inquiries for a wet nurse to be placed in the registry offices in Matlock and Derby. This was not a typical means of hiring on a servant at Pemberley; usually, when the estate had a rare opening, word of mouth would see at least a few qualified applicants express interest well before it could be advertised in any other way.

None on the Pemberley staff knew of a wet nurse seeking employment, however, nor did anyone in the Darcys's social circle. Much of the neighbourhood consisted of older families well past the possibility of needing such a person, and of the families with younger children, none knew of someone who should be coming available. This, then, left the registry offices – the same means by which Charles and Jane had found poor Mrs. Padgett – as their only option.

Fortunately, they received word that applicants at the Matlock office had expressed interest in the position, and following a rather aggravating several rounds of correspondence, it was arranged that Elizabeth and Darcy should meet with the applicants and interview them. They set out for Matlock, stopping in Lambton on the way to see if there had been any new post, which there had – a letter from their aunt, Ellen Fitzwilliam, the Countess of Brandon, who was called Lady Ellen amongst her family.

Elizabeth opened the letter eagerly. It had been some time since she had received any correspondence from Lady Ellen, who was by far her favourite aunt of those she had gained by marriage, although this was hardly a competition, given the other aunt was Lady Catherine.

"She writes that Edward has gone to Paris, to be part of what is expected to be an army of occupation."

"Must everyone go to Paris?"

"I believe only three members of our family are there, now, Darcy –

four if you count Wickham, which I am not sure that I do – so that is a bit of an exaggeration. Although I have not yet heard back from Lydia, and who knows what she shall do." Elizabeth continued to read, until she reached the next piece of news. "Oh, Alice is in the family way again!"

"Is she? I am sure they must be overjoyed at the news. Godsend it will be a boy – they still have ample time, if it is not, but I know it would make them all easier at mind."

Elizabeth sighed, and made to continue reading the letter.

"Do not turn my words into an indictment of you, Elizabeth, or a child who has not yet been born. You know Alice and Andrew are in a very different situation, given the earldom must be inherited through the male line."

Elizabeth felt the comfort of his words, and said, "Thank you, I believe I needed to hear that. I cannot help but think of how my parents must have felt each time my mother was with child, and how they must have reacted to each of us, upon learning they had another girl."

"Yet things have turned out well, even with five girls. Yes, Mr. Collins will take over Longbourn, eventually, but at least four of you will be married by then," he said. "And our situation is different, without an entail – if we have five daughters, the eldest will inherit Pemberley."

"Would you not mind that?"

"Well, I suspect you and I may have a few more spirited debates regarding the necessary accomplishments for females, if we are to have five daughters, but perhaps we can convince Lady Harrison to mediate in the matter."

Elizabeth let out a peal of much-needed laughter, but when she had calmed, said: "I did not mean the five daughters – I meant a female inheriting Pemberley."

"A female is presently the heir presumptive, so nothing would change, in that regard. And if she is *your* daughter, I have no doubt of her being able to manage the estate. I suppose I might request that her husband – if she marries – take the Darcy name."

"I think that perfectly appropriate, for she will be *your* daughter as well, and I should like to see your name carried on, to remind all our future generations of how I married such a wonderful man." With this said, Elizabeth leaned against him, to continue the journey in as much comfort as a woman in her present state could hope to feel.

The Matlock registry office was not a separate entity, but instead a side business of an attorney there whose services were sometimes used by Darcy for matters that needed to be handled more locally than could be done by his London attorneys. They were, therefore, greeted very cordially by the attorney upon entering his offices, but then shown into a side-room, where a clerk indicated he had received two strong applications for their position, and both women were waiting to speak with them.

The side-room had a tall counter where, Elizabeth presumed, those interested in jobs came to see what had been listed in the office. It also had a small sitting area, which could be curtained off; they were shown there, and the curtain drawn for privacy, although nothing about it felt very private to Elizabeth.

Their first applicant was Mrs. Beecham, who had been the wet nurse for Oakerthorpe for some years, but owing to that village having no babes now, nor any foreseen in the future, she was seeking employment with a private family. The clerk told them this, then drew the curtain aside, and Elizabeth's first impression of Mrs. Beecham could not help but be that the woman was slovenly. Ashamed that this was the first description to emerge in her mind, Elizabeth examined Mrs. Beecham more closely to see if it was something beyond the woman's sagging bosom that had prompted this first impression. In doing so, she observed Mrs. Beecham's dress, which was dirty, and torn in at least one visible place, and knew she would never allow someone who could take so little care of her dress to care for their child, particularly when it had been indicated that she sought work because she had no children under her care, currently. Mrs. Beecham should have had time to wash and mend her dress, yet she had not done so.

Elizabeth feared they would still have to go through an extensive interview with the woman, so as not to be impolite, but she could not think of anything to ask, and she was grateful when Darcy began the interview: "Good morning, Mrs. Beecham. I am Mr. Darcy, and this is Mrs. Darcy. How long have you served as a wet nurse?"

"Five and ten years, sir, alwus in Oakerthorpe. I did nae want to leave me place there, sir, but t'aint no babes, and I can nae go so long without nursin' as I 'spect t'will be takin'."

"How many children would you estimate you have nursed?"

"Oh, sir, nigh on five and seventy, I shun reckon."

"Thank you, Mrs. Beecham, that will be all. We are seeking someone who has had a more limited clientele, but we thank you for your time," Darcy said, quite surprisingly handing a few coins over to the woman. "Here is for your trouble to come here today. And you would do best to mend your dress before you interview again."

"Thank ye sir, thank ye kindly, but I dinnae see where the dress needs mendin'."

"The hem," Darcy said, simply, his tone indicating dismissal.

Mrs. Beecham glanced down at her hem in consternation, then made a hasty, embarrassed curtsey, and slipped out from the curtain.

"Did you just pay that woman so as to shorten our interview?" Elizabeth whispered, although she could not say she was upset he had done it; indeed, she was rather glad of it.

"I did. I could never countenance hiring her, nor could you, I expect," he said, glancing at her to ascertain he was correct. "She must have experienced some degree of difficulty to come here, from Oakerthorpe. Given the choice between making her believe the difficulty of the journey was worth the while, or paying for her troubles and saving our own time, I would rather pay for her troubles."

It was a strange philosophy, Elizabeth thought, to compensate for lost hope, but she could not fault it. The clerk, unfortunately, was not the recipient of similar kindness, when he stepped inside the curtained area. He must have had some idea of what was to come, based on the shortness of the interview, for he held a great degree of wariness in his countenance.

"May I ask why that woman was brought out all the way from Oakerthorpe when we were very clear that we did not wish to share our child's nurse with more than ten others, much less half of Derbyshire?" Darcy asked.

"I understand your concern, Mr. Darcy, it is just that such candidates as you look for are not easy to find, and – "

"If they are not easy to find, I would rather you be honest about it, and write to us as such. Do you think the master and mistress of Pemberley not to have better things to do, than travel to Matlock to meet with candidates who do not meet our qualifications? Do you think a woman in Mrs. Darcy's condition should be made to travel needlessly?"

"No, sir, of course not, sir."

"Is the next candidate within the qualifications we asked for?"

"Very nearly, sir. Mrs. Devaney has nursed nineteen children, but aside from that she fits exactly what you have asked for."

"Since we are here, then, we shall see her. But in the future I expect my instructions to be complied with precisely. Are we understood?"

"Yes, of course, Mr. Darcy, perfectly so, sir."

Mrs. Devaney was brought in, and immediately showed herself to be someone more suitable to be hired on at Pemberley, and for such a position. No one would call her figure slim, and her hair was rather greyer than Elizabeth would have expected for such a role, but she was well-kept, and very prompt and proper in making her curtsey.

"Good morning, Mrs. Devaney. I am Mr. Darcy, and this is Mrs. Darcy. How long have you served as a wet nurse?"

"Seventeen years, sir, and I hope to serve at least five more, sir, 'till my boys are fully established in the world."

"You have sons, then?"

"Yes, sir, two of 'em. Jack's been working in a manufactory for two years, and John only just joined him. My husband's been gone these eighteen years, now, and it's only been me and me boys, since."

"Have you always been employed with private families?"

"Very nearly always, sir. When my husband first passed, I took in several children in the village of Holmewood, where we lived at the time, for to make ends meet. After that, though, I sought private employment, and I've had it ever since."

"Whom were you employed with most recently?"

"The Johnsons, sir, of Matlock. Two girls I nursed, with them. Sweetest little things, they is, but the youngest is grown very nearly too old to nurse, and Mrs. Johnson says I should think of moving on, for she's not yet in the family way."

Elizabeth had, until now, been silent during the interview, but sensing that Mrs. Devaney, although perhaps older than they might have expected, seemed otherwise a rather suitable candidate, now asked her: "What made you choose to become a wet nurse?"

"I don't know it was a choice I thought on, ma'am. My husband died, bless his soul, and I had to support two boys while still in mourning. That I could nurse was my best way to earn a living."

Elizabeth found herself disappointed by Mrs. Devaney's response, although now that she heard it, she suspected it was a fairly common reason for choosing such a career. She had been hoping for some manner of enthusiasm about caring for infants, but if this was something Mrs. Devaney had felt at some point, perhaps it had dissipated after nursing nineteen of them.

"And do you find that all – functions – as it should – after so many years of nursing?" Darcy asked, so awkwardly that Elizabeth felt the need to steal a glance over at him, and saw he was utterly discomfited.

"Of course, Mr. Darcy, or I should not be thinking to apply. Allow me to provide a sample for your inspection."

Darcy looked utterly horrified at the thought of it, while Elizabeth felt a full wave of that horror wash over her. Even in the abstract, she did not like the idea of a stranger nursing her own child, and to think of inspecting this woman's milk, as though she was a cow for purchase, turned Elizabeth's stomach in a way that it had not been turned since early in her pregnancy.

"Pardon me," she said, rising. "I am feeling unwell – I believe I have need of a little air. It was good to meet you, Mrs. Devaney."

She slipped out of the curtain, and then out of the office entirely, making her way as near as she could to the Derwent and still remain in sight of the office, for undoubtedly Darcy would be emerging from there with concern, as soon as he could conclude the interview. The sound of the river soothed her a little, but it was not enough to fully ease her mind.

True to her prediction, Elizabeth turned back from the river, and saw her husband exiting the office with a great deal of haste. When he had reached where she was standing, he extended his hand and grasped hers, saying, in a most worried tone: "Are you ill? Should we have them fetch Dr.

Alderman? He lives just down the road."

"I am not ill in that sense, my dear. I just could not stay and listen to more of the interview. Did she – did she display her milk for you?"

"She did not." Darcy looked as disgusted as she was at the thought of it. "We ended things fairly rapidly after your departure. She hopes you will feel better quickly, with some air."

"I do not know that I shall feel better so long as we must continue trying to hire this position. Perhaps I was wrong to dissuade you from seeking a wet nurse in town. I am not sure I have the stomach to travel to Derby for additional interviews."

"Then do not do so. Let me go there and do the first set of interviews, and if there is a candidate better than Mrs. Devaney, you may return for a second interview with her."

"What if there is no candidate better than Mrs. Devaney?"

"We could do worse, I suppose. She is older than I would have expected, but I am more concerned at not knowing of these Johnsons. She mentioned several other families she has worked for, but I do not know any of them."

"Can we truly settle for someone neither of us is at all enthusiastic for? This is not a new housemaid we are seeking, but a woman who will care for and possibly feed our child."

"We may have to. Think on it, Elizabeth. I know you wish to nurse the baby yourself, and her nursing shall merely be a plan in case – in case of other events. If we promised Mrs. Devaney five years of employment, as was her wish – regardless of whether she was required to act as a wet nurse or not – I should think that a good situation for her. We may not find a better candidate."

Elizabeth sighed. "I suppose you are right, but I cannot manage any enthusiasm for the idea, at present."

"Nor should you have to, my dear," he said, squeezing her hand. "Now you have had a far more trying day than you should have. Let us return home and save our concerns over this for another day."

Elizabeth had concerns the day following, but they had nothing to do with finding a wet nurse. With the post on this day was a letter from Kitty, which Elizabeth thought might be a response to her news regarding Mr. Wickham's being alive.

Elizabeth was handed the letter by Mr. Parker as she made her way to the music-room, there to join Sarah, who had been playing for Mary and Bess. She took the letter in with her, finding her sister holding the baby and instructing Sarah on how to read the music.

In such a scene of busyness, Elizabeth was barely acknowledged by Mary, but given a more deferential nod by Sarah. Such an atmosphere was suitable for reading Kitty's letter, although Elizabeth would have preferred for Jane to be there; her elder sister would have been as concerned as she was about what should be contained within, which was:

"My sister and mother are too distraught to write to you in response to your letter at present, and my father will not be troubled to do so with any urgency, but I thought you would want to hear from us as soon as possible.

"Lydia at first denied the truth of what you wrote. She thought perhaps Georgiana had somehow mistaken another man for George Wickham, or for some other reason had made up this story. I assured her that I have always known Georgiana to be most truthful, and that from Mr. Wickham's (I do not see why we should call him George – I have no desire to be familiar with such a man, even if he is family) long association with the Darcys, Georgiana must have known him well enough to be able to clearly recognise him in Paris.

"Once she began to believe it truly was Mr. Wickham that Georgiana and Matthew spoke to, and that he had been in Paris without sending for her, she became violently angry. I regret to tell you that some of the pieces of your favourite tea set here fell victim to her bout of anger, which lasted the better part of the day. Papa made her go outside once she began breaking things – I tried to go with her and console her, but she said I could not be of any help to her when my situation was so different.

"She said some very cruel things following this that I will not repeat, as thinking on them again brings me pain. You must know how the season I spent in London and my engagement to Captain Ramsey had such an influence on me (and I am forever grateful to you and my brother for it). I have known for some time that Lydia and I cannot be so close as we once were, but still, I hate that the sister who was once my most particular friend thinks these things of me.

"Anyway, she would only be consoled by my mother, and finally I believe she stopped being angry – at least in the same way she was – and since then she has seemed mostly sad, and bitter. She is at least able to come out of mourning, but she truly did love Mr. Wickham, and I believe her heart is broken by what he has done.

"I will admit a little jealousy of Mary to be at Pemberley instead of Longbourn, for this is not a happy place right now, with Lydia as she is, and papa realising he will have to support her at least as long as Mr. Wickham lives. I am not seeking an invitation, however. Captain Ramsey's latest indicated that if all goes well, he will be coming home within the month, and while Hertfordshire is not exactly near to Portsmouth, it is still much nearer than Derbyshire. I cannot wait to see him, and to finally be married!

"Please give my sisters and brothers my love. Missing you all very much is,

"CATHERINE BENNET (but soon to be RAMSEY!)"

Elizabeth finished the letter with a mixture of emotions. She was glad Lydia had finally been brought to realise that Mr. Wickham had behaved in an unacceptable manner, although the heartbreak that must necessarily follow this realisation saddened Elizabeth. She had never understood how Lydia could love Mr. Wickham as she did, when he often treated her poorly, but had also thought it for the best that Lydia *had* loved him; it was far preferable to her being miserable, as she was now.

And poor Kitty, who had changed so much for the better over the last year that she had become someone who could not be loved in the same way she had once been by her younger sister. Indeed, from Kitty's letter, it sounded more like Lydia disliked her sister, now, or at the very least that she was jealous of Kitty's situation. Kitty had always followed after Lydia when they were younger; flirting with officers, and spending more of her pin money than she ought on frivolous things. Lydia's unfortunate marriage had undoubtedly been beneficial for her next-eldest sister, for it meant she had no longer been around to corrupt Kitty. Brought to Weymouth and then London to spend time in better company, Kitty had grown tremendously, taking up drawing and watercolours, and eventually even reading, although this latter interest centred largely on naval history. It was no longer a duty to invite Kitty to spend time with them; Elizabeth truly enjoyed her company, and felt her absence now.

"I suppose I should no longer call her Kitty; she always signs her letters Catherine, now, does she not?" Elizabeth murmured.

Mary overheard her, and asked what she had said, and what news was contained in the letter. Elizabeth told her of Lydia's reaction to Mr. Wickham's actions, but did not share the more private parts of Catherine's letter; Mary and Catherine had grown at least a bit closer, but Elizabeth was not certain if they were so close that Catherine would want these parts shared. If Catherine wished to do so, let her do it within her own correspondence to Mary.

Mary confirmed that Catherine's preference these days was to be referred to by her full Christian name, and then said, "As for the rest, it is unfortunate, although I cannot say it is entirely surprising. A man who would tempt a young lady to live in sin, such as he did, is capable of a great measure of sin. Not that I absolve our sister of her own part in the matter; she knew full well what she was doing, when she ran away with him."

Elizabeth wondered what Mary would think if she knew that Georgiana, who was undoubtedly more quiet and rational than Lydia, had very nearly made the same mistake Mary censured her own sister for. Jane was right, that they should put the blame more squarely in Wickham's quarter. Both young ladies, certainly, had been manipulated; Lydia had taken much longer to see the error of her actions, but it seemed she finally saw them now.

The matter of what to do with Lydia would now be what occupied correspondence between Pemberley and Longbourn. Catherine was correct in that she must be supported, and while he lived, it was natural that this support should fall to Mr. Bennet. As part of her marriage contract with Mr. Wickham, largely drawn up by Elizabeth's own husband, Lydia was to be allowed one hundred pounds per annum; this must go to Lydia now, and not her husband, who could not attempt to claim it in any English court. This income should have been sufficient for Lydia to live on, but Elizabeth's sister had always been frivolous with money, and Elizabeth suspected Lydia would be encouraged by her mother so that the hundred pounds were easily exceeded every year.

"Someday, we shall have to support her," Elizabeth thought. "Unless she takes up as someone's mistress, which I suppose is entirely possible. I only hope she can be discreet about it."

CHAPTER 13

Thankfully, even with child, Georgiana was not afflicted with seasickness. They had boarded HMS Rapid at Le Havre early in the morning, but unlike many of the other passengers, as the ship had got underway, she found herself feeling progressively better instead of worse.

The same could not be said for poor Hughes, who, as she had been on the journey to France, was wracked with a violent bout of sickness. Georgiana was glad they had taken this ship, a navy sloop-of-war, rather than the packet ship, where the captain might not have afforded them the courtesy of allowing a maid to lie prostrate on a blanket within his cabin, as Captain Gibson had.

Georgiana, having checked on Hughes again, was making her way back up to the weather deck of the ship. When she reached the companionway, however, the ship lurched violently, and she was forced to wait a moment to allow dizziness to pass before she could climb the steps. She did not like this constant light-headedness, but it seemed that it was going to stay with her during the course of her pregnancy, and she was going to have to take care to compensate.

She found Matthew where she had left him, standing at the stern of the Rapid, alternately looking down at the gently wobbling foam in the wake of the ship, and then up to examine the ship's rigging.

"Gibson is right – she is a crank, fussy little ship," he said, as much to himself as to her. "Whoever thought to name her Rapid clearly had no notion of her sailing qualities. How is Hughes?"

"Much the same," Georgiana said.

"Well, we are nearly there, so at least it shall not be much longer for her. You can see the Spithead anchorage, just up there."

He pointed, and Georgiana could see dozens of masts on the horizon. She watched eagerly as the ships came closer into view, for as they had made the passage over to France by way of Dover, this was her first opportunity to see Spithead, and then Portsmouth beyond it. Georgiana had never seen a naval ship much larger than the one she was on now, and as they drew closer, she was shocked at the size of the big ships of the line, looming over the little Rapid.

"I wish the Jupiter and the Polonais were here, instead of Plymouth, so I might see them," Georgiana said.

"I cannot say I share your wish – you would be shocked at the look of them, with their repairs incomplete."

"Still, I would have liked to get a sense of their relative differences in size."

"Ah, unfortunately I do not think the fleet will oblige you – fourth-rates like the Jupiter are rare. There is the Mars, however, and she is fairly comparable to the Polonais."

Georgiana looked at the ship he pointed to, and tried to imagine a smaller ship, one with twenty-four fewer guns, and the two of them engaged in battle. As she had never seen such a thing, however, merely heard it described, this was generally beyond her imagination. After studying the Mars for some time, she commented on the sky beyond it, which was a great fiery red, in possibly the most spectacular sunset she had ever seen.

"It is very beautiful," Matthew said, in agreement.

"Are they always like this, at sea?"

"They are often beautiful, and benefit from the uninterrupted horizon," he said, "but I have not seen anything like this. The redness is remarkable."

They drifted into the harbour, and Georgiana looked about eagerly, to finally see the place she had only heard described. Matthew was no less eager to show it to her, pointing out Southsea Castle, Spice Island, and then the Victory, rather elegant-looking for her size, and a sharp contrast to the ship Matthew was most eager to show her.

"There she is – there is the Caroline," he said, pointing to a set of ships, tied up side-by-side. "Third from the left."

Georgiana looked at these ships, all of them without their masts and looking faded and stumpy, and counted over to the third one from the left, which looked no more or less stumpy than the others. Georgiana had always longed to see this ship, the frigate Matthew had commanded for five years and held the utmost fondness for, and she felt disappointed by it, as she felt Matthew must have been disappointed by how long it took her to say anything.

"I am so glad to finally have a chance to see her," Georgiana said, when she could think of nothing more complimentary. "I am sure she must bring back many happy memories, for you."

"Indeed, she does," he said, fondly, "although I hope she shall soon enough become the source of new memories."

There being no quay for the Rapid to tie up to, Georgiana and Hughes had their first introduction to what Matthew called a bosun's chair, which was simply a plank of wood tied with rope on either side, on which they were to sit and be lowered down into a boat. Georgiana liked to think that if she had not been wearing a dress, she might have clambered down the side of the ship as her husband and Hawke did, although there was something to be said for the sensation of swinging freely out over the water.

Hughes came after her, looking very pale and eager to be on shore, and they were rowed thither. Georgiana had never been to a town so dedicated to one purpose – there seemed to be officers in uniform everywhere, and even more seamen, many of them staggeringly drunk already, even in the twilight hour. A few of them made some manner of obeisance to her husband, usually bowing and saying, "good evnin', cap'n sir," and Matthew would not pass any that did so without asking how they did, so that what should have been a short walk to the George took a very long time.

They were to stay only overnight, it being too late to set out for London, and Georgiana was so exhausted by the time they came in and took a room that she cared little for the fineness of the apartment. She found herself rather more cross than was proper at their needing to hire a carriage to go on to London, and although she had determined she would not say anything of it until they were in town – for London would certainly be the best place to purchase the equipage and horses – she found she could not help herself.

Poor Hughes had made her apologies and retired early, still feeling the ill effects of her seasickness, which left Matthew to unlace Georgiana's stays before they retired, and as he did so, he said, "I hired the post-chaise for ten, tomorrow morning, so we should depart after your illness is usually over."

"Thank you. I only wish we were not going by hired carriage."

"Dearest, I know we are in a port, but I assure you it would take far longer to go by ship. Even if we were to find a ship sailing for London tomorrow, it would be going quite the long way around, to come in through the Thames from here, and – "

"I meant I did not want to take a *hired* carriage, when it would be much nicer to set up our own."

"Georgiana," he said, stepping around so that he faced her, and putting his hands on her shoulders, "Do you wish to set up a carriage?"

"Yes!" she exclaimed, in exasperation.

"Then just tell me so, plainly. When my ship has need of something, I am told of it directly – I am not accustomed to subtlety, and I find I am not very good at reading it," he said. "I had thought we might wait until I know of my assignment, to see whether we would have need of one immediately, but if you wish that badly to set up a carriage, we shall see to it as soon as we are in London."

Georgiana bowed her head sheepishly. It sounded so simple when he spoke of it now, that she should have just said directly that she wished to set up a carriage. Nor had she thought of what would become of the carriage if Matthew did receive a command, and she was to travel with him.

"You must think me very silly, to be worried over such a thing," she said, finally, looking up to meet his eyes.

"I would never think you silly," he said, and reached out to caress her cheek. "Now that I think on it, I realise how important this is for your independence, particularly if I am from home."

"And I realise how unnecessary it will be, if I am from home with you."

"Do you still wish to live on board the ship? I will admit to some concern about being able to make the accommodations comfortable enough for you, particularly while you are with child."

"Is this because of the first hotel in Paris?" Georgiana asked, with a sinking feeling in her stomach.

"In part, yes, and also in part on having now seen Pemberley. I would fully understand if you would rather live there, or look for a suitable purchase. We shall have to do so eventually – your aunt is right, that the baronetcy must have a seat."

"I do still wish to live on board, or at least to try it. I have different expectations for what comforts I should have on board a ship, than in an hotel," Georgiana said. "And the delegation would have a certain expectation of us, I thought, in how they should be received when they called on us. There is a certain standard of living we should be seen to have, with our income."

"Ah, see, you are thinking of things I have not been required to think of. In the navy, one must only keep a good table to entertain well, and even that is proportionate to how readily one can come by supplies."

"So you are still open to my living on board?" Georgiana asked.

"Yes, of course, if you wish it. But let us see if I am given an assignment, first," he said, kissing her gently. "I am hoping for the Mediterranean; it has been some time since I have been there, and I believe you would like it."

They had any number of options, for houses to stay in while they were in London; Fitzwilliam would have opened up the Darcys's house on Curzon Street, if Georgiana had asked. But Matthew's uncle, the Earl of Anglesey, was active in politics and spent most of his time in town, letting his son and steward see to the running of his estate. His house was already open and ready for visitors, and Georgiana and Matthew were greeted enthusiastically as soon as the carriage had set them down at Margaret Street.

They were shown up to the bedchamber that had been prepared for them, and encouraged to change and then return to the drawing-room, so they might tell Lord Anglesey of all they had seen and done while in Paris. They did so, and he was also informed of Georgiana's being in the family way, and said all that was right and proper in congratulating them. In turn, he told them his son and daughter, also lately married, were expecting a child as well. Georgiana was particularly glad they had told him, for when Matthew took his leave to call on the Admiralty, and she said she thought she might go upstairs to rest for a little while, Lord Anglesey was quite understanding, saying:

"Yes, of course, you should go rest. My late wife was often exhausted, when she was carrying George. And – " he spoke wistfully, and did not complete his thought. Georgiana, not knowing what to say, only nodded gently to him before going up to her bedchamber.

She laid down for a little while, but did not sleep, and returned to an empty drawing-room, taking up her work on Matthew's new shirts. Lord Anglesey's house had not known the touch of a woman for many years, and Georgiana had generally found it lacking in comforts, but the one amenity the earl had installed was a fine new water closet, something Georgiana thought she might suggest to her brother, for Curzon Street as well as Pemberley, for it was exceedingly convenient. The only difficulty of it was that she could not remember which of the doors in the hallway led to it, and the door she tried first was instead Lord Anglesey's study, and it contained a most shocking scene.

There, in a very improper embrace on the chaise in the study, were Lord Anglesey, and the Dowager Viscountess Tonbridge. Georgiana knew very well what they were about, although up until now she would have described it as an act for the marriage bed; Lord Anglesey and Lady Tonbridge were neither making use of a bed, nor were they married. Georgiana's face grew tremendously hot, and she closed the door as quietly as possible, hoping they had not noticed her. She tried the other door, found it did belong to the water closet, and made quick use of it before returning to the drawing-room.

Her return coincided with Matthew's entrance, and he looked at her and immediately asked, "Georgiana, what in the world is the matter?"

"I – I accidentally walked into the study. I did not know your uncle and Lady Tonbridge were – having an affair."

"Oh yes, they have been for several years, now – I should have thought to tell you. And *they* should have locked the door," he said. "I suppose my uncle forgot he had guests."

"How was your call?" Georgiana asked, for she did not wish to think any longer about what she had seen behind the door that should have been locked.

"Lord Melville was out. His clerk made an appointment for me to return tomorrow, however, and did seem to indicate it should have a positive outcome."

"That is good, although I am sorry you have to wait another day."

"I am as well, but there is little to be done about it," he said. "I had actually been thinking of seeing if you wished to go to Clementi's shop as a distraction; it seems now you may be in need of a distraction, as well."

"Looking at music is precisely the sort of distraction I could use right now."

"Let us go, then – the carriage is still outside."

The Clementi & Co. shop was one of Georgiana's favourites in London; beyond the opportunity to purchase music from one of her favourite composers, there was something that delighted her about the smell of fine wood, and the occasional tinkle of pianoforte keys as they were tested. She breathed deeply as soon as they entered, and was making her way to the sheet music, when Matthew called her over to one of the pianofortes in the middle of the shop floor. It was a small square pianoforte, perched atop six spindly little legs, and although it was elegantly painted, it could hardly compete with the great Clementi grands all around it.

"What do you think of this instrument?" he asked, with a pleased countenance, so that Georgiana quickly suspected his intent had not been to bring her here to purchase sheet music, but instead a pianoforte.

Yet he could not be serious, in asking her what she thought of this little thing; he had seen her Clementi grand, at Pemberley. She thought it to be another example of his frugality, and then recalled how he had told her that if there was something she wished for, she should tell him so plainly. So she said, "It is very nice, for a square pianoforte, but I should like to wait until we have established our household, and then send for my grand, from Pemberley. Fitzwilliam has promised it should go with me."

He stared at her incredulously for a moment, then began chuckling, and said: "Oh, Georgiana, the look on your face – you cannot believe I intended this for land, can you? Yes, of course, once our household is in being, you shall have your grand from Pemberley, or a new one, if that is your preference. But I regret to inform you that neither will fit so well in the cabin of a frigate."

"Oh – I had not even thought there was a possibility of my taking a pianoforte on board. I had rather thought I must console myself with my harp."

"Absolutely not – some modifications were required, but I would not see either of us deprived of your playing. There is Mr. Woodson – he sent word to my uncle a fortnight ago that the modifications were complete, and I must admit I was eager to see them."

A young man approached them, and asked Matthew if this was Lady Stanton, come to see her pianoforte, and Matthew replied that she was.

"Well, my lady, you will find the modifications have all been done quite carefully, and there should be minimal effect on the sound."

"You did the same as you did for Admiral Russell, yes?" asked Matthew.

"Almost exactly the same, sir, although his model was much older. All of the legs may be detached, and the pedal swivels just so." Upon saying this, Mr. Woodson knelt down below the unit, to show that the pedal could be folded up underneath it.

"Excellent, then it may be packed up and stowed in the hold whenever we clear for action."

Mr. Woodson looked mildly horrified at the thought, but said nothing in response.

"Would you like to try it, Georgiana?" Matthew asked.

Georgiana was still adjusting to the notion that this pianoforte was not a theoretical instrument, that it was not only intended for her use on board a ship, but that it had already been modified to serve such a purpose. She felt a mixture of tenderness towards Matthew for thinking of it, and embarrassment that she had thought he intended it for a drawing-room, and could only just reply that she would very much like to try it.

She approached the bench, and found both her husband and Mr. Woodson attempting to pull it out for her; Mr. Woodson deferred to Matthew, and once seated, she tried a few scales before deciding she must of course test it with one of Clementi's own sonatas. She was pleasantly surprised to find that although it would not have surpassed the grands surrounding them, the sound was quite fine, and better than some of the other pianofortes she had played in various drawing-rooms. She finished, pleased with the instrument, and turned to Matthew, meaning to express her appreciation, when she saw there was a third gentleman standing with him and Mr. Woodson.

"Well done, madam, although I meant the allegro agitato to be even more *rapido*," he said. "Perhaps once you are more familiar with the instrument, you shall be able to play it so."

Georgiana started, rose from the bench, and curtsied as deeply as she could, for surely the gentleman in front of her was Muzio Clementi. Mr. Woodson confirmed her assumption, introducing them all at Matthew's request.

"Signore Clementi, it is the greatest of honours to meet you, sir," Georgiana said.

"Mister Clementi is perfectly fine for someone who has been in England so long as myself, Lady Stanton," Mr. Clementi said. "I am told your husband bashes about great big French ships, and so we should execute his commission, to take one of our pianofortes and modify it so it may be taken apart. I must admit I feel better about the commission, to know it is for your practise. It seems most young ladies of your age are required to play the pianoforte, but you, madam, you *play*. Do not give it up now that you are married."

"I would never think of doing so," Georgiana said. "I thank you very kindly, Mr. Clementi."

"You are welcome. But you must remember, faster in the allegro agitato. It is within your capabilities. Good day to you all."

Georgiana and Matthew wished him a good day, and Mr. Woodson followed him, asking about some matter of business. After such an event, Georgiana hardly knew how to react, and she was glad Matthew stepped closer.

"I believe I shall have need of your arm in walking away from this bench," she murmured. "I feel nearer to fainting than I ever have before."

"As well you should, to be praised by such a source," he said.

Georgiana took up his arm, and they walked toward Mr. Woodson, who had remembered his customers on the exit of Mr. Clementi. Matthew indicated that all with the pianoforte was satisfactory, and asked that it be sent to Lord Anglesey's house.

As they were leaving the shop, Georgiana, still feeling a little overcome, finally said, "I do not know how to thank you for your thoughtfulness. I will always look upon this instrument with the utmost fondness, although I believe it will be enhanced by my memories of meeting Mr. Clementi."

"The first look on your face was not quite so fond," he said, and although his tone was teasing, Georgiana felt herself blushing. "But you need only thank me by playing it. I thought we might even venture upon some duets."

"Oh, I had been thinking that as well – I would like that more than anything," she said.

This event was recounted over dinner – which, unsurprisingly, Lady Tonbridge was invited to – with a great deal of enthusiasm by those hearing the tale, as well as those telling it. When she and Lady Tonbridge withdrew from the dining-room, Georgiana assumed they would be followed shortly by the gentlemen, with only four in their party. However, before the gentlemen joined them, and in her usual direct manner, Lady Tonbridge raised that topic which was most embarrassing to Georgiana.

"I believe you may have encountered Lord Anglesey and myself in the study, earlier?" asked she.

Georgiana felt her face grow exceedingly hot, and nodded mutely.

"I told Lord Anglesey he needed to put a sign on that water closet when he installed it. It need not be crass; a little gilt sign would do nicely," Lady Tonbridge said. "However, I find I digress from what I wished to say, which is that I apologise for our lack of discretion. I hope you do not think this was a whim of the day; we have been, well, involved, for several years now."

"Yes, Matthew informed me," Georgiana said. "Do you mind if I ask why you do not marry?"

"Oh, we speak of it from time to time. But neither of us has much in the way of motivation to change the present arrangement. There is no chance of my becoming in the family way, and the thought of combining two households so established as ours quite frankly exhausts me."

"But there are so many wonderful things about the married state," Georgiana said, blushing again.

"Ah, I see what you are thinking, but it is different for you than it is for me. What is it you enjoy most about marriage – perhaps being able to spend as much time as you choose with the man you love?"

"Yes, you have described it very well."

"We have several differences, then, you and I, for I may spend as much time as I wish with Lord Anglesey, as a widow, but I cannot say I would call what we have love, at least not the deeper sort. A goodly fondness, perhaps. He and I have both had that deeper love with others in our lives, but one comes to miss the companionship of the other sex – particularly the sort of companionship you witnessed," Lady Tonbridge said. "Now, I believe I hear them coming; you must not speak of this to Lord Anglesey, for he would be terribly embarrassed. That man can be squeamish as a maid, when it comes to these sorts of matters."

CHAPTER 14

The initial correspondence from the registry office in Derby had indicated no candidates meeting their qualifications, which Elizabeth and Darcy had taken as a sign that the office was adhering more strictly to their qualifications than the one in Matlock had done. A second, later letter indicated one suitable candidate had inquired about the position, and Elizabeth – somewhat guiltily – had seen her husband off in the morning to go and interview the woman.

She passed the time working on the household accounts while he was gone, looking over the great ledger book in Darcy's study, as she usually did. There was a study for the mistress of the house's particular use, but like the mistress's bedchambers, it was entirely overdone, and so Elizabeth had taken to sharing her husband's study, just as she had in their house in town.

Elizabeth was still there when he returned, and she knew as soon as he came in that he had not favoured this candidate. Beyond the slightly grim look on his countenance, he had changed out of his travelling clothes, and he would have come to see her immediately, if he felt he had good news to share.

"Mrs. Devaney, then?" she asked him.

"You know me too well," he said, sitting down near the secretaire she had moved into the room some months ago. "And yes, I will not trouble you with the details, but I believe Mrs. Devaney to be our best choice. There is one other possibility I had thought of, and that is to approach Charles and Jane about sharing the services of Mrs. Padgett. We would need additional help in caring for two babies, given how busy Bess keeps her, but they need not have Mrs. Padgett's particular qualifications."

"Yes, I had thought of that as well."

"And what did you conclude?" he asked.

"The same as you, I suspect – that Charles and Jane are much too kind to say they do not favour the arrangement, even if they do not."

"You are correct – that was my conclusion as well, which returns us to Mrs. Devaney. Perhaps we may give it another week or so, and see if there are any other candidates; if there are not, I will write to the Matlock office."

Elizabeth sighed. "It might be best if you just write to them now. There is no guarantee she will still be available in a week's time. As you said, she may be more amenable to being offered five years' employment, with the possibility that she would not need to do any wet-nursing."

"Is that what you wish me to do?"

"I suppose so. I cannot say I am enthusiastic about the decision, but perhaps it is best to just have the decision made."

"Very well, then, I shall write the letter," he said. "I do have some other, more interesting news from Derby. The Camberts are selling more of the land from Barrowmere Park."

"But there is hardly any land to begin with! I am not even certain I would call it an estate – it has less acreage than Longbourn."

"If you might not call it an estate now, you certainly shall not be able to, once this sale is complete. But the reason there is so little in the way of acreage is because much of it has been absorbed into Pemberley over the years."

"Indeed? Was it you or your father who was responsible for this?"

"It has been the work of both of us. Mr. Cambert racked up an extraordinary amount of gambling debts, and began selling his land, parcel by parcel, to my father in an attempt to return the estate to the clear. I thought he might succeed, but then more land came up for sale, and more after that."

"If it has always been you or your father who purchased the land, why does Mr. Cambert not speak to you directly? We are all acquainted. They were here to dine last month."

Last month, however, and not any more recently. Elizabeth did not prefer the company of the Camberts so much as she did the other families in the neighbourhood, and although their home bordered directly on Pemberley's land, that family was most often invited to dine with larger groups. Perhaps, she thought, this mild disfavour was mutual.

"I expect he does not wish to admit it to my face, that he must sell more land," Darcy said. "We have had an excellent harvest this year – Pemberley's returns only increase, while his estate fails, and for good reason. Richardson and I shall have to draw up another plan, for what must be done to this new land so it can bring a decent yield."

"So you intend to purchase the land?"

"Of course. I intend to finance it in part with the twenty guineas you owe me."

Elizabeth at first could not remember what he was speaking of, that she owed him twenty guineas, and then she recalled a bet they had made, sitting in the gardens of Carlton House, as to whether he would still find her beautiful when she was large with child.

"I do not owe you twenty guineas yet. The bet was that you would still find me beautiful when I was ready to enter my confinement. I still have nearly two months before then, so there is ample time for me to grow larger, and you to change your mind."

"I shall not change my mind."

"Let us see about that when the time comes," Elizabeth smiled at him, and found herself – not for the first time – wishing they had not given up marital relations. These exchanges of teazing and wit they so often enjoyed had always carried with them a certain thrill, a promise of something initiated which would be fulfilled later, in the night. Now, they still fell into it naturally, but there would be no fulfilment, not for many more months.

As if plagued by the same distracting thoughts as his wife, Darcy sought to change the subject, noting there had been a letter for her from David Stanton in the post, and handing it over to her. Elizabeth took it with surprise, for this was a very prompt reply to her last, and she had not expected such frequent correspondence from him. She remembered, though, that she had indicated her sister Mary was returning to stay with them, and with a twinge of hope for her sister, broke the seal and unfolded it, although she soon saw that what was contained within was not at all what she had expected:

"I am writing you on a topic you may well find improper, and I must beg your forgiveness in advance for the impropriety of the query I shall eventually put to you. I hope now that we are family, you will allow me a little of what my brother would call leeway."

He opened the letter thus, and proceeded to explain that there was a woman in his parish, Mrs. Nichols, who had been the second wife of Mr. Nichols, a hundred-acre farmer on Lord Winterley's estate. Lord Winterley, Elizabeth recalled, was a baron, and the patron of David's living.

Mrs. Nichols had given birth to a son, several months ago, the first child for both she and Mr. Nichols. The son might have eventually been brought up to take over the lease on the farm, but Mr. Nichols's heart had unexpectedly given out during the harvest, and he had died. Both David and Lord Winterley were concerned for the welfare of poor Mrs. Nichols, who could be allowed to stay in the farm's cottage through the winter, with Lord Winterley's steward supervising the planting of the winter wheat, but must vacate it by spring for new tenants. It was too soon for her to remarry respectably, and so she must find a way to make her living; serving as a wet nurse had seemed the most likely possibility that would allow her to keep her son. David's letter concluded:

"You must by now know why I have written to you particularly of Mrs.

Nichols's situation. I do not know if you have yet hired on any help for your nursery, nor what sort of help you would seek, but thought you my best chance of finding an excellent placement for her. She is, of course, presently qualified to be a wet nurse, but if this is not desired, a position as a head nurse or under-nurse would be of equal interest.

"I realise she has no other qualifications than nursing her own son, but I will tell you that she does so most tenderly and carefully. Lady Winterley has called on her frequently and has written a character, and says she would take her on herself if she still had need of a nurse. In an area in which I am more qualified to speak on, Mrs. Nichols attends church services most dutifully; she is a pious woman who believes in the true Anglican communion and shows this in words and deeds. She seems to me of precisely the sort of character one would want in one who cares for children.

"I hope if you have not yet hired on all the help you desire in your nursery, that you will at least give Mrs. Nichols consideration. Lord Winterley will see her conveyed to Pemberley in one of his carriages, if you wish to interview her. Regardless of what your reply must be as it relates to Mrs. Nichols, I hope I shall hear in your next that Miss Bennet and Mr. Darcy have arrived safely at your home. Please give your entire family my best wishes for your continuing health and happiness,

"Your most humble and obedient servant,

"DAVID STANTON"

Elizabeth finished the letter in a state of shock, for it seemed impossible that he should have written to them with such a neat solution to their search for a nurse. She skimmed the later passages again, and on Darcy's noting that whatever was contained within seemed to have made her happy, handed the letter over to him so he might read it as well. She watched his face carefully as he did so, although she suspected he would react as she had; Lord Winterley's concern on behalf of his tenant was the same as Darcy would have shown, and the baron's working with David to find a solution was exactly the sort of thing Darcy would have done with his own rectors, if faced with a similar situation.

"Well, this is possibly the completest thing that could ever have happened," Darcy said, when he had finished. "Including his listing your sister before me, in hoping we had arrived here safely."

"I did notice that, and as to the rest, I cannot believe it," Elizabeth said. "To have someone so well spoken for, by someone we know – it would make me so much easier at mind, to have her in this role."

"Yes, and with her own child still to nurse, she need only lend her assistance as a wet nurse if – if there is need of it. We would have to make accommodations for her son, of course; for now all of the babies may share the nursery, and hopefully we shall have a spare child's bed-room, once the boy is older."

It would take five of their own children to fill the small bed-rooms bordering the nursery, and Elizabeth was pleased Darcy thought this a possibility.

"Let us interview her, first; I will write to him to have her sent out," she said. "Or – perhaps we should send our own carriage for her, and invite David to accompany her."

"Were your mother to hear you right now, I believe she would be quite proud."

"I have not been the only one to participate in a little scheming for a match for one of our sisters, Mr. Darcy."

Darcy confirmed that what she said was true, and her idea was a good one. They fixed upon having her response carried by a footman in one of Pemberley's carriages, and the footman and under-coachman to wait at the nearest inn until Mrs. Nichols and David Stanton – if he did choose to come – were ready to travel. Darcy then mentioned idly that she might note Pemberley's Guy Fawkes Night bonfire, if David did not have any related duties in his own parish, and wished to time his visit so he might attend.

"What Guy Fawkes bonfire do you speak of?" asked Elizabeth, feeling a little panicked, for it was already the end of October, and she had not ordered any preparations for an event on the estate.

"Oh, we do one every year. You need not worry about it; I am sure Richardson and Mrs. Reynolds have it in hand. Most of the work is on Richardson's end, in seeing the fireworks purchased and the wood assembled for the bonfire – he quite delights in a good bonfire."

"Still, I would have expected Mrs. Reynolds to say something of it." Indeed, it was the sort of thing Mrs. Reynolds would have consulted with Elizabeth on well in advance, typically. Elizabeth had been encouraging Mrs. Reynolds to act with more autonomy, but she thought that perhaps this autonomy was increasing with Elizabeth's belly.

"She likely will, in a day or two. The kitchen's role is minimal; we serve out biscuits and mulled wine. Although of course something different might be done, if you wish it."

"No, staying with the tradition is fine, if it has been well-received. I only – I only hope she is not attempting to coddle me because I am with child. I am still some time away from birth, and it is important to me that I learn all of Pemberley's traditions."

"I do not believe it is a case of coddling, merely that she did not think it an event which should require major notice from you. I only thought of it as a possible incentive for David to make a visit. And yes, before you say so, that is certainly at least a little scheming, Mrs. Darcy."

CHAPTER 15

With Matthew gone to call on the First Lord, and Lord Anglesey off on his own round of calls, Georgiana thought she would spend much of the morning by herself, and was pleasantly surprised when the butler announced Mrs. Gardiner and Miss Catherine Bennet, there to call on her. She asked that they be shown in immediately, and could not even greet Catherine before her friend was saying:

"Oh, I hope you do not mind I did not just leave my card – my aunt and I called on Lady Tonbridge just now, and when she said you had returned to town I could not wait to see you!"

"Of course not – it is a surprise, but the most pleasant of surprises. I had thought you were still at Longbourn!" Georgiana said, and then greeted Mrs. Gardiner, inviting her and Catherine to be seated.

"I only just came to town. Captain Ramsey expects he will come into Portsmouth, but no one is available to take me there. My father did allow me to come here to stay with my aunt and uncle, though, so at least I am a little closer."

"Oh, we were just in Portsmouth," Georgiana said, "although only for a night."

"Even if it was only a night, I am terribly jealous of you!" exclaimed Catherine. "I so long to see it, after hearing so much about it."

"It may be a poor substitute, but I have done a few rough sketches, of what I saw," Georgiana said. "Let me go and get my sketchbook, and I shall show you, although you must not expect much. I believe you have long since surpassed me in drawing skills."

Catherine said all that was polite, as regarded her friend's skills, but Georgiana knew what she said to be true. She had never been enthusiastic about drawing and painting, and had largely given them up. Only upon learning she had the opportunity to visit Paris had she procured a new sketchbook, but only with the aim to capture her travels, not for any particular enjoyment of the art itself.

The sketchbook was retrieved, and Georgiana, Catherine and Mrs. Gardiner spent a good deal of time in looking over all she had drawn, both of Portsmouth, and Paris. Georgiana did not consider it her place to ask for refreshments to be brought in, but brought in they were, the result of a housekeeper who had served under a widower for many years.

When Georgiana mentioned the many shopping outings they had undertaken in Paris, and had sent Hughes upstairs in search of the gifts she had purchased for her friends, Mrs. Gardiner – whose husband earned his money through trade, and a goodly amount of it through textiles – asked a few discreet questions about the state of the shops, and particularly the fabrics. Georgiana answered her as best she could, and then had Hughes bring down her dresses so Mrs. Gardiner could see them for herself.

It was a most delightful call, but despite Georgiana's attempts, she could not convince them to stay beyond what was polite. They would take their leave, and Matthew returned not long after they had gone. Georgiana knew immediately by the set of his face that he was unhappy about something, but she was not certain precisely what it was.

"What is the matter?" she asked. "Were you not given the Caroline? Or no command at all? I cannot see how they could ignore all of the interest in your favour."

He sat beside her, and after some hesitation, said, "It is neither. I have been given a command, of the Caroline."

All of this, Georgiana felt, should have been the most wonderful news, and so she waited for him to continue.

"It is the mission of the ship that proves to be a problem, or perhaps I should say the destination. I am to carry despatches to our ministers in the Baltic ports."

"Now, so near to winter?"

"The despatches must go through, regardless of the season, particularly with such a treaty to be signed."

"I am sure it will be bitterly cold outside, but still, I believe we may manage."

"That is the problem, Georgiana. There is very little difference between inside and outside, in the wooden walls of a frigate, even with the best brazier, and thus there can be no *we*. I could never countenance taking you to the Baltic in the winter, much less while you are carrying a child."

Georgiana felt tears welling in her eyes – this was not a possibility she had considered, that he should be assigned somewhere so inhospitable that she could not go with him. Nor was she entirely certain the Baltic was so cold a place she could not still go; she wondered if perhaps he was still thinking of the hotels in Paris, and assuming she required a higher level of comfort than she truly did. Certainly, there was a level of comfort she *preferred*, but that was well above the level of comfort she *required*.

"How long do you expect you will be there? I believe I can manage, if it is of short duration. I have spent many a winter in Derbyshire."

"Two to four months, I expect, and if you had spent many a winter in the Orkneys, that would prove an equivalent," he said. "Even without that, I would be inclined to have you try it, if that was your choice, but the risk is too great. We are given despatches for four countries – Russia, Prussia, Sweden and Denmark – when in another season four ships might have carried them. The Admiralty will only risk one frigate because the Baltic does freeze over occasionally, and if that happens, they would rather lose one ship than four."

"But what should happen to *you*, if the sea freezes?"

"In the worst case – the very worst case – the ship would be trapped by the ice – possibly crushed," he said, and then, noting her horrified countenance: "If that was to happen, and the odds are not for it, we would take shelter as needed, on the nearest land or the ice itself, and send a party for help. I cannot say it would be a pleasant experience, but now that my injuries have healed, it is not one that overly concerns me. However, I would not place my pregnant wife in a situation where there was the slightest chance she should suffer such a thing."

Despite the constant physical reminders of her condition, Georgiana often found herself forgetting the very strange notion that it meant she was carrying a life in addition to her own. Now, she was most painfully reminded of it, for surely he was right – she had doubts about her own ability to endure what he described, and it could not be risked while she was with child. With this understanding, she could no longer contain her tears. She found herself quickly embraced, and comforted by it, although it was impossible to forget that such comforts would soon be lost to her.

"With the war over, I never thought we would have to be separated," she whispered.

"Neither did I, dearest. It seems my timing was too early, rather than correct. They need someone who may be prepared to leave as soon as the treaty is signed. If I had waited a little longer, I might have been given despatches for somewhere more temperate."

"Is there any chance of Lord Melville's being persuaded to give you one of those assignments instead?"

"It is not likely, not with so many ships returning. If I refuse this assignment, it will be given to another – there are any number of captains returning home who will go on half-pay, and would be most happy for even this mission. And if I did refuse this assignment, it is very likely no other would ever come my way. Such an action is not taken lightly by the Admiralty."

"We must resign ourselves to it, then," Georgiana said, "and hope it is closer to two months, than four."

"Even if it is four, I should still return with plenty of time before the baby is born."

"What if you are given another assignment following this one?" Georgiana asked, feeling a little panicked at the thought of his being away when she was to give birth.

"I will request leave again, if necessary," he said, holding her even more closely. "You would never be alone for the event, given your family, but I promise I shall be there, to greet our son or daughter. You will not give birth without me."

The remainder of the day was spent largely in seeking comfort; they went for a quiet walk in Cavendish Square, and had a rather sober dinner with the earl, who was acquainted with Matthew's assignment and not at all happy over it. He agreed that nothing could be done about it, though, without affecting his nephew's chances for a future command.

The morning following, Matthew told his wife very gently that he would need to go down to Portsmouth in a few days to take command of the ship, and asked if she would prefer to go with him.

"Of course," she said. "I would like to stay with you for as long as I may. I only wish we could bring Catherine with us. I am sure she would love to be able to greet Captain Ramsey upon his return."

"Is there any reason why we may not?" he asked.

"She has no one to attend her there and chaperone – oh, I suppose I am a married woman now, and may chaperone her myself." This, to Georgiana, was a very strange notion, given Catherine was older than she, but Matthew was correct; there was no reason why they might not convey Catherine to Portsmouth, and have her stay with them.

"Send her a note, then, and invite her to come with us," he said. "For I do not know that we shall have time to call on her. I thought we might go to Aldrich's today; we may always try Tattersalls tomorrow, if no suitable purchase appears."

Georgiana smiled sadly, for it appeared he was in earnest about setting up a carriage, which she would surely need now, and yet it seemed an impossible thing to accomplish within a few days. "I thank you for thinking of the carriage," she said. "Yet even if we were to find equipment and a pair of horses, I do not know that the proper servants may be located in such a short time."

"I am not so certain of that, myself, but my uncle will make the attempt on our behalf," he said. "He claims there is always some fool who has put himself in debt and needs to trim his stables, and if he asks around at his clubs, he should be able to find a few candidates."

To Aldrich's they went, in the earl's carriage, and as soon as they had entered the yard, Georgiana felt deeply uncomfortable, quite certain she was the only lady present. "Perhaps I should not have come," she whispered.

"If we were purchasing a boat, I would happily do the deed myself," Matthew said. "However, you are easily a better judge of horseflesh than I, and you will make far more use of the carriage; I could not see making the purchase without you."

Georgiana appreciated the sentiment, if not the stares from a few of the gentlemen present. She stepped even closer to Matthew, as if to tell them she at least was not here by herself, as they examined the carriages on display. She had long wished to set up a carriage, but now found the offerings overwhelming, particularly with the knowledge that the choice must be made quickly.

"I think I would prefer a landau," she said, and could not help but be reminded of her dreams, and Mr. Wickham's promise within that she should have a landau. Yet it *was* what she preferred; there seemed a certain versatility in such a vehicle that could be used for longer distances, and yet also enjoyed in milder weather. Upon explaining this to Matthew, he agreed with her, and they focused their search thus, yet still did not see anything they preferred.

They were similarly disappointed with the horses on offer that day, and Georgiana feared they should have to go to Tattersalls in order to find a sufficiently matched team she approved of; if she found Aldrich's Repository intimidating, she felt sure Tattersalls would be far worse. They left the place with no carriage, and no horses, and Georgiana found they were not even to go directly home, for they must stop at the offices of an attorney, so they could both sign a series of papers, giving her control of their finances beyond her own pin money, should she need it. They then went to Drummonds, so she could be introduced to the bank managers, and copies of the papers handed over to them.

Georgiana was exhausted by the time they returned to the carriage, although she did attend to Matthew's speaking of how his uncle would readily attend her to Drummonds, if she had need of it. He expected his uncle to remain in town through the whole season, save a return to his estate for a few weeks around Christmastime. If Lord Anglesey was unavailable and none of her nearer male relations were in town, Matthew thought perhaps Mr. Gardiner would be willing to assist her, given he was family and resided in town. Georgiana replied that Mr. Gardiner was a genial man, and undoubtedly would do so if she had need of his assistance.

They found Lord Anglesey most eager for their return, and could not even be seated in the drawing-room before he was telling them why.

"You have not yet made any purchase related to the carriage?" he asked, and when they replied they had not, continued, "In that case I believe I have learned of just the thing. Lord Fulton's son looks to trim his stable and hoped to sell the entire shooting match together – a very fine landau, all the rest of the equipage, and a pair of Cleveland Bays. Mr. Fulton also looks to trim staff, and has a groom ready for promotion, and likely to be very interested in a new position as coachman for this team."

"Georgiana had been wishing for a landau," Matthew said, smiling at her.

"Excellent, I had hoped as much, because I have invited him to dinner, and to come in that conveyance, so you might see it. We shall have to put up with his conversation, but I thought it for the best, given how quickly you must make your purchase."

Georgiana feared they might wish to continue to speak of the carriage, and although she was happy at the prospect of it, she also wished to rest before dinner, particularly if she was to meet a new acquaintance and inspect the carriage. Lord Anglesey had nothing further to inform them of, however, and noted she might like to go up and rest, as she had the day before.

Had Mr. Fulton not been arriving in what might become her own landau, Georgiana might have continued to claim fatigue through dinner, and requested a tray instead. She rallied as best she could, and made her way downstairs to be introduced to Mr. Fulton, whose clothes and manners immediately showed him to be the sort of dandy who would find himself in enough debt to require the trimming of his stable. He was, however, quite good about their inspecting the landau, for once he had introduced the promising groom, who was named Murray, he returned inside with Lord Anglesey to consume the earl's brandy, leaving Georgiana and Matthew free to look over the carriage as closely as they wished.

It *was* a very fine landau, pulled by a very fine-looking set of horses. Georgiana approached them and stroked each of their noses, looking them carefully in the eyes, for her father had instilled a belief in both of his children, that you could tell much about a horse from its eyes. She was pleased that they seemed to possess equal parts spirit and kindness, and then made her way around to the side of the horse nearer the house, to feel his front legs for hot spots. She found nothing of concern, there, but was once again overcome by a wave of dizziness when she stood to make her way over to his hind legs. Matthew had by now come to anticipate these spells, and offered his arm for even those few short steps.

Her need to complete the inspection, however, was prevented by one of Lord Anglesey's grooms running up to them and saying the lady should have no need of such dirty work in her dinner dress. He not only felt each leg, but bade the horses to pick up their feet so he might check the condition of their hooves and frogs, and opened their mouths, confirming the teeth of each matched the seven and eight years of age that had been promised.

"Fine cattle," said Murray. "Cared for 'em these four years, I 'ave. Never more than a stone bruise, I promise ye."

"I am glad to hear that," said Matthew. "Would you have interest in continuing to care for them, and taking on a position as our coachman, were we to purchase them?"

Murray replied as a man fond of his charges, desirous of promotion, and well aware of his employer's debts would, and also told them Mr. Fulton had said he might take them around the block in the landau, if they so chose. They were pleased by this, and that the young man seemed a good whip and the carriage well-sprung. These observations took little time, however, and after they had been shared, Matthew indicated concern over his wife's not-infrequent dizziness, asking the name of her sister's accoucheur. Georgiana told him it was Dr. Whittling, that her sister saw, and they agreed she should have an appointment with him.

"If he cannot see you before we go down to Portsmouth, my uncle would host you while you see him before you – we have not discussed where you will go. Shall you go to Pemberley, or would you prefer to stay here? Or do you wish to set up your own household?"

"I do not wish to rush into a purchase, or even a lease," Georgiana said. "If I cannot go with you, I should like to be with Elizabeth for her birth."

"Yes, of course. Then before you go to Pemberley, you will see Dr. Whittling?"

"Yes, I shall see him. Although we should not settle it that I shall go to Pemberley until I have been invited. It is not my home any more, to be dropping in as I choose."

"You cannot possibly think your brother and sister would not invite you."

"I have no doubt that they shall, but it would be proper to wait until the invitation has been made. I will write to them first thing on the morrow and tell them of my situation."

When they had returned to the house, Matthew requested Murray drive the landau past them again, so they might see the way the horses looked. Georgiana and the groom watched them carefully, and Georgiana found she liked them very well; they were fine, but not flashy movers, and she thought if her brother was to see them, he would say they were inclined to soundness.

"I like the horses very much," she said, and found Lord Anglesey's groom nodding in agreement, "and Mr. Murray, and the landau itself. It is the completest thing, that your uncle should find them available."

"If there is a thing in London to be found, my uncle is the person to see to it," he said. "We will need to hire a footman, but I have an idea in that quarter. Shall we go in and tell Mr. Fulton we wish to make the purchase?"

"Yes, let us do so."

Lord Anglesey had been right that Mr. Fulton's conversation was wanting, and through the course of dinner, they were required to listen to a series of stories centred on card games and horse races, Mr. Fulton never seeming to realise as he told these stories that such things were the cause of his needing to trim his stables. Georgiana would have preferred to retire immediately, rather than going to the drawing-room, but to announce such an intent might have invited Mr. Fulton to linger interminably over port. Instead, her presence alone in the drawing-room meant the gentlemen joined her there quickly, and thankfully Mr. Fulton did not stay long after that.

When he had taken his leave, Lord Anglesey said, "I only saw it from the doorway, but it looks to be a fine carriage. Just the thing for a couple newly married. You should at least paint over the arms, before making your way down to Portsmouth; you would not wish to rush drawing up your own."

"Might I not simply use the family arms?" Matthew asked.

"You could, but I would suggest at least some modification – perhaps an anchor, or some rope, or something of the like. Now that you are a baronet, some independence of your arms would be appropriate."

Matthew indicated that they should look in to having something drawn up, and yet Georgiana felt his countenance matched her own thoughts on the subject. They had married for love, without a thought to his new baronetcy, and all that must come with it: a coat of arms on their carriage, a seat to list in the Baronetage, an heir to succeed to the title. At least, Georgiana thought, she might be carrying the heir, but she felt overwhelmed at the thought of trying to make any more progress on their land-based life alone, while her husband was at sea.

CHAPTER 16

While his younger brother was making the journey to Portsmouth, David Stanton was escorting Mrs. Nichols to Pemberley. The fifth of November having fallen on a Sunday that year, by tradition, the bonfire was held a day later, which allowed the carriage to set out early that morning, and arrive well before the event was to take place.

Its arrival was greeted with a good deal of anticipation from several members of the household. Elizabeth and Darcy were eager to see Mrs. Nichols, and desirous of finding she matched with what they hoped for. Mary, although delighted her sister had already contrived a way of inviting Mr. Stanton to stay with them for a few days, greeted him with that shyness which must result from a long separation of two such people.

It was not an unbecoming shyness, however, and having made every proper greeting to his hosts, he offered his arm to Mary so they might go inside together. There they joined the Bingleys in the yellow drawing-room, where the doors had been opened to the music-room so they could hear Miss Kelly practising the pianoforte, occasionally punctuated by a little coo from Bess.

In the larger house party in which they had formerly been in company, Mary and Mr. Stanton had been largely forgotten amongst those who were more dominant in conversation. Today, however, with so few people in the drawing-room, they were not able to converse privately as quickly as Mary would have liked. Bess must be introduced, and then Mr. Stanton's journey, the weather, and his sermon the day prior were required to be inquired after and discussed in some detail before he excused himself to change out of his travelling clothes.

Mary watched him leave the room with the strangest and most unexpected little fluttering of spirits. She would never allow herself to act as her sister Catherine had, when being courted by Captain Ramsey – although nowhere near what their sister Lydia was capable of, Kitty had been more forward and flirtatious than Mary could support – but she understood better the elevated spirits Catherine had shown whenever her beau had come to call. Such thoughts could not help but be followed by the question of whether Mary was in love, but with some reflection on the matter, she decided she was not yet in love. Capable of love, certainly, and perhaps even on the precipice of it, but not yet in love, and she wondered if these few days would be enough to see her heart settled.

Mrs. Nichols could not be interviewed immediately, for she had alighted the carriage with her young son in her arms, and Elizabeth had asked Mrs. Reynolds to show them both up to the nursery, where the boy could be settled in before they would all speak. Still, Elizabeth found she liked the look of this woman very much; she had a kind, straightforward countenance and a trim figure. She had arrived in a simple dress, dyed black and in good repair, and compared to Bess, at least, her son was absolutely silent.

They allowed some time for her to settle in before going to the nursery, and upon entering found she was singing her son to sleep in a voice no one would compliment, although it seemed to be effective. It was a scene of such maternal serenity that Elizabeth felt deeply envious, before reminding herself that it would not be so many more weeks now before she might do the same, with her own child.

Poor Mrs. Padgett was still down in the music-room with Bess, and Mrs. Nichols was reluctant to leave her son alone, even to go to the sitting-room nearest the nursery, so a maid was summoned to sit with the child, and alert them if he awoke. Once Elizabeth, Darcy, and Mrs. Nichols had left the nursery and were all seated, however, Elizabeth felt fully the awkwardness of the situation – this was not an interview like those at Matlock, where Mrs. Nichols might be easily dismissed if some aspect of her was found wanting, for she had come to stay in their home, with her own child. Finally, Elizabeth asked: "What is your son's name? I do not believe Mr. Stanton mentioned it in his letter."

"George, ma'am, after his father," said Mrs. Nichols.

"Of course," Elizabeth said, "and please allow me to say how very sorry we are, for your loss."

"I thank ye very kindly, Mrs. Darcy."

They seemed at risk of falling into silence again, but Darcy now spoke, saying, "Has Mr. Stanton indicated to you the position we seek to fill?"

"Yes, sir. He says ye have a need of a woman, for to look after your child who is coming," Mrs. Nichols said. "He says there is a chance for she who holds the job to keep her own baby, if she has one, which is very important, for myself. I will not give up my boy."

Mrs. Nichols looked at him with a little defiance in her countenance, and Elizabeth loved her for it.

"Yes, as you see, we have more than ample room in the nursery, and would make accommodations for you and your son," Darcy said. "You should know, as well, that Mrs. Darcy intends to do the wet-nursing of the child herself, although in certain circumstances you might be called upon in that quarter. Would that be acceptable to you?"

"Yes, sir. If my own boy is allowed to stay I'd be ready to aid as wet-nurse for another child, were it needed."

"Very well, Mrs. Nichols. Regardless of whether that is needed, if you perform your duties admirably, you shall have little need to worry over your future livelihood. I expect we will have need of a nurse for a great many years."

No longer defiant, Mrs. Nichols now looked exceedingly relieved. She produced her character from Lady Winterley, and Elizabeth and Darcy read it over, although Elizabeth assumed her husband's mind was already settled in the matter, as was hers. Lady Winterley had written a most proper character; she was honest about those of Mrs. Nichols's virtues she felt she could speak on, and about those she had not been able to observe.

The character was returned to Mrs. Nichols, Darcy named a rate of pay which Elizabeth knew to be very generous – although she thought it appropriate, for the woman who would have such a role – and it was agreed to with no negotiation at all. Darcy noted that Mrs. Padgett was already staying in the bed-room usually reserved for the resident nurse, and so Mrs. Nichols should be put up in the room beside it. This traditionally would have been one of the children's rooms, so she would need to stay elsewhere for a few nights, while it was made over for an adult.

They returned to the nursery with a very stunned Mrs. Nichols, who did not seem to believe her good fortune, to have been hired on into such a house with such ease, and with the promise of every accommodation being made for her own son. There they found that Mrs. Padgett had returned with Bess, who was not asleep, but laid quietly in her crib across the room from George, who slept still. Mrs. Padgett and Mrs. Nichols were introduced, and Mrs. Nichols was welcomed most happily by poor Mrs. Padgett, who seemed hopeful the new nurse might be willing to help her with Bess, at least in the weeks before Mrs. Darcy's baby was born. She was having these hopes encouraged by Mrs. Nichols as Elizabeth and Darcy left the nursery.

When they came back out into the hallway, Darcy asked Elizabeth if she would rest a little, before the evening, as they were likely to have a long night of it. Elizabeth's pregnancy had long since reached the point where she preferred to rest even if she had nothing but dinner with the Bingleys planned, and she replied that she would.

"Very well, I will walk with you," he said, and they started toward their apartment. "Are you happy with Mrs. Nichols?"

"Yes, entirely happy. I like her very much, and it is even more pleasing to know she and her son will have a good home here, given their situation."

"Yes, I presume David and Lord Winterley will be most relieved, to know we will take her on."

Darcy opened the door to her bedchamber for her, and saw her settled onto the chaise there, for Elizabeth feared if she laid on the bed she would sleep too deeply, and feel even more tired when Sarah woke her to change.

"Do you require anything? A blanket, perhaps?" Darcy asked.

"Are you to coddle me now, as well?"

"You must allow me to. Whom else may I coddle, but my wife, and the child she carries?"

"You are insufferable," Elizabeth said, shaking her head. "Bring me the blanket, if you must."

The blanket was brought, and bestowed with a chaste little kiss and his hand on her belly, and Elizabeth, exceedingly contented, fell into a deep sleep in spite of her intentions.

They did not keep town hours, at Pemberley, but they did usually dine at six, and as the bonfire's festivities began at twilight, dinner must necessarily be affected. Elizabeth had decided it was best to have a little cold collation in the yellow drawing-room before they set out, and then a more substantial supper when they returned.

Mary found this informal arrangement to be preferable, for when she had taken her plate to a little group of seats on the edge of the drawing-room, she found that – as she had hoped – she was immediately joined there by Mr. Stanton. They were studiously avoided by the rest of the party, who, despite having lived together for many months, managed to engross themselves in conversation in the centre of the room.

"I have finished both Gisborne and Paley," Mary said, a little abruptly, but she could think of no other way to begin the conversation she wished to have.

"Have you?" Mr. Stanton asked, with some degree of surprise. "I will admit, I am not used to young ladies following my recommendations for spiritual reading with such zeal."

Mary thought he must be acquainted with some very frivolous young ladies, for although a few passages had been laborious, she had completed them easily enough.

"I allot quite a bit of time for reading, and of course for practising the pianoforte," Mary said. "I do wonder, however, at your recommending works so very contradictory! I read Paley first, and thought you aligned more with the enlightenment thinkers, yet if I had read Gisborne first, I would have been certain you were an evangelical."

"Ah, yes," he smiled. "I cannot say that I sit firmly in either camp, and I hope I never shall. My enjoyment is in the discourse of these ideas."

Mary had always assumed there was a right camp, just as there was right and wrong, and she found it troubling that he – who had possessed more years in the world than her, in which to make up his mind as to what was right – could comfortably say he had no desire to do so. She had not seen this side of him, before, but then they had discussed less controversial writings, such as those of Fordyce and Gregory.

"Do you not think eventually you shall encounter an argument that settles your mind in one direction, or the other?"

"I have thought I encountered it many times, Miss Bennet, but then I always read something to influence it in another direction," he said. "You must remember that my father is quite a closed-minded man, and I suppose I have always endeavoured to keep my own as open as possible, so as not to be like him."

Mary had not met The Honourable Richard Stanton, but she had heard him described by Georgiana as a cruel man, and such a description from Georgiana, who ordinarily would not say anything so critical of anyone, had very much influenced Mary's opinion of the man. Perhaps if she had grown up in such a family, she might have reacted in a manner similar to David Stanton, but Mary had been raised in a family where no-one could be brought to have much of an opinion one way or the other, when it came to religion. It was not that the Bennets were not devout – they attended church every Sunday and prayed at all the appropriate times. Yet none of them but Mary could be brought to go beyond the common prayer-book.

They had lapsed into silence, although the need to keep eating so they would be ready when the carriages came around meant it was not awkward. Eventually, he asked how she had been, since he had seen her last, and she told him of how things had been during her time back at Longbourn, so the remainder of their time in the drawing-room passed pleasantly enough.

Elizabeth was glad David and Mary had come with Darcy and her in the carriage, for without the presence of a clergyman, she might very well have let slip some blasphemy, upon seeing the tower of wood that was to make up the bonfire. She looked over at Darcy, who was shaking his head in shock, and saying: "This is too much by half. Richardson must have made it much larger last year, with wood more readily available after the peace. I shall tell him this is the limit. It cannot be made any larger than this."

The bonfire would take place on Pemberley's grounds, but it was close enough to Lambton that the inhabitants of the village could make the walk there easily enough, and they were joined by most of Pemberley's staff and tenants, who were brought round by waggonette if they could not walk so far.

Mrs. Reynolds and the footmen were already there, beside one of the kitchen maids, who stirred a great pot of mulled wine, hung over a much smaller fire. They had a table set up, as well, covered with cups, and the biscuits the kitchen had been making for the last three days; beside all of this was a single chair, which Mrs. Reynolds indicated had been brought out for Mrs. Darcy.

"I do not need a chair," Elizabeth protested. "I shall go around with Mr. Darcy and speak with everyone."

"You needn't exert yourself, ma'am," Mrs. Reynolds said. "They all will surely come to you. They would do so even if we had not sat you near the refreshments."

Elizabeth looked to Darcy to make her protest to him, but he was making as though he wished to escort her to the chair.

"I am not an invalid," she whispered fiercely to him, "and yet I find I am being treated as such."

"You may stand or walk with me for a while if you choose to," he murmured. "But it will be a long evening, and Mrs. Reynolds only wishes to ensure your comfort. You must remember that she has hardly known a mistress of Pemberley in her present role, and never one who was expecting a child."

Elizabeth sighed, for his point was a good one. She thanked Mrs. Reynolds, and said she would appreciate use of the chair later, but for now she would walk about a bit with Mr. Darcy. They made their way amongst the gathering crowd, which parted easily at their approach, saying little more than how-do-you-dos to tenants and those from the village. A few of the local genteel families had come out, as well, under the promise of a bonfire, fireworks, and supper at Pemberley, to follow.

When the sun had fully set, Elizabeth sensed the event wanting some formal speech before the bonfire was to be lit, but knew her husband would be loath to speak in front of so many people, even if most of them were in some way dependent on him. Instead, it seemed it was the duty of Lambton's rector, Mr. Clark, to lead them all in a prayer, which began with thankfulness for a good harvest, and then continued on to duty to one's king – or regent – and country. He prayed they should all avoid the sin of treasonous thoughts, and never think evil or speak ill, as regarded their ruler or government, then concluded simply with the Lord's Prayer.

After a lengthy pause, Mr. Richardson walked up to the tower of wood with a lighted torch in his hand, and Pemberley's usually mild-mannered steward raised the torch in the air with a dramatic flourish, and then, with an expression of raw delight, plunged the torch into the wood. Some portion of the wood in the tower had been soaked in tar, and it lit quickly, so quickly there was a great "ooh!" emanating from the crowd, which, fortunately, had known to stand well back of the bonfire from the previous year's blaze.

Mary and Mr. Stanton were standing behind most of the crowd, yet even so, she could feel the heat coming from the fire, and found her eyes dazzled by the bright flames against the night sky, particularly when a round of rather brilliant fireworks began. She was troubled by Mr. Clark's prayer, however, that it was a sin to speak ill of their ruler, and it seemed her concern was noted by Mr. Stanton, who asked her in a tone of great solicitousness if she was cold and wished to move closer to the fire.

"Oh, no, I am perfectly warm here," Mary said. "I was thinking on Mr. Clark's prayer, that it was a sin even to speak ill of a ruler, or our government. I know the King – or now, I suppose, the Prince Regent – is God's representative on earth, yet kings may also be sinners – think of St. Thomas the Martyr, and King Henry II."

"Ah, I will admit it did not sit fully right with me, either," Mr. Stanton said. "Let us go find Mr. Clark, and speak with him of it."

"No, please – I did not mean that we should raise an argument with him." Mary was perfectly comfortable with sermonising to her own family, and attempting to influence their minds, but to critique the prayer offered by an ordained clergyman! The thought of it very nearly made her tremble, even though it was another ordained clergyman who proposed it.

"I do not mean to argue, merely to discuss. You know how I favour discourse," he said, offering his arm in a manner so kind and so direct, Mary could not bring herself to disappoint him.

They found Mr. Clark speaking with some of the local gentry, and waited until he was disengaged from his prior conversation before saying their greetings. Mr. Clark had become acquainted with Mr. Stanton in the course of Georgiana's marriage to Sir Matthew, and Mary had never sensed any strong feelings of either like or dislike between them. After a very cordial beginning, Mr. Stanton said:

"Miss Bennet and I have been discussing your prayer, and I believe we both must admit that it does not sit entirely right with us. Speaking ill of a king or a parliament is treason, of course, yet it does not necessarily follow that treason is a sin."

Mary tensely awaited Mr. Clark's response, which was: "You raise a rather interesting point, sir. Yet I would argue that when the King, or in his place, the Prince Regent, is head of the church, there is little difference between speaking ill of the monarch, and speaking ill of the church."

"But what of cases where a king has gone against the true church? Would you argue that the Glorious Revolution should not have come about – for surely it could not have come about without some manner of speaking ill of James II – and we should all have reverted to papacy?"

"If we lived in such times, perhaps my prayers would be different – I will allow you that. What say you, Miss Bennet? Mr. Stanton says my prayer did not sit right with the both of you, and yet you have been silent, thus far."

"As I told Mr. Stanton, I do not think we can forget that kings may be sinners, as well," Mary said, timidly. She required herself to continue in a louder, if wavering voice, "I gave as my example St. Thomas the Martyr and King Henry II, and I do not believe you may say I am speaking ill of that king, for he readily admitted his sins in the matter, and sought penitence for them."

"Very true, Miss Bennet," Mr. Clark said. "I will allow, then, that in theory, if a monarch acts to put his people off of God's path, it would not be a sin for those people to discuss how that path might be righted."

"Even if that discussion led to the monarch being deposed?" Mr. Stanton asked.

"That is further than I would wish to go, in front of a Guy Fawkes bonfire. And yet you have already given an example where it was so, and caused the restoration of the rightful religion in England," Mr. Clark said. "I will say, however, that you must consider the audience to which I spoke tonight. They live in an era with considerable freedom to worship God as they choose, and they are the beneficiaries of a very good master and landlord. Your other, theoretical people may have reason to speak ill of their monarch or their government, but these people here – they do not."

"But just because they have no reason to, that does not mean it is a sin," said Mary.

"I will allow that perhaps I may have worded my prayer a little better," Mr. Clark said. "I thank you both for giving me something to think on; I did not expect such a lively discussion, tonight."

Mr. Clark bowed and walked away, to speak with others in the crowd, and after he had left them, Mr. Stanton said, "You see, that was not so bad at all, although I will own that he was far more open to the discussion than many men might have been."

"Indeed, he was. It was very good of him," Mary said, and found herself feeling very pleased about the exchange. In the past, she might have just kept her disagreement in, and thought less of Mr. Clark. Now, however, she thought better of him for listening to them, and she found she thought even better of the gentleman who had prompted the conversation.

By the time the crowd had gathered around the mulled wine and biscuits, Elizabeth was ready to admit the wisdom of Mrs. Reynolds's having seen to a chair for her. Mrs. Reynolds was correct, as well, that people would come to her. None would pass the refreshments without stopping to bow or curtsey to her, and she engaged them each in a little conversation, then encouraged them to move on and take up their cups of wine. Eventually, Darcy came over to stand beside her, looking strangely happy for having been in such a large crowd for so long.

"Sinclair had a fox make an attempt on his henhouse, two nights ago," he said.

"You look entirely too pleased by this. Had you and Mr. Sinclair some sort of bet involving the survival of each other's chickens?"

"Oh, no – one of his men heard the commotion before too much damage was done," Darcy said. "I am pleased because it means we should open the hunt season as soon as we may. I believe we might fix a date over supper, for the first hunt."

Elizabeth had not realised he enjoyed foxhunting so much, although it made sense; Darcy favoured anything of the equestrian line, except racing. They had missed the foxhunting season last year, remaining in town for so long as they had, and it seemed Darcy intended to make up for it this year.

"Another tradition I shall have to learn," Elizabeth said. "We may discuss later the order of things, and what is needed for food and drink."

"Certainly. I only wish Georgiana was here for it."

"Georgiana hunts?" Elizabeth had begun learning to ride before her pregnancy had progressed very far, but could never imagine herself participating in a hunt. Georgiana, however, was a far more enthusiastic horsewoman than she, and far more experienced.

"She could now, if she wished. Her jumping has been up to the level required for some years, but it would not have done for her to even follow the hunt, before she was out in society."

"Well, if Matthew is not given a command, perhaps they may return here, and she shall have her chance."

CHAPTER 17

Georgiana and Catherine made their entry into Portsmouth a few days after Matthew, who had determined he could not wait any longer to join his ship, and – to Georgiana's chagrin – taken the mail down. Georgiana had wished to come in their own carriage, pulled by their own horses, and this necessitated a longer journey, so the horses might rest between stages.

She had no fear of their safety as two young ladies travelling alone, however. Before setting out himself, Matthew had sent Hawke down to the docklands, to find an old shipmate named Robert Bowden, and bring him to Lord Anglesey's house. Georgiana had been startled by Bowden's appearance, for he had a strange, milky left eye, and a horrible scar across his forehead, in addition to being tall and thickly built. He had served under Matthew on both the Caroline and the Jupiter, and been injured in battle on the latter ship, losing the sight of his eye, and yet upon hearing that the Caroline was to set out again, he had come eagerly to his summons. Matthew did not wish him to join the ship, however, and noted gently to the man that an incident which would rob him of the sight in his other eye – and therefore his entire livelihood – was much more likely to befall him on the ship, than in the new employment now offered to him.

That employment, which Bowden had accepted, was to serve as their footman, and it would have been a very brave highwayman indeed who would attempt to rob them with such a fearsome-looking man up behind the carriage. Yet in the course of their slow journey, Georgiana had learned that although Bowden looked fierce, and spoke roughly, he was actually a rather kind man. He had clearly been instructed by Matthew to always offer his arm to the young ladies, and although Georgiana had no need of it for walking – she had fallen asleep frequently during the journey, and so was not tired at all – she did accept his assistance down from the carriage. Catherine, all exuberance at finally being in Portsmouth, and exclaiming over every-thing she saw, leapt out of the carriage with no need of any assistance.

The carriage had stopped on the Common Hard, and Bowden looked about the harbour before finally pointing and crying out, "There she is, there's the barky!"

Georgiana followed his arm and saw a ship moored in the harbour, all of its masts up and freshly painted, looking far finer than her first impression of the Caroline.

"Oh! What a beautiful ship!" exclaimed Catherine, echoing Georgiana's thoughts.

Lord Anglesey had loaned them a spare livery for Murray, but had nothing that could fit Bowden, and so he had worn what he called his shore-going rig, a thoroughly naval outfit that had looked very strange in London. Here, however, he matched the other sailors about them, in his black hat and white trousers, and had no difficulty hailing a boat to take them to the ship.

The men on the Caroline must have seen them coming, for Matthew was looking over the side at them when the boat touched against the ship. Georgiana was wholly struck by this first glimpse of her husband in his own command, standing tall on the deck in full uniform, and looking very much like a man other men would follow into battle. Although the bosun's chair was already hanging over the side, Bowden still called out in an impossibly loud voice that he had Lady Stanton and Miss Bennet, for to join the ship. Upon being set down on the deck and greeted very formally by her husband, Georgiana found herself the focus of many inquisitive stares. She supposed this made sense – most of these men would have served with her husband for many years, and must have a goodly amount of curiosity about the lady he had married.

Catherine was deposited on deck with a little giggle of delight, and the stares were halted when someone shouted, "Back to work, ye sorry parcel of lubbers!"

"Lady Stanton, Miss Bennet, would you like to accompany me to the cabin?" Matthew asked.

"That would be lovely, Captain Stanton," Georgiana said, and they followed him down the very steep set of steps in the companionway, and into the great cabin at the stern of the ship.

Only when they were there and the door had closed did Matthew kiss her – chastely, with Catherine present – and ask how their journey had been. Georgiana and Catherine gave him an account of it, Georgiana noting that both Murray and Bowden had done well in their duties, and then were asked if they wished to take up rooms at the George, or to stay on board the ship.

Catherine, who had seated herself on the stern cushions and was looking out the windows there, as though her betrothed's frigate might be seen at any minute, eagerly cried, "Oh, may we stay on board the ship?"

"I would prefer to stay here, as well, if it is possible to accommodate both of us," Georgiana said, mindful now of her role as a chaperone. "And Hughes, of course. She remained behind in the carriage."

"Certainly. You and I shall share the sleeping cabin, and Catherine may take the day cabin. I have a cabin below that Hughes can use, within the wardroom," Matthew said, pointing to the first two spaces he had indicated: the day cabin, which they had walked through to get to the great cabin at the stern of the ship, and the sleeping cabin beside it. He said he would send Bowden back for their trunks, and give them a tour of the ship, if they were not too tired.

Georgiana had explained the cause of her apparent tiredness to Catherine during the journey, and so Catherine left her friend to say that she was not tired at all, and they would very much enjoy a tour of the ship. They walked out through the day cabin, and down the length of the frigate, with its great guns gleaming. Catherine made her way along easily, but Georgiana – like her husband – had to walk in a stooped manner to avoid hitting her head on the wooden beams above. They went down another level, into a much dimmer space, there being no guns here with their ports open to let in the light, and were shown the officers's wardroom and cabins, including the one Hughes was to use, and then the midshipmen's mess. Down yet another level, to what Matthew called the orlop deck, and here it was so dark lanterns were required, for as he told them, they were now below the waterline.

In this space, they met a grey, grizzled old man, who had what appeared to be an operating theatre set up – a set of trunks, upon which had been placed a piece of canvas, and a variety of surgical instruments. Matthew introduced the man as his surgeon, Mr. Clerkwell, and if Georgiana had not already been exceedingly inclined to like him, for successfully treating Matthew's injuries following the battle with the Polonais, she would surely have disliked him. He greeted the ladies brusquely, before saying to Matthew: "An' 'ow am I supposed to work down here, with it so awful dark? T'was twice as bright in t' Jupiter."

"Clerkwell, you managed well enough for five years down here; I have no doubt you shall manage again," Matthew said. "We will send down more lanterns, if you have need of them."

"I just tol' you I 'ave need of more light," grumbled Clerkwell, to which Matthew only shook his head, and invited the ladies to come forward.

He showed them the forepeak, a small little space in the bow of the ship, which he indicated to Georgiana would be where she would go, if ever on board the ship when it went in to action, and then they went back up, all the way to the weather deck of the ship. There, they met with a man in a lieutenant's uniform, who looked every bit as amiable as Mr. Clerkwell was sour. He was introduced as Lieutenant Rigby, now first lieutenant of the ship, as Matthew's longstanding first lieutenant, Campbell, had been promoted to Commander following the action against the Polonais. Rigby was all enthusiasm to meet the ladies he had heard so much about, and made them a very gallant bow.

They returned to the great cabin to find a fine variety of little cakes, fruits, and a pitcher of lemonade being laid down on the table by Hawke, which surprised and pleased Georgiana. Wishing to make up for her lack of a proper response the last time she had seen the ship, she said, "The Caroline is a very beautiful ship. I am glad to have a chance to see her with everything in place."

This elicited the pleased countenance she had wished for, and Matthew said, "Yes, I am very glad to have her again, although we still need to shift the bowsprit. The Caroline likes hers higher, and my new second lieutenant, Holmes, did not know of it."

Neither Georgiana nor Catherine had much opinion on bowsprits, and so they refocused their attention on the food. When she had finished eating, Catherine, perhaps sensing that her companions would wish for some time to themselves, asked if she might take her sketchbook up on the deck, for she was wild to begin to capture all of the things she saw in the harbour.

Bowden was summoned to take her up and find a comfortable place where she would not be disrupted, and once they had left, Georgiana rose to kiss her husband much more thoroughly than she had before. He encouraged her to come sit with him on the stern cushions, and asked if she had been able to see Dr. Whittling before departing London.

"Yes – Lady Tonbridge was very kind to go with me," she said. "Dr. Whittling confirms I am with child, and says the dizziness is normal. One of his patients is a baroness who fainted nearly every day she was in the family way, and yet still has a very large family."

"That is a relief to hear. I am very glad you were able to see him before we sail," Matthew said. "Is there any other news from London?"

"Not from London," Georgiana said. "But I received a troubling letter from Edward – he wrote that he was obliged to dismiss Monsieur Laquerre, and hire on another lawyer to work on Madame Durand's case."

"That is very troubling. Did he explain why?"

"It seems Monsieur Laquerre told Madame Durand that he had not been paid for any of his services."

"But that is complete nonsense. We paid him in full for everything he had done before we left Paris, and made very clear that he was to direct all future bills to us."

"I believe he thought Madame Durand was unaware of this arrangement. It seems the lawyer was quite taken with her and wished to offer her *alternative* means of paying him," Georgiana said, blushing hotly.

"That scoundrel! If only I could sail back to France and show him what I think of propositioning a poor, respectable widow in such a way."

"I believe Edward has already done all you would have wished for, in that quarter. He wrote that he convinced the lawyer to return everything we had paid him already, and is using it to pay the new lawyer. You can imagine the means he used to convince the man."

"I can indeed, and I am very glad he was in Paris and willing to take this on. It is another thing that makes me much easier at mind."

Over the following days, Georgiana and Catherine fell into a strange new pattern of life, on board the Caroline. They were often on deck, watching the activities of the crew as the ship was readied and supplies came on board, and they soon learned where they could and could not sit, so as not to interfere with the crew's work. Occasionally, there was some operation complicated enough that it required Matthew or one of his lieutenants to invite them to go down and sit in the great cabin instead, and they came to treat that space as if it was their drawing-room. When Matthew felt his presence could be spared from the ship, he would take them ashore, to drive about Portsmouth in the landau, pointing out the various sights of the town.

They dined in the great cabin every evening, as well, and Georgiana was once again surprised at the ease with which Matthew kept his table there. He had his own cook, and although the recipes were perhaps heartier and less delicate than might be found on land, it was all quite good. As well, he invited at least some of his officers and acquaintances from Portsmouth to dine every evening, and presided quietly over the conversation, needing to do little to help it along with Catherine at the table, and eager to learn all she could of the ways of the ship and town. A few of the guests enjoyed music, and those who did were invited to remain in the cabin following dinner, to hear Matthew play his cello, and Georgiana her new square pianoforte, which had come in by carrier. Catherine's accomplishments were not ignored on these evenings, either, for their company was always eager to look at her very fine attempts to capture in watercolour the spectacular fiery sunsets that were now a regular occurrence.

Of the officers, Georgiana found she most liked Lieutenants Rigby and Egerton, and the master, Mr. Travis, whose main achievement in Georgiana's eyes was living on board with his wife, an amiable older woman who dined with them when he did. Like Georgiana, Mrs. Travis would be leaving the ship during the mission to the Baltic, but Georgiana was pleased to think she would perhaps have such pleasant company on a future journey. As well, she could not help but be amused by Mr. Clerkwell, who could not go a quarter-hour without grousing about something or other; Matthew had admitted privately to her that the old man grew more irascible every year, but was tolerated because he had been with Matthew since his first command, and was very good at his work.

In this time, there were two events of significance. The first was that Hughes, after having rather shakily dressed Georgiana the first morning of their living on board, said she did not think she could remain on the ship any longer. The immediate solution to this was that she be rowed ashore and a room let for her at the Keppel's Head, within sight of the Caroline. Yet it also meant Georgiana and Hughes could not continue on in optimism that all would work out, with Hughes's seasickness. Bolstered by Matthew's intelligence that even Nelson was seasick for the first few days on board, they had hoped Hughes would eventually become attuned to the swaying of the ship, but she only grew worse, not better, even with the ship merely at anchor. Georgiana had grown teary-eyed, when Hughes had told her she could remain in her position a few months more, while her lady lived on land, but then must look for something new. She could not begrudge poor Hughes for it, though, for the maid had looked every bit as upset as Georgiana had felt.

The second, happier event, came one morning while they were all on deck. One of the sailors called out from his perch, well up on the mainmast, "Small frigate, hull-up off Spithead!"

This caused both Georgiana and Catherine to look up rather sharply, and see Matthew climbing up to the masthead as nimbly as any of the men. Once there, he pulled out a spyglass, peered through it for some time, and then descended rapidly, sliding down one of the stays leading from the mast.

"Lieutenant Holmes, lower the barge and ready the bosun's chair, if you please," he said, and then pointed to something Georgiana could not see. "And when you find the lubber who coiled that line, he is to have his grog stopped for two days, for he must have been drunk to do it thus on a King's ship."

Georgiana took care to hide her smile as Matthew made his way over to where she and Catherine were standing, on the quarterdeck at the stern of the ship. There were times, like this one, when Matthew the ship's captain seemed an entirely different person than Matthew her husband, and she did not think he would appreciate how diverting she found him at these times.

"Miss Bennet," Matthew said, "I believe that ship is the Andromeda. I do not know of any other twenty-eight gun frigates expected in."

Catherine was as thrilled with this news as would be expected, gasping and pressing her hand to her heart. She was still more thrilled when the ship came closer and was proved to be the Andromeda, and when Matthew gave her loan of his spyglass, so she could look through it and see her betrothed, standing there on the quarterdeck of his own ship. Captain Ramsey may have noticed the Caroline, but he had no reason to suspect his future wife to be on board, and he paid it no particular notice until the Caroline's barge approached the Andromeda, carrying Catherine, Georgiana and Matthew.

"Larboard side," Matthew told the men as they rowed. "There is no need for ceremony."

"Would there be a ceremony if we arrived on the starboard side?" asked Catherine, who rather thought seeing Captain Ramsey for the first time in more than half a year deserving of a bit of ceremony.

"Yes, but for myself as captain of another ship, to be received formally," Matthew said. "I feel fairly certain your presence will be the more noteworthy one, and it should not be delayed."

This response pleased Catherine, but could not do so as much as seeing Captain Ramsey standing there on the larboard side of the ship, staring down at them with a look of open delight. Catherine waved at him, blushed prettily, and was highly impatient over the pace at which the bosun's chair was lowered down. When she was on board, however, she found herself received as formally as Georgiana had been, with Captain Ramsey taking her hand and bowing to her, although with the happiest of countenances.

It was only when the couples had retired to the Andromeda's great cabin that Captain Ramsey said, "My lovely Miss Catherine, this is the finest surprise that ever was. I have missed you so very much, and had thought I had at least a few more days before I could be in your presence."

Catherine responded by throwing herself into his arms and exclaiming over how very much she had missed him, as well, which prompted Matthew to murmur, "We are not very intimidating chaperones, are we?"

Georgiana smiled, and agreed, but could not bring herself to say anything against such a happy reunion, particularly for a couple who had been engaged before them, yet had not had opportunity to marry. They allowed Catherine and Captain Ramsey a few more minutes before Matthew finally cleared his throat, prompting them to separate.

Now Captain Ramsey turned his attention to his friend, exclaiming, "Stanton! You lunatic! A French seventy-four?"

"It was not quite so much lunacy as you make it out to be."

"You will have to give me a full account of it, and then I shall judge whether it was or no."

"Dine with us this evening, then, on the Caroline, and you will have your account."

"That would be capital," Captain Ramsey said. "And I in turn shall tell you of the privateer we captured. It is no ship of the line, but I daresay it will pay for a few more pins, for Miss Catherine."

Captain Ramsey's steward came in with the sort of meagre refreshments that could be provided after having been at sea in support of a blockade, although they all partook of them, so as not to slight such a genial host. When they were all seated, Captain Ramsey raised his glass, and said, "Do not think I have forgotten to congratulate you on your marriage. I toast you both. And a damned good thing it is, too. You should have seen him during the carriage ride down to Portsmouth, Lady Stanton, moping about with the longest face in the world."

Georgiana usually enjoyed Captain Ramsey's teasing of his friend, and the good-natured way in which the man who was now her husband took it. The time Captain Ramsey spoke of, however, had been one of a great deal of unhappiness for her, and it was clear by Matthew's countenance that it had been the same for him. She took up his hand silently under the table, by way of reminding him – as well as herself – that at the very least those days were over. They might again be apart, but at least now they would part with the certainty that they loved one another.

CHAPTER 18

For some days, Mr. Darcy's countenance had been a touch lighter than was usual, even for a man happily married and awaiting the birth of his first child. Pemberley's staff knew this to be his usual eager anticipation for the first hunt of the season, an understanding also reached by his quick-witted wife, despite her lack of the same years of experience with Pemberley's foxhunting season.

She was surprised, therefore, to come into his study the day before the hunt, and find him frowning over a letter. She was even more surprised to learn it was from Georgiana, and the news contained within was that Matthew had been given command of the Caroline, and would be going to the Baltic without Georgiana. These things, however, were not what most troubled Darcy.

"She does not indicate where she will go, once Matthew departs. I suppose the London season will be coming up soon enough, so perhaps she will continue to stay with Lord Anglesey. But why would she not think of coming to Pemberley? Particularly with you so near to your birth. I do not understand it."

"I believe she may see it as a matter of more delicacy than you do," Elizabeth said, sitting heavily and resting her hands on her belly. "She is a married woman now; Pemberley is not formally her home."

"That does not mean she is not welcome here."

"No, and nor does it mean she does not wish to come here. But I do not presume I may simply appear at Longbourn whenever I wish – we always write, to arrange it in advance. My father did make a surprise appearance here at Pemberley, but I fully own it was irregular to do so, and I do not see Georgiana behaving thus."

"Do you think she will come, then, if I write to invite her?"

"I think it likely she will, and you may add that I would very much like her here for my birth. It might also be worth noting that Bess is much quieter, these days, and we would enjoy Georgiana's assistance in keeping her so."

"I will do so, then. I shall also mention the hunt, and remind her that Grace is still here."

"I think you are well on your way to making her feel guilty if she does *not* come to Pemberley."

"I cannot say I wish to go that far, but I will make the case for her coming here as best I may."

"And I suspect that even if you do not, she will still accept your invitation," Elizabeth said, then after some hesitation, she continued, "Darcy, I know since your father's death, your role towards Georgiana has been more like a father than a brother, but I suspect now you shall have to find your way back to being more of a brother."

"You are right, and I am well aware of it," said he. "I cannot say that I find it easy, however. Perhaps once I am a father to my own child, it will become easier."

"I suspect it shall. If nothing else, our child will provide a distraction from all else," Elizabeth said, then exclaimed, "Oh!"

"What is it? Is something the matter?"

"No, quite the opposite. The baby just kicked," she said, wishing it would do so again, so Darcy might come over and see if he could feel it as well, but her baby was not nearly so active as Bess had been, keeping poor Jane up half the night with her kicking, even before being born.

"Are we always to call it *the baby*, or might you be willing to discuss names?"

"No names — absolutely not, before he or she is born, and we know whether it is he or she," said Elizabeth, for she had a superstitious fear of naming a child before it was born.

"You fear risking our luck?"

"Yes, I do. I would rather not discuss it until after the birth," she said, groaning as she rose and went over to kiss him, before she would leave his study.

"I understand," Darcy said, "and you needn't leave to close the topic."

"No, I leave for other reasons. You have a letter to write, and I need to speak with Mrs. Reynolds, to ensure all is ready for the hunt. Do give Georgiana my best."

The morning of the hunt dawned crisp and cool, with not even a hint of rain present, a relief to all. Elizabeth could not bring herself to be particularly keen on the idea of her husband and Charles careening across the countryside and over any number of fences and hedgerows even on firm ground, and she had feared rain would turn the pursuit muddy, and even more dangerous.

They were not having a large house party, so the hunt was to comprise only local gentlemen, as well as any farmers who kept a suitable horse and wished to join – their reward in exchange for any upheaval of their fields that might occur. Darcy kept not one but four hunters; his favourite horse, Kestrel, was too valuable as a stud to use for hunting, but the chestnut he rode as he trotted up to the front of the house looked quite fine to Elizabeth's eye. He, Charles, and Richardson came up together, the hounds and their keepers following behind them.

Elizabeth had refused Mrs. Reynolds's offer of a chair, and was standing beside Jane, waiting as their neighbours gathered. Mr. and Mrs. Sinclair were first, the gentleman trotting along beside his wife's carriage. This pleased Elizabeth, for they were among her favourite neighbours: Mr. Sinclair was older, but very pleasant company, and his wife – who was his second wife – was nearer Elizabeth in age, and even more amiable than her husband. Mrs. Sinclair alighted her carriage, followed by her lady's maid, and a footman holding a valise, for Elizabeth had invited wives, sisters, and daughters to sit in the saloon during the hunt, and stay for dinner following, which would require a change of dresses. Most of the other families made similar arrivals, although a few of the ladies did come on horseback, wishing to ride out with the hunt.

"Was Charles disappointed you chose not to ride out?" Elizabeth asked Jane.

"A little, but he knows how long it has been since I have ridden," said Jane, "and I would much rather stay behind and worry over them with you."

"Indeed, I fear we shall be a fretful bunch, in the saloon, but at least we may fret together instead of separately, in our own homes. There is something to be said for that, I suppose."

"And both of our husbands are excellent riders," said Jane. "I take some comfort in that."

The husbands she spoke of, after having greeted all of the men, rode over to where Elizabeth and Jane were standing.

"I believe we have everyone who was expected, although a few more may join in when they hear the horn sound," Darcy said.

Elizabeth walked closer to his horse, and laid her hand on his knee, saying, "Please do be careful out there."

"I shall," Darcy said. "I love a good hunt, but you know I am not one of those neck-or-nothing sporting sorts, and neither, fortunately, are most of these men. Closer to London, you get that type of hunt, but here we all look at it as a fine country outing. If the timing had been different, you might have ridden out with us to get a better sense of it."

"The timing would have needed to be exceedingly different, Darcy, for I believe you would have been rather embarrassed by your wife's riding out on Buttercup," Elizabeth said, referring to Pemberley's stout old pony, on whom she had learned to ride.

Darcy laughed heartily, "Very true. After the baby is born, *and* you have graduated to a cob, perhaps then you might ride out with the hunt."

His countenance became troubled, and Elizabeth followed his gaze to see Mr. and Mrs. Cambert riding up. They had been invited, but neither Elizabeth nor Darcy had expected they would come, as their men of business had been settling the sale of the Camberts's land with nary a word on the matter from that party.

"I expect this shall change the nature of the mood in the saloon," Darcy said. "At least she is riding, so she will not be there the entire time."

"We will manage," Elizabeth said. "I would rather they come; it feels more neighbourly this way. I will follow her lead on whether she wishes to speak of the land."

"I had better go and greet them," Darcy said. "I shall see you before dinner."

Darcy trotted over to the Camberts and greeted them cordially. But Elizabeth, who had not offered anything stronger than claret cup as a pre-hunt refreshment, frowned to see that as soon as her husband left him, Mr. Cambert pulled out a flask and offered it to some of the gentlemen around him. Thankfully, none of them took up the offer, and Elizabeth was soon enough distracted by one of the hounds, who had strayed from the pack and stood looking affectionately at her, as though his greatest wish in the world was to be petted. Elizabeth leaned over as best she could and obliged him, but was eventually interrupted by the keepers calling all of the hounds in, prompting the dog to dash off. This, and a low rumbling of hooves, signalled that the hunt was to begin.

Those who had not been eagerly awaiting this beginning made haste to set down their cups on the trays offered to them by the footmen, and a great long string of riders followed the hounds, hooves clopping over the low stone bridge that crossed the stream. They were visible for quite some time, and all of the ladies who had remained at the house gathered near the door and watched them.

Even when they were out of sight, Elizabeth could still hear the hounds baying, and, eventually, the horn, and she said a quick prayer for the safety of all before making her way into the house, all of the other ladies following her. They were met in the saloon by Mary, who had no interest in the hunt – perhaps she might have, if David Stanton could have been convinced to stay for the event, but he had felt compelled to return to his duties at Wincham, a few days after the bonfire.

One of the ladies expressed a desire to see little Elizabeth Bingley, which was quickly taken up by the rest, and the baby was brought down from the nursery. Bess obliged them by being quiet for a good quarter-hour, as she was passed amongst the ladies to be held, but then made up for this by descending into hysterics, so that she must be quickly carried off by poor Mrs. Padgett.

Following this, the ladies settled into conversation, and their occupations of choice; some had brought needlework, and Elizabeth led an expedition to the library, for any that chose to select a book. From the saloon's broad windows, they could see the approach of the carriages holding the lady's maids for those ladies who had ridden out with the hunt, and later the return of those ladies on their horses. It was some time before they were all dressed and entering the saloon, followed immediately by the footmen with refreshments, and these things caused some rearrangement of the ladies's chosen seats, as well as some enlivening of the conversation.

"I must say, Mrs. Darcy, this is very handsomely done, particularly for someone so much in the family way," said Mrs. Sinclair, who had thoroughly availed herself of the fruit cut from the pinery that morning. "It was good of Mr. Darcy to have his steward arrange a few hunts while you were in town last year, but this is far better, to have some society for the ladies while we wait."

"I fully agree," said Mrs. Kinsley, who was to be the subject of more hospitality than most; her husband's estate bordered that of Clareborne Manor, and was therefore far enough away that the Kinsleys had been invited to stay overnight. "Mr. Kinsley says his father always used to say, you can leave it to the Darcys to do well by the neighbourhood. He was speaking of the previous generation of Darcys, but I believe we may say the same for this one."

Elizabeth would have thanked them for their compliments, but before she could speak, Mrs. Cambert was saying, "Yes, you can always trust the Darcys to do the *best* for the neighbourhood. How very fortunate we all are to have them."

She said it in the coldest possible tone, and as Elizabeth looked around, she could see that many of the ladies present knew what she meant by it. That the Darcys were the party purchasing the land from Barrowmere Park would not yet have been made public, but many of their husbands would have followed that the land had been for sale, and now was removed from the market. Those who knew of this must necessarily assume the party making the purchase was that of Pemberley, as it had been for the prior sales.

"I thank you all," Elizabeth said, but she would go no further in censure of Mrs. Cambert than to say, "Mr. Darcy and I are committed to doing whatever we may to ensure the happiness and stability of the neighbourhood."

"And glad we are to hear it," said Mrs. Sinclair. "The thought of stability makes me think to ask Mrs. Bingley how the construction gets on with the new house at Clareborne Manor."

"It is progressing well," Jane said. "Things will slow during the winter, of course, but we hope before next winter to have at least some portion of the house we may live in."

"Oh, how delightful," Mrs. Sinclair said. "I do rather like the thought of building a house anew – everything exactly suited to your taste."

They discussed the Bingleys's plans for the new house for some time, so that nearly all had forgotten Mrs. Cambert's coldness, although the discussion of a new house caused that lady's countenance to sour even further. And if Mrs. Cambert had been unhappy before, she became far more so when a groom was seen leading a horse up to the house, upon which sat her husband. Mr. Cambert's arm was in a makeshift sling, and as he came closer, they could all see his face contorted in pain.

With a cry, Mrs. Cambert fled to the entrance-hall, and was let outside by Mr. Parker. Elizabeth followed her, but could not move so quickly, and by the time she had come outside, Mrs. Cambert was berating her husband for being a fool who could not even stay on his horse, much less hold on to his fortune. It was left to the groom to inform Elizabeth that Mr. Cambert had taken a fall going over a jump, and thought his arm was broken.

"Mr. Parker, please have a carriage readied and someone sent to Matlock, for Dr. Alderman," Elizabeth said, which alerted Mrs. Cambert to her presence.

"It is not enough for you to take what remains of our estate, is it?" she asked. "No, you must also hold a hunt."

Elizabeth gaped at her for a moment, and thought of a great many things to say in response. These things largely centred on it neither being her fault that Mr. Cambert had gambled away his fortune, nor that he had imbibed something out of a flask that morning, which had likely led to his being unhorsed. She could not bring herself to speak in a way that would be cruel to a woman in Mrs. Cambert's situation, however, and so she said only, "I am terribly sorry to see anyone hurt at a hunt. We are readying a carriage to go for Dr. Alderman. Until he arrives, perhaps Mr. Cambert would be most comfortable waiting in the bed-room belonging to the dressing-room you had been using?"

Mrs. Cambert replied that she supposed he would be, and Elizabeth sent them both off with poor Mr. Parker.

It was perhaps unfortunate to think of it as such, but Mr. Cambert's injury necessarily benefited the rest of the hunt party. It was confirmed to be broken by Dr. Alderman, and dressed according to Larrey's method, and following this it was determined best by the Camberts that they return home, so Mr. Cambert could take his laudanum and rest more comfortably. They went off in their carriage as the remainder of the party was changing for dinner, and Elizabeth found the conversation was made lighter – at least at her end of the dining table – for their absence.

It continued so in the drawing-room, but thankfully on this evening their guests did not wish to linger. The gentlemen had enjoyed a fine hunt and a fine discussion of that hunt over port and brandy, although they had not caught their fox, which perhaps made it an even finer day, as it necessitated another hunt. The ladies had enjoyed all that Pemberley had to offer, and some of them had taken a lovely ride out, yet like the gentlemen, they were all ready enough to return to hearth and home. At an entirely reasonable hour, therefore, they all began calling for their carriages.

Thus, while Elizabeth had expected to be too exhausted to relate the entirety of her interactions with Mrs. Cambert to Darcy, she entered his bedchamber not long after they usually retired, and told him of all that had occurred.

"I must admit her logic baffles me," he said. "They would be even worse off, if we did not purchase the land. This last parcel is nearly entirely surrounded by what remains of their land, and Pemberley's. Do they truly think someone else would have purchased it?"

"I do not believe she is thinking logically, Darcy. It cannot be easy to watch their estate disintegrate, particularly when the debts are her husband's."

"True, but that is not any fault of ours. If she would have paid you any kindness at all, I would be inclined to treat her with a great amount of sympathy and assistance."

"Perhaps we should do so anyway, particularly with his arm now broken; I will send them a basket of fruit tomorrow, with a note of apology for his injury."

"A note of sympathy, not apology. He has a poor enough seat when he is sober – the fall was his fault alone."

"Fine, then, a note of sympathy," Elizabeth said, and then, for she was tired of speaking of the Camberts, "I hope you enjoyed the hunt."

"I did, very much. Would you mind terribly if we scheduled another?"

"Not at all. I know eventually my society will be significantly reduced, and I quite enjoyed today, excepting what happened with the Camberts," she said. "And I doubt they will attend the next hunt."

"Excellent, let us decide on a day tomorrow, then, and send our invitations."

"Yes, although this next time you had better catch your fox, or I will begin to believe you preserve his life so you may have more attempts at chasing after him, and surely someone's poor, innocent chickens must pay the price."

CHAPTER 19

Georgiana awoke to a rasping sound above her head; they were holystoning the deck, and unlike her husband, she had yet to learn how to sleep through such a noise, although she had by now mostly learned to ignore the bells every half-hour. She did not mind, however, for waking in this way allowed her at least a few minutes before nausea set in, where she might lay in her cot, swinging slightly, as sleep left her.

Matthew was in a cot beside her, and this was one problem she thought would need to be rectified, if she was ever to live on board for a longer period of time; she would have much preferred a cot that could hold both of them, for she missed having him immediately beside her. Aside from this detail, however, and her inability to forget that soon they would be separated by far more than the sides of hanging cots, Georgiana might have counted the last week among the happiest of her life.

Not a day had passed when they did not dine with Captain Ramsey, either inviting him over to the Caroline, or going themselves to the Andromeda. He was as talkative and amiable as ever he had been, and it was not possible to look at him and Catherine without feeling happiness for the reunited couple. After some time to discuss their wedding plans, loosely chaperoned by Georgiana in the Andromeda's cabin, the couple had asked if Georgiana thought the Darcys would be amenable to Catherine's being married out of Pemberley.

This had been a surprise, at first, although once Catherine explained their reasons, it had made a great deal of sense. Mr. and Mrs. Bennet would be returning to Pemberley soon enough, anyway, for the birth of Elizabeth's child, and so they might be married soon after Elizabeth's confinement was over. Elizabeth would not wish to stir from Pemberley for some time after her birth, and Catherine could not see herself being married without the presence of the sister who had given her the London season that had seen her meet Captain Ramsey. And, as Catherine confessed later to Georgiana, holding the wedding at Pemberley would lessen Mrs. Bennet's role in the planning, which Catherine, who had grown more short of temper where her mother was concerned, thought perhaps the greatest benefit.

Georgiana – who had received as effusive a letter as her brother ever wrote, inviting her to come to Pemberley – thought Fitzwilliam and Elizabeth would be very much for the scheme, and encouraged Catherine to write to them expressing her wishes. The response to Catherine's letter had, quite handsomely, come delivered by a groom riding on the estate's waggonette, which had been left to their disposal for carrying their belongings north.

The Andromeda was now paid off, and Captain Ramsey had arranged for six months of leave by correspondence with the Admiralty, so were it not for the Caroline's continued presence in port, they might have begun the journey. The Caroline was still in port, however, fully victualled and awaiting only the despatches she was to carry.

Georgiana felt the first stirrings of nausea, and made her exit from the cot much more gracefully than she had during her first few mornings on the ship, using the fire bucket which had been left on the floor for her particular needs. When she finished, she put on her dressing gown and a thick shawl, reflecting on how correct Matthew had been about the wooden walls of a frigate – even with one of the coal braziers going in the sleeping cabin, it was still quite cold. Georgiana made her way into the great cabin and thought to take up a book, but once she had sat down on the stern cushions, she found the action outside the windows far more interesting. Small boats plied the harbour nearly constantly – some pleasure craft, some fishermen, and others bound for some naval ship or another – and there was something beautiful about so many boats under sail on a fine, crisp morning.

"If it were not wholly scandalous, I would ask Catherine to paint you, just as you are now," Matthew said, entering the cabin.

"I believe that would sink us even further as chaperones than we are currently, although I believe some of the Parisian fashions were even more revealing than my dressing gown and shawl."

"Indeed they were," he said, laughing softly. "In truth, I am glad to find you in a quiet moment, for I have been looking for the right time to give you this."

He sat beside her on the stern cushions and astonished her by handing over a little jeweller's box, inside which was a dainty necklace, with an anchor as its pendant, sparkling in the morning sunshine.

"I hope it is to your liking," Matthew said.

"It is very much to my liking," Georgiana said, blinking back tears. "I will wear it every day, and think of you. I feel poorly that I have no similar gift for you."

"But you are not the one leaving for several months, and you have made four shirts for me."

"Shirts are not the same as a necklace, Matthew, particularly one so fine as this," Georgiana said, although tenderly, so charmed was she that he would even think to equate them.

"Not to a lady, perhaps, but you have said you will wear this every day, and I shall wear my shirts every day. So to me they are very much the same, except the shirts have been made by your own hands, and therefore must be classed as better," he said, and then continued, in a tone of some embarrassment: "If you are inclined to be giving, though, I would very much like a lock of your hair."

"Of course you may have a lock of my hair," Georgiana said. "Let me find my scissors, and a little ribbon."

Georgiana searched through her trunk until she found these items, and then returned to the stern cushion, braiding off a section of her hair and tying it with the ribbon. She was struck with a wildly romantic sensation as she made the cut with her scissors, for this was the sort of thing women in novels did, although the man she handed the lock over to was her own husband. She tried not to think of her dream, and how Mr. Wickham had so violently claimed a lock of her hair.

"There you are," she said.

"Thank you, my dearest," he said, holding the lock with an expression that was both tender and sad, and Georgiana knew precisely how he felt.

Georgiana could not have known it at the time, but she had bestowed the lock of hair upon her husband only the day before he left her. It was Catherine who noticed the messenger first, having been sitting on the deck with her sketchbook, so that she saw the man ride down Queen Street as fast as any express rider, and pull his horse to a hard stop just before the beach. This event was exclaimed over by Catherine, and then watched carefully by all on board the ship.

When it became clear the man on horseback had hired a boat, and the boat was rowing with all possible speed toward the Caroline, Matthew said, "Georgiana and Catherine, you had best pack up your trunks. I expect these will be our despatches, and if that is the case, we will sail on the next tide."

Georgiana had never been entirely lulled by these lovely, effortless days on board the ship, and yet the speed with which things changed quite stunned her. She and Catherine had been managing their own trunks and helping each other dress, with an hour or so of assistance from Hughes every day, before the maid grew too ill to do any more. Yet now she felt the urgency in Matthew's voice, and did the best she could in packing up her trunk. When she made her way into the great cabin, she saw Hawke and Bowden had already disassembled her pianoforte, and were wrapping the pieces in canvas, and Matthew was sitting at the large table in the middle of the cabin, with four bundles of waxed silk before him, and the contents of a fifth opened and being read.

"Is this it, then?" she asked.

"It is."

"How long before the tide?"

"A few hours more, but it would be best if we said our farewell now," he said. "Things will be busy right up until we sail."

Georgiana felt her eyes fill with tears, and she willed herself not to cry openly; she would have to bear this, for it was what she had chosen, in becoming a sailor's wife, if not exactly what she had envisioned. She nodded, but did not yet trust herself to say anything.

"Remember that we carry what may well be the fastest mail," Matthew said. "It is very possible that my letters may be few, or that you will not receive any before I return – please do not let this worry you."

"I will worry no matter what, but I will try not to allow it to add to my worries," Georgiana said. "I only hope it will be as quick as possible."

"I share your hope. Perhaps you will hardly notice I am gone."

"I doubt that – you at least will have daily occupation to distract you," Georgiana said, and then, noting his face had fallen further, "There will be Elizabeth's baby, though, and the wedding."

"Yes, and I am glad of it, and that you will be at Pemberley. I wish for you to be happy, always, including while I am gone."

"I will do my best to be so."

They were silent for a few moments, after this, and it felt natural that Matthew should pull her into a tight embrace, and they should share a long, lingering kiss good-bye. Georgiana attempted to absorb every detail of this time, for she knew it would have to sustain her in the months to come. It would not have mattered how long they were thus, for it would always have been too short a time before Matthew released her, and offered his arm so they could walk up to the deck.

Catherine was already waiting in the boat alongside the ship, with an expression far more sombre than was usual for her, and after Georgiana was lowered down and seated beside her, she clasped her friend's hand and said, simply, "I know how you feel."

Georgiana had decided it would be best to send her own team of horses up slowly, with the waggonette, and to order post horses for her landau, so they could make good time in the journey to Pemberley. With both Hughes and Captain Ramsey already staying at the Keppel's Head, it seemed easiest to take rooms there for her and Catherine, and to order the horses through the hotel. There was an additional advantage in the little iron balcony outside her room, from which the Caroline could still be seen, and when Captain Ramsey told her the tide was near, they all went thither to watch.

Even without any assistance, Georgiana could see the Caroline's anchor coming up, but when Captain Ramsey loaned her his glass, she could see the men all around the capstan, pushing with all their might, and her husband, standing there on the quarterdeck. Even before the anchor was stowed alongside the ship, one of the sails dropped down from the foremast, puffing out as the wind hit it. With that, the ship made a little ghostly movement forward; another sail, and with purpose, the Caroline started toward the mouth of the harbour.

Georgiana had been watching the sails, and found when she turned the glass toward the quarterdeck that Matthew was looking back at her through his own glass. He waved to her, she waved back, and that was to be her last glimpse of him for several months.

CHAPTER 20

On such a long journey, and with the day of their departure uncertain, the timing of the arrival of Lady Stanton, Miss Bennet and Captain Ramsey could not be predicted, nor the appearance of the carriage they were to come in. When an unfamiliar landau came up the drive, pulled by the team of horses that had been sent to the last coaching inn, however, it was clear enough to all that these were the expected guests. Further confirmation was given when the landau came closer and a rather rough-looking footman, who could only have been a former seaman, was seen standing up on the back. This intelligence caused happiness on the part of all who heard it, excepting Cook, who was horrified at their coming so close to dinner.

The lateness of the arrival meant they must all become reacquainted over dinner, for there was hardly time for them to change and make their way to the blue drawing-room before it was time to go in. The residents of Pemberley inquired after the journey, which had been just tolerable in the landau, not designed to go such distances regularly. They then turned to all that had happened in Portsmouth, and before, and were treated in great detail to the Andromeda's taking of the French privateer, the young ladies's time aboard the Caroline, and Georgiana's trip to Paris.

It was only well into the second remove that conversation turned to how those at Pemberley had been, and during this time, Charles noted with great enthusiasm that there had been a very fine hunt to begin the season.

"Ah, yes, it was an excellent outing," Darcy said. "We have another planned for next week, Georgiana, if you wish to join us. And Catherine and Captain Ramsey as well, if you wish – we have hunters enough here to provide you all with mounts."

Catherine replied that she did not ride; Captain Ramsey that he did, but had not been in the saddle for years, and was therefore not yet up to a hunt. This left Darcy staring expectantly at Georgiana, who had been largely quiet that evening, and to Elizabeth's eye looked to be a little melancholy, although Elizabeth understood it thoroughly, to be faced with such a long separation from her husband.

"I shall ride out with you, but I do not think I will hunt," Georgiana said.

"I have seen you and Grace clear jumps well over the height of anything we encountered in the last hunt," Darcy said. "I beg you will at least consider participating in the full hunt."

"If circumstances were otherwise, I might," said Georgiana, turning quite crimson. "I am in the family way, and would rather not make my first attempt in that state."

Elizabeth was not entirely certain how many of those seated at the table exclaimed, "So soon?" She knew that she had, however, and was fairly certain Darcy had as well. These exclamations only made Georgiana's apparent mortification worse, but before Elizabeth could bring herself to say anything in comfort to her sister, she was first required to deal with a substantial wave of jealousy. It had taken more than a year before Elizabeth had found herself with child; she had despaired at times of ever having one, and feared herself barren. Yet here was Georgiana, not even a half-year married and barely nineteen years of age, and already expecting her first child.

Jane recovered from the news first, exclaiming, "Oh, congratulations! How wonderful!" This roused the rest of the table into their own congratulations and best wishes, although Darcy seemed too stunned to offer more than the most basic of felicitations.

He was quiet in the drawing-room, but little conversation from him was needed, as they were looking over Georgiana's sketches of Paris, and Catherine's sketches and watercolours of Portsmouth, with all the attendant queries and descriptions over these items, so that the evening passed in a lively manner. It was only when she came into his bedchamber later that Elizabeth learned her husband was rather more angry, than stunned.

"I would not say anything in front of the others, but if Captain Stanton was here, I would give him such a piece of my mind, you would hear me halfway to Matlock," he said.

"Whatever for?"

"Whatever for? My sister is with child!"

"Darcy, when you gave your consent to their marriage, you must have expected this would happen eventually," Elizabeth said. "You make him sound as though he is George Wickham, instead of a baronet, who will of course wish to pass his title down."

"Well, he is hardly at Wickham's level," he said. "But he did get her with child just in time to leave her on her own for several months. You have read Georgiana's letters, what she wrote about the risk of the ship being frozen in. What if something happens to him, and she is widowed before the baby is even born?"

"Darcy, it was clearly for the best that she did not go with him, so I hardly see where he had other options, aside from refusing the command at the risk of jeopardising his career."

"I would rather he risk his career than his life, when the latter must affect Georgiana so much more substantially than the former, given their fortune."

"And yet you put your life at risk without the purpose of a career, unless you count foxhunting as part of touring the estate grounds, which is quite a stretch."

"So now this has turned into an indictment of my hunting?" he cried.

Elizabeth sighed, and shook her head. "Darcy, I am very tired, and not in spirits to argue tonight. I have no desire to ask you to give up something which gives you so much enjoyment. I only wished you would see that Matthew's career also gives him a great deal of enjoyment, although also with a *small* risk to his life, now that there is peace."

Elizabeth had spoken honestly; she was fatigued, and had no energy for the sort of argument two people so passionate as she and Darcy could, on occasion, have. She had not intended for her words to doubly impact him, and yet it seemed they had, for when he spoke, after a pause of some duration, he said:

"You shame me, my dearest Elizabeth, and thankfully you call me out for an unfortunate degree of prejudice, against a man towards whom I should have none, and prevent me from vexing a lady in whose condition I should be loath to vex."

"Let us not go that far, Darcy. I will not deny you have had rather irrational thoughts towards a man who gave you no reason for them, but he is not here, and I am not entirely vexed, merely tired."

"Still, you are in the right of it. You have been attempting to convince me that I must treat Georgiana more as a sister, now, than a girl whose guardianship I have held. I hear her say she is in the family way, and immediately feel the worst, as if she was still unwed."

"And I will allow that she *is* very young to be having a child, but no more so than any of the other ladies her age who have married," Elizabeth said. "It cannot be easy for her, particularly with him from home. But you must remember how low her spirits were, when she was uncertain of his affections, and they are not remotely so low now."

"No, they are not, thank God."

"Then you might turn your energies towards a more useful purpose, and begin convincing her to have the baby here. We shall fill up the nursery, and it will be wonderful."

"Only so long as our newer additions are not so loud as Bess was, in the beginning. There is no guarantee they will all be placated by the pianoforte."

Elizabeth chuckled, and kissed him good-night. "Perhaps for this one, it shall be the cello."

The nursery was the focus of much attention the day following, for Bess had not been seen by Georgiana and Catherine in some time, and she was in a far better state to be seen than she had been during their last residence at Pemberley. Mrs. Padgett had taken her down to the music-room already for a few turns through "Twinkle Twinkle Little Star," and so she was content to be held by them. When she was calm, Bess promised to be every bit as handsome as her parents, although it remained to be seen whether she would become as amiable, once she grew older.

When Elizabeth, Jane, and Mary also came in, Mrs. Nichols, who was always endeavouring to make herself useful before her charge was born, brought in additional chairs from the sitting-room down the hall, and then allowed her son to be passed around and held, as well. Georgiana had not met her Fitzwilliam nieces until they were older, and so her only experience with babies so young as these had come with Bess's birth – and Bess could hardly have been called a model infant, when last Georgiana had seen her. She found herself becoming a little more attuned to the idea of having a baby of her own, holding Bess, then George. There was something exceedingly lovely about the soft, pudgy bundles in her arms, and the distinct, powdery smell of the babies.

"Georgiana, I do not believe you mentioned last night when your child is to come," Elizabeth said.

"June, or possibly July of next year, Dr. Whittling believes. I saw him, in London."

"Was Matthew as fussy about the visit as your brother was? I thought he might wear a path in the carpet of Dr. Whittling's sitting-room."

"Matthew had already gone down to Portsmouth. He had very little time in London, once we learned of his assignment."

"Did you go by yourself?" asked Jane, with an expression of some horror.

"No, Lady Tonbridge went with me," Georgiana said, thinking about what a kind sacrifice it had been for that lady to do so. Lady Tonbridge had confessed a little of her own history with children, which had been fraught with miscarriages, and never seen a baby live more than a few days. It had been very hard on her, although made easier by the kindness of Lord Tonbridge, who could afford to be kind, having already produced an heir with his first wife.

Bess chose this moment to halt Georgiana's recollections, and any discourse in the room, by wriggling in Mary's lap, which prompted her holder to say, "Oh, we must get her back to the music-room immediately," and then, recollecting that Georgiana was now returned to the house, holding out the baby to her and saying, "Should you like to play for her? We have all been taking turns."

"I would, certainly," Georgiana said, "but it might be best if you carried her. I have been inclined to faintness, since I have been in the family way."

Mary said she would, and with that, the ladies all made their way down to the music-room. Reunited with her instrument, Georgiana played for an hour, to Bess's great delight. Georgiana, though, found herself strangely longing for her little Clementi square. It could never be said that it was as fine an instrument as this one, but it was associated with a great many fond recollections for her, now.

They sat quietly when she had finished, until Mr. Parker brought in the post, among which was a letter from Edward, indicating that the new lawyer had thus far been more trustworthy, and made good progress on Madame Durand's case. Elizabeth inquired as to the source of Georgiana's letter, was informed that it was from Edward, and then said, "Darcy will be quite jealous of you – it seems you are now Edward's favoured correspondent."

Georgiana told the ladies of Madame Durand and her legal case, and how Edward had agreed to assist her upon Georgiana's and Matthew's leaving Paris.

"I am sure you must have had quite the task, to convince Edward to look after a beautiful French widow," Elizabeth said, laughing.

"Yes, he teazed us both for not informing him she was beautiful, before he first met her."

"He does love playing the gallant," Elizabeth said. "I expect he calls on her every day, whether there is an update to her legal case or not."

"I hope he does," said Catherine. "It would mean he is back nearer to his usual self, and I believe we may all rejoice in that, except perhaps this Madame Durand. We may never know how *she* feels about his attentions, but I hope for her sake she finds him as amiable as we all do."

CHAPTER 21

With a great deal of contentment did Elizabeth see her sisters settled in at Pemberley, and if she did not feel so uncomfortably large, she would have been thoroughly happy at having all of them – save Lydia – there with her. Lydia was, occasionally, the source of guilty thoughts for Elizabeth, which emerged most substantially whenever Catherine was in her presence.

Catherine had once been very nearly as silly as Lydia. Yet now she was to be found working diligently on watercolours in whatever room they were all seated in, or going on walks with Captain Ramsey and whoever could be roused to chaperone them, on days when the weather was fine. Her conversation at dinner was still lively, but marked with good manners, and sense.

Lydia had been invited to come up with Mr. and Mrs. Bennet, when Elizabeth's birth drew nearer, and Elizabeth wondered what her youngest sister would be like, now, and whether she would still treat Catherine with jealousy and contempt. These thoughts were followed by the greatest measure of guilt, for Elizabeth could not help but think that their mother had led Lydia and Catherine into their silliness, and that removing Catherine from Longbourn for the better part of a year had done her a great deal of benefit. It would be right to give Lydia the same opportunity; although she could not be given a season in town, as Catherine had been, she could at least be invited to stay at Pemberley after her parents returned home. Lydia would never have Catherine's prospects unless her husband died, but perhaps her manners could still be improved in some way.

Catherine would have no opportunity to walk with Captain Ramsey on this day, for Charles and Darcy had been steadily wearing down his resolve not to hunt over port every night following dinner. He had not yet agreed to participate in the next hunt, but had allowed a long ride with Darcy, Charles, and Mr. Sinclair that morning, to attempt a few jumps and see how he did. Mrs. Sinclair had come over in the carriage alongside her husband, to call on them, and she had new intelligence on the Camberts, which she would only share upon learning that all of the ladies in the saloon were family.

"They are in a far poorer way than any of us realised," said she. "It seems they have not even paid Dr. Alderman for treating Mr. Cambert's arm, and now they plan to move in with relations; Barrowmere Park is to be let or sold."

"Oh, dear – we were the ones who summoned Dr. Alderman," Elizabeth said. "If he has not been paid by them, we should do so."

"They would not take kindly to your paying their debts, I do not think," Mrs. Sinclair said. "Perhaps you might send him items of comparable value to his fees – fruit or game, perhaps – and call them gifts. He will understand their purpose."

"Yes, that is a much better course," Elizabeth said. "I do not know if we shall see the Camberts again, but I would wish to minimise the awkwardness as much as I may. Do you know when they are to remove?"

"Within a fortnight, I understand. They are already allowing interested parties to see the house," Mrs. Sinclair said. "You might have a look at it, Lady Stanton. There are few it would be so convenient for."

This idea of the Stantons's taking Barrowmere Park was brought back up over dinner, with increasing enthusiasm among most at the table. Only one of the party expressed any uncertainty about the idea, but as this was Georgiana, this provided a substantial obstacle to the plans of the others, for how she was to let it, or perhaps even purchase it, and furnish it new.

In Matthew's absence, the thought of settling so near her brother and sister did appeal to Georgiana. Yet she was reluctant to do something so substantial as take a house without her husband's approval, and beyond this, she was not entirely certain she wished to settle such a long distance from any port. If Matthew was unable to get a letter back to her, giving some idea as to the date of his return, it would be days before an express could reach her in Derbyshire, and she could travel down to meet him. Still, if he was often from home, it might instead be better to have some delay in their being reunited, so she could stay near family.

She considered all of these things, and was nowhere near making a decision, but did allow herself to be convinced to at least go and see the place with Fitzwilliam on the morrow. As could be expected, Fitzwilliam approached the matter more practically, asking before they would set out if Georgiana even had access to enough of their fortune to be able to let the house before Matthew returned. She told him of the papers she had signed, although it had all happened in such a rush, she was not entirely certain what they were.

"Likely a letter of authorisation, which would be all you would need to produce the funds for a lease," he said, and rang the bell in his study for a footman, to find Hughes and have her seek out the papers in Georgiana's bedchamber.

It was some time before Hughes came in with the papers, and they were handed over to Fitzwilliam, who read through one of them carefully, and then said, "It is not a letter of authorisation. This is a full power of attorney, Georgiana; you have complete control over all of your finances. If you wish, you could purchase the house."

Fitzwilliam seemed a little shocked, but it was not entirely surprising to Georgiana that Matthew would leave her with such powers. He had told her very firmly that if there was a thing she wished for, it should be purchased if it was within their funds, and yet she felt reassured at his confidence that she would make the right decisions while he was absent. This did not make her any more likely to wish to let or purchase the house, but it did do away with some of the worry that if she should do so, it would be the wrong decision, one Matthew would be unhappy about when he returned.

With this all settled, they should have been able to make the journey to Barrowmere without further delay, but as they were coming up the drive, the waggonette could be seen approaching them, Murray up behind the bays and looking rather relieved his long journey was finally coming to an end. It would not end as quickly as he might have liked, however, for Fitzwilliam asked Georgiana if these were her new horses, and upon hearing that they were, ordered Mr. Powell, his coachman, to stop.

Georgiana followed her brother out into the lane, standing there nervously as he looked them over – there was none whose good opinion of her horses mattered so much as his. As she had attempted to, he felt each of their legs, and then stepped back and gazed at them.

"A very fine pair, for your first," he said to Georgiana. "Neither too delicate, nor too coarse. They will do well in town, but they have managed the journey here very nicely."

"Thank you, Fitzwilliam, I am glad to hear you like them."

Fitzwilliam instructed Murray on where he might drive the waggonette, so it could be unloaded, and informed him Mr. Parker would see a groom sent over from the stables to get him and the horses settled in. He then assisted Georgiana back into the carriage, and it set off again.

"Does your coachman serve as your groom, as well?" he asked.

"He does, for now. It was a promotion for him, so he does not mind the extra duties," Georgiana said. "But I think we shall hire on a groom, to care for the bays, and Grace and Phoebe. We have trespassed on your grooms for too long."

"You need not rush, Georgiana – two or even four more horses hardly signify, in Pemberley's stables."

"Still, if you hear of any possible applicants, please do let me know,"

Georgiana said, knowing that inquiries for such positions at Pemberley happened with some frequency.

Fitzwilliam replied that he would, and then they were silent until the carriage stopped in the drive at Barrowmere. Georgiana had seen the house before, an old stone affair, but it had been some time since she had been inside, and she could not remember any of the interiors. It was best she could not, for she suspected it would have made what she saw inside seem even more shabby by comparison. It was apparent that the paintings had been sold, and perhaps even some of the furniture, for all inside looked sparse.

They were shown around by the housekeeper, with no sight of the Camberts, which Georgiana – who had been informed of all that had occurred involving that family by Elizabeth – thought for the best. The principal rooms were faded, but liveable, as were a few of the primary bed-rooms. When they examined the farther wings, however, Georgiana thought them unusable, such poor repair were they in. It seemed Fitzwilliam agreed, for he said:

"I believe these wings would be best to come down. It would make for a cosier house, but I fear it would be more effort to restore them than to rebuild in the future, if you had need of more space."

"I do not know that we would ever need so much more space," Georgiana said. "We were quite comfortable living on board the Caroline together."

"Well, then so long as you have enough bed-rooms for your children, the core house may well suffice."

Georgiana thought she would prefer the cabin of the Caroline over the principal rooms of this house, for the cabin at least was freshly caulked and painted. She said nothing of this, however, until after they had thanked the housekeeper and returned to the carriage.

"I hope it does not disappoint you," she said, "but I do not think I would wish to take the house, even just to let it. The only thing it has to recommend it is that it is close to Pemberley. It might be different if Matthew was home; I daresay he would recruit a great many seamen to see the place freshly scrubbed and painted from top to bottom, and all else returned to better repair. Without him here, though, I would not wish to take it on."

"It does not disappoint me at all, Georgiana; it would have disappointed me if you *had* decided to let it, despite how enthusiastic everyone else has been about it," Fitzwilliam said. "I would hate the thought of your living alone in that miserable house when you might be at Pemberley instead. If you do wish to set up a household, I would rather it be in Derbyshire so you are closer to us, but there is no need to do so immediately, or in such a house."

"Aunt Catherine would not agree with you, on that point. She is adamant that the baronetcy should have a seat."

"Yes, she has written to me of it, as well. But you would do best not to make any decisions on the advice of Lady Catherine," Fitzwilliam said, then added, "And you must never tell her I said thus."

Georgiana laughed. "I shall keep your secret. I know we must settle on a home, eventually, for the sake of our child, if not the baronetcy, but I would rather wait until we have a better sense of how often Matthew is to be from home."

"I think that wise," Fitzwilliam said, and then his countenance turned more serious. "Georgiana, you know you will always have a home here at Pemberley, regardless of whether you set up your own household or not. I would never wish to see you alone when Matthew is from home; you need not wait for an invitation."

"Thank you, Fitzwilliam," Georgiana said, her eyes filling with tears. "That means a great deal to me."

"I only wish I had said so before you were married," he said. "Your old room is not entirely suited for a married couple, so I believe what we shall do is set aside one of the larger apartments on the second floor for your particular use. The one on the east side of the house is very nice – unless you would prefer your old room?"

"No, I believe I would prefer the apartment you speak of," Georgiana said. "You are right that it is better suited for a married couple."

"Excellent, then we shall see you moved there at your convenience, and it will always be yours, whenever you choose to stay here. And do not worry on account of your child; nothing would delight Elizabeth more than to fill the nursery."

Georgiana found herself comforted by all that her brother had said, but this last statement did so most deeply. The thought of her child living in the nursery in which she herself had grown up made her future feel much more secure, and she came into the entrance-hall in a state of reassurement.

Elizabeth had been in the nursery with Jane, when one of the footmen informed her Darcy and Georgiana had returned. Curious to learn how the visit to Barrowmere Park had gone, she made her way downstairs and found Darcy in his dressing-room, just finishing his change of clothes.

"And how was it?" asked she, walking with him into their private sitting-room, where, claiming advantage of her situation, she took the chaise.

"The house itself is in poor repair – if Georgiana were to take it, I recommended the farther wings be pulled down. But she does not intend to take it, either for lease or purchase."

"Do you agree with her decision?"

"I do. It was a pleasant notion to think of her settled so close to us, but with Matthew from home, it makes no sense for her to take a house in such condition, when we have so much space," he said. "I did offer her and

Matthew permanent use of the large apartment on the east side of the house, on the second floor. I hope you do not mind that I did so without speaking to you first."

"I do not mind at all, and I can think of no better use for it," Elizabeth said. "Did you see the Camberts?"

"There was no sign of them, thankfully, but the house shows how poor their situation must have been. The paintings are down from the walls, and some of the furniture is gone as well."

"It will be interesting to see who our new neighbours shall be, then, to take on such a house."

"It will require the right sort of people – they must have income from other sources, and be willing to spend it to make the place comfortable again. I expect the Camberts will need to lower their asking price, before they will find a suitable party."

"You have made things too easy for them, by buying up all of the land whenever it comes on the market."

"Perhaps I have, and perhaps they will think more highly of us when they realise what waiting it saved them, although I doubt it," Darcy said. "Now I am afraid I must leave you – I promised Charles and Captain Ramsey I would meet them for billiards on my return. Are you to stay here and rest?"

"I believe I will, for a little while, and then I will speak to Georgiana about when she wishes to move into the new apartment."

"Would you like me to have Miss Kelly wake you?"

"I do not intend to sleep, but yes, it is probably best, for I may well fall asleep in spite of myself," Elizabeth said. "Would you be so good as to bring me my book?"

Darcy did as he was bade, fetching it from the table beside his bed and handing it to her with a kiss, and the gentlest little caress of her cheek.

"How do you think I should spend my twenty guineas?" asked he.

"You still have several weeks more, Mr. Darcy, which is ample time for my feet and face to swell further still, and my back to pain me even more, which surely must affect my countenance."

"Has your back been paining you?" he asked, his teazing forgotten. "Why did you not say anything?"

"Dr. Alderman said it was natural – after all, I am carrying the weight of what is very nearly an infant in my belly. But there is little that can be done about it."

"I do not agree – here, sit up a little," he said, and then assisted her to do so, sitting on the edge of the chaise beside her and rubbing his hand in little circles on her back.

"That is better," Elizabeth said, although she was not entirely certain whether his actions were helping with the pain, or simply so pleasant they served as a distraction. "You needed to meet Charles and Captain Ramsey for billiards, however."

"It takes only two to play; they may occupy each other for a while."

Sarah did not need to wake Elizabeth, although she did inform her at the appointed hour that Georgiana had just rung for Hughes, as well. Thus Elizabeth knocked firmly on the door with no fear of waking her sister, and walked into the spacious chamber that had been Georgiana's ever since she had moved out of the smaller children's bed-rooms beside the nursery.

Darcy was right that it was not appropriate for a married couple; aside from only possessing a dressing-room adjoining it, there was a girlishness about the room, in its hues and furniture. Presently, there were also several trunks on the floor, and the large, canvas-wrapped object that had stirred Elizabeth's curiosity, upon seeing it brought into the house.

Georgiana, after welcoming Elizabeth to her room, began rummaging through one of the trunks, producing great quantities of lace, a very fine parasol, and a bottle of scent. She gave these over to her sister, saying, "These are for you; I hope you will like them."

Elizabeth did like them all, very much, and thanked her sister by telling her so, then continued, "I had wondered at your bringing so many trunks back, but now I know them to be not your own purchases, and instead the result of your generous nature."

"I had the fortune of an opportunity my family and friends shall not be likely to have for some time," Georgiana said. "I could hardly be in Paris without giving you some benefit of it."

"You must tell me – what is that great object there?" Elizabeth said, motioning to the canvas package, which had been left in the far corner of the room.

"Oh, that is not from Paris; it is from London. It is a Clementi square pianoforte," Georgiana said, and then continued, somewhat defensively, "Matthew had meant it for my use in the great cabin of the Caroline, but since I do not travel with him for now, we thought it best that I take it with me."

"A pianoforte? But must it not have legs to stand on?"

Georgiana walked over to the object and unwrapped it sufficiently, so that Elizabeth could see the detached legs, and below them, the main body of the pianoforte itself. Then Georgiana said, in a tone of sadness, "Matthew had it altered, so it might be taken apart and struck down in the hold. It was so thoughtful of him."

"You must miss him tremendously."

For a moment, Georgiana's countenance appeared overwhelmed, and her eyes filled with tears, but she blinked them away, and said only, "I do, very much."

"I must admit surprise at your package being a pianoforte," Elizabeth said, expecting her sister wished for a distraction. "I had never expected one so small – we have a square at Longbourn, but it is much older, and larger. I believe we must get one for the nursery, so Bess may be entertained there."

"You may use this one there, if you wish, while I am here."

"Oh no, we shall order another. This would go very nicely in the sitting-room of your new apartment, if you still wish to move there. Not, of course, that you may not use the one in the music-room whenever you please – Darcy has indicated it is yours, and will go with you whenever you set up your household. But you may find it nice to have an instrument so convenient."

"Yes, I believe I would like to have it in the sitting-room there, if you do not mind. And I am very appreciative of you and Fitzwilliam setting aside that apartment for us. It is so kind of you."

"It is kind of Fitzwilliam, but I fear it is more selfish of me. I should prefer as many of my sisters near me for as long as possible. I do not know how I shall bear it when Jane finally repairs to her own estate," Elizabeth said. "When would you like to make the move to your new apartment?"

"I suppose whenever it is convenient for the staff. It shall be strange to leave this room, but somehow it does not feel as though it belongs to me, any more. It is as though a different person lived there."

"I know precisely what you mean. When we stay over at Longbourn, your brother and I share what was my bedchamber, when I lived there, and it feels impossibly strange. That room was for being a girl, and wondering with Jane if we would ever marry. It is not a room for my husband to be staying in."

Georgiana smiled, and said she knew what Elizabeth meant, but with a listlessness that worried her sister.

CHAPTER 22

A few days following the hunt – in which Captain Ramsey was said to have ridden well – a succession of servants, supervised by Hughes, made quick work of seeing all that a young lady could acquire in nineteen years transferred from Georgiana's old apartment to her new one. The move came to be a welcome distraction for her, to take over a new space and think of what might be done to make it her own. Georgiana was glad Elizabeth had declined her offer to have her square pianoforte placed in the nursery, for it fit nicely in the little sitting-room. She smiled upon it every time she saw it, and spent a little time in practice on it every morning, thinking always of Matthew as she played.

With this apartment on the east side of the house, rather than the north, Georgiana was beginning to attune herself to using a different staircase than she had for most of her life. She went to the east stairs now, so she could go down and join the ladies in the music-room, and assist in the entertainment of Bess. Fitzwilliam's voice could be heard as she descended, which seemed natural; his study was down the hall from these stairs, and he sometimes began or concluded his business while walking with his guests. As she reached the first storey, she could hear Fitzwilliam more distinctly, saying: "Remember, she must go with you to America. You will not see a shilling of it, unless she agrees."

Georgiana thought it odd that he spoke of someone agreeing to go to America, and thought to ask him of it later; perhaps it was the son of a tenant, although it was odd that someone must agree to go with the son. She was entirely unprepared when she reached the landing.

"Mr. Wickham!" she exclaimed, and fainted dead away.

Georgiana's shock and horror at this revelation were complete. She could never have suspected this had been his plan, in telling her they were going to Jamaica, and that he

148

had intentionally given her the blackberries with her dinner, so as to provide her with the means for making an ink.

"Please do not do this," she whispered. "Please."

These were all the words she could manage, before she collapsed, sobbing, on the floor.

It took her a very long time to recover from this state, and it was well into night before she managed to crawl into her bed and curl up there, considering what she should do. She had always harboured hope that somehow all would come right, that either Mr. Wickham or Fitzwilliam would give in, but now she understood she would never be released from Mr. Wickham's custody, and her only hope was to attempt to free herself. She must do so in time to warn Fitzwilliam, she thought, and she set about creating a plan. It was one borne of desperation, but she found it better to plan than to give in to her desperation.

She began after Mr. Wickham next left the cottage, practising by picking up the battered old chair and swinging it over her head. This she did until her arms tired, and then she rested, and practised again.

When Mr. Wickham returned, she laid on the bed and feigned reading, and when he came in with her food, she did her best to look as though she was as thoroughly defeated as she had felt the night before, thanking him timidly for her meal. Although she had the deepest desire to be off, she did this for some time, practising during the day, and acting deferential and defeated when he returned, until finally he said:

"If I had known this would break your spirit, Georgiana, I would have done it long ago. Perhaps we might live as a more traditional man and wife, someday."

"Do you think so?" she whispered, allowing herself to look just the slightest bit hopeful.

"Perhaps, once your brother is well on his way to Jamaica. It would be better, to have a proper mistress for Pemberley," he said. "I have mailed the letter, so I do not believe it will be long now."

After this, Georgiana felt the deepest inclination to set her plan in motion immediately, but still she waited. She would have one chance only, and she could not risk being unprepared. So she practised still further, until her arms grew stronger, and she thought she could do the deed successfully. When he came in with her dinner that evening and actually smiled a little at her, Georgiana felt this must be when she should spring her trap, such as it was.

"The girls you bring home, what you do with them, they seem to enjoy it," she said, softly. "Is that what you wished to do, the night we were married?"

"It was," he said. "How do you know what I do with those girls?"

"I watch, through the keyhole."

"You do, hmm? And how do you feel, when you are watching? Do you feel a stirring, in unmentionable places?"

"Yes," Georgiana whispered, although in truth she had felt no such thing. "I – I sometimes wish to be doing those things myself."

"If you were to participate willingly in such an act, I assure you, Georgiana, things would be much better for you. Meat and wine for dinner, to start, and we would be well on our way to acting as a true husband and wife."

"If you would bring me some pure wine, to start, and allow me to finish my dinner, I – I will participate willingly," Georgiana said.

Mr. Wickham seemed both delighted and distracted by this, as she had hoped. A little cup of wine was deposited on her floor, and then the door closed and locked, with Mr. Wickham saying, "Change into your nightclothes, and let me know when you are ready for me to enter."

Georgiana trembled, and drank only a little of the watered wine. Distracted by lust, and perhaps having drank down some of the pure wine himself – which had been her hope in asking for her own – Mr. Wickham would prove an easier target for the chair, but in his lustful state Georgiana expected he would have her regardless of how she reacted, if she made her attempt and failed.

She did change into her nightgown, for it would make it easier to move to the next step in her plan. She picked up the chair and went to stand by the door, then called out that she was ready, in a quavering voice. The sound of the key in the lock was less steady than usual, and when the door opened, and she had sighted his head, Georgiana took the very swing she had been practising all this time, and found she had timed it perfectly.

Mr. Wickham fell to the floor, stunned, although not unconscious, and Georgiana swung again, to make him so. She did not think she had done any lasting damage, although she could not be brought to care deeply if she had.

She checked him briefly, and found his purse was not on his person; she would need to search the other room for it, and hope there was at least some money inside. Georgiana had already set aside the things she wished to take with her, and she gathered up this bundle, locking Mr. Wickham inside the room as she left. Doing this gave her some measure of security, but still, she wished to be well on her way when he awoke, and she worked quickly once outside.

The purse was easily enough located, and did, thankfully, contain some money. Georgiana next found his clothes, and dressed herself in what she deemed the best options – buckskin breeches and boots, a shirt, waistcoat, and coat. Her hair was the most difficult matter; she pulled it back tightly on her head and tied it as a man of the older fashion would have done, hoping it would serve when mostly hidden by a hat. Then she finished making up her bundle with items to aid in the journey – the knife she had been threatened with so many times, bread, cheese, and a bottle of wine. In her rapid search of the room for anything else that might be useful, she came across a little strongbox, and found inside a set of letters, written in her brother's hand, as well as the licence for her own marriage. She longed to read the letters, but knew she could not tarry; she would read them when she reached a safe place – if she reached a safe place.

Georgiana left the key just outside the door of the room she had been imprisoned in – close enough that Mr. Wickham should eventually contrive some way to get it, but far enough that it should take him a while to do so – and walked out of the cottage. Mr. Wickham owned a horse, housed in a little shed attached to the side of the cottage, and Georgiana went thither. She had, thankfully, been raised by a horse-loving father and brother; her kind words, which the horse likely had not had from Mr. Wickham, gentled him in her presence. Georgiana was also glad her father had insisted she understand all of the tack involved in saddling a horse, although this was usually done for her by a groom, for now she was able to find saddle and bridle and apply them properly, tying her bundle behind the saddle.

Lacking a name for the horse, she called him Star, for the only marking on his otherwise plain coat. Patting his neck gently, she mounted – feeling very strange to be riding astride – pulled Wickham's greatcoat a little tighter around herself, and nudged Star with her heels to be off.

For now, her only goal was to be away – far, far away – from the cottage. She drove Star as quickly as she dared in the moonlight, passing through a little village and its brightly lit inn. She glimpsed the men inside with their tankards, and presumed it to be the one with the serving girls who were so amenable to Mr. Wickham. The road continued on in darkness, and she was forced to slow to a walk. She rode on in this way for a very long time, until she was struck with a sense of giddy relief and thought she should stop, so she and the horse could rest.

They passed the remainder of the night concealed in a grove of trees just off the road. Georgiana did not sleep, but she allowed herself a little of the wine, hoping it would soothe her, for she feared both Mr. Wickham's pursuit, and the source of the night-time noises all around her. It did not, but at dawn, she saddled Star again and mounted, and felt better for being in motion, continuing down the road. That it led to a larger road could eventually be seen, but Georgiana had no notion of what that road might be, nor whether she was nearer Pemberley, or London.

With every imaginable joy did her eyes fall upon the mile post of the greater road, which informed her she was only nineteen miles from London. She believed, for the first time since her wedding night, that freedom could be hers. Resisting every temptation to gallop the entire way, she set out toward town at a reasonable pace, one Star should be able to maintain for the remainder of the journey. Upon reaching the first set of turnpike gates, she trembled in fear as she handed over her two pence to the operator, concerned he would recognise she was a lady. If he did, however, he said nothing, merely handing her a ticket in return. By the time the sun was setting, she had raised the city, and needed only navigate her way to Mayfair.

When she reined Star to a halt outside her brother's house on Curzon Street, she felt all the strangeness of the situation. To show up on the doorstep, and dressed as a man, after having been gone for so long! The knocker was not on the door, and so she pounded on it with her fist, filled suddenly with a wave of panic that no-one would be there.

The door was opened, hesitantly, by Mr. Miller, who looked at her with an expression of deepest shock, and exclaimed, "My God, I thought I would never see the day!"

There followed some period of confusion, where a groom was sent for the horse, Georgiana was ushered inside, and Mrs. Wright and Miss Hughes were summoned for her. She was assisted into the drawing-room, collapsing in fatigue and relief on the settee, and was engulfed in the attentions of the housekeeper and her maid. Wine, bread, and cold meat were offered to her, and she was informed more food and a posset were being prepared, and a bath drawn, and if there was any other thing poor Miss Darcy wished for, it would be procured for her immediately.

These simple gestures were of the utmost comfort to Georgiana, and their kindness nearly overcame her. What did overcome her, however, was when Mrs. Wright said, "Oh, if only the master would have waited – he could have seen you safe with his own eyes."

"Has he gone to Pemberley?" asked Georgiana.

"No, miss – ma'am, to Jamaica. Left five days ago, and we were not to expect him back for some time."

Georgiana fell prostrate on the settee, sobbing over the knowledge that she had failed. She was free, but Fitzwilliam was not here to see it; he had left already, on that mission designed to endanger him.

"Oh ma'am, it is not so bad as you make it out to be. We shall send word to him and he will be back before you know it," said Miss Hughes.

"No, it is not enough – not nearly enough," Georgiana said. "I must go myself, and assure him of my safety."

"He wouldn't want it, ma'am, you running off, when you only just came back to us safe," Mrs. Wright said. "You had best wait, and let us send word."

"I must insist on this," said Georgiana. "I have failed him in every other way, and I will not fail him in this."

Over the remainder of the evening, they all sought to steer Georgiana from her chosen course, attempting to convince her to send a servant, or hire a man of business, or at the very least wait until she had spoken to one of her Fitzwilliam relations, who were all presently from town. Georgiana held firm; she would allow them to prepare her a meal, and the luxury of a bath and a full night's sleep in her own bed, but Hughes was to pack her a small trunk, and in the morning she would seek her passage. She went into Fitzwilliam's study, to draw the money she would need from the strongbox there, and was disappointed to find less than was usually kept. Georgiana thought Fitzwilliam must have taken some of the money himself, in his rush to be off to Jamaica, and the thought of her brother going immediately thither on the basis of her letter brought on another bout of tears, and further deepened her resolve to follow him.

CHAPTER 23

Fitzwilliam Darcy had prepared himself for any manner of unpleasantness, upon learning that George Wickham had come to the front door and threatened to make a scene there, if he was not allowed to see Mr. Darcy. Mr. Parker had, wisely and quietly, ushered Wickham into Darcy's study, there to wait until the master could be found. By then, it was inevitable that Darcy should have to see him, and find out what it was he wanted – or rather how much it was he wanted, for surely Wickham would not have risked his neck by returning to the country, unless he planned to ask for a substantial sum.

Darcy was correct: Wickham began with ten thousand pounds, as his asking price. He planned to go to America and begin a new life, and would take Mrs. Wickham with him, if only he was afforded the funds. Darcy, who had already at this point in his life deposited far too much into the man, and for no good purpose, would have sent him away with only enough to pay for the passage, but for Lydia, whose welfare concerned him primarily because it would concern his wife; he could not bring himself to care for Lydia as he did his other sisters. And so he said he would give Wickham three thousand pounds, the same sum Wickham *should* have put to better use the first time it had been given to him, and that only if Lydia was willing to rejoin her husband. This sum was protested; Wickham was firmly reminded of his status as an army deserter.

The sum was thus accepted, and Wickham was to travel to Longbourn to seek a reconciliation with his wife. From there, Darcy had only the task of seeing him out of the house quietly; Elizabeth he would inform later of the visit, but he did not wish for Georgiana to encounter Wickham, and thought he might be best smuggled out at the exit by the east stairs, so as to be seen by the fewest possible people while walking to the stables, where he had left a hired horse.

At the time, he had thought there only the slightest of risks that someone might be using the stairs in a house so large, and inhabited by so few people at present. He had forgotten Georgiana's move to the new apartment. The east stairs were the most convenient to her, now, and he had unwittingly given the last person in the house he would want to encounter Wickham the greatest chance of seeing him. In the minutes and hours following his sister's fall, he would criticise himself continually over this.

In the moment, however, he heard Georgiana exclaim Wickham's name, and saw her knees buckle before she tumbled, unconscious, down the stairs. There was nothing he could do in such a horrifying moment but let out a strangled cry and look over to the man beside him, who – to his credit – appeared equally horrified. Georgiana did not wake upon reaching the bottom of the stairwell, and there was the first evidence of a wound on her head, rapidly growing. Darcy went to her, and in his panicked mind, had barely the fortitude to check her pulse, which was at least steady.

It could not be said whether Wickham assisted out whatever thread of benevolence his character possessed, or whether he thought his aid in the matter might eventually procure him some sum greater than three thousand pounds, but assist he did. He called out to some unseen servant in the hallway that Mrs. Bingley should be fetched at once, a command Darcy could not help but find grounded in good thinking, for he did not want Elizabeth, so far along in her pregnancy as she was, to encounter such a shocking scene. Wickham turned to him and asked if Dr. Alderman still lived in the same house in Matlock, and upon being told that he did, said his horse was still saddled, and he would go to summon the physician.

"Do not go on horseback," Darcy said, removing his signet ring and handing it over. "Have Powell prepare the chaise and four. Use this as proof the command comes from me."

It was only after Wickham had run off that Darcy began to doubt the wisdom of giving him such power, but then, he trusted his staff thoroughly, and Wickham would see none of his money if he decided to take some inappropriate action now. As Jane rushed into the stairwell and cried out over what she found, Darcy reverted to only one thought, that there was a frightening amount of blood.

Elizabeth became aware that *something* was the matter in the house well before she was informed of what it was. The others could not be found in any of the usual rooms, and there seemed a strange restlessness among the staff, who were not so attentive to her as they usually were.

The event was finally explained to her by Jane, who found her sitting alone in the music-room, under the assumption that eventually some of the guests in the house would make their way to that space. Jane sat down beside her, and said, tearfully, "Oh, Lizzy, there has been a most terrible accident."

Jane, with all the distress in her countenance which must come from imparting such news, proceeded to explain to her the whole of Georgiana's injuries, and how they had come about, so far as she knew. Jane then explained that Georgiana had been moved back up the stairs to her new bedchamber, it being almost as near as any of the others, and that Kitty, Mary, and Hughes had seen her cleaned and changed. Elizabeth was at first upset that she had not been summoned immediately; she was closer to Georgiana than any of the others, in being directly her sister by marriage. She willed herself to stay calm; they had likely wished to spare her a shock, so near as she was to birth, which would account for the delicate way in which Jane had informed her. Still, the most unfortunate news was what Jane had yet to relate, and she did so now, saying:

"Lizzy, I do not think her baby could have survived, with as much blood as there was, and much of it not from her head. Dr. Alderman should be here soon, and perhaps we may hope for better news, but I fear we should prepare for the worst."

Elizabeth reached out to embrace her sister, and was not sure which of them was in greater need of comfort. They remained thus for some time before Elizabeth finally determined she should see Georgiana for herself, and made her way to that apartment with Jane.

She found her sister there looking very pale, laid out on the bed and changed into her nightgown, being rather ably nursed by Mary, who held a piece of flannel up to Georgiana's head, and told them Catherine had gone to change, her dress having been spoilt. Only after all of this was explained did Elizabeth notice her husband, seated in a chair beside the bed and seemingly overcome with worry. She wished to be of assistance to both brother and sister, but as her sister showed no signs of stirring, she kneeled beside Darcy and embraced him, an attitude that could not be maintained for long before Jane had brought over a chair, and convinced her to sit beside him, instead.

Dr. Alderman arrived, and was shown with all urgency into the room. They could not all stay, for such an examination, and Jane offered to remain, as it would only be appropriate for a married woman to do so. Elizabeth would have protested, at this, but began to sense that Jane had done so not to spare her such a painful task, but because someone needed to lead Darcy from the room, and be of comfort to him, and none would have been so well-suited to do this as Elizabeth.

She led him into the empty bedchamber across the hall, where they were seated, and he explained to her more of the details of how Georgiana had come to be in this state. If Jane had been nearly overcome, Elizabeth feared Darcy was still very much in shock, for although he spoke of the events that had occurred, it was in a strange, disconnected voice that worried her, particularly since Jane had given her cause to fear Dr. Alderman's diagnosis.

The physician was directed into the bedchamber they occupied by someone or other in the hall, and stood in front of them, being silent for a very long time before saying, "I am grieved to inform you that the child has almost certainly been lost. The only fortunate thing, if it can be called that, is that the pregnancy was not so far along that the loss puts the mother's life at risk."

"Poor Georgiana," murmured Elizabeth. "So there is no risk to her life – she will wake?"

"I have explained it poorly," said Dr. Alderman. "The risk to her life comes not from the loss of the child, but from the blow to the head – I understand she struck her head as she fell."

Elizabeth looked to Darcy to confirm this, and he nodded, mutely.

"That she has not awoken gives cause for concern," said Dr. Alderman. "It is possible she is afflicted by a fracture of the skull."

Elizabeth gasped, then reminded herself to be calm, for Darcy's sake, if none else. "What is to be done, if that is the case?"

"First we must ensure it is a fracture of the skull; if she wakes in the next day or two, it may be only that her head is severely bruised. Beyond that, we will have to look at more substantial measures, for in time it will not matter if it is a fracture or not – the greater concern will be that she cannot take any liquid, particularly given how much blood has been lost. She shows a weakness of pulse, at present."

"What should we do for her?"

"She must be watched at all times, and I would like her mouth opened and a spoonful of broth given every half-hour. Her jaw is pliant; I do not believe you will have any difficulty with it, but I will show all who are to nurse her how to do so before I leave."

"You will have no shortage of volunteers in that quarter."

"I am glad to hear it," Dr. Alderman said, and then continued, "I have looked after Lady Stanton since she was a young girl, and it grieves me more than I can say to see her in this state. I promise I shall do everything I may to save her, including praying for her."

"Thank you, Doctor. That means a great deal to all of us," Elizabeth said. "Let me send down to the kitchen for some broth, so you may show us what is to be done."

There were so many people milling about in the hallway, concerned but without direction for their concern, that Elizabeth quickly identified a maid who could be sent down for the broth, and then returned to the bed-room.

"While we wait, you are far enough along, Mrs. Darcy, that I should like to see how your baby does, if you do not mind," Dr. Alderman said.

"Yes, I believe that would be for the best," Elizabeth said, feeling terribly guilty to be thinking about her own birth, with Georgiana in such a state. Yet her child was to come, and soon, and no measure of guilt would make her wish to sacrifice the health of her own baby. "Mr. Darcy, do you wish to wait in the hall? Or perhaps go back and sit with Georgiana?"

"I will go and sit with her," Darcy said, looking as though he had been a little awakened by her formality.

The examination was not as thorough as those done by Dr. Whittling, who was to arrive at Pemberley in less than a week. Dr. Alderman thought Elizabeth better than a fortnight away from her birth, and she was relieved to hear this, both because it corresponded with Dr. Whittling's original assessment of when she should have the child, and because she could hope to see Georgiana restored to health before then.

There was quite a crowd around Dr. Alderman while he demonstrated how Georgiana was to be fed, and Elizabeth felt a little embarrassed on behalf of her sister, to be propped up on pillows and have her mouth opened by the doctor's hand in front of so many people. When he had finished, they bade him farewell, and all but Elizabeth, Darcy, and Jane remained in the room. Jane seemed to linger for a purpose, and kneeled beside where Elizabeth was seated.

"The carriage will have to carry Dr. Alderman back to Matlock," Jane said. "Charles and I thought that when it returns, we should send someone with the news to David Stanton, given he is her brother."

"Yes, we should – it is good of you to think of it. We may send a second carriage to him now, though, rather than waiting. And the message should indicate that we will have a room ready for him, if he wishes to come here and see her himself."

"I will have Charles send word down to the stable to have it readied," Jane said, and then handed over what appeared to be Darcy's signet ring to Elizabeth. "I nearly forgot, Wickham did return this. It was he who went to fetch Dr. Alderman; Fitzwilliam gave it to him so everyone in the stable would believe the command to prepare the carriage came from their master."

"Where has Wickham gone now?"

"Off to Longbourn. He intended to reach there before our family set out for Pemberley, and convince Lydia to go with him to seek their passage to America. In chance he was delayed, I told him of the inns we typically use, so he might meet with them on the journey. And Mrs. Reynolds saw to some food for him to take."

"Good. I cannot say I wish to have him roaming this house, but he did do one good turn for us, in fetching Dr. Alderman, although I cannot be sure he did so out of kindness."

"Lizzy, he has tried to do the right thing, of late. I cannot think him an entirely good man, but let us at least give him credit for that."

Elizabeth nodded, for there was a good deal of rightness to what Jane said, and her sister squeezed her hand and gave her a sad smile, before exiting the room. It was very strange, to be left alone there with Darcy and their silent, lifeless sister. Elizabeth had rarely been at such a loss for what to say: she could not think that everything she had ever said before in life had been the right thing, but never before had she been so lost to make an attempt.

Darcy placed his head in his hands for some time, but finally raised it, and said, "I failed her. There were so many times when I thought I might have done so, and things turned out for the better, and now, when I would have least expected it, when I thought this to be the safest place for her, and her husband's life to be the one at risk, I failed her. How am I to be a father, when I could not even take care of her?"

"Darcy, you cannot blame yourself for an impossible accident."

"Someone must be blamed. Whatever happens, and dear God I hope for the best, Matthew is going to return and someone is going to have to explain to him why his child, possibly his heir, was lost – if not his wife, as well. And who is to blame more than I?"

"Mr. Wickham, for one."

"As much as I hate the man, one cannot blame him for being at the bottom of a staircase."

"Nor can one blame the person standing beside him, for that is all that you were."

"But I am the one who chose to take him out through that exit. I am the one who forgot she had moved to the new apartment. I might have walked him out the back, or the servants's entrance, even the entrance-hall – truly, any other place in the house would have been better than the one I chose."

"Darcy, you cannot do this." Elizabeth laid her hand over his. "It is no help to Georgiana now, and she would not want you to. We must focus all our thoughts, all our force of will, on her condition improving."

Darcy did not seem entirely convinced, but nor did he protest.

"Now here, it has been close enough to half-an-hour. Help me give her the broth, and then we may go down and organise a schedule of when everyone is to watch her, if Jane has not done so already."

Jane *had* organised a schedule for who was to watch Georgiana; Elizabeth's name was not on it, and the others would not allow her to be added, regardless of her protests. She might sit with her sister whenever she wanted, but they would not allow it to be a duty for her, in her present condition.

None of them was much inclined to dinner that evening, so Elizabeth asked Mrs. Reynolds to have Cook prepare a cold collation, and give to the staff anything that would not keep from what had originally been planned. They ate in the winter breakfast-room, it being just down the hall from the room where Georgiana laid, watched by Catherine for now. This would allow them all to know immediately of any improvement to Georgiana's condition, for Catherine would surely run down the hall in jubilation if the event they all hoped for was to occur.

It did not occur during the meal, however. The only news that came to them was by letter, a piece of neglected post given over by Mr. Parker to Elizabeth, when she had finished her food. It was from Mrs. Bennet, and began with an indication that the Bennets might be delaying their journey north. The reason for this was interrupted by a very long passage about Catherine's wedding clothes: what colours looked best on Kitty; little Lambton would never be able to furnish all that was needed; a trip to Matlock or Derby or perhaps even Manchester would be required; and had Captain Ramsey settled on whether he would be wearing his naval uniform?

Following all of this, Mrs. Bennet noted that Mr. Bennet had a little sore-throat and a fever, on account of having been caught in the rain riding back from a tenant's property, and they therefore thought it best to wait at Longbourn until he was fully well. Mrs. Bennet then turned to her daughter's upcoming birth: she hoped they still would have time in plenty before Elizabeth's baby was born; she hoped Lizzy would not leave the succession of so grand an estate as Pemberley in question by having a girl as Jane had done; she did love little Bess, for being her first grandchild, but oh, the thought of endless girls gave her such a fit of nerves!

When she had finished the letter, Elizabeth placed it on the table in bewilderment, and was asked of its contents by the others. She related to them those items that were actually news, which was very little, and determined she would show it to Catherine later, so her sister might read the passages pertaining to her.

Elizabeth related the news of her father's being ill with the same level of import that her mother had placed upon it, and yet she could not help but be worried. Her worries were vague, and distant, and hardly seemed to have merit given Georgiana's condition. Yet no-one would call Mr. Bennet young, and Elizabeth feared that if she had been at Longbourn herself, this sore-throat her mother spoke of would have worried her far more than it did Mrs. Bennet.

However, she could not allow these worries to take precedence, once she had changed for bed and made her way into Darcy's bedchamber. There she must be hopeful, and stroke his cheek and take up his hand in the hopes of soothing him. It was a long night, for Elizabeth; Darcy slept fitfully, if at all, and was often waking her with his frequent turnings in the bed, so much so that she wished she had thought to make him take a little laudanum before they had retired, and even considered going to her own bedchamber, but did not, for fear her absence would lessen his comfort.

When she awoke from a shallow sleep to find the room filled with the grey light of dawn, he was already gone from the bed, and standing over by the window, silently gazing outside. He had not realised Elizabeth was awake, and she watched his profile, feeling the tightness of grief for him in her chest. Elizabeth had always known a full family, a noisy household; she had possessed what she had not then considered a luxury, of numerous sisters and both parents living. But Darcy, although he had gained family by marriage, had only Georgiana left of his nearest relations, and the thought of losing her could only have brought the most tremendous pain.

CHAPTER 24

Georgiana's cabin on the Margaret Poole was cramped and stifling, but she had been used to living locked within a small room, and so it had taken very little for her to become inured to the damp space which was her own for the passage.

The limited funds from the strongbox had forced her to be frugal, to take a berth on this ship, which could hardly be called the finest merchant ship on the seas. Even though she had saved money on her passage, she still had less than ten pounds remaining, together with a hundred pound note from Drummonds, which she had taken, but not attempted to use. The Margaret Poole was to put in at Bermuda first, to unload some of her cargo and then wait for the next convoy to Jamaica, so as to avoid becoming prey to an American privateer.

There was no opportunity for society on the ship, aside from those who might be met while walking on deck. The Margaret Poole was devoted to her cargo; passengers were few, and Georgiana had made no friends among them, all men, save for her. Some of them were nice enough – Mr. Harris never failed to bid her good day and ask how she did – yet without the usual social structures of land, she had no opportunity to become better acquainted with anyone.

She spent much of her time in the little cabin, reading as much as she chose, for although her candle allotment was small, a number of extras had been placed in her trunk by Hughes, who had been exceedingly disappointed she could not come. Georgiana wished she had been able to afford the passage for her maid, if only to provide an additional female presence on the ship.

Georgiana had brought books, but she mostly read Fitzwilliam's letters to Mr. Wickham. They were at once painful and reassuring: painful to read of how badly he had wished to see her restored home; reassuring to know he had never given up.

She was interrupted in her reading by a great convulsion of the ship beneath her, a sound of the most horrific scraping, which left her sitting up in her cot, unsure of what to do. This uncertainty was ended by Mr. Harris, who knocked on her cabin door and told her the ship had grounded, and she had best gather her valuables and wait on deck.

Georgiana did as she was bade, making a little bundle of her reticule and the letters, wrapped in one of her shifts and tied up tight with a ribbon. Once this was done, she went up on deck, where she had the relief of seeing they were within clear sight of the island. She could make out those on shore, frantically launching boats to go to the stricken ship, and she was glad of it, for the ship itself was entirely motionless. The deck that had previously felt so alive beneath her feet was wholly firm, and pounded on by the feet of seamen who seemed to be running about frantically, to little purpose.

They were recalled by the master of the ship, who screamed and cursed at them until they were circling the capstan, and pushing with all their might. Georgiana looked about and saw that an anchor had been dropped out away from the ship, and as the men heaved on the bars of the capstan, the anchor cable tightened. She saw, as well, that Mr. Harris was standing by the railing, and went to join him, thinking it best to stay near the only person who had shown any concern for her welfare.

"Mrs. Wickham," he said, but before he could say more, the ship gave a great rending crack, and shuddered so violently Georgiana would have fallen, if he had not grabbed her arm to hold her upright. When she recovered, she saw the deck was slanting more than it had been, and there was a long crack cutting across the middle of it.

"Her back is broken," Mr. Harris said. "Those boats cannot arrive soon enough."

The boats were close enough that the men rowing them could be seen, big bulky men soaked by the heavy surf, but still making good progress. Georgiana and Mr. Harris waited at the railing as the boats came alongside; once they had, the seamen of the Margaret Poole abandoned what they were about and came over in a crush, seeking to jump into the boats.

"Belay that, all of you!" shouted a man in one of the boats, in a voice that cut through all of the chaos. "Ladies and children first! We have room enough for all."

"We have one lady only!" Mr. Harris called out, and then said to Georgiana, "It looks as though you will have to make a jump of it."

Mr. Harris took the bundle from her, and threw it down to the men, a distance nearly twice Georgiana's height. She looked at the railing, which would not be an easy climb in itself, but with the men on deck all staring at her with furious impatience, she steeled herself against the length of leg she would reveal, picked up her skirts, and climbed over it, with Mr. Harris's assistance. Once standing on the other side, she waited only a moment before jumping down, where she was caught by countless arms, and assisted to a seat.

Mr. Harris sat with her during the journey to the shore, and was kind to give her his coat, to protect her from the surf. They came upon the shore in twilight, a beach before a pretty little town, of which it appeared many inhabitants had come out to watch the rescue. Mr. Harris demanded of one of them the directions to the finest inn that could be found nearby, and offered his arm to Georgiana, seemingly without a doubt that she would come with him.

She did, with concern over his asking for the finest inn, and she spent the walk there thinking of how she would need to make her remaining money last, until the Margaret Poole's master could see her placed on another ship. The inn was a fine little place, and responded favourably to Mr. Harris's inquiry on available rooms. The price named, however, was higher than what Georgiana would have wished, and she indicated she would take her room for one night only, intending to find a less costly place in the morning.

Mr. Harris asked the innkeeper to give them a moment, and drew Georgiana aside. "Mrs. Wickham, if it is the price which causes concern, you need not let it. I should be happy to pay your board. I would, of course, have certain expectations that my kindness be repaid in *other* ways, and if that is how we are to go about things, we may as well take one room, together."

If he had not said it with the same lecherous look Georgiana already knew from Mr. Wickham, she might not have understood what he spoke of. Shocked that someone who had seemed a gentleman would make such a proposal to her, she stood silently for a little while before removing his coat and handing it to him.

She walked back over to the innkeeper, told him she would not be taking a room after all, and went off into the evening, alone.

CHAPTER 25

Mary had taken to rising early, to see if any assistance was needed with Bess, and so it was natural she should be given the time well before breakfast, to watch after Georgiana. She had brought a book with her, but was not reading it; instead she sat, silently, hoping for some sign of movement from her friend.

Mary was not someone who made friends easily, and if pressed to admit it, would say that Georgiana was the only person among her acquaintances she could truly call a friend. Jane and Elizabeth had always been kind to her, and in the last year or so had she grown closer to Catherine. But they were all sisters by blood, which was not the same as a young woman who was indeed family, but whose acquaintance Mary had wished to further, and had done so with every kind reciprocation.

She looked down at Georgiana's hands, which someone must have crossed over her belly, and recalled all of the times they had spent together, practising duets on the pianoforte. This brought her thoughts to the new square pianoforte in the sitting-room of this apartment: she had gone up to admire it, two days previously, and to hear Georgiana's tale of having met Muzio Clementi with equal parts enthusiasm and jealousy.

Perhaps music would rouse Georgiana as none of Dr. Alderman's treatments had, Mary thought. She gave her friend that half-hour's spoonful of broth, then stole away to the sitting-room and found that the pianoforte, on its little brass wheels, was as easy to push through to the bed-room as she had thought it would be. She situated it so she would be able to play and still keep watch on Georgiana.

Playing was comforting to Mary, but proved not to be the panacea it had been for Bess, for Georgiana did not stir as Mary made her way through a few pieces she knew by memory. The square pianoforte had a fine sound, but not the volume of the grand in the music-room, and Mary sensed easily enough the opening of the door to the bed-room. She rose from the bench guiltily, and found it was Elizabeth entering, but that her sister was followed by David Stanton.

"Mr. Stanton!" Mary curtsied awkwardly, trapped between the bench and the pianoforte. "I was – I did not mean to – I thought it might be helpful to play for her."

"It was a fine idea to play for her, Mary," said Elizabeth, soothingly. "I am sure that if she can hear you, she is appreciative. Mr. Stanton wished to see her – he has only just arrived."

"Miss Bennet," he said, but then seemed at a loss for what to say beyond it.

"Mr. Stanton," Mary nodded, and pushed the bench out of the way so she could stand properly.

"I will leave you now," Elizabeth said quietly, and slipped from the room. Mary made to leave as well, but he held up his hand to stop her.

"Please stay. Your sister told me you have all been taking shifts, and that it is your turn. I do not wish to interfere, although I will want a shift of my own."

"It is very early for you to have just arrived. Did you travel all night?"

"Much of it. The moon was sufficient, and I wished to come and make myself helpful as quickly as I could."

"It was very good of you to do so."

"She is my sister – I could hardly have stayed at home after hearing what had befallen her," he said. "And I know it is what Matthew would have wanted, given he cannot be here himself."

Mary checked the clock and found it was again time for the broth. Mr. Stanton was not the sort of man who would watch such an endeavour without offering to lend his assistance, and Mary assigned to him the holding of Georgiana's jaw, while she spooned in the broth, carefully and slowly as Dr. Alderman had instructed. As she was doing so, her hand brushed against his, and despite the seriousness of her task, it made her face grow tremendously hot.

When she had returned the spoon to the table beside the bed, she said, mostly as a means of distraction: "Mr. Stanton, do you think you might lead us in a prayer for her?"

"Of course, Miss Bennet," said he, "but before that, I might note that as you and I are family, and in such circumstances, you would be welcome to call me by my Christian name."

"Very well," she said. "If you will call me Mary, as well."

Downstairs in the saloon, the long absence of the two single people in the household, with only an unconscious chaperone, might have been better noted had an express not arrived from Longbourn. It was addressed to Elizabeth, and she opened it with trembling hands, worried it contained the news she had feared – that her father's illness was not so trifling as her mother had made it out to be.

This was confirmed as she read the hysterical prose, written in the wildest hand she had ever seen from her mother. Mr. Bennet's mild fever had sunk over the two days since Mrs. Bennet's last to a stubborn, putrid fever which both Mrs. Bennet and Mr. Jones thought might very well be the last fever he ever suffered from. All the fears, worries, and nervous symptoms which might be expected from Mrs. Bennet followed this: she was certain to be turned out of her home by Mr. Collins within a fortnight; Lydia was not sympathetic to how deeply she suffered; if only Mrs. Collins would allow her to stay, at least for a little while, she would absolutely give up her bedchamber and dressing-room, so long as she could stay; if the Collinses would not allow her to stay, could she come to Pemberley; and oh, poor Mr. Bennet, how deeply she would miss him!

Elizabeth finished the letter feeling full of dread and drained of spirit, and related the worsening of Mr. Bennet's symptoms to all in the room before giving the letter over to Jane to be read. The sight of his wife in tears of worry over her father roused Darcy as little had since Georgiana's fall, and he came over to sit beside her and clasp her hand tightly. Jane finished the letter, and gave it over to Catherine, who spoke with hope and a good deal of sense when she said: "Our mama has always been prone to exaggeration. We must remember that. I will not say the threat is not real, or that we should not be concerned, but it may not be so bad as she makes it out to be."

This was of some comfort to them all. Jane, looking at her sister with a countenance of deep concern, said, "Lizzy, why do you not go upstairs and rest a little? I know this is a shock, particularly after all that happened yesterday, but you must think of your health. You must preserve your health, for the sake of your child."

Elizabeth nodded, knowing the rightness of what Jane said, and still feeling very tired from having slept so ill. She rose to take her leave, and found herself escorted out by Darcy. He was silent as they made their way upstairs, but still, she was glad of his presence, and knew he was doing what he could, burdened as he was by his own worry.

She quickly came to wish they had not gone by the entrance-hall stairs, for their route now took them through the gallery. Elizabeth always avoided looking at her own portrait, hanging there next to Darcy's, for there was something very strange about knowing she was captured there for posterity. Now, however, she glanced over at Georgiana's portrait, and feared Darcy would, too. Elizabeth was struck with the thought that if her sister did die, it should be given to Matthew, in remembrance of the wife he had known for such a short time. Then she was horrified she had thought it, and wished she was able to walk faster, so they might quit the room more rapidly.

Darcy held her briefly, and then left her when Sarah arrived, for Elizabeth had determined it best to change into her nightclothes and attempt a proper rest, although she was not certain she would be successful. Elizabeth found herself weeping silently as Sarah helped her change, and when her dressing gown had been slipped over her shoulders, Sarah came around to face her and, in the least proper and most welcome thing she had ever done, leaned over and gingerly embraced her employer.

"I am so sorry, ma'am, for all that happens with your family. It is a terrible thing to have to bear at any time, but even more so in your condition."

Elizabeth sobbed, and said, "You must really call me Elizabeth now, of all times."

Mary felt a great deal of embarrassment, upon Jane's entering the room, for she and David were still seated there, talking, but if Jane noted their lack of a proper chaperone, she said nothing on that subject, only, "Mary, I wonder if you might come and join us for a little while. There is some news I must share with you, and then some things we must discuss."

Mary looked over at David, who, before she could even ask it of him, said, "I will stay here with Georgiana."

With that settled, Mary followed Jane into the hallway, and as they walked down to the saloon, Jane shared with her the news that her father's health was much worse than Mrs. Bennet's initial letter had indicated. This was not entirely a surprise to Mary; when Jane had said there was news, it was what she had suspected.

Everyone was in the saloon except for the Darcys, and after they were seated, Jane said, "At least one of us should go to Longbourn, to assist my mother, particularly if the worst does happen. Our aunt and uncle Phillips will be there, and hopefully the Gardiners, but it is not the same as another daughter."

"I will go," said Catherine. "Jane, Lizzy will need you here. I would have liked to stay, for her and Georgiana, but you are right, one of us should go."

"Are you quite certain, Catherine?"

Catherine nodded firmly, and said, "Our father always said I was silly, like Lydia. I hope I shall arrive in time to prove him wrong, and help nurse him back to health."

Mary had never liked her sister more than she did now, for the truth was that Mr. Bennet had called her silly as well, lumping her in with the rest of the younger sisters, but she did not feel the same way about proving him wrong as Catherine did. Someone did need to go, for Lydia would be useless in such a situation, and if Catherine had not volunteered, Mary would have been the other logical choice of the sisters. Mary did not wish to leave – not for a man who had never bothered to know her well enough to understand she was not like Kitty and Lydia. Well, not like Lydia, now – her younger sisters could no longer be classed together. Nor did she have much desire to leave to support the mother who had never paid her so much attention as her other daughters, because she was not interested in the sort of fripperies Mrs. Bennet cared about. Mary hated the circumstances that had caused it, but all of the people she cared most about were in this house, and would remain here, save Catherine and whoever might escort her.

"I will have to attend you there," Charles said. "I hate to leave here with things as they are, but I do not see another way around it."

"There is certainly another way around it," said Catherine, with just the slightest glance over at Captain Ramsey, who gave her a little nod. "If I was a married woman, I could make the journey with my husband."

"Catherine, it is a fine thought, but the banns have not been read," said Charles.

"Nor will they be," said Catherine. "When Mr. Darcy spoke with Mr. Clark about reading the banns, Mr. Clark told him we would need a common licence, instead, because neither of us is a resident of this parish. Captain Ramsey has already seen to the common licence – we may marry whenever we choose."

"Still, are you certain you wish to take such a step?" asked Jane. "It is rather quick to make such a decision, and it will not be as large an event as we all would have hoped for you."

"I have been waiting to be married for *months*. I do not mind at all, to do so sooner than expected."

"If you have a common licence, I believe you may be married in the chapel here, so long as it is consecrated, and within the parish," said Mary.

"We will have to hurry to fetch Mr. Clark, then," said Jane, checking her watch. "It is near eleven already, and if you are to travel today, you must be married before noon."

"You do not need to fetch him, either," Mary said. "You are forgetting that Mr. Stanton arrived here this morning. I am sure he would perform the ceremony."

Jane still looked doubtful, and seemed as though she was going to ask her sister again if she was sure she wished to marry now, but Catherine fixed her with such a strong look that Jane stayed silent, and then Catherine motioned to the bell pull beside her sister, saying, "Well, ring the bell, Jane – there is so much to be done!"

Never before had Pemberley's staff been challenged in such a way, to have perhaps half-an-hour in which to prepare a wedding, but Mrs. Reynolds, upon being told what was needed, put them to work at a most rapid pace. Maids were sent to the chapel to dust, a gardener to the hot house for whatever flowers could be quickly made into a bouquet, and a groom on horseback to Lambton for the parish register. Cook was informed that some manner of wedding breakfast must be on the table shortly after noon, and Sarah put in charge of some of the other maids, to see Mrs. Darcy woken and dressed, and Catherine made to look as much like a bride as could be done in such a short time.

Of the two ladies who last came down the hall to Pemberley's chapel, Elizabeth looked by far to be the more stunned of them, having been awoken from a deep sleep for a most unexpected event. Upon seeing Catherine approaching, Elizabeth checked her watch to ensure there was time, and then waited to speak with her sister before they went in.

"Catherine, are you entirely sure about this?" Elizabeth asked. "I know you wished for a large wedding, and you must go forth now without even our parents here."

"I have already waited so long, Lizzy. I would have waited longer if circumstances were different, but it is better both for my own future and for our family if I do so now."

There was a great deal of sense in what Catherine said: it could not be denied that she and Captain Ramsey were the best choices to go to Longbourn, for Elizabeth did not wish Jane to be parted from her so near her birth, and if the worst did happen to Georgiana, she would much rather Charles be there beside her husband as they bore her out on her final journey. Catherine was also right that it was best for her own future, to ensure she was securely married before the possible death of her father.

"That is all I could ask, for you," Elizabeth said.

"You might – if all turns out as we would hope, for papa and Georgiana – you might hold a large ball in celebration, later, after your baby is born?"

Elizabeth laughed softly, and said, "Catherine, if all turns out as we hope, we shall have the largest ball Pemberley can ever muster in your honour."

They went inside, where David Stanton had been querying Mr. Darcy and Captain Ramsey on the matters he wished to confirm, before he would agree fully to the ceremony. He was assured that Pemberley's chapel had indeed been consecrated, and was within the parish of Lambton; that Mr. Bennet had consented to the wedding; and that the marriage contract had already been seen to. When he had been satisfied on all of these points, he went up to the little altar at the front of the room, and found his place in the prayer book.

The chapel was rather full; all of the staff had been invited to attend, and they comprised equal mixtures of those who had served the bride or groom in some manner and liked them, those who wished to do right by the house, and those who could not resist the curiosity of such a rapid wedding. Sarah and Hughes were the most notable absences; Hughes was still sleeping after staying up much of the night with her mistress, and Sarah had volunteered to sit with Georgiana during the ceremony and wedding breakfast.

As weddings went, it was a more sombre affair than any of their family might have imagined for such a jovial bride and groom. Catherine's hair had been done simply, and she was wearing only her best ball gown, but there was a becoming blush on her face, and if she did not look wholly happy, she did still look satisfied to be going to the altar holding Charles Bingley's arm. As for Captain Ramsey, he stood there waiting for her wearing his naval uniform, which was perhaps the one requirement for her wedding that Catherine would not have been willing to compromise on.

For Mary, it offered the strange opportunity to watch the gentleman she harboured thoughts of marrying perform a marriage ceremony, and she feared she was blushing even more than Catherine, to be listening to him.

Captain Ramsey – who they would all have to grow used to calling Andrew, now – was used to being ordered to sea on short notice. Therefore, following what could only barely be called a wedding breakfast, he had his trunk packed far more quickly than his new bride, and came down to sit with them in the saloon, where he was informed that Dr. Alderman had arrived and was examining Georgiana.

The doctor came down before Catherine did, and sat amongst them, with a most serious expression on his face, saying: "I am afraid there has been no improvement. We still have another day or so to hope she shall wake naturally, but I have done some reading on what must be done if it is a fracture of the skull, and I believe she will need to be trephined."

"Dear God!" exclaimed Andrew, startling them all.

"You are familiar with the operation?" Dr. Alderman asked.

"I have seen it done. We see far more fractures of the skull in the navy than you would in a county such as this."

"You are more familiar with it than I, then. There are some surgical operations I will attempt myself, but not this one, and I do not know of a local surgeon who would have done it. I believe we shall need someone from Manchester."

"Pardon me," Elizabeth said, "but what is this operation?"

His countenance marked with the deepest reluctance, Dr. Alderman said, "The skin of the skull is cut back, and any visible fragments of bone removed. Then a hole is bored into the skull itself, the bone removed, and the causes for damage to the brains alleviated as well as they can be."

At this point, the physician, recognising that everyone in the saloon – Andrew Ramsey included – looked rather ill, stopped his account.

"Is there not still a chance she will wake on her own?" asked Jane.

"There is, Mrs. Bingley, but if she does not, and I do not seek out a surgeon qualified in the operation soon, I fear it will be too late. I believe I must go to Manchester."

"If you go, it should be in our carriage, and we will bear the expense," said Darcy, in something resembling his usual authority. "But is there no other way? Might a servant be sent?"

"I wish to examine the credentials of any possible candidates myself."

"It is a shame Portsmouth is not nearer," said Andrew. "You could find half-a-dozen men who had done the operation within an hour, my old surgeon included."

"It is a shame indeed, but if you are offering your carriage, I will accept it most gratefully, and return as soon as I may with a qualified surgeon."

Catherine came down to the saloon not long after this conversation, to be informed of what Dr. Alderman had said, and to find fresh tears at the plight of the friend she must leave in order to carry out her duty to her family. Two carriages were now ordered around, and Dr. Alderman slipped quietly into his, to carry out his grotesque duty, but Catherine and Andrew had longer good-byes to say.

"Do not go any farther than the Royal Oak tonight," said Elizabeth, to her sister. "I should hate to think of you sheltering at that miserable Fox and Hens on your wedding night. Oh my, your wedding night – has anyone even told you of – "

"Jane spoke to me of it, while I was packing," Catherine said. "But in truth Lydia had given me the details long ago, and I must admit I have been all anticipation for it for quite some time. I know how well Andrew loves me, and the delay in beginning our married life has been so difficult."

"I cannot say this was for the best, then, but I do hope you shall have some manner of happiness, on your journey."

"I wish it was you going, Lizzy," said Catherine. "I know it is impossible, but you are his favourite, and I know he would wish to see you again before the end, if the worst does happen."

Few things could have broken Elizabeth so thoroughly as what Catherine said, and Elizabeth felt fully the maturity of her newly married sister, who would embrace her calmly as she sobbed at the thought of losing her father, without even a chance to see him. Eventually, Elizabeth sniffled, and handed Catherine the letter she had been holding, saying, "Will you see that he reads this, if it is not too late?"

"I will," Catherine said. "But even if it is too late, you cannot doubt that he loves you, and is well aware that you love him."

Elizabeth nodded tearfully, but did not trust herself to speak.

"Good-bye, Lizzy. *When* Georgiana wakes, please tell her I am sorry I was not here for it," Catherine said, and then walked over to her new husband, who assisted her into the post-chaise.

CHAPTER 26

Georgiana had succeeded in finding an inn fitting her limited means. It was shabby, but it was clean, and allowed her to retain far more of her funds than the one selected by Mr. Harris would have.

Following this, her first effort had been to seek out the master of the Margaret Poole, and ask him when she would be placed aboard another ship bound for Jamaica, or given a refund of her fare. His response, from the beach where he watched the remains of his ship battered by the waves, was that neither of these things would be forthcoming until the owner of the ship could be contacted as to the loss, and the insurance company then produced the compensation.

Georgiana railed at him for some time that this was unacceptable, that she had paid for passage to Jamaica, and if she was not to be provided with such, then her money should be returned immediately, so she could book passage anew. Her pleading and her tears would not move him, however, and finally he said he would listen to no more, and strode off.

After she recovered, Georgiana determined she must find some other means of getting herself to Jamaica. The easiest thing would be to turn the hundred pound note from Drummonds into ready money, and she spent the remainder of her day visiting every office in Bermuda said to be capable of processing her note. None would take it, however; none would believe her story, or her papers.

Georgiana returned to her shabby little room, determined to make more progress the next day. She decided she would take all that remained of her ready money down to the harbour, and inquire after passage. It would not be enough, but she hoped to convince some master or owner that she would some money down now, and the remainder plus a bonus would be paid by her brother, upon her arrival in Jamaica.

She rose early, to attempt this plan, and made her way down the unfamiliar streets, not entirely sure she was going the right way to the quays, for it was so early there were no other people to give her a sense of whether she was heading toward a place of greater activity. Still, she did not expect the next event, which was that a young boy, darting out from a passage, ran straight into Georgiana, knocking her down as he snatched her reticule and ran away.

Georgiana, entirely stunned by the event, sat up in the street and realised the boy's footsteps could hardly even be heard now, so far he had run. He was gone, and with him, her reticule and the last ready money to her name. This thought was so overwhelming to her that she sat in shock for some time before descending in to weeping. She was thus when someone spoke to her, from over her shoulder:

"I am sorry, madam. I was not able to catch him. I hope the loss was not great, although I fear by your reaction it must have been."

Georgiana looked up to see a rather tall man standing over her, heavily winded from running. She wiped at her eyes, and found him kneeling beside her and giving over his handkerchief. Raising her hand to take it up, she began to realise that there was a dull ache in her wrist that was growing worse; when the boy had grabbed her reticule, its ribbons had caught around her wrist before he had finally managed to pull it off, and then she had landed on it as she fell. Thus weakened, it had bent most painfully under her weight.

Grimacing in pain, she withdrew her hand. Now that her initial shock had passed, she observed the man was wearing a naval uniform, and he asked, "Are you hurt?"

"It is only my wrist," Georgiana said, explaining how it had come to be injured.

"Are you able to bend it?" he asked, making a few motions with his hand about his neck, before she realised he was removing his cravat.

"It hurts, but yes, I am," Georgiana said.

"It is most likely not broken, then, but you should have it looked over by a surgeon," he said, tying the two ends of the cravat's fabric together in a neat little knot, and then indicating that he would slip the loop of fabric over her head.

It was a strangely intimate gesture, particularly for someone she was not acquainted with, but Georgiana allowed him to do so, and to help place her arm within the sling, murmuring, "You are very kind, but I cannot afford a surgeon."

"You need not worry about that. My surgeon, Clerkwell, will look at it as a favour to me," he said. "But I beg your pardon, for you have no notion of who I am, and I suppose I must beg leave to introduce myself to you, for I see little else in the way of choices for introduction."

Georgiana nodded, finding herself soothed both by his solicitousness, and such gentlemanly manners.

"I am Matthew Stanton, captain of HMS Caroline."

"And I am Georgiana Wickham, of – of Derbyshire."

"You were the lady, were you not, on the Margaret Poole?"

"I was," Georgiana said, looking at him more closely. "It was you, who called out that the women and children should go first, into the boats."

"It was," he said. "Such a lubberly display I have rarely seen, by the men on that ship. But you – you gave a most plucked jump."

Georgiana felt reasonably sure this was a compliment, but was unsure of how to receive it. He saved her any possible embarrassment by standing, and offering his hand to help her rise.

"Come," he said, now offering his arm. "The Caroline is only a short walk from here. Is your father at your inn, still? We may stop there, first, if you would wish to have him with you while the examination is done."

"I cannot go with you – I am sorry," Georgiana said, thinking of Mr. Harris, whom Captain Stanton must have assumed to be her father. "I do not wish to take on an obligation I cannot repay."

"There is no obligation," he said. "If there is any obligation, it is on my end, for not catching the thief. If I had done so, you would have funds enough for a surgeon of your choice."

"You cannot feel yourself obligated to someone so unconnected to you, merely for failing to stop her from being robbed."

"I can, and I do."

"It is very good of you, but I am afraid I cannot give rise to expectations that I would repay this debt in *other ways*," Georgiana said, although even as she spoke, she began to realise that with no ready money remaining, she would have to find some means of paying for her passage. There was still the hundred-pound note, tucked away under her stays, and she regarded it with increasing desperation.

"Dear God!" he exclaimed. "Whom have you encountered in this world, to make you think of such things at your age, Miss Wickham?"

"*Mrs.* Wickham," said Georgiana, and her tone in saying it silenced him, although he continued to offer his arm, and finally she took it up and let him walk her toward his ship. If nothing else, the vehemence of his tone had convinced her that he was, at the least, not another Mr. Harris.

After this first conversation, she found his manners to be rather reserved; they hardly spoke before they reached the ship, a fine, trim-looking ship, tied up against the quay, so that Georgiana could step easily onto the deck. As they came aboard, Captain Stanton called out to someone to pass the word for Mr. Clerkwell, who was to meet the captain in his cabin.

Captain Stanton led Georgiana to a large cabin at the stern of the ship, invited her to sit, and stepped out for a moment to speak with someone outside. The person he spoke to could not be Mr. Clerkwell, for that man entered on the other side of the cabin, and immediately said:

"An' what do ye have need for, that I mus' halt me inventory an' come all this way up to th' cabin?"

"Mr. Clerkwell, this is Mrs. Wickham. She was knocked down by a thief this morning in sight of me, and has hurt her wrist. I informed her you would look it over, as a favour to me."

"A favour to ye! An' what next, as a favour to ye? Am I to look at every man, woman, an' child on this isle as a favour to ye?"

"I am asking you to do an act of Christian generosity for one young lady, which you know I shall reward you for anyway, and which you might have been done with already if you did not tarry by arguing."

With some inaudible grumbling, Mr. Clerkwell walked over to Georgiana, asked her how badly her wrist hurt, proceeded to examine it, and then said, "'Tisn't broke. Ye best keep it still for a little while. I'll send me mate up, to wrap it up tight, and ye may have some laudanum for the pain, if ye wish it."

"No, thank you, I do not believe I need it," Georgiana said, afraid to take any laudanum in unfamiliar surroundings. At least she had found someone who had been kind to her, but she still needed to keep her wits about her.

Mr. Clerkwell left them, and Captain Stanton apologised for his behaviour, saying, "You might ask why I put up with him, but the truth is he is a capital surgeon, when he does finally get down to work. The Caroline sees enough action that the hands must know they have someone to care for them who will see them healed, if ever it can be done."

Georgiana nodded her understanding, but before she could speak, a large, burly seaman came in with a tray of food that thoroughly distracted her. After her meals in the cottage, and then those on the Margaret Poole, which had hardly been better, such an abundance of fresh fruits and cakes held every temptation, and if left alone, Georgiana might have eaten them all. Instead, she thanked Captain Stanton for his hospitality, and made a few delicate selections.

"Now," he said, "I do not wish to be cross, but I am concerned as to whether the loss of your purse allows you and your husband funds enough to live, given you came to be here in a shipwreck."

Georgiana felt the shame of her situation, swallowed hard, and spoke: "My husband is not here with me, and that was the last of my ready funds. I have a hundred-pound note from Drummonds, still, but that is all."

"That should be no difficulty, then. There are several establishments here that will take your note."

"But they will not! I have tried every one I could find, and none would take it."

"Surely Landris did not refuse your note, but you must not have known of him."

"Yes, I did try Mr. Landris, and he refused it, the same as all the rest," she said.

"Did he? Well, then he shall have something to hear about from me. Landris is my prize-agent, and when your wrist has been wrapped, we shall go and speak with him."

CHAPTER 27

Elizabeth had no more opportunities to return to rest, following the wedding, and in her exhaustion that evening, she briefly considered sleeping in her own bed. She did not like the thought of leaving Darcy alone, however, and so she made her way to his bedchamber as usual.

"Has there been any change?" she asked, for he had been the last to sit with Georgiana, relieved now by Charles, and then Hughes.

"None. I fear our hopes may rest on Dr. Alderman's ability to find a good surgeon."

"My God, I hate the thought of that horrible operation."

"I hate the thought of it as well, but I would rather have it done, than try nothing and see her waste away. She is so young – she should have so much more life ahead of her," he said, and then seemed to regret it. "I am sorry, Elizabeth. I did not mean – "

"I know you did not, but even if you did, I could not blame you for it. Papa has had what anyone would consider a long life; married six and twenty years, and five grown daughters," Elizabeth said, struggling to keep herself from weeping. "I only wish I could be there for him, if it is the end."

"Oh, Elizabeth, we must pray they both come through," he said, and moved closer, so he could embrace her.

Elizabeth thought again, too late, of having him take some laudanum, but it seemed he was too exhausted to need it, for he fell asleep beside her quickly, and she was not long to follow.

She awoke in the middle of the night, and thought at first it had been Darcy who had roused her, but when she looked across the bed, she saw that while he had drifted away from her, he was still there, and sleeping calmly. She felt better rested, at least, but her back ached far worse than it had before she fell asleep, and she rose, thinking to take a walk around the apartment in an attempt to stretch it.

The light from the moon was enough to see her way through Darcy's dressing-room, their sitting-room, her own dressing-room, and then her bed-room, but this walking did nothing for the pain in her back, although there was something nice about the cold stillness of the night. She was about to return, when the pain in her back moved around to her belly in the strangest sensation. Elizabeth's pregnancy had been filled with strange new sensations, and upon describing all of them to her physicians, she had always been told they were entirely normal. This one she did not like at all, although thankfully it ended, and she sat down, to wait and see if it happened again.

Just when she thought it was not going to return, she was seized by another pain, this one slightly more intense, and when it had finished, she fled back to Darcy's bedchamber at the quickest pace she could manage.

"Darcy! Darcy!" She shook his shoulder, and it took some time to wake him.

"What – is it Georgiana? Has she awoken?" he asked.

Elizabeth was too frightened to tell him gently that she did not wake him for good news, and said, "No, I believe the baby may be coming."

"Good God! But it is too early, and the doctors – "

"I do not need a reminder that we have no doctors available to us!" Elizabeth gasped, and endured another wave of pain.

"Here, you should rest, and then I will call for help." Darcy sprang from the bed, and all but picked her up in his anxiousness to assist her into the nearest chair, then ran across the room and violently pulled the cord for the bell. Left alone for just that short time, Elizabeth found herself overwhelmed with panic, thinking of Dr. Whittling, who was still days away from leaving London, and Dr. Alderman, who might not have reached Manchester before he stopped for the night, and even if he had, would require much of the day to return, assuming a surgeon could be found quickly. Her breathing grew short, and she felt nearly dizzy with fear.

"Miss Kelly, please have them wake her – and Jane."

"It will be a while before anyone arrives – perhaps I should go myself," he said, coming back over to her, and grasping her hand tightly.

"No, please do not leave me alone."

He said nothing, but leaned over and kissed her forehead, and when he rose and looked at her again, she could see he was every bit as worried as she.

The person who finally knocked on the door – hesitantly, for such a summons in the midst of the night was most unusual – was Darcy's valet, Mr. Mason, who slipped his head inside and asked, "Sir?"

"Mason, the baby may be coming," Darcy said. "Please have Miss Kelly and Mrs. Bingley awoken immediately."

Mason did not even pause to acknowledge the command; he rushed off down the hallway, and the rapidity with which Sarah, fully dressed, came into the room spoke to how seriously he had executed his first task.

"Miss Kelly, I am sorry to have awoken you," Elizabeth said. "But I have the strangest pain in my back and my belly – it feels as though I am being stabbed there. It comes and goes, but it grows a little worse every time."

Sarah had, of course, never borne a child of her own, but she had assisted in the births of other women in her neighbourhood in Ireland, and so far as Elizabeth knew, was the only person with such experience in the house. Jane, Mrs. Padgett, and Mrs. Nichols had each borne one child, and Elizabeth had been there for Jane's birth, but she suspected Sarah had more experience than the rest of them combined.

"'Tis likely the baby, then, but it may be some time. Let me go and have them send for Dr. Alderman," Sarah said.

"You cannot – he has gone to Manchester, to find a surgeon for Lady Stanton. He will not be back until tomorrow evening, at best."

"It takes a very long time, sometimes, for a birth," Sarah said. "He may still return before it is time."

"If he does not, Sarah, we will need you – please, I will need your help," Elizabeth said, weeping, and still very breathless.

"Of course, I shall do all I can to help, ma'am, but you must relax, and breathe. Worry will not help you now."

"But it is much too early! Dr. Alderman said I should have better than a fortnight more."

"A fortnight early is not so bad, ma'am, and you are plenty large enough."

Elizabeth found these words a little soothing, and did attempt to calm her breathing, but before she could speak again, Jane had rushed in and was exclaiming, "Oh, Lizzy, is it the baby?"

"We believe so."

"I was afraid this would happen," said Jane. "It has been too much by far for you, today. They should have let you rest, instead of waking you for the wedding. I know Catherine would have been disappointed, but we should have let you rest."

"Why did you not say anything?" asked Elizabeth.

"I did not wish to worry you further – I thought it would only make things worse."

Elizabeth groaned as the stabbing began again, and felt Darcy clutch her hand more tightly, reaching around with his other hand to rub her back as he had been doing, lately. It provided her with little relief from the pain, but did more to calm her, and she was grateful to him for setting aside his own worry to do so.

There was a knock at the door; Sarah opened it, spoke for a little while to whoever was on the other side, and servants entered some time later, carrying a wash-stand, the birthing chair Jane had used, and the small folding bed that had been purchased for Elizabeth, on Dr. Whittling's instructions.

"I wasn't sure which you would prefer, ma'am," Sarah said, as a maid covered the bed with its new sheets.

Elizabeth contemplated this choice for a little while, a choice she had not expected to need to make. Dr. Whittling had corresponded on what her birthing position would be, on the folding bed, and had been firm in indicating it was the superior method. Yet Elizabeth had actually witnessed Jane's birth in the chair, and it had gone well.

"Is there one you would prefer, Miss Kelly?" she asked.

"I'll manage with either, ma'am. You should choose the one you think you'll be most comfortable with."

"I think the bed, then, as Dr. Whittling intended. But if I find I do not like it, I may wish to change."

"You should be able to change, for a while, but we will reach a time when it would be too late."

Elizabeth nodded her understanding, but worried that she had made the wrong choice, and would realise it too late.

"Do you wish to lay down on the bed now?" Sarah asked. "It might slow the birth, if you were to lie quietly."

"I should prefer to prolong things as much as I can," Elizabeth said. "Although I may think differently after much more of this."

There was much more of it to follow, hours more of waiting, during which Darcy, Jane, and Sarah could do little but take up chairs around the bed and watch Elizabeth with their tense countenances. They determined it best not to wake anyone else in the house, until things were further along, and there was a strangeness to the atmosphere, as though they were all in a drawing-room – most of them in dressing gowns – but with no appropriate topic for conversation. Sarah seemed least comfortable, and was frequently stepping out into the hallway, returning with pieces of flannel, scissors, and what appeared to be another nightgown and dressing gown of Elizabeth's.

Finally Elizabeth, desperate for a distraction, asked Darcy if he would find a book and read a little for them. He released her hand and went off to their sitting-room, where some favourite volumes were kept on a little shelf, and returned with several, holding them up beside his candle so Elizabeth could see the titles.

"Oh, not Wordsworth. I have not the patience for verse right now. *Gulliver's Travels*, perhaps. I should like to be transported to another world, presently."

Their family was not much for reading aloud, but listening to him, Elizabeth wondered why they did not make it more of a habit in their drawing-room, for Darcy had a fine reading voice, more animated than might be expected of him, as he grew more and more caught up in telling the story. The reading seemed to settle Sarah, and Jane even more so, as Elizabeth's sister fell asleep in her chair. Elizabeth could not do so herself, not with her time so punctuated by pain, but the distraction did serve to help, and it was sooner than she would have expected before the room lightened slightly, with the approach of dawn.

CHAPTER 28

In her previous reception by Mr. Landris, Georgiana's hundred-pound note had been swiftly and firmly refused. When she came into his little office a step behind Captain Stanton, however, she found things to be quite different.

"Good morning, Captain Stanton, what may I do for you? I am afraid we have not yet cleared the Phoebe, but I hope it shall be any day now. A fine little prize – five hundred for you, at the least – " the prize-agent faltered now, noticing Georgiana's presence.

"Mr. Landris, did you refuse this young lady's banknote? Can you not recognise a perfectly good note from Drummonds?"

"I – Captain Stanton, you must understand, I do not see so many notes from London, here, and the lady is unknown to me – she comes here *by herself*, with nary but her natural papers and a marriage certificate from Gretna Green to authenticate herself. What am I to do? My business is not so large as to be able to absorb the loss from a false hundred-pound note without some difficulty."

"Shall you accept it, now that she is escorted by myself? Or must I give you a note of hand to guarantee it? You know I have easily brought a hundred times its value through your office, so I hope that at least should suffice."

"Nay, nay, of course that will not be necessary," said Mr. Landris, already unlocking a drawer, and removing both notes and coin.

Georgiana stepped out of Mr. Landris's office stunned that she had done little other than thank him, and yet had left holding a little sailcloth bag containing her hundred pounds. Thankfully, she had little fear of being robbed while walking beside Captain Stanton.

"I am glad he did not push me," Captain Stanton said. "I might have threatened him that I should select a new prize-agent, but in truth, I have not the time to do so."

Georgiana did not know what to say, for he had made much of his time available for a lady he had no prior acquaintance with. Finally, she merely thanked him for assisting in the matter, and noted with relief that she should have no difficulty securing her passage to Jamaica, now. They walked on, and Georgiana realised they were making a return to the Caroline, and were too near the ship for her to politely ask that he instead walk her to her inn.

Returned to his great cabin, they sat there for some time before either of them said anything, and it was him that finally spoke, saying, "If it is passage to Jamaica you seek, you should not worry about that. We leave for Kingston on Thursday, and you may stay in the day cabin, there," gesturing with his hand, "I will have it made over for your particular use during the journey."

"I cannot – I cannot possibly accept such generosity from you, as much as I may appreciate it," she said. It was too generous an offer by far, wholly improper, and yet Georgiana longed to accept. To have what had seemed impossible only that morning offered, and at no cost to her!

"I hope you shall, although I understand your reluctance," he said. "I cannot – I do not know how to say that I worry for you, Mrs. Wickham, when I see someone so young as you, coming from a marriage at Gretna Green, and here without your husband. Please correct me if I am wrong, but I cannot help but think you are here in flight from Mr. Wickham."

The way in which he spoke could not but condemn Georgiana; she might have remained in silent pain, but for the deeply concerned look of his countenance, which seemed to prise out her story in the gentlest manner possible. Unable to meet his eyes, she descended into the whole of her elopement and captivity, and he responded with every bit of shock that such a history should muster, asking how she had come to be free. Georgiana told him of the events that had led her brother to Jamaica, and how she had made her escape, and followed after him.

"My God, I admire your spirit," he said. "But I must ask you again to take your passage on this ship. I do not know how high the risk is, of your husband following you, but it would make me much easier at mind to see you safely to your brother. We are leading the next convoy out, so you shall not find a faster passage – if you do, I would not recommend it, with the Americans about."

His tone was grave, as he spoke, as was his face, when Georgiana looked up at him. She had been so focused on his kindness, that she only now realised he was quite handsome, and she averted her eyes again.

"I assure you there would be absolutely no obligation on your part, except to allow me to see you safely to your brother," he said. "And perhaps, if you wish, to dine with the officers and myself in the evenings, for we are generally lacking in female company."

"Thank you – you have convinced me," Georgiana said. "I do not know how you can wish to be so generous to someone so unconnected to you, nor do I know how to begin to thank you for such generosity, but I would certainly dine with you and your officers, if it pleases you."

She was seized after this acquiescence with the sudden fear that she should not have accepted his offer, that somehow he was only playing kind to her, as other men had done. Yet she could not think of any purpose for his doing so – unless it was the most obvious one, which he had already spiritedly rejected.

As if he knew what she was thinking, he said, "It is not so generous as you make it out to be. There is a thing that should be done, and it is in my power to do it. I hope one day the world will show you it is not so unkind as you have been led to believe through your experiences thus far, Mrs. Wickham."

"I believe it has begun to do so already," she replied, softly.

Restored to some manner of wealth, and with none of it required for her passage, Georgiana returned to town and allowed herself a few purchases, the majority of her hundred pounds now held safely under her stays. Two new dresses were to replace those that had gone down on the ship, and she paid extra for them to be made quickly, to ensure they were ready before the departure of the Caroline.

She did not anticipate needing the dinner dress before this departure, but she learned Captain Stanton had secured her invitation to dinner, which he told her of after she had finished moving her small set of possessions into the day cabin of his ship.

"It is only a family dinner with some friends of mine, the Quintons, but I thought you might enjoy a little society before our journey," he said. "And if you are fond of music, I believe I may promise you some."

"I am very fond of music," said Georgiana, painfully reminded of how long it had been since she had played the pianoforte. "But I believe I must decline, having no prior acquaintance with the Quintons. I wonder at how you even explained *our* acquaintance."

"I did not tell them of your history, if that concerns you. I merely told them you were travelling to Jamaica under my protection. I believe they assumed it to be a favour to someone associated with my uncle; he is quite political, and likes to give out favours that may aid him in the future. And if they do not mind, I hope you will not allow it to trouble you."

"On that point I might be able to accept, but my wrist is far from better," she said. "I am not sure if my gloves will fit over the wrap, and it is still too painful to go without."

"It may be explained easily enough that you fell, without mentioning the thief. They will assume it happened on board the ship, I expect, and we need do nothing to correct them. Indeed, you will have to be careful once we are underway, for normally I would tell you to keep one hand for yourself and the other for the ship, but you will have no hand to spare."

Once again, Georgiana allowed herself to be convinced by him, and when the time came for dinner, she found herself astonished by him, as well. Held in his hand was a cello case, and she could not help but exclaim her surprise at learning that he played. He demurred, and said the enjoyment he found in playing was far higher than the quality of the sound, but explained that his friendship with the Quintons had come about because they, too, were musical.

Mr. and Mrs. Quinton proved to be pleasant company, but the dinner was exceedingly strange for Georgiana, who had never formally come out into society. Her injured wrist was easily accepted by the Quintons, but it left her feeling awkward, and constantly afraid of doing wrong.

It did not seem that she committed any egregious errors, however, for Mrs. Quinton was all kindness as she suggested they retire to the drawing-room. Georgiana followed her there, and was asked if she played the pianoforte. She answered honestly that she did, but had not practised in a while; Mrs. Quinton looked at her wrist and nodded, clearly presuming it to be the cause. Thankfully the gentlemen were not long in joining them, for Georgiana feared any topic raised by Mrs. Quinton might require her to lie, so as to not expose her situation.

Once the gentlemen were seated, Mrs. Quinton was encouraged by them to play the pianoforte. She played beautifully, and not long into the performance, Georgiana found herself overwhelmed with remorse and sadness. It had been so long since she had heard any music, but oh, how she had longed for it during her captivity. She noticed Captain Stanton gazing at her with a concerned expression, and lowered her eyes: concern from another, particularly from him, was unbearable.

Mrs. Quinton was followed by Mr. Quinton, who played the violin in a duet with Captain Stanton. By the time they began, Georgiana found her spirits had settled, and she could listen with true enjoyment.

When it came time to walk back to the ship, Georgiana hoped Captain Stanton would not mention what he had seen, but he did raise the topic, saying, "I must apologise, Mrs. Wickham, for pushing you to attend an event that has caused you distress."

"Please do not apologise. I did enjoy the music – it was only a reminder of how long it had been since I have heard any music, or practised myself."

"So you play, then?"

"Yes, I played both the pianoforte and the harp."

"I see no reason why you must speak of it in the past tense. Surely once you are reunited with your brother, and returned to your home, you may return also to your practise."

"I have lost so much time, though. I despair of ever being able to play so well as Mrs. Quinton does."

"Mrs. Quinton does play very well, but she is at least ten years your senior," he said. "You shall have ample time to catch her."

The remaining time before the departure of the Caroline and her convoy passed quickly, and on the first morning of the ship's being underway, Georgiana was invited to break her fast in the great cabin with the captain. As sometimes happened to her, she found herself forgetting she was a married woman, for her immediate thought was that she should not eat alone with him. Upon remembering that she was, and could, she went in and was seated at the table.

He asked her what she wished to eat, served her requests, and then handed over a rolled-up piece of sailcloth, saying: "I sent Hawke over to make a copy of an octave of Mrs. Quinton's pianoforte keys, with pencil and paper, and then had one of my men copy it out for a full keyboard. I realise it is not the same as a true instrument, but once your wrist is better, perhaps you might practise your fingering, until you have access to one."

Georgiana unrolled the sailcloth to find an entire pianoforte's keyboard had been painted upon it, and was wholly overwhelmed by the thoughtfulness of the gift. It was simple, and had cost him nothing but a little time from two of his men, and yet that he had thought to do so during a most busy time showed once again a terrific generosity.

"Thank you," she whispered, wondering how she had ever been concerned that he had anything governing his actions towards her, other than kindness.

CHAPTER 29

Mary was supposed to be awoken by Annie, the maid who helped her dress, so she could go and relieve Hughes at Georgiana's bedside. The time for her turn was early enough that this should have been done by candlelight, and so when she awoke to sunlight, she felt an immediate rush of guilt over keeping poor Hughes from her sleep. She dressed quickly, having been required to do so herself at Longbourn often enough that she had no difficulties, and made her way down the hall to Georgiana's room.

"Miss Hughes, I am so sorry – oh!" She halted abruptly, upon entering the room, for it was not Hughes seated beside Georgiana, but David Stanton.

"Good morning, Mary. I am very sorry to startle you, but they wished to let you sleep – some of the others have been up half the night, and you may need to spell them," he said. "Your sister's birth has begun; Mrs. Reynolds and I will look after Georgiana today."

Mary felt herself briefly overcome by this latest news, when their family had already suffered so many events, but she was the sort to favour action over worrying, if there was any action to be taken, and she said, "I believe I should go to help Elizabeth."

"Of course," he said. "Mary, I am praying for you – for all of your family."

Mary made her way downstairs to find the hallway outside Mr. Darcy's bedchamber filled with people, and it appeared they had been there long enough to have brought chairs to line the hall so they could sit, waiting. They all rose at her approach; she bade them sit down again, asked if she might go in, and was told by Mrs. Reynolds that she could.

As the room filled with morning light, and Elizabeth was convinced to eat a little from a tray brought in by Sarah, she began to think that perhaps she might very well hold out until Dr. Alderman returned, so at least a physician would attend her. Her pains were intense, but steady, and they had not changed for quite some time. When Mary came in, Jane woke at the disturbance, although Mary did little other than ask Elizabeth how she did, and what she might do to help.

"Nothing, yet, Mary, but thank you for asking," Elizabeth said. "We are a rather dull party, currently, sitting around and waiting."

Mary had not been allowed in the room during Jane's birth, once things had progressed, but Elizabeth was not entirely certain whether she would require her sister to leave when the time came. Mary was an unmarried woman, yet so was Sarah, and it seemed strange to dismiss her sister for the same status as the person upon whom Elizabeth's hopes for a safe delivery currently rested.

Mary was seated, and Elizabeth was about to suggest Darcy begin reading again, when she felt a stronger spasm of pain in her back. She winced, and said she wished to attempt walking again, to see if it made the pain any better. The chairs were moved from her path, and Darcy helped her to rise; as soon as she was standing, Elizabeth did find she felt a little better, and walking served as a distraction, if nothing else. She did nothing but circle the bedchamber, with Darcy hovering worriedly about her, although she had not the heart to scold him for it, in part because she was not entirely certain his hovering would not eventually prove necessary.

The next event was none so dramatic, however. She became aware of dampness, trickling between her legs, and her immediate fear was that it was blood. There was no easy way to check for such a thing, with her belly as big as it was, but when she pulled her nightgown up, she could see that it was soaked, but not with blood.

"We must get you into the bed, ma'am," said Sarah, upon seeing her. "It will move more quickly, now. Let us get you a fresh nightgown first, though. It will be more comfortable."

Although Elizabeth knew full well that Darcy had seen all that would be revealed in her changing nightgowns – many times over – he still took this as a cue to step out. He kissed her temple, and said, "I shall return," and indicated Mary should leave with him, which was a bit of a relief to Elizabeth.

When Elizabeth had been given a few minutes to change, Darcy returned with Mrs. Padgett; Mrs. Nichols, who had attended only her own birth, would stay in the nursery with Bess. It was Darcy who assisted his wife up onto the bed, and once she had laid down on her side in the manner Dr. Whittling had indicated she should, Mrs. Padgett brought a chair back over so he could sit, facing her. He grasped her hand, and she returned his grip; the pains were rapidly becoming both more severe, and more frequent.

"Do you wash your hands for the birth?" Jane asked, and Elizabeth followed her sister's gaze to see Sarah at the wash-stand, cleaning her hands carefully.

"Oh nay, makes no difference for the birth," Sarah said. "But Mrs. Wright always impressed upon us how important our hygiene is. I never attend Mrs. Darcy without my hands are clean, and this time should not be any different. I apologise for not going to my own room to do so, but I would not want to be gone for any length of time."

"Never worry about that, Miss Kelly," Elizabeth said. "Do whatever you must, now, and do not feel you need to apologise over any of it."

Sarah met her eyes, and just for a moment, Elizabeth could see fear. It was startling, for Sarah had seemed so certain of everything thus far. Yet it was a tremendous responsibility, and one Sarah had not expected to be given, to be responsible for the lives of both her employer and her employer's child.

While the others largely watched her in the time that followed, Elizabeth felt the increase in her pain acutely, and – as much as she had wished to hold out until Dr. Alderman arrived – now she wanted the event to be over as soon as it could be. She was wracked then by a pain far worse than those that had come before, and could not help but cry out. Her distress was met with a deeply sympathetic gaze from her husband; her pain seemed to visibly hurt him, as well.

"You are going to be well, Elizabeth. You shall get through this, and then you will be well, and you will meet our child," he murmured, and Elizabeth thought he was attempting to reassure himself as much as her. Still, it helped, as did his stroking her hair with his free hand.

Sarah very quietly draped a sheet over Elizabeth's midsection and then ducked beneath it, lifting up Elizabeth's nightgown and then leg, and this prompted Jane to say, "Miss Kelly, you cannot *look*!"

"But I must see the baby!" Sarah exclaimed, in a startled tone.

"It is most irregular!" Jane's birth had consisted of Dr. Alderman's hands only so far beneath her nightgown as was required to catch the baby as Bess had emerged, and his eyes steadily on Jane's during the entire course of the birth.

"Mrs. Bingley, what Miss Kelly is doing is, I believe, what Dr. Whittling had intended to do," Darcy said, quietly. "He finds it important to see the progress of the child, as Miss Kelly does, and I believe she has been even more careful of my wife's modesty. It was good to think of the sheet, Miss Kelly. Please continue, and do whatever you feel is best to deliver the baby."

Elizabeth was glad Darcy had corrected Jane gently, but shown his support for Sarah's actions. Everything depended on Sarah, now, and it would not do to have her confidence shaken just before the critical moment.

Sarah slipped her head back beneath the sheet and lifted Elizabeth's leg again, eventually asking Mrs. Padgett to come and hold it up by the knee. They were all informed that the baby was head-first, as it should be, but Elizabeth's only response was to cry out again, as she was wracked by an even more severe pain. She found herself incredibly desirous of pushing the child out, and thankfully, Sarah told her she should push, now, as hard as she could. Following this, although the pain was even worse, Elizabeth still found it more bearable, to know that the pain could be ended, if only she could bring her child into the world.

"'Tis close, just a little more, ma'am, and you'll be there!" Sarah cried.

Elizabeth pushed; she made noises she would not have thought herself capable of making; she gripped Darcy's hand so tightly she actually feared hurting him, although she could not bring herself to stop. He merely continued murmuring words of encouragement to her, and these were all she focused on, although she could hear the others doing the same. Through the pain, she could feel the baby emerge, and then there was a strange nothingness for a moment, as Sarah came out from beneath her nightgown.

Silence, silence. Silence was not good; silence was terrible. But then there was something like a cough, and the baby cried, and Elizabeth knew relief and happiness like she had never known before.

"'Tis a boy, ma'am. He's little, but fine and healthy."

"A boy?" Jane had been convinced she would have a girl, and had; Elizabeth had not realised just how convinced she had been of the same until now, when she had been quite certain Sarah would tell her the baby was a girl.

"Yes, ma'am, a boy. Let me do just one thing and then you and Mr. Darcy may hold the next master of Pemberley," Sarah said. "Mrs. Padgett, could you please bring me the scissors and those strips o' cloth?"

Whatever it was Sarah did, it took a few minutes, and during this time, Jane gently washed the sweat from Elizabeth's face; she had not even realised it had formed. Then the little boy was swabbed with felt, wrapped in a blanket, and given over to his mother. Sarah was right, that he was small – notably smaller than Bess had been, when she was born – but he seemed quite healthy. Elizabeth felt the temptation to look under the blanket, to ensure it was true he was a boy, so unbelievable it was still to her. Instead, she held him carefully against her chest, kissed his damp little head, and thought she would never again be so content as she was at this moment.

They all left the room except Darcy and Sarah, who went over to the window and feigned interest in what she saw there, so as to give them privacy.

"If I was not so relieved, I believe I would teaze you about having a boy, when you were so convinced you would have a girl."

"You may teaze me if you wish; it is a topic I will happily be teazed over. But perhaps instead you wish to hold your son," Elizabeth said, giving over the baby at his eager nod.

"He has your eyes," Darcy said, "which means he is going to be a little breaker of hearts. We shall have to watch out for Bess, or she is doomed."

"Let us not have any more matches for those in their cradles," Elizabeth said. "I believe yours caused you a great deal of aggravation."

"Very true," said he. "Now, are you willing to discuss names, since our child is in being, or shall we just refer to him as *him* for the first year or so?"

"I am willing to discuss names. My only requirement in this matter is that it not be Fitzwilliam."

"You *have* thought about names, then."

"Only so far as that I shall not have a child with that mouthful of a name," Elizabeth said. "If you wish to name him after you, William is perfectly suitable."

"I do not know that I wish to name him after myself. I thought – perhaps – you might like to name him after your father."

Elizabeth had been so elated, with the birth of her son, that she had forgotten all else that troubled them, and his statement brought a most painful reminder of her father's and Georgiana's situations, although she appreciated the sentiment of his suggestion.

"That seems the right thing to do," she whispered, reaching out to stroke the soft skin of her son's cheek. "James Darcy, how I do hope you have a chance to know your namesake."

CHAPTER 30

HMS Caroline drifted into Kingston harbour with the air of watchfulness appropriate for a lone frigate assigned to protect so many merchant ships, taller and more elegant than any of those that surrounded her. Having left Bermuda with sixteen ships in consort, she arrived with seventeen, the extra ship an American privateer that had thought to snatch one of the laggards from the convoy, but had instead been roundly run down by the Caroline.

The prize had not made the Caroline's captain as happy as it had his men. The reason for this had been explained to Georgiana one evening after dinner, once the others had left the great cabin. Captain Stanton had told her that the Caroline had already captured well over her share of privateers and merchantmen, and his heart was set on defeating an American frigate. Then he had played Bach, plaintive but lovely, on his cello.

At his invitation, Georgiana had listened to him play every night following dinner, and found that while she did enjoy the music, she enjoyed his company even more; over the course of the journey, any last remnant of reserve in his manners had long since dissolved, and they spoke openly, comfortably, with each other.

Now that Georgiana was about to depart Captain Stanton's company, she realised she would miss him very much. But the sight of the island she had been trying so very hard to reach filled her with the deepest anticipation, and she said a little prayer that she should find Fitzwilliam quickly.

The ship gave her salute, one gun after another, perfectly timed, and then boats began putting out from the shore. Georgiana paid little attention to them until one pulled up alongside the ship, and a well-dressed man inside called out, "Is there a Georgiana Wickham or Georgiana Darcy on this ship, or any in the convoy?"

"I am! I am Georgiana Wickham!" she cried, leaning over the rail and waving her hand. As Captain Stanton had said she should, she kept one hand for herself, and one for the ship, holding tight to the railing; this was no difficulty, now that her wrist had healed.

This exchange was noted by Captain Stanton, who left the quarterdeck and walked over to stand beside Georgiana.

"You seek Georgiana Wickham?" he asked. "Who sent you?"

"Yes, sir. Her brother, Fitzwilliam Darcy, sent me. We have been checking every ship to come into the harbour – she has been expected a week past, now."

"Lieutenant Campbell, may we have a bosun's chair readied for Mrs. Wickham?" Captain Stanton said. "Hawke, Taylor, and Bowden, you are to accompany Mrs. Wickham and ensure she reaches her brother safely."

So excited was Georgiana at the possibility of seeing her brother again, she had not yet considered what Captain Stanton clearly had – that with her delay in reaching Bermuda, there was a possibility her husband had arrived there already, and sought to reclaim her by deception.

"Thank you – I was not thinking," she murmured.

"I wish I could see you safely there myself, but there is too much I need to attend to here, currently, and I am sure you wish to see your brother as soon as you may," he said.

"I do, thank you."

Georgiana was lowered down into the boat, and the men from the Caroline settled around her. As they were rowed to shore, the well-dressed man indicated he was Mr. Warner, a man of business hired on by her brother. Upon their reaching the shore, he led her and the men along to a fine little townhouse. Before any of them could even knock, the door there was opened by Mr. Mason, who exclaimed, "Oh, but he'll be so happy to see you!"

Mason indicated she should come with him up to the first floor, and they were followed, awkwardly, by Hawke, Taylor, and Bowden. Mason opened the door to one of the rooms, and said, "It is her, sir, it is her, safe and sound."

Georgiana stepped into the room, and what she found there was devastating. Fitzwilliam was lying in bed, looking terribly pale and yellow, and he did not even attempt to rise to greet her; he only extended his hand to her, and said, "Oh, thank God. Thank God for this."

Georgiana rushed over to kneel beside the bed and take up his hand, overcome and unable to speak for some time, until finally she said, "Fitzwilliam, what has happened to you?"

"Yellow jack," he said, "and then a dropsy of the heart, but let us not speak of that right now. Let me be happy you are here, and safe, and tell me of how you came to be here so much later than we expected."

"I do not even understand how you knew to expect me."

"Mr. Miller posted a letter, that you were making the passage. You cannot know what relief his letter brought me, for I had expected to find you here, and here you were not," he said. "And then we expected your ship in, and it did not come."

With this explained, Georgiana told him of all that had happened to her, of her escape from Mr. Wickham, the shipwreck, and then her passage on the Caroline. He reacted with dismay at the difficulties she had borne, and then said: "This Captain Stanton seems to have shown you particular kindness."

"He has; he has been exceedingly kind to me."

"It is out of kindness, is it not?" he asked, dubiously. "Georgiana, I dearly hope he had no untoward expectations of you, during the journey here."

"He did not – he is a true gentleman," Georgiana said. "I cannot pretend I do not know what you speak of, but that is because Mr. Wickham would bring home women from the local inn. I have no personal experience in the matter."

"Oh, Georgiana, that is a tremendous relief to me. Wickham wrote that your marriage was not – was not consummated," he said. "But I never could know if he was merely attempting to use this for leverage."

"It was not," she said, although she was unwilling to say any more about that night.

"Those days are over, or they shall be, before you return to England," Fitzwilliam said. "Your uncle and I have been attempting to annul your marriage, for neither Edward nor I gave our consent. But Wickham declared you were dead, and as you were dead, there could be no annulment."

"Oh, Fitzwilliam, I hope you did not believe him!"

"I did not want to, but I did have to prepare myself for the possibility that it was true," he said. "Your letter was a tremendous relief to me, as well as the evidence required to proceed with the annulment. I do not know what you went through, to get it into the post."

Here, Georgiana looked at her brother, who had always seemed so strong and healthy to her, and felt the heavy weight of her guilt. She had avoided this part of the story, telling him only that she had determined to escape, but not what had driven her to do so.

"I did not put it in the post. Mr. Wickham tricked me in to writing it. He told me we would be travelling to Jamaica, and the rest was left to my own foolish hand. His plan was that you should travel here, and be taken ill by some disease you had no immunity to. Then I would inherit Pemberley, and he would control it, as my husband. I fear he very nearly accomplished his aim."

"Not entirely, Georgiana," he said, gently. "You will inherit Pemberley, but Wickham will never have any measure of control over it. I have updated my will to exclude him openly and deliberately, and to make the inheritance contingent upon the annulment. If the annulment is not granted within ten years' time, Edward will inherit, and even if that is to happen, you shall receive a jointure to your name alone, so long as you reside at Pemberley."

"But none of that shall matter," Georgiana said. "You will get better, and marry, and have a child of your own, to inherit the estate."

"I fear not, Georgiana, for I am dying. The yellow jack I survived, and that might have been the end of it, had the dropsy not set in. My physician says one or the other alone I could have lived through, but not both."

"But you cannot die, when I have only just found you again!" Georgiana sobbed.

"There is a chance I shall survive, but it is the slightest one," he said. "I am only glad I had a chance to see you safe before the end. It is such a comfort to know things are settled."

"But my actions caused you to be here, and so ill as you are!"

"You cannot blame yourself for writing the letter, Georgiana. I surely would have done the same in your situation."

"I *can* blame myself for consenting to the elopement in the first place."

"That is an area in which I will not allow you to bear any of the blame," he said. "It is I who hired Mrs. Younge, I who allowed her to take you to Ramsgate, and I who failed to see you educated in the rougher ways of the world."

"But it was of my doing! I am the one who foolishly thought myself in love, and acted upon it in such a way as to ruin both of our lives."

"Georgiana, you must allow me to take the blame in this," he said, weakly. "I do not wish to argue in the short time we have left. Allow me to enjoy your presence, I beg you."

She could not argue with such an entreaty, and she clasped his hand more tightly, and stayed there quietly with him, praying they had more time left together than he seemed to think they did.

Later, Georgiana's possessions were brought into the house by Hawke, and she feared she would not see Captain Stanton again. She did not have the right to expect any additional contact with him: he had wished to see her safely to her brother, and he had done so. Yet she felt the loss of his company with some degree of pain, although it was nothing in comparison to the misery of finding her brother so ill.

It was some relief, though, when Mr. Mason came into Fitzwilliam's bed-room and said there was a Captain Stanton of the Royal Navy, there to call on Mr. Darcy and Mrs. Wickham. Mason asked if Fitzwilliam wished to have him sent away, but Fitzwilliam said he would like to make the captain's acquaintance.

Captain Stanton entered the bed-room, and with his tall, healthy presence, seemed a painful contrast to Fitzwilliam, who only nodded at him, upon being introduced.

"I am very sorry to intrude on you," Captain Stanton said. "I only wished to see that Mrs. Wickham was as properly settled as my men reported she was."

"She is," said Fitzwilliam, "and please allow me to thank you for your role in seeing her here; you have my deepest gratitude for the kindness you have extended to her."

"It is nothing. I am glad to see her returned to where she belongs," said Captain Stanton.

He did not stay long, and when he took his leave, he informed them that the Caroline was to sail to Port Royal for her victuals, and then off to patrol the entirety of the West Indies. Georgiana offered to walk him to the front door, and only when they left the bed-room did she inform him of the extent to which her brother's health was failing.

"I am very grieved to hear that, Mrs. Wickham," he said. "I hope he shall make his recovery, and I will send a note to the governor, to call on you while I am gone and see if there are any matters you need assistance in."

"Thank you – that is exceedingly good of you."

"Goodbye, Mrs. Wickham," he held out his hand. "I will miss your company more than I can say."

Georgiana gave him her hand, and he held it tightly; she returned his grasp, and took what comfort from the gesture she could.

"Goodbye, Captain Stanton," she said, sad that it was very possible she would never see him again. She allowed herself a little time to settle before returning to Fitzwilliam's bedchamber, and when she was seated there, he observed that Captain Stanton was quite gentlemanly.

"Yes, he is. He is the sort of man I should have married," Georgiana said, upset by this observation, for only in saying it aloud had she fully realised it.

"Perhaps you might, still," Fitzwilliam said. "It would be best for you to remarry quickly, if you are able to find a suitable candidate – it would give the scandal less time to brew, and provide you with some protection, and a new name. And a naval captain might be the sort who could be convinced to overlook your history."

"Not this particular naval captain. His uncle is an earl – I am sure there must be some degree of expectations upon him, from his family."

"Still, I would not rule it out entirely. If that is where your heart lies, Georgiana, you should pursue it."

Georgiana was startled by his saying this, for her heart had long since ceased to be a consideration for her.

"I think it might be best not to trust my heart in the future," she said. "In truth, I am not sure I could ever trust anyone enough to marry again."

"If that is the case, you should consider Edward."

"Edward?"

"Yes, Edward. The Fitzwilliams have been affected by the scandal,

Edward included, so there would be little additional impact to his reputation, and as a second son, assisting you with Pemberley would be a fine fit for him. He is your cousin, and cares for you."

"But I have never thought of him in that way."

"If you do not trust your heart, perhaps that is better. You must know you can trust Edward thoroughly."

Georgiana replied that she did.

"And Pemberley will need an heir; that heir should come from you. You will be the last of our father's line," he said. "You need not make a decision now, Georgiana, but you should consider it."

Fitzwilliam was right, Georgiana knew. She could marry Edward, and know she could trust him completely, and yet she was sure she could never love him as a wife should love her husband. She held every affection for him as her cousin and guardian, but her affections ended there, and she did not think they could ever grow. Once she had affirmed such a conclusion, she turned her mind to why this was, and from there it was only a little while before she arrived at the truth: she could never love Edward as a wife, because she was in love with Captain Stanton.

She had told Fitzwilliam she could not trust anyone enough to marry again, and yet she had placed her trust in Captain Stanton to deliver her here, and he had done exactly that, with every kindness and no obligation on her part. She had sat, quite comfortably, alone with him on many evenings; beyond comfort, for she had enjoyed his company more than any other man she had ever met.

Now that she realised this, however, she knew nothing could ever come of it. Even if she did see him again, and if he did return her affections – and she was by no means sure that he did – the annulment was her only choice. She was glad Fitzwilliam and her uncle had seen this, but it would ruin her in the eyes of society, and a man with Captain Stanton's connexions could not be seen to marry someone like her. It was a realisation that only deepened her present sadness, and she was relieved to have a distraction, when the physician came to see her brother.

Fitzwilliam had seemed relatively strong thus far, to Georgiana. Not by any means his usual self, but he had seemed a man who was ill, but could make a recovery. But the physician informed her she should prepare for the worst, and then there came a time when she entered Fitzwilliam's room, and found him much weaker. He was able to speak, still, but it was clear the effort drained him.

She asked Mason that a chaise be moved into the room in the evening, so she could better nurse her brother. Georgiana spent the night on the chaise, never sleeping, in a terror the entire time that he should stop breathing. He did not, but by dawn each breath seemed a painful labour to him.

Fitzwilliam stirred a little, and awoke, although he seemed so tired he could only barely be called awake. "Georgiana," he rasped, and she reached over and took his hand, discomfited by the strange puffiness of it.

"I am here," she said.

"I am so glad. There is nothing I wished for more than to see you safe, before the end."

Georgiana trembled. She could no longer attempt any optimism, could no longer speak with hope that he would still improve.

He asked her to retrieve a leather pouch from the desk nearby, and then, when she had done so, said: "Inside is my updated will – I have sent copies to Edward and our uncle, should anything happen to this one. When you get to London, go immediately to your uncle's house, and do not leave until you are certain the annulment is complete."

"I will," Georgiana said. Her sense of the lonely life she would lead upon her return to England had been growing since Fitzwilliam mentioned the annulment, and it grew further with the thought that she would return alone. She would be mistress of a great estate, but shunned by most of society, hoping only that her children might eventually be accepted and have the sort of life she should have led, and all of this she would suffer without her only sibling in the world, the brother who had been like a father to her.

"Please do consider Edward," he said. "He and I have spoken of it, and he will not press you, but you need only tell him that you wish it, and he will propose."

"I will give him every consideration," Georgiana said, and in truth she was already fairly certain it would be her best course. To have an heir, she must have an husband, and beyond this, she thought she must have some companionship, in such a secluded life. It would be better to share a shallow love with her cousin, rather than be alone, even if her heart was bound to another.

"There is a note of consent, with the papers, if you do choose to marry him. I thought it best, given the annulment, and that he is your other guardian," Fitzwilliam said. "There is also one for Captain Stanton."

"I wish you would not have gone to the trouble, for something so unnecessary."

"Perhaps it will be unnecessary, perhaps not," he said, then was interrupted by a bout of coughing, and continued, sounding winded: "Georgiana, you have had such a horrible time of it in your life, thus far. I wish you to be as happy as you can be, for the rest of it. You must promise me that – you must give me that peace, now."

Georgiana wished to argue, to tell him she did not deserve happiness, not when her actions had led them both here, to this horrible sickroom, but he looked at her with tired, pleading eyes, and she promised him she would seek what happiness she could.

He thanked her, and that was the last he spoke. Drained by their conversation, he fell asleep soon after, his breathing growing ever more laboured, until at last there was one shallow breath which was not followed by another. When she placed her hand on his chest, she could feel no movement, and she knew he was gone.

"I am so sorry, Fitzwilliam," she said, and laid her head down on the bed beside him, crying, for how long she knew not.

CHAPTER 31

Elizabeth had moved to the master's more comfortable bed and was lying there, growing used to the strange sensation of nursing little James, when she became aware of a certain murmuring taking place between Darcy and Sarah, over by the window.

"Are either of you going to tell me what it is you are so concerned about?" she asked.

Elizabeth had not been entirely certain they *were* concerned, until both of them turned to look at her guiltily. Sarah approached first, and softly asked, "Ma'am, have you felt any more pains, like what you felt before you had the baby?"

"No, I have not – why do you ask?"

"I do not know yet if it is a problem, but I haven't ever seen an afterbirth take so long."

"It has hardly been an hour," Elizabeth said.

"In all the births I've assisted in, it usually comes between a quarter-hour and half-hour after, sometimes a little longer – but I've not seen so many to say that it cannot come later, without any danger to your health."

"But there is a chance, that there is a danger to my health."

"There may be."

Darcy reached out and brushed her forehead with his hand, in a gesture that at first seemed meant to be comforting, until she realised he was checking for fever.

"Miss Kelly, do you think you might give us some time alone?" Elizabeth asked. "Mr. Darcy will call you in as soon as I feel anything. And I would be obliged to you if you would share your concerns with my sisters."

"Of course, ma'am," Sarah said, and slipped quietly out of the room.

"How worried is Miss Kelly, truly?" Elizabeth asked.

"*She* is very worried, but as she said, she does not know if she has cause to be worried. We still have at least eight hours until we can even begin to expect Dr. Alderman, I believe, and days more for Dr. Whittling. I had Parker send him an express, informing him you had begun your birth, but even if he sets out immediately upon receiving it, and travels without stopping, it will be three days before we can even begin to expect him."

That he had worked out the timing so exactly was telling in itself. "I do not *feel* ill at all," Elizabeth said. "I feel strange, certainly, but I did just have a baby, and I would think things should feel a little strange, following that."

"I take that as a positive sign, but I think we will all feel much better, once the afterbirth passes."

"Indeed we will," said Elizabeth, and then, realising that if her time truly was limited, she did not wish to spend it in worry, not yet: "Now that Miss Kelly is gone, why do you not come up into bed with us, and spend a little time with your family?"

He looked at her strangely for a moment, and then seemed to understand her request, for he climbed into the bed beside her, and she handed over James, who had finished nursing.

"Here, against your shoulder, in case he is a little sick," she said, helping him position the baby, and placing a cloth, in case James did cough up a little of what he had consumed.

Elizabeth might have wished to enjoy this time, but whenever she glanced over at Darcy, there was a look of deep worry upon his face. She wondered how much more one man could take, to worry over, and for the first time, thought of what would happen to him, should both she and Georgiana pass. It was a strange thing to think about, given it involved her own demise, but rather than filling her with fear for herself, at this time it made her deeply sad and worried for him. He was strong; he would rally, in time, but she hated the thought of the pain he would suffer. At least he would have James, she thought, at least he would have a son, to love and bear responsibility for. For Darcy, both of those things would be critical to his recovery.

She was glad neither of them had ready access to a watch, for she could not tell how quickly time was passing, and there was therefore less to worry her. And thus she did not know how long they had been there together before Sarah burst in, and said:

"Mr. Darcy, please come at once – it is Lady Stanton."

CHAPTER 32

Georgiana was helped, thankfully, in burying her brother, for both her mother and father had died when she was too young to be informed of any of the details of the process. Mason seemed as saddened as she was by his master's death, and it was he who volunteered to prepare her brother for burial, to dress him this one last time.

Mr. Warner knew some of what was to be done next, and the rest was handled by the governor, Sir John Wallis, who had the misfortune of calling shortly after Mason went in, to prepare Fitzwilliam's body. It was Sir John who recommended the church, helped her arrange the burial plot, and promised to see the headstone placed, if Georgiana returned home before it was ready.

Fitzwilliam Darcy was, then, laid to rest in a little churchyard in Jamaica with more mourners than might be expected, for someone so far from home. Georgiana had ordered all three of her dresses to be died black, and it was one of these she wore, to see him as far as the street outside the townhouse, grieved that as a woman, she could go no further. Then she went inside to wait for the church bells to peal, a sound she thought she would forever associate with the most painful loneliness.

After the funeral, Georgiana visited the fresh plot in the churchyard as often as she could, wishing to make amends for her absence from the burial. She could not even begin to think about returning home. It seemed too large a step, too much to manage in her grief, and so she visited the churchyard, and began playing the little square pianoforte in the drawing-room of the townhouse. It grieved her even more, to think Fitzwilliam must have considered it for her, when he had let the house, but in playing again, she found what seemed the best expression for her grief. She played better than she might have otherwise, if she had not benefitted from the use of her practise keyboard, and sometimes she thought of the man who had given it to her, vaguely sad that she would likely never see him again, amidst the greater sadness that pressed upon her mind.

She played without any expectation of ever being interrupted; she had asked Mr. Warner to give Mason twelve months' pay, and the fare for his passage home, and so Fitzwilliam's valet had left, the only servants remaining in the house a more general man-servant, and a maid. She was as alone on this day as she was on every other day, and did not expect to hear, when she completed her last passage:

"I believe you shall best Mrs. Quinton, in time."

It was Captain Stanton, and he so startled Georgiana that she gasped. She turned, saw he was standing in the doorway, and rose hastily to curtsey to him.

"I apologise for entering in this way," he said. "Your butler was not answering the door, but another servant allowed me in."

"My brother's valet was acting as the butler, but I sent him home," Georgiana said. "He was no longer needed, after – after Fitzwilliam died."

"I am so sorry, Mrs. Wickham. I had hoped he would recover."

"I had as well, but it was not to be," Georgiana said, and then found she could not hold up under his concerned gaze.

She collapsed into tears, and found herself very quickly enveloped in his arms. It was improper, terribly improper, and yet she could not bring herself to care as they sat there together on the pianoforte's bench, Georgiana sobbing into his chest. Nothing could ever come of it, but still, it was the most comforting thing imaginable, to be held by the man she loved.

Later, when she had recovered somewhat, Captain Stanton revealed he was returning to Bermuda, although only after a lengthy patrol of the American coastline, and he offered to allow her to resume her place in the day cabin, if she wished it. He would help her find passage back to England once they reached Bermuda, if she so chose.

It would have been wisest for her to refuse his offer, and ask instead that he help her find a more direct passage from Jamaica, but Georgiana could not bring herself to do so. His presence served only to reinforce that she *did* love him, and although she knew nothing could come of it, she could not resist the opportunity to spend so much time in his company, particularly when he had been so soothing to her, in her grief.

When all of her things had been packed up, however, and Georgiana had returned to her place on the ship, she found the Captain Stanton of this journey was not the same as the man she had known before. There was a coldness in his manners towards her during breakfast the first morning, and again during dinner. And when she knocked on the door and entered the great cabin that evening, as she had on so many other nights, she found him leaning over his desk, rather than his cello, and he said, "I apologise, Mrs. Wickham, but I am behind on my logbook," which seemed to her a dismissal.

This was how it was on every evening; he always had some other duty, which must be attended to, and the coldness in his manners continued, so that Georgiana began to regret her decision to take what would be a longer passage on this ship. Even after the much greater pains she had suffered, it still hurt her to be neglected, and sometimes outright dismissed, by him.

One morning, she was walking along the deck, when she happened to be passed by him.

"Mrs. Wickham," he said, bluntly, giving her only the slightest of nods by way of acknowledgement.

"Captain Stanton," she said, hollowly, and curtsied. Georgiana felt it fully now, the loneliness of her future life, to be shunned even by that person who had once been so open in his manners towards her. She would be alone on this ship, and then retire to a lonely life at Pemberley, which only a marriage to Edward could alleviate.

She felt herself on the verge of crying, and fled to her cabin, not wanting any of the men to see her in such a state, and once there, she knelt on the floor, laid her face in her hands, and sobbed. There was a knock at the door, but she did nothing about it, until it was opened hesitantly by Captain Stanton. Then she looked up at him, and said: "Captain Stanton, whatever I have done to offend you, I must apologise for. Unless it is my situation itself which offends you."

He looked at her sadly, but not coldly, at least. "*You* have done nothing, Mrs. Wickham, and I am sorry you think you have. Come, I had hoped to avoid it, but I believe we must talk."

With the gentlest of touches, he helped her rise and led her into the great cabin, where they were seated.

"I hardly know what to say, except that I have done a very foolish thing, and that is to allow myself to fall in love with you," he said. "I am sorry: I did not mean to indicate it was foolish to fall in love with you, but to fall in love with a married woman."

"They are, unfortunately, one and the same," Georgiana said, yet although she spoke bitterly, she still felt a fluttering of spirits, at his admission that he loved her.

"You understand, then," he said. "I thought distancing myself from you might prevent it, but when I returned and saw you at the pianoforte, I had not the strength to push you away. I have been attempting to since, and in so doing, I pained the last person whom I would ever have wished to give pain to, without the benefit of any preservation of my heart. So you see it is I, who must apologise."

"I do not know whether to feel relief, or deeper pain," Georgiana said. "For I love you, too, and yet I know nothing must come of it."

"It is horrible of me to wish a man dead, even one who has used you so ill, and yet for some time, I have been hoping for your husband to find some way of making you a widow."

"I do not think it likely we should be so fortunate, if such a thing can be called fortune," Georgiana said. "And unless such an event would occur soon, my situation is far too inferior, and the expectations of your family must be too high, for me to attempt to convince you into such a degradation."

"I am relieved to hear you understand, although it pains me. Perhaps it is because my father and brothers are clergymen, but I cannot countenance the taking of a mistress. I could not do that to you, dearest Georgiana, as much as I might desire it."

"Nor do I believe I could consider it myself, for I shall already be enough of a pariah, after the annulment."

"I am sorry – Georgiana, did you say *annulment?*"

"I did." They had hardly spoke, since Georgiana had come back on board the ship, and she had told him nothing of the plans for her upon her return to England. "Neither my brother nor my other guardian consented to my marriage. My uncle will see the annulment through, since my brother cannot."

"Oh, thank God," he said, taking up her hand and clasping it. "Why did you not say so? There is no obstacle, as I thought there had been – we may marry!"

"There is every obstacle!" she cried. "In attaching yourself to me, you would expose yourself to the cruellest judgment of society. What would your connexions say, to have you bring such a person into your family? After all your uncle has done to further your career, could you repay him in such a way?"

"My uncle cares for politics, not gossip; it is very likely people will think he has engineered this to gain a favour from *your* uncle, and anyway, I am his nephew, not his son. I am hopeful he will support us, but if he does not, I will not allow it to stop my being with the woman I love."

"But what of your father? What of your career?"

"I have never held my father's good opinion. He may disown me if he so chooses – it would be no loss on my side," he said. "As for my career, the loss of my uncle's influence would undoubtedly hurt, but I do not think I shall lack for a command, so long as there are two wars on."

"I could not bear to see your love turned to resentment because you have been isolated from society, or not given the command you deserve, due to me," Georgiana pleaded, attempting to stay firm in her resolve.

"You have not seen enough of naval society, yet," he said. "You may live on board ship with me, or we shall set you up in a fine house near Portsmouth – I have prize money enough for a small estate, even, if you wish it. You may not be welcomed into the London ton, but many captains have not been very selective in their choice of wives. They will look to your superior manners, not that your name was once Wickham."

"That, I am afraid, is not a possibility. You forget: I am now the heiress to Pemberley – I must take up my position at the estate."

"This does raise a difficulty," he said, looking disconcerted for the first time since she had mentioned the annulment. "I do not like the thought of you living all alone in Derbyshire while I would be at sea. But perhaps you need not live there all the time, so long as you have a competent steward. I could seek a nearer command – something on the channel would see me home more frequently."

"You speak as though it is already settled."

"No, I am well aware that you have not given your consent, nor, I suppose, have I asked properly. Georgiana, will you please marry me? There can be no obstacle greater than the heartache I would suffer, if you will not."

He spoke so earnestly that Georgiana found herself moved by his conviction, and she said, "I will consent to marry you, but I promise I will release you from the engagement if the objections from your family are too strong."

"Then we shall be married, for I will never allow you to do so for that reason." He spoke sternly, but his expression was one of happiness, and he reached out to caress her cheek.

Georgiana leaned into his touch like a flower seeking sun, and when he asked if he might kiss her, she told him yes. Past experience had taught her that she would not like it, but nor would she deny him anything he wanted, and she thought she might at least gain some pleasure out of that which made him happier. She was surprised, then, by the delicate touch of his lips, by how it stirred her heart and sent a pleasing sensation throughout her. It was she who drew closer to him for a second kiss, and when this was finished, she whispered, "I did not know it could be like that."

"I hope it will always be like that for you now, my poor, sweet Georgiana."

"I believe it will," Georgiana said. "Captain Stanton, you should know – my marriage was not consummated. I will not say there was not some unpleasantness on my wedding night, for there was, but Mr. Wickham decided against it. He thought to use it as a means of negotiation with my brother."

"Oh, thank God," said he, looking deeply relieved. "I knew not the full nature of your captivity, and I must say I feared that comprised part of it. But we must be careful now – I should not have asked to kiss you. If your marriage is to be annulled, we must act as though you are Miss Darcy, perhaps even so far as to find a companion for you, when we reach Bermuda."

"You are right, although I shall never regret kissing you," said Georgiana. "And I will not give up my evenings, listening to you play. We may resume our evenings together now, may we not?"

"I would not withhold anything you would wish for. And I promise you,

Georgiana, I shall do everything I may to make your second wedding night far better than the first."

Fitzwilliam had made Georgiana promise to seek happiness in her life, yet after the initial felicity brought on by her engagement to Captain Stanton, she could not help but think guiltily of her brother. She entered thus into a period of alternating between sadness and, if not happiness, at least a degree of comfort, living on board the Caroline as the ship made her way along the coast, and her captain returned to his former intimacy with the young lady travelling under his protection. Georgiana would always mourn her brother, and always think with guilt on her own role in what had happened to him, and yet there was a certain relief she felt, that she should never again be so distraught as she had been in the past year.

Captain Stanton, it seemed, had his own obstacles to feeling truly content in his engagement. As their time at sea went by, he grew increasingly restless, as did his men, and this was explained only when the cause for the restlessness ceased, when a man well up in the masts of the ship shouted: "Two sail, hull up to starboard!"

Upon hearing this, the first lieutenant, Campbell, called out a series of commands. Georgiana, desirous of keeping herself out of the way as these commands were followed, went to the stern of the ship and stood there.

Captain Stanton came up from below, spoke a little to Lieutenant Campbell, and then pulled out his spyglass, to view the ships. Even without such an aid, Georgiana could see them, although she could not identify them as two merchantmen, as Captain Stanton did. Georgiana suspected this meant she would eventually need to go down to the forepeak, so as to be safe during the battle, but no one seemed in any rush to see her there, so she remained at the stern, watching the activity of the ship as the men prepared for battle.

They were all so intently focused on the two ships, growing ever-closer as the Caroline bore down on them, that Georgiana wondered if she was the only person who saw what seemed a ghostly wisp of sails, on the opposite side of the ship. It came and went, but seemed to her to be a definitive thing, and when Captain Stanton walked over to her, and told her it was time to go below, she said, hesitantly pointing: "Shall you capture that ship, also?"

"What ship?" he asked, for the sails had once again disappeared.

"There looks to be a ship, right there – it comes and goes."

To his credit, he did not at all dismiss her, and instead made his way up the mizzenmast, where Georgiana watched him re-open his spyglass, and point it in the direction she had indicated, scanning the horizon and then stopping dead.

"Campbell! Belay the next tack!" he roared out, in a voice like he had used the evening the Margaret Poole had grounded. "Large sail, hull-down off larboard stern."

He slid back down to the deck in a frighteningly rapid fashion, and issued a new series of orders that seemed to cause a good deal of consternation among his men. The ship was turned, the ship was tacked away from the other ships, and only then did one of the men up in the masts call out, "Looks like a man-o-war, sir – an' a frigate, if ever t'was one!"

Captain Stanton made his way back to where Georgiana stood, laid his hand on her shoulder, and said, in a most animated fashion: "God bless you and your pretty young eyes – it is the chance I have always wanted, and we even have the weather-gage."

It seemed the other frigate did not want the chance, however, for it made every manoeuvre it could, to avoid the Caroline. Over time, though, it became clear that the Caroline was drawing ever-closer, and would eventually have her battle. Georgiana sensed she should have to go to the forepeak soon, and was about to make her way to that space, when Captain Stanton called his men around him on deck, and said:

"I know I have asked you to give up two fat prizes, to have our shot against this frigate, but none of you can argue that we have not already had our share of fat prizes. She behaves most cowardly for an American, which may mean she has been injured already, but we must not assume that. She looks to be one of their heavier frigates, and if so, she carries at least forty-four guns, and very likely twenty-four pounders against our own long eighteens. We must not be over-confident; we must not assume she will be as easy as what we have grown used to. She will be the toughest fight of all of our lives. Remember the Guerriere, and the Java. Remember them, and avenge them."

At this, many of the men nodded soberly, and then Captain Stanton continued: "You are good, honourable men serving a good, honourable ship. I know you all shall do your duty, and when you do, we shall earn a far more famous prize."

This statement was met with a good deal of huzzaying, which made clear that Captain Stanton's speech had been effective. Georgiana had already fallen wholly in love with him, and yet she found she could love him more, now, for the way he spoke to his men, the way he seemed to stand tallest among them. Following his speech, he made his way back to Georgiana, and told her he would walk her to the forepeak.

When they arrived there, he clasped her hand, then placed inside it his purse, saying, "If anything happens to me, my officers shall help you. If anything happens to all of us, and we are captured by the Americans – God forbid – you should not worry about any ill-treatment by them, but in addition to your own funds, this will help make your way easier. They will exchange my men for American prisoners – hire on Hawke and a few others to see you safely back to your uncle's house. And Georgiana, if the worst does happen, you will always know my regrets over not being able to begin our life together, and that I loved you until the end."

At that moment, at the thought that he might not survive the engagement, Georgiana regretted ever mentioning the ship she had seen. She knew how not having this fight had haunted him, but she had not thought through the possibility that it could end in his death, and the thought of losing both her brother and him in such quick succession frightened her terribly.

"I love you, too," she whispered, and wished he would kiss her again, but he had been very careful about his promise to treat her as Miss Darcy in that respect, and with one last longing look, he left her.

The forepeak was not a comfortable place, but it *was* safe, below the waterline. The nearest bit of action to Georgiana was the space where Mr. Clerkwell was setting up his surgical station, a process involving much haranguing of the surgeon's mate. This was all the sense of approaching battle she was to have for some time, until she heard the sound of distant guns, and then a few thumps against the side of the ship. Someone called out to hold, there was more thumping and crashing, and then finally the Caroline's guns went off above her head. From the frequent practises Captain Stanton held, Georgiana had grown used to the deafening boom of the great guns, but what she had known before was nothing like this. Over and over again, ceaselessly, the guns roared above her head.

Georgiana became aware, eventually, of noise other than the guns, and this was Clerkwell, yelling to his mate that he must work faster. She stepped out into the surgeon's cockpit, and what she found there horrified her: men who had been brought in with a grievous set of injuries, and blood-soaked patches of sand on the floor. Despite her shock, she asked, "Is there anything I may do to help?"

Clerkwell looked up from whatever operation he was conducting on the man lying before him, and said, "Ye can swab th' blood, if ye have the stomach for it. Flannel o'er there."

Georgiana was not at all certain she could do what he asked, but she could not very well rescind her offer to help without at least attempting it. She took up a cloth, and wiped the blood from a man's stomach as directed by the surgeon, finding that although she was disgusted by it at first, she soon enough grew used to it. She did this until the ship crashed hard against something, and she was required to grasp one of the trunks forming Clerkwell's operating table, to keep from falling.

"Damned long time 'ta board," said one of the men, and another replied, "Rot yer eyes, Jacob Smith, 'tis a forty-four gun frigate. We ain't just goin' to give her a broadside an' board like some half-arse merchant."

Georgiana endeavoured to ignore Jacob Smith and his companion, focusing again on her gruesome work until the sound of distant cheering reached them, and someone came running in, remaining only long enough to shout to them, "She's struck! Oh, she's struck!"

The men around Georgiana all cheered with as much enthusiasm as could be mustered around their injuries, but all she could think of was how the ship's captain had come through the engagement. Georgiana continued swabbing at Clerkwell's direction, grateful now to have an occupation, although worry increasingly clutched at her.

She was made aware of Captain Stanton's status when someone called out, "Make way for th' captain!" above them, and shortly thereafter, he was assisted down on the arms of Campbell and another man. He did not appear gravely injured, yet neither was he at all well. Georgiana could make out a steady stream of blood, running down his right hand, and one of the legs of his breeches was soaked through as well. What concerned Georgiana most was that although he was awake, he seemed dazed, and very pale.

Clerkwell recalled her to her duty, and she wiped the blood away from the wound he had been stitching. When he finished, and the man on the table was carried off, Georgiana found the ship's captain took precedence over everyone else, for he was laid down on the table. She abandoned her duty and made her way to his left side, taking up his hand.

"Georgiana, my sweet Georgiana," he murmured, as Clerkwell cut open what remained of the sleeve of his coat. "It is done. We have taken her: USS President, forty-four guns."

"You have done it – I am so glad of your victory," Georgiana said, although she became distracted as she spoke by what Clerkwell revealed when he peeled back Captain Stanton's tattered shirtsleeve. There was a tremendous amount of blood and torn flesh, and when Georgiana glimpsed what could only be bone, she very nearly fainted.

"Is it that bad, then?" he said, upon seeing her reaction.

"'Tis bad," said Clerkwell. "I dinna think it can be saved, but I wish a few minutes more to make me decision."

Clerkwell spent a little more time swabbing the blood away from Captain Stanton's arm, made a quick inspection of the wound in his leg, and then returned to the arm, considering it, then shaking his head and saying, "Nay, nay, it's to come off."

"If you cannot save it, Clerkwell, I know it cannot be done. Let us have it over with," Captain Stanton said, weakly.

Georgiana had seen everything Clerkwell had been about since she left the forepeak, so when he wiped the blood from his largest saw, she shuddered at the thought of what he would do with it.

"It mus' be done, lass," Clerkwell said, and it was the first time Georgiana had ever heard him approach kindness. "Ye may stay for it if ye wish; ye've a better stomach than most, man or lass."

Things happened with a sort of horrific quickness. Fresh sand was thrown down on the floor, and Captain Stanton was made to take a draught of laudanum by Clerkwell's mate. The mate returned with a thick piece of rolled leather, and went to place it in Captain Stanton's mouth, but before he could do so, the captain told him to wait.

"Release my hand, please, Georgiana – I do not want to hurt you," he murmured.

Georgiana did as she was bade, and laid her hands on his arm so as to be of some comfort. The leather was placed in his mouth, and the mate and some of the other men took up positions around their captain, so they could tighten the leather-covered chains crossing the table, and then further assist in holding him down.

Georgiana watched the beginning of Clerkwell's actions, and felt Captain Stanton's arm grow so tense it shook beneath her hands. When she looked down at it, she found his fist clenched so tight, she knew he was right, that he would have hurt her if she had continued to grasp his hand. Clerkwell raised the saw, and Georgiana looked away; she could not watch this be done to the man she loved. She only heard the worst of the operation, and returned her gaze when she felt Captain Stanton's arm go slack beneath her hands.

"Fainted from the pain," said Clerkwell. "'Tis for the best."

The surgeon worked quickly, leaving his mate to bandage what remained of Captain Stanton's arm, and seeing a bullet removed from his leg. When Clerkwell was done, some of the men who were not too badly injured volunteered to carry their captain to his cabin. Georgiana followed, up into the severely mauled gun deck: there were a tremendous number of holes in the side of the ship, several guns were on their sides, and everywhere Georgiana looked, there was blood. Still, she could see that order was slowly being restored by those men well enough to see to it.

The captain's cabins had suffered less than the gun deck, although it seemed there was no area of the ship that had not undergone some degree of damage. Captain Stanton's cot had been moved into the great cabin, and he was placed inside very gently by the men, who looked at Georgiana and clearly assumed it was her right to nurse him, for they all filed out silently. Georgiana took up a chair and moved it next to the cot, and sat there for some time, interrupted only by one of the midshipmen coming in with a draught glass, which he placed on the table and said was more laudanum, from Mr. Clerkwell.

Then there was only waiting. Georgiana sat beside Captain Stanton, mostly, but she did allow herself to go over to the gun ports and have a look at the captured ship. It was noticeably larger than the Caroline, and although two of its three masts were down, it did not look nearly so mauled as the Caroline was.

Then, finally, Captain Stanton awoke, and groaned. Georgiana clasped his hand, and when he made to get up, put her other hand on his chest.

"Lie still," she whispered. "Your men are seeing to everything."

He made a little movement of what remained of his arm, realisation spread across his countenance, and he said, "Oh – that is going to take some getting used to."

Until now, Georgiana had been too shocked to cry, but cry she did, in sadness for his loss, and relief that at least he had lived.

"Do not cry, my dearest," he said. "Do you not see that not only is this everything I have wished for in my own career, it also eases our way together?"

"No, I do not see it!" Georgiana cried.

"This will be celebrated in the papers, surely – perhaps not so much as the Shannon's victory, since it came first, but then again, the Chesapeake carried only thirty-eight guns. And they gave Broke a baronetcy; I believe I may hope for at least a knighthood, particularly for loss of an arm, if not the same. So you see, Georgiana, the notoriety of the victory shall overshadow whom I choose to marry, and you should be able to make your way in the world as Lady Stanton."

"But look at the cost!"

"It is none other than what Nelson and a great many other men have had to pay."

"But Nelson did not play the cello."

This saddened him, and Georgiana was sorry she had said it, but eventually, he said, "That is a loss I shall mourn, but at least I will always have music in my life, in marrying a lady who plays the pianoforte so sweetly."

"What will become of your career?"

"That I shall have to decide on. Others have continued on as captains after such a loss, but perhaps I should take this as a sign, to retire with you to Derbyshire."

"You would do that?"

"Perhaps it would be best. Although I might favour it more if you were to tell me there was a large enough lake on the grounds to hold a little sailing yacht."

"The estate brings in ten thousand a year," Georgiana said. "We shall make you a lake if that is required for your happiness there."

"*You* are what is required for my happiness there, but I would enjoy a lake, and something to sail upon it," he said, and then winced in pain.

"Oh! I am sorry – there is a laudanum draught for you. I should have had you take it as soon as you woke."

In her rush to rise and get the draught, Georgiana forgot entirely where she was. She rose, and struck her head with such force against the frigate's overhead beam that she fainted dead away.

CHAPTER 33

Georgiana awoke in a most unexpected place, what appeared to be a bed-room at Pemberley, although one less familiar to her, with Mrs. Reynolds asleep in a chair beside her bed. Georgiana could not remember why she was not in the mistress's bed-room, but then she thought she might not have wished to usurp Fitzwilliam's chambers so soon. Perhaps, she thought, she might never choose to do so; she might allow her son or daughter to take them up when it was time, and leave them until then, out of respect that the place she occupied was not really her place.

She sat up, and felt a rather substantial pounding in her head, along with a terrible thirst. There was a pitcher of what appeared to be broth on a tea table beside the bed, and she took a first hesitant sip to ensure that it was, then drank it down, which did make her feel much better. Georgiana rose carefully, so as not to wake Mrs. Reynolds, and found a dressing gown. A pair of chairs had been placed in the hallway, and on one of them was seated a maid. She rose, looking very startled, and exclaimed: "Lady Stanton, you gave me such a fright! Oh, but they'll be so happy to see you awake!"

Georgiana shook her head in confusion – she remembered neither returning to England, nor coming here, nor marrying Captain Stanton, which she must have done, to have such a name.

"So he *was* knighted, then. Or was it a baronetcy, for capturing the President?"

The maid gave her a peculiar look, and said, "A baronetcy, ma'am, for the *Polonais*. Please take a seat here and let me go and find the master – he'll wish to see you straightaway."

Georgiana allowed herself to be ushered into a chair, although she felt well aside from the ache in her head, and was glad to see the maid was outright running. She very much wanted to see Captain Stanton, although she supposed that if they were married, he must be Matthew to her now.

214

Something the maid had said, about the Polonais, prickled at her consciousness, but she was not sure why, and she was distracted when she felt at the sore spot on her head. A large patch had been shaved there, and she could feel the stitches, but the strangeness of it was that it was not where it should have been, to have hit her head on the overhead beam of the Caroline.

"Georgiana!"

She looked down the hallway to find it was Fitzwilliam, not Captain Stanton, calling her name, and after the first moment of complete shock, after she had gasped and felt tears rush into her eyes, Georgiana stood and fled down the hallway to embrace him.

"Fitzwilliam! Thank God, oh, thank God!" she cried. The Polonais, of course, Matthew had captured the Polonais in this world, the real world, the world where she had not married Mr. Wickham. The world in which Fitzwilliam had lived, and still held his rightful place in this house, and was strangely wearing his dressing gown still, in the midst of the day.

"I believe it is I who am supposed to say that," he said, tightly returning her embrace. "We have been terribly worried about you. How do you feel? Do you remember what happened?"

"My head hurts, rather badly, but aside from that, I feel well enough," she said, "and I do not remember what happened." So much had occurred in her dreams that she remembered only vaguely having arrived at Pemberley, and staying there for what must have been some time.

"Georgiana, are you certain you are well? The maid said you were confused, when you awoke."

"I was, but I am not, any longer. I had a horrible dream, and I did not understand, at first, that it had ended."

"Here, if you will sit with me, I shall tell you of what happened," he said.

Once again Georgiana allowed herself to be ushered to one of the chairs in the hallway, and Fitzwilliam sat beside her, but seemed lost as to how to begin.

"George Wickham came here," he said, finally.

"Here? At the risk of being taken up as a deserter?"

"I know not how he slipped into the country, but once here, unless someone who recognised him would turn him in, I believe he thought himself at little risk," Fitzwilliam said. "As he has in the past, he sought money from me, this time in exchange for returning to his wife. He thought to go to America, and begin a new life, and I said I should provide him with some funds, but only if Lydia chose to go with him."

Georgiana received this statement with both relief for herself and sadness for Lydia Wickham, that her husband should seek a bribe from another, merely to do what should have been his natural duty. She nodded to Fitzwilliam to continue.

"I thought I could see him quietly out of the house, but you chanced upon the east stairs just as we approached the exit there. You saw him and fainted, and you fell nearly the length of the staircase."

Until now, Georgiana had not thought about the faintness which had attended her over the last few months, but upon his mentioning it, she realised she felt it no more, and she suspected what Fitzwilliam was to tell her next, even before he spoke.

"The baby was lost, and very nearly you as well," he said, and she realised with some shock that he was weeping; only once before had Georgiana seen her brother cry, when their father was dying, and she followed him easily into tears. "I am so sorry, Georgiana. I made a very foolish mistake, and it has cost you and Matthew so much."

"It is not your fault, Fitzwilliam. If it is anyone's fault, it is mine, for not telling you all of what happened in Paris," Georgiana said, and proceeded to tell him of how Mr. Wickham had accosted her.

"My God, Georgiana, why would you not tell me of this?" he asked.

"I did not wish to worry you, and because of it, you did not know how severely seeing Mr. Wickham again would affect me."

"Still, I can hardly place more blame for this on you than I," he said. "The shock of seeing him might have been too much, regardless."

"Then we must not blame either of ourselves, and accept it as a terrible accident," Georgiana said, although she knew in her own heart she would always feel responsible. She wished for some time to herself, to think on what she had lost, but she knew she must wait a little while for that. "Let us speak of other things for now, particularly why you are dressed so at this hour of the day."

"Elizabeth has had her baby – a boy, James," he said, hesitantly.

"Oh – my congratulations to you both."

"All is not well with the birth, Georgiana. The baby is healthy, but the afterbirth has not yet passed, and until it does, we must worry for Elizabeth."

Georgiana had thought his reluctance to share the news with her to be due to her own loss, and she received this intelligence both with shock, and the thought that these last days must have been terribly wearing on him.

"She is so strong; I believe she will come through it," Georgiana said, reaching over and clasping his hand.

"I should return to her," he said. "Will you come with me? I am sure it would be good for her spirits to see you."

"I would very much like to see her," Georgiana said. "But will you allow me a little time to myself, first?"

"Of course. She is in my bedchamber," he said, rising. "I am so very glad you are well, Georgiana. I know this time will be difficult for you, but it will pass – you will heal."

"I am so very glad you are well, too," Georgiana murmured, and then laid her head in her hands, in a turmoil of emotions.

In the last few days, when neither she nor Darcy had been in a state to take charge of everything that had befallen them, Elizabeth's sister had surprised and impressed her with her command of all that needed to be done. When Jane came in to see her, having had the news that Elizabeth's life was at risk, however, all of that command was utterly gone.

"Lizzy," she said, rushing over to her sister's bedside to lay her hand upon one of the arms that still held little James. It was clear by her face that she had been crying, and was about to do so again. "Oh, Lizzy!"

This was all Jane said for some time, and Elizabeth found herself moved by her sister's distress into a greater degree of worry than she had felt previously. She still did not *feel* ill, but she wondered if perhaps it was something that would come upon her suddenly, and she wondered what it would be like, to die, to be gone from this world and into the next. For the first time, she felt a clutch of panic over these thoughts, and it took her some time to calm herself as much as was possible.

"Darcy insisted on hiring a wet nurse," Elizabeth said. "I did not want one, and we had a terrible row over it, because I was not thinking of this possibility. If the worst does happen, will you tell him, Jane, when the time is right, that I am glad he did? At least now, whatever happens, I need not worry for James."

Jane nodded to her, with a face wet with tears.

"And will you be a godmother to little James? Will you tell him always of how his mother loved him, even if she could not know him for long?"

"Oh, Lizzy, I hate to even think of bearing such a burden, but if I must, I would do so. I would tell him always of your love for him, and of everything about you, so he would know you."

They were silent for some time after this, the only noises made by James, who seemed content, unaware of the danger his entry into the world had brought. Mary came in and joined them after some time, saying nothing, but taking a chair to sit beside Jane. Elizabeth found herself wishing Catherine could have been there as well, and then thought guiltily of Lydia, but she decided now was a time to be allowed at least a few selfish thoughts.

"Actually, Jane, do you think you might take James for a little while? And Mary, could you find me some writing things?"

Her sisters did as they were bade, and when Elizabeth had pen, ink, and paper placed as best as they could be on a travelling desk upon her lap, she set about writing letters. The first was to James, to be read much later in his life, but then as she found she still felt well, other brief notes to Darcy and Catherine followed. She would have written to her father, as well, but she had already expressed all she would have in her last letter to him, and she was struck by the notion that she had worried so over him, when it might be her to die before he did.

When she finished, feeling she had burdened Jane with too much already, she asked Mary if she would deliver the notes, if the worst should happen.

"Of course I shall," said Mary, solemnly.

"Wait a little while, if you will, for Darcy's. A fortnight, perhaps, but use your own judgment," Elizabeth said. "And I have not written a letter for either of you, but you must know how very much I love you. And Mary, if you must go in to mourning, I hope you will not allow it to delay your romance for too long; I would very much want you to have a chance at such happiness as I have had these last two years."

Mary blushed furiously at Elizabeth's last statement, sobbed, and then burst into most uncharacteristic tears, and she was still thus when Darcy came into the room. Mary rose first, and was followed reluctantly by Jane, so that he could be allowed more time alone with his wife. Jane handed the baby over to his father, and then with one last glance back at her sister, left the room.

"How is Georgiana?" Elizabeth asked him.

"Awake, and surprisingly well, although I believe more grieved than she will let on over the loss of the child. She wished for a little time alone before she would come to see you."

Elizabeth felt fully the relief of this news, for it meant that of the lives that most affected Darcy, only hers remained at risk. This would do little to ease his mind at present, but at least it meant he would not suffer both losses.

"So she is no longer confused?" she asked.

"No, it seems she had a rather involved dream, and could not tell at first that it had ended. But she was well when I spoke to her, and perfectly coherent."

"Thank God for that," she said. "I would hate for Georgiana to be grieved over seeing James so soon after learning of her loss, so perhaps you should take him to – oh, but my dressing-room has not been prepared. Where is he to live until it is ready?"

They had intended that James live in Elizabeth's dressing-room, at least through her confinement, so she would be near him when he needed to nurse. Yet moving James necessitated moving Mrs. Nichols and her son, as well, for they would both need to sleep in the dressing-room while James resided there, and none of this had been done.

"Do not worry over it, my love – they are working on preparing your dressing-room presently. Mrs. Nichols can attend James in your bedchamber, until the dressing-room is ready."

Darcy had already begun carrying the baby to the door, when Elizabeth said, "Wait, bring him here, first."

Elizabeth took up her son only briefly, long enough to bestow a kiss upon the crown of his soft little head, and wonder if this was to be her good-bye to him.

There were even more chairs arranged in the hallway outside the master's bedchamber, when Georgiana finally came down, and they comprised a scene of some sadness. Most noticeable was Jane, who was sobbing into her husband's shoulder, and it was upon seeing this that Georgiana felt the full seriousness of Elizabeth's condition.

She hesitated at the doorway, but Miss Kelly, who had been standing beside it with a grim look on her face, encouraged her to go in, saying Mrs. Darcy would be most relieved to see her. There was a strange stillness to the room when she entered; Fitzwilliam was seated beside the bed, and Elizabeth lying there, neither of them speaking. Elizabeth did not look unwell, to Georgiana's eye, merely tired – certainly not nearly as bad as Fitzwilliam had looked in her dream – but Georgiana's knowledge of matters of birth was so slight she did not wish to comment and give false hope, and so she only made her way over to sit beside Fitzwilliam.

"I am very glad to see you awake and walking about," Elizabeth said. "We have all been so worried about you."

Elizabeth's concern caused a sharp pang in Georgiana's breast, at the thought of losing the only sister she had ever known, and she knew not what to say.

It was Elizabeth who spoke again, saying, "I was worried upon hearing that you were confused when you awoke, but then your brother told me it was due to a dream you had difficulty leaving behind. It must have been quite a dream."

Elizabeth had a way of speaking, and of listening, which made Georgiana willing to share far more than someone who was very shy at heart would ordinarily, and she found herself compelled now to tell the story of her dreams. The telling of such a thing, of how she had dreamt of her brother's death, could not be done without a goodly degree of shame, but when she reached this point, he came to understand how it had been that she was as relieved to see him, as he was her.

She told them the whole of it, except what had happened to Matthew at the very end. Both Fitzwilliam and Elizabeth expressed horror over the majority of her dream, and agreed the only redeeming element of it was that Matthew had been there to assist her. This thought struck Georgiana painfully, for he was not there with her, and yet it seemed she had just left his presence. She missed him desperately, particularly after having learned what had befallen their child.

"I must say I very much prefer what truly happened over your dream," said Elizabeth. "Perhaps it should be a reminder of what a blessing the last two years have been for all of us – oh, Georgiana, I am so sorry. I meant excepting what has happened to you, of late."

"Do not worry yourself, Elizabeth, for even if I had the opportunity to choose between that world and this, even with the loss of my – my child – I still would have chosen this world," Georgiana said, although it made her eyes fill with tears, and she was not sure how much these were for the child she had lost, versus the risk Elizabeth now faced, the one Georgiana had unintentionally avoided, in losing the baby.

"I do prefer this world," Elizabeth said. "I am not sure of the likelihood of all that happened, in your dream, but I believe if you had eloped, Darcy and I would have had little chance of meeting. But we did, and we have had such a fine life together, and now we have little James to show for it."

Elizabeth seemed tired as she spoke, now, and Georgiana needed only to glance at her brother to see he feared what she did, that this was the beginning of the fever that would take her sister. Fitzwilliam reached out and felt her forehead, and then said, "You must be exhausted; you have been up most of the night."

"I believe it was less that than birthing a baby which exhausted me, Darcy," Elizabeth said, and this return of her spirit gave Georgiana a little surge of hope. "But yes, I believe I would like to sleep a little. Perhaps that is all I require."

They rose together, but Fitzwilliam lingered to kiss Elizabeth on the forehead before he would follow Georgiana out.

As Georgiana opened the door, Elizabeth said, hoarsely: "Wait – you know I love you both very much, do you not? You shall not forget it, regardless of what happens."

"Of course," said Georgiana, for at the moment, Fitzwilliam seemed too overcome to speak, "and you know we love you very much, as well."

Fitzwilliam, perhaps realising he could not leave his sister to speak for him at such a time, laid his hand on Georgiana's shoulder, and said, "I shall be out in a few minutes."

He was returning to Elizabeth's bedside when Georgiana closed the door behind her, and he remained inside the bedchamber for much longer than a few minutes. When finally he emerged, he looked to Georgiana, and said, "I do not understand – her forehead is not yet warm."

"Then we must hope," Georgiana said, fiercely. "We must pray and hope."

"She fell asleep while I was speaking with her," he said. "We were reminiscing, and then she just closed her eyes and drifted off."

"I am sure she was very tired," Georgiana said. "You said she had been up most of the night, and it must be – it must be very exhausting, to bear a child."

"I want to believe it was merely exhaustion, but Georgiana, what if she never awakens?" he asked, in a tone of the deepest emotion. "What if that was the last I was to speak with her?"

Georgiana did not answer him, for she feared the same thing he did, although she would never voice it to him. Wordlessly, she embraced him, and prayed that if she could awaken when everyone had feared she would not, Elizabeth would do the same.

Part Two
December, 1815

CHAPTER 1

"My dearest Lizzy,

"I find myself very unwell this morning, which, I suppose, is to be imputed to my getting wet through yesterday. My kind friends will not hear of my returning home till I am better. They insist also on my seeing Mr. Jones — therefore do not be alarmed if you should hear of his having been to me — and, excepting a sore-throat and head-ache, there is not much the matter with me. Yours, &c."

Elizabeth could not read such a note from her sister without a great deal of agitation, in worry over Jane, and anger at her mother over having put her in a situation that not only endangered Jane's health, but also imposed on the party at Netherfield.

Her father made some flippant remark, and her mother responded, but Elizabeth only partly attended them, for she was forming in herself a determination to visit Jane. There was some difficulty in this, for the carriage was not to be had, and as she was no horsewoman, walking was her only alternative. She declared her resolution, and was met with some resistance by Mrs. Bennet, but none that could not be overcome.

Walking with the impatience which worry for her sister must cause, Elizabeth made quick work of her journey. It was muddy work, as well, but she spared only a glance at her dirty boots and hem as she was shown into the breakfast-parlour at Netherfield.

She cared not for the good opinion of any of them, excepting Mr. Bingley, who treated with every kindness her concern for her sister, and Mr. Darcy, with whom she had thus far had so little interaction that she had yet to form an opinion of him. It was generally agreed in Meryton that he was the proudest, most disagreeable man in the world, an impression that had been caused largely by his standing at the edge of the ball-room for nearly the entirety of the Meryton assembly, dancing only two sets with the sisters of his friend, and declining to be introduced to any other lady.

This had been Elizabeth's first impression, as well, but then she had overheard a conversation between him and Mr. Bingley, which made her inclined to withhold her judgment of Mr. Darcy for longer than the rest of her neighbours. Having been obliged, by the scarcity of gentlemen, to sit down for two dances, she had been near Mr. Darcy when Mr. Bingley came from the dance for a few minutes, to press his friend to join it:

"Come, Darcy," said he. "You had much better dance; people will notice you more if you stand about in this way."

"I cannot," Mr. Darcy responded. "You know my heart is not in it. I have done my duty by your sisters, but to stand up with anyone else and pretend all is well would be too much a punishment to bear."

This, to Elizabeth, had seemed to indicate some prior wound, one still quite fresh for him, and she wondered if some lady had broken his heart, or something else was the cause. Regardless, she wondered at his coming to an assembly in such a state, when his manners would prejudice the entire neighbourhood against him. She was so little acquainted with him as to feel only a vague sympathy over this, however.

She might, it seemed, have more opportunity to at least observe the gentleman, for when she made her indications to leave, after attending to her poor sister – who had caught a violent cold – her reluctance to go, and Jane's concern in her intent to do so, saw her invited to stay at Netherfield for the present. Elizabeth's relief at the offer was out of concern for her sister, but she could not help but wonder if some of her curiosity about Mr. Darcy might be satisfied.

To stay at Netherfield meant she must also dine with the party there, for thankfully Jane's health was not so poor as to require Elizabeth's constant attendance. Surprisingly, it was Mr. Darcy who made the first inquiry over her sister's health, upon her entry into the drawing-room, although Mr. Bingley and the others followed quickly after with their own questions and expressions of concern. In Mr. Bingley's, she heard a superior solicitude, but there was something striking about Mr. Darcy's quiet inquiry.

They returned to the topic of Jane's illness over dinner, when Miss Bingley said: "Mr. Darcy, poor Miss Bennet's predicament makes me think to ask after dear Georgiana. How is she? Has her health improved?"

There was a degree of desperate over-familiarity in her manners, and stoniness in Mr. Darcy's reaction to her question, which made Elizabeth feel certain that if a lady *had* broken Mr. Darcy's heart, the lady had not been Caroline Bingley.

"Caroline, you forget that Miss Bennet is not acquainted with Miss Darcy's illness, nor is it your role to inform her of it," Mr. Bingley said, in a colder tone than Elizabeth had thought him capable of.

"I will tell Miss Bennet of it, Charles," said Mr. Darcy, then, turning toward Elizabeth: "My sister is ill, as well, although her illness has been of longer duration. She is at Bath currently, taking treatment."

"Oh, I am very sorry to hear that. I hope her health improves." Elizabeth now believed she better understood the soft voice in which he had asked after Jane, and what she had overheard at the assembly, although there was something very odd about it all. How should a gentleman so distracted by the illness of his sister that he would not dance at an assembly be staying here, rather than in Bath, where he could see for himself how Miss Darcy got on in her treatment?

She had no more opportunity to gain a better understanding of his situation, however, for Mr. Darcy was largely silent for the remainder of the evening. He spoke only if spoken to, and even then his answers were short. Elizabeth stole upstairs to check on her sister following dinner, found no improvement, and so sat with Jane for most of the evening, until her sister fell asleep. Following this, Elizabeth could no longer avoid the party downstairs.

They were quite an insipid group; she was informed that Mr. Hurst wished to start up a game of loo, if she had interest in joining. Looking about the room, she found both Mr. Darcy and Miss Bingley reading, and came to suspect that Mr. Darcy had declined cards first, and was followed in his choice of occupation by Miss Bingley. Elizabeth also declined, and walked towards a table where a few books were lying. Mr. Bingley immediately offered to fetch her others – all that his library afforded – and apologised over the size of his collection. Elizabeth assured him that she could suit herself perfectly with those in the room.

"I am astonished," said Miss Bingley, "that my father should have left so small a collection of books. What a delightful library you have at Pemberley, Mr. Darcy!"

"Thank you, Miss Bingley," said Mr. Darcy, with a cold finality that indicated he had nothing further to say on the subject.

"It *is* a delightful library," said Mr. Bingley, "and although the one here is not nearly its equal, I do encourage you to avail yourself of it, Miss Elizabeth. Please feel welcome to all that it has; if not tonight, then during the rest of your stay. Perhaps it might take Miss Bennet's mind off of her illness, were you to read to her."

"That is a fine idea, Mr. Bingley, and I thank you for your hospitality."

When Elizabeth next went up to check on her sister, she found Jane worse, and returned to the drawing-room only long enough to impart this news. There followed some discussion of what should be done, until it was settled that the apothecary should be sent for in the morning.

CHAPTER 2

Jane was, thankfully, somewhat improved in the morning, although not so well that Elizabeth was certain she could be moved. She felt compelled to send for her mother, so Mrs. Bennet could form her own judgment of the situation, although Elizabeth should have known that regardless of how Jane actually did, Elizabeth's mother would wish her to remain at Netherfield.

This Mrs. Bennet indicated, having come with the remainder of Elizabeth's sisters, and causing her second-eldest a goodly degree of mortification during their short time in Netherfield's breakfast-parlour. Mrs. Bennet had found Jane too ill to be moved, and it was agreed – fervently by Mr. Bingley, and with a measure of reluctance by his sisters – that the two eldest Miss Bennets should remain at Netherfield until Jane was better.

With this settled, Elizabeth's younger sisters were free to convince Mr. Bingley to hold a ball at Netherfield, and Mrs. Bennet to effuse on what a charming house it was, and to express her hopes that Mr. Bingley would not quit it in a hurry. Her hopes were not met in a wholly favourable way, for Mr. Bingley replied that whatever he did was done in a hurry, and if he should resolve to quit the house, he should probably be off in five minutes, although at present, he considered himself quite fixed.

"That is exactly what I should have supposed of you," said Elizabeth.

"You begin to comprehend me, do you?" cried he, turning towards her.

"Oh! Yes – I understand you perfectly."

"I wish I might take this for a compliment; but to be so easily seen through I am afraid is pitiful."

"That is as it happens. It does not necessarily follow that a deep, intricate character is more or less estimable than such a one as yours."

"Lizzy," cried her mother, "remember where you are, and do not run on in the wild manner that you are suffered to do at home."

"I did not know before," continued Bingley, immediately, "that you were a studier of character. It must be an amusing study."

"Yes, but intricate characters are the *most* amusing. They have at least

225

that advantage."

Upon saying this, Elizabeth could not help but glance over at Mr. Darcy, who had stood in silence by the window during the whole course of the conversation, and remained so now. She suspected his was the most intricate character in the house, but her opportunities for study had been very thin thus far, and this could not but further stoke her natural curiosity.

Her mother and younger sisters left, and Elizabeth went back up to check on Jane, finding her sister asleep. She then thought to take Mr. Bingley up on his offer to avail herself of the library, to find something Jane might enjoy hearing read aloud, once she awoke. A servant gave her the direction, and Elizabeth entered with no expectation of there being anyone in the room, so that at first she did not even notice Mr. Darcy's presence.

When she did, she felt a deep, unexpected pang of sympathy for the gentleman. He was hunched over in one of the chairs, with his head in his hands, and what looked to be a letter in his lap. Elizabeth wondered what had put him in such a state, but she felt all the indelicacy of the situation, and made to leave before he noticed her.

She was not successful, however. He looked up at her with red-rimmed eyes, and she felt it very possible that he had been crying.

"Mr. Darcy, I am so sorry to intrude on your privacy – I did not think there would be anyone here."

"There usually is not, apart from myself," he replied, in a thick voice.

"I will leave you – I must apologise again. But you do not look well – is there anything I may bring you to give you present relief? A glass of wine; shall I get you one?"

"You are very kind, Miss Bennet, but I am not ill. There is nothing you can bring me for my present relief," he said, "unless you are somehow able to return my sister to me."

It was an exceedingly strange statement; Elizabeth could not understand what he meant by it, for he had said only the evening before that his sister was in Bath.

"Is that a letter from your sister?" she asked, glancing down at the paper in his hand.

"It is a letter from her husband."

"Her husband? I did not realise she was married." Nor, although she would not say it, did she understand why Mr. Bingley would refer to her as *Miss Darcy*, if his sister was married. "Has her illness worsened?"

He stood abruptly, and strode over to the window on the other side of the room. She would have thought him rude, but that he seemed exceedingly agitated. He stayed there for some time before he returned to where she was, and even then, he would not sit.

"I do not know why I just told you of her husband, although I suppose the truth cannot be concealed for much longer."

"You need not tell me anything which brings you discomfort, sir, and I promise I will not speak of what you have just said."

"I feel no doubt of your secrecy, Miss Bennet. In truth, there is some relief to another in this house knowing of it, aside from Charles. About six months ago, my sister eloped. I have not seen her since."

Elizabeth gasped, in spite of herself, and apologised. Her immediate thought, from his words, was that he had cut his sister from his life, but it was clear from his countenance that this was not what he meant.

"Is she still in Scotland?"

"I do not know where she is," he said, striding back over to the window, and then beginning to pace. "The man she eloped with was the son of my late father's steward, who was a good man, and cannot be faulted in all that has happened since. The son – Wickham, is his name – was also my father's god-son, and he supported him in his education."

Thus far, Elizabeth could see nothing so terrible about the man other than his being the son of Mr. Darcy's father's steward, but she felt there must be more, and so she nodded to him to continue. He did, and explained that he had seen a very different side of Wickham the son than was shown to his father, that of a young man with vicious propensities, and a want of principle. A man who, rather than taking a living that had been intended for him by the late Mr. Darcy, had instead asked for alternate compensation, a request the younger Mr. Darcy had met with the sum of three thousand pounds.

"I thought at the time all connection between us was to be dissolved," he said. "For about three years I heard little of him, but on the decease of the incumbent of the living, he applied to me again, having dissipated the funds of his legacy. I refused to comply with his request, and his resentment was in proportion to the distress of his circumstances. If I had known then what would happen, I would have placated him with a great sum of money, to have prevented it. Instead, I dropped his acquaintance."

"How did he come upon your sister's notice?"

"My sister is more than ten years my junior, and was left to the guardianship of my cousin and myself. Earlier this year, she went with her companion to summer at Ramsgate, and thither also went Mr. Wickham, in collusion with her companion, in whose character we had been most unhappily deceived."

He seemed reluctant to continue, but Elizabeth, who had heard too much of the story now to allow it to stop, nodded to encourage him.

"I arrived in Ramsgate, wishing to surprise Georgiana with a visit, to learn they had gone to Gretna Green only two days prior. I and several hired men gave chase, but they had departed that town by the time we arrived. She was only fifteen, which must be her excuse."

"My God, the poor girl!" Elizabeth thought of Lydia and Kitty, who were nearly the same age as Mr. Darcy's sister and likely equally capable of being persuaded into an elopement, without comprehending the consequences. "You are certain they are married?"

"I have his word of it, and the one letter from her which I have been allowed, but I believe they are, although that is not my main worry until she is recovered," Mr. Darcy said. "Wickham's chief object was my sister's fortune of thirty thousand pounds, although I believe the hope of revenging himself on me was also a strong inducement. His revenge has been complete indeed. He writes to me every fortnight to tell me I shall never see her again until I release her dowry to him, which I will not do while she is in the clutches of that man. I know him well enough to be certain he will not return her, despite his promises. If I give him the money, he will only ask for more."

"What has been done, what has been attempted, to recover her?" she asked.

"I have hired a number of men to search for her, but the difficulty is in determining where to search – he has been clever in that. Each of the letters is posted from a different town, usually within Hertfordshire or Bedfordshire; I believe them to be somewhere within one of the two counties. When I learned Charles was to take a house in Hertfordshire, I confessed the whole of the matter to him, and asked if I might stay here, so I would be closer to the search."

"I am sure you will find her," Elizabeth said, attempting to put as much conviction into her voice as she could, for she found herself very worried for this girl she had never met. "This country is not so large that she may be concealed for long."

"I pray you are right, Miss Bennet. My only hope is to find her, and have the marriage annulled. It will likely be scandalous, but that would be nothing if she can be safely restored to her rightful home. I fear, though, what she has been through and will continue to go through, until she is found."

"I will pray for her," Elizabeth said, "and you must have no doubt of my secrecy in this matter."

"I thank you for that. In truth, I know not why I have shared all of this with you. I must apologise if I have burdened you with more than you wish to bear."

"I find my heaviest burdens are always lighter after I have shared them with my sister," Elizabeth said. "If I have in the slightest way eased your own burdens, it is not something you must apologise over, for I do it gladly. And I hope you know that you shall have another ally in this house."

"Thank you for that, Miss Bennet. It is more than I deserve, but I thank you for it all the same."

Elizabeth came away from this conversation shocked at the rapidity with which all of her questions about Mr. Darcy had been answered, and what those answers had been. She was, perhaps, the only person within their neighbourhood to think kindly of him – excepting Jane, who thought kindly of everyone – but Elizabeth did think of him with every kindness which his situation must engender, and was determined to make good on her promise to be an ally of his, at Netherfield.

Her assistance was not needed during dinner, and following that event, they repaired to the drawing-room, where the party once again promised to be dull. Mr. Hurst had given up on his loo-table, and was playing at piquet across the room with Mr. Bingley, while Mrs. Hurst looked on. Elizabeth took up some needlework, and was nearer the conversation between Mr. Darcy and Miss Bingley, which began as an amusement, and only later turned in a concerning direction. Those two were reading again, a task Miss Bingley could not attend to with any focus, when she preferred to laud Mr. Darcy:

"I am amazed you read verse instead of prose, at this time of the evening, Mr. Darcy. I hardly have the focus for it in the morning."

"Yes, it can be quite difficult to focus."

"How uncommonly fast you read, Mr. Darcy!"

"I find, as a rule, that I read faster when I am not also conversing."

At this dismissal, Miss Bingley was silent for a little while, but could not remain so for long.

"I declare, this neighbourhood is entirely too dull," she said. "I think I would rather we all go to Bath, and support your sister in her recovery. Let me bring it up to Charles."

Elizabeth looked up sharply at this, in time to see a brief expression of panic in Mr. Darcy's eyes, as he replied, "My sister would prefer to take her treatment in private, Miss Bingley."

"Oh, yes, of course, away from the ton, but surely such old friends as we would only serve to raise her spirits," Miss Bingley said. "I believe I make an admirable nurse."

Elizabeth could not even allow herself the amusement of this last statement, for she felt she must do something to aid poor Mr. Darcy in dissuading Caroline Bingley from her course. Surely Mr. Bingley would disallow the trip, knowing what he did, but to forbid it outright might lead Miss Bingley to question why it had been forbidden, and seek to get at the cause. Elizabeth had seen enough of the lady to understand she was a thorough gossip, which was no doubt why Mr. Darcy wished to conceal the true story of his sister from her, when he had shared it so freely with Elizabeth.

"Did you mention Bath? My mother has been wild to go to Bath these twenty years at least," said Elizabeth, moving to a seat nearer them, and being rewarded only with a very peculiar look from Mr. Darcy. "My father took her there before we were all born, and she has been on about it ever since; how it is the very height of fashion and society."

"Twenty years ago, perhaps it was," said Caroline. "I suppose your mother would not know – that is not at all the case now."

"But she spoke with such fondness of the pump-room and assembly-rooms, of how they were the finest spaces she had ever seen." In truth, Elizabeth *was* repeating what her mother had said of Bath, with very little embellishment. "And she said she could not pass a lady without admiring her dress, so new were the styles."

"They are still fine spaces, I suppose, but she should not find such fashionable ladies if she went there now. She would find last year's fashions, if that."

"Indeed?"

"Yes, Miss Bennet. The trouble with Bath is that nobody who is anybody goes there any longer," said Miss Bingley, and then, with a nervous look to Mr. Darcy, "excepting those there for treatment, of course."

"Oh yes, of course. If one is there for treatment, I am sure it is an entirely different thing," said Elizabeth, "but otherwise, it sounds as though it would be quite a degradation, to be known as going to Bath. Thank you for informing me, so I can tell my mother she shall have to think of somewhere else to begin convincing Mr. Bennet to take us. Perhaps the seaside would be a better choice."

"You are welcome, Miss Bennet. I suppose it is not the sort of intelligence you would have in this neighbourhood, although I wonder at it, given how close you are to town."

"Perhaps we are *too* close," said Elizabeth. "If we were farther away, we might think to set aside time to go there more often, but instead, we may go there any time we choose, and as a result, rarely ever choose to go."

"I believe you are right, Miss Bennet," said Mr. Darcy, looking at her with a very relieved countenance. "Derbyshire is nearly two days from town, if one is to make the journey in any degree of comfort, and thus my travel is planned far more carefully."

"I wish Charles would buy an estate in Derbyshire," said Caroline. "It is the finest county in England. I do not know why he bothers with Hertfordshire. It is such a dull place, and if you had not come to visit us, Mr. Darcy, I am in horror to think of how little society we would have had."

"I believe you expect too much of a country neighbourhood, Miss Bingley. The society must – by its nature – be more unvarying than you would find in town, but it does not follow that it cannot be pleasurable."

"I have been looking for pleasurable society since we arrived here, and I have found very little of it."

"I hardly know how you can say that, Miss Bingley. We have met with a great many people here who have been hospitable and kind." At the last word, he met Elizabeth's eye, and she gave him the slightest little nod in return.

Having thus been pushed down too many avenues of conversation she did not wish to go down, there was little else for Miss Bingley to do but sigh heavily, and take the dire step of returning to her book.

CHAPTER 3

Jane's health had so improved that she and Elizabeth were in agreement that, if there was no relapse, Jane might go down to the drawing-room for a little while in the evening, and Elizabeth should write to Longbourn requesting the carriage to attend them home the next day. Elizabeth sought, therefore, to return the book she had borrowed from the library. This might have been done by a servant, but in truth, a wish to speak again with Mr. Darcy privately formed part of her motives in doing the task herself.

She was not denied; Mr. Darcy was there, although not in the same saddened attitude she had found him in previously. He was seated in the same chair, however, and rose as soon as she entered.

"I apologise for disturbing you again, Mr. Darcy," she said. "I wished to return this."

"Unless you remember precisely where you got it from, there may be some difficulty in that," he said. "I have yet to find any semblance of organisation in how the shelves are arranged."

"The arrangement was a little haphazard when I found it," she said, crossing the room. "But I know it was on this shelf."

The book was replaced in approximately the same location in which she had found it, and when Elizabeth turned away from the shelf, she found Mr. Darcy standing nearer to her.

"Miss Bennet, I do not know how to thank you for your assistance yesterday," he said. "You manoeuvred Miss Bingley from her course far more skilfully than either her brother or I would have done."

"It was nothing," she said. "I needed only to find something to set Miss Bingley firmly against it, and I suspected my mother's raptures would be the quickest path to provoke such a reaction."

"Ah, yes, you are the great studier of character."

"I did not know you were attending that conversation, in the breakfast-parlour."

"I was, and I must say I am glad you have put your talents to such good use."

"Does Miss Bingley inquire after your sister frequently?"

"Yes, she does. I believe she wishes to match Georgiana to Charles, and so she is always seeking to throw them together. If she knew the truth, she would be horrified, and then see it spread across half of London."

"You might send your sister farther abroad, for her health – somewhere far enough away that Miss Bingley could not think to go to her on a whim."

"I have considered it, although in some ways it feels as though it would be giving up hope that she should be found and recovered soon, and I am not ready to do so," he said. "At least you have put Miss Bingley off of Bath."

"If you have need of reinforcing that, you need only mention Bath while my mother is around, for she *is* truly wild to return there," Elizabeth said.

"I will remember that."

Elizabeth had been alone with him in the library for entirely more than was proper, of late, and felt she could not tarry any longer. She made to take her leave, telling him she wished to check on Jane before dinner, and that her sister was well enough to perhaps make an appearance in the drawing-room in the evening.

"I am very glad to hear her health is improved, Miss Bennet, and I must thank you again for your assistance last night."

"You are very welcome, Mr. Darcy, and if I have opportunity to do so again, I promise you that I shall."

This was the last conversation between the two of them while Elizabeth and her sister were living in the house. Jane improved rapidly, and soon enough they were in the carriage, departing from Netherfield. Elizabeth was relieved to return to Longbourn, for it was home, although it could not be called a peaceful home, and she found it was to become far less peaceful shortly after she and Jane made their return, due to a visitor.

This visitor was their cousin, Mr. Collins, who was to inherit the estate, and had been, like his father, heretofore estranged from them, but had written to Mr. Bennet of his intention to visit and heal the breach. Mr. Collins arrived at Longbourn and very nearly immediately showed himself to be a pompous, empty-headed man, and the only people happy about his visit were Mrs. Bennet, who seemed to think to marry one of her daughters off to him, and Mr. Bennet, who found a great deal of amusement in the man. Elizabeth might have found amusement in him as well, but for her suspicion that she was the daughter Mrs. Bennet wished him to marry.

Elizabeth did not think he had a true preference for her, but that he must have been steered into it by Mrs. Bennet, for she found him always seeking her out in company. This he did one morning when she and her sisters had decided to walk to Meryton; there was no-one else he would walk beside, and he was often encouraging Elizabeth to take up his arm, and Elizabeth then discouraging him by indicating she was not tired, and had no need of it.

The attentions of the youngest Bennet ladies were soon enough taken up in their usual diversions. The two eldest found their own attention diverted, soon enough, for the sound of horses drew their notice, and Mr. Darcy and Mr. Bingley could be seen riding down the street. On distinguishing the ladies of the group, the two gentlemen came directly towards them, and began the usual civilities, with Mr. Bingley indicating they had been on their way to Longbourn to inquire after Miss Bennet's health. Mr. Darcy corroborated this with a bow, and asked if they could be introduced to the new member of the Miss Bennets's party; they were, and then Mr. Darcy surprised them all by dismounting, as though he meant to walk on with them. Mr. Bingley most eagerly followed his lead, and Mary, who had been walking alongside Jane, readily dropped back so Mr. Bingley could take her place.

Excepting Elizabeth, no-one wanted to walk beside Mr. Darcy, and upon finding herself in a trio with the displaced Mary and Mr. Collins, she took the opportunity to walk on ahead to where Mr. Darcy led his horse. He held the horse's reins in one hand, and made to offer his other arm to her, which she noticed in mortification.

"I cannot take your arm, I am afraid," she murmured. "I declined my cousin's, earlier."

"I suppose that is better than your refusing my arm outright," he said. "How have you been, Miss Bennet?"

"Well, I suppose. We have a goodly degree of distraction about our house, currently."

"Ah yes, your cousin."

"We are entertained alternately with readings from Fordyce's Sermons, and stories of the condescension of his highest, most exalted and noble patroness, Lady Catherine de Bourgh."

He looked at her in surprise. "Your cousin holds the living at Hunsford?"

"You know of it?"

"Lady Catherine is my aunt."

In embarrassment, Elizabeth said, "I am sorry, Mr. Darcy – I did not intend to demean your aunt."

"Do not apologise, Miss Bennet. When she learns of the elopement, Lady Catherine will be the very first to cut me, and she shall do so mercilessly."

"Has there been any news, of your sister?"

"None since we last spoke. I wrote my reply, and attempted to trace its delivery, as I always do, but he has things very cleverly arranged in that regard. I am instructed to leave my response at a less-reputable club in London; from there the letters are delivered to one of several brothels, and must exchange hands within, for he never goes to any of them himself."

"It must be terribly frustrating."

"It is. I had, before now, thought I possessed enough fortune to see my way through any problem. But this is not one that can be solved simply by hiring on more men. I still hope they shall eventually find some sort of lead, and locate Georgiana."

They were both of them fast walkers, and had outstripped the rest of the party, already reaching the door to Mr. Phillips's house, at which Elizabeth halted and asked if he and Mr. Bingley would like to come in.

"I think not, but thank you for the invitation," he said, motioning to his horse, whom he held with a very firm hand. "This one will not stand for it."

"I understand," she said. "I would offer up the use of my uncle's groom, but I cannot believe your spirits much attuned to new company, and I will own my aunt Phillips is a rather boisterous sort of new company."

"This is true, although I, in turn, will own that even in happier times new company was not something I sought frequently. I have not the talent which some people possess, of conversing easily with those I have never seen before."

Yet he conversed easily enough with her, Elizabeth thought, but would not say. Before she could reply, the others had caught up with them. Her offer to come into the house was repeated by them, but Mr. Bingley would follow Mr. Darcy's lead in this, and even in spite of Mrs. Phillips's throwing up the parlour window, and loudly seconding the invitation, the gentlemen would defer to their horses.

Elizabeth had opportunity to converse with Mr. Darcy again the next day, however, for he and Mr. Bingley were seen to be riding toward the house, throwing Mrs. Bennet into a flutter.

"It is a fine enough day, Jane, for you to propose a walk to Mr. Bingley. Yes, you must go and have a nice long walk and some fine conversation between the two of you," said she. "Oh! – but one of you will have to go with them, and accompany Mr. Darcy. I hate to burden one of you with such an unpleasant task, but it must be done. It would never do for you to walk as a trio!"

"I will go, mama," Elizabeth said. "I find Mr. Darcy improves upon acquaintance."

"Well! I would not go near so far as that, myself, but that is very good of you, Lizzy," said Mrs. Bennet, with only a glance in the direction of the library, where Mr. Collins had been passing the morning with Mr. Bennet. "Very good indeed."

The gentlemen were shown in, and the walk proposed and agreed to. Elizabeth worried Mr. Collins might emerge from the library and insist on joining them, but as this did not happen, they set off as a very pleasant foursome, which soon enough became two rather distant couples.

Elizabeth and Mr. Darcy walked on in silence for some time, before she finally inquired after how he was.

"I am much the same as I have been," he said, "but perhaps a little better, for the prospect of a fine walk, on a fine day. How are you, Miss Bennet?"

"I share your sentiments regarding a fine walk, on a fine day."

They walked on for some time, before he said, "Have you been to Hatfield House, Miss Bennet? Or is it another of your places that is so close you may visit it at any time, and therefore never do?"

"It is indeed. We have been once, but when I was a little girl, so I remember very little of it."

"Would you have interest in going? Over breakfast at Netherfield, we formed an expedition for tomorrow, and Charles and I would like to see you and your sister attend, if you have no other plans. You would be in the carriage with Mrs. Hurst and Miss Bingley; the gentlemen will ride."

"I cannot speak for Jane, but I believe she would be as delighted as I," said Elizabeth, and in truth she *was* delighted, excepting the prospect of riding in the carriage with Mr. Bingley's sisters.

"Excellent – do you believe your parents will give permission? We may ask when we all return, so long as Miss Bennet has interest."

"My mother will gladly give permission for any sort of event where Jane is able to spend more time in company with Mr. Bingley. Oh – I am sorry, I should not have spoken so."

He was silent for some time, and Elizabeth chanced a look sideways, fearing she had angered him.

"Do not worry over your own statement, Miss Bennet. You have said nothing I could not observe myself, both of your own mother, and others in town. Mr. Bingley is young and amiable, and of good fortune. I have seen a great many young ladies thrown at him."

"Surely you do not think Jane one of them!" Elizabeth exclaimed, turning to face him. "My mother is not subtle about the need for us to marry, but I hope you would exclude my sister's motivations from my mother's actions."

"In truth, I had been hoping to speak with you about this, although it was not my purpose in this conversation. Your sister is always kind to Bingley, and seems pleased by the attentions she receives, but I see no symptoms of any peculiar regard. I would not accuse your sister of being mercenary, but given your mother's behaviour, I also cannot entirely acquit your sister of mercenary motives," he said. "It has become clear to me that my friend prefers your sister to any other woman in the country. In such a case, the inequality of their fortunes cannot be ignored, and I would be loath to see my particular friend in a match where both affection and fortune were unequal."

Elizabeth's first reaction to this speech was one of furious indignation, that he should say and think such things about her family, particularly Jane. A little reflection before she spoke – that Mr. Darcy, given his history, must be far more likely to attribute mercenary motives to those he met than other men – softened her feelings somewhat.

"Mr. Darcy, I must first say that I think you go too far, in speaking of a match – farther, even, than either of the principals of which we speak. They have hardly spent enough time together to be concerned over such things, although I assure you my sister is not mercenary. She cannot afford to marry poorly, but she is too good at heart to be mercenary."

"If I am not concerned now, it will be far too late by the time Bingley comes to me for advice. If he was to propose (and I do not say he would do so now, but at some point in the future, after further acquaintance), could your sister truly ignore your mother's wishes and tell him no, if she felt no affection?"

"I hope he would not do so, without some notion that she returned his affections."

"I wonder if any such notion would ever be forthcoming. She does not seem to be someone whose heart is easily reached, and if that is the case, it is perhaps better for Bingley to cease the attempt."

"I disagree completely with you there, sir. My sister does not show her feelings easily, but it does not follow that she does not have them. In truth, a friend encouraged me to tell Jane to show more affections than she feels to Mr. Bingley, so as to secure his regard. But Jane is not formed for such arts, and I rather think it better that she will not feign regard, simply for the sake of attempting to capture a man's heart before she is sure of her own."

"I had not thought of it in that way."

"I hope that you will. So long as Mr. Bingley allows her behaviour to guide him, he will never be led astray."

"If he seeks my advice, then, I will give him that, for I cannot provide any better."

Satisfied, Elizabeth turned back to face the path, and they walked on.

CHAPTER 4

The Hatfield House expedition began much as Elizabeth would have expected, with the two eldest Miss Bennets picked up in the carriage and received with cold civility by Mrs. Hurst and Miss Bingley. Thankfully, the drive was not a long one, and the sisters had as little desire to converse with Elizabeth as she did with them, so she was free to look out the carriage window while Mr. Bingley's sisters feigned interest in Jane's society.

Elizabeth could not help but notice that all of the gentlemen rode well, including Mr. Hurst, which she thought must have been caused by his being more sober than usual. It was Mr. Darcy who drew most of her attention, though; his mount was the same spirited animal he had ridden into Meryton, but managed with a firm hand. Mr. Darcy seemed preoccupied, however, and not nearly so pleased with the ride as Mr. Bingley clearly was, and Elizabeth wondered if he had received another letter from this Mr. Wickham.

It was Mr. Darcy, as well, who drew her attention back to the conversation, for Miss Bingley indicated the entire expedition had been his idea, and this surprised Elizabeth. Miss Bingley – and this was not a surprise – thought the honour due to her, since she had been complaining about there being so little to do in Hertfordshire, and her complaints had been met with Mr. Darcy's fine idea for an outing. Now, however, Elizabeth thought she understood Mr. Darcy's preoccupation: he had prompted an expedition into a new area of the county, which might put him on Wickham's path, and he was looking about for some sign of the man as he rode.

Their application to see the house was only partly successful; the family was in residence, and as no-one in their party was acquainted with them, they could see only the state rooms, the gardens, and the stables, housed within the old palace. Those in the party who were inclined to be satisfied were satisfied with this, and those who were inclined to complain, did so. Miss Bingley ceased the latter only when she had claimed Mr. Darcy's arm to walk with him through the state rooms.

"How very strange it must be for you to be applying to see the estate of another family, when I am sure you are far more used to receiving applications to see your own house, Mr. Darcy," Miss Bingley said. "How many parties apply to see Pemberley, in a given year?"

"No more than two hundred, I daresay. We receive our share of those visiting the Peak, but not so many as Chatsworth."

"How odious it must be to have people so frequently going through one's house," said Miss Bingley, in a tone that indicated she found it the opposite of odious.

"It is hardly so. My housekeeper always sees to them, and she endeavours to keep them out of sight, unless I am acquainted with the party."

This was an intriguing thought to Elizabeth, that Mr. Darcy lived in a home fine enough to merit visitors, although she supposed she should have assumed this to be the case, given how highly Pemberley had been spoken of. She wondered if this was his greatest draw, where Miss Bingley was concerned; certainly he was handsome, and rich, but Miss Bingley seemed the sort to fancy herself mistress of a great estate.

Elizabeth had the freedom for such thoughts, because in their party of three gentlemen and four ladies, she had been the one left out of the coupling, and she walked amongst them, behind Mr. Bingley and Jane. Rather than joining them and making a trio, for Jane's benefit, she remained alone, and simply enjoyed the splendour of the house.

When they had finished with the state rooms and were strolling through the gardens, Elizabeth indicated her desire to see the old palace, but found it unpopular. Miss Bingley was particularly adamant that she would much rather see more of the grounds, than look through some dirty old horse stable, and when none in the party spoke to contradict her, Elizabeth said, "I do wish to see it. I shall just go and take a quick look, and rejoin you shortly."

"I will go with you, Miss Elizabeth," Mr. Darcy said.

"Ah, now if Darcy is going with you to view stabling, it may not be such a quick look as you had wished, Miss Elizabeth," Mr. Bingley said teasingly, looking as though he might like to see the stables himself, but that Jane did not seem inclined to leave the gardens.

Mr. Darcy offered Elizabeth his arm, and this time she had no reason to reject it, as they walked the short distance to a long brick building, which appeared only slightly worn, considering its age.

"Thank you for coming with me," Elizabeth said.

"It is nothing," he said. "I am a bit surprised none of the others had interest in viewing it. Perhaps it is more relevant for you, though – might I assume you were named for Queen Elizabeth?"

"I believe all we Elizabeths were, to some degree or another. I suppose I do feel some remote connection, but mostly, I would hate to leave such a piece of history without viewing it."

Mr. Darcy opened a door at the end of the building to reveal what at first looked and smelled like any other stable, with a row of stalls on either side of a long aisle. For the viewer who would look up, however, as Elizabeth did, they would be rewarded with the sight of a beautifully curved hammerbeam roof, impossibly far above them. Elizabeth gasped, and even an abundance of cobwebs could not prevent her from imagining Queen Elizabeth dining and dancing within this space, and finding she did now feel a greater connection with the former queen, for sharing her name.

"How remarkable," she whispered.

"Indeed, I admire the Cecils for keeping it up. It must take a tremendous amount of effort."

"Keeping it up?" she cried. "They have turned it into a stable!"

"And were it not a stable, it might not be worth the cost of maintenance," he said. "I am sorry – I think too much like an estate owner now, I find. I see a fine, graceful old thing such as this and immediately begin calculating what it must cost to keep it standing. But I think if it must survive as a stable in order to survive, that is better than the alternative."

"I suppose so," Elizabeth said. She intended to tell him it was a rather dour way to view such a magnificent thing, but there was a cry from the other end of the building, of "loose horse!" and immediately following this, a horse charging down the narrow aisle.

There were few things in the world that could paralyse Elizabeth so effectively as seventy-five stone of horseflesh, galloping directly toward her. She knew she should move, and yet she could not, and did not, until Mr. Darcy's hands firmly grasped her shoulders, spinning her out of the horse's path and pushing her against one of the stalls, just before the horse passed them.

"Stay here, Miss Bennet!" he cried. "I will attempt to help them catch him; I do not wish for him to make my horse's acquaintance."

Elizabeth allowed herself some time to recover, before peering around the stable door to see what was happening outside. There in the yard, she saw several grooms dancing about with their arms far outstretched, attempting to enclose the horse, which she now saw to be a stallion, and better understood Mr. Darcy's concern that the horse not meet with his mount, which was also a stallion.

Unlike the others, Mr. Darcy had taken up a feed bucket from somewhere, and Elizabeth watched as he picked up a handful of gravel from the yard, dropped it in the bucket, and shook it vigorously. The horse, who had heretofore been capering about and evading capture, took notice of the sound, and, perhaps thinking the bucket to be filled with oats, stopped and pricked his ears in Mr. Darcy's direction.

Slowly, the horse walked toward the sound, and Mr. Darcy set the bucket down on the ground as it drew nearer. When the horse dipped his nose near the bucket, sniffing for the oats that were not there, Mr. Darcy took a firm hold of its nose with one hand, pushing his other hand into its neck, so that it was turned at a significant angle, and the horse could do nothing other than spin its hindquarters around at a vigorous pace until one of the grooms came up with a halter and lead line, and they were able to see the animal more firmly secured.

Elizabeth watched of all this with a mixture of fascination and fear, until Mr. Darcy stepped away from the horse, and returned to her with a concerned countenance.

"Miss Bennet, are you well? I did not hurt you, I hope?" he asked, laying his hand on her arm.

"No, not at all, although even if you had, it would have been far less than the horse would have done. I must thank you – I am rather afraid of horses," she admitted.

"May I ask what it is that makes you fear horses so?"

"I had a few bad experiences, when I was learning to ride," she said. "I fell quite a few times, and the last time the horse's hooves were so near to my head I could feel all the force they would have brought had they stepped on me."

"I am sorry you had to suffer such an experience," he said. "We have a gentle old pony at Pemberley. If – if you are ever in Derbyshire when I am in residence, you would be welcome to try again on him."

"Thank you, Mr. Darcy," Elizabeth said, perplexed, although not unpleased, at such an odd offer. "I shall keep that in mind if I am ever in your county. Now, should we be getting back to the others?"

"I believe we should," he said, offering his arm again. "Poor Miss Bennet – I fear you must have determined never to accept an invitation from Mr. Bingley or myself again. You were quite neglected, earlier, in having no one to walk with, and then nearly trampled by a horse."

"I could have done without the horse, but I assure you, aside from that I have enjoyed myself."

"If you are still open to invitations from myself, then, I wonder if you might have any dances still open for the Netherfield ball, and if so, if I might be allowed to claim one."

"I have no claims on my time for the ball thus far, and I would certainly stand up with you. I fear though, that the ball must be a punishment for you, given everything," she said.

"I cannot say it will not be, generally, to dance and pretend all is well, although I must do so for Mr. Bingley's benefit. But you are one person it would not at all be a punishment to dance with. Perhaps we might dance the first set and the supper set?"

"Of course, you may consider them yours."

Following their return to Longbourn, Jane and Elizabeth were thoroughly queried over dinner as to all that had passed during the outing, although as the main person seeking this intelligence was Mrs. Bennet, only what had passed between Jane and Mr. Bingley was of importance. When all of these items had been related, there was nothing remaining for the attention of the family, but the Netherfield ball.

Catherine and Lydia were most vocal in the anticipation of the happiness the event should bring, but the prospect of the ball was extremely agreeable to every female of the family, and they discussed all that was expected at length. No-one asked him of his plans to attend, but Mr. Collins entered the conversation in his usual awkward manner, informing them that he intended to accept Mr. Bingley's invitation, and Elizabeth could not help but express her surprise, to find he entertained no scruples regarding the ball, or in venturing to dance. He put forth that such a ball, given by a young man of character, to respectable people, could have no evil tendency, and reinforced this by indicating he wished for the hands of each of his fair cousins in the course of the evening.

"I take this opportunity of soliciting yours, Miss Elizabeth, for the two first dances especially; a preference which I trust my cousin Jane will attribute to the right cause, and not to any disrespect for her."

Jane nodded her understanding, and Elizabeth was left to reply, "I apologise, Mr. Collins, but I am already promised for the first set. I may dance the second with you."

"Promised for the first set!" cried Mrs. Bennet. "Who could you possibly be promised to for the first set already?"

"Mr. Darcy," said Elizabeth, in a tone of some embarrassment. "He asked for my hand in the dance earlier today."

For those who had seen the workings of Mrs. Bennet's mind over a great many years, it was easy to see her determine that if Mr. Darcy had been free to ask Elizabeth to dance, he had not been interfering with Mr. Bingley's pursuit of Jane, by claiming a share of his friend's attention, and then, following this, that Mr. Darcy – although proud and wholly disagreeable – had ten thousand a year, and was not at all an objectionable man for her daughter to be seen dancing with.

"Mr. Darcy, yes, of course. Well, Mr. Collins, I suppose you should have asked my Lizzy earlier, for you see what a favourite she is among our neighbourhood, and well she should be. But I am sure you shall have a fine second set with her, and the third, Lizzy, if you are not engaged for *that*."

"I am not, mama."

"Well, then it is settled. Now as to the first set, Jane, may I suppose you are promised to Mr. Bingley?"

Jane replied that she was.

"Of course, yes, very well. Then Mr. Collins, perhaps you might dance the first with Mary?"

It was thus settled that Mr. Collins should begin the ball with Mary, and that Elizabeth was very kind to suffer through dancing with Mr. Darcy for the benefit of her sister, the latter being mentioned by Mrs. Bennet as an aside to her second-eldest, later in the evening.

It was only when Elizabeth went to bed that she had the time and quietude for reflection on all that had happened. To think of being singled out so by Mr. Darcy's already requesting two sets of her only enhanced the tenderness she had been feeling towards him for some time. She reminded herself that in dancing the supper set with her, he was spared dancing it with Miss Bingley, and so Elizabeth may merely have been the lesser of two evils. Yet something in the way he had asked, and that he had volunteered to come with her to the stables, indicated he did prefer her company.

Her tenderness shifted to admiration, and gratitude, when she thought of those moments in front of the horse. His actions then were such as any quick-acting gentleman might take to protect a lady in harm's way, and yet Elizabeth recalled most vividly his hands upon her shoulders, pushing her up against the stall. And how cleverly and calmly he had set about catching the horse! Even that he had gone to give his assistance, rather than leaving it to the grooms, she thought worthy of praise. Elizabeth felt herself in a dangerous place, now, for a man in his present situation could not possibly have romance on his mind. It would be best to tamp down her feelings, she thought, before they turned into anything stronger, and she resolved to do so.

CHAPTER 5

Elizabeth entered the drawing-room at Netherfield determined not to be making conquest of any hearts that evening. She had dressed with more than usual care, and did attribute this to her promised dances with Mr. Darcy, but it was strong on her mind that what he would need most at this time was friendship, and that must be what she would provide.

He had not formed part of the receiving line, and her first glimpse of him showed a man utterly miserable in his surroundings. He stood on the edge of the drawing-room in silent observation, well on his way to reinforcing his reputation within the neighbourhood as a proud, disagreeable man. Elizabeth ignored the way this tugged at her heart, and went to him. If any of the guests had been judging him then, they would have found his features softened with a smile for her, which was returned willingly.

"You look very well, Miss Bennet," he said. "Are you in good health?"

"I am. Mr. Darcy, I hope I do not injure you by saying you do not look to be in good spirits this evening."

"Is it that apparent?"

"I am afraid it is."

"I shall have to try harder, then, for Bingley's sake. The truth is, I had another letter from Wickham yesterday, and it weighs heavily on my mind. There was nothing that had not been in his last few, but his timing could not have been worse."

"That is horrible – do you think he knows you are staying here, and of the ball, and timed it intentionally?"

"The county is not so large; it is entirely possible."

"I wish I knew what he looked like. I might pass him in Meryton and never know."

"I doubt he would risk going into Meryton if he does know I am staying at Netherfield," he said. "But I have a miniature of him, commissioned by my father; I will bring it when next I call on you."

"Good. I would like to be of any assistance I may."

"You are very good, Miss Bennet. I do not deserve such friendship, but I am glad of it anyway."

"I see no reason why you do not deserve friendship, Mr. Darcy. Perhaps you might have been more careful in checking the character of your sister's companion, but you cannot blame yourself for the events that followed."

"I cannot agree with you there. My lapses were frequent, and occurred long before that incident. I have been a selfish being all my life, in practise, though not in principle, and it is my sister who has paid the price of it. I acted with wholly improper pride; I did with my sister what society judged best: I sent her away to the finest school known to me, then established her in town, and was often absent from her company. I should have hired on a governess and kept her with me, providing her the familial love my father would have, if he had lived. The elopement would not have happened if I had done so, I am convinced."

The extent of his remorse was so painful, Elizabeth hardly knew what to say, and she could only gaze at him in distressed sympathy.

"I am sorry, Miss Bennet. The last thing I wished to do was upset you on a night which should be formed for your enjoyment. Why do we not go in? I believe the dance will be starting soon."

They did so, and took up their place in the set, dancing for some time in silence. Elizabeth determined she should allow Mr. Darcy to set the pace of conversation, for their most recent topic they could not speak of amongst the other dancers, and she would not have wished to make small pleasantries with a heart as heavy as his. He did eventually make some slight observation on the dance; she replied, and they were again silent.

Even though he was the quietest partner she had ever danced with, Elizabeth found she liked dancing with Mr. Darcy. He danced well, and was extremely attentive to her between the dances of the set; she would have derived a great deal of enjoyment from the set, if only she thought her partner could do the same.

During the second dance, Sir William Lucas appeared close to them, and on perceiving Mr. Darcy, he stopped, bowed, and complimented the gentleman on his dancing and his partner. His speech then flowed into a nearly blatant hint that he would enjoy seeing them dance together again, following the marriage of Elizabeth's sister and Mr. Bingley.

The two of them could scarcely have heard such comments without looking over at Mr. Bingley and Jane, who looked very well together, farther up the set, and when Sir William had left them, Mr. Darcy said: "I have been making a closer study of your sister since we spoke, and I believe I perceive more regard there than I had, originally."

"I am glad of it. Looking at them, I believe there is more regard on both sides," said Elizabeth. "Still, I wish Sir William had not spoken so."

"Do you believe the expectations he expressed are those of the neighbourhood?"

"Mr. Bingley *has* singled her out particularly, to allow her to lead the first set, instead of his sister, as the hostess."

"That, I am afraid, was intentional. Miss Bingley refused to continue with any duties as hostess, when we returned from Hatfield House. When they were in the gardens, she gave her brother leave to dance the first set with Miss Bennet, under the presumption that I would ask her for the set. It seems I managed to anger her twice over – first by seeking your company instead of hers, to go to the old palace, and then by asking you for the first set while we were there."

"If that is the case, I must feel badly for my own role in prompting you to go with me. I could have managed on my own," Elizabeth said. "Well, perhaps up until the horse."

He did not respond to her humour, however, and said: "Do not feel badly, Miss Bennet, for my choice was my own. I did not like to see you so neglected."

There was something about the way he spoke that caused Elizabeth's spirits to flutter, and she was glad the dance was drawing to an end, for she was beginning to fear she would not make it through the evening without her own heart's being affected, and by a man she could harbour no hopes towards.

The next two sets, as mortifying as they were, at least proved a suitable distraction, for Mr. Collins gave her all the shame and misery which a disagreeable partner for a couple of dances can give. Mr. Darcy had chosen the second set to do his duty by Miss Bingley, and whenever they passed each other in the dance, Elizabeth and her previous partner would exchange sympathetic glances.

The moment of her release from Mr. Collins was ecstasy, and she danced next with one of the officers, before being returned to Mr. Darcy for the supper set. She sensed a certain stirring amongst those near her as she took up her place, which must be caused by a lady dancing a second set with someone such as Mr. Darcy. Jane and Mr. Bingley danced this set together as well, and the couples had the advantage of going in to supper together. Before they went in, Mr. Bingley drew Elizabeth a little aside, and said:

"I wished to thank you for looking after Mr. Darcy tonight, Miss Elizabeth. This cannot be an easy event for him, but he did at least have his dances with you to anticipate."

"Of course, Mr. Bingley. I would wish to do whatever I might to make the event easier for him."

There could be no good in sitting near Mrs. Bennet, and Elizabeth was glad to see Mr. Bingley seat them on the opposite side of the room from her. They passed a pleasant supper, therefore, during which Elizabeth occasionally looked up at her mother, talking away in a most animated fashion, and both wondered and feared what Mrs. Bennet was saying. Her mother, in one of these times, looked most particularly and puzzledly at her, and Elizabeth could only presume the gentleman seated beside her to be the cause.

When supper was over, singing was talked of, and Elizabeth had the mortification of Mary's obliging the company, delighted by her opportunity to exhibit. It was no better or worse than Mary's usual performances, but with this audience, it was entirely painful to watch, and Elizabeth did so with impatience, until she felt Mr. Darcy rise beside her, and saw he was going up to turn the pages for Mary.

When she finished the song, Mary needed no more than the hint of a hope that she should favour them again before she made to begin another song. She could not do so, however, for Mr. Darcy stated that although she had played very well, Mr. Bingley wished for each lady to have one song each, so they would all have a chance to exhibit. He assisted Mary in rising from the bench, and escorted her back to her place at the table, seeming to murmur something to her which was intended for comfort and encouragement.

Mr. Darcy did not return to the table, however, and instead quitted the room entirely. Elizabeth wished to follow him, but could not do so immediately; she was required to wait until several other ladies had exhibited, and the room began to take on a certain restlessness which eventually resulted in some starting to make their way back to the ball-room. Mr. Darcy was not in that room, or the drawing-room, though, and Elizabeth, upon seeing this, suspected immediately where he was.

She went to the library, and found him there, weeping, a sight that caused her to cry as well. He looked up at her with a countenance indicating she was not unwelcome, and she made her way over to where he sat.

"I could not help but think of Georgiana," he said. "She loved nothing more than to play the pianoforte."

"Mr. Darcy, I fear you rescued my family from mortification at too high a cost to yourself."

"Turning the pages was perhaps a more painful reminder than I had expected, but it is entirely possible that simply watching other young ladies exhibit would have done the same. In another few years, it is what she should have done – made her entrance into society and showed the world how beautifully she plays. Instead, she will only ever have a limited audience, if she is recovered."

"*When* she is recovered, Mr. Darcy. You must not give up hope."

"You are right, Miss Bennet. Thank you for reminding me."

"I should go back," Elizabeth said. "It would not do for anyone to notice we have both disappeared. If I see Mr. Bingley, I will tell him you are feeling unwell."

"Thank you for that. I do not think myself able to return to company tonight."

The rest of the evening brought Elizabeth little amusement. She was teazed by Mr. Collins, who would not leave her side, and though he could not prevail with her to dance with him again, put it out of her power to dance with others. Elizabeth entreated him to stand up with somebody else, and offered to introduce him to any young lady in the room, but it was all in vain. He sought to remain by her side, and to recommend himself to her, and Elizabeth wished she had the prospect of Mr. Darcy's coming to her rescue, but knew she would not.

CHAPTER 6

A new scene opened at Longbourn, one most mortifying to Elizabeth. Mr. Collins asked Mrs. Bennet for a private audience with her second-eldest daughter, and although Mrs. Bennet might now have wished to steer him towards Mary, instead, knowing Elizabeth to have danced twice with a gentleman who had ten thousand a year at the Netherfield ball, it was too late for such things, and the audience was immediately granted.

Mrs. Bennet marshalled her other daughters upstairs, and Elizabeth was left to the addresses of her cousin. He stated first his reasons for marrying, of which it seemed the wishes of his patroness were of utmost importance, and love or even affection not at all a consideration. She interrupted him, she declined his proposal, and found her rejection either not understood, or not taken seriously. He continued to press his suit, and said, finally:

"I will remind you again that it is by no means certain that another offer of marriage may ever be made you, and if you think it shall come from Mr. Darcy, you are most incorrect on that point. Even if he was not promised to Anne de Bourgh, his family would never allow the match."

Elizabeth might have been struck by the intelligence that Mr. Darcy was promised to his cousin, if she did not, from Mr. Darcy's own statements, feel certain that if such an engagement did exist, it would not continue once Lady Catherine was made aware of Georgiana Darcy's elopement. She would mention none of what she knew regarding that matter by way of dissuading him, however, and said only:

"I have no expectations from that quarter, sir, but nor will I accept your own offer. I thank you again and again for the honour you have done me in your proposals, but to accept them is absolutely impossible. My feelings in every respect forbid it."

"You are uniformly charming!" cried he, with an air of awkward gallantry; "and I am persuaded that when sanctioned by the express authority of both your excellent parents, my proposals will not fail of being acceptable."

The application was made to her parents, and Elizabeth found herself summoned to the library to speak with them. With the greatest relief did she learn that neither of them intended to require her to marry her cousin, although she endured a lengthy chastisement from Mrs. Bennet, for not informing her mother sooner that Mr. Darcy was a suitor, so Mr. Collins could have had his affections encouraged towards Mary, instead of her.

"Mama, Mr. Darcy is not a suitor!" Elizabeth exclaimed, although she would never tell her mother the reasons for her certainty in this.

"Oh well then, Lizzy, if you wish to play coy with us for now, you do so, but surely you only refused such an offer because you anticipate a better one. You just continue to dance with Mr. Darcy whenever he asks you, and go on walking out with him and Jane and Bingley. You *will* promise to do this, at least, or I will require you to go back out there and accept Mr. Collins."

Elizabeth, in a tone of mortification, told her mother she would do as requested, because it was no more than she would have done, anyway. She took leave of her parents, hearing her mother crow about *ten thousand a year* as she closed the library door.

Overcome by agitation, Elizabeth determined she would go for a walk, and left the house as soon as she could don her spencer and bonnet. She set out at a strong pace, utterly preoccupied with all that had passed, and it was some time before she noticed Mr. Darcy riding toward her, and realised he must have waved to her already. In truth, her spirits were too disturbed presently to wish to speak with him, but she could see no way to avoid the encounter.

He rode up to her; they exchanged greetings; he dismounted and made to walk with her, stating he had been sent by Mr. Bingley to give his apologies for that gentleman's inability to call on them, for Bingley had been required to go into town on business.

"Are you well, Miss Elizabeth?" he asked, after they had walked on in silence for some time. "You seem rather distracted."

"My cousin, Mr. Collins, proposed to me this morning," she said. "It was not an event which could pass without causing some agitation of my spirits. Indeed, I should not have told you of it – I believe such matters are supposed to be left between the gentleman and the lady – but it presses so firmly upon my mind, I can hardly think of anything else."

He drew to a halt, but his horse snorted and danced, so that he was required to continue walking, and say, sharply: "When is the happy event to occur?"

She shook her head; he must have misunderstood her, for if she had accepted Mr. Collins, she would have had no qualms about sharing the news of the proposal.

"Never, given I made my refusal," she said. "I was feeling rather too agitated, after, so I decided to go for a walk, and here you find me."

"You refused him, then?" he asked. She nodded in response, and was startled to find him halt entirely, claiming a firmer grip on his horse's bridle with one hand, and taking up her hand with the other.

"In vain have I struggled. It will not do. My feelings will not be repressed. You must allow me to tell you how ardently I admire and love you."

Elizabeth's astonishment was beyond expression. She stared, coloured, doubted, and was silent. She had never allowed herself to imagine that in all the cast of emotions he had been feeling over the last few weeks, such affections would have had a chance to grow amongst them, and yet here he was, declaring they had. She had spent a good deal of time disallowing herself of falling in love with Mr. Darcy, and now that he had made his declaration, it took no time for her own emotions, her own admission of the truth, to come forward: she loved him, so very much that at first, all she could feel was a heady rush of heightened spirits.

"I had determined to remain silent on the matter, but I expect given your family's situation, there may be pressure on you to accept him, and I wish you to know that you do have another choice, although I will own it is not a very good one," he said. "Nothing would make me happier than if you would agree to marry me instead, but you know full well that at some point, my sister's marriage will undergo a scandalous annulment, and we will be ruined in the eyes of society. To ally yourself with me would be to agree to a degradation, one that would cast a long shadow over your own family, when the news is public.

"Indeed, now that I say it aloud, I realise how ridiculous it is. We spoke only yesterday of my having been a selfish man, and here I am, being so again. I must apologise for having put you in a situation where you must refuse two proposals of marriage in one day, and only hope we might be able to continue on as friends, at least until that event which must cause you to sever the acquaintance. You are the very last person to whom I would wish to give discomfort, when it is you who have given me such comfort over the past few weeks."

"Mr. Darcy, am I even to be allowed to speak before you would withdraw your proposal?"

At this, his countenance, with had been heavily marked with dejection, brightened slightly. "Do you mean there is even the slightest chance you would consider it?"

"I would consider it far more seriously than the one I received this morning, as I do very much return your affections," she said. "I will not deny that the scruples you have listed are substantial, but you were right to think of my family's situation. I hate to be so crass as to speak of your income, but ten thousand pounds a year would be far more than what would be necessary to ensure the security of all of us, upon my father's death."

"It would have to be, for our marriage would make it significantly more difficult – if not impossible – for your other sisters to make a successful match."

"That is where my greatest hesitance is," Elizabeth said. "If I had only myself to think about, I would have agreed immediately. But I would not lessen Jane's chances for all the world."

"On that subject, I may speak with hope. Charles went into town to ensure his finances were in order; he wished to be prepared when he spoke with your father, to ask for his consent. Now, there is the possibility that she will refuse him, but if she does wish to marry Charles, he has already stated firmly that he will maintain my acquaintance, once the news is public, so I do not think any further alliance between us would affect *his* actions."

"Then I shall think of her chances with hope, as well, for I do not at all believe he will be refused," she said. "I would wish for my father to know the whole of it, when you ask for his consent. I do not want to deceive him, although you must make him promise not to speak a word of it to my mother. I do not like to deceive her, either, but if she knows – even if she does attempt to keep the secret – it would not be long before she would let it slip, and the whole neighbourhood would know."

"Do you mean, then, that I *may* ask for your father's consent?"

Elizabeth realised that, without him ever formally asking if she would marry him, and her formally accepting, she had just agreed to marry Mr. Darcy, so long as her father consented. The very thing she had thought an impossibility and yet had, deep in her soul, wanted for some time was now likely to happen.

"Yes, Mr. Darcy, you may, and I hope very much that he grants it."

"Shall I do so now?"

"In a little while," she said. "For now, let us walk on. I wish to enjoy this moment, for I must tell you I had found myself falling in love with you, without any hope of that love being returned, given all else that was on your mind."

"I had not expected to fall in love, certainly, and I was not inclined towards it. I admired you from the beginning of our acquaintance, and perhaps that was why I felt compelled to tell you of such a private matter after so little time in your company. I believe it was that admiration, and your kindness regarding my situation, which united to form affections that could not be suppressed."

"I am glad they could not, for otherwise I would have found myself in the circumstance of being in love with you, while needing to carry on as your friend, and that would have been most painful to me."

"The same would have pained me, I assure you."

They walked on, Elizabeth in silent enjoyment of her betrothal; she could not be too outwardly happy, not when there was so much he still suffered under. It was after they turned back to Longbourn that Mr. Darcy recalled the miniature he carried in his pocket, and he gave it over to her for inspection. The man painted there was young, with every appearance of amiability, and if Elizabeth had not known of all the injury he had caused the Darcys, she might have been inclined to think favourably of him.

"So this is Mr. Wickham," she said.

"Yes, if you do ever see him, however, I beg you will take no action of your own. Send word to me of where you sighted him, but no more."

"But that may allow him to make his escape," she said, fully intending to follow him, if ever she did sight this Mr. Wickham.

He grasped at her hand again, taking it up and clutching it very tight. "You must not, Elizabeth. I could not bear to see any harm come to you. I do not believe him a dangerous man, generally, but the prospect of the end of his scheme may change that. Please promise you will not make any attempt to pursue him. He has already taken so much from me."

"I shall, but only if you will also promise to take care when you do so yourself."

"I will give you that promise willingly."

"Very well, then I give you my own promise," she said, slipping the miniature back into his hand, and then, noting their proximity to Longbourn, saying, "When we go inside, I shall say I met you in the lane, and there was a book you wished to borrow from my father's library – he will likely be there. If my mother knows a private audience to have been granted, and consent not given, she will not rest until she knows the reason why."

"I assume you abhor this deception as much as I do, Miss Bennet, and it increases my gratefulness that you are willing to participate in it."

Mr. Bennet was indeed hiding in his library – thankfully alone, for Elizabeth had remembered too late the possibility that Mr. Collins might have gone there to further plead his case. Her cousin was in the parlour with the others, however; Elizabeth noticed Charlotte Lucas had come to call, but was so distracted she could hardly even be pleased by this. She closed the library door behind Mr. Darcy and leaned against the wall outside, overwhelmed that it had come to happen so quickly that so much of her future life awaited the conversation within.

It was not a short conversation. It could not have been hoped to be, with so much of a history to be related. When finally Mr. Darcy returned to the hallway, it was with a grim face, but a book in his hand, which at least assured Elizabeth of her father's secrecy in the matter.

"He has neither given nor denied his consent," Mr. Darcy said. "He wished to have more time to think on the matter. For now, he wants to speak to you. I shall join the rest of your family in the parlour."

Her father was walking about the room, looking grave and anxious. "Lizzy, you need not accept another man's proposal simply to spare yourself from marrying Mr. Collins. In truth, after all he has related to me, I can hardly sort out which would be the better offer, were you to act without any consideration of affections."

"But I am acting with every consideration of affections, papa."

"We all know him to be a proud, unpleasant sort of man, but you have seemed to tolerate his company more than anyone else," Mr. Bennet said. "I hardly thought this went so far as to your really liking him, however."

"I do, I do like him," she replied; "I love him. Our neighbourhood has judged him cruelly for his behaviour during the most difficult of times. If more people knew what he really is, I know I would not be alone in esteeming him."

"It seems your mother was right after all, although she may not ever learn of it. She thought the two of you had affections for each other, and this was your reason for declining Mr. Collins," he said. "May I presume he has told you of the matter involving his sister?"

"He has, papa. I have known of it since early in our acquaintance."

He shook his head. "I had thought you more recently informed, and was going to advise you to think better of this, but now I must assume you have had ample time to think on it."

"I have, papa. I understand fully the benefits and disadvantages of marrying him."

"I would call it more than a disadvantage, Lizzy," he said. "While I appreciate that he did the honourable thing in telling me of it – otherwise I could hardly have avoided giving my consent – it is a matter that requires some deliberation. Once your mother and I gave up hope of having a son, we knew that either all of you must marry, or one of you must marry exceedingly well. Mr. Darcy has presented me with the latter option in as complete a manner as possible; he promises pin money and a home for your mother and any of your sisters that remain unmarried. All of this, he entirely volunteered to write into the marriage contract.

"But the scandal with his sister will effectively end the chances of any of your sisters who have not married, when it breaks. Perhaps Mr. Bingley will have offered for Jane by that time, but I see little hope for the rest of them, although I cannot say that I had much hope for them before, as silly as they are. So you see, Lizzy, I am faced with a choice I should never have thought possible, that of securing the future of all of my daughters, but at the expense of their standing in society. You seem certain of your own happiness, but should you be allowed an unequal share of the happiness in marriage, while the rest must merely hope for security? They will say you are my favourite, and they will be right, and they will never forgive me of it."

"I did not make any claim to happiness, papa," Elizabeth said. "I esteem and love Mr. Darcy, but the event with his sister has necessarily damaged his hopes of happiness, and I expect shall do the same for his wife. Miss Darcy's recovery, I hope, will be cause for restoration of some happiness, but our prospects for such would not be the same as if the elopement had never occurred."

"And this is what you wish to marry into?"

"Yes, papa. It is because I love him that I wish to help him through his difficulties."

This seemed to wound her father, but on reflection, she realised that of course it should. His marriage to her mother must have begun on its best footing, its days of happy trips to Bath, and only grown worse from there.

"Thank you for your candour, Lizzy. I do wish to think on the matter, and it may take me some time to come to my decision. I trust I do not need to worry about a *third* gentleman coming to offer for your hand before I do so?"

"Of course not, papa."

She slipped out quietly, determined not to cry, and made her way to the parlour. There, she was at least a little relieved to see neither Mr. Darcy nor Charlotte had taken their leave, for in addition to their both being dear to her – although one was much dearer than the other – they also increased the number of the party, lessening any awkwardness of Elizabeth's being in the same room with Mr. Collins. Charlotte, who must have had the intelligence of Elizabeth's refusal from someone in the family, was even so kind as to draw his attention in conversation. As for the object of most of Elizabeth's thoughts, however, he took his leave not long after her return. She managed only one painful glance up at him, as she curtsied good-bye, hoping he understood she was afraid she would burst into tears if she looked at him any longer.

CHAPTER 7

Mr. Bennet did not make his decision quickly, and the situation sat heavily on Elizabeth's heart. She was distracted from her worry only when a letter came from Netherfield, causing Jane a great degree of distress. It was from Caroline Bingley, and contained the news that she and the Hursts had left Netherfield by this time, to join her brother in town, and Caroline did not think they had any intention of returning.

This news surprised Elizabeth far more than it had her sister, for it seemed to be in direct opposition to what Mr. Darcy had told her, and she could only attribute it to Miss Bingley's hoping her brother would not marry Jane.

Jane read a few of the passages to her, and concluded, "It is evident by this, that he comes back no more this winter."

"It is only evident that Miss Bingley does not mean he *should*."

"Why will you think so? It must be his own doing – he is his own master."

"Mr. Darcy and I spoke of his going to town only yesterday. He indicated the stay would be of short duration. You can hardly think Mr. Bingley would abandon his house with a guest still there."

"Perhaps Mr. Darcy will follow them later."

"I do not think it likely; he has said nothing that indicates it." Elizabeth regretted that she could not share the two critical things tying Mr. Darcy to Hertfordshire for the foreseeable future, although the secret that most burned inside her was the intelligence of why Mr. Bingley had gone to town. She could only hope Mr. Bingley would make his return quickly, to ease Jane's doubts.

"Lizzy, I hope you do not mind my saying – you seem to be on very intimate terms with Mr. Darcy, perhaps more intimate, even, than Mr. Bingley and I are with each other. I believe my mother has entirely turned her thoughts from Mr. Collins to Mr. Darcy, now."

Elizabeth could not help a wry smile, at the thought of her mother's taking up her cause to marry Mr. Darcy. This did not last long, however: any interference from Mrs. Bennet at this time would only make matters worse.

"I do like Mr. Darcy very much, Jane. I am glad at least I can say that to *you* without your calling him proud, or disagreeable."

"Of course not, Lizzy. He is reserved, of course, but I do not think Mr. Bingley would be such particular friends with him, without seeing a good degree of merit."

"Nor should you think Mr. Bingley would abandon his particular friend here in Hertfordshire."

Elizabeth was very glad to see Mr. Darcy call upon them soon after this conversation; although their secret situation still pained her, she was a better master of her emotions now, and even if she was not, she would never deny Jane the knowledge that he still remained in residence at Netherfield.

She raised the topic immediately, and was most relieved to hear Mr. Darcy refute Miss Bingley's letter. Jane, who had been wan and listless since receiving the letter, grew hopeful again. Mr. Darcy was clear in saying that Miss Bingley and the Hursts had grown desirous of town entertainments, and while they stayed at Mr. Hurst's house, Mr. Bingley was making use of Mr. Darcy's own house there, and was expected to return in a few days, at most.

"He has promised me good shooting here, and as I am usually the one to indulge him in that at Pemberley, he had better make good on his promise," Mr. Darcy said.

"When you have killed all of Mr. Bingley's birds," said Mrs. Bennet, "I beg you will come here, and shoot as many as you please, on Mr. Bennet's manor. I am sure he will be vastly happy to oblige you, and will save all the best of the covies for you."

The relation of some manner of plans upon Mr. Bingley's return brought about a visible revival of Jane's spirits, for which Elizabeth looked gratefully at Mr. Darcy, with a hint of embarrassment over her mother's comment.

They passed some time together, during which Mr. Darcy made every effort to be agreeable to Mrs. Bennet, Jane, and Mary – the others of the household having gone out, excepting Mr. Bennet, who remained in his library. Elizabeth was glad of Mr. Darcy's endeavours, although she suspected it weighed heavily on him to make such pleasantries, and this brought about the fear of what should happen to him if Mr. Bennet refused his consent. To have his hopes raised and then dashed could only further wound a man who already had so much to pain him.

Elizabeth became aware then of her mother's winking at Jane and Mary, which prompted Mary to say: "Mama, if you have something in your eye, you had best get it out at a looking-glass."

"Yes – yes child, you are absolutely right. I have a most bothersome thing in my eye, and I cannot tell what it is. I shall go up to my dressing-room – will you assist me, my love?"

Thus entreated, Mary followed her mother from the room. In a few minutes, Mrs. Bennet half opened the door and called out, "Jane, my dear, I shall require your assistance as well."

If her mother had not affected the very thing she wished for most, Elizabeth would have been mortified, but instead, she smiled gently at the man who might be her husband someday, and said, "My mother has seized upon you as an alternative to Mr. Collins, although I assure you I have done nothing to encourage her. I believe you are expected to be proposing to me."

"Am I? Then I shall have to make my exit fairly quickly, and you will have to say I grew uncomfortable at our not having a chaperone. It would never do for your father to think we are taking liberties."

"True, although I am very glad of a little time in private to speak of our matter," she said. "First, though, I must thank you for your reassurances to Jane. She had been quite disheartened by Miss Bingley's letter, and truly concerned he would not return. I told her as much as I dared, but it was not enough to soothe her worries."

"Was her manner today all due to worry over Bingley's not returning?"

Elizabeth confirmed that it was.

"Then I am sorry for her suffering, but it is more evidence to me of the strength of her attachment. You may be assured, Miss Elizabeth, that if Caroline Bingley seeks to manipulate him in to staying in town, I shall go there and convince him otherwise. He is staying at my house; it will be nothing but Miss Bennet when we break our fast; Miss Bennet over dinner; Miss Bennet over port. With such reminders, I have no doubt he shall be returned to thinking for himself, and to his intentions."

"I am so grateful to you, Mr. Darcy; now you have reassured me, as well."

"If only I could reassure you so easily on our own matter."

"No, there I do not believe reassurance will be so easily come by," she said. "I cannot help but fear what will happen if my father refuses his consent."

He rose, and came to sit beside her, taking up her hand and clasping it tightly.

"If he does refuse his consent, I wish you to know that I would wait for you. I will not ever countenance an elopement, but if you are of age and still wish it, I would gladly marry you. Even if it is later in your life, when your situation changes – if you find you must marry for security, one letter to me would be all that is necessary. My affections and wishes will not change."

Elizabeth was overwhelmed with emotion at what he said, and could not speak for some time. When she finally thought on it, however, she realised the practical aspects which must require her to make him amend his promise.

"It cannot be too much later in my life, I suspect. You own an estate, and it must have an heir. I would not expect you to wait indefinitely," she said, but then, seeing how his countenance had fallen: "Nor do I think I would require so much time to make my decision, after I come of age. Circumstances may change, of course – by then I pray your sister will be returned, so I speak more of my own family – but I see little that would sway my heart. I love you; I shall always love you, and given the time until my majority to contemplate these feelings, I am sure they will only be stronger."

She was surprised, following this declaration, to see him take out his purse, remove what could not be less than twenty guineas, and press the coins into her hand, saying: "If we are parted by distance when you reach your majority, write to me, and I will come to you, wherever you are. If there is any difficulty in that, here is for your travel to come to me. I would never wish money to be an obstacle for you, if you do choose to marry me."

"Mr. Darcy, I cannot take such a sum from you – "

"If you are thinking it creates an obligation, please do not. If your choice is not to marry me, I would ask only that you purchase something fine for yourself, in remembrance of him who loves you now, and will still love you then."

The expression in his eyes was so loving, and so mournful, that Elizabeth found herself weeping as she looked at him. He had drawn even closer to her during his speech, and in the impulse of her emotions, Elizabeth brought her lips close enough to his that he could not mistake her wish, and closed what remained of the distance between them to kiss her. It began with the hesitance of her inexperience, but blossomed rapidly and wonderfully into a very ardent kiss. Elizabeth sought to impress every moment of it upon her mind, so that in the future, in those dreary days, if her father should decline the match, she would always have this memory of how very passionate Mr. Darcy's love for her was.

"I am sorry; I let my emotions get the better of me," he said, after finally drawing back from her.

"Then if we are so fortunate as to marry soon, I would rather you let them get the better of you as frequently as possible."

"Let us part with that hope, but for now I think I must go, before someone in your family walks in on some circumstance likely to damage my suit with your father."

"Yes, of course." Elizabeth stood, and with nothing more than a brief touch of his hand to her cheek to comfort her, he left the house.

Mrs. Bennet returned downstairs with her other daughters, and learned to her disappointment that nothing of note had occurred between her daughter and Mr. Darcy, in the time they had been left alone. Elizabeth was glad of the distraction when Charlotte Lucas came to call and desired a tête-à-tête with her, but learned Charlotte's intelligence was something beyond a distraction, for it was that she was engaged to Mr. Collins. Elizabeth, wholly shocked, exclaimed the impossibility of it; she could not believe he had transferred his affections so easily.

Charlotte described her impending nuptials as a practical matter, one borne out of necessity, rather than love, and Elizabeth could not help but feel her friend was disgracing herself. Such thoughts, however, must be followed with the notion that Elizabeth would readily disgrace herself – although in a far different way – if the match she desired was allowed. She and Charlotte had both chosen marriages in which they would struggle to be tolerably happy, although Elizabeth still had the distress of not knowing whether she would even be allowed her marriage.

The Lucases, when they called later, could do little to alleviate the situation. The news was shared, and received as the greatest misfortune by Mrs. Bennet, who had given Mr. Darcy every opportunity to propose, and yet he had not. Therefore, she could only conclude her second-eldest had ruined not one, but two opportunities for matrimony. Mr. Bennet, upon hearing the news, appeared only thoughtful, and Elizabeth wondered if this would push him in his decision. She could only hope it would not result in her heartbreak, and Mr. Darcy's.

CHAPTER 8

Elizabeth was punished by her mother for some time, but then came the sight of Mr. Bingley, approaching the house on horseback. He arrived alone, and with only Elizabeth certain of his intent.

Mr. Bingley walked into the drawing-room in a more purposeful manner than they had ever seen from him, and requested a private audience with Miss Bennet. Elizabeth's heart fluttered a little, on behalf of her sister, to have been so concerned over his absence, and now to have this, a request almost certain to end in her engagement. Elizabeth envied Jane a little, to have such a straightforward courtship, and to be asked for her hand in marriage by a man Mr. Bennet could have absolutely no objections to. Jane was too good, however, for any true jealousy to be directed towards her, and Elizabeth quitted the drawing-room truly happy for her sister.

The private audience had the outcome desired by all in the house. Mr. Bingley was sent to Mr. Bennet to ask for his consent, and consent was given. Mrs. Bennet's ecstasies over all of this were tremendous, and she invited Mr. Bingley to stay to dinner, an invitation initially declined because he could not very well leave his friend alone to dine at his own house. Mrs. Bennet was thus required to amend the invitation to include Mr. Darcy, and Mr. Bingley to return home in order to give it.

Mr. Bingley's departure provided Elizabeth with a chance to speak with Jane privately, and she found Jane composed of a happiness marked more by giddiness of manner than she had ever known from her elder sister, for both herself and the security she had settled upon her family. Elizabeth heard the latter with a pang of fear, that this security provided by Mr. Bingley would make that which Mr. Darcy could provide far less necessary, but then required herself to focus on Jane, and the happiness for her sister she did truly feel.

"I am certainly the most fortunate creature that ever existed!" cried Jane. "Oh! Lizzy, why am I thus singled from my family, and blessed above them all! If I could but see *you* as happy!"

"Oh, dearest Jane, I never could be so happy as you. 'Till I have your disposition, your goodness, I never can have your happiness. But I hope that I may, in time, have my own sort of happiness."

"Lizzy, is it possible that happiness will be with Mr. Darcy? I promise I will not pry, but you had the strangest look upon your face, when Mr. Bingley mentioned him this morning, and you have seemed so very out of sorts, lately. Did you hope, as my mother did, that he would propose when she left you alone?"

"Oh, Jane, I can hardly tell you of what I hope for," Elizabeth said, and then, despite her every intention of leaving this day as Jane's alone, she found herself breaking down and sharing much of what troubled her. She did not impart the exact details of the scandal that should eventually cloud Mr. Darcy's name, but did think it best that Jane have some awareness of the alliance her betrothed intended to keep.

Jane, however, revealed she already knew of the matter; Mr. Bingley had informed her of it, having gained permission to do so from Mr. Darcy, and after she had revealed this, Jane declared firmly her intention of standing by him as her betrothed would do. She then focused on the matter closer to her heart, that of the suffering her poor sister must have undergone, in finding herself in love with and proposed to by a man in his situation, with the consent of their father still undecided.

Elizabeth allowed herself to be comforted by Jane's concern for only a little while, and then required both herself and her sister to focus on the happier event of the day, which Jane was only partly convinced to do. Dinner, very much celebratory in its nature, helped to serve as a reminder for the both of them, and the most notable thing of it occurred after the ladies had gone to the drawing-room, when the gentlemen were perceived to be lingering over their port for an exceedingly long time.

Elizabeth wondered at the nature of what was being discussed in that room, and an anxious look at Jane showed her sister marked with the same curiosity. She had her answer when the gentlemen finally came into the drawing-room, her father looking visibly perturbed, but Mr. Darcy perhaps happier than she had ever known him to be. He made the slightest little nod of his head *yes*, and Elizabeth felt her heart lift in tremendous relief.

What manner of discussion had passed between the gentlemen she could not yet know, but she felt certain that Mr. Bingley must have had some role in bringing her father around. This was confirmed to her late in the next morning, when Mr. Bennet summoned Elizabeth and Jane to a conference in his library, and said:

"Lizzy, after a good deal of convincing on the part of Mr. Bingley – who turns out to be more stubborn by half than I had thought, so you had best be aware of that, Jane – I have agreed to give my consent to your marriage, but only on one condition. I must hear from Jane that she is comfortable with the alliance she would find herself in."

"I am, papa," said Jane, without any hesitation at all.

"Very well. I requested we wait a few days, so Lizzy's betrothal does not overshadow your own. Then Mr. Darcy will call and request a private audience with you, Lizzy, and you had best keep it short."

Nothing occurred to prevent Mr. Darcy's making his call and requesting the private audience, a request that occurred to the complete and utter delight of Mrs. Bennet. When the others had left them, he took up Elizabeth's hands and said, "My God, these last few days have been unbearable."

"Yes. I am only glad they are over now, and we may be married soon."

"I am glad you say *soon*. I had wondered whether you would be willing to be married quietly, by common licence, in town."

Elizabeth had no desire for a large wedding, nor to wait; she wished only to begin in her role as his wife as soon as she could, to better support him in all he had to bear, and she told him this. They agreed that a town marriage was the best choice, and that if done quietly, it could be done before her elder sister's wedding, without overshadowing that event.

Following this, Elizabeth had only one topic upon which to satisfy her curiosity. She asked him what had transpired in the dining-room after the ladies took their leave, and what made her father say Mr. Bingley was so stubborn.

"Charles surprised even me in his stubbornness," Mr. Darcy said. "I hope you will consider him as much a friend as I do, for he forced your father's hand in as complete a manner as possible. He indicated his family should always be connected to mine, whether by friendship or by marriage, regardless of what your father did, and then outright refused to support the rest of you upon your father's death, unless the burden was shared with me. I intend his share of it to be very small, though, for I will forever be in his debt, and at least in that way I may repay him."

"Oh, I adore him for it!" cried Elizabeth, affectionately. "I shall be so happy to call him my brother."

"I shall as well. I had never thought the two of us might be linked by familial bonds, and I am very glad to be connecting myself in such a way to my two dearest friends."

CHAPTER 9

*Much to Mrs. Bennet's chagrin, the marriage by which her daughter became Mrs.
Darcy was effected in as restrained a manner as the principal parties had desired.
Elizabeth's wedding took place quietly in town, shocking those in the ton, including Mr.
Darcy's aunt, Lady Catherine de Bourgh, who descended on her nephew in a furious
manner, upon seeing the announcement in the papers.*

*Lady Catherine, without even learning of the elopement of Georgiana Darcy, had
cut her ties with her nephew, a breach Elizabeth did not encourage her husband to heal,
presuming they would only be cut again, when the scandal broke. Elizabeth's other new
relations, the Fitzwilliams, were far more welcoming. Whether they truly liked her, or
simply thought Darcy had done well to make some manner of respectable alliance while
he was able to do so, could not entirely be told, but Elizabeth liked them nonetheless.*

*In the very beginning of their marriage, Darcy had clearly endeavoured to make
Elizabeth happy, setting aside his situation and giving her what could be given of her
due as a new bride. But then came the time when he asked her to come into his study,
and told her that he and their Fitzwilliam relations, the Earl of Brandon, Lord
Fitzwilliam, and Colonel Fitzwilliam, were giving serious consideration to going forward
with the annulment, even though Georgiana Darcy had yet to be located. This, Darcy
explained, might be the best course of action to force Mr. Wickham from wherever he
had been hiding.*

"If we are able to push the annulment through, he would no longer have
any rights as a husband. Her being missing would become public. This
would, of course, come at the expense of our standing in society, but
Georgiana would then be a captive held against her will, rather than a wife,"
he said, and then frowned. "I am sorry, Elizabeth, I never meant to indicate
that to be *any* wife was to be – "

"You need not explain yourself. If anything, this is a reminder of my
own good fortune, to have married a man I love, who shall always treat me
with respect and kindness."

264

"I am glad you say that, my love, but if we do go forward with the annulment, I hardly think you can call it good fortune. I think we shall wait until after Charles and Jane are married, but would you mind if we moved forward following that event?"

Elizabeth rose from her seat and kissed him, then said, "Move forward with it whenever you choose. You know I will always support you."

The annulment was required to be pursued in Georgiana Darcy's home diocese, and so they travelled north, to Pemberley. As the proceedings began, Elizabeth grew acquainted with the estate of which she was now mistress. Any intimidation she might have felt, on beginning such a role, was tempered by the quiet life Darcy warned her they would lead soon enough, ostracised by much of their neighbourhood, and even more by his acquaintances in town.

She managed well enough the house's Christmas dinner, but her mind was always on how her husband was bearing up under the annulment. She was utterly unprepared, however, for the letter that felled him.

Few of Pemberley's staff had been informed of the true nature of Georgiana's absence, but the housekeeper, Mrs. Reynolds, was one of them, and she informed Elizabeth that there had been another letter, forwarded express from town, from *that man*. At Netherfield, Darcy had retired to the library, but here, Elizabeth knew his study was his refuge, and he was there, clutching the letter in his fist and sobbing wretchedly.

She pulled him into an embrace that lasted for a very long time, during which she could only murmur words of comfort and wonder what it was that had put him in such a state. When he finally recovered enough to speak coherently to her, he said, "Wickham writes that the annulment cannot take place, because she is dead. She took fever a fortnight ago, and died. She has been buried, but he has enclosed a lock of her hair, to be made into mourning jewellery."

Elizabeth's shock upon hearing this was so great, she knew not what to say, and merely held him closer.

"She must have died in the most miserable situation, to have only that man to nurse her, if she received any nursing at all from him," he said. "I fear he might have left her alone to die."

"Please do not think that, my love. He must have some manner of humanity in him."

"I hope he does, but even so, it must have been horrible for her, to face her end without those who love her."

"We cannot be sure it was her end," she said. "Is this the only way he might escape the annulment going through?"

"It is, but I hardly know how her death benefits him. If she is dead, the marriage cannot be annulled, but nor can she receive her dowry."

"Could he not make the case that he would have the legal right to it, having been her husband for the period of time in which she was alive?"

"He might, but he must know we would tie the case up with so many attorneys that he would die himself – even if of old age – before he would ever see the money."

"Still, I cannot help but think that this is some other scheme of his, one we cannot yet understand," Elizabeth said. "I beg you will not give up hope, only on the word of a dishonourable man, and instead believe he must lie for some purpose. Your sister is young and healthy – I find it difficult to fathom that she should succumb to fever and yet he should be spared."

"What you say is what I think in moments of hope," he said. "But I hardly know whether to hope, or to resign myself to the possibility that he tells the truth, in the fear that eventually my hope will only bring me greater pain. The hair is undoubtedly hers, and if it was not taken from her when she was unable to object, I abhor the thought of how it might have been gotten."

"You must not give up hope," said Elizabeth, in her most convincing tone. "All you have as evidence of her death is the word of a deceiver, and a lock of hair, which may just as easily be taken from a woman who is living, rather than dead. And you must continue with the annulment – perhaps it shall be more difficult, now, but you must push through, for I believe this is what Wickham wishes to do his utmost to discourage you from."

CHAPTER 10

The large complexity now challenging the annulment required town lawyers, and so Elizabeth and her husband made their return to London. It was well into the season, and if she did not have more significant matters on her mind, Elizabeth might have worried more over how she was received by some of Darcy's acquaintances, which was quite coldly.

As word of the annulment's having been sought began to drift south, however, Elizabeth came to see a transition in the way she was seen; she began to receive more looks of sympathy, although the invitations coming to their house still dwindled. No longer was Mrs. Darcy seen to be a reaching woman who had married above her station; she was an object of pity, who had married into a scandalous family.

The dwindling of their social engagements affected Darcy far more than it did her. Although he was not fond of most society, to him, this represented the fall of his family, and when combined with what seemed the increasingly strong possibility that Georgiana was indeed dead, it made him seem to float about the house in an intense state of sadness. There had been no more word from Mr. Wickham, who seemed to consider the matter complete, and with some reluctance, Elizabeth began to wonder when she should suggest the lock of Georgiana's hair be made into jewellery, and they begin to mourn her formally.

It would still be some time, though, before Darcy was ready for it. As the months turned to spring, he again sought their invitation to Netherfield, from which they travelled out together in his phaeton, canvassing the countryside in the hope of glimpsing Wickham. This, too, was unsuccessful, and when Jane and Charles indicated they meant to go to Scarborough for the summer – although the Bingleys would leave the house open for their particular use if they desired it – the Darcys thought it too much of an imposition, and returned to town.

Once there, they found that knowledge of the annulment had become widespread, and although the knocker was on the door, there were few outside of the Fitzwilliams and the Gardiners who called on them. One of these was the Dowager Viscountess Tonbridge, who kept quite liberal company, and had no qualms about retaining their acquaintance.

She called now, and Elizabeth, who had not expected anyone, was required to hastily put away the shirt she had been making for her husband, and take up some finer work. She made the usual pleasantries to Lady Tonbridge while Mr. Miller sought Darcy in his study, and when he had arrived to sit with them, Lady Tonbridge asked: "Are either of you familiar with the Earl of Anglesey?"

They replied that they were not.

"He is an old friend of my family, and is returned to town. I know we have hardly spoken of your private matter, for I do not like to pry, but I wonder if you might like me to introduce you to him. He is active in politics, and might know of a way to help the case along."

"If you think he would be willing to take on the acquaintance, we would be grateful for his assistance," said Darcy, in a tone indicating he did not think it likely an earl would be willing to take on their acquaintance.

"I cannot promise he would acknowledge you publicly," Lady Tonbridge said. "You would not be the first connection he meets with behind closed doors, however. These political men often operate in such a way."

"I would be thankful to you, if he is willing to meet privately with us and aid us in the matter," said Darcy. "I thank you for your consideration, and your discretion."

"Well, now, it has been a long time since anyone called me discreet!" said Lady Tonbridge, chuckling. She returned to her usual good-natured manner, and more frivolous topics of conversation, and was taking her leave when Mr. Miller came in, holding a letter and saying it must be given to Mr. Darcy immediately.

In the resulting confusion, it was Elizabeth who was left to see Lady Tonbridge out, and although the lady's curiosity as to the nature of the letter was clearly evident, she merely made a polite good-bye. Elizabeth's curiosity was even more intense, although she assumed the letter must have had something to do with Georgiana. She returned to the drawing-room, and the sight there could only affect her heart in the most severe way: Darcy was once again weeping, and clutching a letter.

When he spoke, however, she learned they were tears of joy: "It is from her! She lives!"

"Oh, thank God!" she exclaimed, and sat beside him to give him an embrace. "There is still hope, then, that we may recover her."

"No, we *will* recover her. She wrote this herself, without authorisation from Wickham. I have no idea what she must have gone through to get it into the post, but she did. He seeks to take her to Jamaica, and a disruption in their routine must give us an opportunity to find her."

He handed over the letter, so Elizabeth could see it in all of its strangeness, written in pale indigo ink, and the tiniest scrawl. She wondered what Georgiana could have used, to write such a letter, and in what desperate circumstances she must have done so. When Elizabeth had finished the letter, she became aware that Darcy was now reawakened to purpose, and he seemed to have immediately gained strength from it.

Mr. Miller was informed of the contents of the letter, and instructed to send messengers for Lord Brandon, Lord Fitzwilliam, and Colonel Fitzwilliam, to come to Curzon Street immediately. Mr. Mason, meanwhile, was to be sent down to the docklands to inquire about passage to Jamaica. "Anything that leaves within a few days. Comfort is second to speed in this matter," Darcy said.

"Darcy, you cannot seriously be planning to leave for Jamaica in a few days," Elizabeth said.

"Of course I am. If they are not found before Wickham is able to get them on a ship, I will intercept them in Jamaica instead. You see the date on the letter. We have lost a few days – they may already have taken passage."

"But do you not feel all of this is terribly odd? She is said to be dead, there is no word for many months, and now he seeks to leave the country with her?"

"He seeks to smuggle her out – perhaps he thinks it will be more difficult to gain the annulment with her out of the country. But that is where he has erred. This letter is proof she lives. We may proceed now, on this evidence, and then it will only be a matter of finding her, and bringing her home."

"Then send hired men immediately, and let them conduct the search there," she said. "Until you are certain they *have* gone to Jamaica, you should not be flying off there yourself. My uncle Gardiner has contacts in shipping; let him help us first determine what ship they took."

"I will not send only hired men when I may recover her myself."

"Darcy, please, you promised me you would take care, when pursuing Mr. Wickham. If you do find evidence she has been taken from the country, we may both go, together," said Elizabeth. "But your sister was manipulated into the elopement by him, and we cannot be sure that he is not doing so again."

"To what purpose could he be *manipulating* her now?" he asked, harshly.

"I do not know! But something does not sit right with me about all of this. I am only asking that you do not act hastily."

"I will act as I must, to recover my sister. You have never met her, and clearly cannot be brought to care for her as I do, but still, I find it tremendously selfish that you should wish me to stay here with you."

"Is that what you think this is?" she exclaimed. "Do you truly think so low of me that you believe I act in self-interest here? Do you think if I had been acting in self-interest, that I would have married you in the first place? I did so because I loved _you_. I wanted to help _you_."

Elizabeth was too upset to remain in the room, and she fled just before the Fitzwilliams were announced. She went up to her bedchamber: the mistress's bedchamber, not the master's, where she had invariably slept since being wed. She would need to grow used to sleeping alone, now, she thought, and began to contemplate her options, if Darcy held to this stubborn course and went to Jamaica. She had one last point upon which she might negotiate – she was with child, and had been planning to tell him of this, when the time was right. In his present state of mind, however, she feared he would only accuse her of stooping to art in order to get him to stay, and he would not be entirely wrong, although she thought the purpose honourable.

Perhaps she could join Jane and Charles in Scarborough; the comfort of her sister's presence might help soothe her heartache. The thought of heartache, the thought that she might have made a terrible mistake in marrying Mr. Darcy, brought her rapidly to weeping, and by way of distraction, she began to pack her trunk. She was thus when there came a knock at the door. She knew it would be her husband, and she told him to come in, wondering if she had the strength for another row with him.

"Elizabeth, I am so very sorry," he said. "After all you have sacrificed, after all you have done to comfort me, at the first test I doubted you. I have only to say in my defence that I was too impassioned by the letter to think clearly."

"You cannot know how badly it hurt, to think that was your opinion of me."

"I know that it hurt you badly enough to cause me to lose your love – unless that had happened earlier, and I have been so foolish as not to notice it."

"You have not lost my love; it would not have hurt me so badly if I did not love you."

"Oh, thank God," he said, kneeling beside her on the floor, and embracing her tightly. "When you said you married me because you _loved_ me, it was as though I had been stabbed in the chest, to hear you speak of it in the past tense."

Elizabeth allowed herself a little comfort, but knew she still had the task ahead of convincing him to remain in England.

"Elizabeth, why are you packing your trunk?" Darcy asked.

"I intend to meet the Bingleys in Scarborough, if you insist on going to Jamaica. I do not wish to remain here alone."

"I am not going to Jamaica, at least not straightaway," he said. "My uncle and cousins urged a more cautious approach as well, but I must admit

I might not have listened to them, were it not for you."

Elizabeth felt the deepest relief his statement brought, and asked, "How are you to conduct the search? Shall we call on my uncle?"

"Edward is to go to Liverpool, and Andrew to Bristol, to see if they might have taken passage from those ports. I will handle the inquiries in London, and Lord Brandon is going to go north, and deliver the letter to our bishop himself; God-willing, his influence will see the annulment completed quickly. And yes, I would very much like to call on your uncle."

"Then of course we shall," she said, and then added, hesitantly, "There is one other thing I wish to tell you, before we go. It hardly seems the right time, but I am not sure when there will be a better. I believe I am with child."

He stared at her incredulously, then kissed her fervently. "Oh Elizabeth, my dearest, loveliest Elizabeth. You would have had every right to wish to keep me here for your own purposes. I know, of course I know, that you did not, and this only serves to provide me with further confirmation."

"Are you pleased? I know it only adds more complexity to our lives, at a complex time."

"Of course I am pleased! It does add complexity, but it is a most welcome addition. If we are fortunate, by the time our child is born, we shall be able to introduce the baby to his or her aunt."

"Yes, I pray we shall, my love."

CHAPTER 11

Elizabeth did not see much more of her husband than she would have if he had made the journey to Jamaica. He was gone from the house for most of the day, down at the docklands or in the offices of various merchants, seeking anyone who could confirm that a Mr. and Mrs. Wickham, or a couple matching their description, had sought passage. In this search, her uncle's contacts proved most useful, but none of their leads were successful.

News of the annulment was more favourable. Lord Brandon sent an express to them, indicating the ecclesiastical court had found the letter to be sufficient proof of Miss Darcy's being alive, and granted the annulment; their bishop promised to pray for the poor girl's soul.

It would be some time before they could expect word back from the hired men who had been sent to Jamaica, and Elizabeth still lived in fear that the lack of evidence of the passage would eventually drive Darcy to renew his desire to go there himself, so as to be sure his sister was not there. But as the inquiries continued to uncover more and more ships in which Georgiana had not gone to Jamaica, Elizabeth felt increasingly certain that her newest sister was still somewhere in England.

The sun was setting, and Darcy was not yet home, but this did not worry Elizabeth. He had gone down to the docklands again, but with two footmen, as well as a brace of pistols carried on his person. She wondered only if she should delay what little they ate in the way of dinner these days, and she was about to ring the bell to tell Mrs. Wright it should be delayed, when she became aware of a violent rapping on the front door's knocker.

Her immediate thought was that one of the men involved in the search must have found something – or perhaps one of her cousins had returned to town – for there could be no other reason for someone to be calling now. She was utterly shocked, therefore, when Mr. Miller helped a young, thin gentleman into the drawing-room, and assisted him to sitting on the settee. A closer look told her the gentleman was not a man at all, but a young lady, dressed as such.

"My God, are you Georgiana?" she asked, in a tremendous rush of hope. The girl nodded mutely, and appeared ready to cry.

"Send everyone who may be sent down to the docklands, to find Mr. Darcy and bring him back here," Elizabeth instructed Mr. Miller. "And bring whatever you have by way of food and drink immediately."

Elizabeth realised, looking at poor Georgiana, that she hardly knew how to explain her presence in the house. She could not imagine how she would feel, in such a situation, but was certain Georgiana would want the comfort of family she knew, not a sister she was unaware of. The poor girl was quickly given comfort from another quarter, however, for Mrs. Wright and Miss Hughes came in and provided her with every attention, a scene Elizabeth could only watch. Food and wine were brought in, and consumed voraciously, and once these more immediate needs were met, the poor girl descended into a fit of weeping what must have been tears of relief.

"I had Sarah start a bath for her, Mrs. Darcy," said Hughes. "We shall keep it topped up with hot water for whenever she is ready for it, since we know not when the master will be back, and I am sure he will want to see her immediately, and she him."

"That is very good, Hughes. Thank you for thinking of it."

"Hughes, did you say *Mrs. Darcy*?" asked Georgiana, for the first time looking at Elizabeth, most carefully.

"She did," Elizabeth said, drawing up a chair before the settee. "Miss Darcy, I know this must be strange for you to hear, but I am your sister."

Georgiana shook her head, and said, "If you are married to my brother, you must know I am Mrs. Wickham, not Miss Darcy."

"No," said Elizabeth, gently, "you *are* Miss Darcy again. Your brother and uncle have had your marriage annulled."

"Annulled? Then he no longer has any power over me," Georgiana said, and descended into another fit of relieved sobbing, during which Elizabeth awkwardly patted her shoulder, and hoped her husband would arrive home soon.

Her hope was met: never before and likely never since would Fitzwilliam Darcy make such a raucous entry into his home, but he did so now, being heard to loudly ask where Georgiana was, and then dashing into the drawing-room. Elizabeth gave up her seat, so Darcy could take it, and embrace his sister.

"Thank God you are home," he said. "I am sorry, Georgiana, so very sorry for all you must have suffered."

"At least I did not suffer what I had feared, which was that my letter would have lured you to Jamaica. I knew not when I wrote it that such a scheme was Mr. Wickham's aim."

"To *lure* me to Jamaica?"

"Yes. He thought if you went there, you would take ill with some disease and die, and he would thus be master of Pemberley, because he was my husband."

"Good God, what a desperate plan!"

"Yes, but you cannot deny that it might have worked."

"Not so far as he was concerned. Your marriage is already annulled, Georgiana. You are Miss Darcy, again."

"Yes, *Mrs.* Darcy told me of that."

"Georgiana, I am sure it must have come as a shock to you that I have married. I hope you will allow me a little explanation on the matter."

The girl nodded, but said nothing, and Darcy explained how he had been staying with Charles Bingley in Hertfordshire, so as to be nearer the search for her. "While I was there, I met Miss Elizabeth Bennet, and while I promise you I did not go there seeking love, I fell in love nonetheless," he said. "If you must blame anyone in the matter, let it be me; do not hold it against Elizabeth. Indeed, were it not for her, I would likely be halfway to Jamaica by now. It was she who thought clearly enough to find it strange that you should send such a letter, after we had been told you were dead."

"He told you I was dead?"

"Yes, when we first attempted to push the annulment through, Wickham wrote to say you had died of fever," he said.

"Oh, Fitzwilliam, I am so sorry for all of the pain and suffering I have caused you. I was so very foolish, and I have brought ruin to our family for it," Georgiana said. "I do not blame you at all, for marrying. The effort you have expended on my behalf is far more than I deserve, for my actions."

"I cannot allow you to think this way, Georgiana. The blame in the matter is my own, and must be left squarely there. I hired your companion; I did not keep you close as I should have, nor did I better educate you in the rougher ways of the world," Darcy said. "I cannot tell you how it pained me to read your letter, that you should think I no longer had affection for you, when it was I who failed you."

Seeing they might argue this point indefinitely, going on for the rest of the evening on who truly deserved blame in the matter, Elizabeth interjected, gently: "Why do we not put the blame where it truly belongs, which is upon Mr. Wickham?"

This was sufficient to put an end to the topic for the present, and Darcy asked, "How did you come to get free of him, and make your way here?"

Georgiana tentatively offered how this had come to be, and told the story of her captivity, and escape, which Elizabeth listened to with a heavy heart, that one so young should have to endure such an ordeal. Only when her story was complete did Georgiana allow herself to be coaxed upstairs for a bath.

In quiet happiness did they dine at Curzon Street that evening. Elizabeth was well aware that while one set of difficulties had been overcome, another must now be faced. Georgiana would need to be re-established in society as best she could be, although her prospects had substantially lessened. She could either live a quiet life with them at Pemberley, or attempt to make a respectable marriage – Elizabeth knew Darcy and Colonel Fitzwilliam had conversed seriously on the possibility of Georgiana's marrying her cousin, and this was the most likely option for her, if she did wish to remarry. But for now, Georgiana seemed simply content to be home, glancing up periodically at her brother, as if to reassure herself that she was reunited with him.

Elizabeth felt herself to be an awkward third in their dining party, and was not certain what to expect when she found herself pulled aside by her sister as they returned to the drawing-room.

"Mrs. Darcy, thank you, for what you did in keeping Fitzwilliam from going to Jamaica," Georgiana said. "I was so afraid he would do so."

"I am doubly relieved he did not, now knowing Mr. Wickham's aim," Elizabeth said. "And I hope you will call me Elizabeth, whenever you are comfortable in doing so. I know you and I have not begun things in the usual manner, but I hope we can be sisters, and friends."

"I would like that very much. I – I have always wished to have a sister."

"Well you shall have one now, one who is very happy and relieved to finally meet you. Now let us go in and sit – you must be exhausted. Whenever you wish, you should go upstairs to sleep."

"Thank you. I shall, eventually, but it has been so long since I have known all of this, I am reluctant to give it up, even for a night of sleep."

True to her word, Georgiana stayed with them until she was visibly drooping with exhaustion, and Elizabeth suggested they all retire for bed. It was natural that Miss Hughes return to Georgiana's service, so Elizabeth was changed by the young housemaid, Sarah, who did a fine enough job of it that Elizabeth did not feel any need to seek a new lady's maid immediately.

As soon as she entered her husband's bedchamber, Elizabeth found herself embraced tightly by Darcy, who held a countenance happier than she had ever seen on him. He kissed her forehead and said, "Thank God for you, my love. I do not know the odds of his full aim being met, of my taking ill, but I would have been loath to be across the ocean when she came home. You were right to think the letter to have been the result of his manipulation."

"In exchange, I shall own that I never could have thought such a plot to be behind the letter. I believe we must accuse Mr. Wickham of every possible evil, excepting lack of imagination."

He laughed, heartily, and Elizabeth said, "I do not believe I have ever heard you laugh like that. I like it very much."

"I am glad you do. I believe we shall have more laughter in our family, now. We may not be what we could have been, but I believe we may be happy, nonetheless."

"I believe you are right," Elizabeth said, leaning over to blow out her candle. "I believe there will be a much greater share of happiness in our future. Good night, my love."

CHAPTER 12

Elizabeth woke softly, coming back into the room like a puff of powder, wafting through the air. She was not so disoriented as it seemed Georgiana had been; she knew immediately that she had been dreaming, a dream clearly influenced by hearing her sister's account of her own dream, and by reminiscing with Darcy over their life together, just before she had fallen asleep.

Her first thought was relief, to come into a world so preferable to one where the Darcys had suffered in the manner they had in her dream. But then she wondered about the child she would have had, in that world. Would she have borne some other son or daughter, instead of James? Might Dr. Whittling have been able to attend her birth, instead of poor Sarah? This thought led her to hold her palm against her forehead, and find that it did not feel warm to her touch, although she was not entirely sure whether she should be able to feel her own fever.

She rose from the bed, pulled on her dressing gown, and walked over to the window, feeling a little refreshed by the cold chill coming through the glass. There was something beautifully desolate about even grounds so well-tended as Pemberley's at this time of year. She smiled faintly, as she thought about little James, running, or perhaps riding Buttercup across the grounds before her, at four or five years of age. It was strange to think of her son in a future life, a life she could not presently imagine herself to be a part of.

Darcy would raise him well; of that, she had no doubts, even if he did. As regretful as her husband had been over the mistakes he felt he had made in raising Georgiana, he *had* raised her, and she had turned out to be a very lovely young lady. Any true errors in judgment in the raising of his sister he had surely learned from, and would apply to the raising of his son.

Elizabeth wondered now what was to come next for her. Would she look down on the two of them, her husband and her son, as it was commonly thought a departed parent should do? Would she watch James trot across the lawn on Buttercup, with Darcy telling him to keep his hands steady and his elbows in, but from a vantage so very far away she could have no contact with them? Would she be in heaven, but unable to see them at all, in the place that now seemed a terrifying mystery to her? Or would her future be a vast, blank nothingness, with naught but the comfort of knowing her son and husband to be well, before she went there?

She considered these things, and now felt the weight of her situation, the fear that her remaining time might be counted in days, if not hours, clutching painfully at her stomach. Trembling, she turned back toward the door of her bedchamber: she needed to see James again; she needed to see Darcy again.

"Oh!" she exclaimed, and halted, for now a pain very much like those she had experienced before her birth had returned to her back. It hurt, but brought with it a deep sense of relief, that things were perhaps finally progressing as they should. She made her way to the door as quickly as she could, saw Sarah was seated immediately outside, waiting, and said, "I am having the pains again. I hope it is finally time."

This was directed at Sarah, who would need to assist her, but there seemed an audible sigh of relief throughout the whole hallway. In Darcy's countenance, there was something beyond relief, something of the most intense love, and he rose to follow Sarah into the room.

Elizabeth was assisted back up onto the little bed, and found there that the pains came quickly, and seemed just as severe as those of her birth.

"Is it supposed to hurt so badly?" she asked, and then felt silly for doing so; Sarah had never given birth herself, and should not be expected to know the relative differences in pain.

"I don't believe so, but perhaps it's something to do with it taking so long," said Sarah.

Darcy took up Elizabeth's hand and grasped it tightly, but could not do so for long, for after Sarah had put her head under the sheet and lifted Elizabeth's leg slightly, she said, in a strangely calm voice:

"Mr. Darcy, if you please, we shall have need of Mrs. Bingley and Mrs. Padgett again."

"What is the matter with her?" Darcy asked, tensely, for Elizabeth could see he liked no more than her this sudden need for additional assistance.

"There's naught wrong with her," Sarah said. "'Tis another bairn, not the afterbirth."

At this, Darcy ran to the door to get the others, and Elizabeth was left to ask: "Another? How can there be another?"

"The same way there was one, I presume, ma'am," Sarah said.

Elizabeth could not see Sarah's face, but was fairly certain this was not said in jest. Still, it made her giggle, as much in relief that the worry of the last few hours now had a cause to attribute to it as anything else. The pains, intense and progressing much more rapidly than the last time, were possibly the only thing that kept her from descending into hysterical laughter. She could not entirely bring herself to believe she was carrying another child, and thought it possible she might only believe it when she could feel the baby emerging.

It might have been hoped that after birthing one child earlier in the day, Elizabeth would have an easier time with this second baby, having grown used to the pain and what was needed. Despite having slept, however, she found herself fatigued and sore, desperately wishing the whole ordeal was over, and were it not for the coaxing of Darcy and Jane, she knew not how she would have endured it. She *did* feel the baby emerging, she looked in her husband's eyes and drew strength from him, and pushed through her exhaustion until it was done.

"There we are," said Sarah, and this time the child could already be heard to cry. "Another fine little boy, perhaps a wee bit bigger than his brother. They are different, I think."

Elizabeth laid her head down on the bed and chuckled with what spirit she had left. Jane washed the sweat from her face, again, as Sarah and Mrs. Padgett were engaged in preparing the baby behind her. She wondered where Darcy had gone to, but found him approaching her with a blanket, and it seemed most natural that he should do so, that he should be the one to worry over her taking a chill.

She turned over on her back, and he draped it over her, looking so incredibly relieved that it seemed to take him some effort to smile at her. Then the baby was handed over to her by Sarah, and Elizabeth immediately forgot her shock and disbelief over having a second child. This was her son, now, every bit as much as his elder brother. She felt certain Sarah had been right, that her sons were not identical, and she hoped this would be for the best; it would already be strange for this boy to be a second son by mere hours.

Darcy resumed his place in the chair beside the little bed, and upon his doing this, the women all filed out, Sarah saying, "Please call me as soon as she feels the pains again; it shall be the afterbirth, finally, unless there are *three*."

Elizabeth smiled, for this was clearly deliberate humour from Sarah, and therefore a rarity; smiled at the thought of having two sons, now; and smiled particularly at the look on Darcy's face, for he seemed to have recovered a little.

"Perhaps there *is* a third," Darcy said. "Perhaps the girl you have been waiting for is still planning on making her entrance into the world."

"I sincerely hope not. Twice has been quite enough for me today, and I know not how there was even space in me for the both of them."

"How are you feeling, Elizabeth?" he asked.

"Tired, but well, considering. I am glad I slept, although I had the strangest dream."

"Indeed?"

"Yes, I believe I mingled Georgiana's dream, and our own memories," Elizabeth said, and told him of all that had happened in her dream.

"So in addition to bearing two sons today, you also determined to set Georgiana's dream to rights, by saving me from an impetuous decision in your own dream?"

"I would not say I *determined* to do so." Elizabeth smiled, recalling a portion of the dream she had not remembered until now. "And I did owe you in the dream – you had rescued me from a horse."

"A horse?" he asked. "This is all the rescue I am able to manage in your dreams? Not, say, a wolf, or a dragon?"

"There have not been wolves in England for some hundreds of years, Darcy."

"And yet you had no objection to the dragon."

"Very well, you had better rescue me from the next dragon that threatens me in my dreams," she said, laughing. "Or perhaps I should say the first dragon, for I cannot recall one, in all my nights of sleep."

"You tease me even now, and I suppose I deserve it," he said. "Yet in truth, it is you who have the greater responsibility, as it seems your role is to rescue me from my poor behaviour, in both our waking world, and within dreams. It must exhaust you, to be so constantly vigilant, and still you do it, my dearest, loveliest Elizabeth."

They had been teasing each other, in high spirits over the birth of a second son, and then, in the course of his last speech, it became apparent to Elizabeth that this teasing was over, that her husband had grown emotional again, and she was too tired presently to handle such deference well.

She smiled, faintly, and then averted her eyes, deciding to see if the baby had interest in nursing. She found the baby took to it quickly, and showed nothing amiss related to his delayed entrance into the world. That she continued to think of him as *the baby*, as well, provided her with a less emotional topic.

"We are overdue to name this little one," she said. "I feel badly that his brother has a name and he does not."

"Well, I believe I know where you stand on the name *Fitzwilliam*," he said, and she was glad he understood she was not yet ready for any more serious conversation.

"I had been thinking that since James is named for my father, we might name him after yours? Although I own the name George cannot have entirely positive associations in our family, so if you would prefer something else, I am open to it, so long as it is not Fitzwilliam."

"I think that is a fine idea, and I do not believe anyone will think we chose to name him after Wickham. Georgiana will understand – indeed, her name comes from both of my parents, and it might honour her, in part."

"I do like honouring Georgiana, given how much she has been on our minds today. And I had not thought about George and Anne forming her name, before."

"I do not believe they would have named her so, without it already being a common name."

"That is good; I will have to tell you I am equally against Fitzabeth and Elizilliam, as I am Fitzwilliam."

"You might wait for a few more births before you take such a stance on any more names," he said. "If you insist on two children every time, we shall run out of names eventually. Our fourteenth child, perhaps, might be Elizilliam."

Elizabeth laughed. "I assure you, if I have two babies every time, we are going to need to make some adjustments in our marital relations well before we reach that number of children. Are you pleased, though, at our having two sons?"

"I would have been pleased with one daughter, but yes, I will own it is a relief to have two heirs, already."

"I feel the same relief, particularly since there was a time when I feared there would never be any heirs from our union – oh! you had better call Miss Kelly in," Elizabeth said, for she now felt a fainter version of her earlier pains beginning again.

"I will be even more relieved, myself, when this part is done," he said, kissing her forehead and carrying little George Darcy out into the hall with him.

CHAPTER 13

Mary could not bear to wait in the hallway with the others, and so after sitting there restlessly for some time, she had gone to the chapel to pray. It had not really been a place she considered open to her, before – Catherine's wedding was the first time she had been in the space. Yet she thought that due more to its lack of use than it being restricted to her – the family always worshipped in Lambton when she came to visit, although she understood occasional visits to Kympton were made, that living also belonging to Pemberley.

Thus, although with all that was happening in the house no-one should stop her, she thought it likely that she would have been encouraged to go there anyway, if she had asked. And she did very much wish to go there. She liked the high painted ceiling, and the stained glass windows – having grown up at Longbourn, the notion of a room within a *house* having stained glass windows seemed an impossibility to her, and yet this one did possess very fine ones.

Even more, she wished for the quiet stillness of the space, for a place within the house completely devoted to God. She did not wish and had not planned for what she found there, which was that David Stanton, having thought similarly to her, would already be seated at the first row of chairs and offering his own prayers. Mary noticed his presence with a start, and thought for a moment to leave. Yet he was a clergyman, and she was here to pray, and had no wish to disturb him or seek conversation, so instead she attempted to slip in as quietly as she could, and seated herself in the back row.

He noticed her, however, although with some delay in acknowledging her, so that Mary realised he must have been finishing his prayer. When he had done so, he rose, bowed, and said, "It seems you and I had similar thoughts, Mary. There is little else I could think to do now, but pray."

"But Georgiana is well – I have seen her! Has no one told you she is awake?"

"Oh no, I have seen her. She seems as well as can be, considering how long she was asleep, and what she has lost," he said. "But I wished to give thanks, for her waking, and to pray for your sister and father. Has there been any change in Elizabeth's condition?"

"No, she is sleeping, now."

"Perhaps sleep is all that is needed," he said. "I must admit I have very little experience in these matters. I have seldom been called to the bedside of a woman due to her giving birth."

"I am glad of that," Mary said. "Was – did your own wife die in childbirth?"

"No, of typhus – we had not even been married two years," he said, and his countenance was grim enough that Mary regretted having asked. "But my mother did die in childbirth."

"I am very sorry," said Mary. "I should not have pried."

"I know the difference between prying and asking because you care, Mary."

She did care; he was correct. Yet there was such a strangeness to be asking about his wife, when that lady's death had made possible what Mary now considered. She wished she might think of something else to say on the topic, but truly did not wish to pry, and finally, when enough time had passed, said: "Do you ever struggle with what to say, in your prayers? No, I suppose you must not – you must always be ready to speak to God. I do, though. Sometimes, like now, I wish very much to pray for those I love, but know not what to say – I stumble through as best I can. I *want* to pray better, but I cannot."

"I struggle all the time, Mary, particularly when the prayers are for my own family and dear friends. But I believe in a loving God, and I do not think He judges you on the quality of your prayers, only that you do pray. I believe He knows what worries you, even if you do not speak it as well as you might wish to; the important thing is in reaching out to Him. When I am lost, I fall back on the Lord's Prayer; sometimes, there is no greater comfort, and I think He must hear me and know of all I cannot say."

"Will – would you say it with me now?" Mary knew not why she asked this of him; his advice was sound, and she might very well have followed it on her own. But she liked the sound of his voice, and she thought the act would bring the comfort of an embrace, without any actual embrace, which would have been horribly improper. In this, she was right – there was something very soothing about his voice mingled with hers, about the familiar words, which left her feeling peaceful when they had finished.

He made his exit then, but did not go directly to the door, instead walking near where Mary was seated, and placing his hand very gently on her shoulder for a moment. Mary felt the weight of that hand for far longer and in much greater proportion than it had been bestowed. She blushed, and felt a strange flutter in her stomach, even though she knew the gesture must have been meant for comfort.

It was some time before she was able to order her thoughts again, and bolstered by what he had said about prayer, made her prayers as best she could, and did not worry over whether they had been good enough. She was startled to find a footman waiting for her in the hall when she left the chapel, and was provided with the news that her sister had borne another baby, a boy, and that the afterbirth for both babies had passed following this, so Mrs. Darcy was no longer perceived to be in any danger. As this was the very subject upon which Mary had been praying, she would have welcomed the interruption, but she was so overjoyed she made no correction to the footman, and merely thanked him and rushed off to see her sister.

Once she felt well enough, Elizabeth had made her way to her own bedchamber, to begin her confinement, and Mary was not the last of the relieved persons making their way thither to see how she did. This honour went to Dr. Alderman, who arrived with a surgeon, to be informed that no-one in the house had any more need of their services. He and the surgeon were paid, regardless, and he did examine Elizabeth and speak with Sarah about how the birth had gone, a discussion that seemed to embarrass him far more than the maid.

Dr. Alderman pronounced all that had happened to be beyond what he had experienced, but perhaps not abnormal, given he did not deliver many babies; the bulk of his practise came from treating those invalids who came to Matlock for the waters, and the local gentry who could afford his fees. To the relief of all, he found both Elizabeth and her sons to be in good health, and cautioned against exposing the twins to even the slightest draught, given how small they were. He was informed that a good steady fire would be kept going constantly in Mrs. Darcy's dressing-room, and would continue to be until the babies were moved to the nursery, where similar measures would be taken.

It was late by the time Dr. Alderman finished, and he and the surgeon needed little convincing to accept dinner and rooms for the night, particularly the surgeon, who faced the return journey to Manchester in the morning. Elizabeth did not dine with the rest of the household, but took a substantial tray in her own chamber, and found herself feeling much better restored, once she had eaten.

She rose and walked over to her dressing-room, which had now been made up satisfactorily to house Mrs. Nichols and the babies, and made complete with a third cradle, one that was visibly older, but had been polished to a high gloss by someone before George had taken up residence. Dr. Whittling was to bring with him a monthly nurse, but prior to her arrival it was Sarah who filled that role, helping both Mrs. Nichols and her mistress as assistance was needed. Elizabeth noted to herself that she should see if one of the housemaids had interest in becoming a dedicated nursery maid, with an increase to her wages, now that there was one more baby than had been expected. Another housemaid could be found, eventually, but that was not as pressing as ensuring there were enough hands about for the children. She found herself once again glad to have hired Mrs. Nichols, for Elizabeth was not certain of her capacity to nurse two babies by herself and eventually return to managing the household.

"It should be near enough time for them to feed," said Mrs. Nichols. "Would you like to try them both together?"

"I think so. Will you help me get them situated?"

Elizabeth picked up James, and returned to her bed, resting her back against the pillows. Mrs. Nichols followed, with George, and helped her situate both babies. They struggled a little, at first, to find a way where she could hold them both at the same time, but then she found a position that seemed comfortable both for her and for her babies, and quickly found herself in a state of the most perfect maternal bliss.

Mrs. Nichols went about the bed and closed the bed-curtains on all but the side nearest Elizabeth, giving her more privacy. Although anyone who entered the room should have knocked, Elizabeth was still glad of this extra barrier, for it would have been impossible for her to nurse both babies at once and be discreet about it.

She had little expectation of interruptions, anyway, for everyone else – excepting Georgiana – had gone down to dinner, and Elizabeth was glad to be alone. This was her time, with James and George, to make the delightful adjustment to no longer thinking of herself as one who was going to have a baby, but instead a mother. The child she had wanted for so long was in being, and had come into the world followed by his most surprising younger brother. An unexpected sense of satisfaction resulted from these thoughts, for so long as both of her sons lived – and she said a silent prayer now that this would be the case – Pemberley would have two male heirs, a luxury that had been absent for two generations. These thoughts were not so satisfying as the simple pleasure of holding her own sons in her arms as they fed, but neither could they be ignored.

When they had finished, she kissed them both and called out to Mrs. Nichols to help her put them back into their cradles. As they were arranging the blankets, Elizabeth noticed that James wore a blue ribbon around his ankle, and George a green, and asked Mrs. Nichols what they were for.

"Oh, ma'am, to make absolute sure which is which. They are different, sure enough, but not so very different, and it would never do for them to be mixed up. It shan't be fair to Master James if he is denied his birthright."

"Yes, of course. That was very good thinking on your part, Mrs. Nichols," Elizabeth said, and yet she could not help but look with sympathy to little George. It could not be easy to be born a second son in any circumstances, but to be so by only a matter of hours!

For the mistress of a great estate, however, the presence of a second son just born cannot be a troubling one for very long, and by the time she entered her bedchamber, Elizabeth had returned to calmer spirits. Remembering that she had wished to speak with Mrs. Reynolds, but not wishing to further disturb the women in the dressing-room, she rang the bell to see if the housekeeper could be summoned.

Once she and Mrs. Reynolds had made their arrangements, she called Sarah into the room, and found her maid looking very tired, but still ready to take on whatever responsibilities were needed of her that evening.

"I need nothing, at present, Sarah," Elizabeth said. "Mrs. Reynolds will attend me tomorrow morning, and one of the maids will assist Mrs. Nichols – you should sleep as late as you want. I only wished to give you this."

Sarah took the silk purse from her employer, made a little glimpse inside, and said, "Oh no, ma'am, I cannot possibly accept such a sum."

"Dr. Alderman readily accepted the same sum, and he did not do any of the work, Sarah," Elizabeth said, wondering vaguely how her husband would compensate Dr. Whittling, if he made the now-unnecessary journey to Derbyshire. "You saw me and both of my sons through a rather frightening pair of births, and neither Mr. Darcy nor I take that lightly."

"But Elizabeth, I did not do it for money!"

"I know you did not, and that only makes you deserve it more. And I am terribly glad you called me Elizabeth, just now, for if you could not be brought to do so after all you have done today, I hardly know what I should do."

This time, it was Elizabeth who embraced Sarah, and when they had separated, Sarah said: "If you are sure you wish to give me this, I shall take it, and I am grateful to you, for it will be very helpful to my family."

"I hope you will spend at least something of it on yourself, and if you do not, we will have to go into Lambton, and I will not allow you to leave Green's until you have selected something I may buy for your particular use. Now that I think on it, we shall do just that, regardless of what you do with the money."

Sarah, still a little flustered, curtseyed to take her leave, and Elizabeth climbed back into bed. It was still early, but she felt a pervading exhaustion from all she had been through that day, and thought she should at least lie down, although she felt certain Darcy would visit her again before he retired, and did not wish to attempt sleep before then.

When the knock at the door and a muffled, "It is me, Elizabeth," came, however, it was from Mary. Elizabeth called out that she should come in, and saw Mary had all of her letters in hand.

"Oh, I very nearly forgot about those," she said, reminded of the fear and uncertainty in which she had written them, and incredibly relieved she was done with that time.

"I thought I should give them back to you." Mary approached the bed as though to hand them to her.

"I do not think I want them," Elizabeth said. Certainly the sentiments within were those she should express, but she would express them in person, in the course of the life she lived. "Will you throw them in the fire, please, Mary?"

"I will be so very relieved to throw them in the fire, rather than deliver them," Mary said. Once she had completed this task, she came over to the bed and awkwardly hugged her sister, before saying her good-night.

Elizabeth was still feeling tenderly amused by such a display of affection from Mary when Darcy came in, looking even more exhausted than she felt, but smiling a very tired smile to her.

"I hope I did not wake you – I wished to see how you were, and say good-night," he said.

"A little tired, but otherwise well," she said, sitting up in the bed. "And I am glad you came to see me before you retired. If nothing else, we have a bet to settle, and I have an unfortunate suspicion that it is I who owe you twenty guineas."

Elizabeth had begun by teasing, assuming they would transition slowly to that more serious talk she thought he wished to have, but instead, he came over to sit beside her on the bed, taking up her hand and clutching it tightly.

"Consider them paid. Consider them paid a thousand times over," he said, hoarsely. "Elizabeth – oh, Elizabeth, I could not have done this without you."

"You could have, my love. You absolutely would have, if it had been required of you," she said, and wished for a moment that she had not asked Mary to burn the letters, for her note to him had centred on this topic, before she had closed with a reminder of her love for him.

"You say that, now, but your dream would seem to indicate otherwise."

"It was merely a dream."

He shook his head. "It might have been a dream, but both of us know it to be within my character to act precisely as you described, and so I find it yet another example of what I have known for some time: I need you, Elizabeth. I needed you when I proposed in Kent, and I need you now, and for the rest of my life. I need you to tell me when I err, to pull me back when my temper gets the better of me. Most of all, now, I need you to be a parent alongside me."

"And you still have me," Elizabeth said, soothingly. "I am not going anywhere, my love."

"Thank God," he said, his countenance wholly overcome with emotion, as he began to weep. "Thank God I did not lose either of you."

Overcome herself, with how affected he had been, Elizabeth felt her own eyes fill with tears. She held out her arms to him, and he responded immediately, embracing her fervently. Elizabeth had been embraced by her husband on countless occasions, but never had she been held with such desperation, or felt his body wracked with sobs of this intensity. At least they were sobs of relief, she thought; at least this was not prompted by grief, and she pulled his head into her shoulder, murmuring continuously to him that they were all well: her, his sister, his sons.

She could not help but be troubled at the extent to which he seemed lost in her arms, at the number of times she must whisper, "we are well, my love, we are all well," before she got any manner of response, which was merely that he should kiss repeatedly the palm of the hand she had placed on his cheek.

It was as she told him they were all well once more that a reminder intruded painfully on Elizabeth's thoughts: there was one person whose health could not have worried him to the extent it did her, one person whose life was still in doubt. She was more focused on providing comfort, rather than deriving it, yet her father's health weighed heavily on her mind. She held Darcy more tightly, and prayed they were truly *all* well.

CHAPTER 14

Georgiana waited until the next day to see her nephews. Ever since she had awoken, there had been a painful hollowness about her, in addition to a lingering head-ache, and she thought of her baby with every regret over what had happened. She was very relieved over Elizabeth's having come through her birth safely, but it was unsettling to think of her sister having delivered two boys, when Georgiana would not have a child at all.

This was what troubled her mind as she went into her sister's dressing-room. Mrs. Nichols dozed by the fireplace, and Rachel, one of the maids, sat silently beside her, so the room was peaceful, with all of the boys sleeping. The serenity of her sleeping nephews first touched Georgiana's heart, and then one of them, she knew not which, awoke and gazed intensely at her. Expecting him to turn immediately to tears as Bess usually did, she was surprised when he did not, and reached out tentatively to pick him up.

He remained silent as she did so, and she could not help but smile at the soft, sweet, delicate nature of him. In this tenderness, she felt the first real sense that she *did* want a child of her own — not merely to produce an heir, but to have a child she and Matthew had brought into the world, and would love together. Matthew, somewhere out in a horrific cold, perhaps hemmed in by ice, and completely unaware of what had happened. These thoughts overwhelmed her, but she was still exceedingly careful as she placed the baby back in his cradle, and only then did she rush from the room, past Mary, who must have been intending to visit her nephews as well.

She fled to the gallery nearby; there was no reason to expect anyone there at this time of day, although it was strange to be here amongst her ancestors, considering what troubled her. She was not to remain alone there for long, for Mary came in quietly, found where Georgiana had come to sit with her head in her hands, and sat beside her, gently laying an arm across her shoulders.

"I am so sorry about your baby," said Mary. "I have been praying you shall be blessed with another."

"You are likely to pray on that subject for some time, then." For a moment, there was something exceedingly satisfying about indulging in such bitterness, but then Georgiana was given over to regret. Mary could never be described as entirely easy in her interactions with others, and Georgiana had treated her very kind gesture with what Mary might take to be derision. Beyond this, she had made far more allusion to the marriage act than was proper for an unwed lady to hear, even though Mary was older than she. Georgiana had enough worries already without the shame of bad conduct to add to them, yet if Mary was offended, she said nothing, and merely hugged her friend closer.

"I was not sure I was ready, for a child," Georgiana said, hesitantly, wishing to explain herself. "But now I know that I was, and it will be a year or so before I might hope for another."

"You are still young enough to have a great many children, even with this loss," said Mary, soothingly.

Georgiana might have argued that there were other ladies her age who had already borne children, who had borne their husbands heirs, but mindful now of Mary's age, and that her friend was unmarried, she said nothing of this, and instead spoke of the thing that most troubled her mind: "I must write to Matthew today, and tell him of what happened. I hardly know how to give him this news, and I hate to think of him receiving it so far away, and in so inhospitable a place."

"You need not do that if it pains you too much. I am certain David would write to him for you."

Georgiana caught Mary's use of his Christian name, and looked up at her friend more quickly than she should have, prompting Mary to grow a profuse shade of pink. She spoke quickly, to aid in alleviating Mary's embarrassment, although some remote part of her that could still be pleased *was* pleased to know Mary and David must have become more intimate in order for her to be so embarrassed.

"I should be the one to write to him of it. I would not wish to make him worry that I am still not well. That at least I may assure him of; I am sound of body and mind, if not heart."

Mary left her, upon being assured that Georgiana was well enough, and Georgiana began the walk back to her bedchamber, taking a much longer route, so as to avoid the east stairs. She wondered whether it was James or George that she had held, was struck by the thought that both of them would inherit Pemberley ahead of her, now, and was glad of it. It was never something she had thought of, before her dream, and only in having her dream had she realised how little she desired it.

Pemberley belonged to Fitzwilliam, as it had belonged to her father, and would belong to James, someday. She knew now what she wanted, and it was not a grand estate; it was something much closer to what Matthew had described, in her dream: a fine house or a small estate, an intimate home for the two of them and their children. And she wanted the other thing he had offered, to give up his career and spend the rest of his days with her, in that home.

Yet the price she had paid for these things in her dream was far too dear. She meant what she had said to Elizabeth, that she preferred this course of her life, the one it had actually taken, even if it meant she must suffer Matthew's absence, and the loss of their child.

Mary had, by now, admitted to herself that although it was wholly improper, she did like encountering David when they might be alone in each other's company. In the upheaval the two new babies had brought upon the household, she harboured hopes that she might do so again today, although this time her purposes were not entirely her own.

She went to the chapel, hoping he might come in, but her hopes were not satisfied there, nor were they in the yellow drawing-room, when he was indeed there, but they were joined by Jane and Charles. After having sat in conversation with them for some time, he declared his intent to go to the library, and Mary tarried awhile before following him thither. She was in receipt of a particular look from Jane as she made to leave the room, as if her sister at least suspected what she was about, but Jane said nothing. Mary thought they should be glad she was not like Lydia, for the amount of freedom she was allowed in a house so large, but then, perhaps if she *was* like Lydia, everyone would have been more cautious about chaperoning her.

He was there in the library, examining the books on one of the shelves, and did not seem very surprised at her entrance. It took her some time to cross the room, and when she had, she said, "I wished to speak with you about Georgiana. She worries over having to write to Matthew of what happened with the baby. I attempted to convince her to allow you that duty, but she insists on writing, to assure him that she at least is well."

"It is probably for the best that she does, at least as far as he is concerned. She is right in thinking he will wish to see from her own hand that she is recovering."

"I wondered, though, if you might supply more of the details, so she is at least spared in that."

"I certainly shall. In truth, I am not sure of what she knows herself, of the accident. Matthew will wish to know all of it, however, and you are right to wish to spare her that burden."

"Thank you."

"I had actually wished to speak with you of another letter," he said, producing one from his coat, and handing it over to her. "This is an express from my father, in response to my own express to him, regarding the accident. I know he did not even give them the respect of attending their wedding, but still, she is his daughter-in-law, and I thought he should know of what had happened."

Mary opened the letter, and found it was both short and horrible. David's father showed little in the way of care for his daughter, and spent the majority of the letter preaching as to how the loss of the child must have come as the result of the sins of either the father, or the mother – most likely the father. When she had finished, her hand, still holding the letter, fell to her side in silent shock.

"I see your reaction is similar to mine. I wished to know if you thought I should show the letter to Georgiana."

"No, no, she must never see it!"

"I had hoped you would agree with me on that. I do not like deception, but I think in this case it is better that she and Matthew never know the letter was written, nor responded to in such a way."

"How could he possibly think, let alone write, such terrible things?"

"You must understand that my father is a cruel, judgmental man. I know it is not respectful of me as his son to say such a thing, but I am even less inclined to respect him after reading that letter," he said. "His idea of being a Christian is in thinking himself more pious than anyone else, and entirely without sin. There is no kindness and no generosity in his Christianity, and certainly no forgiveness; he shall cast the first stone, every time."

His words cut through Mary painfully, for she recognised in them the way she had thought of herself all these years. Had she not thought herself more pious than her family? Had she not judged Lydia for her actions, without any thought of forgiveness or assistance? Presented with a more egregious version of her own faults, she saw them clearly, and regretted very much the way she had behaved.

"Mary, what is the matter? Are you ill?" he asked, gazing at her with a concerned look upon his face.

She *was* ill, exceedingly ill to her stomach, and this must have reached her countenance. She saw now that his interest in her must not have been romantic interest, but instead that of a clergyman seeking to set her on the right path. A man who valued the qualities he valued could never have any romantic interest in someone such as her.

"I am a little indisposed, I believe," she said, tremulously. "I think I might retire to my apartment and rest for a little while."

"Of course. Do you have want of my arm while you walk there?"

"No. I shall be able to go there without any assistance," Mary said. "I am perfectly fine on my own, but thank you."

She gave a little curtsey and fled the room, back to the bedchamber she used while staying at Pemberley, and there had a very long, regretful cry, before she settled herself enough to gather her writing things and pen a very difficult letter to Lydia.

Mary was not the only person in the house embarking on a difficult letter; Georgiana had spent the better part of half-an-hour with a sheet of paper before her, trying to determine what she should write. The paper was not entirely blank. She had done the easy things: first numbering it, as Matthew had instructed her to, for he expected to receive many of her letters all at once, although this was the second number one she would send him, and so she had added "please read first" beside the numeral. She had written "My dear love," and only after this had her pen hovered in the air, until it had dripped several blotches of ink onto the paper, and she had been required to return it to the inkwell while she decided what she should write.

With some degree of relief, she found herself interrupted by a knock at her door, and that it was Mr. Parker who had knocked.

"If you have a minute, ma'am, Robert wishes to speak with you."

For a brief moment, Georgiana could not recall who Robert was, then realised it was Bowden's Christian name, and if she had not taken to calling him by his surname as her husband did, it was how she would have addressed him, as her footman.

"Of course, please send him in."

Bowden came in, looking deeply uncomfortable as Mr. Parker closed the door behind him, and he stood there for some time before saying: "Milady, I'm verr' sorry. The captain tol' me I 'ad one duty above all else, to keep milady safe, an' I failed. If'n you wish I leave your imploy, jus' say so an' I'll be gone t'night."

"Bowden, please." Georgiana shook her head to stop him speaking any more, and willed herself not to cry, as she had already done in response to Hughes's own tears of relief over her mistress's recovery. "There was nothing you could have done. Neither Captain Stanton nor I had any expectation that you should be helping me down every staircase in my childhood home. What happened was a terrible accident, and there was not anything *you* could have done to prevent it. I hope you will remain in our employ for many years to come."

Bowden nodded, thanked her, and after some awkward combination of salute and forelock tug, backed out of the room. His exit was followed by another knock, which turned out to be David, who asked how she was feeling and very kindly offered to write Matthew of the details of her accident, so she only needed to give her own account in the broadest strokes. She thanked him, and was glad when she returned her attention to the paper before her that it should be a slightly easier letter. Yet she still needed to write it, and if she did not start soon, she might not finish in time to include it with the day's post. Georgiana thought of the little boy she had held earlier, she dabbed at her eyes with her handkerchief, and then picked up her pen and forced her hand into motion:

"Matthew, my love, I know this news must shock you and I am so very sorry for it, but I have lost the baby. You were right to be worried about my light-headedness, and if I had ever thought this might be the outcome, I would have been so much more careful, although I never suspected that which was the cause of my fainting.

"Mr. Wickham, unbeknownst to me, came here seeking money from my brother, so that he might take up with Mrs. Wickham again, by starting a new life in America. Fitzwilliam did agree to give him a sum, if Lydia would go with him, and was seeing him out of the house at the door by the east stairs, when I had the misfortune to be coming down those stairs. I hope you will understand my shock at seeing him there, after all that happened in Paris. I fainted, and fell, and when I awoke, Fitzwilliam told me the baby had been lost.

"I think back now and know I should have told him, of how Mr. Wickham accosted me when we were in Paris. He had no reason to believe I would be shocked to the degree I was by seeing Wickham, and feels guilty for it. I know, however, that the blame for this must fall on myself, for not telling him, and for not being more careful. I am so sorry – my actions, and lack of them, have cost us our child, and possibly your heir.

"I wish I had something else to offer you, some hope, but all I have is that I have been reminded I am young, and there is no reason to expect other children will not follow this one. But this child, that we might otherwise have planned for, and loved, and raised, shall never be. My only wishes now are that you will forgive me, and that you shall return home soon. I hope you are well.

"Love,

"GEORGIANA"

It was a poor letter; the degree of her distress would be as readily apparent from her handwriting as the words she had written, but at least now that it was done, Georgiana could set it aside and cry freely.

While in her confinement, Elizabeth should hardly have gone farther than her own bedchamber and the dressing-room beside it, but after a day in which she had done nothing other than sleep, eat, and nurse her babies, she found herself so restless that it seemed an hour in the blue drawing-room following dinner would do her some good. Sarah came and dressed her, and she was received there with surprise, but not censure. They were a quiet party, however; of her sisters, only Jane seemed to have any interest in conversation. Georgiana's silent sorrow, Elizabeth could understand – she was a bit surprised her sister had returned to company – but Mary also seemed even less inclined for conversation than usual.

This she first attributed to worry over their father, for this was still a strong shadow over Elizabeth's mind. But this possibility was eliminated, when Mr. Parker came into the room with an express from Catherine. It was addressed to Elizabeth, and she looked with hope at the red seal, but then realised that if her father had died, the household might have been too chaotic for Catherine to find black wax. She opened it with trepidation, therefore, and with the greatest relief did she read: "Elizabeth, our father lives, and is expected to make a full recovery."

Elizabeth exclaimed this news to the group, and then read on. Catherine wrote that her father had passed the worst of his illness before the Ramseys had arrived at Longbourn, and while there had been some exaggeration on her mother's part, Mr. Jones had confirmed that there was a truly significant risk to her father's life, to have such a fever at his age.

Mrs. Bennet's nerves had no sooner recovered from the threat of losing her husband and being turned out of her home than they had suffered the shock of having her second-youngest daughter appear on her doorstep late in the evening, informing her mother that she was now Mrs. Ramsey. Mrs. Bennet had been torn between happiness at having one more daughter married, and additional fits of nerves over how quickly it had come off, and what they were to do about the clothes.

Catherine's letter was short, and made no mention of Wickham, but if he had made the whole journey on horseback – which seemed likely, for the public stage or the mail would have carried additional risk for an army deserter – the married couple would have outpaced him in the post-chaise. Elizabeth wondered if her sister had made any manner of warning to their family that he was to come, or if she had warned Lydia of the decision she would need to make, soon.

Her thoughts at present were too happy to dwell on Lydia and George Wickham for long, though, and the mood in the drawing-room was improved substantially by this news. Even Georgiana seemed a little happier, and when they had said all that could be said about Catherine's letter, David asked if any of them might wish to play the pianoforte, and Georgiana had volunteered. Yet this was where Elizabeth thought Mary's behaviour most odd; usually, she would have been eager to play, particularly given who had made the request, but when Georgiana completed her sonata and Mary was applied to, she claimed fatigue over playing too much already for Bess that day.

Elizabeth might have considered Mary's demeanour more, but Mrs. Reynolds entered the room and discreetly informed her that the twins had need of her. Elizabeth excused herself and said she was going to see to her sons, and then to retire for the night.

She found it was George who had immediate need of sustenance, although James awoke not long after she had sat down with her second-eldest, and was handed over to her as well by Mrs. Nichols.

"I cannot tell you how much I appreciate your assistance, Mrs. Nichols," Elizabeth said, well aware that if the nurse had not seen to her sons through the previous night, allowing her to sleep, she would have felt far less recovered from her births. "I could not have managed them both without you."

"'Tis nothing, ma'am. You had quite the ordeal yesterday."

"It could have been worse," Elizabeth murmured, then thought to inquire after the maid who had been selected to assist in the nursery, and in so doing, better see how Mrs. Nichols was bearing up under the care of so many babies. "Has Rachel settled in?"

"Aye, ma'am, she has, an' she's been such a help."

"I hope you will get some sleep tonight, then. Please have her wake me, whenever the boys need to nurse."

"Thank ye, ma'am, that's much appreciated." Mrs. Nichols might have spoken more, but Elizabeth heard her greeting Mr. Darcy, and moments later, he peered behind the bed-curtain.

"Am I allowed to be here with you?"

"There is nothing revealed here that you have not seen many times before," Elizabeth said.

"I completely disagree," Darcy said, taking up a chair and placing it beside the bed. "I have not seen anything like this before. You are the sort of scene the masters carved out of marble."

"I believe that scene is usually Madonna and child, not Madonna and twins."

"Must you always teaze?"

"You should be happy that I teaze. I only teaze when I am in good spirits."

He said nothing, but smiled a sort of pure, contented smile that Elizabeth felt certain was echoed in her own countenance. After some time, he reached out and fingered the ribbon on George's foot, which had slipped out from under his blanket, and asked, "What is this?"

"Mrs. Nichols put ribbons on each of them, in different colours, to ensure they did not become switched, accidentally."

"That was wise of her," he said. "The last thing we need is any doubt about which of them was first-born. Things will be strange enough, as it is."

"Darcy, what if James does not turn out well? What if he becomes one of those wastrel first sons, like the late Viscount Burnley?" The man to which Elizabeth referred had been the elder brother of one of Georgiana's suitors, until he had been killed in a duel, and his younger brother had become the heir apparent.

"We shall both have to do all we can, to raise two sons who behave as gentlemen should," Darcy said. "And I do not want either of them to be idle, as the late Viscount Burnley was. George will obviously need to take on a career, but James will participate in the running of this estate, just as our cousin Andrew does for Stradbroke, and if he chooses to shirk his duties, or his younger brother seems notably worthier, I would not hesitate to change over the inheritance. James shall have the first opportunity, but he will have to be worthy."

"Poor George. I never thought on what it might be like to have two heirs, and to to make plans for a second son."

"I believe we may wait a little while before making plans. He is only a day old."

"I suppose so. He may be given a pass until the end of the week, at least," she said. "He is done, would you like to hold him?"

"Yes, but let me find a cloth, first. Mason is utterly horrified over the notion of having to clean anything emanating from a baby from any of my clothes."

"You ought not to have mentioned that to me. Poor Miss Kelly took the mess on the shoulder of my dressing gown without the slightest complaint, and so now I shall be seeking ways to vex your valet."

"Please do not," said he. "Mason is perhaps overly fastidious, but he has been with me these ten years, and I could not find a more diligent man. And I believe I would have shared his squeamishness over – over the substances a child can produce – before I had children of my own."

"I suppose I shall have to be kind to him, then, although I cannot guarantee James and George will. Mason does tie a rather nice cravat."

CHAPTER 15

Mary's odd behaviour continued through the course of the next day, and no sooner had Elizabeth determined she should seek some time to speak with her alone, than Mary sought her out. Mary's purpose, upon entering Elizabeth's bedchamber the following morning, was to ask if she could help prepare the Christmas baskets and deliver them, because she wished to do more to help the poor. This surprised Elizabeth, for Mary had always preferred to stay at home and read, when Elizabeth and Jane had gone about with their father to visit those dependent on Longbourn.

"I think that is a fine idea, Mary, and although you will not find much in the line of poor amongst Pemberley's tenants, there will be some in Lambton and Kympton who are in need of greater generosity, and I am not at all sure what you may expect of Clareborne," Elizabeth said. "Jane and Mrs. Reynolds will be managing the baskets, for both estates, and I am sure they would be glad of your assistance."

"I would not mind going to see the tenants, then, but I particularly wish to be included in the visits to the villagers. I would like to see if there are any other things they have need of, and help with them. Sewing clothes, perhaps?"

"Yes, please do see who is in need of assistance, and then you may help with whatever you wish," Elizabeth said. "I see you are already preparing yourself to be a clergyman's wife."

With this, Mary coloured, but then looked away, as her eyes filled with tears. "No, I do not think I am going to become a clergyman's wife. At least not with the clergyman I believe you are referring to."

"Oh Mary, whatever happened? Please, sit and let us talk."

Mary did as she was bade, and after some time, finally said: "I have been foolish, and judgmental, and selfish, and while I credit Mr. Stanton with helping me see these things, it cannot have been out of romantic interest."

"Mary, did he say these things to you?" Elizabeth could not deny that there was some truth to what Mary said, but she did not like the idea of someone so new to their family telling her of it in a way that had clearly upset her.

"Oh no, he has been without fault in all of this. Please do not blame him – I am distressed, but it is distress over realising my own failings. And, I suppose, understanding that his role in my life was to be the person who very gently guided me towards understanding them. If I am to tell you of how he did it, however, I must ask for your confidence. There is something I will speak of, which he and I agreed Georgiana and Matthew should not know."

Elizabeth nodded, and was told of the horrible letter Richard Stanton had sent to his eldest son, David's reaction to it, and Mary's realisation that she saw enough of the flaws in his father's character in her own heart and actions as to be wholly ashamed, and repentant. Mary had concluded that his interest in her was as a man of God, seeking to steer her to a better path, and could have nothing to do with romance.

"Oh, Mary, it cannot be easy that he has helped you better understand yourself, and see how your character might be improved," Elizabeth said. "But this does not mean he has no romantic interest in you. I do not believe I have ever seen a gentleman show a young lady such particular attention, without being romantically interested in her."

"But why? What interest could a man of two and thirty years of age have in a foolish young lady like me?"

"Do you not mean, what interest could a clergyman have in a pious young lady who reads the same things he does, and enjoys discussing them?"

Mary was silent, but her countenance indicated she preferred to continue in her self-recriminations.

"I do not believe I have ever told you that the proposal I accepted from Mr. Darcy was his second. He proposed to me first in Kent, and I refused him," said Elizabeth. "In so doing, I led us both on a path of coming to realise our own flaws and acting to improve upon them, and ultimately I believe he would say the same as I, that we are both the better for it."

"But I may not do the same for Mr. Stanton. His character is not flawed at all!"

"I believe there are few – if any – on this earth who may claim a character without flaws. His may not be egregious, I will grant you, and he has been married before, so it is possible his first wife has done some of the duty there."

"Do you truly think he *does* have romantic interest in me?"

"Nothing is ever completely certain in love, Mary, but yes, I do. Let me ask you, has he spoken of his home at all, of his neighbours and his parish?"

"Oh yes, he speaks of Wincham all the time – of those who live in the village and the surrounding estates, although he has not said so much about

Lord and Lady Winterley as Mr. Collins did of Lady Catherine."

"That is likely for the best, Mary; I believe he respects them, but he does not fawn over them. I can tell you that for their role in finding Mrs. Nichols her position here, I favour them."

"And he has told me of the rectory – quite a bit, actually," said Mary.

"You might imagine why he would tell you so much of it."

"Yes, I suppose so. I had not really thought of it in that way. We were merely conversing."

"He has not conversed with me in any detail on that topic, nor Jane, I suspect," Elizabeth said. "Now, let his behaviour be your guide. If he wished merely to correct your character, he would not continue to pay you such attentions. Yet if he does have other purposes, he shall."

It was strange, for Georgiana to wake and feel hunger and a head-ache, rather than the illness that had previously comprised her mornings. Yesterday, she had taken a tray in her room, and broken her fast in silent despondency, and so on this day she determined it would be better to go to breakfast, and be in company. She found the breakfast-room empty, save for David, who chose to linger and have another pot of coffee brought around when she came in, although she felt herself to be making most of the effort in conversation between the two of them. She was thus surprised when he asked if she would like to take a turn through the conservatory, when she had finished.

Once there, she found him more inclined to speak, for after they had walked the length of one of the aisles, he said: "I think to make my return to Wincham on the morrow – I cannot neglect my duties at the parish any longer. I have not yet spoken of it to Mrs. Darcy; I thought I should tell you first, as it was the threat to your health that brought me here."

"Thank you for that – I am very grateful you came here, as I am sure Matthew will be," Georgiana said, although she thought it odd that he considered her the most important person to inform.

"I am sure that were he in the same position, he would have done the same for my wife," David said, sighing. "The truth is, Georgiana, I had hoped to leave Pemberley with the promise of another wife, but it seems it is not to be."

"Oh – did Mary refuse you?" Georgiana asked, before she had time to think that such a question was wholly improper.

"She did not refuse me, for I did not ask," he said. "I do not know what has been the cause, but there has been a coldness in her manner towards me, of late. Given how close our families are, I would be loath to make an unwelcome proposal, which should cause awkwardness whenever we meet."

"I must admit, I had believed a match between the two of you to be inevitable," said Georgiana. "You both seemed so well-suited for each other."

"So I had thought as well. I must admit, I was a bit reluctant with Miss Bennet at first because she seemed so well-suited for me, compared to my late wife. Bless her soul, Isabel was of lively temperament, and I did love her, but I could not help but feel guilty at thinking that Miss Bennet and I are so much more alike."

"I cannot claim acquaintance with your late wife, but I do think you and Miss Bennet are a very good match. Was there something you said to her, to cause this coldness of manner?"

"You ask what I have asked myself many times, but there is naught I can recall."

"Perhaps it was some innocent remark, taken wrong, then – you must understand how we young ladies mull so carefully over everything a suitor says to us, wondering at what each statement might mean. Or perhaps there is something else entirely that is the cause," Georgiana said. "It is strange to ask someone who has been married for a longer time than I have, but I shall ask: may I give you some advice?"

"I would be glad to hear it."

"Please do not do what your brother did, and leave without making your heart known. His situation was very different, but it does not follow that the pain it caused the both of us would be any different from the pain experienced by you and Miss Bennet, if she does return your affections."

He contemplated this for some time, before saying, "You are right, of course. You might think that having put my heart forward once in my life, it would be easier this time around, but I find it is not."

"I do not see why it should become any easier," Georgiana said. "I do not envy gentlemen in this, to be the ones who must put forth an offer, and if it is an offer of the heart, to expose their affections in such an open manner."

"I appreciate your sympathy," he said. "There is also the matter of requesting a private audience, which must be known to the family, and in my instance, if there is a refusal, still being required to sit down to dinner with her and the family that evening."

"In that, at least, I may help you. Now – or later, if you wish for some time to gather your thoughts – I may fetch Mary and bring her to you. You have requested the private audience to me, and I believe my brother and sister would consider that sufficient."

"Would you? That is very good of you," he said. "And you may find her now, if it is convenient for you. My thoughts have been ordered for some time, and would have been shared already, if I thought them at all welcome."

Mary, finding herself soothed by her conversation with Elizabeth, hardly knew where to go after leaving her sister's bedchamber. She thought perhaps to go to the library, hoping that no-one else would be there, and she might have some time to herself to think. She would have done so, but she found herself detained in the hallway by Georgiana.

"Will you come with me to the conservatory?" Georgiana asked.

"I shall," said Mary, with some measure of suspicion at the strangeness of Georgiana's tone. They went thither in silence, and when they were nearly there, Mary asked: "Are you merely wishing to pass the time, or was there something particular you wished to speak to me of?"

"Neither," said Georgiana, halting at the doorway, and murmuring, "David would like to speak with you."

Georgiana held open the door, but did not follow Mary inside, and Mary trembled when she heard it click closed behind her. She knew not what this meant, but that it was most abnormal, and the conservatory was so large that she could not even see David at first, and must make her way amongst the plants before he was visible to her.

He was seated, in a fine space in the midst of the ferns that afforded a view out over Pemberley's grounds, although he rose as soon as he saw Mary approach, and thanked her for agreeing to speak with him. Mary had not agreed to this, and was about to say so, when she thought better of it. If Georgiana had asked it, she would have agreed, whatever was to come of the conversation.

"Miss Bennet, before I say what I mean to say, I wish for you to know that if you find it at all unwelcome, you may tell me to stop at any time. Given the closeness of our families, I would not wish to be indelicate about this."

Mary nodded, thinking perhaps he meant to lecture her, or at the very least to provide some manner of advice.

"I did not expect to find, within my new sister's family, a young lady whose interests so closely matched my own, a lady I thought might be willing to become a clergyman's wife, which is not the easiest of roles, compared to others you might marry into," he said. "There are duties for the parish, in addition to keeping your own house, although things are made easier because my uncle has seen to a good living for me. My income is more than a thousand pounds a year, between the tithe, the glebe land, and what I have in the funds. It is not what your elder sisters have, but I find it very comfortable, and it does have the advantage of being relatively close to them."

Mary stared at him in astonishment, for it seemed rather more like he was proposing marriage than lecturing her. Overcome with a strange quivering in her knees, she found herself forced to sit.

He sat beside her, an expression of concern on his face, and asked if she was well. She nodded tearfully, and when he asked if he should continue, she nodded again.

"I am glad you are at least open to listening to a proposal from me,

Mary, for the truth is that I love you, and it would make me incredibly happy were you to agree – "

"But I do not understand how you could love me!" exclaimed Mary. "I am not at all a good person!"

"Mary! However could you have gotten such a notion into your head? I have seen nothing but goodness in you, ever since we have been acquainted."

"It is you who put it into my head, and it is true! My deeds, perhaps, have been good during the course of our acquaintance, but my thoughts have not. I am judgmental, and unforgiving, and therefore by your own standards not at all a good person."

Having said this, she fully gave in to her tears, and found him pressing a handkerchief into her hand, as he said, "Mary, whatever I have said to make you think such a thing, I must apologise for. It was never my intention."

"You must not apologise, for it was necessary. When you spoke of your father, and how his notion of being a Christian was in thinking himself more pious than anyone else, and how judgmental he was, I for the first time recognised those characteristics in myself, and how inferior they were. I have since been endeavouring to correct myself, and ever will be."

"I will not do you the discredit of not believing your own introspection, but I also believe you do not consider all of the good deeds you have done. I think particularly of your dedication in nursing Georgiana, and in helping with your young niece."

"You see only how I have acted towards someone who has always been a true friend to me, and a baby who requires skills I was once terribly immodest about, and perhaps still am, a little," said Mary. "You have not seen my thoughts, particularly as they regard my youngest sister, Lydia."

Slowly, and painfully, Mary detailed for him her thoughts and treatment of Lydia, both before and after her sister's elopement, and spoke of how a better person might have attempted to steer Lydia toward the correct path, rather than judging her for her faults. She concluded that for these reasons, he should not love her.

"I do, though, Mary. I love you perhaps even more, now, for it is not a little thing to be willing to admit one's faults and wish to improve upon them, although I do not believe them to be as egregious as you make them out to be."

"But you must! I am going to strive every day, now, to be a good person, and I shall need you to tell me if I am not succeeding," she said. "Why are you smiling so?"

"Because you indicated we should see each other every day, or at least it was my hope that you meant this by your words. Does that mean you will marry me?"

"I will," said Mary, once again so overcome that she wept, and felt his hand grasp hers in a gesture meant to be comforting, but which only made her cry all the more. She had known it was possible to cry from happiness, but had never before experienced such emotion, and such relief.

When she had calmed a little, he said, "I would prefer to ask your father for your hand in person, but I need to return to my duties at home for at least a little while, so I think it might be best if I write to him to request his consent. I am glad we met when he was here during the summer, so I am not a complete stranger to him."

"Oh, you need not do that," said Mary. "I mean, I suppose it would be good for you to write to him as well, but he has given Mr. Darcy leave to act in his place, for such matters. I am of age, so their consent would be favourable, but not necessary."

Mary did not believe she needed to tell him that her father had done so at her mother's behest, that when she and Mr. Darcy had been preparing to depart from Longbourn, Mrs. Bennet had said: "Now Mr. Bennet, you must give Mr. Darcy your permission to consent to any proposals of marriage Mary receives, so if Mr. Stanton *does* propose to her, there need not be any delay where he could change his mind. Oh, our Mary, part of a noble family! Who would have thought of such a thing?"

"Even if their consent is unnecessary, I would not feel comfortable in marrying you without it," David said. "Let me seek out your brother now, and if I am so fortunate as to gain his consent, we might announce it to the household this evening."

"He gave his consent to his sister's marrying your brother," said Mary, smilingly. "I believe you may take your suit to him with some confidence."

The express came as they were sitting in the blue drawing-room, and it was fortunate to come during what had become Elizabeth's nightly respite from her confinement, for it was addressed to her. It was from Catherine, again, and if Elizabeth could have delayed opening it, she would have. Her husband had been waiting for her arrival in the drawing-room to make his announcement to the rest of the party, and Elizabeth hated the idea of what must surely be news of the Wickhams overshadowing Mary's betrothal. She might have done so, but the rest of the party was looking at her expectantly, and she realised the letter might instead be about Mr. Bennet's health, so she opened it and read as quickly as she could, then related to the rest of them:

"Lydia has chosen to go to America with Mr. Wickham. They hope to find passage within a fortnight, and have left for town already." She looked at Darcy after saying this, unsure of how Wickham was to get the money he had been promised if he did not return to Pemberley, but Darcy gave her a little nod, and she assumed he would arrange the matter by correspondence with one of his men of business in London.

"We may never see her again," said Jane, softly.

Elizabeth had considered this, of course, in an abstract way, but Jane's saying it aloud struck her in its finality. Lydia had been silly, and on one occasion foolish beyond measure, but still, Lydia was her sister, and it was strange to think of her being across the ocean, of never seeing her again.

"I wish them well," said Mary. "Perhaps they will find opportunities in America, and succeed there as they have not been able to do here."

It was a very strange statement for Mary to make, although she seemed sincere, and Elizabeth thought this evidence of how Mary's introspection and betrothal had changed her. There was a new serenity, and something that might even be described as kindness, about Mary, as she sat there on the sofa beside David and spoke of her sister.

Darcy wisely gave this news some time to settle, waiting until after the tea things had come out and they had all returned to their seats, before asking for their attention and announcing that Mr. Stanton and Miss Bennet had become engaged to be married. To none in the family party did this seem to be news, but the enthusiasm of all was readily expressed at the match.

There followed some discussion of where and when the wedding was to take place, and Mary indicated her wish to be married in Pemberley's chapel, once Mr. and Mrs. Bennet and Captain and Mrs. Ramsey – how odd it was to hear her say that! – had made the journey there. This was readily agreed to by Elizabeth and Darcy, and David indicated he would return to his parish until the time came.

Throughout the discussions, Elizabeth looked between her sisters: Mary, who would marry the elder brother, and was marked with most uncharacteristic – although becoming – blushes and happy smiles; and Georgiana, who had married the younger, and made her best effort at a happy countenance, but was given away by the sadness in her eyes. It had not been so very long ago that Georgiana had been the happy young lady, engaged to be married, and Elizabeth wished both for her sister's return to happiness, and that Mary should never again encounter that which made her so sad. It seemed possible she should not, however; while they had attached themselves to brothers, they had done so to two very different brothers, and Mary would have all the benefits of a settled home and husband.

CHAPTER 16

Dr. Whittling arrived the morning following, accompanied by the monthly nurse, Mrs. Hutchinson. He examined all three of his patients, pronounced them all as healthy as could be expected, then queried Sarah with a great deal of curiosity regarding how the afterbirths had passed, for he had only read of one similar case, and wished to better inform his colleagues.

The accoucheur had been disappointed, upon learning he was not to have a sojourn at Pemberley as planned, for he had been anticipating a little time away from his London practice, spent in country pursuits, and had lowered his expectations for compensation accordingly. Upon being delicately told of this, Darcy had invited him to stay as a guest, and Dr. Whittling did so for a week complete, going out shooting or riding with Charles and some of the other gentlemen of the neighbourhood every day that the weather permitted it. David Stanton participated in the first of these outings, but then departed for Wincham, an event that prompted uncharacteristic tears from his betrothed. Mrs. Hutchinson remained, following the departures of the two gentlemen, and continued to be of such assistance – particularly to Mrs. Nichols – that Elizabeth attempted to convince her to stay on for more than her month, but was told Dr. Whittling could not spare her for longer.

The Christmas baskets were prepared, and distributed amongst both the estates and the villages that supported them by Jane, Mary, and Georgiana, as Elizabeth had not yet been churched. They returned from their outings relating the blessings of all for Mrs. Darcy's safe delivery of two heirs for Pemberley, and Elizabeth found herself wishing she had been able to go with them. Although she often felt tired, for handling the majority of the twins's frequent feedings, her evening visits to the drawing-room were no longer entirely quelling her agitation over spending so much time in the same two rooms, and she intended to cease her confinement as soon as it reached a respectable length of time.

Christmas itself came with four healthy babies in the house, and a quiet dinner for their small family party, for the Bennets and Ramseys had decided to journey north after having Christmas at Longbourn, giving Mr. Bennet more time for his recovery. There was one event of some significance that Christmas evening, which occurred when they had all retired for bed. Darcy entered Elizabeth's bedchamber, somewhat nervously passing a little box from Hadley's back and forth between his hands.

"I have something else to give you," said he, "but it means admitting to a little deception on my part. When I gave you the garnets this autumn, you indicated the original set must have been simpler, for there were no extra pieces to the new set."

"Yes, now that I think on it, you never did confirm it."

"I did not, because there *was* an additional piece, and I did not want to tell you of it at the time. You were so convinced you would have a girl, you had me a bit convinced as well. I held back a few of the stones to be set into a second necklace, one that would have been simple enough for a young girl – for your daughter."

He handed her the box, and Elizabeth opened it to find exactly what he had described, and found herself overcome with emotion at the thoughtfulness of it. Darcy had always said he would be as happy over having a daughter as a son, and if their firstborn child *had* been a daughter, Elizabeth presumed the necklace would have been given to her shortly after the birth, to reaffirm his past statements, and indicate his approval and love. She could think of no sweeter gesture, than to give her something that would match her own set, and would be hers to someday bestow on a very happy young girl.

"If you are worried over the deception, you should not be," she said, kissing him thoroughly. "It was done in a most significant kindness of heart, and I love you all the more for it."

"I do not know what you will wish to do with it now," he said. "But I thought it best to give it to you. Perhaps you will wait until we do have a daughter?"

"I do not wish to tempt fate in that way. Now that we have two sons, I would very much like a daughter, but it must not be assumed we will have one, or we shall be the opposite of my parents, and have five sons."

"If we do, you know I shall teaze you mercilessly for it. But what will you do with the necklace, if you will not hold it for the possibility of a daughter?"

"I shall give it to someone very deserving," Elizabeth said.

By now, all the Christmas gifts that were to be bestowed by the Darcys upon those dependent on Pemberley had been bestowed, with the exception of the boxes for the servants. Elizabeth began her Boxing Day as she did every other day, with Sarah helping her dress, although dressing during Elizabeth's confinement generally meant changing into a new nightgown and dressing gown, save when she went down to the drawing-room.

Once Sarah had finished with her hair and asked if she needed anything else, Elizabeth took the opportunity to hand over the box she was most anticipating. Sarah opened it, glanced discretely inside, and must have seen that in addition to the expected coin, there was also a jeweller's box.

"You may see what is inside now, if you wish," said Elizabeth.

Sarah did so, and removed the necklace from the box, the little garnets glistening in the winter sunlight. "Oh ma'am, it is too much by far! I cannot accept such a thing."

"You must, for I shall not take it back. Mr. Darcy had intended it for a daughter, if I had one, but since I have had sons, and you were the one to bring them into the world, it seems most appropriate for you to have it. I know you will send most, if not all, of the money to your family – and do not think I have forgotten Green's, for we shall still go together, once I am churched – but this is something you must keep and enjoy for yourself."

"I will, then," said Sarah. "I shall wear it every Sunday, and on special occasions, and I will be ever grateful to you for it."

"Then we are perhaps closer to even, for I will be forever grateful to you for all you have done, Sarah."

CHAPTER 17

Elizabeth was churched on a Wednesday, exceedingly pleased to be leaving the house and getting into the carriage, even if it was only to go so far as Lambton's parish church. She had thought there would be little other than family, to attend the service, and was surprised to enter the church and find it entirely filled with tenants and villagers.

After the service, she and Darcy took their time to greet each, and the well wishes that had been passed along to her by her sisters at Christmas were repeated now. Elizabeth had always understood how important Pemberley was to the crowd within the church, but only now did she see what her sons meant to these people: they were stability, and the continuity of a prosperous ownership. She was glad to only realise it now, for she felt certain that if she had sensed it before her birth, she would have been more worried over never having any sons. She thought then about Longbourn, left to the unfortunate Mr. Collins, and felt badly for her father's tenants.

Her thoughts were more pleasantly turned the next day, for it was the day her sons were christened. Although both boys had grown rapidly, so that they were now nearer Bess's size at birth, Elizabeth and Darcy had decided it to be too much of a risk to take them out in January, and so this service was done privately, in Pemberley's chapel. Both boys took the very little water Mr. Clark used without squalling, which all were glad of, for Bess had shrieked for nearly the entire ceremony.

After the ceremony, the twins were taken up to the nursery, and settled in there; Mrs. Hutchinson stayed long enough to assist with this, but was then required to make her preparations to return to town. Elizabeth's dressing-room had been returned to its usual furnishings by the time Sarah changed her that evening, and with hardly a thought about it, she reverted to routine and went to sleep in the master's bedchamber, although she did quietly inform her husband that she was still too sore for marital relations, and likely to be so for some time.

Now that these events were completed, society could fully resume at Pemberley, and Darcy and Charles began speaking again of continuing the hunt season, and setting a date for the next outing. This plan was shared over dinner, and Darcy asked his sister in the gentlest of tones if she wished to participate this time, for none of them could ignore that Georgiana might only reconsider doing so because she was no longer carrying a child.

Georgiana, however, was glad he had asked, and as her head-ache had been entirely gone for some days now, agreed readily to join the hunt. It was a distraction, and something to anticipate, and she took to riding out with her brother and Charles, so as to practise her jumping. Grace, who had been hunt-bred, but thus far mostly used for hacking, took naturally to it, and Georgiana found that between riding and practising the pianoforte, she was able to forget her grief for longer periods of time. It was strange, though, to be occupied with the same pastimes she had enjoyed before marrying, and to do so at Pemberley; sometimes it seemed as though her married life with Matthew was as much a dream as the one in which she had eloped with Mr. Wickham, and then she would remember her husband, freezing up in the Baltic, and their baby, with the sharpest pang in her breast.

The Pemberley household learned from Mrs. Sinclair that they should have a new family to invite to the hunt, for Barrowmere Park had been let to the Bakers, who had taken up residence just after Christmas. The Bakers were duly called upon and invited by Darcy and Charles, who came back to Pemberley with little in the way of enthusiasm at having made the acquaintance. The reason for this became readily apparent when the Bakers returned the call.

Mr. Baker was a true nabob, who had earned a tremendous fortune in India, and had little to recommend himself other than that fortune. Mrs. Baker was an exceedingly pretty woman, of fine figure, much younger than her husband and, if it were to be judged by her conversation, terribly silly. They left after one of the more awkward quarter-hours of Elizabeth's life, and Jane admitted to her later that she feared the Bakers were the very sort of people from trade that would cause society to look down upon the likes of the Bingleys.

Still, they *were* neighbours, and must be treated as such, and if they had one praiseworthy thing about them, it was that Mr. Baker was sinking a small fortune in to returning Barrowmere Park to a liveable state. And so Mr. Baker was among the men who gathered on the morning of the hunt, and Mrs. Baker was admitted to the saloon to sit with the rest of the ladies of the neighbourhood, excepting Georgiana and those who would ride out.

Georgiana felt a touch of nervousness, but could not focus upon it. Thus far, it had been a cold winter, and this day was no exception; the chill and the presence of so many other horses made Grace even more spirited than usual, snorting in the frigid air, and requiring Georgiana to trot her around in little circles periodically to take some of the edge from her energetic manner. Despite her nerves, Georgiana was eager to be off, both to allow Grace her head, and for the warmth the greater exercise would bring.

"Now ain't that a fine piece o' horseflesh!" exclaimed Mr. Baker, who, as a very stout man, at least had the good sense to own a large, calm hunter who seemed capable of accommodating his bulk. "Ye've took on more than I'd be willing to, with yer pretty grey there, Lady Stanton."

"Thank you, Mr. Baker," was all Georgiana could think to say in response, and she was relieved Fitzwilliam rode over then, to tell her they would be setting out soon.

"I told your man he should ride back with the other grooms," Fitzwilliam said, motioning with one hand toward Murray, who sat astride one of Pemberley's hunters, for Matthew's filly, Phoebe, was far too young to be jumped. "I shall stay with you the whole time."

"You should not feel obligated to stay with me," said Georgiana, knowing he would prefer to be up at the front of the group. She noticed he was riding Kingfisher, the oldest and quietest of his hunters. "Indeed, I already fear you have chosen a slower horse than you would have otherwise."

"Nonsense," he said, patting his mount's neck with affection. "I should never be unhappy with a day out on old King. He is not so fast as he once was, I will own, but I doubt there is a finer jumper in the field."

They could speak no more, for the hounds were called up by the keeper, and they all set out, the pace sedate for now. They rode for about a mile, through the fields with their sheep and cattle, foraging for winter swedes, and halted while the master sent the hounds into a thick brushy area.

"They are casting now," Fitzwilliam said. "Let us see if they get the scent here, or if we must ride on."

The hounds spent some time snuffling around in the brush, and then, with sudden violence, they were off, crashing through the brush and dashing through the adjacent field. The horses followed as quickly as their riders could react, and Georgiana was finally able to give Grace her head and allow the mare to run. At first she worried Kingfisher might not be able to keep up, but there were few horses not feeling the crisp air, and although the old gelding might not have been so fast as he once was, he was still faster than a good deal of the pack.

Georgiana had feared there would be constant jumping, but found they began with a long, hard gallop, and only after that needed to clear a series of low hedgerows that bounded the fields they raced across. Fitzwilliam, true to his word, stayed a stride or so behind her, and was such when the field approached a much higher hedge. The difficulty with this obstacle began when Mr. Patterson's horse refused the jump, and a number of horses behind his determined they should do the same, while some of the other riders pulled their horses up in the ensuing confusion.

Georgiana, watching all of this, gripped more tightly with her legs, and Grace, a little to the left of the chaos, snorted and laid her ears back, as though concerned she too would be pulled up, and when she was not, made her way effortlessly over the hedge. Georgiana glanced back at Fitzwilliam just in time to see him clear the jump, and that he appeared every bit as exhilarated by it as she was.

From here, Georgiana felt herself and Grace at the very least equal to the field, and gave herself over to enjoyment of the long gallops and occasional jumps as they trailed the hounds. Her only cause for concern came when the dogs scrambled between the boards of a very high fence. Mr. Sinclair, up ahead of her, was already making to open a gate some distance down from the fence, and Georgiana, not wishing to attempt something of that height, made to steer Grace toward the gate.

She looked over at Fitzwilliam, and found him eyeing the fence, and then asking her, "Would you mind terribly if we had a go at it?"

"Of course not," Georgiana said, for Murray was still trailing behind her, back with the other grooms and Mr. Richardson, who felt his duties as steward required him to ride at the back of the group and make note of any damage done by the hunt, so it might be rectified later.

Fitzwilliam set Kingfisher at the fence, and although Georgiana knew her brother would not have attempted it if he was not sure the horse would make it, her breath still caught in her throat as they went over. Old King jumped it easily, and of the rest of the field, only Charles Bingley saw fit to attempt and clear the fence. With no urging at all, Grace caught Kingfisher, and they galloped on until the hounds came to a scrabbling halt, and Georgiana realised they had caught up with the fox. They had caught him entirely, it seemed, and after a first glance at the bloody spectacle that followed, Georgiana averted her eyes.

This was the only unpleasant element of the hunt, and once it was done, they could all make their way back to Pemberley at a leisurely canter, and Fitzwilliam could turn to ask her: "And how did you like your first hunt?"

"I liked it very much, excepting the end."

"Ah, I should have thought to warn you of it – I am sorry," he said, and then continued, haltingly, "It is good to see you look happy again, Georgiana."

"It is good to feel happy again, if just for a while – " she said, her voice faltering with a half-formed thought: "You do not think Matthew will be upset that I have gone hunting so soon after – after what happened, do you?"

"Absolutely not, Georgiana. You must not think that. If the same were to happen to Elizabeth – God forbid – I would know it was not her fault, and there was nothing that could be done of it, and I would hope very much for her return to happiness."

Georgiana thought that if such a thing had somehow happened to Elizabeth, it would not have been Elizabeth's fault; only Georgiana had caused such a strange situation as to lose her child in the manner she had. But she knew what Fitzwilliam would say if she protested, and so she tried to allow his words to comfort her as best they could.

They rode on in silence, until Mr. Baker came up alongside them, his horse in a muck sweat, and said: "Eh, Lady Stanton, no want of bottom on ye, I should say! I should think ye and yer pretty mare bested at least half 'o the field today."

Georgiana, shocked that he should speak to her so, managed only a nod in response, which was still more than Fitzwilliam could provide, and they rode on together, a bewildered pair watching Mr. Baker's broad back and his horse's labouring hindquarters, as he cantered on up the line in front of them. He had, at least, stayed on his horse through the course of the day, but this was all that could be said in compliment of him.

Elizabeth was at that time having her own struggles with Mrs. Baker, in Pemberley's saloon. She knew not what Mrs. Baker's background had been, but whatever it was, it had certainly not provided her with suitable manners. Elizabeth found herself reminded of her own mother, in Mrs. Baker's constant raptures over every-thing she experienced, from the height of the ceiling in the saloon, to the quality of the muslin of Jane's gown, to the pine-apples that had come out with the refreshments. There was nothing she did not love, and nothing she did not wish to imitate, and she had been forming a plan for Mr. Baker to repair the hothouse, and grow their own pine-apples there, when the hunt party made their return.

They all halted in the saloon only long enough to greet the ladies before retiring to change, and Elizabeth glanced over them to ascertain the health of those she cared most about. Darcy and Charles looked well, but it was Georgiana who most caught her eye, looking flushed from the cold and the exercise, and much better than she had been since the accident.

Georgiana did indeed come down to dinner in a happy state of tiredness, and greeted the ladies, whom she had hardly seen that day. As none of the rest of them had ridden through a complete hunt, she found herself applied to for her impressions of the event while they waited.

They waited longer than they should have, and dinner was in great danger of actually being delayed when Mrs. Baker, the last to come down, did so in a great profusion of diamonds, and a very low-cut dress. She announced her presence by exclaiming, "An' don't all you gentlemen look so much better when your britches ain't covered in mud!" to which most of the objects of her admiration looked at her with a goodly degree of mortification – excepting Mr. Baker, who laughed – and many of the ladies gasped, although a few were heard tittering in the corners of the room.

Georgiana espied Mary, who seemed particularly aghast, and went over to where she sat to engage her in some conversation, by way of distraction. She was thus when they were approached by Elizabeth, who said: "I am afraid we must let Mrs. Baker go in first to dinner. They were married less than two months ago. I hope you do not mind."

Georgiana had only cared about where she went in to dinner before she had married, when her place at the table would determine how close she was to Matthew, and yet it was only after her marriage that she had always been assured of going in first. In Paris and London, she had been a new bride, and here at Pemberley, she was the wife of a baronet, which was uncommon in their particular neighbourhood. She truly did not mind, though, and told Elizabeth so.

With this settled, she watched Elizabeth walk amongst the group, and with her usual quiet discretion, ensure they were all in order to go in. When she reached Mrs. Baker, however, and told her she was to go in first as a new bride, Mrs. Baker exclaimed, "Lord! Me go in first, in a house such as this!"

It was then that Georgiana realised she would care about going in second on this day, only because it meant she would sit near Mrs. Baker, and she gave Fitzwilliam a look of sympathy as he offered the woman his arm.

The food came out with Pemberley's usual efficiency, and it seemed Bowden's education from Mr. Parker on this portion of the footman's role had progressed far enough for Bowden to be allowed to serve here, outfitted in a silk eyepatch that matched the rest of the Pemberley livery, which he had been especially fitted for, and was like as not to become the Stantons's livery, with some token modifications so that it should not be precisely identical. Georgiana gave him a little nod, and then returned her attention to the table, horrified to see Mrs. Baker was serving herself, and Fitzwilliam was looking at his sister in puzzled desperation. She knew no more what to do than he; Elizabeth was much better at handling this sort of situation, but she was at the other end of the very long dining table.

Georgiana thought that perhaps to provide an example was the best way of going about things – and she was famished from riding, anyway – and so she gave Fitzwilliam a look, and then glanced back down at her own empty plate.

"Lady Stanton," he said, slightly more loudly than he would have otherwise, for it was clear he had caught Georgiana's meaning, "would you care for some of the beef?"

"I would, thank you," she said.

They continued at this for a few more dishes on the table, at which point Mrs. Baker finally seemed to understand what they were about. From then on, she took tremendous delight in being served by Mr. Darcy, and asked to try everything on the table within his reach. Each dish was a new discovery to be exclaimed over; that the cook they had hired on at Barrowmere *must* come over to Pemberley and get the recipes was mentioned several times.

Only when they were well into the second remove did they have anything else in the way of conversation from her, and that was to say, "So what do you *do* here in the country, aside from hunting the foxes? I'm so a-feared of boredom!"

"We do not have so many diversions as there are in town, of course, but there are quite a few families in the neighbourhood, so there is some manner of society," Fitzwilliam said.

"Lord, I hope some of 'em play cards," Mrs. Baker said. "And if not I'll start 'em on it, soon as the leaks are all fixed up in the drawing-room. You'd come to a card party, wouldn't you, Mr. Darcy? And you, Lady Stanton?"

A card party was not the sort of society either brother or sister preferred, and yet to be asked so singularly meant they must agree to attend, and could only hope the repairs to Barrowmere Park's drawing-room took a very long time to reach completion.

Dinner was followed by the usual separation of the gentlemen from the ladies, for although the men had spent the better part of the day together, they had no intention of skipping their port and brandy. The ladies, meanwhile, had passed quite enough time together already on this day, particularly where the company of *one* of the ladies was concerned. They settled into a lethargic silence in the yellow drawing-room, which was broken only when Elizabeth asked if any of the ladies would care to play some music, and Mary, after a very long pause during which there were no other volunteers, offered to do so, and was followed by Georgiana. It was during her performance that the gentlemen made their way in, and arrayed themselves across the drawing-room and music-room.

"Oh! Listen to how well Lady Stanton plays, love!" exclaimed Mrs. Baker, as she saw her husband come into the room, in a tone heard not only by Mr. Baker, but by most of the rest of the party. This drew the attention of them all to her, although even if she had not made such an exclamation, it was likely the attention of at least some of the gentlemen would have strayed towards her anyway. Mrs. Baker, like Georgiana, was wearing the very latest of the French fashions, but while Georgiana had trimmed the neckline of her dress with lace, Mrs. Baker had not, and very nearly left more exposed to the world than Elizabeth did when she was nursing her sons.

"Aye, Mrs. Baker, I begin to see Lady Stanton is one of yer accomplished females. Ye should have seen her take the high hedge, that half 'o the field refused, me mount included. Went over it like a rare plucked 'un, she did. But then yer husband is the naval captain who captured that thumpink big Frenchie, ain't 'eee?" asked Mr. Baker.

"He is; it was the Polonais, that he captured," said Georgiana, looking incredibly discomfited.

"T'ain't no lack of courage in yer family, I dare say," said Mr. Baker, descending into a fit of chuckles.

"I must purchase a fine hunter like yours, Lady Stanton, and then learn my riding," said Mrs. Baker. "Perhaps we can ride together, wi' the estates so close!"

Georgiana, to her credit, said all that was right and proper. Her brother, however, watched the entire exchange from the edge of the room, and when it was done, remained there. Elizabeth kept expecting him to make his way into the conversation, but it seemed he was on this night to stand there, silently as he had used to do, and she could not help but be disappointed in him. People such as the Bakers put a great deal of strain on her as a hostess, and she very much wished him to share the burden.

She could only speak to him of it later, after the party had left – the Bakers, as might be expected, the last among them to call for their carriage. Elizabeth had gone up to the nursery to see to the twins, and Darcy was already in bed when she made her way there. He looked exhausted, and Elizabeth thought twice about saying what she wished to say, but she was determined.

"You cannot be so unsocial with the Bakers," she said. "It will not do for you to be standing about on the edge of the room in your own house, as though it is the Meryton Assembly, just because there is a couple from trade present. You were as unsociable as you have ever been; if you wish to hold a hunt, we cannot have you acting so."

"Do you truly think I dislike them because they are from trade? Are you endeavouring to correct my poor behaviour again, as I had indicated you must do?"

"I suppose that I am, and it is clear you dislike them. No-one would have called you your usual self this evening, excepting perhaps myself, back in the earliest days of our acquaintance. I am sure the Bakers think you the proud, disagreeable man I thought you were then, and they have every right to do so."

"I dislike them – that I will not deny," said he. "But it is their manners I find abominable. I would much sooner have Mr. Smith to dinner than the two of them; his manners are much more gentlemanlike."

He referred to the tenant with the largest farm of Pemberley's holdings, a farm recently expanded with the addition of the land purchased from Barrowmere, and Elizabeth could not deny that he was right in this. Mr. Smith's manners were far superior to those of the Bakers, and given the size of his farm now, he might rightly be classed as a gentleman farmer.

"Why do you not invite Mr. Smith to dinner, then?" she challenged.

"I believe we should. Perhaps not to dinner, but certainly to tea."

"Oh, of course we should not sink so low as to have a tenant dine with us!"

He exhaled, in that manner which meant he was far more frustrated than he was letting on, and said, "No, I merely do not wish to give Smith an invitation he does not feel he is able to reciprocate. He is a bachelor, and keeps only a maid of all work; I would not want him to feel as though he must invite us to dine, once we have done so for him."

Mollified that at least if his actions had not been right, his thoughts were, Elizabeth did not respond immediately, and in the silence that followed, he asked:

"Did you truly believe I had reverted to my former pride?"

"No, I suppose I did not. But I think you are in great danger of those who do not know you so well believing you are proud, and that you required myself and others to share the burden of easing things along in the drawing-room. I know you are discomfited by such behaviour – I do not like it, either – but I am going to need for you to help me manage them, in the future."

He was most affected by this argument; his frustration dissipated entirely, and was replaced by remorse: "I am sorry, Elizabeth. You are better at it than I, but you are correct that it is a burden to be shared, and I promise to take my share of it, when next they are here."

Elizabeth, entirely placated by this, made her way closer to him, laid her hand on his chest, and thanked him.

"Must we invite them, however?" he asked. "I cannot say any of our other neighbours had any enjoyment of their company."

"We need not invite them any more than we did the Camberts," Elizabeth said. "But we should invite them to our larger parties, so long as they continue to occupy that house."

"May we all hope Mrs. Baker grows bored of the country, then, and desires their return to town."

"If you think it possible for her to be bored by the country, then we must endeavour to learn what bores her, and make our invitations for it," said Elizabeth, with a conspiratorial smile, before she blew out the candle on her side of the bed.

CHAPTER 18

With the discord regarding the Bakers settled between Mr. and Mrs. Darcy, an agreement was made between them to alter the hunting entertainments, so the next hunt would be held with only the usual refreshments before and after, given out by the footmen on the lawn, and no ladies's waiting party. The ladies might wait in their own sitting-rooms, although an exception was to be quietly made for Mrs. Sinclair.

The hunt would instead be preceded by a dinner a few days beforehand, thus ensuring Pemberley maintained an acceptable level of society for both the ladies and gentlemen of the neighbourhood, but the ladies were spared an entire day in the saloon with Mrs. Baker. The invitations for both events were delivered without remark from any of the parties invited, who – excepting one couple – must have had at least a little understanding of what had prompted the change.

One additional invitation was delivered for the dinner, and this was that Mr. Smith should come to tea following. This invitation was so graciously accepted that Elizabeth immediately began contemplating a way to invite Mr. Smith to a future dinner, in some manner that would not make him feel compelled to reciprocate.

Only after all of the invitations had been given and accepted did Pemberley receive a note from the Earl of Anglesey, proposing in a most delicate fashion that he stop for a night or two at the house on his return to London for the new session of Parliament. He had been as concerned as any in the family of his niece's accident, and wished to see how she got on, and wished equally to become better acquainted with the young lady who would become his niece soon enough.

This was cause for hand-wringing amongst several in the household. Elizabeth and Darcy were concerned that the very evening he proposed arriving was that of the dinner, which was too far along to be put off for another day. Ordinarily, it would have been a fine thing for the neighbourhood, for Pemberley to host an earl to dinner, particularly a different one from the Earl of Brandon, who had been a regular visitor since his sister had married the previous Mr. Darcy. The thought of Lord Anglesey sitting down at the same dinner table as the Bakers, however, made Elizabeth's stomach sink every time she thought of it, and she was certain it did the same for her husband.

Mary worried not about the Bakers, but of Lord Anglesey's interest in becoming better acquainted with her. She had seen the earl on numerous occasions before this one, but it had never been under the expectation that she was to marry into the family the earl undoubtedly headed. Many attempts were made by Georgiana to soothe her concern, but it was only the response back to her frantic letter, asking if David might come out for a short visit at the same time as his uncle, that brought her anything resembling a return to the tranquillity a newly engaged lady should feel. David Stanton would likely have made the journey without such fervent urging, for to see both his betrothed and his uncle for an evening or two, without missing another Sunday service, could hardly be expected *not* to draw him from Wincham.

Before the dinner, there was one more piece of intelligence that should be related, of which only Georgiana was a party to. She had been passing the morning in her private sitting-room, practising idly on the pianoforte there. It felt a selfish occupation, to do so without Bess, and of course Georgiana would take her shift with the child later in the day, on the new square that had been installed in the nursery. This instrument reminded her of Matthew, though, and she thought of him fondly and sadly as she played, and wondered how soon he might return. During a break between songs, she had a letter delivered to her, from Edward, and she remained there on the bench as she read:

"My dear cousin,

"It was such a terrible shock to hear from Fitzwilliam of your accident. I believe there is little I can say that will be of consolation after such a loss, but I hope that you know I grieve for you, and pray you shall make a full recovery. For someone so young and healthy as you, other children will surely follow. I will admit it is a strange thought, to think of the girl I was once guardian to as a mother herself, but I believe you will make an excellent mother, and long to see you in such a role."

Here, Georgiana was required to leave off reading for a little while, and dab at her eyes with her handkerchief before she read the remainder of Edward's kind words regarding her situation, and then found the letter continued on:

"I would have written to you with my condolences regardless, but I must admit there is something else I need to impart. I should not tell you of this; I ought to make it my own private secret, not to be shared with any other except the one who knows it already, but I find I cannot bear that no one else in my family knows, and I feel assured of your discretion, and secrecy.

"I am in love with Marguerite Durand. Now you do not know me so well in matters of love as your brother does, so I will tell you that if I was to write to him of this, he would say it is not the first time I have said I was in love, and he would be correct. I have thought myself in love before, but now that I know the true thing, I see all other attachments I have desired before as trifling, and I have the compleatest understanding of the depth of my heart.

"What is most remarkable in the matter, however, and what I have not yet told you of, is that Marguerite returns my love. Who could ever have thought that such an exquisite creature as her would fall in love with a one-armed soldier, who was until recently an enemy of her country? I did not, certainly, or I would have been much more careful when I called upon her.

"You will be thinking, now, of how Marguerite was in mourning during the time in which we fell in love, and is still. I hope you will not judge her for it – she was fond of Captain Durand, and I daresay would have attempted to make a good marriage with him if he lived. But they were married three and a half years, and during that time, she had hardly four months together with him. I do not say there cannot be a deep and lasting love which forms out of a marriage where the husband is engaged in such a career – I need look no further than you and Matthew for that. I say only that this was not such a marriage."

Georgiana stopped to dab at her eyes again with her handkerchief, and vow fiercely that she and Matthew would never have but four months in three and a half years together. She then continued to read:

"So there you have it. I am in love with Marguerite, and she with me, and we have passed that delicate point where each admitted it to the other. That day was the one which ended one sort of heartache, and began troubles of a new kind. I cannot help but wish I had come from lower connexions. Oh, if I were a colonel of lesser birth, who had worked his way up through the ranks, rather than purchasing in! I would have proposed marriage and we would pass the time until her mourning completes in a secret engagement, with the promise of every happiness before us.

"However, I am not, and I promise you there is no secret engagement, nor could there be, for as you know, I am half-promised to Anne. Even if I was not, it is a match that could not be favoured by my parents. Marguerite is of good family, it is true, but although her land looks to be worth more like eight thousand of our pounds, rather than six, neither is a sum the son of an earl could be seen to live on. Fifty thousand pounds is the sum my parents would desire, and anything less than twenty would be inexcusable.

"Marguerite understands all of this, excellent woman that she is, and you must give her all the credit in what attachment we have, for in my wilder moments, when I have attempted to convince her into an elopement, it has been Marguerite who has reasoned with me that it must not be done, and that a match between us can never be.

"Were I stronger, I would do what I suspect you will recommend, which is to sever the acquaintance. But I am not, and cannot, and so I do what I can for her now, and know that whether I marry Anne or some other heiress, Marguerite will always hold my heart. I will not say that it has never crossed my mind to make her my mistress when I do marry, for I know Anne at least would accept it. Yet I love Marguerite too much to see her put into such a position, and so eventually will come the day when I must leave Paris, and take my last glimpse of my beloved Marguerite.

"I am sorry for placing such a burden upon you, but I hope you will understand the need to share such a matter with someone of your kind nature, for I believe you will be sympathetic to my plight. I hope you continue to improve and recover from what must have been a very difficult loss. You continue to be in the thoughts of –

"Your most affectionate cousin,

"EDWARD"

Georgiana spent a good hour following the reading of this letter conjecturing as to how Edward and Madame Durand had come to fall in love, and thinking guiltily of how she and her husband had been the persons who had set in motion this accidental, doomed courtship.

They must have spent more time in each other's company than they should have, this much was certain. Edward had shown himself to be intimately involved in Madame Durand's affairs, and protective of her, and in order to do so, must have called on her frequently. Madame Durand was a lonely widow, and Edward, pleased with the company of a beautiful woman, must have enjoyed the calls.

"He must not have thought himself at any risk, because of his arm," Georgiana murmured to herself. Poor Edward had indicated to her and Matthew that he thought Madame Durand would have no interest in him because of it, and being wrong in this conjecture, had left his heart more open than it should have been. Georgiana knew not whether to be happy for him, to be proven so wrong in such an assumption, or sad, because in being proved wrong, he had left not only himself but also Madame Durand open to heartbreak. She suspected the affections Edward confessed in his letter had taken both of them by surprise, that they had fallen in love before realising it.

"Poor Edward!" she exclaimed, and felt a sympathetic heartache for her cousin. Of all she and Matthew had suffered, of late, and were not even able to discuss together, at least they *were* married. Things had not been as they were in her dream; there had never been any obstacle to their attachment, aside from a fear on the part of both of them to confess to their affections. Edward and Marguerite had managed what seemed to Georgiana to be the difficult part, and yet they would get no relief from it – rather the opposite. These thoughts burned in her mind, even when she went down to be in company, although she kept Edward's confidence, and would not share them.

CHAPTER 19

Lord Anglesey, upon receiving notice that his intended day of staying over at Pemberley was also one on which a dinner had been planned, although he was of course still welcome, adjusted his time of arrival so that it was early in the morning when his carriage pulled into the drive. To Mary's chagrin, he arrived before his nephew, and she found herself standing with quivering knees beside Georgiana, staring at the arms on a very fine post-chaise.

At least Mary was not the initial object of his attention, for after he had descended the carriage and made his bows to the master and mistress of the house, he focused first on Georgiana. He took up her hands, looked carefully at her head – although Hughes had been taking care to style her hair in a way that did not allow the area that had been shaved to be seen – and asked how she did. Mary did not at all begrudge this initial lack of attention towards her; she thought it proper that he ask after Georgiana's health first, and preferred a little time in his company to settle her nerves before being required to converse.

He did turn toward Mary, eventually, and made a very fine bow before saying, "Miss Bennet, it will be a pleasure to welcome you into my family."

"Thank you, sir," Mary croaked.

With two such family connections, it might be wondered whom he took in, but the earl did not choose to make a choice, and offered an arm each to Georgiana and Mary, and they went into the house and then the saloon thus. There, Mary found that although he asked more questions of her in conversation, he was no less amiable to her than he had been before, and by the time her betrothed arrived, she was telling Lord Anglesey of her efforts with the local poor, and had forgotten her nerves entirely.

Elizabeth was possessed of a far different sort of nervousness, which peaked in that moment when the guests began to arrive for the dinner party, and the Bakers, as might be expected, came in first. Lord Anglesey was not the sort of gentleman to decline any acquaintance that might be met with at a dinner party; anyone might be useful to him politically, and anyone of high enough station to be invited to dine by the Darcys could expect an introduction to be requested.

So it was for the Bakers, and Elizabeth and Darcy worked according to a plan they had set out early that morning, whereby Elizabeth welcomed the couple and engaged them in an intense few minutes of conversation, so Darcy could go stand with Lord Anglesey in anticipation of the introduction being requested. It was their hope that this would prevent the Bakers from attempting to introduce themselves, and the plan was successful, with the introduction made as it should be. Thankfully, Mrs. Baker seemed cowed by Lord Anglesey's title, and said, softly – for her, anyway – that she was pleased to meet him. Mr. Baker, however, surprised them all by saying, "Pleased to meet you, milord. I had the pleasure 'o dining with yer brother, The Hon-rable Harold Stanton, once, in Bombay."

Elizabeth had always known there was a third brother, in Lord Anglesey's generation of the family, but could not ever recall him being mentioned, and had generally assumed he was dead because of this. Now that she knew he was not, she wondered if he had been cut from the family, and should not be spoken of. She looked to Georgiana for some clue as to whether this was the case, but Georgiana seemed as puzzled as her, and Elizabeth was greatly relieved when Lord Anglesey said:

"Indeed? I hope he looked well. I myself have not seen him these five and thirty years, but he sounded so in his last letter."

"Oh, well, t'was three years past, I seen him," said Mr. Baker. "But 'eee did look well, then."

"Well, I am glad of it. I have a great curiosity on how dinners are done, in India, which perhaps you may satisfy me on. Are they very much like dinners here?"

Elizabeth shared a little glance with Darcy, which indicated his thinking was much the same as hers – that Mr. Baker was hardly the best judge of whether dinners in India were the same as those given by polite society in England. But then, she thought, perhaps Mr. Baker's manners had been perfectly acceptable in that outpost, and Lord Anglesey's mysterious other brother might in fact be in possession of manners similar to those of Mr. Baker.

Some of the mystery was removed from The Honourable Harold Stanton shortly before they went in, when Lord Anglesey sought out Elizabeth and Georgiana when they happened to be standing near each other, and said: "You both seemed surprised, at Mr. Baker's mention of Harold. I assure you there is nothing unsavoury in the connexion. He went to India to make his fortune, made his fortune, and chose to stay. If he is rarely spoken of in our family, it is merely because he is oft-forgotten. He and I exchange letters a few times a year, and that is generally the extent to which I hear of him. I believe it is the same for the rest of the family."

Elizabeth could not help but wonder at the family that had produced a generally amiable but highly political earl, a nabob who preferred India to England, and a fiercely religious and generally disagreeable clergyman. As most of her guests were milling in the drawing-room, however, she had little time to dwell on such thoughts, although at least with the earl as the only guest new to some of the party, she had no difficulties in ensuring they understood the order in which to go in to dinner.

Dinner passed without any egregious lapses in manners, at least so far as Elizabeth could see, and every dish coming up from the kitchen in perfect order. The gentlemen were left to their port and brandy, Darcy giving Elizabeth just the slightest nod of understanding that he must carry this portion of the evening, as regarded their most notable guest. The ladies regained the drawing-room, and here Mrs. Baker also regained some of her usual voice, freed from the constraining presence of the earl. Elizabeth was relieved when Mrs. Baker excused herself to utilise the "cab-net day-sanze" in a softer tone, although generally the ladies who had already once been directed to these facilities behind the house simply slipped away and went there as they needed to.

The gentlemen made their return shortly after this, and as they filed in, Elizabeth thought it odd that Darcy did not follow. Five minutes passed, during which Lord Anglesey asked if any of the young ladies had interest in exhibiting on the pianoforte, and Mary, with uncharacteristic shyness, was encouraged to be first by Georgiana.

With the focus of most in the music-room and drawing-room on Mary's playing, Elizabeth took the opportunity to see where her husband had gone to, heard from Mr. Parker that Mr. Darcy had offered to fetch Mr. Patterson a particular book the gentleman had been interested in from the library, and made her way to that space.

She arrived in time to see her husband, with a look of furious indignation upon his face, marching Mrs. Baker through the doorway, with his arm fully outstretched to his hand upon that lady's shoulder. Elizabeth took in further that which she could see in the dim light of the hallway: Mrs. Baker's heaving, overexposed bosom, and the uneven loops of her husband's partially undone cravat. Mrs. Baker gave Elizabeth one long, frightened glance, and then fled past her down the hallway.

Elizabeth made her way to her husband, found her arm taken up by him, and herself ushered rapidly through the library door.

"Darcy, what – "

"*That woman* tried to seduce me!"

Elizabeth felt herself torn between indignation equal to his, towards the woman who had apparently attempted to initiate an affair with her husband, and amusement, at how angry he was over what a great many men would have welcomed, from a woman looking as Mrs. Baker did. In the end, she gave in to both, and burst out laughing, then laid her hands on his cheeks and said, "Oh, my love, whatever happened in here?"

"I came to fetch a book for Patterson, and heard someone else had entered. I saw that it was her, and attempted to direct her toward a more appropriate part of the house, but she would have none of it. She behaved in the strangest manner, and spoke of how fat her husband was, and how you must not yet have made your return to all of your wifely duties, after having the twins, and how it seemed we might be *useful* to each other, and then – "

"Then what?"

"Then she came upon me and attempted to kiss me, and to loosen my cravat, at which you can see that she succeeded."

"I see you were mostly successful at deterring her."

"If I had not been so shocked, I might have been more so," he said. "Now I suppose I must summon someone here, and they may then summon Mason, to tie my cravat again. I can hardly return to the drawing-room as I am."

"It will be at least another quarter-hour, before all of that is done," said Elizabeth. "It is an inexcusable length of absence from your own dinner party, after you have already been gone for so long. People will talk, and I only hope they do not connect your absence with that of Mrs. Baker. Can you not tie it again yourself?"

"I can, but it will not be the same knot Mason does. Any refined gentleman in the drawing-room will note it, which generally means Mr. Baker shall be the last to know his wife attempted to cuckold him."

"So I must explain your absence, then, and you had better ring the bell, for the sooner someone answers it, the sooner they may summon Mason here."

"There is an alternative," said he. "We might give them reason to connect my absence with your own, and then I may tie my own cravat and return shortly after you."

Elizabeth immediately comprehended what he said, found it to be the best course of action, and even raised her hands to her own head to attempt to muss her hair a little, so it might be believed in the drawing-room that the Darcys had partaken of a little romantic sojourn, rather than the true series of events that had occurred.

To her surprise, she found herself pushed back against a bookshelf and kissed very thoroughly by Darcy, who threaded his own fingers up through her hair, loosening her curls. When they had parted, she gave him a questioning – although utterly pleased – look, and he said: "If the drawing-room is to believe I had a romantic liaison with my wife, I would rather I actually had a romantic liaison with my wife."

"I suppose it is a reasonable sacrifice to make, in support of the truth," Elizabeth said, with an arch look. "I had better get back. Do not forget Patterson's book."

In the drawing-room, most of the guests were still seated near the entrance to the music-room, and a few more had made their way into that space entirely. Jane appeared to be completing the setup of a card-table, at which was seated Mrs. Baker, in a more demure attitude than usually became her.

Into this scene walked Elizabeth, with a terribly hot face, murmuring about having to attend to something and imagining that everyone in the room not only saw her entrance, but judged her for it. Mrs. Baker did venture to look up, and Elizabeth fixed on her as stony a glare as she could muster, but felt it was somehow lacking. The woman had attempted an affair with her husband, but was such a foolish woman, and had gone about it in such a foolish way, that Elizabeth felt more pity towards her, than anger. Perhaps if she had any cause, any reason, to be jealous of Mrs. Baker, she would have felt very differently about the matter, but whenever Elizabeth attempted to conjure more ire, she thought of the look upon Darcy's face, and how he had pushed Mrs. Baker out of the library at arm's length, and was more inclined to giggle than seek vengeance.

Darcy made his return a few minutes following her, and although Elizabeth had thought most of the drawing-room watched her return, it was difficult for any of them to miss that of Mr. Darcy, for Mr. Patterson said, "There you are, poor fellow! If I had known it should take so long, I would not have asked."

"It is nothing," Darcy said, handing over the book and looking deeply uncomfortable. "The book was misfiled, so it took longer than I expected. I apologise for my absence."

Elizabeth glanced over the party, to see how they reacted to this statement, and his simpler cravat knot, but could come to no determination on what they thought. The earl, at least, could be seen in the music-room, conversing occasionally with Georgiana and David as they all listened to Mary play, so at least he had been spared most of this little drama, although Elizabeth thought it unlikely that he would fail to notice her husband's cravat.

Shortly after Darcy returned, Mr. Smith and several others from Lambton arrived for tea, the former standing most awkwardly at the entrance to the drawing-room. Those from the village were known to all except the earl, as was generally the case for Mr. Smith. Elizabeth and Darcy made introductions as were necessary, and once this disruption was complete, Mary asked Georgiana to take her turn at the pianoforte, and was obliged for two songs.

When she had finished, a few of the other ladies exhibited, and then the crowd from the music-room generally made their way back into the drawing-room. Another card-table was made up, and Elizabeth noticed both Darcy and Lord Anglesey making every effort to mix into the conversations comprising the rest of the room. Darcy had planted himself very firmly beside Mr. Baker, while the earl moved from conversation to conversation, finding his presence often had a dampening effect in a way that it likely did not in the London drawing-rooms and clubs he frequented, when he was among his equals.

When Elizabeth returned to the room after a brief conversation with Mr. Parker about the readiness of the remaining refreshments, she was surprised to find Lord Anglesey and Mr. Smith talking freely, and, out of curiosity, moved within earshot. They were speaking of what Smith knew best: the husbandry of livestock, winter wheat versus spring wheat, and how Smith had found luck with those crops not typically suited for Derbyshire's climate – and yet Elizabeth found herself incredibly pleased that the earl was so willing to speak with Mr. Smith. They conversed for a full half-hour, during which time the conversation was noted by most in the room, and Mr. Smith's elevated position in the neighbourhood was firmly established, as an acquaintance of the Earl of Anglesey.

When the Bakers showed signs of lingering to the very end of the party again, Elizabeth did finally manage some goodly level of frustration, if not anger, and went over to where Mrs. Baker was seated, murmuring coldly, "Do you not think you are overdue to call your carriage?"

Mrs. Baker had consumed far more ratafia than tea, since both beverages had come out, but was not so drunk nor so foolish as to mistake Elizabeth's meaning, and for once managed to tell her husband that she was tired and wished to leave in a reasonable voice, or at least a reasonable voice for her.

They thus had no guests who lingered for an abnormally long time, for Lord Anglesey retired to the state rooms when those who might have stayed another half-hour remained, signalling as clear an end to the party as might be desired. Elizabeth was therefore able to go up to the nursery and see to her sons at a reasonable hour, without having to contrive another reason to slip away. She felt very content, sitting there with James and George behind the dressing screen, after what had generally seemed a successful dinner party, although she could not entirely ignore the little nagging thoughts at the back of her mind, about what had happened with Mrs. Baker, and what the rest of the party might have noticed.

These thoughts she could not discuss until Darcy had seen the last of the guests out, come to the nursery to see his sons, and met her again in his bedchamber.

"And how much do you believe we scandalised the neighbourhood tonight?" she asked.

"Not by much, as it appears thus far, although we shall see what manner of gossip comes trickling back to us in the next few days," he said. "If they believe it was our actions which led to the state of my dress, there can be little that has not already been attributed to us."

"What do you mean by that?"

"Elizabeth, you had both of our sons in my bedchamber, which was known to most of the servants in the house, and if it was known to most of the servants, and we did not ask them for any discretion on the matter, it must also be known to the servants of the rest of the neighbourhood, and thus their masters."

The thought of this, which was very likely true, took a little time to absorb, and Elizabeth was silent for a while as she thought on it, saying, finally, "I suppose I should note I am glad you have so little interest in a seduction."

"I believe you already noted that when you laughed at me."

"If you had seen the look on your face, you would have laughed as well, I assure you," Elizabeth said. "She is a beautiful woman – many men would have been eager to commence an affair with her."

"Well, then I suppose if this event did amuse you, and assure you of my fidelity, perhaps it had some benefit."

"I do not think I required such assurance; you are capable of many things, Darcy, but a seduction is not one of them."

"I am quite capable of a seduction," said he, defensively. "Has it been so long that you do not remember our times in the secret room, off the library?"

"Of course I remember them. Perhaps I must amend my statement. You are capable of a seduction where you have every assurance of its success, but not when there is any doubt. Fortunately for myself, this leaves your wife as the only possible object of your seductions."

"Then I assure you, madam, when you are ready again, I shall show you such a seduction you will never forget it."

Elizabeth sighed, and said, "That is one point on which Mrs. Baker was unfortunately accurate. I am sorry, but I am still a little sore, and I am not sure when the soreness will finally leave me."

"That is not something you need apologise for, Elizabeth – you bore two babies. We will begin again whenever you are ready."

"Thank you, my love," she said. "Perhaps I shall let you know by seducing you."

"I welcome it, so long as you do not take any lessons from Mrs. Baker."

"You may be assured I will not."

"We are going to have to cut them," Darcy said. "I was willing to overlook their manners so long as they let that house, but this is inexcusable."

"If we cut them, they will find very little society in this neighbourhood, and people may ask why. Can we truly take such a step?"

"They have given any number of reasons why we should not invite them back, beyond that more private event. I will not have that woman in my home again, after she attempted to convince me to break my vows to *you.*"

He said it in a way that could not help but bring a certain flattered tingling over Elizabeth's person, and she kissed him, softly.

"I enjoy it when you defend my honour," she said, "and I will say this for Mrs. Baker – at least this one time she knowingly went after something of the highest quality. Or someone, I suppose I should say."

"Yes, but she should have known this someone belongs completely and entirely to you."

CHAPTER 20

To determine to cut an acquaintance is one thing, to actually go about doing it is quite another. Mr. Baker had been invited to the hunt, an invitation that could not be rescinded without a greater degree of awkwardness than the Darcys wished to undertake, and given he had been innocent in the matter, they agreed to maintain it. The hunt, therefore, took place with Mr. Baker as part of the field, and this was intended to be the last they saw of either Baker.

The Bakers were to be left off of the invitations for every future event at Pemberley, but this was not the difficult action. That came when Mr. and Mrs. Baker came to call the day following the hunt, and must be told that no-one in the family was at home to receive them. They called again the day following, and this time could be overheard in the entrance-hall, for Elizabeth and her sisters were sitting together in the saloon.

When they left, Jane asked quietly why they had been turned away, for while she did not favour their company either, she did not see why this alone should require them to be shunned. Elizabeth gave them the briefest of explanations, of what had happened the night of the dinner, and good-hearted Jane, who before might have risen to their defence, was perhaps the most indignant of all.

They were a silent sewing party, after this ruffling of spirits, all of them having been marshalled by Mary into various projects from the poor basket. They went up to change for dinner at the usual hour, and Elizabeth was surprised to find Mrs. Reynolds there to help her change, instead of Sarah.

"Is Miss Kelly unwell?" she asked.

"'Tis her half-day off," Mrs. Reynolds said. "John took her and a few others into Lambton."

"She just went there three days ago, to purchase stockings for me," Elizabeth said, and then recollected herself. "Of course, that was for her work, and if she wishes to pass her half-day there, she should do so. I suppose there are not so many diversions for her time off here as she had in London, so Lambton will have to do."

"Indeed, ma'am," said Mrs. Reynolds, "although of late she has mostly used her free time for practising the pianoforte on the instrument in the servants's hall. She has been very diligent about it, and the staff rather likes her little concerts."

"I imagine there are few things, if any, that Miss Kelly is not diligent about. Perhaps she desired to get out; I know if I could have borne staying indoors to practise more often, I would have been a much better player than I am."

The Bakers returned again the day following, which Elizabeth thought must have been at Mr. Baker's behest – surely Mrs. Baker knew why they were not being received. When their carriage could be heard leaving the drive, Georgiana's burly footman came in with the day's post, making a rather good bow and shaking his head to his mistress: there was nothing from Captain Stanton in the post, then.

The only letter of interest to the whole party was from Lady Harrison, and indicated a triumph of decorating had taken place at Hilcote, and she was expecting Sir Sedgewick's son and heir.

"I only hope there is still something for him to be heir to, when Caroline finishes the decorating," said Jane. "She will surely feel the need to update the nursery, as well, before the child is born."

Elizabeth also thought it rather presumptuous of Caroline to assume her child would be a son, although she would not say anything on such a topic, not with Jane and Georgiana present.

Mr. Parker came in, then, and asked Elizabeth if she would join her husband in his study. It was a strange summons, and after they had left the saloon and could no longer be overheard by the others, he informed her that an express had come from the Earl of Brandon, and it had been sealed in black. Elizabeth's heart sank at this news, and she strode through the house in a terror over who had caused such a letter. She found Darcy behind his desk, looking deeply troubled, and sat across from him.

"Mr. Parker said you had an express from Lord Brandon, sealed in black."

"I hardly know how to give this news: our cousin Alice has died, in childbirth," he said. "The child was a boy, but was not born live. She took a fever, following the birth, lingered for three days, and then passed."

"My God," Elizabeth said, and she had no speech after that, in the shock of learning her young cousin was dead, and the painful reminder of the risk she herself had faced. She remembered her own fear from that day, and thought Alice must have felt the same. And Alice would not even have possessed the consolation Elizabeth had, of knowing her child had lived, and was well; Elizabeth thought her poor cousin's final days must have been fraught with heartache and fear, and wept for it.

Darcy looked very nearly ill, and Elizabeth knew his thoughts must have been similar to her own; when she had recovered a little, she rose and went to him. He rose as well, and they stood there for a very long time, in the tightest of embraces, Elizabeth softly crying.

Finally, he murmured, simply, "She is gone, just like that, and she was not even five and twenty."

Elizabeth's summons to her brother's study Georgiana found very strange, and it was clear in looking at Jane and Mary that they found it equally so. Elizabeth was gone for a very long time, and when she returned to the drawing-room, it was with Fitzwilliam and Charles, and it appeared Elizabeth had been crying.

Fitzwilliam did not need to announce that he had something terrible to share; it was clear to them all. Once Elizabeth and Charles had seated themselves, he said, "I have had tragic news from Lord Brandon. Lady Fitzwilliam has died, of childbed fever; her child was a boy, but also did not survive. She had her birth in London, but they are taking her to Stradbroke, to be buried."

The news was received with shock and sadness by them all, but aside from her brother, Georgiana had been closest to the Fitzwilliams, and was most overcome by tears. Alice had always been so kind to her younger cousin, had always possessed such elegant manners, and such beauty, and it seemed impossible that she could be gone from the world. Poor Andrew, to have to face the loss of his wife, who had been that impossible achievement for a man of his station – a noble love match, with a fine dowry.

And poor Lady Ellen! Her aunt had lost her only surviving daughter at four years of age, and while a daughter-in-law could not have entirely filled that void, she and Alice had grown very close. Georgiana thought of her poor aunt, grieving without the comfort of any female relations – the companionship she had known for so many years suddenly taken from her.

Georgiana began forming a resolve to go to her aunt, so long as Lady Ellen wished for the company. It was a long journey, but in truth it was a little painful for her to remain at Pemberley, and see the young boys and Bess every day, when they could not help but remind her of what she had lost. She had been living without her husband for so long, she had a lingering feeling that she must ask for permission to go, that someone must accompany her, but she recalled she did not need these things: she was married and had her own carriage, and might go as soon as a few dresses could be dyed.

She announced her intention to the group, and found them very supportive of the idea of going to comfort her aunt. Hughes was summoned to begin on the dresses, and Georgiana wrote a note to her aunt, to be enclosed with her brother's reply to the express.

Only after all of this, and privately, did Fitzwilliam share his concerns with her, over her travelling all that way by herself. Georgiana thought he would have accompanied her if she asked, but she did not ask; his place was here at Pemberley, with his wife and sons. Instead she reminded him of Bowden, who was intimidating enough without the brace of pistols he carried while travelling, and eventually was able to assuage his concerns.

Her aunt replied with a tremulously written express, indicating she would be very grateful for the company of her niece. Following this, Murray was informed he should harness his mistress's bays to make up the first stage, and a trunk containing several dresses dyed black and all those Georgiana owned in lavender and grey strapped on to the landau, so Lady Stanton could make the journey to Stradbroke Castle.

CHAPTER 21

The arrival of the Bennets and Ramseys came shortly after Georgiana's departure. That Mr. and Mrs. Darcy were dressed in mourning to greet the carriage, and a light snow was falling, did little to dampen the spirits of Mrs. Bennet, who, as soon as she had been helped down by Captain Ramsey, exclaimed: "Oh, Lizzy, an heir and a spare, all in one fell swoop! And Mary, engaged! I should never have thought I would marry you all off – now who is to nurse me in my old age?"

Elizabeth, standing there under an umbrella held by one of the footmen, could do little other than sigh over her mother's statements before she was distracted by the descent of her father from the carriage, which showed Mr. Bennet in as much need of Captain Ramsey's assistance in getting down as Mrs. Bennet had been, perhaps more. It was clear he had not yet recovered fully from his illness, and Elizabeth grew teary-eyed at the thought that for the first time, her father truly looked old.

She embraced him tenderly, and heard him murmur as she did so, "That was a very fine letter you wrote to me, Lizzy, and you must know I return all of the sentiments within."

Elizabeth sniffled a little, accepted Catherine's condolences on the death of her cousin, and then led them all inside to the saloon. Here, all of the children were brought down, and Mrs. Bennet had the joy of meeting her grandson, the namesake of her husband, and the heir to Pemberley, and would not give the boy up for a full hour. Elizabeth had given George over to her father for a little while, and then was given him back – Mr. Bennet was pleased to have grandchildren, but not the sort to wish to hold them for an extended period of time – and held her son feeling sympathetic to him, that even his own grandmother exhibited so much preference for the heir.

Mrs. Bennet did take up George, eventually, and then Bess, who had spent much time being held by her grandmother when she was first born, but was now relegated to third-favourite. Rather than accept this, Bess erupted into a crying jag like she had used to do, and required a full half-hour of Mary's playing before she would stop. When Mary came back into the saloon, Mrs. Bennet turned her focus to her middle daughter's upcoming nuptials, now required to be delayed for at least a month, while Pemberley was in mourning.

"Married in a private chapel! Oh, it is just the thing, so long as you do not do it as Catherine did. She very nearly sent me to my grave before Mr. Bennet, showing up as she did with no chaperone, and then announcing she had no need of one, because she was Mrs. Ramsey. What a shock to my nerves! Now, we must go see this chapel, and then Lizzy, we will discuss the flowers. Oh, you should have seen Lady Lucas's face when I told her I was to lose my last daughter, and she was to be married in the *private chapel at Pemberley*. And to one of the *Cheshire Stantons*! And surely the Earl of Anglesey is to be there, for after all, he shall be *her uncle*."

Here, Mrs. Bennet was required to be informed that Lord Anglesey was unlikely to stir from London, now that Parliament was in session, but that he had stayed two nights at Pemberley, so as to become better acquainted with his future niece. This was deemed suitable, by Mrs. Bennet, to retain her superior status over Lady Lucas when it came to daughters, and Elizabeth was fairly certain that when it was told to Lady Lucas, the story would be that Parliament absolutely could not spare Lord Anglesey, even for such a favoured niece.

Catherine and Andrew Ramsey looked on at all of this with amused expressions on their faces, and Elizabeth was glad they could do so, after staying at Longbourn for so long. Indeed, Catherine seemed quite happily married, and spent a little time sitting privately with Elizabeth before dinner, confirming that she was as happy as she looked. After being told her ball must also be delayed by the mourning period, which she took well, she moved on to the event of greatest curiosity for Elizabeth – what had happened after Mr. Wickham made his appearance at Longbourn.

"Mama was very nearly ready to throw him out!" said Catherine. "I think she was even angrier at him than Lydia was. But Lydia asked her to at least let him stay the night, so they could speak, and then they went to her room and had the most furious row I have ever heard! Lyddie was so angry at him, but he did his fair share of the shouting as well. By the time they came down to breakfast the next morning, though, they were reconciled."

"I hope they stay so," said Elizabeth. "I hate the thought of her being abandoned so far from home."

"Do you truly think he would do such a thing?"

"I pray he does not, but I believe him capable of it."

"I was so wild to go to Brighton, do you remember?" asked Catherine, and when Elizabeth had nodded in response, she said, "I think back now and wonder if I would have done something like Lydia did. I thought it was so grand, that she was made love to by Mr. Wickham. I wish now that I had written to discourage her."

"You did not know enough of the world to do so, nor did she."

"You are very right about that, Elizabeth. I wish we had not come out into society so early as we did," said Catherine. "I know how badly I wished to, but I did not know any better, back then. I am only glad I did not make any mistakes that would have prevented my meeting Andrew when I did."

"I am very glad of that, as well, and I wish it could have been the same, for Lydia."

Elizabeth meant this wholeheartedly, as it regarded her youngest sister. However, she could not help but think that the elopement, and Darcy's actions in it, had been the means of bringing them together, and she wondered if they would be married now, without that event having taken place. Then she remembered her dream, and was comforted by it. He loved her, and she him, and they would have come together regardless – perhaps sooner, perhaps later.

Catherine left her to dress for dinner, and once again it was Mrs. Reynolds who came to change Elizabeth.

"My, is it time for Miss Kelly's half-day again?"

"No, ma'am, she went into Lambton to buy new laces for your half-boots, and is not yet back," said Mrs. Reynolds. "Mrs. Darcy, I know 'tisn't my place to say, but 'tis five times in a fortnight, she's gone to Lambton. I find it most irregular."

"I cannot disagree with you – I shall hardly be going out walking in this weather, to need new laces," said Elizabeth. "But I cannot think of why she should go into Lambton so frequently – oh my, do you think she has a secret beau?"

"I should hope not!" exclaimed Mrs. Reynolds, and then, remembering herself, and that the employment of a lady's maid was not under her own purview, "Of course, if she does, it shall be up to you to decide what is to be done about it."

Elizabeth was not at all sure of what should be done about Sarah's possible beau. Sarah was not the sort to take rash action, but forbidding such frequent trips to Lambton might push even her into an elopement, and Elizabeth did not at all like the thought of Sarah acting so precipitously, or leaving her employ. Nor, however, could she begrudge Sarah's wish for romance, if that was the cause of these frequent trips.

"I shall speak to her of it tonight, Mrs. Reynolds. I thank you for bringing it to my attention."

Elizabeth had never been required to confront someone under her employ before, much less someone who had, until now, been a most favoured servant. Sarah came in to change her that night all apologies, saying, "I beg your pardon for missing your dinner dress, ma'am. John took me into Lambton and the waggonette became stuck in the snow. He had to go back for two extra horses, to see it out."

"Yes, Mrs. Reynolds told me you had gone to buy new laces for my half-boots," said Elizabeth, watching as Sarah averted her gaze. "You know I give you freedom to make purchases as are needed, but I hardly see how new laces are needed in this weather, when I recall the old ones being perfectly fine, when last I did wear them."

Sarah looked at her, visibly trembling, and whispered, "I didn't actually buy new laces, ma'am."

"Sarah, please calm yourself. After all you have done for me, I promise I will help you. Do you have a beau in Lambton?" Elizabeth asked, then, with a sudden realisation that it always seemed to be the same under-coachman, who would volunteer to take Sarah into the village, "Or is John your beau?"

"Neither, ma'am! I don't have a beau – I have a sister!" Sarah exclaimed, and then fell into a fit of weeping. Elizabeth encouraged her to sit, and after some time had passed, Sarah said, "I have four sisters – Moll is second-eldest, behind me. My parents arranged a fine marriage for her – Mr. O'Brien is a nice man, and owns his land outright, although he is perhaps a little old – but Moll would have none of it. She kept declaring she would not marry him, but none of us believed she was so serious. The money I send back to my family, some of it is to keep my folks comfortable, but some of it was to be saved up, to pay for passage for my brother Bernard, who was to come over here and enter into service. I was hoping to speak with you of him, when the time was right."

"You may speak with me of him whenever you wish, Sarah. I am certain an opportunity can be found for him here, or elsewhere in the neighbourhood."

"'Tis too late for him," Sarah said. "Moll ran away with the money that was meant for him, and came over herself. I have been housing her at the inn, and trying to teach her of being a maid ever since, but the money is going to run out – the money you gave me so generously – and I know not what to do."

Sarah again descended into a bout of tears very unlike her, and Elizabeth patted her shoulder before going over to ring the bell. Mrs. Reynolds answered it, and must have noticed Sarah weeping, but said nothing of it.

"Mrs. Reynolds, Miss Kelly's sister, Miss Moll Kelly, is staying at the inn at Lambton, currently. Do we have any beds open in the female servants's quarters?"

"We do ma'am, several."

"Very well, may we see Miss Moll transferred there tomorrow morning? And might we see her evaluated for a position in the household?" Elizabeth asked. Mrs. Reynolds had already filled the maid's position left vacant by Rachel's move to the nursery, but they could easily afford the additional help, wherever Moll was found to fit best.

"Yes, of course, ma'am," said Mrs. Reynolds, who gave Elizabeth a look of some understanding, made her curtsey, and left.

Sarah looked up at Elizabeth with a countenance overcome with emotion, and whispered, "I do not know how to thank you, ma'am."

"Sarah, why did you not come to me in the first place?" Elizabeth scolded, ever so gently. "I certainly would have helped you in this."

"I did not wish to trouble you."

"But you did trouble me. I thought for certain you had a beau, and were going to quit your employment."

"Oh, I would never do that!"

"Never say never, Sarah. I once told a man he was the last man in the world I would marry."

Sarah smiled faintly, at this, and said, "Perhaps he was not the last man, but of course you did not marry him."

"Oh no, I did – he was Mr. Darcy."

At this, Sarah giggled a most uncharacteristic giggle, and smiled again at her employer, with a very relieved countenance.

"Now, we will see Moll trained, and a position found for her, either here, or elsewhere," Elizabeth said. "Look at how Lady Stanton's footman progressed, while he was here. I have no doubt that if Moll is anything like you, she shall come along rapidly."

"But that's just the thing, ma'am – Moll is nothing like me."

CHAPTER 22

No one knew precisely when the first stone for Stradbroke Castle had been laid, but family lore held it to be sometime early in the twelfth century, well before the brick house that was now the family's primary living space had been added to the side of the large stone castle. The latter still stood in good repair, however, and was a true and legitimate castle, not like its more modern counterparts, which were castle by name only.

The gatehouse was intact, although it was no longer manned, and it was through this that Georgiana's carriage rolled, in the steady rain that had been coming down since heavy snow had required her to stay at an inn for two nights. The postilions were used to working in such weather, and outfitted for it, but in vain had Georgiana attempted to convince Bowden to come inside the carriage during the journey. "An' what would the captain say, was he to hear o' me shirking me duties o'er a little rain an' snow?" he had asked. "What would me ol' messmates say, I tell ye what they'd say: Bowden think hisself too fine now to stand on the back 'o a carriage in wet weather. Milady, there ain't no weather ol' Brittania can produce as is bad as what I've took in tops'uls in."

And so Bowden, dripping in oilskins, and seemingly none the worse for having ridden better than a hundred miles behind the carriage in such weather, helped her out onto the slick old cobbled courtyard, and held the umbrella over her head as she was greeted by her uncle, aunt, and cousin, who formed a sombre party. Lady Ellen embraced her, and said, "It was so thoughtful of you to come here, and I am very sorry for your own loss."

Lady Ellen led her to her usual bed-room, which was thankfully already being warmed by a fire, so Hughes could help her change out of her travelling dress, its hem sodden despite her pattens. She went down to the great hall, but once there, she found the family absent, and was informed by the butler, Mr. Pearson, that they were all in the drawing-room. Georgiana looked at him in scepticism, for Stradbroke did not possess a drawing-room, so far as she knew. He led her down the hall, though, to a large room that must have been recently fitted up, for in place of the usual dark, sombre feel of the timbered ceilings and panelled walls that comprised the rest of the house, this room was all elegance and light, newly plastered and furnished.

"Oh, aunt Ellen, this is very prettily done," Georgiana said. Her aunt had always spoken of updating Stradbroke, and it appeared she had finally begun to act on her plans.

"Alice and I worked on it together," her aunt said, quietly. "I had hoped to have the whole place done before she took up her position as mistress here."

Georgiana regretted having spoken; of course the two ladies of the household would have both been involved in the updating of the room, and now only one of them remained. She looked nervously to Andrew, to see if he had been hurt by the reminder, but he had a sad, vacant look on his face, as though he hardly even noticed the rest of the family.

Georgiana did not know how to comfort her cousin after such a loss, but she did what she could for her aunt in the days that followed, which generally consisted of playing appropriately sombre songs on the pianoforte, helping sew more mourning clothes for the little girls, and visiting those little girls – who were still too young to understand what had happened – in the nursery.

"I feel so badly for them," said Georgiana on one such occasion, in a tone of deep emotion.

"Yes, of course you must, even more than the rest of us," said Lady Ellen. "You were not too much older than they, when Lady Anne passed."

"They at least have you, who can give them a grandmother's love, as you gave me an aunt's," said Georgiana.

"That may be all they have in life – I do not think they will ever know a stepmother," Lady Ellen said. "You see how devastated poor Andrew is – I do not know if he can bring himself to remarry, and we will not push him to do so, even for the sake of an heir. Perhaps in time he shall heal, and meet someone, but it is possible Edward will be our only hope for the succession."

"Then he will not marry my cousin Anne," Georgiana said, hesitantly.

"No, that is no longer a possibility. In some ways it is a shame, for it would have seen his future secure," Lady Ellen said, and then sighed. "My father was right, after all."

"What do you mean?" Georgiana asked. Lady Ellen's father had been the Marquess of Hayle, a title that had passed to a distant cousin, for Lady Ellen possessed no surviving brothers, nor even sisters. As her father had not favoured the cousin, and left all that was not entailed to his daughter, she had brought a tremendous inheritance to her marriage.

"When I married your uncle, the estate was doing very poorly – his father was a horrific gambler, and they were deeply in debt. My father said most of my inheritance would be spent in getting the estate out of debt, and I would have little remaining even for my own pin money, but I was young, and in love, and would have no-one but Andrew," she said. "I did have my pin money, but if so much of my fortune had not gone towards reestablishing my first son's birthright, I would have been able to see to much more for Edward than purchasing a commission in the army. Now, an heiress of childbearing age is the only wife for him, and such a lady who will take interest in a second son is not easily found."

"But if you had not married Lord Brandon, you would have had some other son, rather than Edward," said Georgiana, comfortingly. "Will he be coming here?"

"Yes. He had not yet decided whether to resign his commission, or to request leave, in his last, but he will make his decision and then come home to us."

"I will be glad to see him, although I wish it was not under these circumstances," said Georgiana, although her mind was on the sad parting in Paris that must take place before she would see her cousin.

Although Georgiana had used post horses after the first stage of her journey, she had asked Murray to follow after her with the bays, so she could have the use of them while at Stradbroke. He came in, riding one and leading the other, a few days after her arrival, and so when her aunt proposed they go to Lynn for her final fitting of the additional mourning dresses she had ordered for herself, Georgiana volunteered her own carriage. The Fitzwilliams had several carriages, at least one of them much finer than Georgiana's, but Lady Ellen was not so old that she could not remember the pride with which a lady begins to set up her own establishment, and agreed readily to use her niece's equipage, although extra warm bricks were required to see it comfortable in the chill that had followed the rain.

Murray set them down at the modiste, and after a few final adjustments had been made, they had a little walk about the town. When they passed a shop with a tidy, fine-painted sign that read, "R. J. Smithson, Portraitist," Georgiana halted, touched the anchor pendant hanging upon her neck, and was struck by the thought that she should have a miniature done for Matthew.

"Do you know if Mr. Smithson's work is any good?" she asked her aunt.

"Oh yes, very good. Edward had a miniature done by him a few years ago. It was my great comfort, in the last war."

"I think I shall inquire with him about painting mine, then – I should like to have something to give Matthew when he returns."

"I expect he would like that very much."

Georgiana stepped into the shop, and made an appointment with Mr. Smithson to return. They walked back, then, to the market place, where Murray was waiting with the carriage. Lady Ellen, looking at the blank door of the landau, said, "Perhaps we should have seen about having Matthew's arms painted on your carriage, but then, you will be back here soon enough."

"Matthew does not yet have arms. He was going to use the family arms, but Lord Anglesey thought he should make some alteration, to reflect the baronetcy."

"Yes, I quite agree. Do you have a copy of the Anglesey arms?"

Georgiana replied that she did, for Lord Anglesey had provided her a little canvas of them, and she had been carrying it with her since, aware that at some point she should have the new arms created.

"Well, then when we return, let us sketch something out."

Lady Ellen was serious when she said it. She had all of the expected accomplishments of the ladies of her generation, but had always possessed a true talent for drawing and painting – many of the screens and pictures hung within Stradbroke had been painted by her hand. She might not have had the practise necessary in the delicate work required to paint Georgiana's miniature, but Georgiana was certainly willing to have her aunt try her hand at the arms.

When they returned, then, Lady Ellen called for her drawing and painting things, and asked Georgiana for the loan of her anchor necklace. After some time, she called her niece over to see her work.

"Oh, it is perfect!" exclaimed Georgiana. Lady Ellen had retained the three lions within the shield that comprised the Anglesey arms, but replaced the crest with the anchor of Georgiana's necklace.

"Would you mind terribly if I attempted painting this on the carriage?" asked Lady Ellen. "I must admit I prefer this project far more than sewing."

Georgiana would have been in favour of anyone volunteering to accomplish this task she had never pursued, but agreed to it even more readily, with the thought that it was providing a distraction from her aunt's grief.

CHAPTER 23

If a family such as the Bennets could produce two daughters so dissimilar as herself and Lydia, it should not have been such a surprise to Elizabeth that Sarah and Moll were so different. Mrs. Reynolds introduced Moll to her, with Sarah standing beside them, once the young woman had been settled into the servants's quarters.

"Good to meet ya, Mrs. Darcy. Molly Kelly, at yer service, but I don' let anyone call me Molly Kelly – sounds right ridiculous, don' it? So I'm Moll, to all who know me. An' thank ye for lettin' me stay here, 'stead that old inn. Right bor'n, that inn was, but this place, now this is proper grand! 'Tis twice as big as Alverstone Hall! I ain't never seen anything half so fine!"

Having thus spoke more before Elizabeth could reply than Sarah had in her entire first day of service to her mistress, Moll allowed herself to be welcomed by Mrs. Darcy, and then rapidly ushered away by Sarah and Mrs. Reynolds.

In the days that followed, Mrs. Reynolds's reports back to Elizabeth indicated that there was no difficulty where Moll was concerned, in hard work. There was nothing she would not dust or scrub, no number of times she could be asked to remake a bed, until she had got it right. But sizing down Moll's outsized personality into the manners expected of a maid was proving difficult, and Mrs. Reynolds was beginning to wonder if she might be better suited for the dairy. Elizabeth suspected this was why Sarah had kept her hidden away for so long, and she wondered how many rough edges Sarah had already smoothed away.

Still, if Moll proved a source of exasperation for her sister and Mrs. Reynolds, when she was found guffawing to a footman's stories while she was dusting the chandeliers in the saloon, or heard to be pressing every single key on the pianoforte in the state rooms, it had been worth bringing her into the house, if just to have relieved Sarah of the sole burden of her.

Elizabeth passed the sisters on her way to Darcy's study, and could not help but see Sarah digging her elbow into her younger sister's side as she made her own curtsey, which prompted a haphazard curtsey from Moll. Elizabeth greeted them both, and continued on her way, quite bemused. She slipped into the study, and looked expectantly at Darcy, for she had been summoned here, although Mr. Parker had been careful to note the summons was of less urgency than the last time.

"I have had two interesting pieces of correspondence," Darcy said. "The first, which I suppose we might have suspected would come eventually, is from Mr. Baker, asking why we will no longer receive him and his wife. I know not whether to reply back and tell him the reason."

"I gather his wife has not confessed, then."

"I certainly hope not. If she has and he still expects us to maintain our acquaintance, his manners are even more erratic than I had suspected."

"Will you truly write to tell him of what Mrs. Baker did?"

"I hardly know. I do not feel it my place to tell a man his wife made every attempt to be unfaithful to him, but nor am I certain that this knowledge should be kept from him."

"I think I am for keeping it a secret. When the neighbourhood begins to understand they are no longer invited to Pemberley, I suspect it will not be long before many other families follow. If they are to have so little society, at least they may have each other."

"I am not sure leaving Mr. Baker to the society of the wife who attempted to cuckold him after only a few months of marriage – and will likely attempt again – is quite the nicest thing to do to him."

"That is true. His manners leave much to be desired, but I would be open to him coming here, so long as it is without his wife."

"If I tell him of it, it cannot be in a letter," Darcy said. "Perhaps I shall write back, and invite him to ride out with me one day, and broach the subject."

"I think that a good course of action. There is no need to commit yourself until you have a better sense of how he will react. What was the other letter?"

"It is from Lady Catherine," he said. "She has cut the Fitzwilliams, and expects us to side with her."

"What?"

He reminded her of the discussions, to have Edward marry Anne, and then said, "It seems Lady Catherine wrote to them, following our cousin's death, expressing her sympathy, and *reminding* them of the engagement – I suspect in a wholly inappropriate way. Lord Brandon replied and indicated it was no longer an option that could be considered, given Anne's health. Any lady Edward marries now must have a legitimate chance of bearing an heir."

"And Lady Catherine disagreed with this? I should hate to see Anne attempt to have a child – look at what happened to poor Alice, who had ten times her health."

"Lady Catherine insists Anne will have a son and heir."

"It would kill her!" Elizabeth exclaimed.

"I agree completely, and I suspect she does not truly believe Anne should attempt to bear a child. But my aunt has been very desirous of bringing this marriage about, and perhaps she believes that if she is able to push the marriage into being, Edward will be too cautious of Anne's health to attempt to consummate it."

"So that is two letters, which you must decide how to respond to."

"Oh, no. I have already written my response to this one. You may read it if you like."

"You are so decisive! What did you write?"

"I wrote that if I was called upon to choose, I would choose the side of the family who welcomed you, when I announced our engagement, rather than insult you as she did. I then recommended she think again about any actions that might leave her estranged from all her blood relatives in the world, excepting Anne."

Elizabeth approached him, and ran her fingers through his hair. "You are defending me again, I see. I still enjoy it."

"I do not like that it is required, but I shall always do so, if it is," he said softly, taking up her hand. "Do you ever wonder what the Fitzwilliams must think of us?"

"What do you mean?"

"We unexpectedly have two heirs already, and you – despite the scare you gave me – are still with us, and entirely healthy," he said. "Sometimes I feel guilty, over our good fortune."

"I understand what you mean," Elizabeth said. "If I could have chosen before I had our boys – if I would have been presented a choice, for us to only have one son, or a daughter, and for Alice to live, I would have chosen so a thousand times over."

"So would I." He sighed. "I cannot say I ever had a strong desire for my children to be in line for a title, but I must admit I wish this earldom could be passed through the female line. I hate that they must worry over having an heir, in addition to their grief."

"Who is in the line, after Andrew and Edward?"

"There is no one beyond them. Lord Brandon's uncle had one son, George. He was a major in the army, and died of fever in the West Indies. There are no other, more distant cousins."

"I am surprised they did not steer Edward towards a less dangerous career, given this."

"You know Edward – could you see him as a barrister, or a clergyman?"

"No, I suppose not."

"It seemed unnecessary, as well, that Edward should need to marry and attempt to father a son," he said. "Alice's daughters were born so easily, no one could have expected this."

Elizabeth's heart was heavy when she left the study, as it was whenever she thought of her cousin's death, and she decided to go to the library for a little while, wishing to be soothed by that space. When she entered, she found she had more cause to be soothed than she had expected, for her father was seated there with a book.

She came in quietly and made her own selection, and would have been content enough to sit near him and read, as she had used to do at Longbourn. He greeted her when she was seated, however, and said, "I have learned that there was just as much fear over your life, for a time, as there was over mine."

"There never was true cause for concern, papa – at least, specific concern," Elizabeth said, once again reminded of her cousin. "It was merely that none of us understood what was happening."

"Still, it is not a thing I like to think of happening," he said. "It will not be this time around, much to your mother's surprise, but you are meant to mourn me, not the other way 'round."

"Papa!" she exclaimed, her eyes filling with tears, for she recognised the rightness of what he said, but she did not like to think of it.

"Nay, nay, do not cry, Lizzy. You know it is the way things should be, and I hope I have some time left. I know I do not look so well, but I do *feel* a little better every day."

"Perhaps you should go over to Matlock, and take the waters. Our Dr. Alderman could see you there, or we could have him attend you here."

"This is the physician who left you in the care of your lady's maid during your births?"

Elizabeth laughed, and said, "Yes, perhaps his timing is unfortunate, but he has much experience with recovering invalids."

"I would rather flatter myself in believing I am healthy enough not to be classed as an invalid, now, but I suppose I should go to Matlock, if just to distract your mother from Bath. You are going to need to keep her at Pemberley for quite some time, if the Ramseys are to have any sort of privacy to begin their married life. She is still wild to go there again."

"We shall do so, then, if that is required to aid the Ramseys. Certainly the lure of so many grandchildren cannot be resisted."

"No, it cannot," he said, looking a little perturbed. "The Ramseys – how odd that sounds. Our Kitty is now Mrs. Ramsey."

"It does sound odd to me, as well. We brought off the wedding so quickly, and so much happened after, I believe I did not entirely adjust to it."

"You should have seen her, when they came in. Your mother had quite the fit of nerves, but Catherine took charge of everything – helped your mother to her bed, sent for Mr. Jones, so he could see to Frances, and so Catherine could consult with him on the giving of my physic. I was wrong about her, Lizzy, terribly wrong. I am only glad you and Mr. Darcy and Captain Ramsey saw the potential in her, where I did not."

"Have you told her so, papa?"

"I have," he said. "I am not so old that I cannot learn a thing or two from nearly dying, my dear child."

Mary had hoped that Catherine would arrive at Pemberley carrying a letter for her elder sister, a response from Lydia to Mary's letter of contrition, but Catherine had arrived with no such note. Mary had feared that Lydia did not favour her letter, and had no desire to make a response, but a response was delivered on this day, and as soon as it could be done, Mary slipped out of the drawing-room, to go to the conservatory and read:

"Lord, Mary, there's no reason to be half so dramatic. I think your letter was the dourest one I've ever got before. I forgive you, I suppose, but I can't say I ever thought there was anything to forgive you for.

"My Wickham and I are living at an inn on Gracechurch Street, now, awaiting our passage to America. My uncle Gardiner would not let us stay with him, on account of the misunderstanding about my husband deserting the Army, but my uncle did find us a place on a ship that didn't cost too much. We don't know yet when the ship is to leave, so my husband has to go down to the docklands and inquire every day as to when it will sail.

"Oh! But that is not the most interesting news – Mr. Darcy was going to give Wickham and me 3,000 pounds, to start our life in America, and his business-man arranged a meeting with me at my uncle's house. The business-man said our passage was to be paid for, and then the money was to come to us as an annewitty of 150 pounds a year, not a lump sum like my husband thought, and that it was to my name alone! George got so angry over it, but my uncle said that because my husband is presumed dead, the money can't go to him.

"So now with what papa gives us, and my widow's pension, we have 286 pounds a year. I think my husband will have to find a position with the Army in America, for who can live on 286 pounds a year, or whatever that is in Yankee money? I hope the regimentals there are fine enough – I do not even know if they wear red coats, or another colour!

"Well, I must say ta to you, for my aunt and I are to go shopping now. I am going to buy a new bonnet and pelisse, so I will look well when I am walking about on the deck of the ship.

"Thank you, Mary, for it was nice of you to write to me, even if you were so grim. Oh, and congratulations on your engagement. I always knew you would get a clergyman for a husband. I'll miss you when I am in America –

write to me if you wish. I'll send my direction once we are settled.

"Yours, &c.,

"LYDIA WICKHAM"

It was difficult to avoid being disappointed at Lydia's not giving her apology the import Mary thought it deserved, but since she had determined not to be judgmental of her sister, Mary told herself to be happy that she had, at least, been forgiven. She said a little prayer for her sister to have a safe passage and find a good place in America, and then decided to write to David, for she knew *he* would not disappoint her in his response.

CHAPTER 24

Lady Ellen began the work on Georgiana's carriage after her niece had returned from Lynn with a little silk-wrapped miniature securely held in her reticule. The landau having been washed and dried sufficiently, two carpets were laid out in the carriage house, alongside the doors of the carriage, and two little stools – also delicately painted by Lady Ellen's hand – were set on one side.

Georgiana sat upon one of the stools, continuing with her sewing, and keeping her aunt company as she began the careful work of pencilling the design onto the door.

"Are you pleased with your miniature?" Lady Ellen asked.

"Yes. I hope Matthew will be, as well."

"I am sure he will be. Do you expect to hear from him soon?"

"I do not know – it could be any day, or it could be another month, if not more."

"You poor thing – I do not know how you bear it. I am not sure that I could."

"I bear it because I have no other choice," said Georgiana. "The waiting would not be so bad if I was not also awaiting his reaction to my losing the baby."

"I would assume sadness to be his reaction – have you reason to expect anything else?" Lady Ellen asked.

"I lost his child, and possibly his heir – I have failed in my duty as his wife. He would have every cause to be upset with me."

"Georgiana!" Lady Ellen exclaimed. "How could you possibly think such a thing? You see poor Andrew, how he grieves – do you think he is at all upset that Alice did not *do her duty*?"

"Of course not," Georgiana whispered.

"I will admit that there are some men who would be upset by what

350

befell you for that reason, and I do not presume to know your husband so well as I know my son, but I do not doubt that Matthew loves you, and I do not believe he will be thinking about your *duty* when he reads of your news. I suspect that if he thinks anything like I do, he will in some ways be relieved that no one else in this family is carrying a child right now, because I cannot bear to lose another of you so soon."

With this, Lady Ellen dropped her pencil on the carpet, and brought her hands to her face in a bout of tears. Georgiana was already of a sentimental and sympathetic nature, and the sight of her aunt so grieved caused her to rapidly follow Lady Ellen in to weeping. She managed to move her stool closer, so as to embrace her aunt, and they remained thus for a very long time.

The carriage project was set aside on that day, but they returned to it in the days following, and Georgiana watched her new family arms form under her aunt's careful hand. On one day, however, they were interrupted by Mr. Pearson, who came in and said, "Pardon me, my lady, but there has been a thick packet forwarded express from Pemberley, for Lady Stanton, and Lord Brandon said she was to be informed of it immediately."

"Oh!" Georgiana exclaimed, and she trembled at the thought that it should not be what she had so long desired. But she could think of nothing else that would have been forwarded on from Pemberley by express, and would have run back to the house if it was not wholly improper. She settled for walking as fast as she could, forcing poor old Mr. Pearson to struggle to keep up with her, but still, it seemed an excruciating amount of time before she was inside, and the thick bundle directed in her brother's hand given over to her.

When she reached the hallway that led to her room, Georgiana did run outright, seating herself by the fire once she had reached it, and somewhat guiltily tossing aside Fitzwilliam's covering letter to be read later, and then the oiled silk that covered a very thick bundle of papers, the topmost of which began with:

"My God, Georgiana, my heart aches for you. You must not spend another moment blaming yourself for what happened, and if you will not do so for yourself, then do so for me, for I cannot bear that in addition to the natural grief which you must feel (and I do, as well), you have added on feelings of guilt for an event you were in no way to blame for.

"If there is anything I would admonish you for, it is only that you told me of losing the baby without any indication of the risk to your own life, although perhaps you did not understand the extent of it. I have been sorting through a very difficult set of correspondence here in Copenhagen, and had to learn from my brothers that I very nearly lost my Georgiana.

"My dearest, there is something I think I should confess now, and it is that before I came to town last year, the thought of marriage had not crossed my mind. When we first met in the park, Captain Ramsey had been telling me of how with the peace, he intended to take a wife, and he thought Miss Catherine Bennet just might suit him very well. What he spoke of had little appeal to me – I thought with my uncle's influence I should be returned to a command eventually, and would continue on in bachelorhood indefinitely.

"That changed only because I came to know you, and in so doing, fell in love with you. My interest in marriage was only in being bound to you, and I thought not of carriages, or a home, or heirs. I know because of this I have not been a good husband, and I will also admit that when I sailed from Portsmouth I felt a certain relief, in being back at sea on the Caroline, in command of the ship I know, master of the world I know.

"But it was not the same without my Georgiana. I used to love this world so, and I do still, in a way, but I will never go to sea again without you. I had decided on this even before receiving your letters.

"I confess all of this both because you should know, and because I hope you understand that having an heir is the farthest thing from my worries. If you want children – if they will make you happy – then I wish for them as well, but I had no expectations in that area. I am deeply saddened by the loss of the baby, but while there may be another baby, someday, there will never be another you.

"You, my dearest Georgiana, you are irreplaceable, and of all the emotions I have felt, upon reviewing all of this correspondence, sadness, for you, and relief, that you are alive, have been chief among them. If I could send for you, and have you join me here in Copenhagen, I would surely do so, for I would feel inexpressible relief in having you in my arms, but by the time you read this, I hope our repairs will be mostly complete.

"Yes, repairs, but please do not worry. We struck ice off the isle of Gotland. When you read all I have written prior to this, you will know that I had my doubts about Lieutenant Holmes, and it was during his watch that it happened. It is possible we would have done so regardless of who had the watch, for although the sea has not frozen entirely, there are vast patches of ice. But the violence with which we struck left the Caroline badly damaged, the pumps going all the way to Copenhagen, and now the poor ship undergoing enough in the way of repairs to see her back to Britain.

"I am going to put in at Chatham, rather than brave the channel. Please do not trouble yourself with an unfamiliar port, however. Once the ship is docked for her final repairs, I shall meet with you at Pemberley, a reunion I long for constantly. Until then, I have little to add by way of consolation. If you find music to be healing, as I do, I have enclosed the pianoforte part for Beethoven's Sonata No. 2 for Pianoforte and Cello, which I found in a little shop here, and have begun to learn. Perhaps once we are returned to each other's company, we may finally play our first duet.

"I hope your health continues to improve, and you have found whatever happiness you can in such a time. I hardly know what else to add, except that I love you, and it pains me greatly to think of what you have been through.

"Yours, always,

"MATTHEW"

It should be little wonder that Lady Ellen found her an hour after reading this, having made no attempt on the additional correspondence. This time it was Georgiana's turn to be comforted by her aunt, although she tried to tell Lady Ellen she had no need of it, that she had been curled up on the bed weeping tears of relief and love, not sadness. Her aunt still rubbed her back in a gentle, motherly way, and it was with some regret of absenting herself from Stradbroke that Georgiana told Lady Ellen she had already determined to go to Chatham despite Matthew's instructions, for to see him even just a few days earlier than she might otherwise would lift her spirits more than anything had in months.

CHAPTER 25

The poor weather seemed determined to continue on through the end of the winter – it was mostly cold, but there seemed also to be snow and rain in undue proportions. In such a winter, Pemberley's gallery and ball-room became the primary places for exercise, and Elizabeth had on this day seized on the idea of walking with her sons, as she would have preferred to do out of doors. Darcy had readily agreed to go along with her scheme, once good fires had been lit in her chosen space, and so they were circling the gallery, Darcy pushing James in the carriage that had been purposely purchased for the new baby, and Elizabeth pushing George in an old equipage scavenged from the attic.

As always, Elizabeth studiously avoided looking at her portrait, for now it was even stranger to think of the children and grandchildren of James and George coming into this room and looking at her, perhaps with the same curiosity she held when she considered Darcy's ancestors. They walked along in silence for some time, before Darcy said, "They are very quiet, for babies."

"Either that, or your point of comparison is Bess," Elizabeth replied. "I believe she has the capacity to be louder than the both of them put together."

"I would certainly agree with you there. James is very nearly asleep."

"George is not," Elizabeth said, looking down at her son, and smiling at him. She was utterly thrilled when, for the first time, he responded to her with a smile back, and she leant down over the old carriage, saying, "No, you are not, are you, my sweet boy? You are awake and smiling at your mama, yes you are!"

"I believe I can see how this is going to go, with the twins," Darcy said. "You are going to feel guilty over having a second son, and you will make up for it by spoiling him always."

"I cannot say that I aim to spoil him, but I do not wish him to be left out. Already he is given a handed-down carriage."

"Only until someone can be spared to go to Derby and purchase another."

"I know, but still – he will always come second to his brother, unless his brother errs grievously. And I know not who would make the better heir, but they *are* beginning to show their differences. James is the sleepier of the two, and he can be fussier when he is upset. George is the first to smile at me."

"Would you like me to make over my will to George, for being the first to smile at his mother? I am tremendously fond of her, but that does seem a little excessive."

"Do not tease about this, Darcy."

"I will not, if you wish it, but nor can you take it so seriously. We cannot spend their formative years wondering if every single thing James does will make him a poor estate manager, and every single thing George does makes him better qualified to be the heir. We must assume it is James, unless he does something that truly merits changing the inheritance, and if he does so, it would likely not be until he is much older."

"Assuming for his sake he does not – what becomes of George?"

"There are any number of options for him, and we shall ensure he has ample funds to pursue whichever of them he chooses. We already have several successful examples, in our family, of men who have pursued such careers. We must assume our George can achieve similar success in his choice," he said. "Still, I cannot help but wonder if I have made the right choices in my recent decisions."

"What do you mean?"

"Purchasing the land from Barrowmere Park. I must admit, I have spent so much time as the only male heir for Pemberley that I assumed heirs would not be so easily come by."

"I assumed the same, or perhaps worse, for having grown up under Longbourn's entail."

"Now that we have two heirs, I wonder if I might have held back on expanding Pemberley, and set the money aside for the purchase of a small second estate."

"You did not know, though, and nor did I," Elizabeth said. "I believe it feels different, because they were born so close together. If they were born a year or two apart, I do not think I would feel so conflicted, but these two – if they had arranged themselves in the womb differently, their legacies would be completely altered. George would be the heir, and James the spare."

"That is true. You might bear even more sons, if just to vex your mother, but I do not believe we will be so conflicted over them as we are these two."

"Oh yes, my mother," Elizabeth said, chuckling at the thought. "Whatever would she do if I had five sons?"

"I am not entirely certain, but I suspect it would involve an attack of her nerves."

"Fitzwilliam Darcy, are you jesting at my mother's expense?" she asked, in her most teasing tone.

He might have responded by teasing her in return, or making amends as regarded Mrs. Bennet, were it not for the carriage's sudden refusal to move. For several minutes, Elizabeth watched as he attempted to push it forward, leaned over to inspect it, and muttered over there being some defect in the axle, or the wheel, all the while becoming ever more frustrated.

"Is this to be my punishment for speaking of your mother's nerves?" he asked. "For I believe myself in danger of a nervous fit, if I cannot get this carriage to move."

"Darcy, James is not attached to the carriage. Someone may come and get it later, and see what the issue is."

He looked once more at the carriage wheels, and then at her, chuckled, and picked up his son. "Perhaps George had the better carriage, after all."

Elizabeth pushed at her carriage, so they could begin walking again, and when she looked over at Darcy, she could not help but be struck by how well he looked, walking along with his son cradled in his arms.

"What are you smiling about?"

"I am smiling to be here, walking with my three handsome boys," she said, and halted again to kiss him deeply, feeling the warmth of the child in his arms. She felt blissfully content, and also something more: those stirrings of desire to return to marital relations, which grew stronger daily, and could not be set aside for much longer.

CHAPTER 26

Georgiana said good-bye to her family at Stradbroke, and made her way to Chatham, glad the distance was short enough to use her own horses, which required Murray and Bowden to rest overnight in a fine, warm inn. She felt, upon entering the town, that pervading discomfort that can accompany a new place, particularly for a lady who has not often travelled on her own.

She might have been utterly lost were it not for Bowden, who knew the town, and asked permission to change out of his livery into his old shore-going rig. He might have done so out of comfort, but it did feel more right to Georgiana to be attended by someone dressed like the other sailors of the town, and it was Bowden who suggested the Admiral's Arms as the most appropriate inn for Lady Stanton to take an apartment within, which she did.

After this, Georgiana entered into a strange, lonely period of waiting. She knew no-one in the town except the innkeeper, Mr. Norris, and his wife, and while they were friendly, they ran a busy inn, and had time for only the most basic pleasantries towards her.

Soon enough, she was deprived even of her lady's maid. Hughes, upon entering such a marine town, had determined she could wait no longer to seek new employment, and begun perusing the advertisements for positions in the London papers. Within a week, she had found a suitable position and was encouraged to take it, parting from her employer in an event prompting tears from both parties.

It was after Hughes left that Georgiana was reminded of how she had sympathised with aunt, over having no female relations around her, for Georgiana was now deprived of very nearly all female companionship. She dressed herself in the morning, struggling to manage her own stays and hair, breakfasted by herself in her apartment, and then went down to ask the innkeeper, Mr. Norris, if there had been any sightings of the Caroline, or any correspondence for her, which might include a response to the advertisement she had placed in the London papers for a lady's maid.

There were no sightings of the Caroline, however, and no responses to the advertisement, which Georgiana could only attribute to the line within stating that the position might require significant time at sea, for she thought it a desirable enough post otherwise. After Mr. Norris made his negative response to her, Georgiana would don her pelisse, and go out for a long walk, along the Medway. Bowden would walk a few steps behind her when the weather was fair, and when it was not, he walked beside her holding an umbrella. He was, despite only having the sight of one eye, the person best suited for first recognising the Caroline, having served on the frigate, but there were few naval ships to come in, and none that remotely resembled the only ship Georgiana wished to see.

She would then return to her room for a few quiet hours, during which she had no callers, and wished desperately that Mr. Norris had seen fit to place a pianoforte somewhere amidst his establishment. She had written to Fitzwilliam, asking that her little square be sent down, but until it arrived, she could only look through the music Matthew had sent, and consider what the fingering might be. This reminded her of her dream, and how he had given her the canvas painted with a full keyboard, for such an item would have been very welcome to her.

Lacking this, she spent the majority of these hours reading through the very long set of correspondence Matthew had written to her, prior to his very tender covering letter. In it, she was able to read of his doubts of Lieutenant Holmes, of a cold so bitter one of the sails had frozen and shattered to pieces when they tried to take it in, and of the daily workings of the ship. There were some passages where a lady not so tender of heart towards her husband might have thought him rambling on, but Georgiana saw in it a wish to write something to her regularly, even if there was little to impart. She longed for him, and wished she had a better sense of when the ship was to come in.

Then she dined alone at the little table in her apartment, and more evenings than not, allowed herself to succumb to the loneliness that seemed to permeate her existence. She missed the Fitzwilliams, and sometimes thought of returning to Stradbroke, but the thought of losing even one day in Matthew's company quickly tempered these impulses.

She had been in Chatham well over a week when she made her way down the stairs, prepared to ask the questions to which she now assumed the answers would be *no*. The inn had no dedicated coffee-room, but many locals liked to take their coffee and newspaper in its front room. There was one man seated there, presently, in addition to Mr. Norris.

"I apologise, Lady Stanton," said Mr. Norris, before Georgiana could even speak. "No sign of 'er as last I heard, but I do have a letter for you."

The letter was not from an applicant for Georgiana's position, but instead from Lord Anglesey, and she was about to thank Mr. Norris and retire to her apartment to read it, when the man seated there asked, "Lady Stanton? Are you Matthew Stanton's wife? Oh, I am sorry – it is Sir Matthew now, of course."

"I am," answered Georgiana hesitantly, wondering if this man was going to ask her about the Polonais, and perhaps even request she recount the battle, which she had been required to do a great many times in company at Pemberley.

"Norris!" exclaimed the man. "You have Lady Stanton staying here, and you did not *once* think perhaps we should be introduced? Have I not been speaking of Captain Stanton ever since the Polonais?"

Mr. Norris gaped at him, and then received a pointed look from the man, whom Georgiana now scrutinised more carefully, and found was dressed as a gentleman, although his face showed signs of weather well beyond the age his greying hair indicated.

Turning to Georgiana, Mr. Norris asked, in a voice that could not but be overheard by the other man, "Lady Stanton, it appears I've failed to ask if you would wish to be introduced to Admiral Russell."

Relieved that the man must be some sort of naval connexion, Georgiana requested the introduction, and it was given. Admiral Russell rose, and made her a bow that might have been deeper, had it not been marked with the stiffness of age. "Very pleased to meet you, Lady Stanton. I was captain of the Iris when he came on as a captain's servant – terribly young fellow, he was then, eight or nine years of age, although of course to the navy he was eleven. He was with me six years complete – one of the better midshipmen I've ever had," Admiral Russell said. "I thought him destined for good things, and he had quite a run in the Caroline, but the Polonais, what a stroke that was. Taking on a French seventy-four with a fifty-gun ship – I cannot say I should have had the pluck to go about it, but I am damned proud of him."

As he spoke, Georgiana moved rapidly from hesitance towards making his acquaintance, to eagerness to converse with someone who had known Matthew in his formative years. To hear him conclude with such praise for her husband, someone far less starved for conversation than she would still have wished to further the acquaintance.

"I am very glad to make your acquaintance, sir. I would love to hear more of Captain Stanton's time with you."

"You may now, if you like, unless you wish to read your letter."

Lord Anglesey's letter appeared unremarkable, and had come by the regular post, so Georgiana assured him it could wait. Admiral Russell nodded, and rose from his seat, picking up his coffee cup, and saying,

"Norris, bring 'round another pot of coffee, and whatever Lady Stanton will have to drink, to your private parlour."

When they were seated in that faded space, and one of the maids had deposited a pot of coffee and a tray of tea things in front of them, Georgiana asked, "What was Matthew like, as a boy?"

"Terribly serious."

Georgiana laughed, and said, "He is like that as a grown man, as well."

"Most boys I had from gentlemen's homes were exceedingly homesick, but not him. Seemed happy to be on board, and set in to hard work right away – I rated him midshipman within two years."

"I expect most of your young recruits did not get it into their own heads to join the navy," Georgiana said.

"Very true – I did not at first believe Lord Anglesey, that it had been Matthew's own choice, but over time it became clear that it was," said Admiral Russell. "And it was for the best that he was a tall lad for his age, else the older boys might have taunted him more – if there is one thing a midshipman most dislikes, aside from being denied shore leave, it is another boy more earnest than himself. Still, they did get him quite good with the ghost."

"The ghost?"

"Oh yes, they had him convinced there was a ghost in the hold of the ship. Unbeknownst to me, they had been winding him up about it for the better part of a week, and when I sent him there to check our stores, it was the first time I ever saw him reluctant to obey a command," he said. "You may guess, with boys, what happened – one of them raced ahead of him and hid there, and scared him damned good, until Matthew figured out what he was about. I had to send them both up into the masthead for a day, they got into such a scrape. But you needn't worry about how your husband acquitted himself – he gave better than he got."

Georgiana could not say she had been worried about how her husband had acquitted himself in a fight nearly twenty years ago, but she did smile over the story of the ghost. Admiral Russell followed with other stories, and from there the conversation flowed into Matthew's return to commanding the Caroline, and how he and Georgiana had become acquainted, before Georgiana could seek to learn more about Admiral Russell. He told her he had not sought another command after returning from the last war, on account of his rheumatism, and was effectively retired on half-pay. He had done well in prize money, and had purchased a town house in Chatham, where he and Mrs. Russell could still see many of their naval acquaintances. It was to this house that he invited Georgiana for dinner the day following, an invitation she readily accepted, pleased not only to have made an acquaintance, but one who was fine company, and had such a connection to her husband.

She retired to her apartment to finally read her letter from Lord Anglesey, and found it contained the news, carefully given, that her cousin Lucy had borne a son – who had been named George, after his father – and both mother and child were well. Although Georgiana attempted to feel happiness for her cousins, the news that another of her female relations had brought a child to birth could not help but bring her low. However, she found herself relieved the letter had not been delivered while she was at Stradbroke, where the contents would need to be immediately shared with the Fitzwilliams, if she had received it in company. It would be better to prepare a gentle way to tell the Fitzwilliams of how the Anglesey title, which already held a long line of male heirs, had now gained that security of a son born to the heir apparent, and his healthy wife.

CHAPTER 27

The day Moll Kelly was found in Mr. Darcy's study was not one that would be readily forgotten, in the annals of Pemberley. It might have been known only to a few others, if Mr. Darcy had not been walking thither with Mr. Mason, discussing the purchase of a new greatcoat, when they walked in and found Moll seated primly behind the desk, apparently pretending to be the master of the estate.

Mr. Mason's having seen this ensured that the entire staff knew of the incident within a few hours of its occurring, and Elizabeth found herself receiving profuse apologies from everyone who could possibly apologise for the incident, including Mrs. Reynolds, Mr. Parker, Moll herself, and of course Sarah. She had been required to strike the proper balance between being suitably stern, but not too censorious, when in truth she wanted to burst out laughing at the thought of her husband walking in to find Moll seated at his desk.

She determined she should write to Georgiana of the incident, for surely her sister would see the humour in it, and Georgiana's first letter since she had settled at Chatham had been quite long, which Elizabeth took to mean she was bored, and would greatly enjoy such an anecdote. First, though, she wished to go to the nursery, to see her boys and nurse them, if they had need of it.

Elizabeth found Jane there, playing with Bess, who had become more active in the last few weeks, and had even begun her first attempts at speaking. The child's first word, to poor Jane's chagrin, had been "pa," which hardly seemed fair when Charles – although a good father – could not visit his daughter as often as her mother did, due to his needing to ride to Clareborne regularly to see to his tenants and the construction of his new house.

The boys were sleeping, so Elizabeth settled into a chair and watched

Jane kneeling on the floor with her daughter, encouraging Bess's early efforts at crawling.

"Pa!" exclaimed Bess, inching forward, and eliciting a sigh from Jane. "Pa!"

"Perhaps she asks for her papa because he is often away, at the estate," said Elizabeth. "She does not need to ask for her mama because you are here with her."

"Perhaps," said Jane, seeming a little consoled by this idea.

Bess continued to inch her way forward, asking for her *pa*, and it was only when her little fingers wrapped around one of the legs of the new square pianoforte, and she once again shrieked, "pa!" that Elizabeth understood what was truly happening, and was overcome with laughter.

"Lizzy, what is it?" asked Jane.

"My poor, dear Jane, she is not asking for her papa. She is trying to say *pianoforte*. I fear you and Charles have both been upstaged by a musical instrument."

"Pa!"

"Oh, Lizzy, I am not sure whether that is better or worse," said Jane, laughing, and making her way over to the pianoforte, to pick up Bess. With some assistance from Mrs. Padgett, Jane was situated on the pianoforte's bench, with her daughter in her lap, and Bess, with absolutely no hesitance, was slapping her hand down on one of the keys, squealing with delight at the sound it made, and proceeding to slap at more of the keys, exclaiming, "Pa! Pa! Pa!"

It must have been the greatest ruckus that had been made at Pemberley in some time, and Elizabeth thoroughly loved it, right up until both of the boys awoke, and James scrunched up his face in disgust, while George began to cry.

"Oh, Lizzy, I am so sorry!" Jane exclaimed.

"Do not worry yourself over it, Jane," Elizabeth said, walking over to George's cradle, so she could pick him up and soothe him. "We may have the pianoforte moved to another room near here, and then Bess may pound away as much as you have patience for, which – knowing you – will be interminably."

Elizabeth waited a few days to attempt her seduction. She did so both to ensure she was truly ready for the physical act, but even more because she was not entirely sure how to go about it. Such doubts were new to her; before, she and her husband had always come together naturally, with no conscious effort on her part, but nearly four months had passed since their last time together. She expected some manner of awkwardness, and yet also knew that the one to initiate matters must be her; Darcy would hardly go beyond a kiss, unless she made it clear to him that she was ready to return to marital relations.

She *was* ready, mostly. She was barely able to eat enough to sustain her part of nursing twins, and no-one would call her heavy, but the old litheness of figure she had always possessed seemed elusive, now. Her hips had changed, her belly had changed, and added to all of this she felt the lack of her usual amount of activity. The weather this winter had left her with few opportunities to walk out of doors, and she was required to make do with taking turns about the gallery or the ball-room, which grew boring far too soon, and thus was not nearly enough to return her figure to what it had been.

This was, at least, another opportunity for physical activity, she thought, and then blushed quite thoroughly as she pulled her dressing gown on over her favourite nightgown. She had waited until as late as she possibly could, and then nursed the twins again, hoping to avoid any embarrassment in that quarter, although the possibility of it was still on her mind, and she hoped her husband would leave that part of her to her sons, for now.

She was late in coming to bed, and when she came into the master's bedchamber, Darcy was reading a book, and looked up to smile at her. Elizabeth removed her dressing gown very slowly, very deliberately, and stood there briefly after she had draped it over a chair, looking at him with desire and anticipation for so long she took a deep, shuddering breath, extinguished her candle, and then climbed into bed.

Elizabeth had thought of at least a dozen things to say in this moment, and none of them seemed right now that it had arrived – the straightforward ways of saying she was ready, the little witticisms, the bolder statements of what she wanted. In the end she just breathed deeply and looked at him again – surely he could read everything in her eyes – and kissed him, very ardently. He responded, with that wonderful mouth of his, and the kiss wound to a very lovely, leisurely end, at which he whispered, "that was very nice – good night, my love," and then turned over in bed, facing away from her.

Elizabeth stared at him in exasperation for a moment, and then thought she must not have made it clear to him that she wished for something beyond a kiss, and if that was the case and she had aroused him, the gentlemanly thing to do would have been to turn away from her, so she did not see it.

"Are you so very tired, Mr. Darcy?" she asked, reaching over his side to run her hand down his chest, then his belly, and then lower. It was bold of her, terribly bold, but there must be a degree of boldness to a seduction, she thought.

"Elizabeth," he said, grasping her wrist to still her hand, "it hardly feels right while we are still in mourning for our cousin."

All the desire fled from her, and she felt cold and sober. They were in half-mourning, and while she *did* mourn Alice, she had not seen her cousin's death as something that should affect their return to marital relations. Yet Alice had been Elizabeth's cousin by a relatively recent marriage; Darcy had known her longer, and Elizabeth would never say it was inappropriate for him to think as he apparently did.

"Yes, of course," she whispered, withdrawing her hand, and turning on her side in the opposite direction, so she faced away from him. For a moment, she felt tears spring to her eyes, but she blinked them away, although she drifted off to sleep feeling guilty, sorely disappointed, and a little unwanted.

CHAPTER 28

Georgiana liked the Russells very much. It was not merely that they were her only acquaintances in town, although until they had hosted a small dinner party, enabling her to meet some of their friends, they had been. Admiral Russell was just what she would have expected of good naval company – a genial host, and always ready with a story of some battle, or of Matthew's younger days.

It was Mrs. Russell who rapidly became Georgiana's closer friend, however, for she had lived aboard ship with her husband for many years, and had a good deal of advice for a younger captain's wife. She also played the pianoforte – Georgiana learned that in addition to the newer instrument in their drawing-room, a sitting-room upstairs housed an old battered square pianoforte that had been adapted for naval use, and made her recall her husband's mentioning Admiral Russell, when they had first gone to see her own instrument. Georgiana was encouraged to call on them whenever she wished, so she might practise on either instrument, and even when her own pianoforte did arrive, she still called on them daily.

In Mrs. Russell, she also found a regular walking companion, and they became a fixture down along the Medway, Bowden and Mrs. Russell's footman trailing behind them with umbrellas, in case the rain started again. They were thus on this particular day, watching the river in the hopes of sighting a new frigate in the distance, and as they were walking along, Mrs. Russell said, "Lady Stanton, there is a gentleman over there who appears to be waving to us. Do you know him?"

Georgiana was puzzled by this until she followed Mrs. Russell's gaze, and saw the gentleman was Edward, and then she was even more puzzled. He came striding up to her, and exclaimed, "Finally I find you! I thought I should have to search every inn."

"Edward, what is the matter – is someone in your family ill? Lady

Ellen, is she well?"

Georgiana found, however, that she did not need an answer to her question, for walking up behind him was Marguerite Durand, and her son.

"Edward, what have you done?" she whispered, pulling him a few steps away from Mrs. Russell.

"Nothing, as yet, beyond selling my commission. But when her mourning is complete, I intend to make Madame Durand my wife," he said, suddenly conscious of Mrs. Russell. "I apologise, may I be introduced to your friend?"

"How do you prefer to be addressed, now, if you have sold your commission?"

"Colonel Fitzwilliam, still, I suppose."

Georgiana introduced him as such, and they both said all that was proper. During this time, Madame Durand and her son had reached them, and Georgiana was completely lost as to how to introduce her. Explaining the source of their acquaintance hardly seemed right, nor was it proper to call her Edward's betrothed. She was glad Edward made the introduction, saying only that Madame Durand was visiting from France, and although Mrs. Russell must have overheard enough of his earlier conversation with Georgiana to know there was more to the Frenchwoman than that, her response was vague, and discreet.

"I will assume you wish to see your cousin and Madame Durand settled into the Arms," said Mrs. Russell. "Perhaps you might all come to dinner tomorrow, and we may become better acquainted."

"Colonel Fitzwilliam has an engagement prior," said Madame Durand. "But I would be please to dine with you."

"Very well, then," said Mrs. Russell. "I shall see you and Lady Stanton tomorrow. It was lovely to make your acquaintance."

It was a strange, awkward party that made the walk back to the inn, and stranger still when they arrived and Edward asked Mr. Norris for lodging for Madame Durand and her son, but not for himself. When they went upstairs, Madame Durand and her son went to their apartment to settle in, and Georgiana led Edward to the sitting-room of her space, prepared to chastise him for living in sin with the widow before they could be married.

He spoke before she could, however, holding up his hand to her and saying, "I know how badly this must look, but I assure you, my intentions are honourable. In fact, that is why I am here – why I sought you out when my mother's letter indicated you had come here."

"Why do you need me?"

"Marguerite has no acquaintances in England, except for you. I had hoped you would look after her – keep her company – while I am gone."

"And where are you to go?"

"To Stradbroke, to speak with my parents. I do not want to appear there with Marguerite in tow – I wish to acclimate them to the idea, to bring them around to the thought of my marrying a woman with only eight thousand pounds."

"In your letter, you were certain such a marriage was not an option."

"It was not, then. I mourn my poor sister – do not doubt me in that – and I feel horribly that her death has brought about the possibility. Believe me, I shall always feel guilty over it, but I will not allow my guilt to be the obstacle that prevents my marrying the woman I love. Do you not see, Georgiana? Before, my duty was to marry Anne, further unite our families, and manage Rosings more firmly. Now, my duty is to ensure there is an heir to the earldom, and I do not mind if I do it on seven hundred a year, if I do so with Marguerite. There are no certainties in having children, but my chances must be best with a young widow who has already borne a son, despite her husband being at sea for much of their marriage."

Georgiana flinched at this last statement, and he said, "Oh Georgiana, I am so sorry – I spoke without thinking." He reached out to embrace her with his lone arm, and said, "I am so very sorry for your loss, and I am remiss in not saying so immediately. Has Matthew not returned yet?"

"No, but I expect him any day," she said, although the truth was that she had been expecting him any day for a fortnight, now, and she had been disappointed on each and every one of those days.

"I am sure it will be soon."

"When are you leaving for Stradbroke?"

"As soon as I am sure Marguerite is settled. My mother will worry if there is too much of a delay in my journey."

"I will look after Madame Durand," Georgiana said, "and of course Matthew and I shall welcome her into the family, although you must understand it will always be a little strange for us – particularly for him – given how we were connected in the first place. I am sure over time it will become less strange."

"That means a great deal to me, Georgiana."

"I know what it is to love, and fear you may not be able to be with the one you love," she said. "I am glad there is a chance, for you." Given her conversations with Lady Ellen, Georgiana felt it was a fairly good chance, so long as Edward was willing to live on so little, but she would not say so – she did not wish to give him hope, when it might turn out to be false.

"Marguerite is everything to me," he said, simply. "I would never have thought I would find love, and with one so beautiful, particularly after – after Waterloo. I do not know how I could have given her up."

Thus far, Georgiana had only Edward's statements as proof of the love he shared with Marguerite Durand, but when a few hours later she had opportunity to witness their parting, she found herself wishing even more fervently that they should have a chance to marry.

She and Madame Durand both came down to see Edward off in one of the inn's post-chaises, despite a new bout of rain. But while Georgiana grasped his hand and wished him well under the protection of Bowden's umbrella, Madame Durand stood in the rain for some time, with her hand upon his cheek, gazing into his eyes before finally saying, "Travel good, mon chéri." Edward broke into a most uncharacteristic blush, reached up with his hand, and covered hers. Only then did Madame Durand step back under the umbrella.

They both stood and watched the carriage set off, and as it did so, Madame Durand said, "It must be strange for you, and you know I do mourn my husband, but you leave Edward to look after me is best thing to happen ever in my life."

CHAPTER 29

It was perhaps not noticeable to anyone else in the house, but there was a degree of awkwardness, between Mrs. Darcy and Mr. Darcy. On her part, there was a distance, which began on the night of her rejection, and grew every night thereafter, when he made clear she was to get no more than a kiss before he turned away from her. On his part, during the daylight hours, there was a solicitousness towards her that seemed aimed at making up for it, but Elizabeth could not fully allow it to do so.

Matters were not helped by the return of the Bakers to their attention. The weather being generally poor, Darcy and Mr. Baker were unable to set a fixed date for their ride, and instead, after a flurry of notes between Barrowmere Park and Pemberley, met between the two houses one morning when the weather had cleared. They had ridden only as long as the skies held, but this was long enough for Darcy to return, and tell Elizabeth of how he had informed Mr. Baker of his wife's attempts at infidelity, and Mr. Baker had been far less upset than he should, by rights, have been. "Eh, well, look at her, an' look at me," he had told Darcy. "I'll speak to her of it – I must, of course – but I ain't too surprised by it. I thank ye for not lettin' her succeed."

Thus the Bakers might have continued on in whatever peculiar manner of marital bliss it was they had, in Derbyshire, but for Mrs. Baker's no longer being welcome at Pemberley. Such a thing could not help but be noticed by the rest of the neighbourhood, and as most of the rest of the neighbourhood did not favour the Bakers's company, they followed suit rapidly. Elizabeth felt badly for Mr. Baker, although less so than she might have, knowing how casually he had received the news of what his wife had done. She had no remorse for Mrs. Baker, but thinking about what that woman had done turned her thoughts in very unpleasant directions.

On this day, Elizabeth was walking in the ball-room – hiding, in essence, from the others, who had gone to the gallery – and once again considering the subject Mrs. Baker had made her think of, which was whether her husband would ever take a mistress. When the incident had happened, Elizabeth had laughed over it, so secure in her husband's love she had been, her security reaffirmed by his reaction to the event.

He had told her then that he belonged completely and entirely to her, but those were mere words, and his actions said far more than his words had done. While she still did not doubt that he loved her, she had come to understand that love and desire were two different things. While her husband might always love her wholly, he had made it clear he no longer desired her, and in time, desire might indeed drive him to seek out a mistress – one with better manners and sense than Mrs. Baker, certainly, but a mistress nonetheless. She paced the ball-room, absorbed in these thoughts, but when the door opened from the saloon, it echoed throughout the space, and she looked over at Darcy – for it was he who had entered – with a bit of defiance in her gaze, over what she had been contemplating.

"There you are," Darcy said, striding across the room to where she had halted. "You are looking very well this morning."

"Thank you, as are you." Elizabeth glanced down at her figure, and wondered if he was lying – to good purpose, of course, to be kind to her, but lying nonetheless.

"May I walk with you?" he asked.

"Of course." She took up his arm and they set out, walking at a good pace, but slower than Elizabeth had been before.

"It seems the Bakers have given up on the neighbourhood. They have gone to town, and are seeking a party to take over the lease."

"I suppose that was inevitable – Mrs. Baker had fears of being bored in the country even before she was cut off from society."

"I cannot help but think that house is cursed, when it comes to us," he said. "I have half a mind to purchase it myself."

"You wish to purchase a house you think cursed?"

"I do not think the house itself cursed, merely the company within. I fear some new party will take over the lease, and find another way to vex us. If we own the house, we control who leases it, and someday it may be needed for what I truly intend it for."

She asked him what that was.

"A dower house. It is inexcusable that an estate of this size lacks one."

"Are you already planning to die before me? For if so, I must raise an objection."

It was very strange to think about the estate needing a dower house, to think of Darcy gone, and James succeeding him as master of the estate, with his own wife to take over as mistress and supplant Elizabeth in that role. Even as uneasy as things were between Elizabeth and her husband now, she did not like the thought of it at all.

"I am not *planning* it, but neither would I like to not plan for such an event, if that is how it is to be."

"Had you not a little while ago been lamenting buying up Barrowmere's land, instead of saving for an estate for George?"

"I had, and it did cross my mind to purchase the house and restore some of the land to it," he said, "but it does not feel right to take away some of James's birthright. There is a reason why things are done the way they are, why all must pass to the first son, and I cannot ignore that. The dower house might be to George's benefit, however – if his career is compatible, he might use it as his household, rent-free, until you are to take it over."

"*If* I am to take it over."

"Yes, *if* you are to take it over. If he chooses the navy or the army as his profession, his poor wife might set up her household there, so she is not shuttling all about the country, as Georgiana does now."

"Georgiana had her chance at the house, and chose not to take it."

"True, and it will still need quite a lot of work. The Bakers made some progress, but not much, in the amount of time they were there."

"I believe I see what this is about now. You are jealous because Charles is building a house, and wish for yourself a similar project."

"Running this estate is more than enough of a project for me," he said, "but I do think this will better Pemberley, in the long run. If you do not have need of it, some lady will, at some point along the family line. Do I have your blessing to make inquiries on the purchase?"

"You do. I only hope this does not bring us back into contact with the Camberts."

"I share your hope," he said, kissing her on the cheek before he left her to continue to pace the ball-room.

If Elizabeth had felt odd of late when she changed for bed, she did so particularly on this night, at the thought of how her husband had so thoughtfully planned for her future, should anything happen to him, and then kissed her so chastely on the cheek. She dismissed Sarah, and stood there in her dressing-room for some time, thinking.

Eventually, she removed her dressing gown, and then nightgown, and stood in front of the looking-glass, staring at her changed body: the widened hips, the stubborn bulge of her belly, and her breasts, sagging slightly so soon after nursing. She sighed, and put her nightgown back on, and when out of habit she started toward the master's bedchamber, rather than the mistress's, she caught herself, and for the first time since her sons had been christened, contemplated sleeping in her own bed. It would be easier, she thought, to not have to pretend all was well, and get into bed and watch her husband turn away from her. It would be easier, and he had no interest in her, anyway. He might wait up for her, for a little while, but she had never asked him if he preferred her return to his bed; perhaps now that he had his heirs, he wished for them to use their separate bedchambers, but had been too polite to say so. Certainly, his kisses had been growing less enthusiastic. With these thoughts, she turned around, and went through the door to her own bedchamber.

It was strange, very strange, to climb up into this bed, to not see him before she went to sleep, and she ached at the thought of what she had lost. But there was another advantage to sleeping alone: she could cry over it, and cry she did, softly, gently, lying there with tears streaming down her face and soaking the pillow, until at last she drifted off to sleep.

She awoke in the middle of the night, to the light of a candle, and thought at first with a rush of guilt that she had left one burning. She rose, and pulled open the bed-curtains to extinguish it, but then she saw Darcy, seated in a chair beside her bed, very much awake, his countenance wholly sad.

"You never came to bed," he said, softly. "I walked through the whole house, looking for you – I thought perhaps you had fallen asleep in the nursery, or the library, or one of the sitting-rooms. This was the last place I expected to find you. I know it is your right to sleep here, but it has never been our way. What is the matter, Elizabeth, that you would not come to my bed?"

Elizabeth wiped a tear from her face. "I cannot bear it any more, to be rejected by you. I know you said it was because of our mourning for Alice, but I do not believe that was really your reason – I am well aware of what has happened to my body, but I have had two babies, now, and there is only so much I can do about it, although I have done all I can while the weather is so poor."

"Oh, Elizabeth, is that truly what you think? Of course it is, and it is my fault. You must not doubt that I find you beautiful – all of you. If I must confess, I find you more beautiful now that you have borne my children, and you are not so thin as you were in London last year. It has been absolute torture sleeping beside you every night for the past few months – both when you were with child, and after – but nor would I suggest you come here to sleep, for I know how much I would miss your presence."

"Then why have you been so cold in your manners towards me in our bed? Even now, when we are very nearly out of half-mourning."

"It is because I must be cold, or it would be even greater torture, and it is entirely because of Alice," he said. "I thought when I mentioned her, that you understood. It was not the mourning; it was because of what *happened* to Alice."

As soon as he said it, Elizabeth understood all. How worried he had been for her, both before and during her births, and then to have that followed by the death of his cousin, from childbirth. They had two male heirs now; they need not have any more children to see the estate's future more secure than it had been for two generations, and if they no longer did the act that might result in more children, her life would never again be at risk in that manner. So determined upon this course he had been, he had intended to purchase a dower house, had planned for her to outlive him. All of this she understood, and she broke down in a series of great heaving sobs, of relief and tenderness towards him.

He rose from the chair and climbed into bed with her, and held her in a way he had not in some time. "I was so terrified for your life, when the twins were born, and then – "

"Shhh, you do not need to explain," she whispered. "I know why you did what you did. I understand, now."

For a very long time, Elizabeth luxuriated in the simple closeness of the man who had not been close to her for some time, in contentedness at being once again secure of his affections – of all of his affections. Then, finally, she said:

"We cannot sustain what you wished to do. There is less risk of it now, anyway, while I am nursing, but I do want more children. I would like a daughter very much, although I would not mind more sons, and I do not want to give it up – not yet. We must live our lives, Darcy. We must live our lives in hope for the best, and not in fear. We never know what may happen – we might give up marital relations only to have you killed hunting, or me in – oh, oh, a carriage accident, perhaps. Your own sister nearly died falling down the stairs."

Elizabeth could see the effect of her argument upon his countenance, and was glad of it. After some time, he said, "Then what are we to do?"

"I believe that depends upon how tired you are, my love," she said.

He responded by kissing her as passionately as he had used to do, a kiss which she returned with some urgency, and was most aroused to find broken only by his desire to kiss his way down her throat. Elizabeth gasped, and then found herself giggling in relief.

"What do you laugh about, my darling Elizabeth?" he murmured.

"I laugh because – neither of us is very good at seduction, are we?" she asked, tracing her fingertips along the muscles of his back.

"Presently, I find seduction to be very overrated," he said, chuckling with her, and then proceeding to touch with convincing fervency those places she had been so ashamed of. He mostly left her bosom alone, as she had wished, but made up for it by lavishing both attention and kisses on her belly, as if to reinforce his words about bearing his children. Elizabeth responded in turn by removing his nightshirt and reacquainting herself with that body which had turned away from her for so many nights. He had not changed as much as she, of course, but she had missed him so very much.

For Elizabeth, it was as though everything was new again, to be experienced after such a change to her body, and to their lives. Seduction, she thought, required confidence – and confidence was not so very far from pride – when what she truly wanted was what she experienced now, to be fully desired by her husband, and to return that desire most ardently. It was certainly not a seduction, but it was one of the sweetest nights of Elizabeth's life.

CHAPTER 30

It was not long before Georgiana was also calling Marguerite Durand by her Christian name. Marguerite's maid had refused to leave France, and so she had been faced with the same difficulties as Georgiana, in dressing herself. They had worked out a system where one of them would dress herself as best she could, and make her way to the other's apartment, where her stays could be properly tightened, and then she could be of assistance herself.

On this morning, Georgiana was helping Marguerite with her hair, when the Frenchwoman said, "You know what Edward says to me, that make me most angry? I think it will make you angry, too."

"What did he say?"

"He says he is not an whole man because he have lost his arm," Marguerite said.

"It must be very difficult for him."

"It should not be! He have life, and health!" Marguerite cried, passionately. "C'est incroyable, for him to think he is not an whole man. I tell him this. And I tell him it is not his *arm* that make him a *man*."

Georgiana coughed, and was fairly certain she blushed from head to toe.

Marguerite reached up and patted her hand, and said, "Ah, you English are so modern – no, no, modest. I will have to mind things I say if I live here."

"I hope you shall live here, Marguerite. I would very much like to call you my cousin, someday."

"You will, Georgiana," Marguerite said. "Even if parents of Edward do not give blessing, he say we will elope. I tell him I would not for very long time, but now I am in England I do not think I can go back. I love him too much."

The weather once again being poor, Marguerite chose to stay in her apartment with her son, while Georgiana went downstairs to learn from Mr. Norris that there had been no sightings of the Caroline and no response to her advertisement, but that there was a letter for her from Elizabeth. Georgiana had become so accustomed to complete disappointment from Mr. Norris that this cheered her spirits substantially, and she returned to her apartment to read the letter.

Georgiana found herself giggling over Elizabeth's description of Moll Kelly, and how Fitzwilliam had come upon her, seated behind the desk in his study. It was not until she was penning her response, however, that she was struck with a thought. She refreshed her pen, and wrote, "Can you tell me, when Moll made the passage from Ireland, was she at all seasick?"

For the thought was that Moll, more adventurous than her sister by far, but hopefully in possession of at least some of the same qualities that made Sarah Kelly such a good lady's maid for Elizabeth, might not merely be convinced to serve as a lady's maid on board the Caroline – she might actually enjoy it. Georgiana noticed as she finished her letter that the rain appeared to be lessening, and this coincided with Marguerite's knocking on her door, and asking if she wished to call on Mrs. Russell, and then perhaps have a walk, if the rain lessened further.

By the time they left the inn, the rain had let up entirely, and as they found upon calling that both Admiral and Mrs. Russell were out, they decided to walk on as a duo. On their first such walk, Georgiana had inquired delicately as to whether Marguerite minded her usual destination, down the hill to the dockyard, to walk along the Medway. As Marguerite had indicated she did not mind, they went that way now without speaking of it, walking slowly, so little Jean-Charles could keep pace.

"I spent more time in dockyard now than I did when I was wife of capitaine marine," said Marguerite, quietly.

"It must be strange for you to be here."

"All is strange for me," Marguerite said. "I never think I can be in England, now, with hope to marry cousin of man who is enemy of Charles. I hope you understand."

"I understand love."

"But you do not understand how love come in different types. You know only strong type of love. I know weak type, with Charles – I care for him, but I do not know if I would have marry him, if I did not need protection, with war happen. I was good wife to him, when he was home, but he was not home much, and when he was home last, we disagree about important things, about Emperor, and King. I was sad when he die – I am sad, still, but is weak sad, like weak love."

"Do you think strong love is still possible, when – when you are often separated, from the one you love?"

"Ah, yes, I know what you think, and you should not think it! I think strong love happen when you do not seek love. Edward and me, we do not seek love – love happen to us as accident. Weak love happen when you seek love. It matters not much if you are separate, when love is strong in beginning."

It might not have been said eloquently, but Georgiana very much saw the truth in what Marguerite had said, and might have ruminated on it further, had Admiral Russell not come up to them at a little bowlegged run, and said, "There you are, Lady Stanton! 'Tis a frigate up the river that just might be her."

Georgiana felt her pulse quicken, and very much wanted to run down to the river immediately. "Do you wish to go?" she asked Marguerite.

"I think no. I will call him cousin, gladly," Marguerite said, "but I will not go on board his ship. I hope you have understanding."

"I do," Georgiana said. "Bowden, will you see Madame Durand back to the inn?"

Bowden looked hesitant to leave his employer, but finally deferred to the fact that she was to be escorted by an admiral, and thus Georgiana was freed to take up Admiral Russell's arm and walk at a rapid clip with him down to the waterfront.

"See her there?" Admiral Russell asked, pointing to the frigate drifting in on the slightest ghost of a breeze. "It must be her – you said she struck ice, and the larboard side has clearly been patched up. Here, let us go and hire a boat."

Admiral Russell did hire a boat, and would not let her pay for it, although he did tell the men rowing that the lady would supplement their wages if they rowed hard but dry, and this they did. Georgiana watched the ship with a keen eye, certain by now that it *was* the Caroline, her pulse pounding as they came closer.

How her heart soared, at that first glimpse of him! He was standing on the quarterdeck, and it was almost as though Georgiana had forgotten how handsome he was, as though he had faded a little in her memory, so struck was she by the sight of him. He had no reason to be looking for her – no reason to suspect her to be in Chatham at all, much less among the small boat traffic all about the Medway.

Eventually, however, someone on the ship must have realised that their boat was headed directly toward the Caroline's battered larboard side, and by the time they were near enough for Admiral Russell to call out, "Admiral Russell, and a lady, who shall require a bosun's chair!" winking to her after he did so, there were several faces peering over the rail at them.

Georgiana had lived on board the ship long enough that this ruse could not last long – surely at least some of these men recognised her, even with her bonnet obscuring part of her face. But it did last long enough for

Matthew himself to peer over the railing as the boat hooked on to the ship, with a look of open happiness to see his former captain, which transformed into something far more emotional when he noticed who was sitting beside Admiral Russell in the boat.

Once he had seen Georgiana situated in the bosun's chair, Admiral Russell climbed up the side of the ship with the pace and skill of a man who had done so for a half-century of his life, and he was being greeted by Matthew when Georgiana was lowered onto the deck.

"Lady Stanton," Matthew said, his voice formal, but his gaze so intense that Georgiana felt all he could not say, in front of his men.

"Captain Stanton."

He helped her out of the bosun's chair, and gave her his hand, which she squeezed tightly, but then was required to release. As happy as she was to be returned to his presence, it was not enough, and would not be until he had seen the ship in, and could meet her in the privacy of his cabin.

"Admiral Russell, perhaps you might like to accompany Lady Stanton to the great cabin? Hawke will see to some refreshment while you wait, and I will be in once matters are settled here."

Georgiana felt tears well in her eyes at the realisation that it was only proper for him to offer some hospitality to Admiral Russell, and she would have to wait to see him privately.

"Nay, nay. If any man had sat, drinking my port and delaying my reunion with Mrs. Russell in the manner you recommend, I should have been entirely irate over it," Admiral Russell said. "I have been in your boots and I shall not be the cause of such a delay. But Lady Stanton was engaged to dine with us tomorrow: if you will come with her, we may reacquaint ourselves then."

Georgiana gazed at Admiral Russell with unmitigated fondness, for having come here with little purpose other than to deliver her, and watched as he clapped Matthew on the shoulder once, and then went back over the side. Matthew then leaned in close to Georgiana, and said, "Why do you not go to the cabin? I will be there as soon as I may."

Georgiana did not want to go to the cabin; she wanted to stay there and not allow him to leave her sight. She realised that these last manoeuvres of the ship must require his attention, however, and if it had been her in his place, she would have been utterly distracted by the presence of the one she loved. She went to the cabin, therefore, and greeted Hawke when he placed a pitcher of what was likely lemonade down on the table. Georgiana was in no mood to sit and drink lemonade, however, and she paced about the cabin in what seemed the longest half-hour of her life, removing her gloves, bonnet, and pelisse one by one in her agitation. Finally, there came a loud, rapid flurry of orders from the boatswain outside, and she felt the ship touch against the quay.

Georgiana stood there trembling, waiting for one of the doors to open, and when it did, she ran to him and threw herself into a crushing embrace. She cried almost immediately – tears of happiness over being reunited, tears of sadness over the baby – and when she looked up at him, she realised he was weeping as well.

"I did not wish for you to trouble yourself to come here, and yet I am so very glad you did," he said, his voice hoarse.

"I would not delay seeing you again for so much as a day," she said, and meant it fully. All of her time waiting here, both the lonely days and those after, in the company of the Russells and then Marguerite, seemed an easy sacrifice now.

"Did you travel here from Pemberley by yourself?"

"No, I came from Stradbroke."

"Visiting your aunt and uncle at this time of year?"

He must have left Copenhagen before receiving her letter informing him of what had happened to Alice, Georgiana realised, and she told him of it now, gently.

"My God, our poor cousin," he said, and pulled her close again, this time for an embrace that ended in a very long kiss. He laced his fingers through her hair, and stopped suddenly when he reached the section where it was still very short, where her wound had been. "You are well, are you not, Georgiana? You look well, but – there have been no lasting effects, have there?"

"None but sadness," she whispered.

"I am going to endeavour to make that go away, as much as I am able," he said, caressing her cheek.

"You have already," she said, and then, feeling the roughness of his touch, "Matthew, what has happened to your hands?"

She took one of them up for inspection, and was a little horrified by what she saw. He could never entirely have been said to have a gentleman's hands, but what she held now was rough and dry, and deeply calloused.

"The captain must take his turn at the pumps, same as any of the men, when the ship is imperilled."

"Was there that much danger?" It had not seemed so in his letters, but Georgiana realised he might not have indicated it, for fear of worrying her.

"To the ship, yes – to our lives, no," he said. "We might have sent our boats off at any time, for assistance, or at the worst, rescue. I am glad we saved her, though. She is not the most important *she* in the world to me, but I am very fond of her."

What he said, and the way he said it, made Georgiana swell with love again, and she sought a tighter embrace. At some point, she knew they would have to leave each other's arms, and go about the remainder of the day – at some point it would not be so novel to be held again by her husband. But for now she wanted to remain just so, and he showed every indication of desiring the same.

Eventually, he asked, "Where is Bowden? I would have thought he would accompany you, for I am sure he would like to see his old messmates. He did not leave our employ, did he?"

Georgiana stared at him for a moment, perplexed as to how she was going to impart what it seemed she now needed to impart. She informed him there was news she must tell him of, to explain Bowden's whereabouts, and then told him of Edward and Marguerite, and how Bowden had accompanied the Frenchwoman back to the inn.

He was silent for a very long time, absorbing this news, and Georgiana finally said, "I know it shall be very strange for you, but I like Marguerite ever so much, and they are truly in love."

"It will be very strange indeed," he said. "I cannot help but think I am responsible for it – I think I will be reminded of it every time I see them. We were the ones who asked Edward to look after her, but beyond that, none of this would have happened if I had not engaged the Polonais. I caused the event that made Madame Durand a widow."

"I believe your mind will be easier about it when you see them together," Georgiana said. "But you have done nothing wrong, and nor have they, for they will not marry until they have both completed their mourning."

"I am sure I will attune myself to the idea eventually," said he. "It is just a bit of a shock."

There was a knocking at the door, then, and Georgiana forced herself to step away from him, as Matthew called out that the person knocking should come in. It was Lieutenant Rigby, who had several things the captain needed to attend to, and Georgiana scowled at the thought that he should have to leave her.

"Do not look so angry, my dearest," Matthew said. "We will be back together soon enough."

"Shall I pack my trunk and have Bowden bring it here?" Georgiana asked, pleased at the thought of living with him again, but not that she should have to sleep in a cot beside him.

"No, no you shall not," he said. "Tonight I am going to have Rigby mind the ship, and I am going to do what I have been longing to do for some time, which is to sleep beside my sweet, gentle wife in a fine, warm bed."

Anyone who had seen Lady Stanton walking through Chatham over the past few weeks must have noticed the change in her countenance now, as she did so on the arm of her husband. They arrived back at the inn to find Edward just stepping out of a carriage with the Brandon arms upon it, and both coachman and footman dressed in mourning. In the time it took the

Stantons and Edward to say their greetings, Marguerite had come rushing out, with her son in her arms and an hopeful expression upon her face, as she set Jean-Charles down before the man who might one day be his stepfather. Georgiana, as well, saw the carriage as a sign for hope, and this was confirmed when Edward took up Marguerite's hand, kissed it fervently, and said:

"They have given their blessing. They will be pleased to welcome you into the family – when the time is right, of course."

"Dieu merci!" whispered Marguerite. "Yes, of course, when time is right."

Edward then turned to retrieve something from the carriage, and kneeled down in front of Jean-Charles to hand him a faded old wooden toy soldier, saying, "I brought this for you – it was mine, as a boy."

"Merci beaucoup," said the boy, who clutched it to his chest in the manner of a child whose mother had not been able to afford much by way of toys, thus far in his life.

"Je t'en prie," Edward said, ruffling the boy's hair before he stood.

Georgiana had been surprised enough by the notion of Edward in love, but this more paternal side of him startled her, pleased her, and made her wonder if Matthew, observing this, wished for the same opportunity for himself.

"Shall we dine together?" Edward asked. "I will take a room here, if one is available."

Georgiana found she was glaring at him momentarily, before she caught herself. She might have preferred to be alone with Matthew for weeks upon end, before any of the obligations society could impose on them, but Edward was family, and Marguerite would be eventually; it was right that they all dine together. Nor could she entirely approve of the thought of Edward and Marguerite dining alone as a couple, as she suspected they would if Edward's offer was refused.

Matthew clearly thought the same, for after a quick glance towards her, for her acquiescence, he offered to order the dinner, and that they should dine in the Stantons's apartment. With all of this settled, and the first fat drops of fresh rain beginning to fall, they all went inside.

"We still need to have our arms drawn up and painted on the landau," Matthew said, absently, looking back at the carriage.

"We do not," Georgiana replied. "They have been completed, and by a countess, no less."

Although Georgiana might have preferred to dine alone with her husband, it certainly could not have been called an unpleasant dinner, that they had with Marguerite and Edward. For a supplement to her wages, Jean-Charles had been entrusted to one of the maids of the establishment, and so the four adults could dine together, sitting close around the little table, but of such convivial spirits as to not mind at all. It became clear to Georgiana that Marguerite and Edward had already dined together, quite frequently by the look of it, for Marguerite quietly ignored propriety and served both herself and Edward, even reaching over at one point with fork and knife to carve his mutton into smaller pieces. Edward looked not the least embarrassed by this event; he gazed fondly at Marguerite before, during, and after the carving of his meat, and through most of the course of the meal, and Georgiana was delighted, to see him so smitten.

They were all better informed of Edward's time at Stradbroke, that not only had Lord and Lady Brandon blessed the marriage, but that Andrew had done so as well, relieved at the thought of a match that should lessen his own need to remarry and father a son. They learned also that Lady Ellen had offered up what little remained of her own inheritance, to supplement the couple's income, which should enable them to live a bit more comfortably, if not exactly as should become the married son of an earl.

It was a strange dinner, there being no separation of the sexes; Matthew and Edward partook of a little port as the conversation continued, and Edward, noting both the square pianoforte and Matthew's cello, resting against the wall beside it, said, "Will you not play for us a little? I have been a soldier for too long to take for granted such musical company."

Georgiana looked at Matthew hesitantly – she hardly knew how he could play at all, with his hands in such a state, but she did know he had been practising the sonata he had sent her. He gave her a little nod, and she said, "We do have a piece we have been practising, but not together – "

"Never worry about that," Edward said. "You are among family, and eventual family. Let us be your first audience."

They were in an apartment within a rather large inn, and so Edward and Marguerite would not be their only audience, but Georgiana pushed this thought aside and went to the pianoforte to arrange her music, while Matthew took out his cello and tried a few notes.

"Georgiana, may I trouble you for a low C?" he asked. When she gave it to him, he reflected it on the cello, and they proceeded to tune his cello thus. Although it sounded well, Georgiana was not entirely sure that the tone of her pianoforte was true, it having travelled all the way from Pemberley untouched by a tuner, but at least if they were off, they would be off together.

They began with the opening note, Georgiana looking over at him to ensure they timed it together, and then the piece was such that she must continue on alone. She did, entirely unsure of how things should go, and wishing they had not attempted this first in front of an audience, even a small and kind one. Matthew's next notes, when they came, were a little ill-timed, a little awkward, but then a strange and beautiful thing happened: everything united, perfectly, to Georgiana's heart, and perhaps even to her ear. She did not know the part that had been missing from what she had been practising, but she trusted it would be there, and it would be right, and it was. They flowed through the piece, plaintive at the beginning, growing hopeful and even triumphant by the end.

It had been so beautiful – to her, at least – she was nearly in tears, and when she looked over to Marguerite, she saw that lady was weeping, as well.

"It make me feel all sad things that ever happen," said Marguerite, "and then all happiness that follow."

That was why Matthew had chosen it, Georgiana thought, with an intensely tender gaze towards him. She had enjoyed dining with Edward and Marguerite, but now she wanted them to leave her sitting-room as soon as it could be done; thankfully, they seemed to sense this, and did so.

It was Matthew, and not Marguerite, who helped with her stays that night, who helped remove all of the pins from her hair, and when he had finished, Georgiana took a step back from him, standing there in her shift and feeling suddenly overwhelmed by shyness. She had been so long without him that it was strange to now be on the precipice of this sort of intimacy, and she felt a little as she had on her wedding night.

"Georgiana, what is the matter?" he asked, quietly. "Do you worry over what happened to your cousin? For if you do, I shall remind you of what I wrote – that the choice is yours. Only if you want children, shall we attempt to have them. There are – other ways – of being together, if you do not."

"But what do *you* want? Do you want children?"

"My own mother died in childbirth, and now so has your cousin," he said. "I do not send a landsman up to take in a topsail, Georgiana."

"Matthew, what on earth are you talking about?"

"I mean that for a man to be a topman, for him to work at those heights, he will never be ordered to do so on my ship. There is a reward, of course, in being rated an able seaman, and earning pay as such, but the risk is his, and so must the choice be."

"But I need to know, so that I may choose, if you have any desire for a child."

"I would very much like to have a child, if it is your choice, Georgiana," he said. "If it is not, I would be perfectly happy to spend the rest of my life with the woman I love. Thank God I did not lose my chance at that – thank God I did not lose you."

Georgiana felt her eyes fill with tears yet again, and said, "I do want a child. I want a little boy who will be brave and good like his papa, and carry on his title. And if he is ever in being, he should know his papa was very, very wrong to write that he had not been a good husband, for what you just said is more important than any carriage."

"No more or less wrong than his mama was, to blame herself for something so completely out of her control."

Georgiana was still weeping when he first kissed her, but like their sonata, their first pairing in so long began with sadness, but it changed, slowly. She felt herself shaking off those forlorn months at Pemberley, of feeling only half-married, with a husband so distant, and it was not too long before things felt as natural to her as they had been in Paris. His hands were rougher, it was true, but Georgiana found she liked this more than she would have expected, and when they had finished, and he was tracing those toughened fingertips up and down her arm, she sighed a deep, contented sigh, and felt whole again.

"I did not ask you – have your dreams returned at all?" he said.

"They returned, but only while I was asleep, after I hit my head," Georgiana said. "You were in them. You helped me, when I most needed it."

"I am glad of it, although I hardly see how I might have become acquainted with you, if you had married that man."

"It would have been most unlikely," Georgiana said, drifting off into a peaceful silence for some time. "Matthew, your horse, Phoebe – why did you choose that name for her?"

"The Caroline's sister ship is the Phoebe," he said. "Oh, and there was a fine privateer I took off Bermuda, with the name. She was painted all black, and the horse reminded me a bit of her."

Georgiana felt a strange, cold chill run over her for a moment, and she could not help herself – she shuddered. He asked her why she did so, and she said: "I met you in Bermuda, and you had just captured the Phoebe."

"I must have mentioned it sometime before, and you forgot I had told you of it," he said.

"Perhaps you did," Georgiana said. "Matthew, sometimes I wonder – "

"Yes, my dearest?" he said, when Georgiana could not quite bring herself to continue.

"Sometimes I wonder if there is a world where this is my cousin Andrew's nightmare, and somewhere he will wake to find his wife and son are still alive, and be as relieved as I was."

"Who is to say there is not?" he asked, thoughtfully. "Will you tell me more of this dream of yours, or do you not wish to speak of it? I will admit I am terribly curious to find out how you came to be acquainted with me."

"No, I will tell you of it, if you wish," she said, and she did. Georgiana did not spare him the ending, but when she had finished, he said:

"I feel a bit guilty that I came out better than the rest of our family in your dream," he said. "Poor Fitzwilliam and Elizabeth, Mary and David – even Edward and Marguerite – would never have met. All for the actions of that scoundrel, and Georgiana, you must not try to shift the blame from where it truly belongs, for George Wickham *is* a scoundrel, in this world, and in your dream."

"I shall not, but Matthew, you cannot possibly feel guilty over how you came out in my dream. You lost your arm, and entered into a scandalous marriage!"

"There were times in my life, Georgiana, when I would have easily given up an arm to capture a frigate such as the President, or to secure your affections."

CHAPTER 31

Sarah entered Elizabeth's dressing-room, having been summoned there, and with a look upon her face as though she intended to make another apology for the incident that had taken place a week prior. That incident had nothing to do with Moll, and was instead that Sarah, in her usual morning routine, had checked both the mistress's dressing-room and bedchamber, to ensure all was set to rights within, and had – instead of encountering the empty, made-up bed of every other morning – found both mistress and master in the mistress's bedchamber, unclothed and not at all asleep.

They might not even have noticed, if Sarah had not let out a little yelp of surprise, although Elizabeth was glad that if it had to happen, she was aware of Sarah's having seen them, so Elizabeth could reassure her it was not at all her fault. For her own part, Elizabeth was embarrassed over it, but not at all remorseful; that morning, and the night that had preceded it, meant too much to her.

She felt settled again, felt fully loved and desired, both for what they had spoken of that night, and just before Sarah had walked in, when she had made her husband give her a very important promise. She had begun by asking him that very thing, if he would give her a promise:

"And what is it you wish me to promise?" he asked.

"If you ever again get it into your head to give up marital relations, you will discuss it with me, openly."

"I will, Elizabeth. I will admit that speaking of the possibility of your death is a most difficult topic for me, but it is even more painful to think of what resulted from my inability to speak of it. I promise I will not do so again."

"I understand it is difficult, but you might speak of whether we should have more children, without broaching the risk they bring. I will understand, now, what you are about. And Darcy?"

"Yes, my love?"

"If we do – together – ever decide not to seek any more children, we need not give *everything* up."

"Elizabeth Darcy, you wicked, wanton woman."

"Would you prefer I were otherwise?"

"I most certainly would not."

Sarah had walked in just after this, thankfully before things had progressed too far, but she had seen – and heard – more than enough to still be greeting her employer with some embarrassment, a week following the incident. Elizabeth had not summoned her here to speak of that, however, and thought the sooner it was as forgotten as could be, the better.

"You asked for me, Mrs. Darcy?"

"Sarah, how many times must I tell you that you may call me by my Christian name?"

"I did, sometimes," Sarah said, "but I cannot, for now – I might slip and do so in front of Moll, and I must set a good example for her."

"Ah, I understand," Elizabeth said. "In truth, it was Moll I wished to speak with you about."

"Oh, ma'am, what has she done now?"

"She has done nothing," Elizabeth reassured Sarah. She saw no need to embarrass Sarah further by telling her that she had written the story of Darcy's desk to Georgiana as a humorous anecdote, and said only, "I had a letter from Lady Stanton. Miss Hughes has left her employ – it seems she was prone to terrible seasickness – and Lady Stanton has had a difficult time finding applicants open to the possibility of living on board a ship for significant periods of time. She wanted to know if Moll was seasick, when she made the passage to England."

"Not that I know of, ma'am, and I expect she would have told me about it, for she told me about all else that happened during the passage," said Sarah, who seemed little enthused by what Elizabeth had indicated.

"Do you think you could train Moll for the position?"

"I could, ma'am, or at least I hope I could, but – well, you've seen her manners. May I speak freely?"

Elizabeth assured her she could.

"It isn't fair, for Moll to be given such a post straightaway. I worked for years as a housemaid before I had my promotion, and many of the other girls could be trained for the post much faster than Moll could. I am ever so grateful you've given her board and a position here, but I would not wish Rachel or Annie to be passed over in her favour."

"I understand," said Elizabeth, "but I think you are neglecting the most important part of the position – that she may have to live at sea. I do agree Rachel and Annie have done well in dressing Mrs. Ramsey and Miss Bennet when they visit, and Rachel in her new position in the nursery, but could you see them leaving Pemberley to live on board a ship?"

"Perhaps not, ma'am."

"Could you see Moll leaving Pemberley to live on board a ship?"

Sarah smiled, slightly. "I could, ma'am. She'd think it a grand adventure, to go see the world."

"I do understand your point about giving the others a chance, however," said Elizabeth. "I shall put it to them, and all who are interested may train with you, and then have a trial with Lady Stanton, who may choose whomever she prefers for the post."

Elizabeth and Sarah went down to the servants's hall, and Elizabeth asked Mrs. Reynolds to call all of the maids in; as Moll was newest, she determined they should all have opportunity to participate, if they so chose. It would take some time for them all to gather from their duties across the house, and while they waited, Elizabeth drew Mrs. Reynolds aside and explained the purpose of the summons.

"Oh, they'll be pleased you look within the house, for the position," she said. "Miss Hughes started as a housemaid here, as well, and when she started dressing Miss Darcy full-time, Mr. Darcy started paying her as a lady's maid, although she wasn't truly, until Miss Darcy married. 'Tis a shame about her seasickness, but I am sure she found a good place, and it gives one of our girls a chance at her step."

The girls all formed a neat line along the opposite side of the dining table, almost as though they were to be inspected, and looked expectantly at Elizabeth.

"I thank you all for stepping away from your duties," Elizabeth said. "Some of you may be aware that Miss Hughes was required to leave Lady Stanton's employ, due to seasickness. Lady Stanton has advertised for a new lady's maid, but the position may require living on board a ship for long periods of time, and travelling anywhere the Royal Navy requires Captain Stanton to sail. She has thus far not received much interest in the position, and so I thought to put it to all of you: anyone who would wish to serve as her lady's maid may train with Miss Kelly, until such time as you are ready for a trial with Lady Stanton, and she may choose whom she prefers."

Elizabeth watched as this information was absorbed by their faces – terribly young faces, for the most part. Possibility of promotion, to hold the coveted post of lady's maid, warred with the thought of unknown living conditions that would surely not be as comfortable as their quarters at Pemberley, and the possibility of travelling far from home. Hughes had been, in essence, a lady's maid for even longer than Sarah, and she – despite a goodly degree of loyalty towards Lady Stanton – had left the post, which must indicate something about its desirability. Rachel and Annie might also have been contemplating whether Mrs. Ramsey or Miss Bennet – once she became Mrs. Stanton – intended to hire on a lady's maid.

"Does anyone have interest in the position?"

Elizabeth had been expecting Moll to step forward, but was still a little surprised that out of all of them, she was the only one to do so.

"I do, Mrs. Darcy. I don't mind living on a ship, 'specially if it's a chance to see the world!" Moll said. "And I ain't been – I mean, I have travelled on a ship before and I wasn't seasick."

Elizabeth waited to see if any of the rest of them stepped forward, now that Moll had done so, but they did not, and she felt certain that Georgiana's advertisement would have gone a very long time without any applicants, if a group of maids this large could only produce one person interested in being promoted to the position. Georgiana had been correct in her conjecture as to which maid it would be.

"Very well, Moll, you shall train with Miss Kelly until you are ready for a trial with Lady Stanton."

Elizabeth left the hall to a line of curtseys – at least this Moll was doing properly now – and went back upstairs. She intended to locate her guests, and encountered Jane almost immediately, looking for her. Jane asked Elizabeth if she would walk with her in the ball-room, and Elizabeth replied that of course she would.

Jane may not have been transparent to most of her acquaintances, but there were few people Elizabeth knew so well as her elder sister: Jane was upset over something, but needed some time to work up to speaking about it. So she made two full laps of the ball-room with her sister, until Jane finally said, "Lizzy, all this horrid weather has delayed the construction at Clareborne. We were meant to have a liveable house before next winter, and now Charles does not think it shall be so."

Elizabeth was relieved; of all the things that might have been vexing Jane, she suspected this one could be easily resolved. "I am glad at least that neither of you is considering the old house liveable, Jane. I cannot even imagine what it is like, with all of this rain."

"Oh, Lizzy, there is very nearly a river running through the dining-room!" Jane giggled, the sort of distressed giggle of a woman who has one half-constructed house, and another with a river running through its dining-room.

Elizabeth laughed with her, and said, "If either of you is worried over trespassing on our hospitality – and I suspect that is why you wished to speak with me, Jane – you should not. This house is so large you might live with us for years. Indeed, Darcy has given Georgiana and Matthew permanent use of one of the apartments, and you should feel you have the same of your own. If anything, I will be upset when you finally must leave us, and I am without my Jane, and Darcy his particular friend."

"Oh, Lizzy, that is very kind of you, but it is the nursery I am worried over. I am in the family way again, and after Bess – "

"Jane, congratulations, my dear sister, and do not worry yourself over the nursery. I *had* made it my goal to fill it with babies."

"But Lizzy, you cannot deny that your two sons put together, even your two sons and Mrs. Nichols's boy, are quieter than Bess."

"'Tis true, perhaps, but all of the babies you speak of are in being. Perhaps the one you carry now shall be the quietest of them all," said Elizabeth, continuing before Jane could protest: "Even if he or she is not, by virtue of being my nephew or niece, your unborn child is absolved of everything. And if this baby also develops a strange love of the pianoforte, at least we will recognise it sooner."

"Oh, Lizzy, do you truly mean that?"

"I do, Jane. It is a very large house – there will *always* be room here for two of the dearest people in my heart, and their children."

Elizabeth awoke the morning following a little surprised to find her husband still in bed with her, and that by all appearances, he had been awake for some time, and waiting for her to reach the same state.

"It is rather late for you to still be abed," she said.

"I am in no hurry to be up this morning," he said. "It seems this infernal rain has turned to sleet, and we have hardly talked this week."

Elizabeth felt her face grow hot. "It is not for lack of time together."

"No, it certainly is not," he chuckled, but then his face turned serious, and Elizabeth could see there was something specific he wished to talk about, even before he said, "I have been thinking – you and I made a promise to each other, last summer, that we should never withhold anything that was troubling us. And, if you do not mind my saying so, we have both failed soundly at it."

"I do not mind you saying it – you are right."

"On my part, I will admit that there is no subject more difficult than the subject of – of your death, for me to speak of. I do not believe it will ever be easy."

"It would be no easier for me to speak of the same for you, but I will own that the possibility must have been much more on your mind, because of all that has happened," Elizabeth said. "You do not want me to die first, and I do not want you to die first, and so we must live together until our old age, and then be killed in that carriage accident together."

"That is rather unfair to the coachman and footman."

"Then it shall have to be you, driving the curricle."

"It is still rather unfair to the horses."

"You are insufferable," she said. "But I am glad you can tease a little on this subject now."

"A little, perhaps. The thought of us living until our old age is an exceedingly pleasing one," he said. "But I also wanted to raise this topic, because I wanted to talk a little more about what it was you feared."

"It feels so very silly, now – you have been very convincing in that regard," she said, growing warm again at the remembrance of their evenings together over the past week.

"I am glad of it, although I cannot say that has been my primary motivation. It has all been my natural feelings and desires," said he. "I wanted to raise the subject because I began to think this was just as unspeakable to you as what troubled me had been, particularly when my foolish actions provided what must have seemed supporting evidence."

"Yes, I do not know that I ever could have broached the fear that you no longer desired me."

"Then do not ever feel you need to broach it again, and do not doubt that I do, ever," he said. "The idea of us growing old together does please me very much, and I do not care if you grow old and thin, or old and fat, or you grow old and stay exactly as you are. You will always be my Elizabeth, and I will always desire you."

He reached out to caress her cheek, and once he had done so, Elizabeth turned her mouth to kiss his palm, too overcome to speak.

"If I was required to choose my favourite feature of yours, I would choose your fine eyes," he said, staring very intently into that which he had said he most admired. "Your eyes are beautiful because your mind is beautiful, and that will not ever change, my clever, lovely Elizabeth."

"That is the most wonderful thing you have ever said about me," she said, tearfully, "and not for lack of saying wonderful things."

"Then I am sorry I did not say it sooner."

"Do not be. It would not have meant as much to me sooner."

CHAPTER 32

After a night during which neither she nor Matthew had slept very much, Georgiana awoke late, luxuriously late, and found he was already gone. There was a note in his place on the bed, indicating he had gone to check on his ship, but would be back. Georgiana thought for a moment to return to sleep, but then guiltily remembered Marguerite.

She dressed herself with loose stays, and went to knock on Marguerite's door, but found Marguerite must have already gone out, for there was no answer. She went downstairs, and there was informed by Mr. Norris that Colonel Fitzwilliam and Madame Durand were breaking their fast in the inn's private parlour, and would be pleased if she would join them.

"Good morning, Georgiana," Edward said, rising to get his cousin's chair upon her entrance into the parlour. "You look very well."

"Yes, you have happy glow of love," said Marguerite.

Georgiana felt herself enveloped in a warm wave of embarrassment, sure everything she had done in the night was visible on her countenance, yet *happy glow of love* did seem the best description for her present state. There was a steady rain drumming outside, and even after everyone had finished eating, they were not inclined to stir, having more coffee and tea brought around as they lingered, discussing Edward's and Marguerite's plan to leave for Stradbroke on the morrow.

Into this Matthew entered, dripping wet in oilskins, and very nearly prompting Georgiana to fret over his catching a chill. Then she thought of Bowden, no worse the wear for riding behind her carriage for so long in the rain, and that if Matthew had not caught a chill over two and a half months in the Baltic, he was not likely to do so now.

"They are moving her into dry dock tomorrow, and then I will be without a ship for at least a month," he said.

"The timing is very good, then, to go back to Pemberley for your

393

brother's wedding, and the ball," said Georgiana, and Matthew agreed that it was.

"It is not entirely on your way, but I hope you will come to Stradbroke for a few nights," said Edward. "I will admit some selfishness in the offer, as it would be far more preferable for Marguerite to arrive in a separate carriage from myself. I do not want word to get out of our intent to marry until our mourning is over."

Georgiana recalled her former suitor, Viscount Burnley, whom they had all judged harshly for becoming engaged while in mourning for his elder brother, and knew Edward must have also remembered this. The stop was agreed to, and now only Edward planned to leave on the morrow; Marguerite and her son would travel with Georgiana and Matthew, a few days later.

Matthew went to their apartment to change, following this, and Georgiana went with him, searching for the miniature in her trunk and failing to find it in the brief time it took him to do so.

"Have you lost something?" he asked.

"How did you do that? Hawke was not even here to help you!" Georgiana said, looking up over her shoulder.

"My clothes are not nearly so complicated as yours, dearest, and I spent my formative years being required to rise from my hammock and dress as quickly as I could."

Her fingers finally closed around the little silk-wrapped oval, and although this was not at all how Georgiana had imagined giving the miniature to him, she rose and turned to face him, holding it out.

"I had this done, for you, in Lynn," she said, suddenly feeling embarrassed by it, for there seemed something immodest about giving him a picture of herself, although he *had* asked for a lock of her hair.

He unwrapped it carefully, and smiled as soon as he saw it, reassuring her, before he said, "Oh, Georgiana, this was very nicely done, and would absolutely be my great comfort if I was ever on another voyage like the one I just faced. And if we are ever apart for a few days, or perhaps a week, I shall keep it close at hand and treasure it, but I mean to make good on what I promised you in my letter. We will never be parted for that long again, so I shall always have my real Georgiana to look at, and I will always prefer her, despite the fineness of what you have just given me."

Upon hearing this, Georgiana burst into tears, and was immediately embraced. "You manage always to give me the better gift," she whispered.

"I have given you nothing."

"You know that is not true. You have given me the thing I most wanted, which is to never be parted from you for so long again."

"If that is something I have given to you, it has been a gift to myself, as well," he said, his hand running up and down her back. "Do you still need help with your stays?"

"Yes, please."

He moved around to her back, and unbuttoned her dress, and then Georgiana felt his hands on the laces, although she thought they were growing looser, rather than tighter, and this was confirmed when he slipped her dress down on her shoulders, and kissed the base of her neck.

Georgiana shivered, and whispered, "Was this your purpose in asking about my stays?"

"No, I had fully intended to tighten them, right up until I undid your knot, and realised we shall not be going anywhere in this rain, and I would much rather loosen them. That is, if you wish to – "

"I do wish to, very much," Georgiana said, and she thought that perhaps this time might be the time they made another baby. Then he kissed her neck again, and she found it very difficult to think at all.

It was raining, again, when the landau containing Georgiana, Matthew, Marguerite, and Jean-Charles came into the courtyard at Stradbroke, to be greeted by the family and a profusion of footmen holding umbrellas.

"Perhaps you should all come inside, and then we may be introduced properly," said Lady Ellen, which Georgiana was glad of, for the awkwardness of the situation could only increase, to be done under umbrellas in a steady rain.

In the entrance-hall, Lord Brandon formally requested the introduction, and it was given by Edward, who introduced his future wife as simply Madame Marguerite Durand of Aquitaine, who stood in front of them all with a goodly degree of tension on her face. Georgiana's uncle and cousin, who appeared no less haggard than he had been when she left Stradbroke, made their pleasantries in English, but Lady Ellen gave Marguerite a substantial curtsey, and said: "Enchantée de faire votre connaissance."

"De même, Lady Brandon," said Marguerite, looking visibly relieved. Georgiana had suspected that Marguerite's acceptance into the family had been led by Lady Ellen, and thought this exchange further confirmed her suspicion. Lady Ellen and Marguerite, now that she saw them together, seemed to have something similar in their bearing that made Georgiana hopeful they should become fast friends, even before Marguerite became Lady Ellen's daughter.

They were to be shown to their rooms to change, and Lady Ellen asked Georgiana if she would mind if Marguerite was given her usual bedchamber, and Georgiana and Matthew one of the newly updated ones. Georgiana replied that they would not mind at all, but was still surprised when it seemed Edward was to lead them into the old castle, while Lady Ellen took Marguerite up the usual stairs.

"The rooms are very nicely done," Edward said. "I think my mother would have put you up here when last you stayed, Georgiana, but it *is* a little strange to be on this side of the house when no one else is here. At least now it will be the two of you. Marguerite and I are to live in the apartment above this one, once we are married."

He led them into a large, circular room in one of the towers, newly plastered, like the drawing-room had been, and with enlarged windows cut in the stone. The spacious fireplace had been left intact, dwarfing the coal grate within, and it was sided by a pair of ancient chairs, the only medieval touches in what was otherwise a very modern room.

"It is beautiful," said Georgiana, although she was not sure she would compliment her aunt on it, for surely Alice must have assisted in modernising this room, as well, and perhaps she and Andrew had originally intended to live in the apartment that was now to be Edward's and Marguerite's.

There was indeed a certain silent emptiness within the old castle as they made their way back to the main house, particularly when contrasted with some commotion that could be heard in the entrance-hall. They had hardly been seated in the drawing-room before the source of the commotion was revealed, when Lady Catherine strode in, exclaiming:

"Where is she? Where is this French hussy who is to steal my Anne's husband?"

The whole family, excepting Andrew, was in the drawing-room, but Georgiana looked at her aunt and uncle, who in turn looked guiltily at each other. It was clear one of them had written to Lady Catherine of Edward's intended betrothal, but they could not have expected this, since Lady Catherine had, by all indications, already cut them.

"I am Marguerite Durand, if that is who you are seek," said Marguerite, rising with rather more grace and dignity than most ladies would, to be so confronted by Lady Catherine.

Lady Catherine looked Marguerite up and down, and said, "Well, now I suppose I understand why my nephew wishes to marry you. You will have a string of lovers before the first year is up, I expect! You will undoubtedly breed an heir, but whether it is legitimate or not, we shall never know. The Brandon title, passed down to some half-breed son of a French harlot. Oh, that the shades of Stradbroke should be so corrupted!"

Marguerite merely stood and glared at Lady Catherine, but neither Edward nor Lord Brandon would allow such an insult – they both stood, but Lord Brandon deferred to his son's right to speak in defence of his intended, and was seated again.

"You have no right to come here and say such things about a wholly respectable woman!" Edward thundered. "If things had been arranged, with Anne, I would have done my duty, but they were not settled, and you know they were not. Do not malign Madame Durand because things did not go according to your wishes, and think on your manners, madam, to disturb a family while they are in mourning."

"Mourning! Ha! This frog harlot wearing black under your roof is not what I should call *mourning*! Let us say she is faithful, and I hope for the sake of the earldom you are not cursed with daughters. But who is she? The widow of some Mr. Durand, with no fortune to recommend her. Is everyone in this family determined to marry an undesirable connection?" Lady Catherine sniffed, then pointed at Matthew. "You excluded. You at least are from a noble line, and had the good sense to win a fortune and a baronetcy, although not enough sense to purchase a suitable seat. Shuttling about like gipsies, the two of you!"

Matthew's face went completely blank, in his discomfort, but Georgiana knew he – and everyone in the room who knew – was thinking of precisely how he had earned his baronetcy, and how it made Marguerite able to marry Edward. Neither he nor Georgiana made any attempt to respond, and it was Marguerite who was finally incensed enough to make her reply:

"And who are you? Who did you marry?" she cried. "A de Bourgh? Des éleveurs de porcs! Not even worth of cutting off of head during terror! I was a Rochechouart-Châtilloux before I marry. That is who I am, you misérable old cow!"

Lady Catherine yelped in shock, and made one last, red-faced reply: "To be thus treated, in the house of my ancestors! I cut you all! I will not acknowledge your marriage, and if I see you in town, I will not give you so much as a nod, especially *her*."

"Do you think Marguerite Rochechouart-Châtilloux Fitzwilliam will care for nod from a de Bourgh? I will not!"

Lady Catherine visibly shook, so angry was she, but then she retreated, in a flurry of skirts. They all sat in stunned silence in the drawing-room for some time, before Lord Brandon finally managed to say to Marguerite, "I apologise, madam, at your having been treated thus in this house, and by my own sister."

"Colonel Fitzwilliam warn me his aunt would take badly the news," said Marguerite. "I hope you are not angry at how I speak to her."

"On the contrary, madam. You would have been warranted in saying far more than you did, given how she spoke of you," said Lord Brandon.

The party did not disperse immediately, but disperse they did; it could hardly be helped, following such an event. Marguerite and Edward indicated their intent to go to the nursery, where Jean-Charles had taken up residence with the two girls who were to be his step-cousins, and Lord Brandon left for his study.

"I do have a little correspondence I must attend to, as well," Matthew said to Georgiana, and then leaned closer, murmuring, "What are *éleveurs de porcs*?"

"Pig farmers," Georgiana whispered in his ear, which caused him to leave the room with a great deal of coughing, and Georgiana to cover her mouth, attempting to suppress her laughter.

Lady Ellen, the only person left in the room with her, said, "If you are wishing to laugh over *pig farmers*, let us just have it done together."

Georgiana looked at her aunt, who seemed far more amused than she had been for some time, burst into laughter, and took a seat closer to Lady Ellen, who was laughing as well.

"Oh, I must admit I am exceedingly glad Edward will not also call that woman his mother," Lady Ellen said.

For a very long time, Georgiana had wondered how similar her own mother had been to her sister, Lady Catherine, and she realised there was no better time to ask about this than now, when Lady Ellen had finally voiced the distaste for her sister-in-law that had always been slightly apparent in their interactions.

"Was my mother very much like her?" she asked.

"Oh, Georgiana, I am sorry. I forget sometimes of your connection to her," Lady Ellen said.

"She was, then, was she not? You would have denied it, if they were different."

Lady Ellen sighed. "It is not so simple, Georgiana. When I first met her, I would have said Lady Anne was very much like her sister. But that was more because I presumed she was so. She was shy, like you, but once I came to know her better, we became very good friends. I was deeply saddened by her death."

Georgiana felt a rush of emotion, for the account Lady Ellen gave her was different from what she had always feared, and she said, "But my brother always speaks more highly of my father, than my mother."

"Your mother died well before your father, and your brother is not so old as to fail to be influenced by that proportion," Lady Ellen said. "Even if their deaths had come closer together, it is natural that your brother would look up to his father more than his mother. Your father made a great deal of profitable improvements to Pemberley, and he was a very upstanding man. He had qualities a young man such as your brother should admire; if your mother had lived long enough for you to know her better, I believe you would have admired her for her adeptness at her own role."

Georgiana stared out the drawing-room window, so as to avoid her aunt's gaze while she thought. Lady Anne *was* a good woman, and for her to be described as such by Lady Ellen meant a great deal to Georgiana. She wondered what it would have been like, to have her mother still as an influence in her life, and then thought of her nieces, deprived of the same thing she had been. She was glad they would gain Marguerite Durand as an additional aunt, one who would live in the same household with them.

"Georgiana, you are terribly quiet. I apologise if I have said anything to upset you," Lady Ellen said.

"I am just thinking, that is all. I am emotional – but I am not upset," Georgiana said. "I will admit, I had not expected such a positive account of my mother."

"Then I am very sorry none of us have ever given you one. Lady Anne would certainly deserve it. I fear those of us who loved her were so pained by her early passing – although thank God it was not so early as poor Alice's death – that we rarely spoke of her, even to you," said Lady Ellen, her voice thick with tears. "I hope you will understand that such a topic would be difficult for me to speak of, presently. I promise you, though, at some other time, I will tell you more of your mother."

The strange stillness of the old castle became a foreboding, dark stillness when Georgiana and Matthew retired, for although their way had been lit, the old sconces in the hallways seemed not quite close enough together, so that long shadows danced along the walls as they walked to their apartment. The room leading to their bedchamber had also been updated to serve as a dressing-room, and it was here that Hannah, one of Stradbroke's maids, helped Georgiana change.

Matthew was already changed when Georgiana knocked and went inside the bedchamber, and she found him looking even more discomfited than her, as the echoing sounds of Hawke's and Hannah's footsteps grew softer and softer in their departure. Other parts of the old castle were still in use; the kitchen had never moved from its original location, and Georgiana thought there were some servants's bed-rooms near it, but inside the thick stone walls, they could hear no other creature alive except themselves, and Georgiana had never thought about how unnerving such a thing could be. Pemberley was large, certainly, but even when she and Fitzwilliam had been the only members of their family, there had always been enough people around for there to be some life and movement to the house, even in the night. It must have been stranger still for Matthew, used to living with several hundred men separated from him by nothing more than a bulkhead, and the natural noises of a ship under sail all around him.

They each made their way about the room, blowing out the candles save those beside the bed, and although they left it unspoken, it was clear to Georgiana when they climbed into bed that neither of them was in the mood for marital relations on this night. Still, after she had blown out her bedside candle, and he his, she nestled in close to him.

"Do you believe there is any chance the castle is haunted?" he whispered.

Georgiana smiled faintly in the dark, as she realised that Matthew – tall, strong Matthew, who never seemed to have any fear of taking on an enemy ship, regardless of its size – was very likely afraid of ghosts.

"No, I do not know of any reason to suppose it haunted," Georgiana said, attempting to infuse as much confidence into her tone as she could, and drawing even closer to him in the hope that her presence would be of some comfort.

The Stantons were not visited by any ghosts in the night, and in the morning following, there seemed some manner of conspiracy among the gentlemen, to leave the ladies in the drawing-room, and even Matthew was not immune to it, wishing to go to the library to see to more correspondence. He did have a good deal of correspondence to attend to, having just returned, but Georgiana suspected the gentlemen had agreed the night before that Lady Ellen and Marguerite might best become acquainted if left to more feminine conversation, and that Georgiana, who knew them both, might help things along.

They conversed in French, which must have helped Marguerite feel more comfortable. Although Lady Ellen had said she wished to practise the language, Georgiana presumed this to be an intentional kindness on her aunt's part, to let Marguerite speak in the tongue she was fluent in, putting the countess instead at a disadvantage. They sewed, and spoke of the late war, and what it had been like in France, until Mr. Pearson came in with a letter for Marguerite. She indicated it was from her attorney in Paris, and asked if they would mind if she read it, for the case had been nearly complete when last he wrote, and she hoped for good news.

Marguerite read it through, and seemed very pleased by its contents, which she imparted when she had finished: the case had gone in her favour, and the lands were hers to sell now; the attorney had, acting under her instructions, already put them on the market.

"Une offre a déjà été faite, pour deux millions de francs," she said.

Georgiana responded with enthusiasm, that an offer had been made after such a short time, but Lady Ellen looked thoughtful.

"Deux millions de francs?" she asked.

"Oui, deux millions de francs," Marguerite said. "Cela correspond à quatre-vingt mille livres sterling."

Lady Ellen asked if she was quite certain about the amount, and Marguerite replied that she was not entirely, for she might have got the exchange rate a little wrong.

"Oh no, Madame Durand," Lady Ellen said, lapsing into English. "You have the exchange rate very right, but the number of pounds is not at all what we or Edward were expecting."

"Quatre-vingt mille livres is eight thousand pounds, no?" Marguerite said, and then fear overtook her countenance. "Is not enough, to marry Colonel Fitzwilliam?"

"Oh, no, no, please do not have a moment's worry over it," Lady Ellen said. "It is not that at all. Quatre-vingt mille livres is *eighty* thousand pounds, not *eight*. Your fortune is ten times what my son thought it was. Votre fortune est beaucoup plus importante."

Seeing that Marguerite still did not comprehend her, Lady Ellen procured pen and paper, and proceeded to do the figures for her, in both pounds and francs, and it was only after this was complete that Marguerite said: "Oh, I have wrong English numbers! I am wondering why Edward say we must rub together our pennies, but I think after war it is more expensive to live here than in France."

"Let me have someone go and find my son," Lady Ellen said. "He should hear of this immediately."

Mr. Pearson was called back in, and sent a footman off in search of Edward, who came into the drawing-room with a puzzled expression on his face.

"Is anything the matter?" he asked.

"Mon chéri, I have eight-y thousand pounds, not eight," Marguerite said. "I hope you are not too upset."

"I – *eighty* thousand pounds?"

"Oui. There was offer made for two million francs, for lands. Is eight-y thousand pounds, your mother tell me."

Georgiana was deeply curious about the conversation that must come from this revelation, but when Lady Ellen rose to leave the drawing-room, she recognised it was right to give them some privacy.

"I thought it was a little strange she was a Rochechouart-Châtilloux and her father's land was worth so little, if she was the last of the line," said Lady Ellen, closing the door behind her. "But with the revolution and the war, it was difficult to surmise what land was left, and what it was worth."

"I am so very happy for them," Georgiana said. "It speaks well of you that you would have accepted her with eight thousand pounds, but this must certainly make things easier."

"A great deal easier, I should say. It is a shame Lady Catherine has cut us, for I would have quite enjoyed her response to this news."

It was not entirely easy on Lady Ellen, Georgiana thought, for her aunt had offered up her remaining inheritance, and there would be some delicacy in determining whether the offer still stood. Knowing her family, however, she suspected that Edward would tell his mother she should keep her money, Lady Ellen would insist she had given it, and it did not matter that his situation had changed, and eventually some manner of compromise would be reached between them all.

Edward and Marguerite should rightfully have taken joy in the knowledge that their married life together would be far more comfortable than had been expected, but although presumably they did so, it was not visible on their countenances during dinner. The presence of Andrew at the table was a constant reminder that while one couple had found good fortune, the fortunes of the other had been so horrific as to make them cease to be a couple, at least in this life.

The news of Marguerite's land was, however, still news, and so there was a rather lengthy recounting of all of the times Edward had conferred with Marguerite on the subject of her land: he had nearly always been present when she spoke to the attorney, but the conversation had been carried on so rapidly in French that he had never heard any number of millions of francs spoken of, and Marguerite had always mentioned it to him in pounds, and had always got it wrong.

The gentlemen did not linger over their port, and when they entered the drawing-room, Edward and Matthew both paused beside Georgiana, Edward looking at Marguerite from across the room.

"Look at her," he said, and anyone in the room could see that Marguerite was looking very well that evening, even if she was wearing black, and would still be for some time. "Would you ever think a woman such as her could love the likes of me, even if she had no fortune at all?"

"I would," said Georgiana. "You do not give yourself enough credit for your good qualities, and good, honourable men are not so easy to come by, present company excepted."

"So Marguerite has a vast fortune, and beauty, and intelligence, and youth, and it is enough that I am a good man, without even all of his limbs?"

"You are much more than that, and I am certain Marguerite would tell you the same," Georgiana said. "And you were there for her, when she most needed someone who would be there for her."

"Still, sometimes this seems as though it is an impossible dream," Edward said. "Setting aside all the love I bear for her, I could not have found a more perfect woman to marry, for my own situation, or my family's."

"But you loved her before that, and that is what matters," said Georgiana.

Matthew said nothing during this exchange, but he was quiet like that sometimes, and so Georgiana was not overly worried. They were compelled by Edward and Marguerite to play their duet again, and although it was perhaps not so magical to Georgiana, now that they had practised it together more, it was still very roundly applauded by their small audience.

She was changed again by Hannah, and came into the bedchamber, which did not seem so eerie on this, their second night there. Matthew was standing in front of the fireplace, and when he turned toward her, she was surprised by how sad he looked.

"What is the matter?" she asked, approaching him.

"I am sorry, Georgiana. I am so sorry I was not there for you."

It took her some time to remember what had prompted this, and then she realised it must have been her words to Edward.

"Oh, Matthew, that was not meant for you. I never meant to injure you, when I spoke to Edward. It is I that am sorry, for speaking so carelessly," she said, taking up his hand.

"I do not doubt that – you are too kind for that," he said. "But it is the truth: I was not there when you needed me."

"You told me I should not blame myself for what happened, and I think you should not blame yourself for being gone this winter," Georgiana said. "In truth it was you, in part, whom I was thinking of when I spoke to Edward, for how you helped me in my dream."

"I hardly think I may take credit for assisting you in a dream."

"If you may fault George Wickham for acting according to his character in dreams, I may laud you for doing the same," Georgiana said. "There are men in this world who take advantage of the weak and unprotected, and there are men in this world who help them. You may not have been able to help me this time, but it was only because of distance. You are still a man who helps, and I love you for it."

Georgiana embraced him, then, and thought she could still feel his sadness, even when she could not look upon his countenance. She hoped her words had eased his mind, and regretted they had not spoken of this sooner. The strongest relief had come of his absolving her of losing the baby, but she had not understood how strong the weight of his own guilt was, in having been gone when it happened.

"Georgiana," he said, stepping back to look at her, "in your dream, I intended to give up my career, and we were to live together at Pemberley. And yet you have never asked, not before and not after I went to the Baltic, if I would retire from the navy."

"I could not ask that of you," she said. "I know how important it is to you."

"It is not more important than *you*. If you wish it, I would give it all up, and we might buy that little estate you spoke of, and stay there together."

Georgiana felt her eyes fill with tears, at the sacrifice he had offered her, and yet she could not bring herself to take it.

"I am not ready to ask that of you," she said. "All I ask is that we always be together, whether we are on land or at sea, and if you are given another assignment that would part us, that you refuse it."

"I will promise you that easily, for it is no more than I have wanted myself."

"And – I think I would like for us to purchase that little estate outside Portsmouth. Not because the baronetcy needs a seat, but because the children I hope for will need some home of permanence – I need a home of permanence. I need to know that wherever we should travel, there is still a place of our own, that we shall come home to."

"You will have it, then," he said. "Are you certain you would prefer Hampshire instead of Derbyshire, though?"

"Pemberley will always be there to visit, but you have promised me all I have asked for," she said. "I will not ask you for more, to live so far away from the sea."

CHAPTER 33

The Darcys had, without entirely thinking through the ramifications, agreed to hold Mary's wedding at Pemberley, followed a few days after by the celebratory ball for both Mary and Catherine. They had done such a set of events in the past for Georgiana, to great success, and it had seemed logical to repeat them.

Elizabeth had not considered the guest list for Mary's wedding, however. The Honourable Richard Stanton, having not attended his middle son's first wedding, replied to his invitation indicating that not only did he intend to be there for his eldest son's second wedding, but that as it was being held in a private chapel, he expected he would be officiating the ceremony. Mr. Clark's services had already been engaged for this purpose, but after consulting with Mary and her intended, Elizabeth had concluded that David's father must be allowed to perform the service, and she would have to smooth the situation over with Mr. Clark.

Mr. Clark was most understanding in giving up the office; he was still, of course, invited to the event, and found this perfectly sufficient, given his role was being usurped by the groom's father. Once this had been settled, Elizabeth had the curiosity on one part, and pleasure on the other, of learning that both of David Stanton's brothers intended to come to Pemberley for the wedding. Jacob Stanton she had never met, nor had Georgiana, although her sister had given the sense that he sounded rather too much like his father to have high expectations of. But Georgiana's and Matthew's return to the house she looked forward to very much, and she had Moll Kelly sent to thoroughly clean their apartment before they arrived, hoping this also served as fair warning to Moll that she had but days until her potential employer arrived.

Of Andrew Ramsey's family, only the youngest brother, Herbert, a curate, was able to attend; the rest of the Ramseys might have managed to leave the family's shop in Salisbury for the wedding itself, but could not bring themselves to do so for what was merely a distant ball. The newly married Ramseys would visit Salisbury instead, to receive the family's blessings, and then continue on to Bath. Young Herbert Ramsey was the first to arrive of their house guests, looking rather wide-eyed at his surroundings, and showing a tendency to be intimidated by his company. It was Catherine, his new sister, who took charge of making him comfortable, and providing him with quiet guidance whenever he seemed a little lost in the drawing-room, or at dinner.

However Catherine, still designated a new bride and taking a goodly degree of pleasure from the recognition, would soon enough be sitting too far away from Herbert to be of much assistance to him, as the additional guests arrived. She and Mary had, thankfully, settled on how precedence should be handled between the two of them, and informed Elizabeth of what they preferred, which was that after her wedding, Mary should go in first to dinner, but Catherine would lead off the ball.

Mary awoke two days before her wedding with something beyond the usual nervousness of a soon-to-be bride, for this was the day she expected to meet the men who would become her father-in-law and youngest brother-in-law, both of them intending to travel to Pemberley in the same carriage, their livings being near. Georgiana and Matthew were expected in, as well, and while she had nothing but pleasant thoughts about seeing them again, she was far too distracted to stay focused on pleasant thoughts while she waited.

With the rain continuing, Elizabeth had decided that the outdoor receiving line should be done away with, and new guests met in the drive by footmen with umbrellas, to be received in the entrance-hall. Mary took up her position there, when it was announced that there was an unfamiliar carriage in the drive, and she waited for some time with her hand on David's arm, in a state of great trembling nervousness.

She should not be so nervous, she told herself, for she had already met and conversed easily with the Earl of Anglesey, and he was the head of the family. But she had been given enough indication by David and Georgiana that their father was to be the more difficult of the acquaintances, and she would not move beyond her worries until she had actually met and interacted with the man.

The carriage did belong to Mr. Stanton and his son, who came into the entrance-hall, had their boots wiped dry by a footman, and were then announced by Mr. Parker. Any hopes Mary might have had about blending into the background of their family unit were set aside when Mr. Stanton was introduced to her, and gave her as sceptical a gaze as anyone ever had. Mary had worn the most austere dress in a wardrobe filled with austere dresses, and had Annie do her hair in a most conservative style, and still she feared his reaction.

In tremulous silence did Mary await what he would say, which was, "I am pleased to meet you, Miss Bennet. You have the look of a clergyman's wife, at least."

"I am pleased to make your acquaintance as well, Mr. Stanton," she said, relieved she had passed this first test.

Jacob Stanton came along to her next, and was introduced by his brother. As they exchanged their greetings, Mary thought that although he was the youngest of the brothers, he was also the least handsome, which might have been caused by her not being able to detect even the slightest hint of kindness in his countenance.

He and his father were shown to their apartments to change, and returned to the saloon when they had done so, where they seated themselves with Mary and David.

"I understand from my son that your main accomplishments are that you play the pianoforte, and you are very well-read," said Mr. Stanton.

Mary had some of the other accomplishments of ladies her age – she could sew and embroider, of course, and she could dance, although she did not really like it unless David was her partner – but not nearly so many as a lady like Georgiana, who spoke several languages and could draw and paint, in addition to her musical talents. Mary's stomach sank, that this was the first thing he should ask her about, for her accomplishments sounded meagre indeed when he spoke of them, and she finally choked out, "Yes, Mr. Stanton, those are my primary accomplishments."

"Very good. I see no reason for a young lady to be painting, which may lead her to make a greater study of the human form than is appropriate," Mr. Stanton said. "And there is absolutely no reason for her to be learning languages, unless she and her husband intend to gallivant about Paris, as my middle son and his wife chose to do."

"I understand they are to arrive today," said Jacob Stanton. "I suppose we shall see for ourselves how corrupted they are from their time there."

Mary grew tense over how they were speaking about Georgiana and Matthew, but she was afraid to speak in her friends's defence, and stayed silent.

"It takes near nothing to corrupt a sailor," Mr. Stanton said. "But I would rather speak more of Miss Bennet. Have you read Fordyce's Sermons, Miss Bennet?"

"Yes, sir, several times through."

"Indeed? I am pleasantly surprised." Mr. Stanton followed his surprise by engaging her in a discussion on several key passages, and Mary was thankful to find she remembered them all, and had a ready response for each of his questions. It was not remotely so comfortable a conversation on the topic as she had grown used to having with David, however, and it concluded in a most horrible manner, when he turned to his eldest son and said, "She seems a good choice, David. Far more appropriate than Isabel."

Mary did not at all like how he had spoken of David's first wife, both for her own sake, and for his, but she did not know what to say, and so she only gave David a sympathetic look as he said, quietly, "I would beg you not to speak ill of the dead, sir."

"You will respect your father." Mr. Stanton rebuked him in a low, cold voice, and they all fell into silence.

Mary was very glad that Elizabeth – perhaps by design – had servants come in with refreshments shortly after this, so she and David might separate themselves a little from father and younger son. She realised that while she had begun this day wishing for Mr. Stanton's good opinion, now that she seemed to have it, she did not care for it. It was not so very desirable to be approved of by such a man.

Elizabeth had overheard enough of the exchange between David and his father to be concerned even before Georgiana and Matthew arrived that she had invited a powder keg into her house, one that made the Bakers seem a simple problem by comparison. Once everyone had partaken of the refreshments in the saloon, she whispered in Darcy's ear that he should take Richard and Jacob Stanton on a tour of Pemberley, in the hopes that the rest of the party in the saloon would break up and find other occupation about the house.

Her hopes were met. Mr. Bennet, as was to be expected, took this as his cue to remove to the library. Mrs. Bennet – who, to her credit, had received the new members of her family politely, and not sat near enough to them to commit any blunders – was eager to go to the nursery with Jane. Mary seemed a little agitated by what had passed, and wished to take a few turns about the ball-room with her betrothed. Charles went with them, to act as a chaperone, for they were all aware without speaking of it that Mr. Stanton would not approve of the laxities in propriety that Mary and David had been allowed previously, because no-one could remotely fathom either of them doing anything improper.

Only Catherine and Andrew Ramsey remained in the saloon with her, which Elizabeth was glad of, for she knew they would receive Georgiana and Matthew every bit as enthusiastically as she would. Catherine, as it turned out, received Georgiana with even greater enthusiasm, pummelling her friend with an embrace as soon as she was in the entrance-hall.

"Oh, I am so glad you are well!" she exclaimed. "The last I saw you, you were lying in that bed and so horribly pale. You look very well now."

"Thank you," said Georgiana. "Congratulations to you both – I wish I could have been there to see your wedding."

"I wish you could have been, too," said Catherine. "And I wish I could have been here when you awoke."

Catherine seemed restless for a moment, and slipped off to one of the tables siding the entrance-hall, upon which were two little square objects wrapped in canvas.

"I have wedding presents for you both," she said, handing the objects over to Georgiana. "It is not much, but I did want to do something, especially since you were so generous with your shopping in Paris."

"You did not need to get us anything," Georgiana said. "We did not even attend your wedding."

"I know you would have, if you could," Catherine said, and motioned to Georgiana to unwrap the items.

Georgiana did so, and first revealed a very striking watercolour of what must have been the Caroline, the sky behind the ship a magnificent reddish sunset. Georgiana's eyes filled with tears, and these were renewed when she unwrapped the second, and showed it to be another watercolour, of Pemberley.

"Catherine, they are beautiful," she said. "You do yourself a disservice in saying they are not much."

Elizabeth seconded Georgiana's compliment, and thought tenderly of Catherine's similar presents for her and Darcy: watercolours of Longbourn and Pemberley. Rushed to marry before she could purchase her wedding gifts, and then largely tied to the house during Mr. Bennet's illness, Catherine had thought herself to be making do with using her talents to produce them, when in truth, Elizabeth treasured her painting far more than she would have another pair of gloves, or a fan.

"I am sorry there are not more of us here to receive you," Elizabeth said, once Georgiana had handed the paintings to Matthew, and hugged Catherine again. "Mr. Stanton and Mr. Jacob Stanton are touring the house with Darcy."

"You need not apologise," said Matthew. "I prefer a small and truly welcoming party."

"Well you are, as always, very much welcome. Georgiana will know the way to your apartment, if you would like to change, but she must embrace me first." Elizabeth hugged her sister, and said, "Catherine is right – you look very well."

And Georgiana did look very well. Gone was all of the worry and grief that had marked her countenance, and there was a happiness and a handsomeness to her that Elizabeth realised she only saw in her sister when Matthew was around. Elizabeth wondered if the same was true for her, when she was in her husband's presence, and felt guiltily glad he was so rarely parted from her.

Georgiana had grown increasingly tense in the last miles of their journey, and had seen Matthew do the same, that they must greet his father and younger brother, and she had been relieved, to find only those among her favourite people there to receive them in the entrance-hall. They would have to face the less-pleasant guests at some point in the day, but she would much rather do so after refreshing herself following such a long journey. She led Matthew up to their apartment, and showed him the rooms there, which were quite fine. They even had separate dressing-rooms, and so, after having complimented how nicely done it all was, he promised to meet her downstairs, and Georgiana went to her dressing-room, awaiting the curiosity that was Moll Kelly.

When Moll came into the dressing-room, Georgiana found herself a little disappointed. She had expected a young woman with an enormous personality, and was instead greeted by a thin freckled girl who gave her a deep and proper curtsey, then went gingerly through her trunks as though each dress was made of old parchment, nervously recommending a perfectly appropriate dinner dress.

Quite efficiently changed, Georgiana paused for a moment at the top of the east stairs. She had avoided these stairs after the accident, but had concluded in her time away from Pemberley that it was silly to think strangely of a staircase, for this one was no more or less dangerous than the other stairs in the house. She steeled herself and was about to descend, when someone spoke behind her:

"May I offer you my arm, Lady Stanton?"

It was her father-in-law, and Georgiana dropped into a curtsey as soon as she had turned to face him. In truth, the absolute last thing she would have wished for was to have to take his arm and walk down two storeys, but it *had* been politely offered, and so Georgiana said: "It is good to see you again, Mr. Stanton. I would appreciate your arm."

"Good. You should get into the habit of it now. You must be more careful, the next time you are in the family way. You will not forget that you are carrying one of God's creatures, and you will take more responsibility for its life, next time."

He might have stabbed her in the heart, and only caused a little more pain than what Georgiana felt now. It would have pained her anywhere, but to be said *here*, where it had happened, was unbearable. She could not even attempt to take up his arm or hold her composure; she burst into tears, and fled back to her apartment.

Mary, who had been coming up the stairs to change for dinner, heard all, and saw most of what had happened. She stopped, frozen, halfway down the stairwell from Mr. Stanton, and was noticed by him after Georgiana had rushed off.

Seemingly unperturbed by how he had upset Georgiana, he looked to Mary and said, "Well! I would give you the same advice, but I expect *you* will never be so careless as her."

Mary was frozen, still, but she felt herself on the precipice of a decision she had been wholly unprepared to make. She wished, badly, to side with Georgiana, who had always been her true friend, but to do so would surely anger her future father-in-law. Her old self would have gone with him and sought his greater favour, would have been proud at gaining his good graces. As soon as she realised this, Mary knew what she needed to do, regardless of the repercussions.

"No," she said. "You have upset my friend, and I must go to her."

Mary gathered her skirts and hurried up the stairs, past him and down the hallway to Georgiana's apartment. She found there that her friend had barely made it a few steps into the room before she had collapsed on the floor in tears. Mary knelt down beside her, put her hand on one of Georgiana's shoulders, and said, "You must not listen to him. What he said was cruel, and unfair. What happened was not your fault."

Georgiana heaved a shuddering sob, and said, "Oh, Mary, it is so good of you to say that, but you must be very careful of what you do and say around him. I do not want things to be as difficult for you as they have been for Matthew and me."

"You are my friend, and soon enough you will be my sister. I would rather things be difficult for me than stand by and watch you be treated thus," said Mary, and it was only as she acknowledged Georgiana was to become her sister that she realised the full potential of her actions. Even as she continued to comfort her friend, she considered what should happen if Mr. Stanton had been offended – and it seemed to take little to offend him – and would rebuke David for his choice of a wife.

She did not want to give David up, but nor did she want to be married to a man who would not approve of what she had just done, and she was faced with the dizzying thought that she might *not* be married in two days' time, as had been her every expectation. This was more than she was prepared to consider, and so she returned her attention to Georgiana's comfort.

"Would you like for me to go and find Matthew?" she asked, for Mary was in love, and near enough to marriage to understand there would be no one else so comforting to Georgiana at this time.

"In a little while. I need to – I must calm myself more, first," Georgiana said. "Anything that man has done will upset him in undue proportion."

"You would spare his feelings at the price of your own discomfort?" Mary asked.

"In this instance, I will," Georgiana said. "It is near time for dinner. Will you tell them I am feeling a little unwell after my travels and wish for a tray here? It should be enough of a sign for Matthew to come to me, but it shall give me a little more time."

"Are you sure?" asked Mary.

"I am," said Georgiana. "And Mary?"

"Yes?"

"It was very kind of you to come to my aid. I hope you do not suffer for it – I would feel horribly if you did."

"I would much rather come to your aid and suffer than stand by and do nothing," said Mary, and she meant it fully.

As it happened, Mary did not need to provide a sign to Matthew amongst the rest of the group, for when she descended the stairs and was making her way to the yellow drawing-room, she saw him approaching her.

"Have you seen Georgiana?" he asked. "She should have been down by now, unless this trial maid of hers is terribly slow."

"She – she encountered your father on the stairs, and he said something very hurtful to her," Mary said. "I was going to make her excuses for dinner, and she was hoping this would be a sign for you to come to her."

"Thank you, Miss Bennet, please make my excuses as well," he said, and rushed off toward the stairs.

Georgiana managed to get herself up off of the floor, although her attempts to dry her eyes were futile, as her tears continued. She seated herself on the chaise in her bedchamber and took deep breaths, trying to think happier thoughts, for she had meant what she said to Mary about attempting to spare Matthew's feelings in the matter.

He came in much sooner than she had expected, though, and at first said nothing but, "Oh, Georgiana, I am so sorry," as he sat beside her on the chaise and embraced her. This offering of comfort – and that he was there, at Pemberley, to give it – only strengthened her tears.

When she had finally calmed to just the occasional sob, she separated from him and, noting the dampness on his shoulder, said, "Your coat – I am sorry, I should have been more careful. You shall need a new one to go back down to dinner."

"I am not going back down to dinner. I told Mary to make my excuses," he said, softly. "Georgiana, what was it he said, that upset you so?"

Georgiana realised Mary must have encountered Matthew in private, and informed him that his father had been the cause of her distress. She told him of Richard Stanton's encountering her, and what he had said.

"My God, that is cruel, even for him," Matthew said. "Please do whatever you can to put it out of your mind, my dearest."

"I shall," she said, and sought another embrace.

"I have been thinking," said he, after some time. "It is madness, to continue his acquaintance. We gain nothing from it, except continuing pain. Where it was my own pain I was more willing to make the attempt, but I will not have you hurt by him, not in a season when you have already had so much to pain you."

"But he is our father," she whispered.

"Fathers disown their sons frequently enough, so why may a son not disown his father?" he asked. "In truth, the only portion he has ever formed of my will has been the approximate sum of my room and board, up until I was eight and a half, and left his charge. I see no reason not to cut the acquaintance entirely."

"Matthew, what was it that made you leave home at that age? Was there some specific thing he said, or did?"

Georgiana had expected the question to sadden him, but instead, his face hardened in an expression of lingering anger.

"He said my mother had been a whore."

Georgiana had held no expectations as to what it was he was going to say, and yet she still found herself utterly shocked by this. "What a horrid man, and how horrible that you should have heard such a thing at that age. I do not believe I would have even understood what it meant."

"You would have, if you had listened to him preach during your formative years," Matthew said. "I believe he considers every woman a whore, in part, for being descended from Eve."

"What did you do?"

"I hit him for it as best I could, at my age," he said. "I assure you, he did not spare the rod over it, but if it had been merely that, I might have borne it. He had other ways of making my life even more of a misery, however. I had been enamoured with the navy for some time, and I wrote to my uncle as soon as I was allowed, begging his assistance in going to sea."

Georgiana trembled, her own reaction a mixture of sadness, and anger, but she reached out with her unsteady hand and touched his cheek, and then kissed him tenderly. "I am so sorry you had to go through that, Matthew, and now I cannot help but think that cutting his acquaintance has been long overdue. Let us do so, together."

Elizabeth felt certain that some sort of incident must have taken place outside of her observation. Her first evidence of this came when Mary entered the yellow drawing-room and said with some degree of agitation that Lady Stanton was feeling a little unwell after her travels and wished for a tray in her room, and Captain Stanton was attending her there, and would also not be attending dinner.

Mary then proceeded to behave in a most subdued and downcast manner through the entire course of dinner, and Elizabeth struggled more in her duties as hostess than she had since her earliest days in that role, so distracted was she. When the ladies retired to the drawing-room, she knew it might be her only opportunity before the morning to learn what had happened, and she pulled Mary aside at the doorway.

"Mary, what is it? I can see something has happened to upset both you and Georgiana. She did not look at all unwell when she arrived."

Elizabeth was surprised to see even this question prompt watery eyes from Mary, and heard from her sister the story of what Richard Stanton had said to Georgiana, and how Mary had reacted, and feared her actions had put her wedding at risk. Elizabeth set aside her anger over the incident and concern for Georgiana to focus on reassuring Mary that she had done the right thing, and surely her betrothed would see this. She thought to tell her of how Darcy had stood up to Lady Catherine, before Elizabeth's wedding, but it was quite a different thing to stand up to a father, than to an aunt, and so Elizabeth kept herself to more general reassurances.

"Would you like me to find some opportunity for you to speak with him privately this evening?" she asked.

"No, no, that would only make it worse, if Mr. Stanton noticed both of us gone from the drawing-room."

"I or Jane could chaperone you."

"No, let me speak with him tomorrow, when it will not be so noticeable."

"Very well, but please let me know if I may help facilitate a private audience between the two of you."

"I would appreciate that, Lizzy." Mary drew a deep, shaky breath, and squared her shoulders to go into the drawing-room.

"Mary, come here, my child," said Mrs. Bennet. "I am still not happy about the trim on your wedding dress, and we must speak of it."

Mary actually looked a little relieved to be called over on such a mundane topic, and even endeavoured to participate in the conversation over dress trim, although with a despondency Elizabeth knew must have been that of a bride who was not entirely sure she would still be wearing her wedding dress in two days' time.

It was a relief to her, to go up to the nursery on this evening, for as soon as the gentlemen had entered, there had been an oppressive atmosphere in the drawing-room that even the Ramseys's conversation and Mary's playing on the pianoforte could not do away with. At least Mary had looked a little better, after being encouraged by her betrothed to play, but there was an unmissable coldness in the manners of her future father-in-law towards her, and perhaps playing served as a distraction from this.

The situation would get worse before it got better, Elizabeth was certain – if indeed it did get better – and she was very glad for her time in the nursery. There was something about sitting there with her boys, while they nursed, that she found intensely peaceful and comforting at all times, and on this night, it provided her with a much-needed escape. There were some disadvantages in having the two of them – if she had been nursing only one son, she might have liked to stroke the soft hair on his little head while she did so – but there was something even more pleasing about having a babe in each of her arms.

Her time was over much too soon, it seemed; she would have preferred for both of her sons to be exceedingly hungry on this evening. But there was Darcy at the door, coming in to take up George, with a cloth laid very precisely over his shoulder. Elizabeth had noticed him being much more careful about giving the boys equal attention since they had discussed their expectations; she half suspected someone so organised as Darcy kept a tally somewhere that listed whom he had held every evening.

Tonight was not a night to talk about such things, though, and once he had got George settled, he asked, "Do you have any idea what is going on?"

Elizabeth told him all that she knew, and as she had expected, he grew furious.

"To have Georgiana treated thus, in this house – I shall not support it! I shall not allow it!"

"I agree with you, my love, but he is to officiate a wedding in our house," Elizabeth said. "I hardly know what to do. I had thought perhaps to speak to Georgiana and Matthew of it, if they are still awake."

It was easy to determine that the Stantons were still awake, for the rich, low hum of a cello could be heard in the hallway. Elizabeth knocked on the door to Georgiana's bedchamber, and Matthew opened it slowly, with a look of suspicion on his face until he saw the Darcys, and stepped aside so they could come in.

"We wished to check on Georgiana," Elizabeth said. "Mary told me of what happened."

"I am better," said Georgiana. Elizabeth knew well the look of her sister after she had endured a long cry, and this was it, although she looked more grim, now, than sad. "Is Mary well? I hope she has not suffered for her role in what happened."

"Her situation is a little undecided, at the moment. Mr. Stanton was noticeably colder towards her, this evening, but I do not believe anything irrevocable has happened," said Elizabeth.

"It has, in our instance," said Matthew, but before he could continue, Darcy asked:

"Why are your trunks not unpacked, Georgiana? I was in favour of giving Miss Kelly's sister a trial, but this is inexcusable."

"They were unpacked, and then repacked," said Georgiana.

"In truth, your coming here saves me the note of warning I had planned to have Hawke give your valet," said Matthew. "I intend to cut my father tomorrow, in direct proportion to the degree of pain he has caused my wife today. After that event, we assumed it would be best to repair to the inn at Lambton. I apologise that it must occur in your home, but I cannot acknowledge him ever again, and so it must be done."

Elizabeth stared at him in shock, but Matthew appeared even more serious than he usually did. In a house party, and with his own father, the only cut he could give would be a cut direct. She hardly knew what to say, but she was saved from needing to respond by Darcy, who exclaimed:

"Under no circumstances, and absolutely not this one, will my sister ever be forced from this house!"

"Fitzwilliam," said Georgiana, softly, "I appreciate your care, but we thought this best for Mary's sake. We would return after the wedding, if it pleases you."

"Will you even attend the wedding?" asked Elizabeth, hoping there would still be a wedding, after all that had occurred, and would in the future.

"That will be at David's and Mary's discretion," said Matthew.

"Is there any way we might find another course?" asked Elizabeth, certain she was the only person in the room with interest in healing the breach. "What if he could be persuaded to apologise?"

Matthew laughed bitterly, and said, "He has never apologised for a thing in his life, so I believe that would take something even beyond your skills of persuasion, Elizabeth. And in truth, his offences towards me have been so many that they are beyond apology."

"Perhaps there might be another way – if you did not have to see each other except in a way in which the cut might be indirectly given – we would have to contend with dinner, of course, but – "

"Elizabeth," Darcy laid his hand on her arm. "It must be done, and in truth it is better that it be done in the privacy of our house."

They bade Georgiana and Matthew good night, and Elizabeth retreated into unhappy meditation as Sarah changed her. As absurd as her family could be, she could never imagine being treated so poorly by any of them as to wish to cut them out of her life. No-one would ever have accused Matthew of determining on a course of action he had not carefully thought through, however, and this made her think sadly of her brother and sister, to have been treated so by their father.

She came into Darcy's bedchamber oppressed by these thoughts, and she could see by his heavy countenance that although he believed the cut was the right course of action, it saddened him as well.

"Oh, how I wish Lord Anglesey was here," Elizabeth said, climbing into bed beside him. "I begin to think he was the only thing holding all together in that family."

"I am not sure it would have helped," Darcy said. "I suspect this would have happened sooner, if Matthew had not been at sea for so much of his life."

"I am not so sure of that. It was not until Mr. Stanton injured Georgiana that Matthew chose to act."

"Very true, and I am glad he did. That he has been absent is unfortunate, but my sister did undoubtedly marry an honourable man, and I am glad he acts, for if he did not, I would be compelled to," Darcy said. "Regardless, were Mary not also my sister, I would have requested the father leave this house immediately."

"Thank you for considering her, in all of this. I know your relationship with Georgiana is very different, because the two of you were on your own for so long, and it must not be easy to have to balance your actions between the two of them."

"True, but Georgiana reminded me that this will be most difficult for Mary."

Elizabeth sighed. "Oh, Darcy, I fear an entire family is about to cleave in half under our roof, and I fear no matter which half Mary finds herself in, things are going to be very difficult for her."

CHAPTER 34

In the days leading up to the wedding, Jane had been spelling Mary on the pianoforte more frequently with Bess, to allow her sister to focus on the upcoming event. Although Jane still played poorly, more often than not Bess preferred to play for herself, now, and Mary was thankful for this, for it allowed her to go in to breakfast early, intending to wait as long as was necessary until David came in, and she could seek some opportunity to speak with him in private.

Elizabeth came in before him, and Mary was glad of her sister's presence, for she knew Elizabeth would aid her in the private conversation she required. She was surprised, therefore, when, despite their being the only two people in the room, Elizabeth stopped beside Mary on her way to the sideboard, leaned close, and murmured:

"You should know that Matthew intends to cut his father's acquaintance in the course of the day, over what happened yesterday. I am sorry to have to tell you of it – I fear it will make things even more difficult for you."

Mary hardly knew what to feel, upon hearing this, and sat there in silent shock. It seemed right that Matthew should do so, based on what she knew of the situation, and yet she feared it would further injure her own position. She did not doubt that Mr. Stanton would react angrily over the event, and it seemed very possible that he should require his other sons – and daughter – to choose sides. If he even did have an additional daughter, Mary reminded herself, for she was very much in doubt over whether that would come to be.

As though he had been summoned by her thoughts, Mr. Stanton came into the room, and gave her and Elizabeth the barest of nods. He proceeded to make himself a plate, and sat in silence, only responding to Elizabeth's question about what he preferred to drink in the morning, which was tea, no milk or sugar. Elizabeth poured it for him, and then they descended into silence.

David came in perhaps five minutes later, and Mary sensed almost immediately that he had been speaking with his father about her, for his face still bore traces of redness and anger. She trembled, unsure of whom he was angered by, and earned no relief when he gave her what seemed a forced smile.

Mary had hardly eaten anything that morning, and now with her stomach clenched in turmoil, she knew she could eat no more until she had spoken with him. She took slow sips of her tea, to pass the time, and was relieved to see David's father ate quickly, as though he wished to be free of their presence, and perhaps he did. When he had left, Mary, her courage bolstered by an encouraging look from Elizabeth, turned to David and said: "Mr. Stanton, I wonder if you might walk with me in the conservatory, whenever you are finished?"

"I have your permission for this?" he asked Elizabeth.

"You do," Elizabeth said.

"Let us go now, then," he said, drinking down the rest of his tea and rising from the table, where his half-eaten plate still sat.

Mary hardly knew what to make of his eagerness to have this conversation with her, but she did not think it boded well for her. They went into the conservatory, and were required to walk the length of it before talking, to ensure no one else was there.

"Do you wish to sit?" he asked her, motioning towards where they had been seated when he proposed to her.

"No, I think I would rather walk," Mary said, for the last thing she wanted to do was sit in the place where he had once made her so happy.

"Will you tell me of what happened yesterday?" he asked. "I have had my father's version of it, but I suspect it not to have been an accurate recounting of events."

Truth and accuracy he would have from her, Mary vowed, and she told him of what she had heard and witnessed on the stairs, and then of her own actions in going after Georgiana.

"I am sorry I had to do something that would cause conflict with your father, but I believe the course I took was right, for me," Mary said. "I know once a man has made his offer of marriage, he cannot honourably rescind it, and so I will release you from our engagement if you wish it. The wedding is private enough that it is not too late to call it off."

"Do you truly wish to call off the wedding, Mary?"

"No, it is the absolute last thing I wish," Mary said, her voice wavering with the tears she was struggling to suppress. "But nor will I force you into a marriage your father is against."

"Then you are still willing to marry into a family where such a man would be your father?"

"Yes," Mary whispered, "but only if you wish it."

He stopped walking, and took hold of her hand. "Oh, Mary, I do wish it. I am sorry if you have been in any doubt of that."

"I thought you were angry with me, when you came into the breakfast-room."

"No, I was angry with my father, and we had just had quite a row," he said. "It was right of you to stand by your friend, particularly when she had just been so cruelly treated, and I told him that. It was among my greatest regrets, that I did not stand up to him when he maligned Isabel, and you may bet he did so frequently, and for no good reason. I will do better by you, Mary, I promise."

"Thank you." Mary's tears finally spilled over, and she knew in that moment that she did not care if her new father was a horrible man, so long as she was to be married to David. Yet she knew there was something further she needed to impart, before things could be fully settled between them.

"There is one more thing you must know. Elizabeth told me this morning that Matthew intends to cut his father's acquaintance today."

He ran his hand through his hair, looking very troubled. "I suppose this was inevitable. It has been a long time coming."

"David, I need to know – if we are required to choose, between your father, and Matthew and Georgiana, I must know what your choice would be. I think you already know mine."

"I do not at all like the thought of making a choice, and I would attempt to avoid it, if at all possible. But if we were required to, it would be better for us to side with the more powerful part of my family, which is Matthew and Lord Anglesey. They have the fortune, and the titles."

"You believe your uncle will side with Matthew?"

"It is usually his way to attempt to repair a rift, rather than to take sides, but I do not think even he can repair a cut direct, and yes, if he must, I have no doubt he will side with Matthew. He always has."

"But what of family in all of this?" Mary said, a little disappointed in him, although she agreed with his choice. "Should the decision be made entirely on fortune, and power?"

"No, Mary, my heart had already decided on those who have treated myself, and you, as a Christian family should. My mind merely needed to rationalise my choice, and I will admit that it does make the decision easier. It would be much more difficult if the more reasonable members of our family were the poorer ones."

Matthew had called Moll up to repack Georgiana's trunks the day before with nary a word of explanation – although Moll, to her credit, had done so without the slightest questioning of why – and Georgiana felt compelled to explain to her now why she would be leaving Pemberley. After Moll finished her hair, Georgiana told her to wait before she would leave the room, and then said, "At some point during the day, we will order our trunks, so as to repair to the inn at Lambton for a few days. Captain Stanton intends to cut his father's acquaintance today, and we thought it best to leave the house for a little while, following that event."

"That is just what he deserves, that cruel old sod!" Moll exclaimed, and then clapped her hand over her mouth, looking very upset. "I knew I couldna do it, ma'am. I tried so hard to be proper-like, and now I ain't goin' to see the world. But he's been terrible mean to all the servants, and he hasn't even been here that long!"

"Oh, Moll, he *is* a cruel old sod," Georgiana said, smiling a little for the first time since Mr. Stanton had spoken to her. "I would like for you to come to the inn with us, and continue to assist me, but that will be your choice, since you are still employed here at Pemberley. I do not think Mrs. Darcy will have any objections to your continuing in your trial there."

"Thank you ma'am, oh thank you!" exclaimed Moll, and for a moment it seemed as though she was going to embrace Georgiana, but then thought better of it. She bobbed a brief curtsey and all but skipped out of the dressing-room, and Georgiana, glad for a few moments of levity, returned her thoughts to the seriousness of the day.

Matthew was waiting for her outside her dressing-room, with an expression on his face that seemed vaguely familiar, until Georgiana realised he had looked like this when he had been threatening George Wickham with the sword. He offered her his arm, and she took it, saying, "It will be over soon enough."

It was not over soon enough for her liking, however, for she found only Elizabeth and the Bingleys in the breakfast-room, and Elizabeth, although she did so casually, informed them of who had already been in before them, including Mr. Stanton.

Neither she nor Matthew could eat much, and Elizabeth and the Bingleys waited for them to finish, then they all went downstairs together. The quickest way to the saloon was down the east stairs, and as they approached the stairwell, Georgiana tightened her grip on Matthew's arm, not for any fear of falling, but for comfort, and he silently reached over and touched her hand with his free one. They went down the stairs quietly, and then through the ball-room, their footsteps echoing loudly through the open space. Georgiana felt her pulse quicken as they drew up to the saloon doors, for if Mr. Stanton had stayed with the rest of the party, he was most likely there.

He was there, and he rose as they entered, saying, "In this house since yesterday, and you finally see fit to greet your father, is that it, Matthew?"

Elizabeth halted as Mr. Stanton spoke, and looked back to her brother and sister, bracing herself for what was to come. Georgiana only glanced at the man, but Matthew looked him very dispassionately in the eye, and walked on, towards the doors on the other side of the room, Georgiana still on his arm. It became clear to all they would make their exit, and Mr. Stanton, rather than take the cut as a gentleman would, shouted:

"Are you trying to cut me, boy? Your road to hell will be that much faster, for not honouring your father! You will think of this day often, over the eternity you spend burning!"

For a moment, Elizabeth feared he would attempt to force Matthew to turn around, which would have been a horrible error. Matthew had youth, strength, and years of fighting experience to his advantage, and the last thing Elizabeth wanted was Mr. Stanton's being put on the floor to add to the mortification of those in the saloon.

He did not, thankfully, and as Matthew and Georgiana walked out, Elizabeth glanced around to get a better sense of who was there. Mrs. Bennet, for perhaps the first time in her life, looked completely and utterly speechless, although Elizabeth was not sure she would be so once she returned to Hertfordshire, and resolved to speak to her mother about what she had seen and its impact to Mary, should it become public. Poor Herbert Ramsey looked as though he did not know precisely what he had witnessed, but he understood it was bad. Jane and Charles sat down with expressions of mild horror on their faces, and Darcy looked as though he was trying to hide how satisfied he was, and not entirely succeeding. Both Mr. Stanton and his youngest son wore expressions of livid fury, and Elizabeth grew a little concerned that to top it all, the father might have an apoplexy.

While none except the remaining Stantons seemed too much the worse for what they had witnessed, she was eager they begin to forget it as much as they could, and so she attempted a smile, and said, "Would anyone care to join me for a turn about the ball-room?"

Georgiana and Matthew exited into the entrance-hall, and once there, she asked Mr. Parker to have their trunks carried down, and their carriage brought around. The butler gaped a little at this request, although he must have overheard Mr. Stanton's shouting in the saloon, and he did go off to see to her requests.

When he had gone, and they were alone in the hall, Georgiana embraced her husband and whispered, "You did well."

"I thought I would be at least a little sad," he said, "but I am not. I feel instead as though a great weight has been lifted from me."

"I feel the same."

"I am sorry, though, Georgiana, at your having to leave what has been your home for so many years – "

She interrupted him with a kiss, and said, "Do not be. You have not been back for so long that I have any complaints over having you very nearly to myself for a few days."

It was an uneasy house party, that Elizabeth managed through the rest of the day. Her thought to encourage the others to take a turn about the ball-room immediately after the cut had been a good one, for it allowed the group that followed her an opportunity to circle the room in disturbed silence, rather than remaining in the saloon and staring at each other. Even Mrs. Bennet, who would not have desired so much walking, had taken the opportunity to vacate the saloon, muttering of plans to go to the nursery, so that Richard and Jacob Stanton had been left alone for whatever manner of furious discussion they wished to have.

Mary and David came into the ball-room not long after they had all begun walking, looking confused to find so many people in this space rather than the saloon, and Elizabeth was required to draw them aside and inform them that the cut had occurred. Poor Mary, who had entered the room wearing a relieved countenance, returned to her tense, worried look of earlier in the morning, but when David said he should go in and speak with his father and brother, Mary bravely said she would go with him.

What exactly was said in the saloon could not at all be heard. Elizabeth took this to be a good sign, that at least voices were not being raised, but had no better opportunity to see where things stood among the remaining Stantons in the house until they all gathered in the drawing-room before dinner. Then, she could see Richard and Jacob Stanton treating Mary and David with a degree of politeness, and that the father otherwise sat and fumed quietly, now that some time had passed since the event.

Still, it was a tense and awkward dinner for everyone; the conversation was light, and stilted, something that seemed to affect even Captain and Mrs. Ramsey, who had not been present when the cut had occurred, but had likely heard of it from their brother. There was some alleviation for the ladies, when they left the gentlemen to their brandy and port, and Elizabeth gave Darcy a deeply sympathetic look as she left, that he should have to preside over the table with its present occupants, when no-one would have doubted that he sided with Georgiana.

Everyone retired early on this evening, but Elizabeth felt far more exhausted than usual as she sank down into her husband's bed, and saw that he looked the same.

"I am so glad this day is over," she said.

"I agree wholeheartedly with you, my dear – it has been quite trying. Do you know what we spoke of, once the ladies went through?"

"I hope you are going to tell me of it now, rather than teazing me over it."

"Curricles. Andrew introduced the topic – he said he is thinking of purchasing one, although I suspect it to be a rather idle thought, and that he presented it as an innocuous topic. It was good thinking on his part, for we proceeded to have the most lengthy and inane conversation on curricles that has likely ever been had, and from there Charles brought us on to carriage horses."

"Well, I know you and Charles have the capacity to talk about horses for hours upon end. I trust that saw your time through?"

"It did. Were circumstances better, I would have liked to do more for Andrew's brother. Herbert Ramsey seems a good, earnest young man, and some discussion of the clergyman's profession would have been helpful for him, in making some additional connexions in the church. But I feared any mention of the church would have led to some insulting statement on its superiority as a career over the navy. Andrew is a jovial man, but I do not think he would have taken such an affront well, particularly since he and Matthew are old friends."

"I am not sure it would have helped young Mr. Ramsey much, anyway. I believe all three Stanton men owe their livings to Lord Anglesey," Elizabeth said. "You do have your own preferments in the church, although I suppose both of the present incumbents are too young to be of much benefit to him."

"Yes, but I can keep an ear open for something more beneficial for him than his present curacy."

"It is very good of you to do so," Elizabeth said, even more pleased than she had let on, that he should be so willing to help a relation only connected to him by marriage, twice over.

"It is nothing. He – and David – are the sort of clergyman this country should have more of, rather than the two more unfortunate examples under our roof."

"Darcy?"

"Yes?"

"When your wife gives you praise, you should enjoy it a little, and say, *thank you, my dear*, and then kiss her good-night."

"Ah, but you know that I am ever-vigilant against pride, thanks to your counsel."

He said it with a lightness of tone, but Elizabeth felt her heart further touched, that he would indicate he was still mindful of what she had said to him, back before they were married, and again early in their acquaintance with the Bakers.

"Darcy, I give you full leave to take any measure of pride you wish, when it comes to assisting a distant relation to a better position in life," she said. "However, there is one thing I would fault you on."

"What is it?" he asked, concerned.

"You *still* have not kissed your wife good-night," she said, glad she once again felt secure enough to teaze on this sort of topic.

Her security was reaffirmed, for this particular criticism was very quickly and repeatedly rectified.

CHAPTER 35

Mary awoke on her wedding day with the simple, happy thought that she was still to have a wedding day. She and David had not – at least for now – been required to choose between his father and brother. Mary had been deeply uncomfortable to witness Mr. Stanton's initial fury, when she and David had gone into the saloon, particularly for fear it might be directed at her over her role in the event that had precipitated the cut. He had largely ignored her during that conversation, however, and after his initial anger had passed, Mr. Stanton had seemed disturbed that one of his sons should disown him so completely and irrevocably, and had no interest in pressing his eldest son to choose sides – perhaps he understood the risk of this ending in a second cut. Although she had no doubt that he was still furious at Matthew and Georgiana, and would likely be until the end of his days, he had treated Mary and David politely, if not kindly, throughout the remainder of the day.

She rose and pulled on her dressing gown, and went to the window. A steady drizzle was falling, but she did not mind it – only Georgiana, Matthew, and Mr. Clark would even have to travel in the rain, with the wedding and breakfast held in the house. Turning back toward the bed, she was struck with the thought that she would not sleep alone tonight; she would sleep with her husband, after the act Elizabeth had blushingly described as pleasurable, following the initial pain, and her mother had said was a burden to be borne. Mary hoped Elizabeth was the more accurate one, but it was all still a mystery to her, and she was a little glad David had been married before, and had experience in these matters, although she hoped he would not compare her to Isabel Stanton.

The only thing she did know about was kissing: most of the married couples she knew, save her parents, were not so good about only doing it when they were alone, and so Mary had seen her share of kissing. The thought of being kissed by David in that way left her with a strange trembling in her belly. "Stop being so silly," she told herself, but the trembling would not entirely go away, nor did she find it wholly unpleasant.

Her thoughts were interrupted by a ferocious pounding on her door, and Mary went over to open it, finding Catherine waiting there, fully dressed.

"Oh, it is entirely too early in the morning! May I come in?" she asked, and then, when Mary had stepped aside: "We haven't got much time before mama storms in here with your dress and half the maids of all Pemberley. Has anyone talked to you about tonight?"

"Lizzy, and mama."

"Well, then of the two sources, you should consider whose advice you would prefer, were it another matter."

"Lizzy's – but she was so vague."

"Jane was vague, too, when she spoke to me. Lydia wasn't, but I found what she said did not entirely align with my own experience, either," Catherine said. "What do you want to know? I will tell you anything."

"I do not even know what I do not know. Am I supposed to wear my nightgown? Should I – or will he – remove it? I do not think I would be comfortable being so – so *naked*," Mary whispered.

"Hmm, in that, my experience may be different from yours, Mary. After all, I married a naval captain, and you are marrying a clergyman. I expect your husband may be more conservative about some things, as are you, which is why you are such a good match. But if something makes you uncomfortable – or if you like something – I think you should say so."

"Will it truly hurt so much I'll bleed?" Mary asked, her face burning.

Catherine nodded sympathetically, and said, "That was my experience, and Lydia's."

"Then how could it possibly be pleasurable?"

"Because everything before and after that moment will be so, and it is only the first time that it hurts," Catherine said. "It will be easier if you are relaxed, though, and there are things he can do to make you more relaxed. He has been married before, so he probably knows of them, but if not – "

"I do not want to know that much!" Mary cried, waving her hands to encourage Catherine to stop talking.

"Of course," Catherine laughed. "But you might have a glass or two of wine, before. This is Pemberley – you can send for it easily enough, if Elizabeth does not see a decanter placed in your chamber, which she likely will, knowing her. In that I envy you – the wine at the inn was so bad, that first night, Andrew gave me some rum to drink, and I thought my nose was going to burn off!"

"It was quite a sacrifice you made, to marry in the way you did, and travel immediately," said Mary, thoughtfully.

"In some ways, yes, but in others, no. I was married more quickly than I would have been otherwise, and to be married was what I wanted most of all, after having to wait so long as I did," Catherine said. "And even though my wedding night was in a coaching inn, and we were worried about papa, there was still something very wonderful about it."

"I think you could say nothing else on the subject that is better," Mary said, embracing her sister. "Thank you, Catherine. I do appreciate it, very much."

"Did you ever think all of us would be married, and so well?" Catherine asked. "Mama is going to need a new hobby-horse."

As though she had been summoned, Mrs. Bennet burst into the room, flanked by several maids, and shouting, "Up, child, if you are not already! Oh – five daughters married!"

Georgiana awoke from a sweet, dreamless sleep, and rolled over in the tangle of bedclothes surrounding them to face her husband, who slept soundly still. She smiled. Everyone had been acting as though it was a great sacrifice on her part, to come here to the inn, and yet it was as she had told Matthew – exactly what she had been wanting, to have so much time alone with him.

David had called on them a few hours after they had taken up this apartment, wishing to ensure they knew their presence was still desired at the wedding, which they had promised, and then they had been left blissfully alone for the rest of the day. Georgiana blushed at how early they had dined, and retired, and thought briefly that it was even better than Paris, although she knew after a few days she should come to miss music. Matthew had been kind to play for her two nights ago, when she had been so upset, but his cello had been left at Pemberley, and her pianoforte in Chatham.

The church bell rang, and reminded her of her own wedding day. Catherine had been married in the private chapel at Pemberley, and Mary would be thus today, but even though she had desired a small, private wedding, Georgiana was glad she had been married here in Lambton, with the church bells pealing and everyone from the village coming out to see her and Matthew ride by in her brother's landau. She smiled again, seeing he had awoken.

"How is it you sleep so soundly on your ship, and yet church bells wake you?" Georgiana asked.

"It is not that the bells ring," he said. "It is that eight bells sound, and no one says all is well."

Georgiana laughed softly at his answer, and asked, "How are you, after – after yesterday?"

"I am very well," he said. "I have no regrets over it – none at all. And how are you?"

"You need not even ask. Today I am going to see my good friend marry our brother, and then I am going to come back here with you."

"True, it is easy for you. I am the one who has to figure out how to smuggle a Darcy out of this inn."

Georgiana giggled. Not wishing to cause consternation from the innkeeper, Mr. Roddinghouse, as to why the former Miss Darcy would be staying in his establishment rather than Pemberley, Matthew had registered as Mr. Staunton, and said his wife would be arriving later. Then, with Moll's delightedly conspiratorial assistance, he had Georgiana come up the back staircase when no one else was there to see her.

"I am sure Moll Kelly will help you again."

"I am sure she will, as well. I like her – she would do well on board ship."

"She called your father a *cruel old sod* yesterday."

"Oh, then she would do very well indeed, and I like her even more."

Georgiana thought back to what Moll had said about Mr. Stanton being awful mean to the other servants, and decided not to share this particular piece of intelligence, but rather to increase her own vails, and give Moll some extra money to distribute to those who had been done the most injury.

"The wedding begins at ten, does it not?" he asked.

"It does. We should have an early wedding breakfast, since there will be no travel, other than to cross the house."

"In that I believe you shall be disappointed, Georgiana. We may have cut my father, but I assure you, we will not be spared his sermonising today; he will use every moment he possibly can."

Elizabeth had not been warned of the sermonising. She had planned for a wedding breakfast at half-eleven, assuming a ceremony of the same length as the others she had attended, and she had rapidly begun to realise that if things continued on the way they were now, which was Mr. Stanton preaching fire, brimstone, sin, fornication, corruption, &c. at them with no seeming indication of when he was to stop, she would surely be serving a cold wedding breakfast, and if it went on too long, she might merely be serving breakfast, without a wedding. Her only hope was that Mrs. Reynolds, seated at the back of the chapel, could find opportunity to slip out and tell Cook to delay things as much as possible.

Things had begun so very well, too. Georgiana and Matthew had quietly returned to the house and seated themselves inconspicuously beside the Ramseys, and Mary, looking quite pretty, had walked down the aisle on Mr. Bennet's arm, her father looking much stronger than when he had arrived at Pemberley. It was Elizabeth and her husband who had stood up with the betrothed couple, perhaps because they were the least politically troublesome choice, and she looked across the chapel and gave Darcy a look of impatience and aggravation, finding all she felt mirrored on his face.

The most difficult thing was that she had no idea how much time had actually passed. Mr. Stanton's lecture seemed interminable, but Elizabeth had no notion of how close to noon they were now, for she could hardly look at her watch in front of everyone. She watched Mrs. Reynolds slip out and return, glad that at least the breakfast should not be entirely cold, but aside from this, she could do nothing but feign attending to what Mr. Stanton was saying.

Finally, it was Mrs. Bennet who acted, and her action was to stand and say: "Sir, there is barely half-an-hour left before twelve, and I will not wait another day to see my last daughter married."

It was perhaps the rudest thing her mother had ever done, and Elizabeth was wholly glad of it. Mr. Stanton did not rebuke Mrs. Bennet, and instead opened the prayer book, seeing the ceremony completed with three minutes to spare before noon.

There had been more than a few cold dishes served at the wedding breakfast, but no one seemed to mind very much. Elizabeth did wish that Georgiana and Matthew had stayed for the meal, although she recognised the rightness in their reason for going: they could not countenance any sort of scene marring what should be a happy day for Mary, and their party was not so large that their presence would not have made things uncomfortable, at the very least.

Thus she was glad when Mr. Stanton approached her in the yellow drawing-room following the breakfast, and informed her that he and Jacob would be leaving first thing on the morrow. Elizabeth did not work very hard to keep her pleasure at hearing this from reaching her countenance, although she thanked him for performing the ceremony.

"You are welcome, although of course it was my duty to do so," he said. "You would do well to reconsider this Mr. Clark who holds your living. I spoke to him, and I would hate for such a soft man to bear responsibility for the religious education of your young sons."

"My sons will be educated as Mr. Darcy and I see fit," replied Elizabeth.

"I see I shall make no progress in this house," he said, and strode back over to where his youngest son was seated, without so much as a nod.

Mr. Bennet came to stand at Elizabeth's side, and murmured, "I am amazed, Lizzy, at the range of ways in which clergymen may be ridiculous. I am only glad Mary managed to find one of what seems the very few rational ones out there."

"Yes, she did," said Elizabeth, looking over to where Mary and David were seated, both of them looking happy, and perhaps a little relieved. "What are you and mama going to do, now that we are all gone from home?"

"I know not, Lizzy. We went so long thinking we should struggle to see any of you married, I believe I always assumed at least some of you would remain at home. You may see us here at Pemberley more often, particularly if you and Jane continue to have more grandchildren."

"You are welcome here at any time, papa."

Elizabeth became aware of Darcy's looking to gain her attention from a corner of the room, and when her father seemed to have no more to say, she went to her husband, and saw he was holding a letter. He informed her it was from Lady Catherine, and she asked after its contents.

"You had better read it for yourself. I hardly know what to make of it."

Elizabeth unfolded the letter, and read of Lady Catherine's wrath that not only had the Fitzwilliams broken their promise of a betrothal to her daughter, Anne, but now Edward was going to marry some French harlot. She once again requested that her nephew join her in cutting the Fitzwilliams.

"I have seen and been involved in more cutting of acquaintances in the past few months than I was my entire life before," she said.

"Lady Catherine cuts people all the time, and just as readily un-cuts them, if it suits her," he said. "I am more curious about this French harlot she speaks of."

"Georgiana and Matthew became acquainted with the widow of the captain of the Polonais, when they were in Paris. There was some matter involving her father's land, and whether she should inherit, and they asked Edward to look after her when they left," Elizabeth said. "Georgiana noted she was beautiful – I wonder if it could have been her."

"They left *Edward* to look after a beautiful French widow?" Darcy asked, incredulous. "That is rather like asking a fox to look after a hen."

"Come, Darcy, he is a very good man, if one who enjoys a flirtation."

"Yes, you are right. It is rather more like asking a loyal dog to look after a shoulder of mutton. Given enough time, it will not end well for both the dog and the mutton, despite the dog's best intentions."

Elizabeth laughed. "I hope if she is the one who is to be our cousin, she never learns you compared her to a shoulder of mutton."

"I wonder at Georgiana and Matthew not saying anything of it, whether this woman is the widow or not. They stayed over at Stradbroke on their journey here. Surely they must know something of this, and they have said nothing."

"We have hardly spoken to them, except of the other matter, but I will send a note over inviting them to return here tomorrow. Mr. Stanton told me of his intent to leave early tomorrow morning."

"Good, I am glad he took my hint," he said, "and do not worry, it was given after breakfast."

"Your hint? Pray tell, what was your hint?"

"I told him I would have little patience to continue to find him under my roof after tonight."

"Darcy, at some point in your life, you seem to have picked up the wrong definition of the word *hint*. A hint would be: I am sure you are eager to return to your parish and provide further guidance to your own flock, Mr. Stanton."

"Well, my first choice for a hint was to have Parker ask him what time he wished for his carriage to be ready tomorrow morning, but when I put it to him, poor Parker acted as if I had asked him to put his head in a guillotine," Darcy said. "Mr. Stanton has injured my sister and castigated my servants, and now that Mary is safely wed, there is only so polite I am willing to be."

"I did not say I disagreed with your words, merely that they did not constitute a hint."

"You are teazing me again."

"And it took you a rather long time to realise it, my dear," she said. "But I think we shall all be better tomorrow, once that man's carriage leaves the drive. I will write my note this evening and have it carried over to Georgiana and Matthew as soon as their father is gone."

"Do not send a note – let us call on them tomorrow and invite them to return ourselves."

"You and I cannot call on them, Darcy."

"Whyever not?"

"Because you are Mr. Darcy, and they are trying not to draw attention to the fact that they are staying there, so the whole village is asking why Georgiana had to leave Pemberley for a few days. Nothing could possibly draw more attention than *you* appearing there to call on them."

CHAPTER 36

It gave Mary a terrible start when she woke, that there was a man in her bed. In a moment, of course, it had all come back to her, that she was a married woman – she was Mary Stanton – and it was David, her husband, in the bed beside her. Then she thought of what they had done in this bed, and flushed most completely.

She was still wearing her nightgown, but when she turned over to face David, she found the hem had drifted up her legs in the night, and she hastened to pull it down. She did not know whether he had sensed she would be uncomfortable, in removing it, or whether Catherine was right about a clergyman being more conservative in the marriage bed, but either way, she was glad they had retained their nightclothes. It was strange enough, that for so long they were not even supposed to be in the same room together, unchaperoned, and now they could sleep in the same bed, and kiss, and touch each other in all those different places underneath their nightclothes.

Mary thought it all seemed a little too much, too quickly, but nor could she say she disliked anything they had done together – except the one part that had hurt – and some things she had liked much more than she had expected. She thought a little guiltily that it was all much nicer than the coaching inn Catherine had stayed in, this beautiful, spacious apartment, and the decanter of very fine wine that had indeed been placed in the bedchamber.

David awoke, smiling immediately at her, and said, "So you are an early riser as well, then?"

"I am." Mary wished very much that he would kiss her, was seized with the sudden thought that she could kiss him instead, doubted herself, and then did it anyway.

"That was lovely, Mary," he said. "I hope I may take it as a sign that you are happy?"

432

"You may, for I am very happy. Are you?"

"I am." He returned her kiss, then rose from the bed and said, "I always begin my day with a prayer. You are welcome to join me if you wish, but do not feel you must depart from your own routine, if you do not wish to."

"Oh, but I would be even happier, if I could join you."

In a far less fine, but passable bedchamber in Lambton, the other couple bearing the name of Stanton had none of the shyness of a newly wed couple in their marriage bed. As much as she liked the parts that came before this time, Georgiana particularly enjoyed the feeling of being sated, of Matthew's leg still draped over her own, and his arm heavy on her belly.

"You have been very eager, lately," Matthew said. "I begin to wonder how we might stay at inns more often."

They had been married long enough for Georgiana to understand this was praise, not censure, although it still made her blush, and she could not think of what to say in response.

"Did you truly miss me in this way so much, or are you more desirous of making another baby?" he asked.

"A bit of both," she murmured.

He brought his hand up to caress her cheek, and said, "It will happen, Georgiana. Perhaps not so quickly as it did the first time, but I have faith that it will happen. We will have a child."

Georgiana allowed his words to soothe her, and as Matthew drifted back to sleep, she realised that she was happy. Not so happy as she expected she would be, when she could finally become a mother, but happy nonetheless, and for someone who had spent a very long time dreaming about a place where all hope was lost, this was more than enough for her – for now, at least.

She did not fall back asleep so easily as Matthew, but she laid there in a state of contentedness, and when the church bell began to toll again, she counted until the eighth ring and said: "All is well."

And meant it, fully.

Georgiana and Matthew made their return to Pemberley late in the morning. Elizabeth greeted them, inviting them to come with her to Darcy's study, and felt a little badly about having given this summons, for surely they must have thought it related to the cutting of Mr. Stanton.

When they arrived, though, Darcy immediately rose, and said, "I am very glad to see you both back in this house."

"We are glad to be back," said Matthew, sitting beside his wife, "and I apologise again for bringing such a disruption upon your house."

"Let us trouble ourselves with that no more," said Darcy. "We wished to speak with you on something else entirely. I had a letter from Lady

Catherine, claiming Edward is to marry a French harlot."

"She is not a harlot!" cried Georgiana. "She is honourable, and beautiful, and she and Edward are very much in love."

"Well, that does answer our question as to whether this was the French widow you introduced him to."

Georgiana confirmed that she was, and told them more of Marguerite Durand, and how they had asked Edward to assist her. In response to the dubious expression forming on her brother's face, she protested: "He said he was able to admire a pretty woman, while knowing he may do nothing but admire."

"It seems he was wrong."

"I suppose he was, for he did fall in love, as did she," Georgiana said. "He thought for a time to give her up, but when Alice passed without an heir, his situation changed – Madame Durand has already borne a son, and is the best hope right now for continuing the earldom."

"And the Fitzwilliams will accept her, with eight thousand pounds to her name?"

"That is a strange matter, as well," Georgiana said, smiling. "It seems Marguerite is not so good with her English numbers. While we were at Stradbroke, Lady Ellen realised the land was worth *eighty* thousand pounds, not *eight*. She was a Rochechouart-Châtilloux, before her first marriage. Edward is marrying a true and legitimate French heiress."

"Accidentally," said Darcy, so drily that he very nearly made Elizabeth laugh. She was glad she suppressed her amusement, for the expression on Matthew's face indicated he had not yet grown wholly comfortable with the situation. Elizabeth was glad that at least Marguerite Durand's possession of an independent fortune meant Edward's marrying her was no longer completely dependent on Alice's death. If Alice had lived, there would have been certain difficulties in breaking off negotiations with Lady Catherine, but Elizabeth thought her aunt and uncle would have sided with their son, if he had presented them with the alternative of a love match with eighty thousand pounds. Even considering the more unfortunate series of events that had occurred, Elizabeth was still very pleased for Edward.

"I very much wish to meet this Marguerite Durand," she said.

"I think you will like her very much," said Georgiana. "I have not even told you yet of what she said to Lady Catherine."

CHAPTER 37

There was something Catherine Ramsey had not told her sister about the marriage bed, and this was that one's husband could snore, quite loudly. She was a heavy sleeper, and so mostly did not mind, but on mornings like this one, she might have liked to go back to sleep for another hour or so, but knew it would be futile. Still, she could have few complaints on a day of so much happiness, for the day of her promised ball had finally arrived.

She slipped out of bed and pulled on her dressing gown against the morning chill, and then danced herself a waltz around their bedchamber. She knew she would dance it tonight with Andrew: Lizzy had indicated that after it was included in Georgiana's ball, it should be included in Catherine's and Mary's, as well, and although Mary did not intend to dance it, she knew of its importance to her sister, and had readily blessed its inclusion. Catherine did not notice the snoring had stopped until she found herself grabbed by the hips, and twirled around so she was facing Andrew.

"I think you would dance better with a partner, pretty Cat," he said.

Catherine had been trying very hard to do away with her old nickname, Kitty, but she liked this one, because he only ever called her that when they were alone, and he always said it in a way that made her feel mature, and womanly. He obliged her in a little pirouette, up and down the room, but then said, "We should not dance too much, or we will be tired for tonight."

"Oh yes. Had you something else in mind?"

He did have something else in mind, the very same thing Catherine did, and she giggled tremendously when he picked her up and carried her back over to the bed, for that occupation she much preferred to another hour of sleep.

When they had finished and she had begun to cool from the flush of the act, Catherine regretted her discarded dressing gown, but saw it had fallen on the floor, and so instead she pulled the covers up around them.

"It *is* quite a big day for you," he said. "A ball in your honour – it was very good of your sister to do it. And I am glad of it, for a bride should have her time to be singled out as special."

Catherine agreed wholly with him, but thought it immodest to say so, and so instead she said, "I wish Lydia could have been here. I know we do not get on as well as we used to, but still, she is the only one of my sisters absent, and I suppose now she always shall be."

"America is not so very far away – you may well see her again."

"Not so very far away? They have been gone nearly two months, and we still have not even heard from them!"

"And likely will not for another fortnight, if not another month, so you mustn't worry about it," he said. "I suppose the world seems a little smaller to me, for having seen so much of it."

"I hope you do not see much more of it, at least not without me," said Catherine. She did not like at all what Georgiana had gone through, over the winter. The fall and losing the baby were particularly tragic circumstances, of course, but even just that she had been without her husband for so long seemed a heavy burden to endure. Catherine had been prepared in the abstract to be a naval wife, but now that she was married and the war was over, she was not so sure she wished for Andrew to have another command.

"I suspect we shall not be seeing much more beyond England's shores, unless you wish to travel," he said.

"But your leave will be over soon."

"Yes, it will be, and I shall call on the Admiralty, as I am obligated to do," he said. "But unless another war breaks out, which seems unlikely now, I will not be offered another command. They gave Matthew despatches to the Baltic, and he is the nephew of two earls. Someone with my connexions has no hope of a command, with so many turned on shore."

"That hardly seems fair," said Catherine. She might not have wished for him to have another command, but nor did she like the thought of him being passed over for these reasons.

"It is the way the world works, including the naval world," he said, "and I can hardly complain of it, for the navy did allow me to rise further in the world than I would have otherwise. Ten years ago, if anyone had told me I was to marry a gentleman's daughter, I'd have laughed in his face. I am content with my lot – I have earned a good fortune, and married my pretty Cat, and I am more than ready to settle down on land."

Elizabeth did not know precisely why she had been required to invite everyone to come down early for what was already an early dinner, preceding the ball. However, she adored a surprise as much as anyone, so long as it had the promise of being something good, and she could hardly see how it would be anything else, with Georgiana and Mary behind it.

Certainly it had something to do with the fact that the two of them had spent a fair amount of their free time since Georgiana's return to the house sequestered in the music-room, and it could thus be presumed to be something of a musical nature. In truth, Elizabeth cared less about precisely what piece of music it was, and more that her two young married sisters could still manage some girlish enthusiasm over their surprise, particularly when they had each been through events in the last few months that had necessarily made them both even less girlish than they were already.

So she had gladly given the summons to her houseguests, and found it very punctually followed, so all were assembled in the yellow drawing-room at the designated time. When they had, Mary pushed open the doors to the music-room, smiled as broadly as she ever could, and said, "If everyone would follow me through, please, my *sister* and I have something we would like to play for you."

They all did as they were bade, and found Georgiana seated there at the harp, which was usually relegated to a corner of the room, but had been moved to a position of importance, before both the old harpsichord and the pianoforte.

"Mrs. Stanton and I have been waiting for some time to perform this piece together, for want of having all those we would have liked to hear it together," Georgiana said, thinking briefly of those who were not there, most notably Lord Anglesey and Lady Tonbridge, who had too many engagements in town at this time of year to get away, but had, Mary said, sent a very fine note of congratulations. "We do not know when we shall all be together again, and so we wished to play Scarlatti's Fandango for you."

A murmur of approval indicated they should begin, and so Georgiana did. She had been practising so much in the short time they had before this evening that the tips of her fingers were quite sore, but capable of one more performance. And there was something important about this performance, at least for her – it was something remnant and incomplete from her life before marriage, a performance that would have been done well before now if it had not been interrupted by the departure of some of the most important members of her prospective audience, to go and fight in the Hundred-Day War.

Matthew and Andrew – an aficionado of Spanish music – were those that had departed. Yet now David must be considered with them as most important among the audience, standing there and watching his wife perform. Mary, playing with great spirit on the castanets beside Georgiana, had been her friend at that time, but was now her sister, a notion that pleased both of them very much.

Young ladies embarking on a performance, in any drawing-room or music-room, shall generally be congratulated by their audience on completion of that performance. In Georgiana's and Mary's case, however, their audience had truly appreciated and enjoyed the piece, and they were applauded most enthusiastically.

They still had a little time before they should go in to dinner, and Georgiana went to stand by Matthew, to learn what his opinion of the song had been.

"I have waited a very long time to hear this performance, and I find it has been every bit as exceptional as I had thought it would be," he said.

"Yes, you once promised you would come back, so you could hear it – a promise you very nearly broke."

"I will not break such a promise again," he said softly, taking up her hand and running his thumb over her fingertips. "Although I find I may need to fret over the state of your hands, as you did mine."

"They are not nearly so bad as yours were," Georgiana said defensively, intending to discreetly put her gloves back on as soon as she could.

"Good, then you will be well enough to waltz with me?"

"Of course. That dance will always belong to you, whether you ask for it or not."

"I intend always to ask for it," he said. "Georgiana – all *is* well?"

She grasped his hand, despite the mild discomfort it brought. "All is very well."

Elizabeth caught Georgiana and Matthew holding hands from across the room, and averted her eyes from what seemed a private moment, turning her attention back to Jane and Charles, who had stood with her and Darcy as they watched the performance.

When she looked over again, she saw the Ramseys had approached both Stanton couples, and were indicating their enjoyment of the performance. It seemed appropriate, to her, that they were grouped in this way. They were all linked to her by some sort of familial bond, but she and Jane had married men who were particular friends, while the men of that group were all linked to Matthew – one a friend, one a brother.

Her dream during those tense hours before George's birth had been very nearly forgotten, but she thought of it now, and how it was possible none of the couples in that group would have come to be, if her dream had continued. Lady Tonbridge had retained their acquaintance, so it was possible Catherine and Andrew Ramsey might still have met in town, and that he would have overlooked the scandalous family of Catherine's sister. Matthew and Georgiana might have met in London, as well, but Elizabeth thought it likely that any affections he felt towards the young lady at the centre of the scandal would have been discouraged by his uncle well before they could have turned into love. And it was very possible that Georgiana would have already been wed to Edward by that time, and met him as Mrs.

Fitzwilliam, rather than Miss Darcy. There would be no meeting, therefore, of Mary and David Stanton, nor even Edward and his delightful Frenchwoman.

But no, all had come out as it should, with four of her sisters all happily married, and anticipating the pleasures of the ball that evening. She thought, with a pang, of Lydia – for Lydia was the one sister who might have come out better in that world. Yet Lydia had willingly reconciled with her husband, and perhaps she and Wickham would make a better life in America.

Elizabeth refocused her attention on the happiness of her sisters in this room, smiled contentedly, and nodded to Mr. Parker to go and open the dining-room doors.

CHAPTER 38

It was a rare day that Elizabeth awoke before her husband, and this was not one of them. He had been awake long enough to take up a book, which he discarded upon seeing her stir.

"Good morning, my love," he said.

Elizabeth kissed him good morning, and then settled back into the pillows, yawning.

"Do you wish to sleep longer? I doubt the others will wake anytime soon."

"No, I would rather stay up and speak with you. We hardly had a chance to talk last night."

"We did dance."

They had danced indeed, the first set and then the waltz to close the ball. Elizabeth, however, pleased to be doing so again, had danced all but two sets, and Darcy very nearly all of them, to ensure their female relations always had partners. The two sets Elizabeth had been required to skip had been to allow her to go and nurse her sons, and she had made her escape from the ball-room in perfect understanding with her husband, who had nodded to her from across the room, as he led Catherine to the front of the line.

"I am glad you obliged me in a few dances," she said. "I know it is not your favourite pastime."

"It is never my favourite pastime, but I do enjoy dancing with you," he said. "And truly, last night was not so bad – I mostly danced with our sisters."

"Ah, true. They did all look very well, did they not? Although Catherine must be allowed to be the belle. I have never seen her so happy, to be leading off a ball."

Catherine *had* looked tremendously happy, wearing the first ball gown of a yet-unfinished wedding trousseau, and Elizabeth had been so pleased for her, to have her moment after marrying in a cloud of worry. Next in the set had come the latest bride, Mary, looking newly confident to be dancing with her husband. Beyond them, Georgiana and Matthew, looking as well as ever together, and then Jane and Charles, the lady of that couple enjoying what was likely to be her last dancing before the birth of her next child.

"I should be hard-pressed to call anyone but you the most beautiful woman at a ball, but I will say that she looked very well, and it was much deserved, for the sacrifice she made."

"Indeed it was."

"I thought it came off well," said he. "No one seemed scandalised at all by our including the waltz again, and I am glad Cook had an event where the timing of the meal could be set precisely in advance."

"Yes, she was so upset over the wedding breakfast, and it was not at all her doing," Elizabeth said. "And it was a good idea you had, to put up the awning."

In truth she was not sure what they would have done without the awning. With so many guests, they had not enough footmen and not enough umbrellas to see to everyone arriving in the drizzle, and so to allow them to come up to the house under an awning had been a very good idea on Darcy's part.

"I would rather I did not need such an idea," he said. "I am glad we still have ample time before the spring planting, but I worry over how the winter wheat is doing with all of this damp. We may have to replant more than is usual."

"But is it not better to have too much rain now, rather than in the spring?"

"So long as we do not spend *all* our rain now, and find ourselves with drought later on."

He touched the wood of the bedpost after he said it, and Elizabeth looked at him sceptically. "Fitzwilliam Darcy, are you superstitious?"

"In this matter, I am."

"I learn something new of you, even now," she said, running her hand across the stubble on his jawline. "But I do hope you will not let the rain worry you too much. We are still so far from spring."

"True." He took her hand, and brought it up to his lips so he could kiss her palm, and then the inside of her wrist. Elizabeth was terribly sensitive there, something he was well aware of, and she thought perhaps he desired a distraction, one she was entirely happy to provide him with.

It was not long before his fingertips were tracing her legs in delightfully languid caresses, and then grasping the hem of her nightgown so he could help her remove it. When Elizabeth had discarded it over the side of the bed, however, she found he did not make any immediate move to proceed, and instead looked at her for a very long time, so long she grew slightly uncomfortable, until he said, "Oh, Elizabeth, that you could think I no longer found you desirable."

His words were lovely, but his eyes said even more, and Elizabeth was so overcome she could do little more than hold her arms out to him, and whisper, "I love you."

"I love you, as well, my darling Elizabeth, and I promise you will never again have cause to doubt how very much I desire and adore you," he said, and then he kissed her again.

IN MEMORIAM

Although poor Alice (Lady Fitzwilliam) had to pass in order to further the plot, it was realistic that in an era with a maternal mortality rate of nearly 20 percent from childbirth, one of the women in this story would not survive her birth.

Unfortunately, for all of our medical advances and technology today, this is still a tragedy that many families suffer. According to the World Health Organization, approximately 830 women still die every day in childbirth, often from preventable causes – the same causes women were dying from two hundred years ago.

I would like to ask readers to please take a moment to remember those who have died to bring children into the world, both then and now.

AUTHOR'S NOTES

Language

I can speak only a few phrases in French, and owe a great deal of gratitude to Caroline Bozec for her assistance with French translations. As this is meant to be an English-language story, I have tried to keep the French phrases to a minimum, and to use words that were moderately decipherable for English readers, but I felt it important to include at least a bit for authenticity.

Many thanks are owed to my "proofreading squad," as well, including: Bryanne Colvin, Ann Marie Colyer, Jennifer Elchisak, Pallavi Rachakonda, and Pip. Any mistakes remaining, of course, are mine.

One of the things I enjoy about reading Austen's work are those little inconsistencies that show she was writing in a time when the notion of a dictionary, and universal spelling for words, was still a relatively new concept. Therefore, I've tried to retain a few inconsistencies in this spirit, particularly in characters' letters. The most egregious of these, of course, is Lydia spelling "annuity" in the manner I imagine she would have sounded it out. I have also peppered in a few random hyphenations, for the same reason. Similarly, there are a few "an h–" instances that align with Austen's usage, and not our more modern application, and other similar adjustments to grammar in an attempt at greater alignment with the original. And there are, of course, passages and phrases from the original included within Elizabeth's dream.

"Voilder" is the most elegant-sounding and subtle word I have been able to find for "chamber pot." The "cab-net day-sanze" Mrs. Baker refers to is properly spelled "cabinet d'aisance," and is, again, a more elegant way to say "outhouse," so long as one does not say it in Mrs. Baker's accent.

"Papacy" would have been commonly used by Anglicans at the time to refer to Catholicism, and no slight is meant to modern Catholics.

444

People

All of the noble titles used within this story were either extinct during the Regency, or are entirely made up, and any resemblance of any of the names within to actual people is entirely coincidental, with the exception of a brief, fictitious encounter with Muzio Clementi, references to the Cavendish and Cecil families, and the use of Rochechouart, a major noble family in France, as part of Marguerite Durand's maiden name. Châtilloux is a creation, but we may assume a family of enough status to marry a Rochechouart daughter, and have land worth 80,000 pounds.

The two sons of earls in this story, because they are in families lacking a second title, have the precedence of viscount, with their surnames used in place of the courtesy title, and their wives take comparable titles. Again, this was done to avoid the confusion of introducing additional titles.

I have not been able to find definitive evidence of what Colonel Fitzwilliam should have been called in this era, after resigning his commission. Modern Debrett's indicates retired officers above the rank of captain may use their former rank. As well, Colonel Brandon in *Sense and Sensibility*, who is generally presumed to be retired (although I am not sure he is formally mentioned as such, in the novel), continues to be addressed by his rank. Going on this, and because I think he would have preferred it (having retired due to a war wound, and not entirely by choice) I have had Edward opt to continue to be addressed as Colonel Fitzwilliam.

Places

The Matlock registry office is entirely based on conjecture, as I have not been able to find any details on what these offices were actually like, particularly in a more remote outpost from London.

Visitors to the Old Palace at Hatfield House may find it rather unbelievable that the palace was serving as a stable during this time (and into the 20th century), but that is indeed the case.

What is known as King's Lynn today was displayed as Lynn Regis on maps of that time. I am presuming that, like Lyme Regis, the "Regis" would have been dropped in common reference to the town.

After a 1692 earthquake, Kingston became the primary port for commercial activity within Jamaica, but Port Royal generally continued to be, and eventually grew as, the site for the Royal Navy's dockyard. I am assuming a merchant convoy would have been brought into Kingston.

While Jane Austen often referenced real inns she would have known, that has not always been possible in this work. The George and the Keppel's Head in Portsmouth are real, and the latter still in operation as a hotel today. The Admiral's Arms in Chatham, however, is fictitious; I was not able to find enough detail on the historic inns within Chatham to find one suitable for use. The inns listed by Elizabeth for the journey from Pemberley to Longbourn are similarly fictitious.

Elopements and Wives

Georgiana's situation in her dreams does have a historical basis, known as the "Shrigley abduction," although it dates from 1826. Ellen Turner, also a 15-year-old heiress, was abducted by Edward Gibbon Wakefield, told her father's business had failed, and convinced into a marriage at Gretna Green. Wakefield took her to France, where they were found by her uncle. The marriage was annulled, and Wakefield and his accomplices spent time in prison for their actions. Turner married a neighbour, and died in childbirth at the age of 19.

Both Georgiana's and Miss Turner's situations underscore what Wickham said about his wife being his property. In this time, once a woman married, she became the property of her husband; part of the proceedings for obtaining a divorce due to adultery required the husband to sue the adulterer, for damages to his property. So while we may read Austen with lighter, more romantic thoughts in mind, it truly was imperative for a woman to be certain she was making a good match before she married, because following the wedding day, she essentially lost what few rights she had possessed, as a single female.

Childbirth and Medicine

Childbirth was, at this time, undergoing a change in terms of the assistance available to women. Midwives, for the very rich, were replaced by accoucheurs, who were willing and experienced in intervening with a birth (forceps and similar instruments were already being used in this time). Most births took place in London, where these new specialists were readily available, although it was not abnormal for them to attend the particularly rich elsewhere.

The prior, more modesty-preserving method of using a birthing chair, with the physician or midwife making eye contact with the woman through the whole birth and catching the baby as it came out, gave way to new methods. Women used a lightweight folding bed, such as is described for Elizabeth's birth, and laid on their side in what is known today as the Sims position, where the accoucheur could see everything, but the woman did not have to face him as he did so. This position was commonly used in hospitals in Britain into the 1970s.

There was no social taboo against appearing visibly pregnant while in public, even up into the ninth month. If Georgiana had decided to hunt while pregnant, it would not have been considered outlandish, as some women did so.

Husbands were generally in attendance during the birth, and

"confinement" was really recovery time for these epidural-less births. Breast-feeding was fairly common, and it was understood then that it lessened the chances of a woman becoming pregnant.

I had not known all of this, when I set out to write this book, and owe a huge debt to Judith S. Lewis's *In the Family Way: Childbearing in the British Aristocracy, 1760-1860*, which also showed that Darcy was far from the only husband in that era to worry over his wife's pregnancy. Lewis's work, in turn, led me to read *An Introduction to the Practice of Midwifery*, by Thomas Denman, a leading accoucheur of the time.

As for the twin birth, twins can be born hours, and even days, apart. Elizabeth's birth, where both placentas for fraternal twins follow the twins themselves, is more rare, but medically possible. However, it would have been more dangerous than our characters realised, due to risk of infection: thank goodness for Sarah and her handwashing.

I was surprised to learn from Denman's book that catheters were actually used during that time, and we can presume one was used at some point in the course of all of that broth being spooned into Georgiana's mouth. I thought I'd leave the poor young lady *some* privacy, however, and keep it out of the story.

Finances

Matthew is careful to ensure there are men available to go with his wife to Drummonds, because it was considered inappropriate for a woman to go into a bank by herself. This, in part, also accounts for why Georgiana was not well received when she tried to exchange her hundred-pound note for ready money.

David Stanton's income of more than a thousand pounds a year would have been made up of yet-undetermined proportions between: the tithe, the actual income collected from the living itself; the glebe land, which was land belonging to the living that he would have made farming income from; and interest from money he references in the funds, which in his instance would largely be comprised of his late wife's dowry. Mary's dowry will increase the income from the latter source.

Lydia's 286 pounds a year would be made up of the 150 pound annuity (the interest of the 3,000 pounds Darcy gave her, presuming it to be in the five per cents), the 100 pounds a year Mr. Bennet had agreed to give her and Wickham in *Pride and Prejudice*, and her 36 pound per year pension, as the supposed widow of an ensign.

The 700 pounds a year Colonel Fitzwilliam thought he and Marguerite Durand would have to live on would have been made up of 400 pounds a year, the interest from the 8,000 pounds made from the sale of her land, and the interest from approximately 6,000 pounds, which he would have received from the sale of his commission. Again, the five per cents are presumed for both.

Finding an accurate exchange rate for this time did not prove easy, but somewhere around 25 francs to 1 pound sterling came up most often in my research, making Marguerite's 2 million francs worth approximately 80,000 pounds.

Funerals

Women were also not allowed to attend funerals, although they usually did the preparation of the body. Because Georgiana would never have done this, and because it seemed right that a loyal valet of many years would volunteer to keep her from needing to, I had Mason do so in her dream.

Marriages

Unlike the special licence, which I believe is far more popular in fiction, a common licence was relatively easy to acquire, and allowed a couple to marry anywhere, so long as it was on consecrated ground. A special licence, meanwhile, allowed them to marry anywhere they wished, consecrated ground or not.

One requirement of a common licence that David Stanton did not touch on was time spent in the parish by one of the couple, which did need to be of some duration. I am assuming that the time Catherine spent at Pemberley during the summer, as well as more recently, fulfilled this requirement.

I did take a *bit* of creative licence, in that the planned location of the wedding was filled in on the licence. So let us just presume that it read only "Lambton parish," as opposed to "parish church of Lambton," and Pemberley's chapel, being consecrated and also within the parish, could fit that looser definition.

Then, as now, the *Book of Common Prayer* actually puts the sermon, if given, well after the vows are actually spoken in the marriage ceremony. But we can assume that Mr. Stanton, never one for sticking to the prayer book, began sermonising before he even opened it.

The Navy

Carrying despatches would have been a common task for a frigate. The need for despatches to go to foreign ministers with new instructions as a result of the second Treaty of Paris is conjecture, but seemed logical to me.

What is referred to as the "day cabin" on HMS Caroline is more commonly called the "coach." I have opted to use the former term to avoid any confusion with the land-based vehicles.

Military and nautical jewellery, clothing, and decorative items were highly popular at the time, for patriotic reasons, and so Georgiana's anchor pendant, while personally symbolic, would also have been fashionable.

HMS Rapid was actually sold out of the service in 1814.

The USS President was captured by a British squadron many months after the action in the dream world took place, so although this dream world battle would have been an accomplishment equivalent to Captain Stanton's taking the Polonais in the "real" fictional world, it would have no effect on the outcome of the war, aside from an additional bolstering of British naval pride. Georgiana observes that the President is not as mauled as the Caroline is, and we can presume this is because the most severe damage was done by firing into the President's stern, the same method Captain Stanton used in the battle against the Polonais.

Foxhunting

I fully recognise that scenes involving foxhunting may be upsetting to some, and indeed, the end result is upsetting to me, as well. However, as a key part of English country life at that time, and an equestrian pursuit I think many of our characters would have participated in, I have decided to include and portray it.

The Pemberley hunt as described is a very unaggressive hunt, and this refers both to what they hunt, as well as how they go about it. While the Pemberley hunt goes after a fox that has been a legitimate nuisance, the popularity and frequency of foxhunting led to an actual shortage of foxes in some places, to the point where foxes were purchased (often after being imported from the continent) and then released. As well, those participating are not "neck-or-nothing" riders, as Darcy refers to them, who would ride their horses (and sometimes themselves) to the death.

For my knowledge of this and other country pursuits, I am indebted to E.W. Bovill's excellent *English Country Life 1780-1830*.

Arms and Heraldry

Although today the College of Arms closely regulates the use of heraldry in the United Kingdom, regulation essentially stopped after the Glorious Revolution up until the mid-twentieth century. This resulted in a considerable drop in the number of registered coats of arms, and so the Stantons may or may not have chosen to eventually register their new arms. This is why Georgiana and her aunt had no qualms about putting the new arms into immediate use, particularly since Lord Anglesey, whose arms they were modifying, had suggested the variation.

The Cut Direct

There were numerous ways to cut an acquaintance, including more indirect methods, such as pretending not to see them – or, as Elizabeth and Darcy do, not being "at home" when they called. This was an era where there was a difference between being physically at home and socially at home, and sometimes people would not be socially at home to any callers, including those they would have no desire to sever their acquaintance with. In this instance, however, they were only socially not home to the Bakers, and also ceased inviting them to social engagements at Pemberley, thus indirectly cutting them.

The cut direct was, as it indicates, direct and more irrevocable – a ritualistic method of severing an acquaintance. It required making eye contact with the person being cut, and deliberately not acknowledging them. It was not supposed to be done to a social inferior; however, as an earl's younger son, Matthew's father would still outrank him. Presumably, though, it was still not something often done by sons to their fathers.

Further Reading

In addition to the books already listed in these notes and *A Constant Love*, I have found the following titles to be particularly useful: *The Complete Servant*, by Samuel and Sarah Adams; *The Gentleman's Daughter: Women's Lives in Georgian England*, by Amanda Vickery; *Wives and Daughters: Women and Children in the Georgian Country House*, by Joanna Martin; *Behind Closed Doors: At Home in Georgian England*, by Amanda Vickery; *Turnpike Roads*, by Geoffrey N. Wright; *Admiral Sir P. B. V. Broke ... a memoir*, by John George Brighton and Philip Bowes Vere Broke; and *The Frigate Surprise : The Complete Story of the Ship Made Famous in the Novels of Patrick O'Brian*, by Brian Lavery and Geoff Hunt.

ABOUT THE AUTHOR

Sophie Turner worked as an online editor before delving even more fully into the tech world. Writing, researching the Regency era, and occasionally dreaming about living in Britain are her escapes from her day job.

She was afraid of long series until she ventured upon Patrick O'Brian's 20-book Aubrey-Maturin masterpiece, something she might have repeated five times through. Alas, the Constant Love series is only planned to be seven books right now.

She blogs about her writing endeavours at sophie-turner-acl.blogspot.com, where readers can find direction for the various social drawing-rooms across the Internet where she may be called upon.

Printed in Great Britain
by Amazon